Everyman, I will go with thee,
and be thy guide

THE CHEKHOV OMNIBUS: SELECTED STORIES

Translated by
CONSTANCE GARNETT

Revised, with additional material,
introduction and notes by
DONALD RAYFIELD
Queen Mary and Westfield College

EVERYMAN
J. M. DENT · LONDON
CHARLES E. TUTTLE
VERMONT

This edition first published in Everyman by
J. M. Dent in 1994

J. M. Dent
Orion Publishing Group
Orion House, 5 Upper St Martin's Lane
London WC2H 9EA
and
Charles E. Tuttle Co. Inc.
28 South Main Street
Rutland, Vermont 05701, USA

Typeset in Sabon by Deltatype Ltd, Ellesmere Port, Cheshire
Printed in Great Britain by
The Guernsey Press Co. Ltd, Guernsey, C.I.

British Library Cataloguing-in-Publication Data
is available upon request.

ISBN 0 460 87472 1

CONTENTS

Note on the Author, Translator and Editor vii
Chronology of Chekhov's Life and Times x
Introduction xvii

SELECTED STORIES

Steppe 3
A Dreary Story 85
The Duel 134
Ward No. 6 222
The Black Monk 268
The Student 295
Ariadna 299
The House with the Mezzanine 320
My Life 335
Peasants 412
A Visit to Friends 443
Ionych 458
The Little Trilogy 474
An Official Duty 502
The Lady with the Dog 516
In the Ravine 531
The Bishop 565
The Bride 579

Notes 595
Chekhov and His Critics 611
Suggestions for Further Reading 613

NOTE ON THE AUTHOR,
TRANSLATOR AND EDITOR

ANTON CHEKHOV was born the son of a shopkeeper and ex-serf in Taganrog (southern Russia) in 1860. He began studying medicine in Moscow in 1879 and practised as a doctor for most of his life. Like his elder brother Alexsandr, he began as a freelance writer of titbits and comic stories, but his talent was widely recognised by prestigious editors, and by 1886 he was writing serious stories in Maupassant vein. His debut as a serious writer was *Steppe* in 1888, followed by a score of major stories of between fifteen and one hundred pages each over the next fifteen years. Periodically he indulged his love–hate for the theatre with eccentric plays: *The Seagull* was his first unequivocal success in 1897, when the new methods of Stanislavsky's Moscow Arts Theatre made it performable. Three subsequent plays, *Uncle Vania* (1897/9), *Three Sisters* (1901), *The Cherry Orchard* (1904) gave Chekhov fame and notoriety, but in Russia his narrative prose brought even more acclaim for his genius than did his dramas.

Chekhov travelled to Sakhalin, Hong Kong and Ceylon in 1890, bought himself an estate near Moscow in 1892 and enjoyed a frantic life feted in Moscow until the TB that decimated his family forced him to sell the estate. Retreating to Yalta, he built himself a remarkable house and garden. He married the last of his actress-loves, Olga Knipper in 1901, but most of their married life was spent apart. Olga Knipper miscarried in 1902 and in 1904 Chekhov died, childless, of TB, in a hotel room in Badenweiler.

CONSTANCE GARNETT (née Black) born in 1861, was the youngest student (gaining a first class in Classics) in Newnham College, Cambridge, and almost the first woman librarian in Britain. She married the critic Edward Garnett, son of the superintendent of the British Museum reading room, in 1889. A series of friendships with Russian exiles inspired her to learn to read (if not to speak) Russian. In 1892 she began translating Goncharov. Over the next thirty years, with phenomenal industry, she translated most of Russia's great prose writers: while she was best with the more contemplative Turgenev and Chekhov, her Gogol, Tolstoy and Dostoevsky are imposing achievements. On two visits to Russia (the second in 1904, with her twelve-year-old son) she met Tolstoy and Korolenko. She was on friendly terms with G. B. Shaw and D. H. Lawrence. Her son David Garnett became a major short-story writer. She died in 1946.

DONALD RAYFIELD, born 1942, is Professor of Russian and Georgian at Queen Mary & Westfield College (University of London). His books include *Chekhov: The Evolution of his Art* (1975), *The Dream of Lhasa: Nikolay Przhevalsky, Explorer of Central Asia* (1976) and *The Literature of Georgia: A History* (forthcoming). He has written articles on Georgian and Russian literature, notably on Osip Mandelstam. He is currently working on a new biography of Chekhov.

CHRONOLOGY OF CHEKHOV'S LIFE

Year	Age	Life
1860		After Alexsandr (1855–1913) and Nikolai (1859–89), Anton is born to Pavel Chekhov, a shopkeeper, and his wife Evgenia in Taganrog
1870	10	Anton begins Taganrog's *gimnazia* (grammar school)
1873	13	Sees first theatre performance: Offenbach's *La belle Hélène*
1875	15	His brothers Alexsandr and Nikolai leave for Moscow, one to University, the other to Art School
1876	16	Family business is bankrupt. Father, then mother and younger children flee to Moscow. Anton stays in school at Taganrog
1879	19	Matriculates, with 'excellent' in Religious Knowledge, Geography and German; wins fellowship to Moscow medical school. Sends first story to *Strekoza* ('Dragonfly'), begins to finance studies and family
1883	23	Writes regularly for Nikolai Leikin's Petersburg *Oskolki* ('Fragments') as Antosha Chekhonte. Shelves his first play *Platonov*
1884	24	Publishes 20 of 200 pieces written so far as *Tales of Melpomene*. Graduates as a doctor. Publishes his one novel, *A Shooting Party*. Traumatic death of infant niece

CHRONOLOGY OF HIS TIMES

Year	Literary Context	Historical Events
1856–61	Turgenev, *Rudin, Nest of Gentlefolk, On the Eve, Fathers and Sons*	Russian serfs are promised freedom and land by Tsar Alexander II; control is relaxed over press and universities
1868–9	Dostoevsky, *Crime and Punishment* Tolstoy completes *War and Peace*	Factories, banks, railways, foreign capital begin to spread all over Russia
1875–8	Tolstoy, *Anna Karenina* Death of Russia's best-loved 'civic' poet, Nekrasov	Russian support for Serbs leads to victorious war with Turkey, isolation in Europe, terrorism and reaction at home
1879–80	Dostoevsky, *Brothers Karamazov*	
1881	Death of Dostoevsky Tolstoy abandons fiction for theology	Alexander II's murder leads to Alexander III's grim regime Pogroms of Jews begin
1883	Death of Turgenev	Russia completes conquest of Central Asia
1884–5	Zola, *Germinal* (in Russian, then French)	

Year	Age	Life
1886	26	Commissioned to write serious stories, in a Maupassant vein, for St Petersburg newspaper *Novoe vremia* ('New Times'). Begins a long friendship with the owner of *Novoe vremia*, Aleksei Suvorin (1834–1912), tyrant, womaniser, publisher, dramatist and self-made provincial. Love affairs with Natalia Golden (later his sister-in-law) and Dunia Efros. Symptoms of tuberculosis are unmistakable
1887	27	Revisits Taganrog and the now ruined southern Russian landscape. *Ivanov*, his first controversial play, his only 'tragedy', puzzles critics
1888	28	Awarded the Academy's Pushkin prize for his masterpiece *Steppe*. One-act farces, *The Bear* and *The Proposal*, have runaway success. Tours the Crimea and Caucasus with Suvorin's son Aleksei
1889	29	Publishes *A Dreary Story*: Critics allege cynicism and plagiarism. *The Wood Demon*, a prototype of *Uncle Vania*, is a theatrical fiasco. His brother Nikolai, an artist of genius, dies of tuberculosis
1890	30	Travels to Sakhalin, carries out single-handed survey of convicts. Returns and recuperates via Hong Kong, Sri Lanka. Publishes collection of stories, *Dismal People*
1891	31	Travels with the Suvorins to western Europe. Writes *The Duel*. Attacks Moscow Zoo. Involved in famine relief
1892	32	Buys an estate at Melikhovo for himself, his parents and his sister. Builds schools, gives pet mongoose to Moscow Zoo, plants trees. Writes *Ward No. 6*, and is politicised
1893	33	Publishes *The Island of Sakhalin*
1895	35	Meets Tolstoy. Publishes *The Black Monk*
1896	36	Stages *The Seagull* in St Petersburg. Publishes *The House with the Mezzanine* and *My Life*

Year	Literary Context	Historical Events
1886	Death of Russia's greatest playwright, Alexsandr Ostrovsky Tolstoy, *The Power of Darkness*	
1887	Tolstoy, *The Death of Ivan Ilyich* Maupassant, *Le Horla* Death of poet Nadson	Access to education for lower classes and Jews restricted
1888	Suicide of Vsevolod Garshin	
1889	Saltykov-Shchedrin dies	
1891	Tolstoy, *The Kreuzer Sonata*	Famine on the Volga. Trans-Siberian railway begun
1893	Briusov, *Russian Symbolists* Death of Maupassant	Death of Tchaikovsky
1894		Accession of Tsar Nicolas II: liberalisation and *entente* with France
1895	Nikolai Leskov dies	
1896		Strikes in St Petersburg Russo-Chinese pact

Year	Age	Life
1897	37	Unfinished *Peasants* mutilated by censors, denounced by Tolstoy. Collapses with haemorrhage of lungs: quits Melikhovo for France. Breaks for a time with the anti-semitic Suvorin
1898	38	Father dies. Moves to Yalta. Befriends Gorky and Bunin. Trilogy *The Man in a Case, Gooseberries, About Love*
1899	39	*Uncle Vania* a success. Publishes *Lady with the Dog*. Illness confines him to Yalta
1900	40	Prints *In the Ravine*
1901	41	Marries Olga Knipper. Takes mare's milk cure in Urals. *Three Sisters* written and staged
1902	42	Writes *The Bishop*
1903	43	Writes *The Bride*
1904	44	Completes and sees *The Cherry Orchard* staged. Leaves Russia to die in Badenweiler, Germany, 15 July

Year	Literary Context	Historical Events
1898	Stanislavsky takes over *The Seagull* and founds Moscow Arts Theatre Gorky's first collection of stories	Dreyfus affair: Zola's *J'accuse* Revolutionary underground SDP founded by Lenin
1899	Tolstoy completes *Resurrection*	Student riots in St Petersburg
1900	Tolstoy excommunicated Vladimir Soloviov dies after writing *The Tale of the Antichrist* Painter Levitan dies of TB	
1901	Andrei Bely's first poems printed Rozanov, *In the World of the Obscure and the Uncertain* Bunin given Pushkin prize for *Leaf-fall*	
1902	Gorky, *The Lower Depths* Gorky banned by Tsar from Academy	Interior Minister Sipiagin assassinated
1903	Alexsandr Blok's first poems printed	Kishiniov pogrom
1904	Innokenti Annensky, *Quiet Songs*	Russo-Japanese war begins Azef takes over Socialist Revolutionary terrorists

INTRODUCTION

In the West Chekhov's reputation as the founder of modern drama is unassailable; the plays of Beckett, Pinter, Adamov, Ionesco, however unChekhovian their ideas or themes, are daughters of the Chekhovian revolution. But in Russia it is almost unanimously agreed that his achievement in the short story is still greater. Russian critics such as Lev Tolstoy, Ivan Bunin or Osip Mandelstam might even have denounced the Chekhovian play as incompetence mistaken for genius.

The key to understanding his plays has always been his stories, even for those who regard Chekhov as a supremely international genius on the stage (where good actors and directors make the barrier of translation a more surmountable hurdle). The plays lack authorial presence, and the apparent contradictions between hope and disillusion, between tragic material and comic approach, are more easily resolved when we see the author in his natural setting, fully in control of his material from conception to consumption – that is as a story-writer, not a dramatist.

No modern reader can doubt that Chekhov's narrative prose is the culmination of classical Russian literature: what Tolstoy took nine hundred pages to resolve in *Anna Karenina* is distilled into twenty pages of *The Lady with the Dog*. Yet, at the same time, Chekhov's prose is the hearth on which a new, modern, ambiguous and laconic fiction has been forged in many other languages as well as Russian. It is not only Katherine Mansfield or John Cheever who are indebted to Chekhov's prose in translation; Chekhovian techniques of subtlety and economy, a refusal to preach or to waste words, have influenced almost every major writer of this century: compare Thomas Mann's *Death in Venice* with Chekhov's *The Bishop*.

Chekhov's work is not confessional or autobiographical; but the chronology shows the importance of three themes that link his life to his art – disease, family and love. His first love, the sharp-witted and irrepressible 'skeleton' Natalia Golden, identified two of them in her sole surviving letter to him of 1885: 'you have two things wrong with you, one is a susceptibility to falling in love, the other is spitting blood. The first is not serious, the second is.' Chekhov was involved with disease as a doctor, but above all as a life-long sufferer from TB. Many of his stories are structured around the triumph of bacteria, or of schizophrenia, over healthy bodies and minds, just as he is intensely aware of social sickness among peasantry and middle classes: the powers of diagnosis are matched by a doctor's self-protective irony and caution. Doctors in Russian society had a powerfully incorruptible image, and their role in literature and the arts as the nation's conscience-keepers was as formidable as in science and government. For Chekhov's self-esteem, being a worthy doctor was more reassuring than being a revered writer.

The Chekhov family was a perpetual turbulence from which the writer never escaped. Only recently released archival material shows how deep the conflicts were between brothers and sister, between parents and children: it was a family which took more from the writer than it gave. It also gave the writer almost intolerably raw material. Never seen to weep, even when his brother Nikolai died in spiritual and physical agony, Chekhov mourned in fiction. His stories transmute the grieving for his shattered childhood, his elder brothers' wrecked lives, his women friends' unhappy love lives and his male friends' untimely deaths from suicide or tuberculosis. The cult of privacy and tolerance that makes Chekhov seem so English is a reaction to the intolerable pressures from which he could only escape by travelling abroad, often in the company of an old roué like the publisher Suvorin. Chekhov's daringly modern morality is in part born of bitter experience.

More puzzling still are the swings from misogyny (*Ariadna*) to feminism (*The Bride*), until we read not Chekhov's evasive letters to his women friends, but their letters to him, in which they explain their trust in his non-judgmental attitudes by his sheer indifference to them as individuals. A man as familiar with brothels as Chekhov was could not fail to have a dual attitude, sympathy for women as exploited and frustrated human beings, impatience with them when sexual encounters were no longer simple transactions but emotional entanglements. Chekhov's thirst for freedom made him sympathise with women's parallel struggles but also resist involvement. A 'Don Juan's catalogue' has yet to be compiled for Chekhov, but from his student days to his marriage in sickness to Olga Knipper a succession of aborted involvements with women fed his fiction and his philosophy of life. The taxonomy of women that Gurov devises in *The Lady with the Dog* must have much in common with the author's. Chekhov enjoyed the affection, not always self-interested, of a wide range of women: Jewish girls, like Natalia Golden and Dunia Efros, living on their wits on the margins of the literary demi-monde; actresses, of socially committed optimists. Only since *perestroika* have previously suppressed letters and biographical material been released to show a much more complex, ambiguous and human figure.

The Germans were the first foreigners to understand that Chekhov was a serious new star in the literary constellation. Writers, rather than ordinary readers, were quick to realise the implications of Chekhov's innovations for their art. The English and the French followed their opinions and a succession of translations from the 1890s to this day have left the English-speaking reader with an enormous choice. One might think that each successive translation would be the best so far. Certainly each one should be more accurate and more authoritative. But a translator has to have a writer's gift, as well as a linguist's skills, and we are often forced to choose between a talented writer who is an amateur linguist and a professional linguist who is an amateur writer. In the case of this selection of Chekhov's stories, the deciding factor has been that the errors of an amateur linguist can be corrected, while the style, the subtle flow of a talented writer is inimitable.

It is this subtle flow that has led me to prefer Constance Garnett's translations as a basis for a new edition. Working in the 1910s, Constance Garnett suffered from many disadvantages: she had a patchy knowledge of Russian mores and religion, and little acquaintance with the seamy side of life anywhere; she had been taught Russian imperfectly by the anarchist refugee Stepniak-Kravchinsky, who in 1895 fell under a London underground train in mysterious circumstances. Constance Garnett spent only two seasons in Russia and was never a confident speaker; she had no good dictionaries and few experts to consult; she worked under enormous pressure, attempting to provide the entire corpus of Russian prose for the English-speaking reader; the Russian editions of Chekhov available to her were slightly defective. While she makes elementary blunders, her care in unravelling difficult syntactical knots and her research on the right terms for Chekhov's many plants, birds and fish are impressive. Above all she was a natural writer, as proven by the genes she bequeathed to her son, the short-story writer David Garnett. Her English is not only nearly contemporaneous to Chekhov's, it is often comparable.

Modern translators – Ronald Hingley and Ronald Wilkes, for instance – make very few mistakes. But their English belongs to a later age and is marked by a personality and style often at odds with Chekhov's original. Constance Garnett's fidelity to Russian word order and to Chekhov's convoluted punctuation is a strength, not a weakness: she keeps nuances and continuity which more orthodox

English style loses. Her original versions are generally prolix and I have shortened her text, without losing anything to be found in the original, by about three per cent.

I have corrected Constance Garnett's howlers (one every two or three pages), such as 'apathetically' for 'with appetite', 'copse' for 'ladder', 'was it solid?' for 'he read it' (*prochen on* misread as *prochel on*). She omits sentences, copies Russian syntax and word order too frequently, and has far too cumbersome a system of transliterating in full proper names. I have filled the omissions in her versions, replaced the more strikingly unEnglish or antiquated constructions and rendered Russian names in just two forms, an intimate Christian name and a formal surname, with the middle 'patronym' given only when it plays an important part in the story.

In choosing which stories to include, I decided to begin with the first story that Chekhov wrote as he wished, with no consideration for his market or editor: had he died in 1888 before writing *Steppe* he would have occupied a mere paragraph, rather than a whole chapter, in literary history. None of Chekhov's less innovative Zolaesque 'naturalist' stories of 1893–5, such as *Three Years*, have been included, interesting though they are. *Ariadna* and *The Black Monk* might be considered artistically inferior to Chekhov's greatest, because of their sensational subjects (atavist femininity, mad intellectuals), but, apart from their genius, they contribute so much to the overall picture of Chekhov's development that they seemed obligatory. Two of Chekhov's ecclesiastical stories, his own favourite, *The Student*, and his valedictory triumph, *The Bishop*, are of crucial importance: his view of the priest as novice and as dying man are the key to his view of the writer's role. Like Leskov, Chekhov sees the priest as the only way of reflecting on his own gifts and purpose in the world.

I have added to this revision of Constance Garnett my own translation of the two last chapters of *Peasants*, which were published after Chekhov's death, and my version of *A Visit to Friends*, a story which Chekhov disliked, for all its indisputable qualities. He recycled its plot and much of its phrasing as *The Cherry Orchard* and Constance Garnett probably did not know of its existence.

Few writers were so diffident about titles as Chekhov: in English the situation is confused by the different choices made by each translator. I have kept Constance Garnett's conservative approach, and not improved on the original understatements. But occasionally the title is embodied in the narrative itself: thus I have reinstated *The House with the Mezzanine*, where Garnett uses the subtitle *An*

Artist's Story, because the obscure architecture of the house is part of the story's atmosphere. I have preferred *The Bride* to *Betrothed* for Chekhov's *Nevesta*, since the heroine is teased by boys who call out 'The Bride!'

Over the last fifty years Russian scholars have reinstated Anton Chekhov's stories in the form which we can safely assume he wished to see them published, with censor's deletions and typographer's errors corrected. The entire English text has therefore been carefully checked against the text of the authoritative 1973–83 *Polnoe sobranie sochinenii* Moscow edition. This was done by processing Constance Garnett's original versions through a scanner before totally revising and resetting them. It is a pleasant irony that this revision has been carried out at Queen Mary and Westfield College, whose first librarian (when it was known as the People's Palace) was in 1887 Constance Garnett (then Black).

DONALD RAYFIELD

SELECTED STORIES

Steppe
(The Story of a Journey)

I

Early one morning in July a shabby covered chaise, one of those antediluvian chaises without springs in which no one travels in Russia nowadays, except merchants' clerks, cattle dealers and the less well-to-do among priests, drove out of N—, the principal town of the province of Z—, and rumbled noisily along the main highway. It rattled and creaked at every movement; the pail, tied on behind, chimed in gruffly, and from these sounds alone and from the wretched rags of leather hanging loose about its peeling body one could judge that it was decrepit and ready for the scrap yard.

Two of the inhabitants of N— were sitting in the chaise; they were a merchant of N— called Ivan Kuzmichov, a man with a shaven face, wearing glasses and a straw hat, more like a government clerk than a merchant, and Father Khristofor Siriysky, the priest of the Church of St Nikolai at N—, a little old man with long hair, in a grey canvas cassock, a wide-brimmed top-hat and a coloured embroidered girdle. The former was absorbed in thought, and kept tossing his head to shake off drowsiness; in his countenance an habitual business-like reserve was struggling with the genial expression of a man who has just said good-bye to his relatives and has had a good drink at parting. The latter gazed with moist eyes wonderingly at God's world, and his smile was so broad that it seemed to embrace even the brim of his hat; his face was red and looked frozen. Both of them, Father Khristofor as well as Kuzmichov, were going to sell wool. At parting with their families they had just eaten heartily of pastry puffs and cream, and, although it was so early in the morning had had a glass or two. Both were in the best of humours.

Apart from the two persons described above and the coachman Deniska, who tirelessly lashed the pair of frisky bay ponies, there was another figure in the chaise – a boy of nine with a sunburnt face, wet with tears. This was Yegorushka, Kuzmichov's nephew. With the sanction of his uncle and the blessing of Father Khristofor, he was now on his way to go to school. His mother, Olga, who was the widow of a collegiate secretary and Kuzmichov's sister, was fond of educated people and refined society, and had entreated her brother to take Yegorushka with him when he went to sell wool and to put him to school; and now the boy was sitting on the box beside the coachman Deniska, holding on to his elbow to keep from falling off, and dancing up and down like a kettle on the hob, with no notion where he was going or what he was going for. The rapid motion through the air blew out his red shirt like a balloon on his back and made his new hat with a peacock's feather in it, like a coachman's, keep slipping on to the back of his head. He felt he was an intensely unhappy person, and wanted to cry.

When the chaise drove past the prison, Yegorushka glanced at the sentries pacing slowly by the high white walls, at the little barred windows, at the cross shining on the roof, and remembered the week before, on the day of the Holy Mother of Kazan, being with his mother at the prison church for the Dedication Feast, and before that, at Easter, going to the prison with Deniska and Ludmila the cook, and taking the prisoners Easter bread, eggs, cakes and roast beef. The prisoners had thanked them and made the sign of the cross, and one of them had given Yegorushka pewter cufflinks of his own making.

The boy gazed at the familiar places, while the hateful chaise flew by and left them all behind. After the prison he caught glimpses of black grimy foundries, followed by the snug green cemetery surrounded by a wall of cobblestones; white crosses and tombstones, nestling among green foliage of the cherry trees and looking in the distance like patches of white, peeped out gaily from behind the wall. Yegorushka remembered that when the cherries were in blossom those white patches melted with the flowers into a sea of white; and that when the cherries were ripe the white tombstones and crosses were dotted with splashes of red like bloodstains. Under the cherry trees in the cemetery Yegorushka's father and granny, Zinaida, lay sleeping day and night. When Granny had died she had been put in a long narrow coffin and two copper coins had been put upon her eyes, which would not keep shut. Up to the time of her death she had been lively, and used to bring soft rolls covered with poppy seeds from the market. Now she just slept and slept.

Beyond the cemetery came the smoking brickyards. From under the long reed-thatched roofs that looked as though pressed flat to the ground, thick black smoke rose in great clouds and floated lazily upwards. The sky was murky above the brickyards and the cemetery, and great shadows from the clouds of smoke crept over the fields and across the roads. Men and horses covered with red dust were moving about in the smoke near the roofs . . .

The town ended with the brickyards and the open country began.

Yegorushka looked at the town for the last time, pressed his face against Deniska's elbow, and wept bitterly . . .

'Come, not done howling yet, cry-baby!' cried Kuzmichov. 'You are blubbering again, little milksop! If you don't want to go, stay behind; no one is making you come!'

'Never mind, never mind, Yegor my boy, never mind,' Father Khristofor muttered rapidly – 'never mind, my boy . . . Call upon God . . . You are not going for your harm, but for your good. Learning is light, as the saying is, and ignorance darkness . . . That is so, truly.'

'Do you want to go back?' asked Kuzmichov.

'Yes . . . yes . . .' answered Yegorushka, sobbing.

'Well, you'd better go back then. Anyway, you are going for nothing; it's a day's journey for a spoonful of porridge.'

'Never mind, never mind, my boy,' Father Khristofor went on. 'Call upon God . . . Lomonosov* set off with the fishermen in the same way, and he became a man famous all over Europe. Learning acquired in conjunction with faith brings forth fruit pleasing to God. What are the words of the prayer? For the glory of our Maker, for the comfort of our parents, for the benefit of our Church and our country . . . Yes, indeed!'

'The benefit is not the same in all cases,' said Kuzmichov, lighting a cheap cigar; 'some study twenty years and no sense comes of it.'

'That does happen.'

'Learning is a benefit to some, but others only muddle their brains. My sister is a woman who does not understand; she is set upon refinement, and wants to turn Yegorushka into a learned man, and she does not understand that in my line of business I could make Yegorushka's fortune for the rest of his life. I tell you this, that if everyone were to go in for being learned and refined there would be no one to sow the corn and do the trading; they would all die of hunger.'

'And if all go in for trading and sowing corn there will be no one to acquire learning.'

And considering that each of them had said something weighty and convincing, Kuzmichov and Father Khristofor both looked serious and cleared their throats simultaneously.

Deniska, who had been listening to their conversation without understanding a word of it, shook his head and, rising in his seat, lashed at both the bays. A silence followed.

Meanwhile a wide boundless plain encircled by a chain of low hills lay stretched before the travellers' eyes. Huddling together and peeping out from behind one another, these hills melted together into rising ground, which stretched right to the very horizon and disappeared into the violet distance; one drives on and on and cannot discern where it begins or where it ends ... The sun had already peeped out from beyond the town behind them, and quietly, without fuss, set to its accustomed task. At first in the distance before them a broad, bright, yellow streak of light crept over the ground where the earth met the sky, near the burial mounds and a windmill, which in the distance looked like a tiny man waving his arms. A minute later a similar streak gleamed a little nearer, crept to the right and embraced the hills. Something warm touched Yegorushka's spine; the streak of light stealing up from behind, darted between the chaise and the horses, moved to meet the other streak, and soon the whole wide steppe flung off the early morning penumbra, and was smiling and sparkling with dew.

The cut rye, the coarse steppe grass, the milkwort, the wild hemp, all withered from the sultry heat, turned brown and half dead, now washed by the dew and caressed by the sun, revived, to fade again. Arctic petrels flew across the road with joyful cries; marmots called to one another in the grass. Somewhere, far away to the left, lapwings uttered their plaintive notes. A covey of partridges, scared by the chaise, fluttered up and with their soft 'trrr!', flew off to the hills. In the grass crickets, locusts and grasshoppers kept up their churring, monotonous music.

But a little time passed, the dew evaporated, the air grew stagnant, and the disillusioned steppe began to wear its jaded July aspect. The grass drooped, everything living was hushed. The sun-baked hills, brownish-green and violet in the distance, with their quiet shadowy tones, the plain with the misty distance and, flung above them, the sky, which seems terribly deep and transparent in the steppes, where there are no woods or high hills, seemed now endless, petrified with dreariness ...

How stifling and oppressive it was! The chaise raced along, while Yegorushka saw always the same scene – the sky, the plain, the low hills ... The music in the grass was hushed, the petrels had flown away, the partridges were out of sight, rooks hovered idly over the withered grass; they were all alike and made the steppe even more monotonous.

A black kite flew just above the ground, with an even sweep of its wings, suddenly halted in the air as though pondering on the dreariness of life, then fluttered its wings and flew like an arrow over the steppe, and there was no telling why it was flying and what it wanted. In the distance a windmill waved its sails ...

Now and then a glimpse through the tall weeds of a white skull or of cobble-stones broke the monotony; a grey stone stood out for an instant or a parched willow with a blue crow on its top branch; a marmot would run across the road and – again there flitted before the eyes only the high grass, the low hills, the rooks . . .

But at last, thank God, a wagon loaded with sheaves came to meet them; a peasant wench was lying on the very top. Sleepy, exhausted by the heat, she lifted her head and looked at the travellers. Deniska gaped, looking at her; the horses stretched out their noses towards the sheaves; the chaise, squeaking, kissed the wagon, and the prickly ears passed over Father Khristofor's hat like a brush.

'You are driving into people, fatty!' cried Deniska. 'What a swollen lump of a face, as though a bumble-bee had stung it!'

The girl smiled drowsily, and moving her lips lay down again; then a solitary poplar came into sight on the low hill. Someone had planted it, and God only knows why it was there. It was hard to tear the eyes away from its graceful figure and green drapery. Was that lovely creature happy? Sultry heat in summer, in winter frost and snow-storms, terrible nights in autumn when nothing is to be seen but darkness and nothing is to be heard but the senseless angry howling wind, and, worst of all, alone, alone for the whole of life . . . Beyond the poplar stretches of wheat extended like a bright yellow carpet from the road to the top of the hills. On the hills the corn was already cut and laid up in sheaves, while at the bottom they were still cutting . . . Six mowers were standing in a row swinging their scythes, and the scythes gleamed gaily and uttered in unison together 'Swish, swish!' The movements of the peasant women binding the sheaves, the faces of the mowers, the glitter of the scythes showed that the sultry heat was baking and stifling. A black dog with its tongue hanging out ran from the mowers to meet the chaise, probably with the intention of barking, but stopped halfway and stared indifferently at Deniska, who waved his whip at him; it was too hot to bark! One peasant woman got up and, putting both hands to her aching back, followed Yegorushka's red shirt with her eyes. Whether it was that the colour pleased her or that he reminded her of her children, she stood a long time motionless staring after him . . .

But now the wheat, too, flashed by; again the parched plain, the sunburnt hills, the sultry sky stretched before them; again a black kite hovered over the earth. In the distance, as before, a windmill whirled its sails, and still it looked like a little man waving his arms. It was wearisome to watch, and it seemed as though one would never reach it, as though it were running away from the chaise.

Father Khristofor and Kuzmichov were silent. Deniska lashed the horses and kept shouting to them, while Yegorushka had stopped crying, and gazed around listlessly. The heat and the tedium of the steppes overpowered him. He felt as though he had been travelling and jolting up and down a long time, that the sun had been baking his back a long time. Before they had gone six miles he began to feel 'It's time to rest.' The geniality gradually faded out of his uncle's face, and nothing else was left but the air of business reserve; and to a gaunt shaven face, especially when it is adorned with spectacles and the nose and temples are covered with dust, this reserve gives a relentless, inquisitorial appearance. Father Khristofor, on the other hand, never left off gazing with wonder at God's world, and smiling. Without speaking, he was musing over something pleasant and nice, and a kindly, genial smile remained imprinted on his face. It seemed as though some nice and pleasant thought were imprinted on his brain by the heat . . .

'Well, Deniska, shall we catch the wagons up today?' asked Kuzmichov.

Deniska looked at the sky, rose in his seat, lashed at his horses and then answered:

'By nightfall, please God, we shall catch up with them.'

There was a sound of dogs barking. Half a dozen steppe sheep-dogs, suddenly leaping out as though from ambush, with ferocious howling barks, flew to meet the chaise. All of them, extraordinarily vicious, surrounded the chaise, with their shaggy spider-like muzzles and their eyes red with anger, and jostling one another in their anger, raised a hoarse howl. They were filled with passionate hatred of the horses, of the chaise, and of the human beings, and seemed ready to tear them into pieces. Deniska, who was fond of teasing and beating, was delighted at the chance, and with a malignant expression bent over and lashed at the sheep-dogs with his whip. The brutes growled more than ever, the horses flew on; and Yegorushka, who had difficulty in keeping his seat on the box, realised, looking at the dogs, eyes and teeth, that if he fell down they would instantly tear him to bits; but he felt no fear and looked at them as malignly as Deniska, and regretted that he had no whip in his hand.

The chaise came upon a flock of sheep.

'Stop!' cried Kuzmichov. 'Pull up! Whoa!'

Deniska threw his whole body backwards and pulled up the horses.

'Come here!' Kuzmichov shouted to the shepherd. 'Call off the dogs, damn them!'

The old shepherd, tattered and barefoot, wearing a fur cap, with a dirty sack round his loins and a long crook in his hand – a regular figure from the Old Testament – called off the dogs, and taking off his cap, went up to the chaise. Another similar Old Testament figure was standing motionless at the other end of the flock, staring without interest at the travellers.

'Whose sheep are these?' asked Kuzmichov.

'Varlamov's,' the old man answered in a loud voice.

'Varlamov's,' repeated the shepherd standing at the other end of the flock.

'Did Varlamov come this way yesterday or not?'

'He did not; his clerk came, though . . .'

'Drive on!'

The chaise rolled on and the shepherds, with their angry dogs, were left behind. Yegorushka gazed listlessly at the violet distance in front, and it began to seem as though the windmill, waving its sails, were getting nearer. It became bigger and bigger, grew quite large, and now he could distinguish clearly its two sails. One sail was old and patched, the other had only lately been made of new wood and glistened in the sun. The chaise drove straight on, while the windmill, for some reason, began retreating to the left. They drove on and on, and the windmill kept moving away to the left, and still did not disappear.

'A fine windmill Boltva has put up for his son,' observed Deniska.

'And how is it we don't see his farm?'

'It is that way, beyond the river bed.'

Boltva's farm, too, soon came into sight, but yet the windmill did not retreat, did not drop behind; it still watched Yegorushka with its shining sail and waved. What a sorcerer!

II

Towards midday the chaise turned off the road to the right; it went on a little way at walking pace and then stopped. Yegorushka heard a soft, very caressing gurgle, and felt a different air breathe on his face with a cool velvety touch. Through a little pipe of hemlock stuck there by some unknown benefactor, water was running in a thin trickle from a low hill, which nature had assembled out of huge monstrous stones. Water fell to the ground, and limpid, sparkling gaily in the sun, and softly murmuring as though fancying itself a great tempestuous torrent, flowed swiftly away to the left. Not far from its source the little stream spread itself out into a pool; the burning sunbeams and the parched soil greedily drank it up and sucked away its strength; but a little further on it must have mingled with another rivulet, for a hundred paces away thick reeds showed green and luxuriant along its course, and three snipe flew up from them with a loud cry as the chaise drove by.

The travellers got out to rest by the stream and feed the horses. Kuzmichov, Father Khristofor and Yegorushka sat down on a mat in the narrow strip of shade cast by the chaise and the unharnessed horses. The nice pleasant thought that the heat had imprinted in Father Khristofor's brain craved expression after he had had a drink of water and eaten a hard-boiled egg. He gave Yegorushka a gentle look, munched, and began:

'I studied too, my boy; from the earliest age God instilled into me reason and understanding, so that while I was just a lad like you I was beyond others, a comfort to my parents and preceptors by my good sense. Before I was fifteen I could speak and make verses in Latin, just as in Russian. I was the crosier-bearer to his Holiness Bishop Khristofor. After mass one day, as I remember it was the patron saint's day of His Majesty Tsar Alexandr Pavlovich* of blessed memory, he disrobed at the altar, looked kindly at me and asked, "Puer bone, quam appelaris?" And I answered, "Christophorus sum". He said, "Ergo connominati sumus" – that is, that we were namesakes . . . Then he asked in Latin, "Whose son are you?" To which I answered, also in Latin, that I was the son of deacon Siriysky of the village of Lebedinskoe. Seeing my responsiveness and the clarity of my answers, his Holiness blessed me and said, "Write to your father that I will not forget him, and that I will keep you in mind." The holy priests and fathers who were standing round the altar, hearing our discussion in Latin, were not a little surprised, and everyone expressed his pleasure and praised me. Before I had moustaches, my boy, I could read Latin, Greek, and French; I knew philosophy, mathematics, secular history, and all the sciences. The Lord gave me a marvellous memory. Sometimes, if I read a thing once or twice, I knew it by heart. My preceptors and patrons were amazed, and so they expected I should make a learned man, a luminary of the Church. I did think of going to Kiev to continue my studies, but my parents did not approve. "You'll be studying all your life," said my father; "when shall we see you finished?" Hearing such words, I gave up studying and took a post . . . Of course, I did not become a learned man, but then I did not disobey my parents; I was a comfort to them in their old age and gave them a creditable funeral. Obedience is greater than fasting and prayer.'

'I suppose you have forgotten all your learning?' observed Kuzmichov.

'I should think so! Thank God, I am over seventy! Something of philosophy and rhetoric I do remember, but languages and mathematics I have quite forgotten.'

Father Khristofor screwed up his eyes, thought a minute and said in an undertone:

'What is a substance? A creature is a self-existing object, not requiring anything else for its completion.'

He shook his head and laughed with feeling.

'Spiritual nourishment!' he said. 'Truly, matter nourishes the flesh and spiritual nourishment the soul!'

'Learning is all very well,' sighed Kuzmichov, 'but if we don't catch up with Varlamov, learning won't do much for us.'

'He's a man, not a needle – we shall find him. He must be going his rounds in these parts.'

Over the sedge were flying the three snipe they had seen before, and in their cries there was a note of alarm and vexation at having been driven away from the stream. The horses were steadily munching and snorting. Deniska walked about by them and, trying to appear indifferent to the cucumbers, pies, and eggs that the gentry were eating, he concentrated on killing the gadflies and horseflies that were fastening upon the horses' backs and bellies; he squashed his victims with relish, emitting a peculiar, maliciously triumphant guttural sound, and when he missed them cleared his throat with an air of vexation and his eyes followed every lucky one that escaped death.

'Deniska, where are you? Come and eat,' said Kuzmichov, heaving a deep sigh, a sign that he had eaten his fill.

Deniska diffidently approached the felt mat and picked out five thick yellow cucumbers (he did not venture to take the smaller and fresher ones), took two hard-boiled eggs that looked dark and were cracked, then irresolutely, as though afraid he might get a blow on his outstretched hand, touched a pie with his finger.

'Take them, take them,' Kuzmichov urged him on.

Deniska took the pies resolutely, and, moving some distance away, sat down on the grass with his back to the chaise. At once there was such a sound of loud munching that even the horses turned round to look suspiciously at Deniska.

After his meal Kuzmichov took a sack containing something out of the chaise and said to Yegorushka:

'I am going to sleep, and you mind that no one takes the sack from under my head.'

Father Khristofor took off his cassock, his girdle, and his kaftan, and Yegorushka, looking at him, was dumbfounded. He had never imagined that priests wore trousers, and Father Khristofor had on real canvas trousers thrust into high boots, and a short striped jacket. Looking at him, Yegorushka thought that in this costume, so unsuitable to his dignified position, he looked with his long hair and beard very much like Robinson Crusoe. After taking off their outer garments Kuzmichov and Father Khristofor lay down in the shade under the chaise, facing one another, and closed their eyes. Deniska, who had finished chewing, stretched himself out on his back and also closed his eyes.

'You keep an eye and see that no one steals the horses!' he said to Yegorushka, and at once fell asleep.

Stillness reigned. There was no sound except the chewing and the snorting of the horses and the snoring of the sleepers; somewhere far away a lapwing wailed, and from time to time there sounded the shrill cries of the three snipe that had flown up to see whether their uninvited visitors had gone away; the rivulet babbled, lisping softly, but all these sounds did not break the stillness, did not stir the stagnation, but, on the contrary, lulled all nature to sleep.

Yegorushka, gasping with the heat, which was particularly oppressive after a meal, ran to the sedge and from there surveyed the country. He saw exactly the same as he had in the morning: the plain, the low hills, the sky, the violet distance; only the hills stood nearer; and he could not see the windmill, which had been left far behind. From behind the rocky hill from which the stream flowed rose another, smoother and broader; a little hamlet of five or six homesteads clung to it. No people, no trees, no shade were to be seen about the huts; it looked as though the hamlet had expired and dried up in the burning air. To while away the time Yegorushka caught a grasshopper in the grass, held it in his closed hand to his ear, and spent a long time listening to the creature playing on its violin. When he was weary of the music he ran after a flock of yellow butterflies who were flying to drink the water by the sedge, and found himself again beside the chaise, without noticing how he came there. His uncle and Father Khristofor were sound asleep; their sleep would be sure to last two or three hours, till the horses rested . . . How was he to get through that long time, and where was he to get away from the heat? A tricky problem . . . Mechanically Yegorushka put his lips to the trickle that ran from the water pipe; there was a chill in his mouth and there was the smell of hemlock. He drank at first eagerly, then went on with effort till the sharp cold had run from his mouth all over his body and the water was spilt on his shirt. Then he went up to the chaise and began looking at the sleeping figures. His uncle's face wore, as before, an expression of business-like reserve. Fanatically devoted to his work, Kuzmichov always, even in his sleep and at church when they were singing, 'Like the cherubim', thought about his business and could never forget it for a moment; and now he was probably dreaming about bales of wool, wagons, prices, Varlamov . . . Father Khristofor, now, a soft, frivolous person, easily amused, had never in all his life been conscious of anything which could, like a boa-constrictor, coil about his soul. In all the numerous enterprises he had undertaken in his day what attracted him was not so much the business itself, but the bustle and the contact with other people involved in every undertaking. Thus, in the present expedition, he was not so much interested in wool, in Varlamov, and in prices, as in the long journey, the conversations on the way, sleeping under a chaise, and eating at odd times . . .

And now, judging from his face, he must have been dreaming of Bishop Khristofor, of the Latin discussion, of his wife, of cream puffs and all sorts of things that Kuzmichov could not possibly dream of.

While Yegorushka was watching their sleeping faces he suddenly heard a soft singing; somewhere at a distance a woman was singing, and it was difficult to tell where and in what direction. The song was subdued, dreary and melancholy, like a dirge, and hardly audible, and seemed to come first from the right, then from the left, then from above, and then from underground, as though an unseen spirit were hovering over the steppe and singing. Yegorushka looked about him, and could not make out where the strange song came from. Then as he listened he began to fancy that the grass was singing; in its song, withered and half-dead, it was without words, but plaintively and passionately, urging that it was not to blame, that the sun was burning it for no fault of its own; it urged that it ardently longed to live, that it was young and might have been beautiful but for the heat and the drought; it was guiltless, but yet it prayed for forgiveness and protested that it was in anguish, sad and sorry for itself . . .

Yegorushka listened for a little, and it began to seem as though this dreary, mournful song made the air hotter, more suffocating and more stagnant . . . To drown the singing he ran to the sedge, humming to himself and trying to make a noise with his feet. From there he looked about in all directions and found out who was singing. Near the furthest hut in the hamlet stood a peasant woman in a short petticoat, with long thin legs like a heron. She was sifting something. A white dust floated languidly from her sieve down the hillock. Now it was evident that she was the singer. A couple of yards from her a little bare-headed boy in nothing but a smock was standing motionless. As though fascinated by the song, he stood stock-still, staring away into the distance, probably at Yegorushka's red calico shirt.

The song ceased. Yegorushka sauntered back to the chaise, and to while away the time went again to the trickle of water.

And again there was the sound of the mournful song. It was the same long-legged peasant woman in the hamlet over the hill. Yegorushka's boredom came back again. He left the pipe and looked upwards. What he saw was so unexpected that he was a little frightened. Just above his head on one of the big clumsy stones stood a chubby little boy, wearing nothing but a shirt, with a bulging belly and thin legs, the same boy who had been standing before the peasant woman. He was gazing with open mouth and unblinking eyes at Yegorushka's red shirt and at the chaise, with a look of blank astonishment and even fear, as though he saw before him creatures of the next world. The red colour of the shirt had charmed and allured him. But the chaise and the men sleeping under it excited his curiosity; perhaps he had not noticed the agreeable red colour and curiosity luring him down from the hamlet, and now probably he was surprised at his own boldness. For a long while Yegorushka stared at him, and he at Yegorushka. Both were silent and conscious of some awkwardness. After a long silence Yegorushka asked:

'What's your name?'

The stranger's cheeks puffed out more than ever; he pressed his back against the rock, opened his eyes wide, moved his lips, and answered in a husky bass: 'Tit!'

The boys said not another word to each other; after a brief silence, still keeping his eyes fixed on Yegorushka, the mysterious Tit kicked up one leg, felt with his heel for a niche and clambered up the rock; from that point he ascended to the next rock, staggering backwards and looking intently at Yegorushka, as though afraid he might hit him from behind, and so made his way upwards till he disappeared altogether behind the crest of the hill.

Watching him till he was out of sight, Yegorushka put his arms round his knees and leaned his head on them . . . The burning sun scorched the back of his head, his neck, and his spine. The melancholy song died away, then floated again on the stagnant stifling air. The rivulet gurgled monotonously, the horses munched, and time dragged on endlessly, as though it, too, were stagnant and had come to a standstill. It seemed as though a hundred years had passed since the morning . . . Could it be that God's world, the chaise and the horses would come to a standstill in that air, and, like the hills, turn to stone and remain for ever in one spot?

Yegorushka raised his head, and with drowsy eyes looked in front; the violet distance, which till then had been motionless, began heaving, and with the sky floated away into the distance . . . It drew after it the brown grass, the sedge, and with extraordinary swiftness Yegorushka floated after the flying distance. Some force noiselessly drew him onwards, and the heat and the wearisome song flew after in pursuit. Yegorushka bent his head and shut his eyes . . .

Deniska was the first to wake up. Something must have bitten him, for he jumped up, quickly scratched his shoulder and said:

'Plague take you, you damned idolater!'

Then he went to the brook, had a drink and slowly washed. His splashing and puffing roused Yegorushka from his lethargy. The boy looked at his wet face with drops of water and big freckles which made it look like marble, and asked:

'Shall we soon be going?'

Deniska looked at the height of the sun and answered:

'I expect so.'

He dried himself with the tail of his shirt and, making a very serious face, hopped on one leg.

'I say, which of us will get to the sedge first?' he said.

Yegorushka was exhausted by the heat and drowsiness, but he raced off after him all the same. Deniska was in his twentieth year, was a coachman and going to be married, but he had not left off being a boy. He was very fond of flying kites, chasing pigeons, playing knuckle-bones, running races, and always took part in children's games and disputes. No sooner had his master turned his back or gone to sleep than Deniska would begin doing something such as hopping on one leg or throwing stones. It was hard for any grown-up person, seeing the genuine enthusiasm with which he frolicked about in the society of children, to resist saying, 'What a baby!' Children, on the other hand, saw nothing strange in the invasion of their domain by the big coachman. 'Let him play,' they thought, 'as long as he doesn't hit us!' In the same way little dogs see nothing strange in it when a simple-hearted big dog joins their company uninvited and begins playing with them.

Deniska outstripped Yegorushka, and was evidently very much pleased at having done so. He winked at him, and to show that he could hop on one leg any distance, suggested to Yegorushka that he should hop with him along the road and from there, without resting, back to the chaise. Yegorushka declined this suggestion, for he was very much out of breath and exhausted.

All at once Deniska looked very grave, as he did not look even when Kuzmichov gave him a scolding or threatened him with a stick; listening intently, he dropped quietly on one knee and an expression of sternness and alarm came into his face, such as one sees in people who hear heretical talk. He fixed his eyes on one spot, raised his hand curved into a hollow, and suddenly fell on his stomach on to the ground and slapped the hollow of his hand down upon the grass.

'Caught!' he wheezed triumphantly, and, getting up, lifted a big grasshopper to Yegorushka's eyes.

The two boys stroked the grasshopper's broad green back with their fingers and touched his antennae, supposing that this would please the creature. Then Deniska caught a fat fly that had been sucking blood and offered it to the grasshopper. The latter moved his huge jaws, that were like the visor of a helmet, with the utmost unconcern, as though he had been long acquainted with Deniska, and bit off the fly's stomach. They let him go. With a flash of the pink lining of the wings, he flew down into the grass and at once began his churring notes again. They let the fly go, too. It preened its wings, and without its stomach flew off to the horses.

A loud sigh was heard from under the chaise. It was Kuzmichov waking up. He quickly raised his head, looked uneasily into the distance, and from that look, which passed over Yegorushka and Deniska without concern, it could be seen that his thought on awaking was of the wool and of Varlamov.

'Father Khristofor, get up; it is time to start,' he said anxiously. 'Wake up; we've slept too long as it is! Deniska, harness the horses.'

Father Khristofor woke up with the same smile with which he had fallen asleep; his face looked creased and wrinkled from sleep, and seemed only half the size. After washing and dressing, he proceeded without haste to take out of his pocket a little greasy psalter; and standing with his face towards the east, began in a whisper repeating the psalms of the day and crossing himself.

'Father Khristofor,' said Kuzmichov reproachfully, 'it's time to start; the horses are ready, and here are you . . . upon my word.'

'In a minute, in a minute,' muttered Father Khristofor. 'I must read the psalms . . . I haven't read them today.'

'The psalms can wait.'

'Ivan, that is my rule every day . . . I can't . . .'

'God wouldn't mind.'

For a full quarter of an hour Father Khristofor stood facing the east and moving his lips, while Kuzmichov looked at him almost with hatred and impatiently shrugged his shoulders. He was particularly irritated when, after every 'Hallelujah', Father Khristofor drew a long breath, rapidly crossing himself and repeated three times, intentionally raising his voice so that the others might cross themselves, 'Hallelujah, hallelujah, hallelujah! Glory be to Thee, O Lord!' At last he smiled, looked upwards at the sky, and, putting the psalter in his pocket, said:

'*Fini!*'

A minute later the chaise had started on the road. As though it were going backwards and not forwards, the travellers saw the same scene as they had before midday.

The low hills were still plunged in the violet distance, and no end could be seen to them. There were glimpses of high grass and heaps of stones; strips of stubble land passed by them and still the same rooks, the same black kite, moving its wings with slow dignity, moved over the steppe. The air was more sultry than ever; from the sultry heat and the stillness submissive nature was spellbound into silence . . . No wind, no fresh cheering sound, not a cloud.

But at last, when the sun was beginning to sink into the west, the steppe, the hills and the air could bear the oppression no longer, and, all patience gone, exhausted, tried to fling off the yoke. A fleecy ashen-grey cloud unexpectedly appeared behind the hills. It exchanged glances with the steppe, as though to say, 'Here I am', and frowned. Suddenly something burst in the stagnant air; there was a violent squall of wind which whirled round and round, roaring and whistling over the steppe. At once a murmur rose from the grass and last year's dry herbage, the dust curled in spiral eddies over the road, raced over the steppe, and carrying with it straws, dragonflies and feathers, rose up in a whirling black column towards the sky and darkened the sun. The tumbleweed ran stumbling and leaping in all directions over the steppe, and one plant got caught in the whirlwind, turned round and round like a bird, flew towards the sky, and turning into a little black speck, vanished from sight. After it flew another, and then a third, and Yegorushka saw two of them meet in the blue height and clutch at one another as though they were wrestling.

A bustard flew up by the very road. Fluttering his wings and his tail, he looked, bathed in the sunshine, like an angler's glittering tin fish or a pond butterfly flashing so swiftly over the water that its wings cannot be told from its antennae, which seem to be growing before, behind and on its sides . . . Quivering in the air like an insect with a shimmer of bright colours, the bustard flew high up in a straight line, then, probably frightened by a cloud of dust, swerved to one side, and for a long time the gleam of his wings could be seen . . .

Then a corncrake flew up from the grass, alarmed by the hurricane and not knowing what was the matter. It flew with the wind and not against it, like all the other birds, so that all its feathers were ruffled up and it was puffed out to the size of a hen and looked very angry and impressive. Only the rooks who had grown old on the steppe and were accustomed to its vagaries hovered calmly over the grass, or taking no notice of anything, went on unconcernedly pecking with their stout beaks at the hard earth.

There was a dull roll of thunder beyond the hills; there came a whiff of fresh air. Deniska gave a cheerful whistle and lashed his horses. Father Khristofor and Kuzmichov held their hats and looked

intently towards the hills . . . How pleasant a shower of rain would
have been!

One effort, one more push, and it seemed the steppe would have
got the upper hand. But the unseen oppressive force gradually riveted
its fetters on the wind and the air, laid the dust, and the stillness came
back again as though nothing had happened, the cloud hid, the sun-
baked hills frowned, the air grew submissive and calm, and only
somewhere the troubled lapwings wailed and lamented their
destiny . . .

Soon after that the evening came on.

III

In the dusk of evening a big house of one storey, with a rusty iron roof
and with dark windows, came into sight. This house was called a
posting-inn, though it had nothing like a stable yard, and it stood in
the middle of the steppe, with no kind of enclosure round it. A little to
one side of it a wretched little cherry orchard shut in by a hurdle fence
made a dark patch, and under the windows stood sleepy sunflowers
drooping their heavy heads. From the orchard came the clatter of a
little toy windmill, set there to frighten away hares by its rattle.
Nothing more could be seen near the house, and nothing could be
heard but the steppe. The chaise had scarcely stopped at the porch
with an awning over it, when from the house there came the sound of
cheerful voices, one a man's, another a woman's; there was the creak
of a swing-door, and in a flash a tall gaunt figure, swinging its arms
and coat-tails, was standing by the chaise. This was the innkeeper,
Moisei, a man no longer young, with a very pale face and a handsome
beard as black as charcoal. He was wearing a threadbare black coat,
which hung flapping on his narrow shoulders as though on a hat
stand, and fluttered its skirts like wings every time Moisei flung up his
hands in delight or horror. Besides his coat the innkeeper was
wearing full white trousers, not tucked into his boots, and a velvet
waistcoat with brown flowers on it that looked like gigantic bedbugs.

Moisei was at first dumbfounded by a surge of feelings on
recognising the travellers, then he clasped his hands and uttered a
moan. His coat-tails swung, his back bent double, and his pale face
twisted into a smile that suggested that to see the chaise was not
merely a pleasure but agonisingly sweet to him.

'Oh my God! my God!' he began in a thin sing-song voice,
breathless, fussing about and preventing the travellers from getting
out of the chaise by his antics. 'What a happy day for me! Oh, what
am I to do now? Mr Kuzmichov! Father Khristofor! What a

handsome little gentleman sitting on the box. God strike me dead! Oh, my goodness! Why am I standing here instead of asking the visitors indoors? Please walk in, I humbly beg you . . . Welcome to my house! Give me all your things . . . Oh, my goodness me!'

Moisei, who was rummaging in the chaise and assisting the travellers to alight, suddenly turned back and shouted in a voice as frantic and choking as though he were drowning and calling for help:

'Solomon! Solomon!'

'Solomon! Solomon!' a woman's voice repeated indoors.

The swing-door creaked, and in the doorway appeared a rather short young Jew with a big beak-like nose, with a bald patch surrounded by rough curly hair; he was dressed in a short and very shabby jacket, with rounded flaps and short sleeves, and in short woollen trousers, so that he looked skimpy and short-tailed like an unfledged bird. This was Solomon, the brother of Moisei. He went up to the chaise, smiling rather oddly, and did not speak or greet the travellers.

'Mr Kuzmichov and Father Khristofor have come,' said Moisei in a tone as though he were afraid his brother would not believe him. 'Dear, dear! What a surprise! Such honoured guests to have come to us so suddenly! Come, take their things, Solomon. Walk in, honoured guests.'

A little later Kuzmichov, Father Khristofor, and Yegorushka were sitting in a big gloomy empty room at an old oak table. The table was almost in solitude, for, except for a wide sofa covered with torn oil-cloth and three chairs, there was no other furniture in the room. And, indeed, not everybody would have given the chairs that name. They were a pitiful semblance of furniture, covered with oil-cloth that had seen better days, and with backs bent backwards at an unnaturally acute angle, so that they looked like children's sledges. It was hard to imagine what had been the unknown carpenter's object in bending the chair-backs so mercilessly, and one was tempted to imagine that it was not the carpenter's fault, but that some athletic visitor had bent the chairs like this as a feat, then had tried to bend them back again and had made them worse. The room looked gloomy, the walls were grey, the ceiling and the cornices were grimy; on the floor were chinks and yawning holes that were hard to account for (one might have fancied they were made by the heel of the same athlete), and it seemed as though the room would still have been dark if a dozen lamps had hung in it. There was nothing approaching an ornament on the walls or the windows. On one wall, however, there hung a list of regulations of some sort under a two-headed eagle in a grey wooden frame, and on another wall in the same sort of frame an engraving with the inscription, 'The Indifference of Man'. What it was to which men were indifferent it was impossible to make out, as the engraving was very dingy with age and was extensively flyblown. There was a smell of something decayed and sour in the room.

After showing the visitors into the room, Moisei went on wriggling, gesticulating, shrugging and uttering joyful exclamations; he considered these antics necessary in order to seem polite and agreeable.

'When did our wagons go by?' Kuzmichov asked.

'One party went by early this morning, and the other, Mr Kuzmichov, put up here for the midday meal and moved on towards evening.'

'Ah! . . . Has Varlamov been by or not?'

'No, Mr Kuzmichov. His clerk, Grigori, went by yesterday morning and said that he had to be today at the Molokans'* farm.'

'Good! so we will follow the wagons directly and then on to the Molokans'.'

'Mercy on us, Mr Kuzmichov!' Moisei cried in horror, flinging up his hands. 'Where are you going for the night? You will have a nice little supper and stay the night, and tomorrow morning, please God, you can go on and catch up anyone you like.'

'There is no time for that . . . Excuse me, Moisei, another time; but now I must make haste. We'll stay a quarter of an hour and then go on; we can stay the night at the Molokans'.'

'A quarter of an hour!' squealed Moisei. 'Have you no fear of God, Mr Kuzmichov? You will force me to hide your caps and lock the door! You must have a cup of tea and a snack of something, anyway.'

'We have no time for tea,' said Kuzmichov.

Moisei bent his head to one side, crooked his knees, and put his open hands before him as though warding off a blow, while with a smile of agonised sweetness he began imploring:

'Mr Kuzmichov! Father Khristofor! Do be so good as to take a cup of tea with me. Surely I am not such a bad man that you can't even drink tea in my house? Mr Kuzmichov!'

'Well, we may just as well have a cup of tea,' said Father Khristofor, with a sympathetic smile, 'that won't keep us long.'

'Very well,' Kuzmichov assented.

Moisei, in a fluster, uttered an exclamation of joy, and shrugging as though he had just stepped out of cold water into warm, ran to the door and cried in the same frantic voice in which he had called Solomon:

'Rosa! Rosa! Bring the samovar!'

A minute later the door opened, and Solomon came into the room carrying a large tray in his hands. Setting the tray on the table, he looked away sarcastically with the same queer smile as before. Now, by the light of the lamp, it was possible to see his smile distinctly; it was very complex, and expressed a variety of emotions, but the predominant element in it was undisguised contempt. He seemed to be thinking of something ludicrous and silly, to be feeling contempt and dislike, to be pleased at something and waiting for the favourable moment to utter a wounding sarcasm and to burst into laughter. His long nose, his thick lips, and his sly prominent eyes seemed tense with the desire to laugh. Looking at his face, Kuzmichov smiled ironically and asked:

'Solomon, why did you not come to our fair at N— this summer, and act some Jewish scenes?'

Two years before, as Yegorushka remembered so well, at one of the booths at the fair of N—, Solomon had performed some scenes of Jewish life, and his acting had been a great success. The allusion to this made no impression whatever upon Solomon. Making no answer, he went out and returned a little later with the samovar.

When he had done what he had to do at the table he moved a little aside, and, folding his arms over his chest and thrusting out one leg, fixed his sarcastic eyes on Father Khristofor. There was something defiant, haughty, and contemptuous in his attitude, and at the same time it was comic and pitiful in the extreme, because the more impressive his attitude the more vividly it showed up his short trousers, his bobtail coat, his caricature of a nose, and his bird-like plucked-looking little figure.

Moisei brought a footstool from the outer room and sat down a little way from the table.

'I wish you a good appetite! Tea and sugar!' he began, trying to entertain his visitors. 'I hope you will enjoy it. Such rare guests, such rare ones; it is years since I last saw Father Khristofor. And will no one tell me who is this nice little gentleman?' he asked, looking tenderly at Yegorushka.

'He is the son of my sister, Olga,' answered Kuzmichov.

'And where is he going?'

'To school. We are taking him to a high school.'

In his politeness, Moisei put on a look of wonder and wagged his head expressively.

'Ah, that is a fine thing,' he said, shaking his finger at the samovar. 'That's a fine thing. You will come back from the high school such a gentleman that we shall all take off our hats to you. You will be wealthy and wise and so grand that your mamma will be delighted. Oh, that's a fine thing!'

He paused a little, stroked his knees, and began again in a jocose and deferential tone.

'You must excuse me, Father Khristofor, but I am thinking of writing to the bishop to tell him you are robbing the merchants of their living. I shall take a sheet of stamped paper and write that I suppose Father Khristofor is hard up, as he has taken up trade and begun selling wool.'

'H'm, yes . . . it's an odd notion in my old age,' said Father Khristofor, and he laughed. 'I have turned from priest to merchant, brother. I ought to be at home now saying my prayers, instead of galloping about the country like a pharaoh in his chariot . . . Vanity!'

'But it will mean a lot of money.'

'Oh, I dare say! More kicks than kopecks, and serve me right. The wool's not mine, but my son-in-law's, Mikhailo's!'

'Why doesn't he go himself?'

'Why, because . . . His mother's milk is scarcely dry upon his lips. He can buy wool all right, but when it comes to selling, he has no sense; he is young yet. He has wasted all his money; he wanted to grow rich and cut a dash, but he tried here and there, and no one would give him his price. And so the lad went on like that for a year, and then he came to me and said: "Papa, you sell the wool for me; be kind and do it! I am no good at the business!" And that is true enough. As soon as there is anything wrong then it's "Papa", but till then they could get on without their dad. When he was buying he did not consult me, but now when he is in difficulties it's up to papa. And what does his papa know about it? If it were not for Mr Kuzmichov, his papa could do nothing. I have a lot of worry with them.'

'Yes; one has a lot of worry with one's children, I can tell you that,' sighed Moisei. 'I have six of my own. One needs schooling, another needs doctoring, and a third needs nursing, and when they grow up they are more trouble still. It is not only nowadays, it was the same in Holy Scripture. When Jacob had little children he wept, and when they grew up he wept still more bitterly.'

'H'm, yes . . .' Father Khristofor assented pensively, looking at his glass. 'I have no cause myself to rail against the Lord. I have lived to the ends of my days as any man might be thankful to live . . . I have married my daughters to good men, my sons I have set up in life, and now I am free; I have done my work and can go where I like. I live in peace with my wife. I eat and drink and sleep and rejoice in my grandchildren, and say my prayers and want nothing more. I live on the fat of the land, and don't need to curry favour with anyone. I have never had any trouble from childhood, and now suppose the Tsar were to ask me, "What do you need? What would you like?", why, I don't need anything. I have everything I want and everything to be thankful for. In the whole town there is no happier man than I am. My only trouble is I have so many sins, but there – only God is without sin. That's right, isn't it?'

'No doubt it is.'

'I have no teeth of course; my poor old back aches; there is one thing and another . . . asthma and that sort of thing . . . I ache . . . The flesh is weak, but then think of my age! I am over seventy! One can't go on for ever; one mustn't outstay one's welcome.'

Father Khristofor suddenly thought of something, spluttered into his glass and choked with laughter. Out of politeness Moisei also laughed and cleared his throat.

'So funny!' said Father Khristofor, and he waved his hand. 'My eldest son Gavrila came to pay me a visit. He is in the medical line, and is a district doctor in the province of Chernigov . . . Very well . . . I said to him, "Here I have asthma and one thing and another . . . You are a doctor; cure your father!" He undressed me on the spot, tapped me, listened, and all sorts of tricks . . . kneaded my stomach, and then he said, "Papa, you ought to be treated with compressed air." '

Father Khristofor laughed convulsively, till the tears came into his eyes, and got up.

'And I said to him, "Heaven take your compressed air!" ' he brought out through his laughter, waving both hands. ' "Heaven take your compressed air!" '

Moisei got up, too, and with his hands on his stomach, went off into shrill laughter like the yap of a lap dog.

'Heaven take the compressed air!' repeated Father Khristofor, laughing.

Moisei laughed two notes higher, and so violently that he could hardly stand on his feet.

'My goodness!' he moaned through his laughter. 'Let me get my breath . . . You'll be the death of me.'

He laughed and talked, though at the same time he was casting timorous and suspicious looks at Solomon. The latter was standing in the same attitude, still smiling. To judge from his eyes and his smile, his contempt and hatred were genuine, but that was so out of keeping with his plucked-looking figure that it seemed to Yegorushka as though he were putting on his defiant attitude and biting sarcastic smile to play the fool for the entertainment of their honoured guests.

After drinking six glasses of tea in silence, Kuzmichov cleared a space before him on the table, took his bag, the one which he kept under his head when he slept under the chaise, untied the string and shook it. Wads of banknotes were scattered out of the bag on the table.

'While we have the time, Father Khristofor, let us reckon up,' said Kuzmichov.

Moisei was embarrassed at the sight of the money. He got up, and, as a man of delicate feeling unwilling to pry into other people's secrets, he went out of the room on tiptoe, swaying his arms. Solomon remained where he was.

'How many are there in the packets of roubles?' Father Khristofor began.

'The rouble notes are done up in fifties . . . the three-rouble notes in nineties, the twenty-five and hundred-roubles in thousands. You count out seven thousand eight hundred for Varlamov, and I will count out for Gusevich. And mind you don't make a mistake . . .'

Yegorushka had never in his life seen so much money as was lying on the table before him. There must have been a great deal of money, for the roll of seven thousand eight hundred, which Father Khristofor put aside for Varlamov, seemed very small compared with the whole pile. At any other time such a mass of money would have impressed Yegorushka, and would have moved him to reflect how many bagels, buns and poppy cakes could be bought for that money. Now he looked at it listlessly, only conscious of the disgusting smell of kerosene and rotten apples that came from the heap of notes. He was exhausted by the jolting ride in the chaise, tired out and sleepy. His head was heavy, his eyes would hardly keep open and his thoughts were tangled like threads. If it had been possible he would have been relieved to lay his head on the table, so as not to see the lamp and the fingers moving over the heaps of notes, and to have let his tired sleepy thoughts get still more tangled. When he tried to keep awake, the light of the lamp, the cups and the fingers grew double, the samovar heaved and the smell of rotten apples seemed even more acrid and disgusting.

'Ah money, money!' sighed Father Khristofor, smiling. 'You are nothing but trouble! Now I expect my Mikhailo is asleep and dreaming that I am going to bring him a heap of money like this.'

'Your Mikhailo is a man who doesn't understand business,' said Kuzmichov in an undertone; 'he undertakes what isn't his work, but you understand and can judge. You had better hand over your wool to me, as I have said already, and I would give you half a rouble above my own price – yes, I would, simply out of regard for you . . .'

'No, Ivan,' Father Khristofor sighed. 'I thank you for your kindness . . . Of course, if it were for me to decide, I shouldn't think twice about it; but as it is, the wool is not mine, as you know . . .'

Moisei came in on tiptoe. Trying from delicacy not to look at the heaps of money, he stole up to Yegorushka and pulled at his shirt from behind.

'Come along, little gentleman,' he said in an undertone, 'come and let me show you the little bear! Such a terrible cross little bear! Oo-oo!'

The sleepy boy got up and listlessly dragged himself after Moisei to see the bear. He went into a little room, where, before he saw anything, he felt he could not breathe from the smell of something sour and decaying, which was much stronger here than in the big room and probably spread from this room all over the house. One part of the room was occupied by a big bed, covered with a greasy quilt and another by a chest of drawers and heaps of rags of all kinds from a woman's stiff petticoat to children's little breeches and braces. A tallow candle stood on the chest of drawers.

Instead of the promised bear, Yegorushka saw a bit fat Jewess with her hair hanging loose, in a red flannel skirt with black dots on it; she turned with difficulty in the narrow space between the bed and chest of drawers and uttered drawn-out moaning as though she had toothache. On seeing Yegorushka, she made a doleful, woebegone face, heaved a long drawn-out sigh, and before he had time to look round, put to his lips a slice of bread smeared with honey.

'Eat it, dearie, eat it!' she said. 'You have no mama here, and no one to feed you. Eat it up.'

Yegorushka did eat it, though after the goodies and poppy cakes he had every day at home, he did not think very much of the honey, which was mixed with wax and bees' wings. He ate while Moisei and the Jewess looked at him and sighed.

'Where are you going, dearie?' asked the Jewess.

'To school,' answered Yegorushka.

'And how many brothers and sisters have you got?'

'I am the only one; there are no others.'

'O-oh!' sighed the Jewess, and turned her eyes upward. 'Poor mama, poor mama! How she will weep and miss you! We are going to send our Naum to school in a year. O-oh!'

'Ah, Naum, Naum!' sighed Moisei, and the skin of his pale face twitched nervously. 'And he is so delicate.'

The greasy quilt quivered, and from beneath it appeared a child's head on a very thin neck; two black eyes gleamed and stared with curiosity at Yegorushka. Still sighing, Moisei and the Jewess went to the chest of drawers and began talking in Yiddish. Moisei spoke in a low bass undertone, and altogether his talk in Yiddish was like a continual 'gal-gal-gal-gal . . .', while his wife answered him in a shrill voice like a turkey-cock's, and the whole effect of her talk was something like 'Too-too-too-too!' While they were consulting, another little curly head on a thin neck peeped out of the greasy quilt, then a third, then a fourth . . . If Yegorushka had had a fertile imagination he might have imagined that the hundred-headed hydra was hiding under the quilt.

'Gal-gal-gal-gal!' said Moisei.

'Too-too-too-too!' answered the Jewess.

The consultation ended in the Jewess's diving with a deep sigh into the chest of drawers, and, unwrapping some sort of green rag there, she took out a big rye cake made in the shape of a heart.

'Take it, dearie,' she said, giving Yegorushka the cake; 'you have no mama now – no one to give you nice things.'

Yegorushka stuck the cake in his pocket and backed towards the door, as he could no longer stand breathing the foul, sour air in which the innkeeper and his wife lived. Going back to the big room, he settled himself more comfortably on the sofa and gave up trying to check his straying thoughts.

As soon as Kuzmichov had finished counting out the notes he put them back into the bag. He did not treat them very respectfully and stuffed them into the dirty sack without ceremony, as indifferently as though they had not been money but waste paper.

Father Khristofor was talking to Solomon.

'Well, Solomon the Wise!' he said, yawning and making the sign of the cross over his mouth. 'How is business?'

'What sort of business are you talking about?' asked Solomon, and he looked as fiendish as though it were a hint of some crime on his part.

'Oh, things in general. What are you doing?'

'What am I doing?' Solomon repeated, and he shrugged his shoulders. 'The same as everyone else . . . You see, I am a menial, I am my brother's servant; my brother's the servant of the visitors; the visitors are Varlamov's servants; and if I had ten millions, Varlamov would be my servant.'

'Why would he be your servant?'

'Why, because there isn't a gentleman or millionaire who isn't ready to lick the hand of a scabby Jew for the sake of making a kopeck. Now, I am a scabby Jew and a beggar. Everybody looks at me as though I were a dog, but if I had money Varlamov would play the fool before me just as Moisei does before you.'

Father Khristofor and Kuzmichov looked at each other. Neither of them understood Solomon. Kuzmichov looked at him sternly and dryly, and asked:

'How can you compare yourself with Varlamov, you blockhead!'

'I am not such a fool as to put myself on a level with Varlamov,' answered Solomon, looking sarcastically at the speaker. 'Though

Varlamov is a Russian, he is at heart a scabby Jew; money and gain are all he lives for, but I threw my money in the stove! I don't want money, or land, or sheep, and there is no need for people to be afraid of me and to take off their hats when I pass. So am I wiser than your Varlamov and more like a human being!'

A little later Yegorushka, half asleep, heard Solomon in a hoarse hollow voice choked with hatred, in hurried stuttering phrases, talking about the Jews. At first he talked correctly in Russian, then he fell into the tone of a Jewish recitation, and began speaking as he had done at the travelling theatre at the fair with an exaggerated Jewish accent.

'Stop! . . .' Father Khristofor said to him. 'If you don't like your religion you had better change it, but to laugh at it is a sin; it is only the lowest of the low who will make fun of his religion.'

'You don't understand,' Solomon cut him short rudely. 'I am talking of one thing and you are talking of something else . . .'

'One can see you are a foolish fellow,' sighed Father Khristofor. 'I admonish you to the best of my ability, and you are angry. I speak to you like an old man quietly, and you answer like a turkey-cock: "Bla-bla-bla!" You really are a queer fellow . . .'

Moisei came in. He looked anxiously at Solomon and at his visitors, and again the skin on his face quivered nervously. Yegorushka shook his head and looked about him; he caught a passing glimpse of Solomon's face at the very moment when it was turned three-quarters towards him and when the shadow of his long nose intersected all of his left cheek; the contemptuous smile mingled with that shadow; the gleaming sarcastic eyes, the haughty expression, and the whole plucked-looking little figure, dancing and doubling itself before Yegorushka's eyes, made him now not like a buffoon, but like something one sometimes dreams of, like an evil spirit.

'What a ferocious fellow you've got here, Moisei! God bless him!' said Father Khristofor with a smile. 'You ought to find him a place or a wife or something . . . There's no knowing what to make of him . . .'

Kuzmichov frowned angrily. Moisei looked uneasily and inquiringly at his brother and the visitors again.

'Solomon, get out of here,' he said harshly. 'Get out!' and he added something in Yiddish. Solomon gave an abrupt laugh and went out.

'What was it?' Moisei asked Father Khristofor anxiously.

'He forgets himself,' answered Kuzmichov. 'He's rude and thinks too much of himself.'

'I knew it!' Moisei cried in horror, clasping his hands. 'Oh my God, oh my God!' he muttered in a low voice. 'Be so kind as to excuse it, and don't be angry. He is such a queer fellow, such a queer fellow! Oh dear, oh dear! He is my own brother, but I have never had anything but trouble from him. You know he's . . .'

Moisei twisted his finger against his forehead and went on:

'He is not in his right mind; he's doomed. And I don't know what I am to do with him! He cares for nobody, he respects nobody, and is afraid of nobody . . . You know he laughs at everybody, he says silly things, speaks familiarly to anyone. You wouldn't believe it, Varlamov came here one day and Solomon said such things to him that he gave us both a taste of his whip . . . But why whip me? Was it my fault? God has robbed him of his wits, so it is God's will, and how am I to blame?'

About ten minutes passed; Moisei was still muttering in an undertone and sighing:

'He does not sleep at night, and is always thinking and thinking and thinking, and what he is thinking about God only knows. If you go to him at night he is angry and laughs. He doesn't like me either . . . And there is nothing he wants! When our father died he left us each six thousand roubles. I bought myself an inn, married, and now I have children; and he burnt all his money in the stove. Such a pity, such a pity! Why burn it? If he didn't want it he could give it to me, but why burn it?'

Suddenly the swing-door creaked open and the floor shook under footsteps. Yegorushka felt a draught of cold air, and it seemed to him as though some big black bird had passed by him and had flapped its wings right by his face. He opened his eyes . . . His uncle was standing by the sofa with his sack in his hands ready for departure; Father Khristofor, holding his broad-brimmed top hat, was bowing to someone and smiling – not his usual soft, kindly smile, but a respectful forced smile which did not suit his face at all – while Moisei looked as though his body had been broken in three parts, and he were balancing and doing his utmost not to drop to pieces. Only Solomon stood in the corner with his arms folded, as though nothing had happened, and smiled contemptuously as before.

'Your Excellency must excuse us for not being tidy,' moaned Moisei with the agonising sweet smile, taking no more notice of Kuzmichov or Father Khristofor, but swaying his whole person so as to avoid dropping to pieces. 'We are plain folks, your Excellency.'

Yegorushka rubbed his eyes. In the middle of the room there really was standing an Excellency, in the form of a young plump and very beautiful woman in a black dress and a straw hat. Before Yegorushka had time to examine her features the image of the solitary graceful poplar he had seen that day on the hills for some reason came into his mind.

'Has Varlamov been here today?' a woman's voice inquired.

'No, your Ladyship,' said Moisei.

'If you see him tomorrow, ask him to come and see me for a minute.'

All at once, quite unexpectedly, Yegorushka saw half an inch from his eyes velvety black eyebrows, big brown eyes, delicate feminine cheeks with dimples, from which smiles seemed to radiate all over the face like sunbeams. There was a glorious scent.

'What a pretty boy!' said the lady. 'Whose boy is it? Kazimir, look what a charming fellow! Good heavens, he is asleep! My chubby little pet.'

And the lady kissed Yegorushka warmly on both cheeks, and he smiled and, thinking he was asleep, shut his eyes. The swing-door squeaked, and there was the sound of hurried footsteps, coming in and going out.

'Yegorushka, Yegorushka!' he heard two bass voices whisper. 'Get up; it is time to start.'

Somebody, it seemed to be Deniska, set him on his feet and led him by the arm. On the way he half-opened his eyes and once more saw the beautiful lady in the black dress who had kissed him. She was standing in the middle of the room and watched him go out, smiling at him and nodding her head in a friendly way. As he got near the door he saw a handsome, stoutly built, dark man in a bowler hat and in leather gaiters. This must have been the lady's escort.

'Whoa!' he heard from the yard.

At the front door Yegorushka saw a splendid new carriage and a pair of black horses. On the box sat a groom in livery, with a long whip in his hands. No one but Solomon came to see the travellers off. His face was tense with a desire to laugh; he looked as though he were waiting impatiently for the visitors to be gone, so that he might laugh at them without restraint.

'The Countess Dranitskaia,' whispered Father Khristofor, clambering into the chaise.

'Yes, Countess Dranitskaia,' repeated Kuzmichov, also in whisper.

The impression made by the arrival of the countess must have been very great, for even Deniska spoke in a whisper, and only ventured to lash his bays and shout when the chaise had driven a few hundred yards away and nothing could be seen of the inn but a dim light.

IV

Who, then, was this elusive, mysterious Varlamov of whom people talked so much, whom Solomon despised, and whom even the beautiful countess needed? Sitting on the box beside Deniska, Yegorushka, half asleep, thought about this person. He had never seen him. But he had often heard of him and pictured him in his imagination. He knew that Varlamov possessed several tens of thousands of acres of land, about a hundred thousand sheep, and a great deal of money. Of his manner of life and occupation Yegorushka knew nothing, except that he was always 'doing his rounds in these parts', and he was always being looked for.

At home Yegorushka had heard a great deal of the Countess Dranitskaia, too. She, too, had some tens of thousands of acres, a great many sheep, a stud farm and a great deal of money, but she did not 'do rounds', but lived at home in a splendid house and grounds, about which Ivan, who had been more than once at the countess's on business, and other acquaintances told many marvellous tales; thus, for instance, they said that in the countess's drawing-room, where the portraits of all the kings of Poland hung on the walls, there was a big table-clock in the form of a rock, on the rock a gold horse with diamond eyes, rearing, and on the horse the figure of a rider also of gold, who brandished his sword to right and to left whenever the clock struck. They said, too, that twice a year the countess used to give a ball, to which the gentry and officials of the whole province were invited, and to which even Varlamov used to come; all the visitors drank tea from silver samovars, ate all sorts of extraordinary things (they had strawberries and raspberries, for instance, in winter at Christmas), and danced to a band which played day and night . . .

'And how beautiful she is,' thought Yegorushka, remembering her face.

Kuzmichov, too, was probably thinking about the countess. For when the chaise had driven a mile and a half he said:

'But doesn't that Kazimir plunder her right and left! The year before last when, do you remember, I bought some wool from her, he made over three thousand from my purchase alone.'

'That is what you would expect from a Polack,' said Father Khristofor.

'And little does it trouble her. Young and foolish, as they say, her head full of nonsense.'

Yegorushka, for some reason, longed to think of nothing but Varlamov and the countess, particularly the latter. His drowsy brain utterly refused ordinary thoughts, was in a cloud and retained only fantastic fairy-tale images, which have the advantage of springing into the brain of themselves without any effort on the part of the thinker, and completely vanishing of themselves at a mere shake of the head; and, indeed, nothing that was around him disposed to ordinary thoughts. On the right were the dark hills which seemed to be screening something unseen and terrible; on the left the whole sky about the horizon was covered with a crimson glow, and it was hard to tell whether there was a fire somewhere, or whether it was the moon about to rise. As by day the distance could be seen, but its tender violet tint had gone, quenched by the evening darkness, in which the whole steppe was hidden like Moisei's children under the quilt.

Corncrakes and quails do not call at night in July, the nightingale does not sing in the woodland river beds, and there is no scent of flowers, but still the steppe is lovely and full of life. As soon as the sun goes down and the darkness enfolds the earth, the day's weariness is forgotten, everything is forgiven, and the steppe breathes a light sigh from its broad bosom. The grass, it seems, cannot see in the dark that it has grown old: a gay youthful twitter rises up from it, such as is not heard by day; chirruping, twittering, whistling, scratching, the basses, tenors and sopranos of the steppe – everything mingles in an incessant, monotonous roar of sound in which it is sweet to brood on memories and sorrows. The monotonous twitter soothes to sleep like a lullaby; you drive and feel you are falling asleep, but suddenly there comes the abrupt agitated cry of a wakeful bird, or a vague sound like a voice crying out in wonder 'A-aah, a-ah!' and slumber closes one's eyelids again. Or you drive by a little river bed where there are bushes and hear the bird, called by the steppe dwellers 'the sleeper', call 'Asleep, asleep, asleep!', while another laughs or breaks into trills of hysterical weeping – that is the tawny owl. For whom do they call and who hears them on that plain? God only knows, but there is deep sadness and lamentation in their cry . . . There is a scent of hay and dry grass and belated flowers, but the scent is heavy, cloyingly sweet and soft.

Everything can be seen through the mist, but it is hard to make out the colours and the outlines of objects. Everything looks different from what it is. You drive on and suddenly see standing before you right in the roadway a dark figure like a monk; it stands motionless, waiting, holding something in its hands . . . Can it be a robber? The figure comes closer, grows bigger; now it is on a level with the chaise, and you see it is not a man, but a solitary bush or a great stone. Such motionless expectant figures stand on the low hills, hide behind the old barrows, peep out from the high grass, and they all look like human beings and evoke suspicion.

And when the moon rises the night becomes pale and dim. The mist seems to have passed away. The air is transparent, fresh and warm; one can see well in all directions and even distinguish the separate stalks of grass by the wayside. Stones and bits of pots can be seen at a long distance. The suspicious figures like monks look blacker against the light background of the night, and seem more sinister. More and more often in the midst of the monotonous chirruping there comes the sound of the 'A-ah, a-aah!' of astonishment troubling the motionless air, and the cry of a sleepless or delirious bird. Broad shadows move across the plain like clouds across the sky, and in the inconceivable distance, if you look long and intently at it, misty monstrous shapes rise up and huddle one against another . . . It is rather uncanny. You glance at the pale green, star-spangled sky on which there is not a cloud nor a spot, and you understand why the warm air is motionless, why nature is on her guard, afraid to stir: she is afraid and reluctant to lose one instant of life. Of the unfathomable depth and infinity of the sky one can only form a conception either at sea or on the steppe by night, when the moon is shining. The sky is terribly lonely and caressing; it looks down languid and alluring, and its caress makes one giddy.

You drive on for one hour, for another . . . You meet upon the way a silent old barrow or a stone figure put up God knows when and by whom; a night bird floats noiselessly over the earth, and little by little those legends of the steppes, the tales of men you have met, the stories of some old nurse from the steppe, and all the things you have managed to see and treasure in your soul, come back to your mind. And then in the churring of insects, in the sinister figures, in the ancient barrows, in the blue sky, in the moonlight, in the flight of the night bird, in everything you see and hear, triumphant beauty, youth, the fullness of power, and the passionate thirst for life begin to be apparent; the soul responds to the call of her lovely austere fatherland, and longs to fly over the steppes with the night bird. And in the triumph of beauty, in the exuberance of happiness you are conscious of tension and yearning, as though the steppe knew she was solitary, knew that her wealth and her inspiration were wasted for the world, unsung, unwanted; and through the joyful clamour one hears her mournful, hopeless call for singers, singers!

'Whoa! Good evening! Pantelei! Is everything all right?'

'First rate, Mr Kuzmichov!'

'Haven't you seen, Varlamov, lads?'

'No, we haven't.'

Yegorushka woke up and opened his eyes. The chaise had stopped. On the right the train of wagons stretched for a long way ahead on the road, and men were moving to and fro near them. All the wagons being loaded up with great bales of wool looked very high and fat, while the horses looked short-legged and tiny.

'Well, then, we shall go on to the Molokans'.' Kuzmichov said aloud. 'The Jew told us that Varlamov was putting up for the night at the Molokans'. So good-bye, lads! Good luck to you!'

'Good-bye, Mr Kuzmichov,' several voices replied.

'I say, lads,' Kuzmichov cried briskly, 'you take my little lad along with you! Why should he go jolting off with us for nothing? You put him on the bales, Pantelei, and let him come on slowly, and we shall catch you up. Get down, Yegorushka! Go on; it's all right . . .'

Yegorushka got down from the box-seat. Several hands caught him, lifted him high into the air, and he found himself on something big, soft, and rather wet with dew. It seemed to him now as though the sky were quite close and the earth far away.

'Hey, take this thing, it's his coat!' Deniska shouted from somewhere far below.

His coat and bundle, flung from far below, fell close to Yegorushka. Anxious not to think of anything, he quickly put his bundle under his head and covered himself with his coat, and stretching his legs out and shrinking a little from the dew, he laughed with content.

'Sleep, sleep, sleep . . .' he thought.

'Don't be unkind to him, you devils!' he heard Deniska's voice below.

'Good-bye lads; good luck to you,' shouted Kuzmichov. 'I'm relying on you!'

'Don't you worry, Mr Kuzmichov!'

Deniska shouted to the horses, the chaise creaked and started, not along the road, but somewhere off to the side. For two minutes there was silence, as if the wagons were asleep and there was no sound except the clanking of the pails tied on at the back of the chaise as it slowly died away in the distance. Then someone at the lead of the wagons shouted:

'Kiriukha! Sta-art!'

The foremost of the wagons creaked, then the second, then the third . . . Yegorushka felt the wagon he was on sway and creak also. The wagons were moving. Yegorushka took a tighter hold of the cord with which the bales were tied on, laughed again with content, shifted the cake in his pocket, and fell asleep just as he did in his bed at home . . .

When he woke up the sun was already rising; it was screened by an ancient barrow, and, trying to shed its light upon the earth, it scattered its beams in all directions and flooded the horizon with gold. It seemed to Yegorushka that it was not in its proper place, as the day before it had risen behind his back, and now it was much more to his left . . . And the whole landscape was different. There were no hills now, but on all sides, wherever one looked, there stretched the brown cheerless plain; here and there upon it small barrows rose up and rooks flew as they had done the day before. The belfries and huts of some village showed white in the distance ahead; as it was Sunday the Ukrainians were at home baking and cooking – that could be seen by the smoke which rose from every chimney and hung, a dark blue transparent veil, over the village. In between the huts and beyond the church there were blue glimpses of a river, and beyond the river a misty distance. But nothing was so different from yesterday as the road. Something extraordinarily broad, spread out and titanic, stretched over the steppe by way of a road. It was a grey streak, well trodden-down and covered with dust, like all roads. Its width puzzled Yegorushka and brought thoughts of fairy tales to his mind. Who travelled along that road? Who needed so much space? It was strange and unintelligible. It might have been supposed that giants with immense strides, such as Ilia Muromets and Nightingale-Robber, were still surviving in Russia, and that their gigantic steeds were still alive. Yegorushka, looking at the road, imagined some half a dozen high chariots racing along side by side, like some he used to see in pictures in his Scripture history; these chariots were each drawn by six wild furious horses, and their great wheels raised a cloud of dust to the sky, while the horses were driven by men such as might arise in dreams or in fabulous thoughts. And if those figures had existed, how perfectly in keeping with the steppe and the road they would have been!

Telegraph poles carrying two wires stretched along the right side of the road to its furthermost limit. Growing smaller and smaller, they disappeared near the village behind the huts and green trees, and then again came into sight in the violet distance in the form of very small thin sticks that looked like pencils stuck into the ground. Hawks, falcons, and crows sat on the wires and looked indifferently at the moving wagon train. Yegorushka was lying in the last of the wagons, and so could see the whole string. There were about twenty wagons, and there was a driver to every three wagons. By the last wagon, the one in which Yegorushka was, there walked an old man with a grey beard, as short and lean as Father Khristofor, but with a sunburnt, stern and brooding face. It is very possible that the old man was not stern and not brooding, but his red eyelids and his sharp long nose gave his face a stern frigid expression such as is common with people in the habit of continually thinking of serious things in solitude. Like Father Khristofor he was wearing a wide-brimmed top hat, not like a gentlemen's, but made of brown felt, and in shape more like a cone with the top cut off than a real top hat. He was barefoot. Probably more a habit acquired in cold winters, when he must more than once have been nearly frozen as he trudged beside the wagons, he kept slapping his thighs and stamping his feet as he walked. Noticing that Yegorushka was awake, he looked at him and said, huddled as though from the cold:

'Ah, you are awake, youngster! So you are the son of Mr Kuzmichov?'

'No; his nephew . . .'

'Nephew of Mr Kuzmichov? Here I have taken off my boots and am hopping along barefoot. My feet are bad; they are swollen, and it's easier without boots . . . easier, youngster . . . without boots, I mean . . . So you are his nephew? He is a good man; no harm in him . . . God give him health . . . No harm in him . . . I mean Mr Kuzmichov . . . He has gone to the Molokans' . . . O Lord, have mercy upon us!'

The old man talked, too, as though it were very cold, pausing and not opening his mouth properly; and he mispronounced his labial consonants, stuttering over them as though his lips were frozen. As he talked to Yegorushka he did not once smile, and he seemed stern.

Two wagons ahead of them there walked a man wearing a long reddish-brown coat, a cap and high boots with sagging bootlegs, and carrying a whip in his hand. This was not an old man, only about forty. When he looked round Yegorushka saw a long red face with a scanty goatee and a spongy looking swelling under his right eye. Apart from this very ugly swelling, there was another peculiar thing about him which caught the eye at once: in his left hand he carried a whip, while he waved the right as though he were conducting an unseen choir; from time to time he put the whip under his arm, and then he conducted with both hands and hummed something to himself.

The next driver was a long rectangular figure with extremely sloping shoulders and a back as flat as a board. He held himself as stiffly erect as though he were marching or had swallowed a yardstick. His hands did not swing as he walked, but hung down as if they were straight sticks, and he strode along in a wooden way, after the manner of toy soldiers, almost without bending his knees, and trying to take as long steps as possible. While the old man or the owner of the spongy swelling were taking two steps he managed just one, and so it seemed as though he were walking more slowly than any of them, and would drop behind. His face was tied up in a rag, and on his head something stuck up that looked like a monk's skullcap; he was dressed in a short Ukrainian coat, with dark blue oriental trousers and bast shoes.

Yegorushka could not even make out the men who were further on. He lay on his stomach, picked a little hole in the bale, and, having nothing better to do, began twisting the wool into a thread. The old man trudging along below him turned out not to be so stern as one might have supposed from his face. Having begun a conversation, he did not let it drop.

'Where are you going?' he asked, stamping with his feet.

'To school,' answered Yegorushka.

'To school? Aha! . . . Well, may the Queen of Heaven help you. Yes. One brain is good, but two are better. To one man God gives one brain, to another two brains, and to another three . . . To another three, that is true . . . One brain you are born with, one you get from learning, and a third with a good life. So you see, my lad, it is a good thing if a man has three brains. Living is easier for him, and, what's more, dying is, too. Dying is, too . . . And we shall all die for sure.'

The old man scratched his forehead, glanced upwards at Yegorushka with his red eyes, and went on:

'Maxim Nikolaich, the gentleman from near Slavianoserbsk, brought his little lad to school, too, last year. I don't know how he is getting on there in studying the sciences, but he was a nice little lad . . . God give them health, they are fine gentlemen. Yes, he, too, brought his boy to school . . . In Slavianoserbsk there is no establishment, I suppose, for study. No . . . But it is a nice town . . . There's an ordinary school for simple folks, but for the higher studies there is nothing. No, that's true. What's your name? . . .'

'Yegorushka.'

'Yegori, then . . . The holy martyr Yegori, the Bearer of Victory, whose day is the twenty-third of April. And my Christian name is Pantelei . . . Pantelei Zakharov Kholodov . . . We are Kholodovs . . . I am a native of – maybe you've heard of it – Tim in the province of Kursk. My brothers are artisans and work at trades in the town, but I am a peasant . . . I have remained a peasant. Seven years ago I went there – home, I mean. I went to the village and to the town . . . To Tim, I mean. Then, thank God, they were all alive and well, but now I don't know . . . Maybe some of them are dead . . . And it's time they did die, for some of them are older than I am. Death is all right; it is good so long, of course, as one does not die without repentance. There is no worse evil than an impenitent death; an impenitent death is a joy to the devil. And if you want to die penitent, so that you may not be forbidden to enter the mansions of the Lord, pray to the holy martyr Varvara. She is the intercessor. She is, that's the truth . . . For God has given her such a place in heaven that everyone has the right to pray to her for penitence.'

Pantelei went on muttering, and apparently was not bothered whether Yegorushka heard him or not. He talked listlessly, mumbling to himself, without raising or dropping his voice, but managed to tell him a great deal in a short time. All he said was made up of fragments that had very little connection with one another, and was quite uninteresting for Yegorushka. Possibly he talked only in order to reckon over his thoughts aloud after the night spent in silence, in order to see if they were all there. After talking of repentance, he spoke again about a Maxim Nikolaich from near Slavianoserbsk.

'Yes, he took his little lad . . . he took him, that's true . . .'

One of the waggoners walking in front darted from his place, ran to one side and began lashing on the ground with his whip. He was a stalwart, broad-shouldered man of thirty, with curly flaxen hair and a look of great health and vigour. Judging from the movements of his shoulders and the whip, and the eagerness expressed in his attitude, he was beating something alive. Another waggoner, a short stubby little man with a bushy black beard, wearing a waistcoat and a shirt outside his trousers, ran up to him. The latter broke into a deep guffaw of laughter and coughing and said: 'I say, lads, Dymov has killed a snake!'

There are people whose intelligence can be gauged at once by their voice and laughter. The man with the black beard belonged to that class of fortunate individuals; impenetrable stupidity could be felt in his voice and laugh. The flaxen-headed Dymov had finished, and lifting from the ground with his whip something like a cord, flung it with a laugh into the cart.

'That's not a viper; it's a grass snake!' shouted someone.

The man with the wooden gait and the bandage round his face strode up quickly to the dead snake, glanced at it and flung up his stick-like arms.

'You jail-bird!' he cried in a muffled wailing voice. 'What have you killed a grass snake for? What had he done to you, you damned brute? Look, he has killed a grass snake; how would you like to be treated so?'

'Grass snakes ought not to be killed, that's true,' Patelei muttered placidly, 'they ought not . . . They are not vipers; though it looks like a snake, it is a gentle, innocent creature . . . It's friendly to man, the grass snake is.'

Dymov and the man with the black beard were probably ashamed, for they laughed loudly, and not answering, slouched lazily back to their wagons. When the hindmost wagon was level with the spot where the dead snake lay, standing over it the man with his face tied up turned to Pantelei and asked in a tearful voice:

'Grandfather, what did he want to kill the grass snake for?'

His eyes, as Yegorushka saw now, were small and dingy looking; his face was grey, sickly and looked somehow dingy too while his chin was red and seemed very much swollen.

'Grandfather, what did he kill it for?' he repeated, striding along beside Pantelei.

'A stupid fellow. His hands itch to kill, and that is why he does it,' answered the old man; 'but he oughtn't to kill a grass snake, that's true . . . Dymov is a ruffian, we all know, he kills everything he comes across, and Kiriukha did not interfere. He ought to have taken its part, but instead of that, he goes off into "Ha-ah-ha!" and "Ho-ho-ho!" . . . But don't be angry, Vasia . . . Why be angry? – They've killed it – well, never mind them. Dymov is a ruffian and Kiriukha acted from foolishness – never mind . . . They are foolish people without understanding – but there, don't mind them. Yemelian here never touches what he shouldn't; he never does, that is true . . . because he is a man of education, while they are stupid . . . Yemelian, he leaves things alone.'

The waggoner in the reddish-brown coat and with the spongy swelling on his face, who was conducting an unseen choir, stopped. Hearing his name, and waiting till Pantelei and Vasia came up to him, he walked beside them.

'What are you talking about?' he asked in a husky, muffled voice.

'Why, Vasia here is angry,' said Pantelei. 'So I have been saying things to him to stop him being angry . . . Oh, how my bad, chilled feet hurt! Oh, oh! They're itching more than ever for Sunday, God's holy day!'

'It's from walking,' observed Vasia.

'No, lad, no. It's not from walking. When I walk it seems easier; when I lie down and get warm . . . it's deadly. Walking is easier for me.'

Yemelian, in his reddish-brown coat, walked between Pantelei and Vasia and waved his arms, as though they were going to sing. After waving them a little while he dropped them, and croaked out hopelessly:

'I have no voice. It's a real misfortune. All last night and this morning I have been haunted by the trio "Lord, have Mercy" that we sang at the wedding at Marinovsky's. It's in my head and in my throat. You'd think I could sing it, but I can't; I have no voice.'

He paused for a minute, thinking, then went on:

'For fifteen years I was in the choir. In all the Lugansk works there was maybe no one with a voice like mine. But, damn it, I bathed two years ago in the Donets, and I can't get a single note true ever since. I caught a chill in my throat. And without a voice I am like a workman with one arm.'

'That's true,' Pantelei agreed.

'I think of myself as a ruined man and nothing more.'

At that moment Vasia chanced to catch sight of Yegorushka. His eyes grew moist and smaller than ever.

'There's a little gentleman driving with us,' and he covered his nose with his sleeve as though he were bashful. 'What a grand coachman! Stay with us and you can drive the wagons and deliver wool.'

The incongruity of one person being at once a little gentleman and a wagon driver seemed to strike him as very curious and witty, for he giggled loudly, and went on enlarging upon the idea. Yemelian glanced upwards at Yegorushka, too, but coldly and cursorily. He was absorbed in his own thoughts, and had it not been for Vasia, would not have noticed Yegorushka's presence. Before five minutes had passed he was waving his arms again, then describing to his companions the beauties of the wedding anthem, 'Lord, have Mercy', which he had remembered in the night. He put the whip under his arm and waved both hands about.

A mile from the village the wagons stopped by a well with a pump handle. Letting his pail down into the well, black-bearded Kiriukha lay on his stomach on the framework and thrust his shaggy head, his shoulders, and part of his chest into the black hole, so that Yegorushka could see nothing but his short legs, which scarcely touched the ground. Seeing the reflection of his head far down at the bottom of the well, he was delighted and went off into his deep bass stupid laugh, and the echo from the well answered him. When he got up his neck and face were as red as beetroot. The first to run and drink was Dymov. He drank laughing, often turning from the pail to tell Kiriukha something funny, then he turned round and uttered aloud, to be heard all over the steppe, half a dozen bad words. Yegorushka did not understand the meaning of such words, but he knew very well they were bad words. He knew the revulsion his friends and relations silently felt for such words. He himself, without knowing why, shared that feeling and was accustomed to think that only drunk and disorderly people enjoyed the privilege of uttering such words aloud. He remembered the murder of the grass snake, listened to Dymov's laughter, and felt something like hatred for the man. And as ill luck would have it, Dymov at that moment caught sight of Yegorushka, who had climbed down from the wagon and gone up to the well. He laughed aloud and shouted:

'I say, lads, the old man has had a baby boy in the night.'

Kiriukha laughed his bass laugh till he coughed. Someone else laughed too, while Yegorushka crimsoned and made up his mind finally that Dymov was a very nasty man.

With his curly flaxen head, with his shirt open on his chest and no hat on, Dymov looked handsome and exceptionally strong; in every movement he made you could see a reckless dare-devil and an athlete who knew his value. He shrugged his shoulders, put his arms akimbo, talked and laughed louder than any of the rest, and looked as though he were going to lift up something very heavy with one hand and astonish the whole world by doing so. His mischievous mocking eyes glided over the road, the wagons, and the sky without resting on anything, and seemed looking for someone to kill, just as a pastime, and something to laugh at. Evidently he was afraid of no one, would stick at nothing, and most likely was not in the least interested in Yegorushka's opinion of him . . . Yegorushka with his whole heart hated his flaxen head, his clear face, and his strength, listened with fear and loathing to his laughter, and kept thinking what word of abuse he could pay him out with.

Pantelei, too, went up to the pail. He took out of his pocket a little green icon lamp glass, wiped it with a rag, filled it from the pail and drank from it, then filled it again, wrapped the little glass in the rag, and then put it back into his pocket.

'Grandfather, why do you drink out of a lamp,' Yegorushka asked him, surprised.

'Some drink out of a pail and others out of a lamp,' the old man answered evasively. 'Everyone has his own taste . . . You drink out of a pail – well, drink, and may it do you good . . .'

'My darling, you beauty!' Vasia said suddenly, in a caressing plaintive voice. 'My darling!'

His eyes were fixed on the distance; they were moist and smiling, and his face wore the same expression as when he had looked at Yegorushka.

'Who is it you are talking to?' asked Kiriukha.

'A lovely vixen . . . she's rolled on her back, she's playing like a dog.'

Everyone began staring into the distance, looking for the vixen, but no one could see it, only Vasia with his grey lacklustre eyes, and he was enchanted by it. His sight was extraordinarily keen, as Yegorushka learnt afterwards. He was so long-sighted that the brown steppe was for him always full of life and interest. He had only to look into the distance to see a fox, a hare, a bustard, or some other animal which avoids men. There was nothing strange in seeing a hare running away or a flying bustard – everyone crossing the steppes could see them; but it was not vouchsafed to everyone to see wild animals in their own haunts when they were not running nor hiding, nor looking about them in alarm. Yet Vasia saw foxes playing, hares washing themselves with their paws, bustards preening their wings and hammering out their hollow nests. Thanks to this keenness of sight, Vasia had, besides the world seen by everyone, another world of his own, accessible to no one else, and probably a very beautiful one, for when he saw something and was in raptures over it you could not help envying him.

When the wagons set off again, the church bells were ringing for morning service.

v

The train of wagons drew up on the bank of a river on one side of a village. The sun was blazing, as it had been the day before; the air was stagnant and depressing. There were a few willows on the bank, but the shade from them did not fall on the earth, but on the water, where it was wasted; even in the shade under the wagon it was stifling and wearisome. The water, blue from the reflection of the sky in it, was alluring.

Stiopka, a waggoner whom Yegorushka noticed now for the first time, a Ukrainian lad of eighteen, in a long shirt without a belt, and oriental trousers that flapped like flags as he walked, undressed quickly, ran along the steep bank and plunged into the water. He dived three times, then swam on his back and shut his eyes in his delight. His face was smiling and wrinkled up as though he were being tickled, hurt and amused.

On a hot day when there is nowhere to escape from the sultry, stifling heat, the splash of water and the loud breathing of a man bathing sounds like good music to the ear. Dymov and Kiriukha, looking at Stiopka, undressed quickly and one after the other, laughing loudly in eager anticipation of their enjoyment, dropped into the water, and the quiet modest little river resounded with snorting and splashing and shouting. Kiriukha coughed, laughed and shouted as though they were trying to drown him, while Dymov chased him and tried to catch him by the leg.

'Ha-ha-ha!' he shouted. 'Catch him! Hold him!'

Kiriukha laughed and enjoyed himself, but his expression was the same as it had been on dry land, stupid, bewildered, as though someone had, unnoticed, stolen up behind him and hit him on the head with a blunt instrument. Yegorushka undressed, too, but did not let himself down by the bank: he took a running jump from a height of ten feet. Describing an arc in the air, he fell into the water, sank deep, but did not reach the bottom: some force, cold and pleasant to the touch, seemed to hold him up and bring him back to the surface. He popped out and, snorting and blowing bubbles, opened his eyes; but the sun was reflected in the water quite close to his face. At first blinding spots of light, then rainbow colours and dark patches, flitted before his eyes. He made haste to dive again, opened his eyes in the water and saw something cloudy green like the sky on a moonlight night. Again the same force would not let him touch the bottom and stay in the cool, but lifted him to the surface. He popped out and heaved a sigh so deep that he had a feeling of space and freshness, not only in his chest, but in his stomach. Then, to get from the water everything he possibly could, he allowed himself every luxury; he lay on his back and basked, splashed, frolicked, swam on his face, on his side, on his back and standing up – just as he pleased till he was exhausted. The other bank was thickly overgrown with reeds; it was golden in the sun, and the flowers of the reeds hung drooping to the water in lovely tassels. In one place the reeds were shaking and nodding, with their flowers rustling – Stiopka and Kiriukha were hunting crayfish.

'A crayfish, look, lads! A crayfish!' Kiriukha cried triumphantly and in fact held up a crayfish.

Yegorushka swam up to the reeds, dived, and began fumbling among the roots. Burrowing in the slimy, liquid mud, he felt something sharp and unpleasant – perhaps it really was a crayfish. But at that minute someone seized him by the leg and pulled him to the surface. Spluttering and coughing, Yegorushka opened his eyes and saw before him the wet grinning face of the devilish Dymov. The mischief-maker was breathing hard, and from a look in his eyes he seemed inclined for more. He held Yegorushka tight by the leg, and was lifting his hand to take hold of his neck. But Yegorushka tore himself away with repulsion and terror, as though disgusted and afraid that the bully would drown him. He said:

'Fool! I'll punch you in the face.'

Feeling that this was not sufficient to express his hatred, he thought a minute and added:

'Bastard! You son of a bitch!'

But Dymov, as though nothing were the matter, took no further notice of Yegorushka, but swam off to Kiriukha, shouting:

'Ha-ha-ha! Let's catch fish! Mates, let's catch fish!'

'To be sure,' Kiriukha agreed; 'there must be a lot of fish here.'

'Stiopka, run to the village and ask the peasants for a net!'

'They won't give it to me.'

'They will, you ask them. Tell them to give it to us for Christ's sake, because we are just the same as pilgrims.'

'That's true.'

Stiopka clambered out of the water, dressed quickly, and bare-headed he ran, his full trousers flapping, to the village. The water lost all its charm for Yegorushka after his encounter with Dymov. He got out and began dressing. Pantelei and Vasia were sitting on the steep bank, with their legs hanging down, looking at the bathers. Yemelian was standing naked, up to his knees in the water, holding on to the grass with one hand to prevent himself from falling while the other stroked his body. With his bony shoulder-blades, with the swelling under the eye, bending down and evidently afraid of the water, he made a ludicrous figure. His face was grave and severe. He looked angrily at the water, as though he were just going to upbraid it for having chilled him in the Donets and robbed him of his voice.

'And why don't you bathe?' Yegorushka asked Vasia.

'Oh, I don't care for it,' answered Vasia.

'How did your chin get swollen?'

'It hurts . . . I used to work at the match factory, master . . . The doctor used to say that it would make my jaw rot. The air is bad there. There were three lads beside me who had their jaws swollen, and with one of them it rotted away altogether.'

Stiopka soon came back with the net. Dymov and Kiriukha were already turning blue and getting hoarse by being so long in the water, but they set about fishing eagerly. First they went to a deep place beside the reeds; there Dymov was up to his neck, while the water went over squat Kiriukha's head. The latter spluttered and blew bubbles, while Dymov, stumbling on the prickly roots, fell over and got caught in the net; both flopped about in the water, and made a noise, and nothing but mischief came of their fishing.

'It's deep,' croaked Kiriukha. 'You won't catch anything.'

'Don't tug, you devil!' shouted Dymov, trying to put the net in the proper position. 'Hold it up.'

'You won't catch anything here,' Pantelei shouted from the bank. 'You are only frightening the fish, you fools! Go more to the left! It's shallower there!'

Once a big fish gleamed above the net; they all drew a breath, and Dymov struck the place where it had vanished with his fist, and his face expressed vexation.

'Ugh!' cried Pantelei, and stamped his foot. 'You've let the perch slip! It's gone!'

Moving more to the left, Dymov and Kiriukha picked out a shallower place, and then fishing began in earnest. They had wandered off some three hundred paces from the wagons; they could be seen silently trying to go as deep as they could and as near the reeds, moving their legs a little at a time, drawing out the nets, beating the water with their fists to drive the fish towards the nets. From the reeds they got to the further bank; they drew the net out, then, with a disappointed air, lifting their knees high as they walked, went back into the reeds. They were talking about something, but what it was no one could hear. The sun was scorching their backs, the flies were stinging them, and their bodies had turned from purple to crimson. Stiopka was walking after them with a pail in his hands; he had tucked his shirt right under his armpits, and was holding it up by the hem with his teeth. After every successful catch he lifted up a fish, and, letting it shine in the sun, shouted: 'Look at this perch! We've five like that!'

Every time Dymov, Kiriukha, and Stiopka pulled out the net they could be seen fumbling about in the mud in it, putting some things into the pail and throwing other things away; sometimes they passed something that was in the net from hand to hand, examined it inquisitively, then threw that, too, away.

'What is it?' people on the bank shouted to them.

Stiopka made some answer, but it was hard to make out his words. Then he climbed out of the water and, holding the pail in both hands, forgetting to let his shirt drop, ran to the wagons.

'It's full!' he shouted, breathing hard. 'Give us another!'

Yegorushka looked into the pail: it was full. A young pike poked its ugly nose out of the water, and there were swarms of crayfish and little fish round about it. Yegorushka put his hand down to the bottom and stirred up the water; the pike vanished under the crayfish, and a perch and a tench swam to the surface instead of it. Vasia, too, looked into the pail. His eyes grew moist and his face looked as caressing as before when he saw the vixen. He took something out of the pail, put it to his mouth and began chewing it.

'Mates,' said Stiopka in amazement, 'Vasia is eating a live gudgeon! Ugh!'

'It's not a gudgeon, but a minnow,' Vasia answered calmly, still chewing.

He took the fish's tail out of his mouth, looked at it lovingly, and put it back again. While Vasia was chewing and crunching with his teeth it seemed to Yegorushka that he was watching something not human. Vasia's swollen chin, his lustreless eyes, his extraordinarily sharp sight, the fish's tail in his mouth, and the affectionate way in which he crunched the gudgeon made him like an animal.

Yegorushka felt bored beside him. And the fishing was over, too.

He walked about beside the wagons, thought a little, and, to escape the boredom, strolled off to the village.

Not long afterwards he was standing in the church, and with his forehead leaning on somebody's back, listened to the singing of the choir. The service was drawing to a close. Yegorushka did not understand church singing and did not care for it. He listened a little, yawned, and began looking at the backs and heads before him. In one head, red and wet from his recent battle, he recognised Yemelian. The back of his head had been cropped in a straight line higher than is usual; the hair in front had been cut unbecomingly high, and Yemelian's ears stood out like two dock leaves, and seemed to feel themselves out of place. Looking at the back of the head and his ears, Yegorushka, for some reason, thought that Yemelian was probably very unhappy. He remembered the way he conducted with his hands, his husky voice, his timid air when he was bathing, and felt intense pity for him. He longed to say something friendly to him.

'I am here, too,' he said, tugging at his sleeve.

People who sing tenor or bass in the choir, especially those who have at any time in their lives conducted, are accustomed to look with a stern and unfriendly air at boys. They do not give up this habit, even when they leave off being in a choir. Turning to Yegorushka, Yemelian looked at him with a frown and said:

'Behave in church!'

Then Yegorushka moved forwards nearer to the iconostas. Here he saw interesting people. On the right side, in front of everyone, a lady and a gentleman were standing on a carpet. There were chairs behind them. The gentleman was wearing a freshly pressed shantung suit; he stood as motionless as a soldier saluting, and held high his bluish shaven chin. There was a very great air of dignity in his winged collar, in his blue chin, in his small bald patch and his cane. His neck was so strained from excess of dignity, and his chin was drawn up so tensely, that it looked as though his head were ready to fly off and soar upwards any minute. The lady, who was stout and elderly and wore a white silk shawl, held her head on one side and looked as though she had done someone a favour, and meant to say: 'Oh, don't trouble yourself to thank me; I don't like it . . .' A thick wall of Ukrainians stood all round the carpet.

Yegorushka went up to the iconostas and began kissing the local icons. Before each image he slowly bowed down to the ground, without getting up, looked round at the congregation, then got up and kissed the icon. Touching the cold floor with his forehead gave him great satisfaction. When the beadle came from the altar with a pair of long snuffers to put out the candles, Yegorushka jumped up quickly from the floor and ran up to him.

'Have they given out the holy bread?' he asked.

'There is none; there is none,' the beadle muttered gruffly. 'It is no use your . . .'

The service was over; Yegorushka walked out of the church in a leisurely way, and began strolling about the market place. He had seen a good many villages, market places, and peasants in his time, and everything that met his eyes was entirely without interest for him. At a loss for something to do, he went into a shop over the door of which hung a wide strip of red calico. The shop consisted of two roomy, badly lit parts; in one half they sold drapery and groceries, in the other there were tubs of tar, and there were horse collars hanging from the ceiling; from both came the savoury smell of leather and tar. The floor of the shop had been painted; the man who painted it must have been a very whimsical and original person, for it was covered in patterns and mysterious symbols. The shopkeeper, a well-fed man with a broad face and round beard, apparently Russian not Ukrainian, was standing with his belly propped against the counter. He was nibbling a piece of sugar as he drank his tea, and heaved a deep sigh at every sip. His face expressed complete indifference, but each sigh seemed to be saying:

'Just you wait; I'll give you something to remember.'

'Give me a kopeck's worth of sunflower seeds,' Yegorushka said to him.

The shopkeeper raised his eyebrows, came out from behind the counter, and poured a kopeck's worth of sunflower seeds into Yegorushka's pocket, using an empty pomade pot as a measure. Yegorushka was reluctant to leave. He spent a long time examining the box of cakes; thought a little and asked, pointing to some little cakes covered with the rust of ages:

'How much are these cakes?'

'Two for a kopeck.'

Yegorushka took out of his pocket the cake given him the day before by the Jewess, and asked him:

'And how much do you charge for cakes like this?'

The shopman took the cake in his hands, looked at it from all sides, and raised one eyebrow.

'Like that?' he asked.

Then he raised the other eyebrow, thought a minute, and answered:

'Two for three kopecks . . .'

A silence followed.

'Whose boy are you?' the shopman asked, pouring himself out tea from a copper teapot.

'The nephew of Mr Kuzmichov.'

'There are all sorts of Kuzmichovs,' the shopkeeper sighed. He looked over Yegorushka's head towards the door, paused a minute and asked: 'Would you like some tea?'

'Please . . .' Yegorushka assented not very readily, though he felt an intense longing for his morning tea.

The shopkeeper poured him out a glass and gave him with it a bit of sugar that looked as though it had been nibbled. Yegorushka sat down on the folding chair and began drinking it. He wanted to ask the price of a pound of sugar almonds, and had just broached the subject when a customer walked in, and the shopkeeper, leaving his glass of tea, attended to his business. He led the customer into the other half, where there was a smell of tar, and was there a long time discussing something with him. The customer, a man apparently very obstinate and sharp, was continually shaking his head to signify his disapproval, and retreating towards the door. The shopkeeper had persuaded him of something and begun pouring oats into a big sack for him.

'Do you call these oats?' the customer said gloomily in Ukrainian. 'Those are not oats, but chaff. It's a mockery to give that to the hens; enough to make the hens laugh . . . No, I will go to Bondarenko's.'

When Yegorushka went back to the river a small camp fire was smoking on the bank. The waggoners were cooking their dinner. Stiopka was standing in the smoke, stirring the cauldron with a big notched spoon. A little on one side Kiriukha and Vasia, with eyes reddened from the smoke, were sitting cleaning the fish. Before them lay the net covered with slime and water weeds, and on it lay gleaming fish and crawling crayfish.

Yemelian, who had not long been back from the church, was sitting beside Pantelei, waving his arms and humming just audibly in a husky voice: 'To Thee we sing . . .' Dymov was moving about by the horses.

When they had finished cleaning them, Kiriukha and Vasia put the fish and the living crayfish together in the pail, rinsed them, and from the pail poured them all into the boiling water.

'Shall I put in some fat?' asked Stiopka skimming off the froth with a spoon.

'No need. The fish will make their own gravy,' answered Kiriukha.

Before taking the cauldron off the fire Stiopka scattered into the water three big handfuls of millet and a spoonful of salt; finally he tried it, smacked his lips, licked the spoon, and gave a self-satisfied grunt, which meant that the stew was done.

All except Pantelei sat down near the cauldron and set to work with their spoons.

'You there! Give the little lad a spoon!' Pantelei observed sternly. 'I dare say he is hungry too!'

'Ours is peasant fare,' sighed Kiriukha.

'Peasant fare is just as good when you're hungry.'

They gave Yegorushka a spoon. He began eating, not sitting, but standing close to the cauldron and looking down into it as into a hole. The grain smelt of fish and fish-scales were mixed up with the millet. The crayfish could not be hooked out with a spoon, and the men simply picked them out of the cauldron with their hands; Vasia did so particularly freely, and wetted his sleeves as well as his hands in the mess. Yet the stew seemed to Yegorushka very nice, and reminded him of the crayfish soup which his mother used to make at home on fast days. Pantelei was sitting apart chewing bread.

'Grandfather, why aren't you eating?' Yemelian asked him.

'I don't eat crayfish . . . Nasty things,' the old man said, and turned away with disgust.

While they were eating they all talked. From this conversation Yegorushka gathered that all his new acquaintances, in spite of the differences of their ages and their characters, had one point in common which made them all alike: they were all people with a splendid past and a very poor present. Of their past they all – every one of them – spoke with enthusiasm; their attitude to the present was almost one of contempt. The Russian loves reminiscing, but he does not love living. Yegorushka did not yet know that, and before the stew was finished he firmly believed that the men sitting round the cauldron were the injured victims of fate. Pantelei told them that in the past, before there were railways, he used to go with trains of wagons to Moscow and to Nizhni, and used to earn so much that he did not know what to do with his money; and what merchants there used to be in those days! What fish! How cheap everything was! Now the journeys were shorter, the merchants were stingier, the peasants poorer, the bread dearer, everything had shrunk and was on a smaller scale. Yemelian told them that in the old days he had been in the choir in Lugansk works, and that he had a remarkable voice and read music splendidly, while now he had become a peasant and lived on the charity of his brother, who sent him out with his horses and took half his earnings. Vasia had once worked in a match factory; Kiriukha had been a coachman in a good family, and had been reckoned the smartest driver of a three-in-hand in the whole district. Dymov, the son of a well-to-do peasant, lived at ease, enjoyed himself and had known no trouble until he was twenty, when his stern harsh father, anxious to train him to work, and afraid he would be spoiled at home, had sent him to a carrier's to work as a hired labourer. Stiopka was the only one who said nothing, but from his beardless face it was evident that his life had been a much better one in the past.

Thinking of his father, Dymov frowned and left off eating. Sullenly from under his brows he looked round at his companions and his eye rested upon Yegorushka.

'You heathen, take off your hat,' he said rudely. 'You can't eat with your hat on, and you a gentleman too!'

Yegorushka took off his hat and did not say a word, but the stew lost all savour for him, and he did not hear Pantelei and Vasia intervening on his behalf. A feeling of anger against the bully was rankling oppressively in his breast, and he made up his mind that he would do him some injury, whatever it cost him.

After dinner everyone sauntered to the wagons and lay down in the shade.

'Are we going to start soon, Grandfather?' Yegorushka asked Pantelei.

'In God's good time we shall set off . . . There's no starting yet; it is too hot . . . O Lord, Thy will be done. Holy Mother . . . Lie down, little lad.'

Soon there was a sound of snoring from under the wagons.

Yegorushka meant to go back to the village, but on reflection, yawned and lay down by the old man.

VI

The wagons remained by the river the whole day, and set off again when the sun was setting.

Yegorushka was lying on the bales again; the wagon creaked softly and swayed from side to side. Pantelei walked below, stamping his feet, slapping himself on his thighs and muttering. The air was full of the churring music of the steppes, as it had been the day before.

Yegorushka lay on his back, and, putting his hands under his head, gazed upwards at the sky. He watched the glow of sunset kindle, then fade away; guardian angels covering the horizon with their gold wings disposed themselves to slumber. The day had passed peacefully; the quiet peaceful night had come, and they could stay tranquilly at home in heaven . . . Yegorushka saw the sky by degrees grow dark, the mist fall over the earth and the stars light up, one after the other . . .

When you gaze a long while fixedly at the deep sky thoughts and feelings for some reason merge in a sense of loneliness. One begins to feel hopelessly solitary, and everything one used to look upon as near and akin becomes infinitely remote and valueless; the stars that have looked down from the sky thousands of years already, the mists and the incomprehensible sky itself, indifferent to the brief life of man, oppress the soul with their silence when one is left face to face with them and tries to grasp their significance. One is reminded of the solitude awaiting each one of us in the grave, and the reality of life seems awful, full of despair . . .

Yegorushka thought of his grandmother, who was sleeping now under the cherry trees in the cemetery. He remembered her lying in the coffin with copper coins on her eyes, and afterwards shut in and lowered into the grave; he even recalled the hollow sound of the clods of earth on the coffin lid . . . He pictured his granny in the dark and narrow coffin, helpless and deserted by everyone. His imagination pictured his granny suddenly awakening, not understanding where she was, knocking upon the lid and calling for help, and in the end swooning with horror and dying again. He imagined his mother dead, Father Khristofor, Countess Dranitskaia, Solomon. But however much he tried to imagine himself in the dark tomb, far from home, outcast, helpless and dead, he could not succeed; for himself personally he could not admit the possibility of death, and felt that he would never die . . .

Pantelei, for whom death could not be far away, walked below, reckoning up his thoughts.

'All right . . . Nice gentlefolk . . .' he muttered. 'Took his little lad to school – but how he is doing now I haven't heard . . . In Slavianoserbsk, I say, there is no establishment for making them very learned . . . There really isn't . . . A nice little lad, no harm in him . . . He'll grow up and be a help to his father . . . You, Yegorushka, are little now, but when you grow up you'll keep your father and mother . . . So it is ordained by God, "Honour your father, and your mother." . . . I had children myself, but they were burnt . . . My wife was burnt and my children . . . That's true . . . the hut caught fire on the night of Epiphany . . . I wasn't at home, I was driving to Oriol. To Oriol . . . Maria dashed out into the street, but remembered the children were asleep in the hut, ran back and was burnt with her children . . . Next day they found nothing but bones.'

About midnight Yegorushka and the waggoners were again sitting round a small camp fire. While the dry twigs and stems were burning up, Kiriukha and Vasia went off somewhere to get water from a creek; they vanished into the darkness, but could be heard all the time talking and clanking their pails; so the creek was not far away. The light from the fire laid a great flickering patch on the earth; though the moon was bright, everything seemed impenetrably black beyond that red patch. The light was in the waggoners' eyes, and they saw only part of the great road; almost unseen in the darkness the wagons with the bales and the horses looked like a mountain of undefined shape. Twenty paces from the camp fire at the edge of the road stood a wooden cross that had fallen aslant. Before the camp fire had been lighted, when he could see things in the distance, Yegorushka had noticed that there was an identical old slanting cross on the other side of the great road.

Coming back with the water, Kiriukha and Vasia filled the cauldron and fixed it over the fire. Stiopka, with the notched spoon in his hand, took his place in the smoke by the cauldron, gazing dreamily into the water for the scum to rise. Pantelei and Yemelian were sitting side by side in silence, brooding over something. Dymov was lying on his stomach, with his head propped on his fists, looking into the fire . . . Stiopka's shadow was dancing over him, so that his handsome face was covered with darkness one minute, lit up the next . . . Kiriukha and Vasia were wandering about at a little distance gathering dry grass and bark for the fire. Yegorushka, with his hands in his pockets, was standing by Pantelei, watching the fire devour the grass.

All were resting, musing on something, and they glanced cursorily at the cross over which patches of red light were dancing. There is something melancholy, pensive, and extremely poetical about a solitary tomb; one feels its silence, and the silence gives one the sense of the presence of the soul of the unknown man who lies under the cross. Is that soul at peace on the steppe? Does it grieve in the moonlight? Near the tomb the steppe seems melancholy, dreary and mournful; the grass seems more sorrowful, and one fancies the grasshoppers chirrup less freely, and there is no passer-by who would not remember that lonely soul and keep looking back at the tomb, till it was left far behind and hidden in the mists . . .

'Grandfather, what is that cross for?' asked Yegorushka.

Pantelei looked at the cross and then at Dymov and asked:

'Nikola, isn't this the place where the reapers killed the merchants?'

Dymov reluctantly raised himself on his elbows, looked at the road and replied:

'That's it . . .'

A silence followed. Kiriukha broke up some dry stalks, crushed them up together and thrust them under the cauldron. The fire flared up brightly; Stiopka was enveloped in black smoke, and the shadow cast by the cross ran along the road in the dusk beside the wagons.

'Yes, they were killed,' Dymov said reluctantly. 'Two merchants, father and son, were travelling, selling holy images. They put up in the inn not far from here that is now kept by Ignat Fomin. The old man had a drop too much, and began boasting that he had a lot of money with him. We all know merchants are a boastful set, God preserve us . . . They can't resist showing off before the likes of us. And at the time some reapers were staying the night at the inn. So they overheard what the merchants said and took note of it.'

'Oh Lord! . . . Holy Mother!' sighed Pantelei.

'Next day, as soon as it was light,' Dymov went on, 'the merchants were about to set off and the reapers insisted on coming with them. "Let us go together, your worship. It will be more fun, and there will be less danger, for this is a remote place . . ." The merchants had to travel at a walking pace to avoid breaking the images, and that just suited the reapers . . .'

Dymov rose into a kneeling position and stretched.

'Yes,' he went on, yawning. 'Everything went all right till they reached this spot, and then the reapers let fly at them with their scythes. The son, he was a fine young fellow, snatched the scythe from one of them, and he used it, too . . . Well, of course, they got the best of it because there were eight of them. They hacked at the merchants so that their bodies were nothing but wounds: when they had finished they dragged both of them off the road, the father to one side and the son to the other. Opposite that cross there is another cross on this side . . . Whether it is still standing, I don't know . . . I can't see from here . . .'

'It is,' said Kiriukha.

'They say they did not find much money afterwards.'

'No,' Pantelei confirmed; 'they only found a hundred roubles.'

'And three of them died afterwards, for the merchant had cut them badly with the scythe, too. They bled to death. One had his hand cut off, so that they say he ran three miles without his hand, and they found him on a mound close to Kurikovo. He was squatting on his heels, with his head on his knees, as though he were lost in thought, but when they looked at him there was no life and he was dead . . .'

'They found him by the trail of blood,' said Pantelei.

Everyone looked at the cross, and again there was a hush. From somewhere, most likely from the creek, floated the mournful cry of the bird: 'Sleep! sleep! sleep!'

'There are a great many wicked people in the world,' said Yemelian.

'A great many,' assented Pantelei, and he moved closer to the fire as though he were awe-struck. 'A great many,' he went on in a low voice. 'I've seen an awful lot in my time . . . Wicked people! . . . I have seen a great many holy and just men, but more sinners than I can count . . . Queen of Heaven, save us and have mercy on us. I remember once thirty years ago, or maybe more, I was driving a merchant from Morshansk. The merchant was a jolly handsome fellow, with money, too . . . the merchant was . . . A nice man, no harm in him . . . So we put up for the night at an inn. And in Russia the inns are not what they are in these parts. There the yards are roofed in and look like the ground floor, or let us say like threshing barns in good farms. Only a barn would be a bit higher. So we put up there and were all right. My merchant was in a room, while I was with the horses, and everything was as it should be. So, lads, I said my prayers before going to sleep and began walking about the yard. And it was a dark night, I couldn't see anything; it was no good trying. So I walked about a bit up to the wagons, or nearly, when I saw a light gleaming. What could it mean? I thought the people of the inn had gone to bed long ago, and besides the merchant and me there were no other guests in the inn . . . Where could the light have come from? I felt suspicious . . . I went closer . . . towards the light . . . The Lord have mercy upon me! and save me, Queen of Heaven! I looked and there was a little window with a grating . . . close to the ground, in the house . . . I lay down on the ground and looked in; as soon as I looked in a cold chill ran all down me . . .'

Kiriukha, trying not to make a noise, thrust a handful of twigs into the fire. After waiting for it to leave off crackling and hissing, the old man went on:

'I looked in and there was a big cellar, black and dark . . . There was a lighted lantern on a tub. In the middle of the cellar were about a dozen men in red shirts with their sleeves turned up, sharpening their long knives . . . Ugh! So we had fallen into a nest of robbers . . . What's to be done? I ran to the merchant, woke him up quietly, and said: "Don't be frightened, merchant," said I, "but we are in a bad way. We have fallen into a nest of robbers," I said. He turned pale and asked: "What are we to do now, Pantelei? I have a lot of money that belongs to orphans. As for my life," he said, "that's in God's hands. I am not afraid to die, but it's dreadful to lose the orphans' money," said he . . . What were we to do? The gates were locked; there was no getting out. If there had been a fence one could have climbed over it, but with the yard shut up! . . . "Come, don't be frightened, merchant," said I, "but pray to God. Maybe the Lord will not let the orphans suffer. Stay still," said I, "and make no sign, and meanwhile, maybe, I shall think of something . . ." Right! . . . I prayed to God and the Lord put the thought into my mind . . . I clambered up on my cart and softly, . . . softly so that no one should hear, began pulling out the straw in the thatched roof, made a hole and crept out, crept out . . . Then I jumped off the roof and ran along the road as fast as I could. I ran and ran till I was nearly dead . . . I ran maybe three miles without taking a breath, if not more. Thank God I saw a village. I ran up to a hut and began tapping at the window. "Good Christian people," I said, and told them all about it. "Do not let a Christian soul perish . . ." I woke them all up . . . The peasants gathered together and went with me . . . one with a cord, one with an oak stick, others with pitchforks . . . We broke in the gates of the inn yard and went straight to the cellar . . . And the robbers had just finished sharpening their knives and were going to kill the merchant. The peasants took them, every one of them, bound them and carried them to the police. The merchant gave them three hundred roubles in his joy, and gave me five gold pieces and put my name down for commemoration. They said that they found human bones in the cellar afterwards, heaps and heaps of them . . . Bones! . . . So they robbed people and then buried them, so that there should be no traces . . . Well, afterwards they were flogged to death at Morshansk.'

Pantelei had finished the story, and he looked round at his listeners. They were gazing at him in silence. The water was boiling by now and Stiopka was skimming off the froth.

'Is the lard ready?' Kiriukha asked him in a whisper.

'Wait a little . . . Soon.'

Stiopka, his eyes fixed on Pantelei as though he were afraid that the latter might begin some story before he was back, ran to the wagons; soon he came back with a little wooden bowl and began kneading pork lard in it.

'I went on another journey with a merchant, too . . .' Pantelei went on again, speaking as before in a low voice and with fixed unblinking eyes. 'His name, as I remember now, was Piotr Grigorich. He was a nice man . . . the merchant was. We stopped in the same way at an inn . . . He indoors and me with the horses . . . The people of the house, the innkeeper and his wife, seemed a friendly good sort of people; the labourers, too, seemed all right; but yet, lads, I couldn't sleep. I had a queer feeling in my heart . . . a queer feeling, that was just it. The gates were open and there were plenty of people about, and yet I felt afraid and not myself. Everyone had been asleep long ago. It was in the middle of the night; it would soon be time to get up, and I was lying alone in my chaise and could not close my eyes, as though I were an owl. And then, lads, I heard this sound, "Toop! toop! toop!" Someone was creeping up to my covered wagon. I poked my head out, and there was a peasant woman in nothing but her shift and with her feet bare . . . "What do you want, good woman?" I asked. And she was all of a tremble; her face was terror-stricken . . . "Get up, good man," said she; "the people are plotting evil . . . They mean to kill your merchant. With my own ears I heard the master whispering to his wife . . ." So it was not for nothing, the foreboding of my heart! "And who are you?" I asked. "I am their cook," she said . . . Right! . . . So I got out of the wagon and went to the merchant. I woke him up and said: "Things aren't quite right, Piotr Grigorich . . . Catch up on your sleep later, your worship, but dress now while there is still time," I said; "and while we can, let's get away from trouble." He had no sooner begun dressing when the door opened and, mercy on us! I saw, Holy Mother! the innkeeper and his wife come into the room with three labourers . . . So they had persuaded the labourers to join them. "The merchant has a lot of money, and we'll go shares," they told them. Every one of the five had a long knife in their hand . . . each a knife. The innkeeper locked the door and said: "Say your prayers, travellers, and if you begin screaming," they said, "we won't let you say your prayers before you die . . ." As though we could scream! I had such a lump in my throat I could not cry out . . . The merchant wept and said: "Good Christian people! you have resolved to kill me because my money tempts you. Well, so be it; I shall not be the first nor shall I be the last. Many of us merchants have been murdered at inns. But why, good Christian brothers," says he, "murder my driver? Why should he have to suffer for my money?" And he said that so pitifully! And the innkeeper answered him: "If we leave him alive," said he, "he will be the first to bear witness against us. One may just as well kill two as one. In for a penny, in for a pound. Say your prayers, that's all you can do, and it's no good talking!" The merchant and I knelt down side by side and wept and said our prayers. He thought of his children. I was young in those days; I wanted to live . . . We looked at the icons and prayed, and so pitifully that it brings a tear even now . . . And the innkeeper's wife looks at us and says: "Good people," said she, "don't bear a grudge against us in the other world or pray to God to punish us; it's poverty that drives us to it." We prayed and wept and prayed and wept, and God heard us. He had pity on us, I suppose . . . At the very minute when the innkeeper had taken the merchant by the beard to slash his throat with the knife suddenly someone tapped hard at the window from outside! We all started, and the innkeeper's hands dropped . . . Someone was tapping at the window and shouting: "Piotr Grigorich," he shouted, "are you here? Get ready and let's go!" The people saw that someone had come for the merchant; they were terrified and took to their heels . . . And we made haste into the yard, harnessed the horses, and were out of sight in a minute . . .'

'Who was it that knocked at the window,' asked Dymov.

'At the window? It must have been a holy saint or angel, for there was no one else . . . When we drove out of the yard there wasn't a soul outside . . . It was the Lord's doing.'

Pantelei told other stories, and in all of them 'long knives' figured and all sounded equally made up. Had he heard these stories from somewhere else, or had he made them up himself in the remote past, and afterwards, as his memory grew weaker, mixed up his experiences with his imaginings and become unable to tell one from the other? Anything is possible, but it is strange that on this occasion and for the rest of the journey, whenever he happened to tell a story, he showed a clear preference for fiction, and never told what he really had experienced. At the time Yegorushka took it all for the genuine thing, and believed every word; later on it seemed to him strange that a man who in his day had travelled all over Russia and seen and known so much, whose wife and children had been burnt to death, so failed to appreciate the wealth of his life that whenever he was sitting by the camp fire he was either silent or talked of what had never happened.

Over their porridge they were silent, thinking of what they had just heard. Life is terrible and marvellous, and so, however terrible a story you tell in Russia, however you embroider it with nests of robbers, long knives and such marvels, it always finds an echo of reality in the soul of the listener, and only a man who has been a good deal affected by education looks distrustfully askance, and even he will be silent. The cross by the roadside, the dark bales of wool, the wide expanse of the plain, and the lot of the men gathered together by the camp fire – all this was of itself so marvellous and terrible that the fantastic colours of legend and fairy tale were paled and blended into life.

All the others ate out of the cauldron, but Pantelei sat apart and ate his porridge out of a wooden bowl. His spoon was not like those the others had, but was made of cypress wood, with a little cross on it. Yegorushka, looking at him, thought of the little icon glass and asked Stiopka softly:

'Why does the old man sit apart?'

'He is an Old Believer,'* Stiopka and Vasia answered in a whisper. And as they said it they looked as though they were speaking of some secret vice or weakness.

All sat silent, thinking. After the terrible stories there was no inclination to speak of ordinary things. All at once in the midst of the silence Vasia drew himself up and, fixing his lacklustre eyes on one point, pricked up his ears.

'What is it?' Dymov asked him.

'Someone is coming,' answered Vasia.

'Where do you see him?'

'Yo-onder! There's something white . . .'

There was nothing to be seen but darkness in the direction in which Vasia was looking; everyone listened, but they could hear no sounds of steps.

'Is he coming by the highroad?' asked Dymov.

'No, over the open country . . . He is coming this way.'

A minute passed in silence.

'And maybe it's the merchant who was buried here walking over the steppes,' said Dymov.

All looked askance at the cross, exchanged glances and suddenly broke into a laugh. They felt ashamed of their terror.

'Why would he be walking?' asked Pantelei. 'Only those whom the earth will not take to herself walk at night. And the merchants were all right . . . The merchants took the crown of martyrs.'

But all at once they heard the sound of steps; someone was coming in haste.

'He's carrying something,' said Vasia.

They could hear the grass rustling and the dry twigs crackling under the feet of the approaching wayfarer. But from the glare of the camp fire nothing could be seen. At last the steps sounded close by, and someone coughed. The flickering light seemed to part; a veil dropped from the waggoners' eyes, and they saw a man facing them.

Whether because of the flickering light or because everyone wanted to make out the man's face first of all, it happened, strangely enough, that at the first glance they all saw first, not his face nor his clothes, but his smile. It was an extraordinarily good-natured, broad, soft smile, like that of a baby on waking, one of those infectious smiles to which it is difficult not to respond with a smile. The stranger, when they did get a good look at him, turned out to be a man of thirty, ugly and in no way remarkable. He was a tall Ukrainian, with a long nose, long arms and long legs; everything about him seemed long except his neck, which was so short that it made him seem stooping. He was wearing a clean white shirt with an embroidered collar, white trousers, and new high boots, and in comparison with the waggoners he looked quite a dandy. In his arms he was carrying something big, white, and at first glance strange-looking, and the stock of a gun also peeped out from behind his shoulder.

Coming from the darkness into the circle of light, he stopped short as though petrified, and for half a minute looked at the waggoners as though he would have said: 'Just look what a smile I have!'

Then he took a step towards the fire, smiled still more radiantly and said:

'Bread and salt, friends!'

'You are very welcome!' Pantelei answered for them all.

The stranger put down by the fire what he was carrying in his arms – it was a dead bustard – and greeted them once more.

They all went up to the bustard and began examining it.

'A fine big bird; what did you kill it with?' asked Dymov.

'Grapeshot. You can't get him with small shot; he won't let you get near enough. Buy it, friends! I will let you have it for twenty kopecks.'

'What use would it be to us? It's good roasted, but I bet it would be tough boiled; you could not get your teeth through it . . .'

'Oh, what a pity! I would take it to the gentry at the farm; they would give me half a rouble for it. But it's a long way to go – nine miles!'

The stranger sat down, took off his gun and laid it beside him.

He seemed sleepy and languid; he sat smiling, and, screwing up his eyes at the firelight, apparently thinking of something very agreeable. They gave him a spoon; he began eating.

'Who are you?' Dymov asked him.

The stranger did not hear the question; he made no answer, and did not even glance at Dymov. Most likely this smiling man could not savour the porridge either, for he seemed to eat it mechanically, lifting the spoon to his lips sometimes very full and sometimes quite empty. He was not drunk, but he seemed to have something nonsensical in his head.

'I'm asking you who you are,' repeated Dymov.

'Me?' said the stranger, starting. 'Konstantin Zvonik from Rovnoe. It's about three miles from here.'

And anxious to show straight off that he was not quite an ordinary peasant, but something better, Konstantin hastened to add:

'We keep bees and fatten pigs.'

'Do you live with your father or in a house of your own?'

'No; now I am living in a house of my own. I've taken my share. This month, just after St Peter's Day, I got married. I am a married man now! . . . It's eighteen days since the wedding.'

'That's a good thing,' said Pantelei. 'Marriage is a good thing . . . God's blessed you.'

'His young wife sits at home while he rambles about the steppe,' laughed Kiriukha. 'Odd fellow!'

As though he had been pinched on the tenderest spot, Konstantin started, laughed and flushed crimson.

'But, Lord, she is not at home!' he said quickly, taking the spoon out of his mouth and looking round at everyone with an expression of delight and wonder. 'She is not; she has gone to her mother's for three

days! Yes, indeed, she has gone away, and I feel as though I were not
married . . .'

Konstantin waved his hand and turned his head; he wanted to go
on thinking, but the joy which beamed in his face prevented him. As
though he were not comfortable, he changed his attitude, and again
waved his hand. He was ashamed to share his happy thoughts with
strangers, but at the same time he had an irresistible longing to
communicate his joy.

'She has gone to Demidovo to see her mother,' he said, blushing
and moving his gun. 'She'll be back tomorrow . . . She said she would
be back for dinner.'

'And do you miss her?' said Dymov.

'Oh, Lord, yes; I should think so. We've been married only a few
days, and she has gone away . . . Eh! Oh, she's lovely, God strike me
dead! She is such a fine, splendid girl, such a one for laughing and
singing, full of life and fire! When she is there your brain is in a whirl,
and now she is away I wander about the steppe like a fool, as though I
had lost something. I have been walking since dinner, God help me.'

Konstantin rubbed his eyes, looked at the fire and laughed.

'You love her, then . . .' said Pantelei.

'She is so fine and splendid,' Konstantin repeated, not listening,
'such a good housewife, clever and sensible. You wouldn't find
another like her among simple folk in the whole province. She has
gone away . . . But she is missing me, I kno-ow! I know the little
magpie. She said she would be back tomorrow by dinner-time . . .
And just think how odd!' Konstantin almost shouted, speaking a note
higher and shifting his position. 'Now she loves me and is sad without
me, and yet she refused to marry me.'

'Eat,' said Kiriukha.

'She would not marry me,' Konstantin went on, not heeding him. 'I
struggled with her for three years! I saw her at the Kalachik fair; I fell
madly in love with her, was ready to hang myself . . . I live at Rovnoe,
she at Demidovo, fifteen miles apart, and there was nothing I could
do. I sent matchmakers to her, and all she said was: "I won't!" Ah,
the magpie! I sent her one thing and another, earrings and cakes, and
twenty pounds of honey – but still she said: "I won't!" What could you
do? If you think about it, I was no match for her! She was young and
lovely, full of fire, while I am old: I shall soon be thirty, and a regular
beauty, too; a fine beard like a goat's, a clean face all covered with
pimples – how could I be compared with her! The only thing to be said
is that we are well off, but then her people, the Vakhramenkos, are well
off, too. They've six oxen, and they keep a couple of labourers. I was
in love, friends, as though I were plague-stricken. I couldn't sleep or

eat; my brain was full of thoughts, and in such a maze, Lord preserve us! I longed to see her, and she was in Demidovo. What do you think? God be my witness, I am not lying, three times a week I walked over there on foot just to have a look at her. I gave up work! I was so frantic that I even wanted to get taken on as a labourer in Demidovo, so as to be near her. I was in misery! My mother called in a wise-woman; my father tried thrashing me a dozen times. For three years I was in this torment, and then I made up my mind. "Damn my soul!" I said, "I will go to town and be a cabby . . . Fate's against it." At Easter I went to Demidovo to have a last look at her . . .'

Konstantin threw back his head and went off into a mirthful tinkling laugh, as though he had just taken someone in very cleverly.

'I saw her by the river with the lads,' he went on. 'I was overcome with spite . . . I called her aside and maybe for a full hour I said all manner of things to her. She fell in love with me! For three years she did not love me! She fell in love with me for what I said to her . . .'

'What did you say to her?' asked Dymov.

'What did I say? I don't remember . . . How could I remember? My words flowed at the time like water from a tap, without stopping to take breath. Ta-ta-ta-ta! And now I can't utter a word . . . Well, so she married me . . . She's gone now to her mother's, the magpie, and while she is away here I wander over the steppe. I can't stay at home. I can't stand it!'

Konstantin awkwardly released his feet, on which he was sitting, stretched himself on the earth, and propped his head on his fists, then got up and sat down again. Everyone by now thoroughly understood that he was in love and happy, poignantly happy; his smile, his eyes, and every movement, expressed languid happiness. He could not settle, and did not know what attitude to take to keep himself from being overwhelmed by the multitude of his delightful thoughts. Having poured out his soul before these strangers, he settled down quietly at last, and, looking at the fire, sank into thought.

At the sight of this happy man everyone felt depressed and longed to be happy too. Everyone was dreamy. Dymov got up, walked about softly by the fire, and from his walk, from the movement of his shoulder blades, it could be seen that he was weighed down by depression and yearning. He stood still for a moment, looked at Konstantin and sat down.

The camp fire was going out; there was no flicker, and the patch of red had grown small and dim . . . And as the fire went out the moonlight grew clearer and clearer. Now they could see the full width of the road, the bales of wool, the shafts of the wagons, the horses chewing; on the further side of the road there was the dim outline of the second cross . . .

Dymov leaned his cheek on his hand and hummed some plaintive song. Konstantin smiled drowsily and chimed in with a thin voice. They sang for half a minute, then sank into silence. Yemelian started, jerked his elbows and wriggled his fingers.

'Lads,' he said in an imploring voice, 'let's sing something sacred!' Tears came into his eyes. 'Lads,' he repeated, pressing his hands on his heart, 'let's sing something sacred!'

'I can't,' said Konstantin.

Everyone refused, so Yemelian sang alone. He waved both arms, nodded his head, opened his mouth, but nothing came from his throat but a discordant gasp. He sang with his arms, with his head, with his eyes, even with the swelling on his face; he sang passionately with anguish, and the more he strained his chest to extract at least one note from it, the more discordant were his gasps . . .

Yegorushka, like the rest, was overcome with depression. He went to his wagon, clambered up on the bales and lay down. He looked at the sky, and thought of happy Konstantin and his wife. Why did people get married? What were women in the world for? Yegorushka put the vague question to himself, and thought that a man would certainly be happy if he had an affectionate, merry and beautiful woman continually living at his side. For some reason he remembered the Countess Dranitskaia, and thought it would probably be very pleasant to live with a woman like that; he would perhaps have married her with pleasure if the idea had not been so embarrassing. He recalled her eyebrows, the pupils of her eyes, her carriage, the clock with the horseman . . . The soft warm night moved softly down upon him and whispered something in his ear, and it seemed to him that it was that lovely woman bending over him, looking at him with a smile, about to kiss him . . .

Nothing was left of the fire but two little red eyes, which kept growing smaller and smaller. Konstantin and the waggoners were sitting by it, dark motionless figures, and it seemed as though there were many more of them than before. The twin crosses were equally visible, and far, far away, somewhere by the highroad there gleamed a red light – other people cooking their porridge, most likely.

'Our Mother Russia is the head of all the world!' Kiriukha sang out suddenly in a harsh voice, choked and subsided. The steppe echo caught up his voice, carried it on, and it seemed as though stupidity itself were rolling on heavy wheels over the steppe.

'It's time to go,' said Pantelei. 'Get up, lads.'

While they were harnessing the horses, Konstantin walked by the wagons and talked rapturously of his wife.

'Good-bye, brothers!' he cried when the wagons started. 'Thank you for your hospitality. I shall go on again towards the light. It's more than I can stand.'

And he quickly vanished in the mist, and for a long time they could hear him striding in the direction of the light to tell other strangers of his happiness.

When Yegorushka woke up the next day it was early morning; the sun had not yet risen. The wagons were at a standstill. A man in a white cap and a suit of cheap grey material, mounted on a little Cossack stallion, was talking to Dymov and Kiriukha beside the foremost wagon. A mile and a half ahead there were long low white barns and little houses with tiled roofs; there were neither yards nor trees to be seen beside the little houses.

'What village is that, Grandfather?' asked Yegorushka.

'That's the Armenian farmers, youngster,' answered Pantelei. 'The Armenians live there. They are a good sort of people . . . the Armenians are.'

The man in grey had finished talking to Dymov and Kiriukha; he pulled up his little stallion and looked across towards the farms.

'What a business, only think!' sighed Pantelei, looking towards the farms, too, and shivering at the morning freshness. 'He has sent a man to the farm for some papers, and the man hasn't come back . . . He should have sent Stiopka.'

'Who is that, Grandfather?' asked Yegorushka.

'Varlamov.'

My goodness! Yegorushka jumped up quickly, to a kneeling position, and looked at the white cap. It was hard to recognise the mysterious elusive Varlamov, who was sought by everyone, who was always 'on his rounds' and who had far more money than Countess Dranitskaia, in the short, grey little man in big boots, who was sitting on an ugly little nag and talking to peasants at an hour when all decent people were asleep.

'He is all right, a good man,' said Pantelei, looking towards the settlement. 'God give him health – a splendid gentleman, Semion Varlamov . . . The salt of the earth. That's true . . . The cocks are not crowing yet, and he is already up and about . . . Anyone else would be asleep, or gallivanting with visitors at home, but he is on the steppe all day . . . on his rounds . . . He doesn't let things slip . . . No-o! He's a fine fellow . . .'

Varlamov was talking about something, while he kept his eyes fixed. The little stallion shifted from one leg to another impatiently.

'Mr Varlamov!' cried Pantelei, taking off his hat. 'Let us send Stiopka! Yemelian, call out and have Stiopka go.'

But now at last a man on horseback could be seen coming from the settlement. Bending very much to one side and brandishing his whip above his head like a gallant young Caucasian, and wanting to astonish everyone by his horsemanship, he flew towards the wagons with the swiftness of a bird.

'That must be one of his circuit men,' said Pantelei. 'He must have a hundred such horsemen or maybe more.'

Reaching the first wagon, he pulled up his horse, and taking off his hat, handed Varlamov a little book. Varlamov took several papers out of the book, read them and cried:

'And where is Ivanchuk's note?'

The horseman took the book back, looked at the papers and shrugged his shoulders. He began saying something, probably justifying himself and asking to be allowed to ride back to the settlement again. The little stallion suddenly stirred as though Varlamov had grown heavier. Varlamov stirred too.

'Get out of here!' he cried angrily, and he waved his whip at the man.

Then he turned his horse round and, looking through the papers in the book, moved at a walking pace alongside the wagons. When he reached the hindmost, Yegorushka strained his eyes to get a better look at him. Varlamov was an elderly man. His face, a simple Russian sunburnt face with a small grey beard, was red, wet with dew and covered with little blue veins; it had the same expression of business-like coldness as Ivan Kuzmichov's face, the same look of fanatical zeal for business. But yet what a difference could be felt between him and Kuzmichov! Uncle Ivan always had on his face, together with his business-like reserve, a look of anxiety and apprehension that he would not find Varlamov, that he would be late, that he would miss a good price; nothing of that sort, so characteristic of small and dependent persons, could be seen in the face or figure of Varlamov. This man made the price himself, was not looking for anyone, and did not depend on anyone; however ordinary his exterior, yet in everything, even in the manner of holding his whip, there was a sense of power and habitual authority over the steppe.

As he rode by Yegorushka he did not glance at him. Only the little stallion deigned to notice Yegorushka; he looked at him with his large foolish eyes, and even he showed no interest. Pantelei bowed to Varlamov; the latter noticed it, and without taking his eyes off the sheets of paper, lisped:

'How are you, old man?'

Varlamov's conversation with the horseman and the way he had brandished his whip had evidently made an overwhelming impression on the whole party. Everyone looked grave. The man on horseback, downcast at the anger of the great man, remained stationary with his hat off, and the rein loose by the foremost wagon; he was silent, and seemed unable to grasp that the day had begun so badly for him.

'He is a hard old man . . .' muttered Pantelei. 'It's a pity he's so hard! But he is all right, a good man . . . He doesn't abuse men for nothing . . . It's no matter . . .'

After examining the papers, Varlamov thrust the book into his pocket; the little stallion, as though he knew what was in his mind, without waiting for orders, started and dashed along the highroad.

VII

On the following night the waggoners had halted and were cooking their porridge. On this occasion there was a sense of overwhelming oppression over everyone. It was sultry; they all drank a great deal, but could not quench their thirst. The moon was intensely crimson and sullen, as though it were sick. The stars, too, were sullen, the mist was thicker, the distance more clouded. Nature seemed as though languid and weighed down by some foreboding.

There was not the same liveliness and talk round the camp fire as there had been the day before. All were dreary and spoke listlessly and without interest. Pantelei did nothing but sigh and complain of his feet, and continually alluded to sudden death.

Dymov was lying on his stomach, chewing a straw in silence; there was an expression of disgust on his face as though the straw smelt unpleasant, a spiteful and exhausted look . . . Vasia complained that his jaw ached, and prophesied bad weather; Yemelian was not waving his arms, but sitting still and looking gloomily at the fire. Yegorushka, too, was weary. This slow travelling exhausted him, and the sultriness of the day had given him a headache.

While they were cooking the porridge, Dymov, to relieve his boredom, began quarrelling with his companions.

'Here he lolls, the lumpy face, and is the first to put his spoon in,' he said, looking spitefully at Yemelian. 'Greedy! always working out how to get to the pot first. He's been a chorister, so he thinks he is a gentleman! There are a lot of choristers like you begging along the highroad!'

'Why are you getting at me?' asked Yemelian, looking at him angrily.

'To teach you not to be the first to dip into the pot. Don't overreach yourself!'

'You are a fool, and that is all there is to it!' wheezed out Yemelian.

Knowing by experience how such conversations usually ended, Pantelei and Vasia intervened and tried to persuade Dymov not to quarrel over nothing.

'A chorister!' The bully would not desist, but laughed contemptuously. 'Anyone can sing like that – sit in the church porch and sing "Give me alms, for Christ's sake!" Ugh!'

Yemelian did not speak. His silence had an irritating effect on Dymov. He looked with still greater hatred at the ex-chorister and said:

'I don't want to get near you, or I'd show you what you really are.'

'But why are you pestering me, you Mazepa?'* Yemelian cried, flaring up. 'Am I doing anything to you?'

'What did you call me?' asked Dymov, drawing himself up, and his eyes were suffused with blood. 'Eh! I'm a Mazepa, am I? Take that, then; go and look for it.'

Dymov snatched the spoon out of Yemelian's hand and flung it far away. Kiriukha, Vasia, and Stiopka ran to look for it, while Yemelian fixed an imploring and questioning look on Pantelei. His face suddenly became small and wrinkled; it began twitching, and the ex-chorister began to cry like a child.

Yegorushka, who had long hated Dymov, felt as though the air all at once were unbearably stifling, as though the fire were scorching his face; he longed to run quickly to the wagons in the darkness, but the bully's angry, bored eyes drew the boy to him. With a passionate desire to say something extremely offensive, he took a step towards Dymov, and brought out, gasping for breath:

'You are the worst of the lot; I can't bear you!'

After this he ought to have run to the wagons, but he could not stir from the spot, and went on:

'In the next world you will burn in hell! I'll complain to Mr Kuzmichov. Don't you dare insult Yemelian!'

'Say what you like,' laughed Dymov; 'every little sucking pig wants to lay down the law. Suppose I box your ears?'

Yegorushka felt that he could not breathe; and – it had never happened to him before – he suddenly began shaking all over, stamping his feet and crying shrilly:

'Beat him, beat him!'

Tears gushed from his eyes; he felt ashamed, and ran staggering back to the wagon. The effect produced by his outburst he did not see. Lying on the bales and twitching his arms and legs, he whispered:

'Mama, mama!'

And these men and the shadows round the camp fire, and the dark bales and the far-away lightning, which was flashing every minute in the distance – all struck him now as terrible and unfriendly. He was overcome with terror, and asked himself in despair why and how he had come into this unknown land in the company of terrible peasants? Where was his uncle now, where was Father Khristofor, where was Deniska? Why were they so long in coming? Had they forgotten him? At the thought that he was forgotten and cast out to the mercy of fate, he felt such a cold chill of dread that he had several times an impulse to jump off the bales of wool and run back full speed along the road; but the thought of the huge dark crosses, which would certainly meet him on the way, and the lightning flashing in the distance, stopped him . . . And only when he whispered, 'Mama, mama!' he felt, he thought, a little better.

The waggoners must have been full of dread, too. After Yegorushka had run away from the camp fire they sat at first for a long time in silence, then they began speaking in hollow undertones about something, saying that it was coming and that they must make haste and get away from it . . . They quickly finished supper, put out the fire and began harnessing the horses in silence. From their fluster and the broken phrases they uttered it was apparent they foresaw some trouble. Before they set off on their way, Dymov went up to Pantelei and asked softly:

'What's his name?'

'Yegorushka,' answered Pantelei.

Dymov put one foot on the wheel, caught hold of the cord which was tied round the bales, and pulled himself up. Yegorushka saw his face and curly head. The face was pale and looked grave and exhausted, but there was no expression of spite in it.

'Yegorushka!' he said softly, 'go on, hit me!'

Yegorushka looked at him in surprise. At that instant there was a flash of lightning.

'It's all right, hit me,' repeated Dymov. And without waiting for Yegorushka to hit him or to speak to him, he jumped down and said: 'God, I feel sad.'

Then, swaying from one leg to the other and moving his shoulder blades, he sauntered lazily alongside the string of wagons and repeated in a voice half weeping, half angry:

'God, I feel sad. Oh Lord! Don't you take offence, Yemelian,' he said as he passed Yemelian. 'Ours is a wretched cruel life!'

There was a flash of lightning on the right, and, like a reflection in the looking glass, at once a second flash in the distance.

'Yegorushka, take this,' cried Pantelei, throwing up something big and dark.

'What is it?' asked Yegorushka.

'Matting. There will be rain, so cover yourself up.'

Yegorushka sat up and looked about him. The distance had grown perceptibly blacker, and now oftener than every minute winked with a pale light. The blackness was being bent towards the right as though by its own weight.

'Will there be a storm, Grandfather?' asked Yegorushka.

'Ah, my poor chilled feet, how they ache!' Pantelei said in a high-pitched voice, stamping his feet and not hearing the boy.

On the left someone seemed to strike a match in the sky; a pale phosphorescent streak gleamed and went out. There was a sound as though someone very far away were walking over an iron roof, probably barefoot, for the iron gave a hollow rumble.

'It's going to be heavy!' cried Kiriukha.

Between the distance and the horizon on the right there was a flash of lightning so vivid that it lighted up part of the steppe and the spot where the clear sky met the blackness. A terrible cloud was swooping down, without haste, a compact mass; big black shreds hung from its edge; similar shreds pressing one upon the another were piling up on the right and left horizon. The tattered, ragged look of the storm cloud gave it a drunken trouble-making air. There was a distinct, not smothered, growl of thunder. Yegorushka crossed himself and began quickly putting on his greatcoat.

'God, I feel sad!' Dymov's shout floated from the foremost wagon, and it could be told from his voice that he was beginning to turn nasty again. 'I feel sad.'

All at once there was a squall of wind, so violent that it almost snatched away Yegorushka's bundle and mat; the mat fluttered in all directions and flapped on the bale and on Yegorushka's face. The wind dashed whistling over the steppe, whirled round in disorder and raised such an uproar from the grass that neither the thunder nor the creaking of the wheels could be heard; it blew from the black storm cloud, carrying with it clouds of dust and the scent of rain and wet earth. The moonlight grew mistier, as it were dirtier; the stars were even more overcast; and the clouds of dust could be seen hurrying along the edge of the road, followed by their shadows. By now, most likely, the whirlwind, eddying round and lifting from the earth dust, dry grass and feathers, was mounting to the very sky; the tumbleweed must have been flying by that very black storm cloud, and how frightened they must have been! But through the dust that clogged the eyes nothing could be seen but the flash of lightning.

Yegorushka, thinking it would pour with rain in a minute, knelt up and covered himself with the mat.

'Pantelei-ei!' someone shouted in the front. 'A . . . a . . . va!'

'Can't hear!' Pantelei answered in a loud voice. 'A . . . a . . . va! Arya . . . a!'

There was an angry clap of thunder, which rolled across the sky from right to left, then back again, and died away near the foremost wagon.

'Holy, holy, holy, Lord Sabaoth,' whispered Yegorushka, crossing himself. 'Heaven and earth are filled with Thy glory.'

The blackness in the sky yawned wide and breathed white fire. At once there was another clap of thunder. It had scarcely ceased when there was a flash of lightning so broad that Yegorushka suddenly saw through a slit in the mat the whole highroad to the very horizon, all the waggoners and even Kiriukha's waistcoat. The black shreds had by now moved upwards from the left, and one of them, a coarse, clumsy monster like a paw with fingers, stretched to the moon. Yegorushka made up his mind to shut his eyes tight, to pay no attention to it, and to wait till it was all over.

The rain was for some reason long in coming. Yegorushka peeped out from the mat in the hope that perhaps the storm cloud was passing over. It was fearfully dark. Yegorushka could see neither Pantelei, nor the bale of wool nor himself; he looked sideways towards the place where the moon had lately been, but there was the same black darkness there as over the wagons. And in the darkness the flashes of lightning seemed more violent and blinding, so that they hurt his eyes.

'Pantelei!' called Yegorushka.

No answer followed. But now a gust of wind for the last time flung up the mat and hurried away. A quiet regular sound was heard. A big cold drop fell on Yegorushka's knee, another trickled over his hand. He noticed that his knees were not covered, and tried to rearrange the mat, but at that moment something began pattering on the road, then on the shafts and the bales. It was the rain. As though they understood one another, the rain and the mat began prattling of something rapidly, gaily and most annoyingly, like two magpies.

Yegorushka knelt up or rather squatted on his boots. While the rain was pattering on the mat, he leaned forward to screen his knees, which were suddenly wet. He succeeded in covering his knees, but in less than a minute was aware of a penetrating unpleasant dampness behind on his back and calves. He returned to his former position, exposing his knees to the rain, and wondered what to do to rearrange the mat, which he could not see in the darkness. But his arms were already wet, the water was trickling up his sleeves and down his collar, and his shoulder blades felt chilly. And he made up his mind to do nothing but sit motionless and wait till it was over.

'Holy, holy, holy!' he whispered.

Suddenly, right over his head, the sky cracked with a fearful deafening din; he huddled up and held his breath, waiting for the fragments to fall upon his head and back. He inadvertently opened his eyes and saw a blinding intense light flare out and flash five times on his fingers, his wet sleeves, and on the trickles of water running from the mat upon the bales and down to the ground. There was a fresh peal of thunder as violent and awful; the sky was not growling and rumbling now, but uttering short crashing sounds like the crackling of dry wood.

'Trrah! tah! tah! tah!' the thunder hammered distinctly, rolled over the sky, seemed to stumble, and somewhere by the foremost wagons or far behind to fall with an abrupt angry 'Trrrah!'

The flashes of lightning had at first been only terrible, but with this thunder they seemed sinister and menacing. Their magic light pierced through closed eyelids and sent a chill all over the body. What could he do so as not to see them? Yegorushka made up his mind to turn over on his face. Cautiously, as though afraid of being watched, he got on all fours, and his hands slipping on the wet bale, he turned back again.

'Trrah! tah! tah!' floated over his head, rolled under the wagons and exploded 'Kraa!'

Again he inadvertently opened his eyes and saw a new danger: three huge giants with long pikes were following the wagon! A flash of lightning gleamed on the points of their pikes and lighted up their figures very distinctly. They were men of huge proportions, with covered faces, bowed heads, and heavy footsteps. They seemed gloomy and dispirited and lost in thought. Perhaps they were not following the wagons with any harmful intent, and yet there was something awful in their proximity.

Yegorushka turned quickly forward, and trembling all over, cried: 'Pantelei! Grandfather!'

'Trrah! tah! tah!' the sky answered him.

He opened his eyes to see if the waggoners were there. There were flashes of lightning in two places, which lighted up the road to the far distance, the whole string of wagons and all the waggoners. Streams of water were flowing along the road and bubbles were dancing. Pantelei was walking beside the wagon; his tall hat and his shoulder were covered with a small mat; his figure expressed neither terror nor uneasiness, as though he were deafened by the thunder and blinded by the lightning.

'Grandfather, the giants!' Yegorushka shouted to him in tears.

But the old man did not hear. Further away walked Yemelian. He was covered from head to foot with a big mat and was triangular in shape. Vasia, without anything over him, was walking with the same wooden step as usual, lifting his feet high and not bending his knees. In the flash of lightning it seemed as though the wagons were not moving and the men were motionless, that Vasia's lifted foot was rigid in the same position . . .

Yegorushka called the old man once more. Getting no answer, he sat motionless, and no longer waited for it all to end. He was convinced that the thunder would kill him in another minute, that he would accidentally open his eyes and see the terrible giants, and he stopped crossing himself, calling the old man and thinking of his mother: he was simply numb with cold and the conviction that the storm would never end.

But at last there was the sound of voices.

'Yegorushka, are you asleep?' Pantelei cried below. 'Get down! Is he deaf, the silly little thing? . . .'

'That's a real storm!' said an unfamiliar bass voice, and the stranger cleared his throat as though he had just tossed off a good glass of vodka.

Yegorushka opened his eyes. Close to the wagon stood Pantelei, Yemelian, looking like a triangle, and the giants. The latter were by now much shorter, and when Yegorushka looked more closely at them they turned out to be ordinary peasants, carrying on their shoulders not pikes but pitchforks. In the space between Pantelei and the triangular figure gleamed the window of a squat peasant house. So the wagons were halting in the village. Yegorushka flung off the mat, took his bundle and made haste to get off the wagon. Now when close to him there were people talking and a lighted window he no longer felt afraid, though the thunder was crashing as before and the whole sky was streaked with lightning.

'It was a good storm, all right . . .' Pantelei was muttering. 'Thank God . . . my feet are a little softened by the rain. It was all right . . . Have you got down, Yegorushka? Well, go into the house it's all right . . .'

'Holy, holy, holy!' wheezed Yegorushka, 'it must have struck something . . . Are you of these parts?' he asked the giants.

'No, from Glinovo. We belong to Glinovo. We are working for the Plater gentry.'

'Threshing?'

'All sorts. Just now we are getting in the wheat. The lightning, the lightning! It is long since we have had such a storm . . .'

Yegorushka went into the hut. He was met by a lean hunchbacked old woman with a sharp chin. She stood holding a tallow candle in her hands, screwing up her eyes and heaving prolonged sighs.

'What a storm God has sent us!' she said. 'And our lads are out for the night on the steppe; they'll have a bad time, poor dears! Take off your things, little sir, take off your things.'

Shivering with cold and shrugging squeamishly, Yegorushka pulled off his drenched overcoat, then stretched out his arms and straddled his legs, and stood a long time without moving. The slightest movement caused an unpleasant sensation of cold and wetness. His sleeves and the back of his shirt were sopping, his trousers stuck to his legs, his head was dripping.

'What's the use of standing there, with your legs apart, little lad?' said the old woman. 'Come, sit down.'

Holding his legs wide apart, Yegorushka went up to the table and sat down on a bench near somebody's head. The head moved, puffed a stream of air through its nose, made a chewing sound and subsided. A mound covered with a sheepskin stretched from the head along the bench; it was a peasant woman asleep.

The old woman went out sighing, and came back with a big water melon and a little sweet melon.

'Have something to eat, my dear! I have nothing else to offer you . . .' she said, yawning. She rummaged in the table and took out a long sharp knife, very much like the one with which the brigands killed the merchants in the inn. 'Have some, my dear!'

Yegorushka, shivering as though he were in a fever, ate a slice of sweet melon with black bread and then a slice of watermelon, and that made him feel colder still.

'Our lads are out on the steppe for the night . . .' sighed the old woman while he was eating. 'Jesus on the cross! I'd light the candle under the icon, but I don't know where Stepanida has put it. Have some more, little sir, have some more . . .' The old woman gave a yawn and, putting her right hand behind her, scratched her left shoulder.

'It must be about two o'clock now,' she said; 'it will soon be time to get up. Our lads are out on the steppe for the night; they are all wet through for sure . . .'

'Granny,' said Yegorushka, 'I am sleepy.'

'Lie down, my dear, lie down . . .' the old woman sighed, yawning. 'Lord Jesus Christ! I was asleep, when I heard a noise as though someone were knocking. I woke up and looked, and it was the storm God had sent us . . . I'd have lit the candle, but I couldn't find it.'

Talking to herself, she pulled some rags, probably her own bedding, off the bench, took two sheepskins off a nail by the stove, and began laying them out for a bed for Yegorushka. 'The storm's not dying down,' she muttered. 'You never know your luck, something

could be struck by lightning . . . Our lads are out on the steppe for the
night. Lie down and sleep, my dear . . . Christ be with you, my
child . . . I won't take away the melon; maybe you'll have a bit when
you get up.'

The sighs and yawns of the old woman, the even breathing of the
sleeping woman, the half-darkness of the hut, and the sound of the
rain outside, made Yegorushka sleepy. He was shy of undressing
before the old woman. He only took off his boots, lay down and
covered himself with the sheepskin.

'Is the little lad lying down?' he heard Pantelei whisper a little later.

'Yes,' answered the old woman in a whisper. 'Jesus on the cross! It
thunders and thunders, and there is no end to it.'

'It will soon be over,' wheezed Pantelei, sitting down; 'it's getting
quieter . . . The lads have gone into the huts, and two have stayed
with the horses. The lads have . . . They can't . . . the horses would be
taken away . . . I'll sit here a bit and then go and take my turn . . . We
can't leave them; they would be taken . . .'

Pantelei and the old woman sat side by side at Yegorushka's feet,
talking in hissing whispers and interspersing their speech with sighs
and yawns. And Yegorushka could not get warm. The warm heavy
sheepskin lay on him, but he was trembling all over; his arms and legs
were twitching, and his whole inside was shivering . . . He undressed
under the sheepskin, but that was no good. His shivering grew more
and more acute.

Pantelei went out to take his turn with the horses, and afterwards
came back again, and still Yegorushka was shivering all over and
could not get to sleep. Something weighed upon his head and chest
and oppressed him, and he did not know what it was, whether it was
the old people whispering, or the heavy smell of the sheepskin. The
melon he had eaten left an unpleasant metallic taste in his mouth.
Moreover he was being bitten by fleas.

'Grandfather, I am cold,' he said, and did not know his own voice.

'Go to sleep, my child, go to sleep,' sighed the old woman.

Tit came up to the bedside on his thin little legs and waved his arms,
then grew up to the ceiling and turned into a windmill . . . Father
Khristofor, not as he was in the chaise, but in his full vestments with
the sprinkler in his hand, walked round the mill, sprinkling it with
holy water, and it left off waving. Yegorushka, knowing this was
delirium, opened his eyes.

'Grandfather,' he called, 'give me some water.'

No one answered. Yegorushka felt it insufferably stifling and
uncomfortable lying down. He got up, dressed, and went out of the hut.
Morning was beginning. The sky was overcast, but it was no longer

raining. Shivering and wrapping himself in his wet overcoat, Yegorushka walked about the muddy yard and listened to the silence; he caught sight of a little shed with a half-opened door made of reeds. He looked into this shed, went into it, and sat down in a dark corner on a heap of dry dung.

There was a tangle of thoughts in his heavy head; his mouth was dry and unpleasant from the metallic taste. He looked at his hat, straightened the peacock's feather in it, and thought how he had gone with his mother to buy the hat. He put his hand into his pocket and took out a lump of brownish sticky paste. How had that paste come into his pocket? He thought a minute, smelt it; it smelt of honey. Aha! it was the Jewish cake! How sodden it was, poor thing!

Yegorushka examined his coat. It was a little grey overcoat with big bone buttons, and cut in the shape of a frock coat. At home, as a new and expensive ariticle, it had not been hung in the hall, but with his mother's dresses in her bedroom; he was only allowed to wear it on holidays. Looking at it, Yegorushka felt sorry for it. He thought that he and the greatcoat were both abandoned to the mercy of destiny; he thought that he would never get back home, and began sobbing so violently that he almost fell off the heap of dung.

A big white dog with woolly tufts like curl-papers about its face, soaked from the rain, came into the shed and stared with curiosity at Yegorushka. It seemed to be hesitating whether to bark or not. Deciding that there was no need to bark, it went cautiously up to Yegorushka, ate the sticky mess left from the cake and went out again.

'There are Varlamov's men!' someone shouted in the street.

After weeping his fill, Yegorushka went out of the shed and, walking round a big puddle, made his way towards the street. The wagons were standing exactly opposite the gateway. The drenched waggoners, with their muddy feet, were sauntering beside them or sitting on the shafts, as listless and drowsy as flies in autumn. Yegorushka looked at them and thought: 'How miserable and comfortless to be a peasant!' He went up to Pantelei and sat down beside him on the shaft.

'Grandfather, I'm cold,' he said, shivering and thrusting his hands up his sleeves.

'Never mind, we shall soon be there,' yawned Pantelei. 'Never mind, you will get warm.'

It must have been early when the waggoners set off, for it was not hot. Yegorushka lay on the bales of wool and shivered with cold, though the sun soon came out and dried his clothes, the bales, and the earth. As soon as he closed his eyes he saw Tit and the windmill again.

Feeling a sickness and heaviness all over, he did his utmost to drive away these images, but as soon as they vanished the daredevil Dymov, with red eyes and lifted fists, rushed at Yegorushka with a roar, or there was the sound of his complaint: 'God, I feel sad!' Varlamov rode by on his little Cossack stallion; happy Konstantin passed, with a smile and the bustard in his arms. And how tedious these people were, how sickening and unbearable!

Once – it was towards evening – he raised his head to ask for water. The wagons were standing on a big bridge across a broad river. There was black smoke over the river, and through it could be seen a steamer with a barge in tow. Ahead of them, beyond the river, was a huge mountain dotted with houses and churches; at the foot of the mountain a locomotive was being shunted along beside some goods trucks . . .

Yegorushka had never before seen steamers, locomotives, or broad rivers. Glancing at them now, he was not alarmed or surprised; there was not even a look of anything like curiosity in his face. He merely felt sick, and made haste to turn over to the edge of the bale. He was sick. Pantelei, seeing this, cleared his throat and shook his head.

'Our little lad's taken ill,' he said. 'He must have got a chill to the stomach. The little lad . . . Away from home . . . It's a bad business!'

VIII

The wagons stopped at a big inn for merchants, not far from the quay. As Yegorushka climbed down from the wagon he heard a familiar voice. Someone was helping him to get down, and saying:

'We arrived yesterday evening . . . We have been expecting you all day. We meant to overtake you yesterday, but it was out of our way; we came by the other road. I say, how you have creased your coat! You'll catch it from your uncle!'

Yegorushka looked into the speaker's mottled face and remembered that this was Deniska.

'Your uncle and Father Khristofor are in the inn now, drinking tea; come along!'

And he led Yegorushka to a big two-storied building, dark and gloomy like the almshouse at N—. After going across the entry, up a dark staircase and through a narrow corridor, Yegorushka and Deniska reached a little room in which Mr Kuzmichov and Father Khristofor were sitting at the tea-table. Seeing the boy, both the old men showed surprise and pleasure.

'Aha! Yegorushka!' chanted Father Khristofor. 'Mr Lomonosov!'

'Ah, the gentry,' said Mr Kuzmichov, 'pleased to see you!'

Yegorushka took off his greatcoat, kissed his uncle's hand and Father Khristofor's, and sat down at the table.

'Well, how did you like the journey, *puer bone*?' Father Khristofor pelted him with questions as he poured him out some tea, with his radiant smile. 'Sick of it, I've no doubt? God save us all from having to travel by wagon or with oxen. You go on and on, God forgive us; you look ahead and the steppe is always lying stretched out the same as it was — you can't see the end of it! It's not travelling but regular torture. Why don't you drink your tea? Drink it up. In your absence, while you have been trailing along with the wagons, we have settled all our business capitally. Thank God we have sold our wool to Cherepakhin, and no one could wish to have done better . . . We have made a good bargain.'

At the first sight of his own people Yegorushka felt an overwhelming desire to complain. He did not listen to Father Khristofor, but thought how to begin and what exactly to complain of. But Father Khristofor's voice, which seemed to him harsh and unpleasant, prevented him from concentrating his attention and confused his thoughts. He had not sat at the table five minutes before he got up, went to the sofa and lay down.

'Well, well,' said Father Khristofor in surprise. 'What about your tea?'

Still thinking what to complain of, Yegorushka leaned his head against the wall and broke into sobs.

'Well, well!' repeated Father Khristofor, getting up and going to the sofa. 'Yegorushka, what is the matter with you? Why are you crying?'

'I'm . . . I'm ill,' Yegorushka brought out.

'Ill?' said Father Khristofor in amazement. 'That's not the right thing, my boy . . . One mustn't be ill on a journey. Ay, ay, what are you thinking about, boy . . . eh?'

He put his hand to Yegorushka's head, touched his cheek and said:

'Yes, your head is feverish . . . You must have caught cold or else have eaten something . . . Pray to God.'

'Should we give him quinine? . . .' said Mr Kuzmichov, troubled.

'No; he ought to have something hot . . . Yegorushka, have a little drop of soup? Eh?'

'I . . . don't want any,' said Yegorushka.

'Are you feeling chilly?'

'I was chilly before, but now . . . now I am hot. And I ache all over . . .'

Mr Kuzmichov went up to the sofa, touched Yegorushka on the head, cleared his throat with a perplexed air, and went back to the table.

'I tell you what, you undress and go to bed,' said Father Khristofor. 'What you want is sleep now.'

He helped Yegorushka to undress, gave him a pillow and covered him with a quilt, and over that Mr Kuzmichov's greatcoat. Then he walked away on tiptoe and sat down to the table. Yegorushka shut his eyes, and at once it seemed to him that he was not in the hotel room, but on the highroad beside the camp fire. Yemelian waved his hands, and Dymov with red eyes lay on his stomach and looked mockingly at Yegorushka.

'Beat him, beat him!' shouted Yegorushka.

'He is delirious,' said Father Khristofor in an undertone.

'It's a nuisance!' sighed Mr Kuzmichov.

'He must be rubbed with oil and vinegar. Please God, he will be better tomorrow.'

To be rid of bad dreams, Yegorushka opened his eyes and began looking towards the fire. Father Khristofor and Mr Kuzmichov had now finished their tea and were talking in a whisper. The first was smiling with delight, and evidently could not forget that he had made a good bargain over his wool; what delighted him was not so much the actual profit he had made, as the thought that on getting home he would gather round him his big family, wink slyly and go off into a chuckle; at first he would deceive them all, and say that he had sold the wool at a price below its value, then he would give his son-in-law, Mikhailo, a fat wallet and say: 'There you are! That's the way to do business!' Kuzmichov did not seem pleased; his face expressed, as before, a businesslike reserve and anxiety.

'If I'd known that Cherepakhin would give such a price,' he said in a low voice, 'I wouldn't have sold Makarov those five tons at home! It is vexing! But who'd have known that the price had gone up here?'

A waiter in a white shirt cleared away the samovar and lit the little lamp before the icon in the corner. Father Khristofor whispered something in his ear; the man looked, made a serious face like a conspirator, as though to say, 'I understand', went out, and returned a little while afterwards and put something under the sofa. Mr Kuzmichov made himself a bed on the floor, yawned several times, said his prayers lazily, and lay down.

'I think of going to the cathedral tomorrow,' said Father Khristofor. 'I know the sacristan there. I ought to go and see the bishop after mass, but they say he is ill.'

He yawned and put out the lamp. Now there was no light in the room but the little lamp before the icon.

'They say he can't receive visitors,' Father Khristofor went on, undressing. 'So I shall go away without seeing him.'

He took off his full coat, and Yegorushka saw Robinson Crusoe reappear. Robinson stirred something in a saucer, went up to Yegorushka and whispered:

'Lomonosov, are you asleep? Sit up; I'm going to rub you with oil and vinegar. It's a good thing, only you must say a prayer.'

Yegorushka roused himself quickly and sat up. Father Khristofor pulled off the boy's shirt, and shrinking and breathing jerkily, as though he were being tickled himself, began rubbing Yegorushka's chest.

'In the name of the Father, the Son, and the Holy Ghost,' he whispered, 'lie on your stomach – that's it . . . You'll be all right tomorrow, but don't do it again . . . You are as hot as fire. I suppose you were on the road in the storm.'

'Yes.'

'Let's hope you don't get really ill! In the name of the Father, the Son, and the Holy Ghost . . . Let's hope you don't get really ill!'

After rubbing Yegorushka, Father Khristofor put on his shirt again, covered him, made the sign of the cross over him, and walked away. Then Yegorushka saw him saying his prayers. Probably the old man knew a great many prayers by heart, for he stood a long time before the icon murmuring. After saying his prayers he made the sign of the cross over the window, the door, Yegorushka, and Mr Kuzmichov, lay down on the little sofa without a pillow, and covered himself with his full coat. A clock in the corridor struck ten. Yegorushka thought how long a time it would be before morning; feeling miserable, he pressed his forehead against the back of the sofa and stopped trying to get rid of the oppressive misty dreams. But morning came much sooner than he had expected.

It seemed to him that he had not been lying long with his head pressed to the back of the sofa, but when he opened his eyes slanting rays of sunlight were already shining on the floor through the two windows of the little hotel room. Father Khristofor and Mr Kuzmichov were not in the room. The room had been tidied; it was bright, snug, and smelt of Father Khristofor, who always smelt of cypress and dried cornflowers (at home he used to make the holy water sprinklers and decorations for the icon stands out of cornflowers, and so he was imbued with the smell of them). Yegorushka looked at the pillow, at the slanting sunbeams, at his boots, which had been cleaned and were standing side by side near the sofa, and laughed. It seemed strange to him that he was not on the bales of wool, that everything was dry around him, and that there was no thunder and lightning on the ceiling.

He jumped off the sofa and began dressing. He felt splendid;

nothing was left of his yesterday's illness but a slight weakness in his legs and neck. So the vinegar and oil had done him good. He remembered the steamer, the railway engine, and the broad river, which he had dimly seen the day before, and now he made haste to dress, to run to the quay and have a look at them. When he had washed and was putting on his red shirt, the latch of the door clicked, and Father Khristofor appeared in the doorway, wearing his top hat and a brown silk cassock over his canvas coat and carrying his staff in his hand. Smiling and radiant (old men are always radiant when they come back from church), he put a roll of holy bread and a parcel of some sort on the table, prayed before the icon, and said:

'God has sent us blessings – well, how are you?'

'Quite well now,' answered Yegorushka, kissing his hand.

'Glory to God . . . I've been to mass . . . I've been to see a sacristan I know. He invited me to breakfast with him, but I didn't go. I don't like visiting people too early, God bless them!'

He took off his cassock, stroked himself on the chest, and without haste undid the parcel. Yegorushka saw a little tin of caviar, a piece of dry sturgeon, and a French loaf.

'See; I passed a fish shop and brought this,' said Father Khristofor. 'There is no call to indulge in luxuries on an ordinary weekday; but I thought, I've an invalid at home, so it is excusable. And the caviar is good, real sturgeon . . .'

The waiter in the white shirt brought in the samovar and a tray with tea things.

'Eat some,' said Father Khristofor, spreading the caviar on a slice of bread and handing it to Yegorushka. 'Eat now and enjoy yourself, but the time will soon come for you to be studying. Mind you study with attention and application, so that good may come of it. What you have to learn by heart, learn by heart, but when you have to tell the inner sense in your own words, without regard to the outer form, then say it in your own words. And try to master all subjects. One man knows mathematics excellently, but has never heard of Piotr Mogila;* another knows about Piotr Mogila, but cannot explain about the moon. But you study so as to understand everything. Study Latin, French, German, . . . geography, of course, history, theology, philosophy, mathematics . . . and when you have mastered everything, not with haste but with prayer and with zeal, then go and work. When you know everything it will be easy for you in any time of life . . . You study and strive for divine blessing, and God will show you what to be. Whether a doctor, a judge or an engineer . . .'

Father Khristofor spread a little caviar on a piece of bread, put it in his mouth and said:

'The Apostle Paul says: "Do not apply yourself to strange and diverse studies." Of course, if it is black magic, unlawful arts, or calling up spirits from the other world, like Saul, or studying subjects that can be of no use to yourself or others, better not learn them. You must undertake only what God has blessed. You think about it . . . The Holy Apostles spoke in all languages, so you study languages. Basil the Great studied mathematics and philosophy – so you study them; St Nestor* wrote history – so you study and write history. Consider the saints' example.'

Father Khristofor sipped the tea from his saucer, wiped his moustaches, and shook his head.

'Good!' he said. 'I was educated in the old-fashioned way; I have forgotten a great deal by now, but still I live differently from other people. Indeed, there is no comparison. For instance, in company at a dinner, or at an assembly, one says something in Latin, or makes some allusion from history or philosophy, and it pleases people, and it pleases me myself . . . Or when the circuit court comes and one has to take the oath, all the other priests are shy, but I am quite at home with the judges, the prosecutors, and the lawyers. I talk intellectually, drink a cup of tea with them, laugh, ask them what I don't know . . . and they like it. So that's how it is, my boy. Learning is light and ignorance is darkness. Study! It's hard, of course, nowadays study is expensive . . . Your mother is a widow; she lives on her pension, but there, of course . . .'

Father Khristofor glanced apprehensively towards the door, and went on in a whisper:

'Mr Kuzmichov will assist. He won't desert you. He has no children of his own, and he will help you. Don't worry.'

He looked grave, and whispered still more softly:

'Only mind, Yegorushka, don't forget your mother and Mr Kuzmichov, God preserve you from it. The commandment bids you honour your mother, and Mr Kuzmichov is your benefactor and takes the place of a father to you. If you become learned, God forbid you should be impatient and scornful with people because they are not so clever as you, then woe, woe to you!'

Father Khristofor raised his hand and repeated in a thin voice:

'Woe to you! Woe to you!'

Father Khristofor's tongue was loosened, and he was, as they say, warming to his subject; he would not have finished till dinner-time but the door opened and Mr Kuzmichov walked in. He said good morning hurriedly, sat down to the table, and began rapidly swallowing his tea.

'Well, I have settled our business,' he said. 'We might have gone home today, but we have still to think about Yegorushka. We must arrange for him. My sister told me that Nastasia Petrovna, a friend of hers, lives somewhere here, so perhaps she will take him in as a boarder.'

He rummaged in his pocket book, found a crumpled note and read:

'Little Lower Street: for Nastasia Petrovna Toskunova, living in a house of her own. We must go at once and try to find her. It's a nuisance!'

Soon after breakfast Mr Kuzmichov and Yegorushka left the inn.

'It's a nuisance!' muttered his uncle. 'You are sticking to me like a burr. You and your mother want education and gentlemanly breeding and I have nothing but worry with you both . . .'

When they crossed the yard, the wagons and the drivers were not there. They had all gone off to the quay early in the morning. In a far-off corner of the yard stood the chaise.

'Good-bye, chaise!' thought Yegorushka.

At first they had to go a long way uphill by a broad street, then they had to cross a big market place; here Mr Kuzmichov asked a policeman for Little Lower Street.

'Aha,' said the policeman, with a grin, 'it's a long way off, out that way towards the town common.'

They met several cabs but Mr Kuzmichov only permitted himself such weakness as taking a cab in exceptional cases and on great holidays. Yegorushka and he walked for a long while through paved streets, then along streets where there were only wooden planks at the sides and no pavements, and in the end got to streets where there were neither planks nor pavements. When their legs and their tongues had brought them to Little Lower Street they were both red in the face, and taking off their hats, wiped away the perspiration.

'Tell me, please,' said Mr Kuzmichov, addressing an old man sitting on a little bench by a gate, 'where is Nastasia Petrovna Toskunova's house?'

'There is no one called Toskunova here,' said the old man, after pondering a moment. 'Perhaps it's Timoshenko, you want.'

'No, Toskunova . . .'

'Excuse me, there's no one called Toskunova . . .'

Mr Kuzmichov shrugged his shoulders and trudged on further.

'You needn't look,' the old man called after them. 'I tell you there isn't, and there isn't.'

'Listen, Auntie,' said Mr Kuzmichov, addressing an old woman who was sitting at a corner with a tray of pears and sunflower seeds, 'where is Nastasia Petrovna Toskunova's house?'

The old woman looked at him with surprise and laughed.

'Why, Nastasia Petrovna lives in another house now!' she cried. 'Lord! it is eight years since she married her daughter and gave up the house to her son-in-law! It's her son-in-law lives there now.'

And her eyes expressed: 'How is it you didn't know a simple thing like that, you fools?'

'And where does she live now?' Mr Kuzmichov asked.

'Oh, Lord!' cried the old woman, flinging up her hands in surprise. 'She moved ever so long ago! It's eight years since she gave up her house to her son-in-law! Upon my word!'

She probably expected Mr Kuzmichov to be surprised, too, and to exclaim: 'You don't say so,' but Mr Kuzmichov asked very calmly:

'Where does she live now?'

The old woman tucked up her sleeves and, stretching out her bare arm to point, shouted in a shrill piercing voice:

'Go straight on, straight on, straight on. You will pass a little red house, then you will see a little alley on your left. Turn down that little alley, and it will be the third gate on the right . . .'

Mr Kuzmichov and Yegorushka reached the little red house, turned to the left down the little alley, and made for the third gate on the right. On both sides of this very old grey gate there was a grey fence with big gaps in it. The first part of the fence was tilting forwards and threatened to fall, while on the left of the gate it sloped backwards towards the yard. The gate itself stood upright and seemed to be still undecided which would suit it best – to fall forwards or backwards. Mr Kuzmichov opened the little gate at the side, and he and Yegorushka saw a big yard overgrown with weeds and burdocks. A hundred paces from the gate stood a little house with a red roof and green shutters. A stout woman with her sleeves tucked up and her apron held out was standing in the middle of the yard, scattering something on the ground and shouting in a voice as shrill as that of the woman selling fruit:

'Chick! . . . Chick! . . . Chick!'

Behind her sat a red dog with pointed ears. Seeing the strangers, he ran to the little gate and broke into a tenor bark (all red dogs have a tenor bark).

'Whom do you want?' asked the woman, putting up her hand to shade her eyes from the sun.

'Good morning!' Mr Kuzmichov shouted, too, waving off the red dog with his stick. 'Tell me, please, does Nastasia Toskunova live here?'

'Yes! But what do you want with her?'

'Perhaps you are Nastasia?'

'Well, yes, I am!'

'Very pleased to see you ... You see, your old friend Olga
Kniazeva sends her love to you. This is her little son. And I, perhaps
you remember, am her brother Ivan Kuzmichov ... You are one of us
from N— ... You were born among us and married there ...'

A silence followed. The stout woman stared blankly at Mr
Kuzmichov, as though not believing or not understanding him, then
she flushed all over, and flung up her hands; the oats were scattered
out of her apron and tears spurted from her eyes.

'Olga!' she screamed, breathless with excitement. 'My own
darling! Ah, holy Saints, why am I standing here like a fool? My
pretty little angel ...'

She embraced Yegorushka, wetted his face with her tears, and
broke down completely.

'Heavens!' she said, wringing her hands, 'Olga's little boy! How
delightful! He is his mother all over! The image of his mother! But
why are you standing in the yard? Come indoors.'

Crying, gasping for breath and talking as she went, she hurried
towards the house. Her visitors trudged after her.

'The room has not been done yet,' she said, ushering the visitors
into a stuffy little drawing-room adorned with many icons and pots
of flowers. 'Oh, Mother of God! Vasilisa, go and open the shutters
anyway! My little angel! My little beauty! I did not know that Olga
had a boy like that!'

When she had calmed down and got over her first surprise Mr
Kuzmichov asked to speak to her alone. Yegorushka went into
another room; there was a sewing machine; in the window was a cage
with a starling in it, and there were as many icons and flowers as in the
drawing-room. Near the machine stood a little girl with a sunburnt
face and chubby cheeks like Tit's, and a clean cotton dress. She stared
at Yegorushka without blinking, and apparently felt very awkward.
Yegorushka looked at her and after a pause asked:

'What's your name?'

The little girl moved her lips, looked as if she were going to cry, and
answered softly:

'Atka ...'

This meant Katka.

'He will live with you,' Mr Kuzmichov was whispering in the
drawing-room, 'if you will be so kind, and we will pay ten roubles a
month for his keep. He is not a spoilt boy; he is quiet ...'

'I really don't know what to say, Mr Kuzmichov!' Nastasia sighed
tearfully. 'Ten roubles a month is very good, but it is a dreadful thing
to take another person's child! He may fall ill or something ...'

When Yegorushka was summoned back to the drawing-room

Mr Kuzmichov was standing with his hat in his hands, saying good-bye.

'Well, let him stay with you now, then,' he said. 'Good-bye! You stay, Yegorushka!' he said, addressing his nephew. 'Don't be troublesome; mind you obey Mrs Toskunova ... Good-bye; I am coming again tomorrow.'

And he went away. Nastasia once more embraced Yegorushka, called him a little angel, and with a tear-stained face began preparing for dinner. Three minutes later Yegorushka was sitting beside her, answering her endless questions and eating rich hot cabbage soup.

In the evening he sat again at the same table and, resting his head on his hand, listened to Nastasia. Alternately laughing and crying, she talked of his mother's young days, her own marriage, her children ... A cricket chirruped in the stove, and there was a faint humming from the burner of the lamp. Nastasia talked in a low voice, and was continually dropping her thimble in her excitement; and Katia, her granddaughter, crawled under the table after it and each time sat a long while under the table, probably examining Yegorushka's feet; and Yegorushka listened, half dozing and looking at the old woman's face, her wart with hairs on it, and the stains of tears ... and he felt sad, very sad. He was put to sleep on a wooden trunk and told that if he was hungry in the night he must go out into the little passage and take some chicken, put there under a plate in the window.

Next morning Mr Kuzmichov and Father Khristofor came to say good-bye. Nastasia was delighted to see them, and was about to set the samovar; but Mr Kuzmichov, who was in a great hurry, waved his hands and said:

'We have no time for tea! We are just setting off.'

Before parting they all sat down and were silent for a minute. Nastasia heaved a deep sigh and looked towards the icon with tear-stained eyes.

'Well,' began Mr Kuzmichov, getting up, 'so you will stay . . .'

All at once the look of businesslike reserve vanished from his face; he flushed a little and said with a mournful smile:

'Mind you work hard . . . Don't forget your mother, and obey Mrs Toskunova . . . If you are diligent at school, Yegor, I'll stand by you.'

He took his purse out of his pocket, turned his back to Yegorushka, fumbled for a long time among the smaller coins, and, finding a ten-kopeck piece, gave it to Yegorushka.

Father Khristofor, without haste, blessed Yegorushka.

'In the name of the Father, the Son, and the Holy Ghost . . . Study,' he said. 'Work hard, my lad. If I die, remember me in your prayers. Here is a ten-kopeck piece from me, too . . .'

Yegorushka kissed his hand, and shed tears; something whispered in his heart that he would never see the old man again.

'I have applied at the high school already,' said Mr Kuzmichov in a voice as though there were a corpse in the room. 'You will take him for the entrance examination on the seventh of August . . . Well, good-bye; God bless you, good-bye, Yegor!'

'You might at least have a cup of tea,' wailed Nastasia.

Through the tears that filled his eyes Yegorushka could not see his uncle and Father Khristofor go out. He rushed to the window, but they were not in the yard, and the red dog, who had just been barking, was running back from the gate with the air of having done his duty. Yegorushka, he could not have said why, leapt up and flew out of the room. When he ran out of the gate Mr Kuzmichov and Father Khristofor, the former waving his stick with the crook, the latter his staff, were just turning the corner. Yegorushka felt that with these people all that he had known till then had vanished from him for ever. He sank helplessly on to the little bench, and with bitter tears greeted the new unknown life that was beginning for him now . . .

What would that life be like?

1888

A Dreary Story
(from the notes of an old man)

There is in Russia an emeritus professor Nikolai Stepanovich, a chevalier and privy councillor; he has so many Russian and foreign decorations that when he has occasion to put them on the students nickname him 'The iconostas'. His acquaintances are of the most aristocratic; for the last twenty-five or thirty years, at any rate, there has not been one single distinguished man of learning in Russia with whom he has not been intimately acquainted. There is no one for him to make friends with nowadays; but if we turn to the past, the long list of his famous friends winds up with such names as Pirogov,* Kavelin,* and the poet Nekrasov,* all of whom bestowed upon him a warm and sincere affection. He is a member of all the Russian and of three foreign universities. And so on, and so on. All that and a great deal more that might be said makes up what is called my 'name'.

That is my name as known to the public. In Russia it is known to every educated man, and abroad it is mentioned in the lecture room with the addition 'honoured and distinguished'. It is one of those fortunate names, for to abuse it or to take it in vain, in public or in print, is considered a sign of bad taste. And that is as it should be. You see, my name is closely associated with the conception of a highly distinguished man of great gifts and unquestionable usefulness. I have the industry and power of endurance of a camel, and that is important, and I have talent, which is even more important. Moreover, while I am on this subject, I am a well-educated, modest, and honest fellow. I have never poked my nose into literature or politics; I have never sought popularity in polemics with the ignorant; I have never made speeches either at public dinners or at the funerals of my friends . . . In fact, there is no slur on my learned name, and there is no complaint one can make against it. My name is fortunate.

The bearer of that name, that is I, see myself as a man of sixty-two, with a bald head, with false teeth, and with an incurable *tic douloureux*. I am myself dingy and unsightly as my name is brilliant and splendid. My head and my hands tremble with weakness; my neck, as Turgenev says of one of his heroines,* is like a double bass's;

my chest is hollow; my shoulders narrow. When I talk or lecture, my mouth turns down at one corner; when I smile, my whole face is covered with aged-looking, deathly wrinkles. There is nothing impressive about my pitiful figure; only, perhaps, when I have an attack of *tic douloureux* my face wears a peculiar expression, the sight of which must arouse in everyone the grim and impressive thought, 'Evidently that man will soon die.'

I still, as in the past, lecture fairly well; I can still, as in the past, hold the attention of my listeners for a couple of hours. My fervour, the literary skill of my exposition, and my humour, almost efface the defects of my voice, though it is as harsh, dry, and monotonous as a Pharisee's at prayer. I write poorly. The bit of my brain which controls authorship refuses to work. My memory has grown weak; there is a lack of sequence in my ideas, and when I put them on paper it always seems to me that I have lost the instinct for their organic connection; my construction is monotonous; my phrasing is poor and timid. Often I write what I do not mean; I have forgotten the beginning when I am writing the end. Often I forget ordinary words, and I always have to waste a great deal of energy in avoiding superfluous phrases and unnecessary parenthesis in my letters, both unmistakable proofs of a decline in mental activity. And it is noteworthy that the simpler the letter, the more painful the effort to write it. At a scientific article I feel far more intelligent and at ease than at a letter of congratulation or a minute of proceedings. Another point: I find it easier to write in German or English than to write Russian.

As regards my present manner of life, I must give priority to the insomnia from which I have suffered of late. If I were asked what constituted the chief and fundamental feature of my existence now, I should answer, 'Insomnia.' As in the past, from habit I undress and go to bed exactly at midnight. I fall asleep quickly, but before two o'clock I wake up and feel as though I have not slept at all. Sometimes I get out of bed and light a lamp. For an hour or two I walk up and down the room looking at familiar photographs and pictures. When I am weary of walking about, I sit down at my desk. I sit motionless thinking of nothing, conscious of no desires; if a book is lying before me, I mechanically move it closer and read it without any interest – in that way not long ago I mechanically read through in one night a whole novel, with the strange title *The Song the Lark was Singing*;* or to occupy my attention I force myself to count to a thousand; or I imagine the face of one of my colleagues and begin trying to remember in what year and under what circumstances he entered the service. I like listening to sounds. Two rooms away from me my daughter Liza says something rapidly in her sleep, or my wife crosses the drawing-room with a candle and invariably drops the matchbox; or a warped cupboard creaks; or the burner of the lamp suddenly begins to hum – and all these sounds, for some reason, excite me.

To lie awake at night means to be at every moment conscious of being abnormal, and so I look forward with impatience to the morning and the day when I have a right to be awake. Many wearisome hours pass before the cock crows in the yard. He is my first bringer of good tidings. As soon as he crows I know that within an hour the porter will wake up below, and, coughing angrily, will go upstairs to fetch something. And then a pale light will begin gradually glimmering at the windows, voices will sound in the street . . .

The day begins for me with the entrance of my wife. She comes in to me in her petticoat, before she has done her hair, but after she has washed, smelling of flower-scented eau de Cologne, looking as though she had come in by chance. Every time she says exactly the same thing: 'Excuse me, I have just come for a minute . . . Have you had a bad night again?'

Then she puts out the lamp, sits down near the table, and begins talking. I am no prophet, but I know what she will talk about. Every morning it is exactly the same thing. Usually, after anxious inquiries concerning my health, she suddenly mentions our son who is an officer serving in Warsaw. After the twentieth of each month we send him fifty roubles, and that serves as the chief topic of our conversation.

'Of course it is not difficult for us,' my wife would sigh, 'but until he is completely on his own feet it is our duty to help him. The boy is abroad, his pay is small . . . However, if you like, next month we won't send him fifty, but forty. What do you think?'

Daily experience might have taught my wife that constantly talking of our expenses does not reduce them, but my wife refuses to learn by experience, and regularly every morning discusses our officer son, and tells me that bread, thank God, is cheaper, while sugar is two kopecks dearer in a tone as though she were telling me something new.

I listen, mechanically assent, and, probably because I have had a bad night, strange and inappropriate thoughts intrude themselves upon me. I gaze at my wife and wonder like a child. I ask myself in perplexity, is it possible that this old, very stout, ungainly woman, with her dull expression of petty anxiety and alarm about daily bread, with eyes dimmed by continual brooding over debts and money difficulties, who can talk of nothing but expenses and who smiles at nothing but things getting cheaper . . . is it possible that this woman is no other than the slender Varia whom I fell in love with so passionately for her fine, clear intelligence, for her pure soul, her beauty, and, as Othello his Desdemona, 'that she did pity' me for my studies? Could that woman be no other than the Varia who once bore me a son?

I looked with strained attention into the face of this flabby, spiritless, clumsy old woman, seeking in her my Varia, but of her past self nothing is left but her anxiety over my health and her manner of calling my salary 'our salary', and my hat 'our hat'. It is painful for me to look at her, and, to give her what little comfort I can, I let her say what she likes, and say nothing even when she passes unjust criticisms on other people or pitches into me for not having a private practice or not publishing textbooks.

Our conversation always ends in the same way. My wife suddenly remembers with dismay that I have not had my tea.

'What am I thinking about, sitting here?' she says, getting up. 'The samovar has been on the table ever so long, and here I stay gossiping. My goodness! how forgetful I am growing!'

She goes out quickly, and stops in the doorway to say:

'We owe Yegor five months' wages. Did you know? You mustn't let the servants' wages mount up; how many times I have said it! It's much easier to pay ten roubles a month than fifty every five months!'

As she goes out, she stops to say:

'The person I am sorriest for is our Liza. The girl studies at the Conservatoire, always mixes with people of good position, and goodness knows how she is dressed. Her fur coat is in such a state she is ashamed to show herself in the street. If she were somebody else's daughter it wouldn't matter, but of course everyone knows that her father is a distinguished professor, a privy councillor.'

And having reproached me with my rank and reputation, she goes away at last. That is how my day begins. It does not improve as it goes on.

As I am drinking my tea, my Liza comes in wearing her fur coat and her hat, with her music in her hand, quite ready to go to the Conservatoire. She is twenty-two. She looks younger, is pretty, and rather like my wife in her young days. She kisses me tenderly on my forehead and on my hand, and says:

'Good morning, Papa; are you quite well?'

As a child she was very fond of ice cream, and I used often to take her to a confectioner's. Ice cream was for her the measure of every delight. If she wanted to praise me she would say: 'You are as nice as cream, Papa.' We used to call one of her little fingers 'pistachio ice', the next, 'cream ice', the third, 'raspberry', and so on. Usually when she came in to say good morning to me I used to sit her on my knee, kiss her little fingers, and say:

'Creamy ice . . . pistachio . . . lemon . . .'

And now, from old habit, I kiss Liza's fingers and mutter: 'Pistachio . . . cream . . . lemon . . .', but the effect is utterly different. I am cold as ice and I am ashamed. When my daughter comes in to me and touches my forehead with her lips I start as though a bee had stung me on the head, give a forced smile, and turn my face away. Ever since I have been suffering from sleeplessness, a question sticks in my brain like a nail. My daughter often sees me, an old man and a distinguished man, blush painfully at being in debt to my footman; she sees how often anxiety over petty debts forces me to lay aside my work and to walk up and down the room for hours together, thinking; but why is it she never comes to me in secret to whisper in my ear: 'Father, here is my watch, here are my bracelets, my ear-rings, my dresses . . . Pawn them all; you need the money . . .'? How is it that, seeing how her mother and I are placed in a false position and do our utmost to hide our poverty from people, she does not give up her expensive pleasure of music lessons? I would not accept her watch nor her bracelets, nor the sacrifice of her lessons – God forbid! That isn't what I want.

I think at the same time of my son, the officer at Warsaw. He is a clever, honest, and sober fellow. But that is not enough for me. I think if I had an old father, and if I knew there were moments when he was put to shame by his poverty, I should give up my officer's commission to somebody else, and should go out to earn my living as a workman. Such thoughts about my children poison me. What is the use of them? It is only a narrow-minded or embittered man who can harbour evil thoughts about ordinary people because they are not heroes. But enough of that!

At a quarter to ten I have to go and give a lecture to my dear boys. I dress and walk along the road which I have known for thirty years, and which has its history for me. Here is the big grey house with the chemist's shop; at this point there used to stand a little house, and in it was a beer shop; in that beer shop I thought out my thesis and wrote my first love letter to Varia. I wrote it in pencil, on a page headed 'Historia morbi'. Here there is a grocer's shop; at one time it was kept by a little Jew, who sold me cigarettes on credit; then by a fat peasant woman, who liked the students because 'every one of them has a mother'; now there is a red-haired shopkeeper sitting in it, a very stolid man who drinks tea from a copper teapot. And here are the gloomy gates of the university, which have long needed doing up; I see the bored porter in his sheepskin, the broom, the drifts of snow . . . On a boy coming fresh from the provinces and imagining that the temple of science must really be a temple, such gates cannot make a healthy impression. Altogether the dilapidated condition of the university buildings, the gloominess of the corridors, the griminess of the walls, the lack of light, the dejected aspect of the steps, the hat stands and the benches, take a prominent position among predisposing causes in the history of Russian pessimism . . . Here is our garden . . . I fancy it has grown neither better nor worse since I was a student. I don't like it. It would be far more sensible if there were tall pines and fine oaks growing here instead of sickly-looking lime trees, yellow acacias, and skimpy pruned lilacs. The student, whose state of mind is in the majority of cases created by his surroundings, ought in the place where he is studying to see facing him at every turn nothing but what is lofty, strong, and elegant . . . God preserve him from gaunt trees, broken windows, grey walls, and doors covered with torn oil-cloth!

When I go to my own entrance the door is flung wide open and I am met by my colleague, contemporary and namesake, the porter Nikolai. As he lets me in he clears his throat and says:

'A frost, your Excellency!'

Or, if my greatcoat is wet:

'Rain, your Excellency!'

Then he runs on ahead of me and opens all the doors on my way. In my study he carefully takes off my fur coat, and while doing so manages to tell me some bit of university news. Thanks to the close intimacy existing between all the university porters and beadles, he knows everything that goes on in the four faculties, in the office, in the rector's private room, in the library. What does he not know? When in an evil day a rector or a dean, for instance, retires, I hear him in conversation with the young porters mention the candidates for the post, explain that one would not be confirmed by the minister, that another would himself refuse to accept it, then drop into fantastic details concerning mysterious papers received in the office, secret conversations alleged to have taken place between the minister and the trustee, and so on. With the exception of these details, he almost always turns out to be right. His estimates of the candidates, though original, are very correct, too. If one wants to know in what year someone read his thesis, entered the service, retired, or died, then summon to your assistance the vast memory of that soldier, and he will not only tell you the year, the month and the day, but will furnish you also with the details that accompanied this or that event. Only one who loves can remember like that.

He is the guardian of the university traditions. From the porters who were his predecessors he has inherited many legends of university life, has added to that wealth much of his own gained during his time of service, and if you care to hear he will tell you many long and intimate stories. He can tell one about extraordinary sages who knew *everything* about remarkable students who did not sleep for weeks, about numerous martyrs and victims of science; with him good triumphs over evil, the weak always vanquish the strong, the wise man the fool, the humble the proud, the young the old. Take all these fables and legends with a pinch of salt; but filter them, and you will have left what is wanted: our fine traditions and the names of real heroes, recognised as such by all.

In our society the knowledge of the learned world consists of anecdotes of the extraordinary absent-mindedness of certain old professors, and two or three witticisms variously ascribed to Gruber,* to me, and to Babukhin.* For the educated public that is not much. If it loved science, learned men, and students, as Nikolai does, its literature would long ago have contained whole epics, records of sayings and doings; unfortunately, it doesn't have them.

After telling me a piece of news, Nikolai assumes a severe expression, and conversation about business begins. If any outsider could at such times overhear Nikolai's free use of our terminology, he might perhaps imagine that he was a learned man disguised as a soldier. And, by the way, the rumours of the erudition of the university porters are greatly exaggerated. It is true that Nikolai knows more than a hundred Latin words, knows how to put the skeleton together, sometimes prepares the apparatus and amuses the students by some long, learned quotation, but the by no means complicated theory of the circulation of the blood, for instance, is as much a mystery to him now as it was twenty years ago.

At the table in my study, bending low over some book or preparation, sits Piotr Ignatievich, my demonstrator, a modest and industrious but untalented man of thirty-five, already bald and pot-bellied. He works from morning to night, reads a lot, remembers well everything he has read – and in that way he is not a man, but pure gold; in all else he is a cart-horse or, in other words, a learned dullard. The cart-horse characteristics that show his lack of talent are these: his outlook is narrow and sharply limited by his speciality; outside his special branch he is simple as a child.

'Fancy! What a misfortune! They say Skobelev* is dead.'

Nikolai crosses himself, but Piotr turns to me and asks:

'What Skobelev is that?'

Another time – somewhat earlier – I told him that Professor Perov* was dead. Good Piotr asked:

'What did he lecture on?'

I believe if Patti* had sung in his very ear, if a horde of Chinese had invaded Russia, if there had been an earthquake, he would not have stirred a limb, but screwing up his eye, would have gone on calmly looking through the microscope. What is he to Hecuba* or Hecuba to him, in fact? I would give a good deal to see this dry stick sleeping with his wife at night.

Another characteristic is his fanatical faith in the infallibility of science, and, above all, in everything written by the Germans. He believes in himself, in his preparations, knows the object of life, and knows nothing of the doubts and disappointments that turn the hair of talent grey. He has a slavish reverence for authorities and a complete lack of any desire for independent thought. To change his convictions is difficult, to argue with him impossible. How is one to argue with a man who is firmly persuaded that medicine is the finest of sciences, that doctors are the best of men, and that the traditions of the medical profession are superior to those of any other? Of the evil past of medicine only one tradition has been preserved – the white tie is still worn by doctors; for a scholar, in fact, for any educated man, the only traditions that can exist are those of the university as a whole, with no distinction between medicine, law, etc. But it would be hard for Piotr to accept these facts, and he is ready to argue with you till the Day of Judgment.

I have a clear picture in my mind of his future. In the course of his life he will prepare many hundreds of chemicals of exceptional purity; he will write a number of dry and very accurate memoranda, will make some dozen conscientious translations, but he won't win a Nobel prize. To do that one must have imagination, inventiveness, the gift of insight, and Piotr has nothing of the kind. In short, he is not a master of science, but a journeyman.

Piotr, Nikolai, and I talk in subdued tones. We are not quite ourselves. There is always a peculiar feeling when one hears through the doors a murmur like the roar of the sea from the lecture theatre. In the course of thirty years I have not grown accustomed to this feeling, and I experience it every morning. I nervously button up my coat, ask Nikolai unnecessary questions, lose my temper . . . It is just as though I were frightened; it is not timidity, though, but something different which I can neither describe nor find a name for.

Quite unnecessarily, I look at my watch and say: 'Well, it's time to go in . . .'

And we march into the room in the following order: foremost goes Nikolai, with the chemicals and apparatus or with a chart; after him I come; and then the cart-horse follows humbly, with hanging head;

or, when necessary, a dead body is carried in first on a stretcher, followed by Nikolai, and so on. On my entrance the students all stand up, then they sit down, and the roar of the sea is suddenly hushed. Stillness reigns.

I know what I am going to lecture about, but I don't know how I am going to lecture, where I am going to begin or with what I am going to end. I haven't a single sentence ready in my head. But I have only to look round the lecture-hall (it is built in the form of an amphitheatre) and utter the stereotyped phrase, 'Last lecture we stopped at . . .', when sentences spring up from my soul in a long string, and I am carried away by my own eloquence. I speak with irresistible rapidity and passion, and it seems as though there were no force which could check the flow of my words. To lecture well – that is, with profit to the listeners and without boring them – you must have, besides talent, experience and a special knack; you must possess a clear conception of your own powers, of the audience to which you are lecturing, and of the subject of your lecture. Moreover, you must be a man who knows what he is doing; you must keep a sharp lookout, and not for one second lose sight of what lies before you.

A good conductor, interpreting the thought of the composer, does twenty things at once: reads the score, waves his baton, watches the singer, makes a motion sideways, first to the drum then to the wind instruments, and so on. I do just the same when I lecture. Before me a hundred and fifty faces, all unlike one another; three hundred eyes all looking straight into my face. My object is to dominate this many-headed hydra. If every moment as I lecture I have a clear vision of the degree of its attention and its power of comprehension, it is in my power. The other foe I have to overcome is in myself. It is the infinite variety of forms, phenomena, laws, and the multitude of ideas of my own and other people's conditioned by them. Every moment I must have the skill to snatch out of that vast mass of material what is most important and necessary, and, as rapidly as my words flow, clothe my thought in a form in which it can be grasped by the hydra's intelligence, and may arouse its attention, and at the same time one must keep a sharp lookout that one's thoughts are conveyed, not just as they come, but in a certain order, essential for the correct composition of the picture I wish to sketch. Further, I endeavour to make my diction literary, my definitions brief and precise, my wording, as far as possible, simple and eloquent. Every minute I have to pull myself up and remember that I have only an hour and forty minutes at my disposal. In short, you have your work cut out. At one and the same minute you have to play the part of savant and teacher and orator, and it's a bad thing if the orator gets the upper hand of the savant or of the teacher, or vice versa.

You lecture for a quarter of an hour, for half an hour, when you notice that the students are beginning to look at the ceiling, at Piotr; one is feeling for his handkerchief, another shifts in his seat, another smiles at his thoughts . . .

That means that their attention is flagging. Something must be done. Taking advantage of the first opportunity, I make some pun. A broad grin comes on to a hundred and fifty faces, the eyes shine brightly, the roar of the sea is audible for a brief moment . . . I laugh too. Their attention is refreshed, and I can go on.

No kind of sport, no kind of game or diversion, has ever given me such enjoyment as lecturing. Only at lectures have I been able to abandon myself entirely to passion, and have understood that inspiration is not an invention of the poets, but exists in real life, and I imagine Hercules after the most piquant of his exploits felt just such voluptuous exhaustion as I experience after every lecture.

That was in old times. Now at lectures I feel nothing but torture. Before half an hour is over I am conscious of an overwhelming weakness in my legs and my shoulders. I sit down in my chair, but I am not accustomed to lecture sitting down; a minute later I get up and go on standing, then sit down again. There is a dryness in my mouth, my voice grows husky, my head begins to go round . . . To conceal my condition from my audience, I continually drink water, cough, often blow my nose as though I were hindered by a cold, make puns inappropriately, and in the end break off before I ought to. But above all I am ashamed.

My conscience and my intelligence tell me that the very best thing I could do now would be to deliver a farewell lecture to the boys, to say my last word to them, to bless them, and give up my post to a man younger and stronger than me. But, God be my judge, I have not enough courage to do what my conscience tells me.

Unfortunately, I am not a philosopher nor a theologian. I know perfectly well that I cannot live more than six months; it might be supposed that I ought now to be chiefly concerned with the question of the shadowy life beyond the grave, and the visions that will visit my slumbers in the tomb. But for some reason my soul refuses to recognise these questions, though my mind is fully alive to their importance. Just as twenty, thirty years ago, so now, on the threshold of death, I am interested in nothing but science. As I yield up my last breath I shall still believe that science is the most important, the most splendid, the most essential thing in the life of man; that it always has been and will be the highest manifestation of love, and that only by means of it will man conquer himself and nature. This faith is perhaps naive and may rest on false assumptions, but it is not my fault that I believe that and nothing else; I cannot overcome in myself this belief.

But that is not the point. I only ask people to be indulgent to my weakness, and to realise that to tear from the lecture theatre and his pupils a man who is more interested in the history of development of bone marrow than in the final purpose of creation would be equivalent to taking him and nailing him up in his coffin without waiting for him to be dead.

Sleeplessness and the strain of combating increasing weakness leads to something strange in me. In the middle of my lecture tears suddenly rise in my throat, my eyes begin to smart, and I feel a passionate, hysterical desire to stretch out my hands before me and break into loud lamentation. I want to cry out in a loud voice that I, a famous man, have been sentenced by fate to the death penalty, that within six months another man will be in control here in the lecture theatre. I want to shriek that I am poisoned; new ideas such as I have not known before have poisoned the last days of my life, and are still stinging my brain like mosquitoes. And at that moment my position seems to me so awful that I want all my listeners to be horrified, to leap up from their seats and to rush in panic, in terror, with desperate screams, to the exit.

It is not easy to get through such moments.

II

After my lecture I sit at home and work. I read journals and monographs, or prepare my next lecture; sometimes I write something. I work with interruptions, as I have from time to time to see visitors.

There is a ring at the bell. It is a colleague come to discuss some business matter with me. He comes in with his hat and his stick, and, holding out both objects to me, says:

'Only for a minute! Only for a minute! Sit down, *collega!* Only a couple of words.'

To begin with, we both try to show each other that we are extraordinarily polite and highly delighted to see each other. I make him sit down in an arm-chair , and he makes me sit down; as we do so, we cautiously pat each other on the back, touch each other's buttons, and it looks as though we were feeling each other and afraid of scorching our fingers. Both of us laugh, though we say nothing amusing. When we are seated we bow our heads towards each other and begin talking in subdued voices. However affectionately disposed we may be to one another, we cannot help adorning our conversation with all sorts of Chinese mannerisms, such as 'As you so justly observed', or 'I have already had the honour to inform you'; we cannot help laughing if one of us makes a joke, however unsuccessfully. When we have finished with business my colleague gets up impulsively and, waving his hat in the direction of my work, begins to say good-bye. Again we paw one another and laugh. I see him into the hall; then I assist my colleague to put on his coat, while he does all he can to decline this high honour. Then when Yegor opens the door my colleague declares that I shall catch cold, while I make a show of being ready to go even into the street with him. And when at last I go back into my study my face still goes on smiling, I suppose from inertia.

A little later another ring at the bell. Somebody comes into the hall, and is a long time coughing and taking off his things. Yegor announces a student. I tell him to ask him in. A minute later a young man of agreeable appearance comes in. For the last year our relations have been strained; his answers at examinations are disgraceful, and I fail him. Every year I have some seven such hopefuls whom, to express it in the students' slang, I 'plough' or 'floor'. Those of them who fail in their examination through incapacity or illness usually bear their cross patiently and do not haggle with me; those who come to the house and haggle with me are always youths of sanguine temperament, or hedonists, whose failure at examinations spoils their appetites and hinders them from visiting the opera with their usual regularity. I let the first class off easily, but the second I plough the whole year through.

'Sit down,' I say to my visitor; 'what have you got to tell me?'

'Excuse me, Professor, for troubling you,' he begins, hesitating, and not looking me in the face. 'I would not have ventured to trouble you if it had not been . . . I've taken your examination five times, and have been ploughed . . . I beg you, please give me a pass, because . . .'

The argument which all the sluggards bring forward on their own behalf is always the same; they have passed well in all their subjects and have only come to grief in mine, and that is the more surprising because they have always been particularly interested in my subject and knew it so well; their failure has always been entirely owing to some incomprehensible misunderstanding.

'Excuse me, my friend,' I say to the visitor; 'I cannot give you a pass. Go and read up the lectures and come to me again. Then we shall see.'

A pause. I feel an impulse to torment the student a little for liking beer and the opera better than science, and I say, with a sigh:

'To my mind, the best thing you can do now is to give up medicine altogether. If, with your abilities, you cannot succeed in passing the examination, it's evident that you have neither the desire nor the vocation for a doctor's calling.'

The sanguine youth's face lengthens.

'Excuse me, Professor,' he laughs, 'but that would be odd of me, to say the least of it. After studying for five years, all at once to give it up.'

'Oh, well! Better to have lost your five years than have to spend the rest of your life in doing work you do not care for.'

But at once I feel sorry for him, and I hasten to add:

'However, as you think best. And so read a little more and come again.'

'When?' the idle youth asks in a hollow voice.

'When you like. Tomorrow if you like.'

And in his good-natured eyes I read:

'I can come all right, but of course you will plough me again, you pig!'

'Of course,' I say, 'you won't know more science for going in for my examination another fifteen times, but it is training your character, and you must be thankful for that.'

Silence follows. I get up and wait for my visitor to go, but he stands and looks towards the window, fingers his beard, and thinks. It grows boring.

The sanguine youth's voice is pleasant and mellow, his eyes are clever and ironical, his face is genial, though a little bloated from frequent indulgence in beer and long periods lying on the sofa; he looks as though he could tell me a lot of interesting things about the opera, about his love affairs, and about comrades whom he likes. It's a pity it's not the thing to discuss these subjects: I should have been glad to listen to him.

'Professor, I give you my word of honour that if you give me a pass I . . .'

As soon as we reach the 'word of honour' I wave my hands and sit down to the table. The student ponders a minute longer, and says dejectedly:

'In that case, good-bye . . . I beg your pardon.'

'Good-bye, my friend. Good luck to you.'

He goes irresolutely into the hall, slowly puts on his outdoor things, and, going out into the street, probably ponders for some time longer; unable to think of anything, except 'old devil' inwardly addressed to me, he goes into a wretched restaurant to dine and drink beer, and then home to bed. Peace be to thy ashes, honest toiler.

A third ring at the bell. A young doctor, in a new black suit, gold spectacles, and of course a white tie, walks in. He introduces himself. I beg him to be seated, and ask what I can do for him. Not without emotion, the young devotee of science begins telling me that he has passed his examination as a doctor of medicine, and that he has now only to write his dissertation. He would like to work with me under my guidance and he would be greatly obliged to me if I would give him a subject for his dissertation.

'Very glad to be of use to you, colleague,' I say, 'but just let us come to an understanding as to the meaning of a dissertation. That word is taken to mean a composition which is a product of independent creative effort. Is that not so? A work written on another man's subject and under another man's guidance is called something different . . .'

The doctor says nothing. I fly into a rage and jump up from my seat.

'Why is it you all come to me?' I cry angrily. 'Do I keep a shop? I don't deal in subjects. For a thousand and one times I ask you to leave me in peace! Excuse my bluntness, but I am sick of it!'

The doctor remains silent, but a faint flush is apparent on his cheek-bones. His face expresses a profound reverence for my fame and my learning, but from his eyes I can see he feels a contempt for my voice, my pitiful figure, and my nervous gesticulation. I impress him in my anger as an eccentric.

'I don't keep a shop,' I go on angrily. 'And it is a strange thing! Why don't you want to be independent? Why have you such a distaste for independence?'

I say a great deal, but he still remains silent. By degrees I calm down, and of course give in. The doctor gets a subject from me for his thesis not worth half a kopeck, writes under my supervision a dissertation of no use to anyone, with dignity defends it in a dreary discussion, and receives a degree of no use to him.

The rings at the bell may follow one another endlessly, but I will confine my description here to four of them. The bell rings for the fourth time, and I hear familiar footsteps, the rustle of a dress, a dear voice . . .

Eighteen years ago a colleague of mine, an oculist, died leaving a little daughter Katia, a child of seven, and sixty thousand roubles. In his will he made me the child's guardian. Till she was ten years old Katia lived with us as one of the family, then she was sent to a boarding-school, and only spent the summer holidays with us. I never had time to look after her education. I only kept an occasional eye on it, and so I can say very little about her childhood.

The first thing that I remember, and which I recall with so much affection, is the extraordinary trustfulness with which she came into our house and let herself be treated by the doctors, a trustfulness which was always shining in her little face. She would sit somewhere out of the way, with her face bandaged, invariably watching something with attention; whether she watched me writing or turning over the pages of a book, or watched my wife bustling about, or the cook peeling potatoes in the kitchen, or the dog playing, her eyes invariably expressed the same thought – that is, 'Everything that is done in this world is nice and sensible.' She was curious, and very fond of talking to me. Sometimes she would sit at the table opposite me, watching my movements and asking questions. It interested her to know what I was reading, what I did at the university, whether I was not afraid of the dead bodies, what I did with my salary.

'Do the students fight at the university?' she would ask.

'They do, dear.'

'And do you make them go down on their knees?'

'Yes, I do.'

And she thought it funny that the students fought and I made them go down on their knees, and she laughed. She was a gentle, patient, good child. It happened not infrequently that I saw something taken away from her, saw her unjustly punished, or her curiosity left unsatisfied; at such times a look of sadness mingled with the constant expression of trustfulness on her face – that was all. I did not know how to take her part; only when I saw her sad I had an inclination to draw her to me and to commiserate with her like some old nurse: 'My poor little orphan!'

I remember, too, that she was fond of fine clothes and of sprinkling herself with scent. In that respect she was like me. I, too, am fond of pretty clothes and good scent.

I regret that I had not time nor inclination to watch over the rise and development of the passion which took complete possession of Katia when she was fourteen or fifteen. I mean her passionate love for the theatre. When she used to come from boarding-school and stay with us for the summer holidays, she talked of nothing with such pleasure and such warmth as of plays and actors. She bored us with her continual talk of the theatre. My wife and children would not listen to her. I was the only one who had not the courage to refuse to pay attention to her. When she had a longing to share her transports, she used to come into my study and say in an imploring tone:

'Nikolai, do let me talk to you about the theatre!'

I pointed to the clock, and said:

'I'll give you half an hour – begin.'

Later on she used to bring with her dozens of portraits of actors and actresses which she worshipped; then she attempted several times to take part in private theatricals, and the upshot of it all was that when she left school she came to me and announced that she was born to be an actress.

I had never shared Katia's inclinations for the theatre. To my mind, if a play is good there is no need to bother actors for the right effect to be produced; it is enough to read it. If the play is poor, no acting will make it good.

In my youth I often visited the theatre, and now my family takes a box twice a year and drags me off for a change of scene. Of course, that's not enough to give me the right to judge the theatre. In my opinion the theatre has become no better than it was thirty or forty years ago. Just as in the past, I can never find a glass of clean water in the corridors or foyers. Just as in the past, the attendants fine me twenty kopecks for my fur coat, though there is nothing reprehensible in wearing a warm coat in winter. As in the past, for no sort of reason, music is played in the intervals, which adds something new and uncalled-for to the effect of the play. As in the past, men go in the intervals and drink spirits in the buffet. If no progress can be seen in trifles, it is pointless to look for it in what is more important. When an actor wrapped from head to toe in stage traditions and conventions tries to recite a simple ordinary speech, 'To be, or not to be,' not simply, but invariably with the accompaniment of hissing and convulsion movements all over his body, or when he tries to convince me at all costs that Chatsky,* who talks so much with fools and is so fond of folly, is a very clever man, and that *Woe from Wit* is not a dull play, the stage gives me the same feeling of conventionality which bored me so much forty years ago when I was regaled with the classical howling and beating on the breast. And every time I come out of the theatre more conservative than I go in.

The sentimental and trusting public may be persuaded that the stage in its present form is a school; but anyone who is familiar with a school in its true sense will not be caught with that bait. I cannot say what will happen in fifty or a hundred years, but in its present conditions the theatre can serve only as entertainment. But this entertainment is too costly to be frequently enjoyed. It robs the state of thousands of healthy and talented young men and women, who, if they had not devoted themselves to the theatre, might have been good doctors, farmers, schoolmistresses, officers; it robs the public of the evening hours – the best time for intellectual work and social intercourse. I say nothing of the waste of money and the moral damage to the spectator when he sees murder, fornication, or false witness unsuitably treated on the stage.

Katia was of an entirely different opinion. She assured me that the theatre, even in its present form, was superior to the lecture-hall, to books, or to anything in the world. The stage was a power that united in itself all the arts, and actors were missionaries. No art nor science was capable of producing so strong and so certain an effect on the soul of man as the stage, and it was with good reason that an actor of medium quality enjoys greater popularity than the greatest savant or artist. And no sort of public service could provide such enjoyment and gratification as the theatre.

And one fine day Katia joined a troupe of actors, and went off, I believe, to Ufa, taking away with her a good supply of money, a store of rainbow hopes, and aristocratic views of her cause.

Her first letters on the journey were marvellous. I read them and was simply amazed that those small sheets of paper could contain so much youth, purity of spirit, holy innocence, and at the same time subtle and apt judgments which would have done credit to a fine masculine intellect. It was more a paean of praise she sent me than a mere description of the Volga, the country, the towns she visited, her companions, her failures and successes; every sentence was fragrant with that confiding trustfulness I was accustomed to read in her face – and at the same time there were a great many grammatical mistakes, and there was scarcely any punctuation at all.

Before six months had passed I received a highly poetical and enthusiastic letter beginning with the words, 'I have come to love . . .' This letter was accompanied by a photograph representing a young man with a shaven face, a wide-brimmed hat, and a plaid flung over his shoulder. The letters that followed were as splendid as before, but now commas and stops made their appearance in them, the grammatical mistakes disappeared, and there was a distinctly masculine flavour about them. Katia began writing to me how splendid it would be to build a great theatre somewhere on the Volga, on a cooperative system, and to attract to the enterprise the rich merchants and the steamer owners; there would be a great deal of money in it; there would be vast audiences; the actors would play on co-operative terms. Possibly all this was really excellent, but it seemed to me that such schemes could only originate from a man's mind.

However that may have been, for a year and a half everything seemed to go well: Katia was in love, believed in her work, and was happy; but then I began to notice in her letters unmistakable signs of falling off. It began with Katia's complaining of her companions – this was the first and most ominous symptom; if a young scientist or literary man begins his career with bitter complaints about scientists and literary men, it is a sure sign that he is worn out and unfit for his work. Katia wrote to me that her companions did not attend the rehearsals and never knew their parts; that one could see in every one of them an utter disrespect for the public in the production of absurd plays, and in their behaviour on the stage; that for the benefit of the

Actors' Fund, which they only talked about, actresses of serious drama demeaned themselves by singing chansonettes, while tragic actors sang comic songs making fun of deceived husbands and the pregnant condition of unfaithful wives, and so on. In fact, it was amazing that all this had not yet ruined the provincial stage, and that it could still maintain itself on such a frail and rotten footing.

In answer I wrote Katia a long and, I must confess, a very boring letter. Among other things, I wrote to her:

'I have more than once happened to converse with old actors, very worthy men, who showed a friendly disposition towards me; from my conversations with them I could grasp that their work was controlled not so much by their own intelligence and free choice as by fashion and the mood of the public. The best of them had had to play in their day in tragedy, in operetta, in Parisian farces, and in extravaganzas, and they always seemed equally sure that they were on the right path and that they were of use. So, as you see, the cause of the evil must be sought, not in the actors, but, more deeply, in the art itself and in the attitude of the whole of society to it.'

This letter of mine only irritated Katia. She answered me:

'You and I are talking at cross-purposes. I wrote to you not of the worthy men who showed a friendly disposition to you, but of a band of knaves who have nothing worthy about them. They are a horde of savages who have got on on the stage simply because no one would have taken them elsewhere, and who call themselves artists simply because they are impudent. There are numbers of dull-witted creatures, drunkards, intriguing schemers and slanderers, but there is not one person of talent among them. I cannot tell you how bitter it is to me that the art I love has fallen into the hands of people I detest; how bitter it is that the best men look on at evil from afar, not caring to come closer, and, instead of intervening, write ponderous commonplaces and utterly useless sermons . . .' And so on, all in the same style.

A little time passed, and I got this letter: 'I have been brutally deceived. I cannot go on living. Dispose of my money as you think best. I loved you as my father and my only friend. Good-bye.'

It turned out that *he*, too, belonged to the 'horde of savages'. Later on, from certain hints, I gathered that there had been an attempted suicide. I believe Katia tried to poison herself. I imagine that she must have been seriously ill afterwards, as the next letter I got was from Yalta, where she had most probably been sent by the doctors. Her last letter contained a request to send her a thousand roubles to Yalta as quickly as possible, and ended with these words:

'Excuse the gloominess of this letter; yesterday I buried my child.' After spending about a year in the Crimea, she returned home.

She had been about four years on her travels, and during those four years, I must confess, I played a rather strange and unenviable part in regard to her. When in earlier days she had told me she was going on the stage, and then wrote to me of her love; when she was periodically overcome by extravagance, and I continually had to send her first one and then two thousand roubles; when she wrote to me of her intention to die, and then of the death of her baby, every time I was at a loss, and all my sympathy for her sufferings found no expression except that I thought a lot and wrote long, boring letters which I might just as well not have written. And yet I was like a father to her and loved her like a daughter!

Now Katia is living less than a mile off. She has taken a flat of five rooms, and has installed herself fairly comfortably and with her innate taste. If anyone were to undertake to describe her surroundings, the predominant mood in the picture would be indolence. For the indolent body there are soft sofas, soft stools; for indolent feet soft rugs; for indolent eyes faded, dim, or mat colours; for the indolent soul the walls are hung with a number of cheap fans and trivial pictures, in which the originality of the execution is more conspicuous than the subject; and the room contains a multitude of little tables and shelves filled with utterly useless articles of no value, and shapeless rags in place of curtains . . . All this, together with the dread of bright colours, of symmetry, and of empty space, bears witness not only to spiritual indolence, but also to a corruption of natural taste. For days together Katia lies in the lounge reading, principally novels and stories. She only goes out of the house once a day, in the afternoon, to see me.

I go on working while Katia sits silent not far from me on the sofa, wrapping herself in her shawl, as though she were cold. Either because I like her or because I was used to her frequent visits when she was a little girl, her presence does not prevent me from concentrating. From time to time I mechanically ask her some question; she gives very brief replies; or, to rest for a minute, I turn round and watch her as she looks dreamily at some medical journal or review. And at such moments I notice that her face has lost the old look of confiding trustfulness. Her expression now is cold, apathetic, and absent-minded, like that of passengers who have to wait too long for a train. She is dressed, as in the old days, simply and beautifully, but carelessly; her dress and her hair show visible traces of the sofas and rocking-chairs in which she spends whole days at a stretch. And she has lost the curiosity she used to have. She has ceased to ask me questions now, as though she had experienced everything in life and expected nothing new from it.

Towards four o'clock there are sounds of movement in the hall and in the drawing-room. Liza has come back from the Conservatoire, and has brought some girl-friends in with her. We hear them playing on the piano, trying their voices and laughing; in the dining-room Yegor is laying the table, with the clatter of crockery.

'Good-bye,' said Katia. 'I won't go in and see your people today. They must excuse me. I haven't time. Come and see me.'

While I am seeing her to the door, she looks me up and down grimly, and says with vexation:

'You are getting thinner and thinner! Why don't you see a doctor? I'll call at Sergei Fiodorovich and ask him to have a look at you.'

'There's no need, Katia.'

'I can't think why your family's so blind! They are a nice lot, I must say!'

She puts on her fur coat abruptly, and as she does so two or three hairpins drop unnoticed on the floor from her carelessly arranged hair. She is too lazy and in too great a hurry to do her hair up; she carelessly stuffs the falling curls under her hat, and goes away.

When I go into the dining-room my wife asks me:

'Was Katia with you just now? Why didn't she come in to see us? It's really strange . . .'

'Mama,' Liza says to her reproachfully, 'let her alone, if she doesn't want to. We are not going down on our knees to her.'

'It's inconsiderate, anyway. To sit for three hours in the study without remembering our existence! Anyway, she can do as she likes.'

Varia and Liza both hate Katia. This hatred is beyond my comprehension, and probably one would have to be a woman in order to understand it. I am ready to stake my life that of the hundred and fifty young men I see every day in the lecture theatre, and of the hundred elderly ones I meet every week, hardly one could be found capable of understanding their hatred and aversion to Katia's past – that is, for her having been a mother without being a wife, and for her having had an illegitimate child; and at the same time I cannot recall one woman or girl of my acquaintance who would not consciously or unconsciously harbour such feelings. And this is not because woman is purer or more virtuous than man: why, virtue and purity are not very different from vice if they are not free from evil feeling. I attribute this simply to the backwardness of woman. The mournful feeling of compassion and the pang of conscience experienced by a modern man at the sight of suffering is, to my mind, far greater proof of culture and moral elevation than hatred and aversion. Woman is as tearful and as coarse in her feelings now as she was in the Middle

Ages, and to my thinking those who advise that she should be educated like a man are quite right.

My wife also dislikes Katia for having been an actress, for ingratitude, for pride, for eccentricity, and for the numerous vices which one woman can always find in another.

Besides my wife and daughter and me, there are dining with us two or three of my daughter's friends and Alexandr Adolfovich Gnekker, her admirer and suitor. He is a fair-haired young man under thirty, of medium height, very stout and broad shouldered, with red whiskers near his ears, and little waxed moustaches which make his plump smooth face look like a toy. He is dressed in a very short jacket, a coloured waistcoat, breeches very full at the top and very narrow at the ankle, with a large check pattern on them, and yellow shoes with low heels. He has prominent eyes like a crab's, his cravat is like a crab's neck, and I even fancy there is a smell of crab soup about the young man's whole person. He visits us every day, but no one in my family knows anything of his origin nor of the place of his education, nor of his means of livelihood. He neither plays nor sings, but has some connection with music and singing, sells somebody's pianos somewhere, is frequently at the Conservatoire, is acquainted with all the celebrities, and is a steward at the concerts; he criticises music with great authority, and I have noticed that people are happy to agree with him.

Rich people always have hangers-on; the arts and sciences have the same. I believe there is not an art nor a science in the world free from 'foreign bodies' like this Mr Gnekker. I am not a musician, and possibly I am mistaken about Mr Gnekker, of whom, indeed, I know very little. But his air of authority and the dignity with which he takes his stand beside the piano when anyone is playing or singing strike me as very suspect.

You may be a gentleman and privy councillor a thousand times over, but if you have a daughter you cannot be immune from that lower middle-class atmosphere which is so often brought into your house and into your mood by the attentions of suitors, by matchmaking and marriage. I can never reconcile myself, for instance, to the expression of triumph on my wife's face every time Gnekker is in our company, nor can I reconcile myself to the bottles of Lafite, port, and sherry which are only brought out on his account, that he may see with his own eyes the liberal and luxurious way in which we live. I cannot tolerate the habit of spasmodic laughter Liza has picked up at the Conservatoire, and her way of screwing up her eyes whenever there are men in the room. Above all, I cannot understand why a creature utterly alien to my habits, my studies, my whole manner of life, completely unlike the people I love, should come and see me every day, and every day should dine with me. My wife and my servants mysteriously whisper that he is a suitor, but still I don't understand his presence; it rouses in me the same wonder and perplexity as if they were to put a Zulu next to me at the table. And it seems strange to me, too, that my daughter, whom I am used to thinking of as a child, should love that cravat, those eyes, those soft cheeks . . .

In the old days I used to like my dinner, or at least was indifferent about it; now it excites in me no feeling but weariness and irritation. Ever since I became an 'Excellency' and have served as faculty dean, my family has for some reason found it necessary to make a complete change in our menu and dining habits. Instead of the simple dishes to which I was accustomed when I was a student and when I was in practice, now they feed me with a purée with little white things like circles floating about in it, and kidneys stewed in madeira. My rank as a general and my fame have robbed me for ever of cabbage soup and savoury pies, and goose with apple sauce, and bream with boiled grain. They have robbed me of our maid-servant Agasha, a chatty and laughter-loving old woman, instead of whom Yegor, a dull-witted and conceited fellow with a white glove on his right hand, waits at dinner. The intervals between the courses are short, but they seem immensely long because there is nothing to occupy them. There is none of the gaiety of the old days, the spontaneous talk, the jokes, the laughter; there is nothing of mutual affection and the joy which used to animate the children, my wife, and me when in the old days we met together at meals. For me, the celebrated man of science, dinner was a time of rest and reunion, and for my wife and children a fête – brief indeed, but bright and joyous – in which they knew that for half an hour I belonged, not to science, not to students, but to them alone. Our real exhilaration from one glass of wine is gone for ever, gone is Agasha, gone the bream with boiled grain, gone the uproar that greeted every little startling incident at dinner, such as the cat and dog fighting under the table, or Katia's bandage falling off her face into her soup.

To describe our dinner nowadays is as distasteful as to eat it. My wife's face wears a look of triumph and affected dignity, and her habitual expression of anxiety. She looks at our plates and says, 'I see you don't care for the joint. Tell me, you don't like it, do you?' and I am obliged to answer: 'There is no need for you to trouble, my dear; the meat is very nice.' And she will say: 'You always stand up for me, Nilolai, and you never tell me the truth. Why is Alexandr eating so little?' And so on in the same style all through dinner. Liza laughs spasmodically and screws up her eyes. I watch them both, and it is only now at dinner that it becomes absolutely evident to me that the inner life of these two has slipped away out of my ken. I have a feeling as though I had once lived at home with a real wife and children and that now I am dining as the guest of a sham wife, and am looking at a sham Liza. A startling change has taken place in both of them; I have missed the long process by which that change was effected, and it is no wonder that I can make nothing of it. Why did that change take place? I don't know. Perhaps the whole trouble is that God has not given my wife and daughter the same strength of character as me. From childhood I have been accustomed to resisting external influences, and have steeled myself pretty thoroughly. Such catastrophes in life as fame, the rank of general, the transition from comfort to living beyond our means, acquaintance with celebrities, etc., have scarcely affected me, and I have remained intact and unashamed; but on my wife and Liza, who have not been through the same hardening process and are weak, all this has fallen like an avalanche of snow, overwhelming them. Gnekker and the young ladies talk of fugues, of counterpoint, of singers and pianists, of Bach and Brahms, while my wife, afraid of their suspecting her of ignorance of music, smiles to them sympathetically and mutters: 'That's exquisite . . . really! You don't say so! . . .' Gnekker eats with solid dignity, jests with solid dignity, and condescendingly listens to the remarks of the young ladies. From time to time he is moved to speak in bad French, and then, for some reason or other, he thinks it necessary to address me as 'Votre Excellence'.

And I am glum. Evidently I embarrass them and they embarrass me. I have never in my earlier days had a close knowledge of class antagonism, but now I am tormented by something of that sort. I am on the lookout for nothing but bad qualities in Gnekker; I quickly find them, and fret at the thought that a man not of my circle is sitting here as my daughter's suitor. His presence has a bad influence on me in other ways, too. As a rule, when I am alone or in the society of people I like, I never think of my own achievements, or, if I do recall them, they seem to me as trivial as though I had qualified only yesterday; but in the presence of people like Gnekker my achievements in science seem to be a lofty mountain the top of which vanishes into the clouds, while at its foot Gnekkers are running about scarcely visible to the naked eye.

After dinner I go into my study and there smoke my pipe, the only one in the whole day, the sole relic of my old bad habit of smoking from morning to night. While I am smoking my wife comes in and sits down to talk to me. Just as in the morning, I know beforehand what our conversation is going to be about.

'I must talk to you seriously, Nikolai Stepanovich,' she begins. 'I mean about Liza . . . Why won't you pay attention?'

'To what?'

'You pretend to notice nothing. But that isn't right. We can't shirk responsibility . . . Gnekker has intentions towards Liza . . . What will you say?'

'That he is a bad man I can't say, because I don't know him, but that I don't like him I have told you a thousand times already.'

'But you can't . . . you can't!'

She gets up and walks about in excitement.

'You can't take that attitude to a serious step,' she says. 'When it is a question of our daughter's happiness we must lay aside all personal feeling. I know you do not like him . . . Very good . . . if we refuse him now, if we break it all off, how can you be sure that Liza will not have a grudge against us all her life? Suitable men don't grow on trees, goodness knows, and maybe no other match will turn up . . . He is very fond of Liza, and she seems to like him . . . Of course, he has no settled position, but that can't be helped. Please God, in time he will get one. He is of good family and well off.'

'Where did you learn that?'

'He told us so. His father has a large house in Kharkov and an estate in the neighbourhood. In short, Nikolai, you absolutely must go to Kharkov.'

'What for?'

'You will find out all about him there . . . You know the professors there; they will help you. I would go myself, but I am a woman. I cannot . . .'

'I am not going to Kharkov,' I say morosely.

My wife is frightened, and a look of intense suffering comes into her face.

'For God's sake, Nikolai,' she implores me, with tears in her voice – 'for God's sake, take this burden off me! I am in agony!'

It is painful to look at her.

'Very well, Varia,' I say kindly, 'if you wish, then, all right, I'll go to Kharkov and do whatever you want.'

She presses her handkerchief to her eyes and goes off to her room to cry, and I am left alone.

A little later lights are brought in. The arm-chair and the lamp mantle cast familiar shadows that have long grown wearisome on the walls and on the floor, and when I look at them I feel as though the night had come and with it my accursed sleeplessness. I lie on my bed, then get up and walk about the room, then lie down again. As a rule it is after dinner, at the approach of the evening, that my nervous excitement reaches its highest pitch. For no reason I begin crying and burying my head in the pillow. At such times I am afraid that someone may come in; I am afraid of suddenly dying; I am ashamed of my tears, and altogether there is something unbearable in my soul. I feel that I can no longer bear the sight of my lamp, of my books, of the shadows on the floor. I cannot bear the sound of the voices coming from the drawing-room. Some force unseen, incomprehensible, is roughly thrusting me out of my flat. I leap up hurriedly, dress, and cautiously, that my family may not notice, slip out into the street. Where am I to go?

The answer to that question has long been ready in my brain. To Katia.

III

As a rule she is lying on the sofa or in a lounge-chair, reading. On seeing me, she raises her head languidly, sits up, and offers me her hand.

'You are always lying down,' I say, after pausing and taking breath. 'That's not good for you. You ought to occupy yourself with something.'

'What?'

'I say you ought to occupy yourself in some way.'

'With what? A woman can be nothing but a simple worker or an actress.'

'Well, if you can't be a worker, be an actress.'

She says nothing.

'You ought to get married,' I say, half in jest.

'There is no one. There's no reason to, either.'

'You can't live like this.'

'Without a husband? Much that matters; I could have as many men as I like if I wanted to.'

'That's ugly, Katia.'

'What is ugly?'

'Why, what you have just said.'

Noticing that I am hurt and wishing to efface a bad impression, Katia says:

'Let's go; come this way.'

She takes me into a very snug little room, and says, pointing to the writing table:

'Look . . . I got it ready for you. You will work here. Come here every day and bring your work with you. They only get in your way at home. Will you work here? Would you like to?'

Not to wound her by refusing, I answer that I will work here, and that I like the room very much. Then we both sit down in the snug little room and begin talking.

The warm, snug surroundings and the presence of a sympathetic person do not, as in the old days, arouse in me a feeling of pleasure, but an intense impulse to complain and grumble. I feel, for some reason, that if I lament and complain I shall feel better.

'Things are in a bad way with me, my dear – very bad . . .'

'What is it?'

'You see how it is, my dear; the best and holiest right of kings is the right of mercy. And I have always felt myself a king, since I have made unlimited use of that right. I have never judged, I have been indulgent, I have readily forgiven everyone, right and left. Where others have protested and expressed indignation, I have only advised and persuaded. All my life it has been my endeavour that my presence should not be a burden to my family, to my students, to my colleagues, to my servants. And I know that this attitude to people has had a good influence on all who have happened to be around me. But now I am not a king. Something is happening to me that is only excusable in a slave; day and night my brain is haunted by evil thoughts, and feelings such as I never knew before are brooding in my soul. I am full of hatred, and contempt, and indignation, and loathing and dread. I have become excessively severe, exacting, irritable, ungracious, suspicious. Even things that in the old days would have provoked me only to an unnecessary jest and a good-natured laugh now arouse an oppressive feeling in me. My reasoning, too, has undergone a change: in the old days I despised money; now I harbour an evil feeling, not towards money, but towards the rich, as though they were to blame: in the old days I hated violence and tyranny, but now I hate the men who make use of violence, as though they were alone to blame, and not all of us who do not know how to educate each other. What is the meaning of it? If these new ideas and new feelings have come from a change of convictions, what is that change due to? Can the world have grown worse and I better, or was I blind before and indifferent? If this change is the result of a general decline of physical and intellectual powers – after all, I am ill, and every day I am losing weight – my position is pitiable; it means that my new ideas are morbid and abnormal; I ought to be ashamed of them and think them of no consequence . . .'

'Illness has nothing to do with it,' Katia interrupts me; 'it's simply that your eyes are opened, that's all. You have seen what in the old days, for some reason, you refused to see. To my thinking, what you ought to do, first of all, is to break with your family for good, and go away.'

'You are talking nonsense!'

'You don't love them, why act against your conscience? Can you call them a family? Nonentities! If they died today, no one would notice their absence tomorrow.'

Katia despises my wife and Liza as much as they hate her. One can hardly talk nowadays of people having a right to despise one another. But looking at it from Katia's standpoint and if one recognises such a right, one can see she has as much right to despise my wife and Liza as they have to hate her.

'Nonentities,' she goes on. 'Have you had dinner today? How was it they did not forget to tell you it was ready? How is it they still remember your existence?'

'Katia,' I say sternly, 'please be quiet.'

'You think I enjoy talking about them? I should be glad not to know them at all. Listen, my dear: give it all up and go away. Go abroad. The sooner the better.'

'What nonsense! What about the university?'

'The university, too. What is it to you? There's no sense in it, anyway. You have been lecturing for thirty years, and where are your pupils? Are many of them celebrated scientific men? Count them up! And to multiply the doctors who exploit ignorance and pile up hundreds of thousands for themselves, there is no need to be a good and talented man. You are not wanted.'

'Good heavens! how harsh you are!' I cry in horror. 'How harsh you are! Be quiet or I will go! I can't answer the harsh things you say!'

The maid comes in and summons us to tea. At the samovar our conversation, thank God, changes. After having had my grumble out, I have a longing to give way to another weakness of old age, reminiscences. I tell Katia about my past, and to my great astonishment tell her incidents which, till then, I did not suspect of being still preserved in my memory, and she listens to me with tenderness, with pride, holding her breath. I am particularly fond of telling her how I was educated in a seminary and dreamed of going to the university.

'At times I used to walk about our seminary garden . . .' I would tell her. 'If from some far-away tavern the wind floated sounds of a song and the screech of an accordion, or a troika with bells dashed by the garden fence, it was quite enough to send a rush of happiness, filling not only my heart, but even my stomach, my legs, my arms . . . I would listen to the accordion or the bells dying away in the distance and imagine myself a doctor, and paint pictures, one better than another. And here, as you see, my dreams have come true. I have had more than I dared to dream of. For thirty years I have been a much-loved professor, I have had splendid comrades, I have enjoyed fame and honour. I have loved, married for passionate love, have had children. In fact, looking back upon it, I see my whole life as a fine composition arranged with talent. Now all that is left to me is not to spoil the end. For that I must die like a human being. If death is really a danger, I must meet it as a teacher, a man of science and a citizen of a Christian country ought to meet it, in good cheer and with an untroubled soul. But I am spoiling the end; I am sinking, I fly to you, I beg for help, and you tell me: "Sink; that's what you ought to do." '

But here there comes a ring at the front door. Katia and I recognise it, and say:

'It must be Mikhail.'

And a minute later my colleague, the philologist Mikhail Fiodorovich, a tall, well-built man of fifty, clean-shaven, with thick grey hair and black eyebrows, walks in. He is a good-natured man and an excellent comrade. He comes of a fortunate and talented old noble family which has played a prominent part in the history of literature and enlightenment. He is himself intelligent, talented, and very highly educated, but has his oddities. To a certain extent we are all odd and all queer fish, but in his oddities there is something exceptional, apt to cause anxiety among his acquaintants. I know a good many people for whom his oddities completely obscure his good qualities.

Coming in to us, he slowly takes off his gloves and says in his velvety bass:

'Good evening. Are you having tea? Just what I need. It's diabolically cold.'

Then he sits down to the table, takes a glass, and at once begins talking. What is most characteristic in his manner of talking is a continually jesting tone, a mixture of philosophy and drollery as in Shakespeare's gravediggers. He is always talking about serious things, but he never speaks seriously. His judgments are always harsh and railing, but, thanks to his soft, even jesting tone, the harshness and abuse do not jar upon the ear, and one soon grows used to them. Every evening he brings with him some five or six anecdotes from the university, and he usually begins with them when he sits down to table.

'Oh, Lord!' he sighs, twitching his black eyebrows ironically. 'What clowns there are in the world!'

'Well?' asks Katia.

'As I was coming from my lecture this morning I met that old idiot N. N— on the stairs . . . He was going along as usual, sticking out his chin like a horse, looking for someone to listen to his grumbling at his migraine, at his wife, and his students who won't attend his lectures.

"Oh," I thought, "he has seen me – I am done for now; it is all up . . ." '

And so on in the same style. Or he will begin like this:

'I was yesterday at our friend Z. Z—'s public lecture. I wonder how it is our alma mater – don't speak of it after dark – dare display in public such noodles and patent dullards as that Z. Z—. Why, he is a European fool! Upon my word, you could not find another like him all over Europe! He lectures – can you imagine? – as though he were sucking a sugar stick – sue, sue, sue. He is in a nervous funk; he can hardly decipher his own manuscript; his poor little thoughts crawl along like a bishop on a bicycle, and, what's worse, you can never make out what he is trying to say. The deadly dullness is awful, the very flies expire. It can only be compared with the boredom in the assembly hall at the yearly meeting when the traditional address is read – damn it!'

And at once an abrupt transition:

'Three years ago – Nikolai here will remember it – I had to deliver that address. It was hot, stifling, my uniform cut me under the arms – it was deadly! I read for half an hour, for an hour, for an hour and a half, for two hours . . . "Come," I thought; "thank God, there are only ten pages left!" And at the end there were four pages that there was no need to read, and I reckoned to leave them out. "So there are only six really," I thought; "that is, only six pages left to read." But, only fancy, I chanced to glance before me, and, sitting in the front row, side by side, were a general with a ribbon on his breast and a bishop. The poor beggars were numb with boredom; their eyes were popping with the effort to keep awake, and yet they were trying to put on an expression of attention and to pretend that they understood what I was saying and liked it. "Well," I thought, "since you like it you shall have it! Out of spite!"; so I gave them those four pages too.'

As is usual with ironical people, when he talks nothing in his face smiles but his eyes and eyebrows. At such times there is no trace of hatred and spite in his eyes, but a great deal of humour, and that peculiar foxy slyness which is only to be noticed in very observant people. Since I am speaking about his eyes, I noticed another peculiarity in them. When he takes a glass from Katia, or listens to her speaking, or his eyes follow her as she leaves the room for a moment, I notice in his eyes something gentle, beseeching, pure . . .

The maid-servant takes away the samovar and puts on the table a large piece of cheese, some fruit, and a bottle of Crimean champagne – a rather poor wine of which Katia had grown fond in the Crimea. Mikhail takes two packs of cards off the whatnot and begins to play patience. According to him, some varieties of patience require great concentration and attention, yet while he lays out the cards he does not leave off distracting his attention with talk. Katia watches his cards attentively, and more by gesture than by words helps him in his play. She drinks no more than a couple of glasses of wine the whole evening; I drink a quarter of a glass, and the rest of the bottle falls to the share of Mikhail, who can drink a great deal and never get drunk.

Over our patience we settle various questions, principally of the higher order, and what we care for most of all – that is, science and learning – is more roughly handled than anything.

'Science, thank God, has outlived its day,' says Mikhail emphatically. 'Its song is sung. Yes, indeed. Mankind begins to feel impelled to replace it by something different. It has grown on the soil of superstition, been nourished by superstition, and is now just as much the quintessence of superstition as its defunct grandams, alchemy, metaphysics, and philosophy. And, after all, what has it given to mankind? Why, the difference between the learned Europeans and the Chinese who have no science is trifling, purely external. The Chinese know nothing of science, but what have they lost thereby?'

'Flies know nothing of science, either,' I observe, 'but what of that?'

'There is no need to be angry, Nikolai. I only say this here between ourselves . . . I am more cautious than you think, and I am not going to say this in public – God forbid! The superstition exists in the multitude that the arts and sciences are superior to agriculture, commerce, superior to handicrafts. Our sect is maintained by that superstition, and it is not for you and me to destroy it. God forbid!'

After patience the younger generation comes in for a dressing-down too.

'Our audiences have degenerated,' sighs Mikhail. 'Not to speak of ideals and all the rest of it, if only they were capable of work and rational thought! In fact, it's a case of "I look with mournful eyes on the young men of today." '*

'Yes; they have degenerated horribly,' Katia agrees. 'Tell me, have you had just one outstanding man during the last five or ten years?'

'I don't know how it is with the other professors, but I can't remember any among mine.'

'I have seen in my day many of our students and young scientists and many actors – well, I have never once been so fortunate as to meet – I won't say a hero or a man of talent, but even an interesting man. It's all the same grey mediocrity, puffed up with self conceit.'

All this talk of degeneration always affects me as though I had accidentally overheard offensive talk about my own daughter. It offends me that these charges are wholesale, and rest on such worn-out commonplaces, on such wordy vapourings as degeneration and absence of ideals, or on references to the splendours of the past. Every accusation, even if it is uttered in ladies' society, ought to be formulated with all possible definiteness, or it is not an accusation, but idle disparagement, unworthy of decent people.

I am an old man, I have been lecturing for thirty years, but I notice neither degeneration nor lack of ideals, and I don't find that the present is worse than the past. My porter Nikolai, whose experience of this subject has its value, says that the students of today are neither better nor worse than those of the past.

If I were asked what I don't like in my pupils of today, I should answer the question, not straight off and not at length but quite specifically. I know their failings, and so have no need to resort to vague generalities. I don't like their smoking, drinking hard liquor, marrying late, and often being so irresponsible and careless that they will let one of their number starve in their midst while they neglect to pay their subscriptions to the Students' Aid Society. They don't know modern languages, and they express themselves badly in Russian; only yesterday my colleague, the professor of hygiene, complained to me that he had to give twice as many lectures, because the students had a very poor knowledge of physics and were utterly ignorant of meteorology. They are readily carried away by the influence of the latest new writers, even when they are not first-rate, but they take absolutely no interest in classics such as Shakespeare, Marcus Aurelius, Epictetus,* or Pascal, and this inability to distinguish the great from the small betrays their ignorance of practical life more than anything. All difficult questions that have more or less a social character (for instance the migration question) they settle by studying monographs on the subject, but not by way of scientific investigation or experiment, though that method is at their disposal and is more in keeping with their calling. They gladly become ward surgeons, assistants, demonstrators, external teachers, and are ready to fill such posts till they are forty, though independence, a sense of freedom and personal initiative are no less necessary in science than, for instance, in art or commerce. I have pupils and listeners, but no successors and helpers, and so I love them and am touched by them, but am not proud of them. And so on, and so on . . .

Such shortcomings, however numerous they may be, can give rise to a pessimistic or abusive mood only in a faint-hearted and timid man. All these failings have a casual, transitory character, and are completely dependent on conditions of life; in some ten years they will have disappeared or given place to other fresh defects, which are all inevitable and will in their turn alarm the fainthearted. The students' sins often vex me, but that vexation is nothing in comparison with the joy I have been experiencing now for the last thirty years when I talk to my pupils, lecture to them, observe their relationships, and compare them with people of other circles.

Mikhail speaks evil of everything. Katia listens, and neither of them notices into what depths the apparently innocent diversion of finding fault with their neighbours is gradually drawing them. They are not conscious how by degrees simple talk passes into malicious mockery and jeering, and how they are both beginning to drop into the habits and methods of slander.

'Killing types one meets with,' says Mikhail. 'I went yesterday to our friend Yegor's, and there I found a studious gentleman, one of your medicals in his third year, I believe. Such a face! . . . in the Dobroliubov style,* the imprint of profound thought on his brow; we got into talk. "Such doings, young man," said I. "I've read," said I, "that some German – I've forgotten his name – has created from the human brain a new kind of alkaloid, idiotine." What do you think? He believed it, and there was positively an expression of respect on his face, as though to say, "See what we fellows can do!" And the other day I went to the theatre. I took my seat. In the next row directly in front of me were sitting two men: one of "us fellows" and apparently a law student, the other a shaggy-looking figure, a medical student. The latter was as drunk as a cobbler. He did not look at the stage at all. He was dozing with his nose on his shirt-front. But as soon as an actor begins loudly reciting a monologue, or simply raises his voice, our friend starts, pokes his neighbour in the ribs, and asks, "What is he saying? Is it decent?" "Yes," answers one of our fellows. "B-r-r-ravo!" roars the medical student. "Decent! Bravo!" He had gone to the theatre, you see, the drunken blockhead, not for the sake of art, the play, but for decency! He wanted noble sentiments.'

Katia listens and laughs. She has a strange laugh. She catches her breath in rhythmically regular gasps, very much as though she were playing the accordion, and nothing in her face is laughing but her nostrils. I grow depressed and don't know what to say. Beside myself, I fire up, leap up from my seat and cry:

'Do leave off! Why are you sitting here like two toads, poisoning the air with your breath? Give over!'

And without waiting for them to finish their gossip I prepare to go home. And, indeed, it is high time: it is past ten.

'I will stay a little longer,' says Mikhail. 'Will you allow me, Katia?'

'I will,' answers Katia.

'*Bene*! In that case send for another bottle.'

They both see me out with candles to the hall, and while I put on my fur coat, Mikhail says:

'You have grown dreadfully thin and older looking, Nikolai. What's the matter with you? Are you ill?'

'Yes; I am a little ill.'

'And you are not doing anything for it . . .' Katia puts in grimly.

'Why don't you? You can't go on like that! God helps those who help themselves, my dear fellow. Remember me to your wife and daughter, and make my apologies for not having been to see them. In a day or two, before I go abroad, I shall come to say good-bye. I shall be sure to. I am going away next week.'

I come away from Katia, irritated and alarmed by what has been said about being ill, and dissatisfied with myself. I ask myself whether I really ought not to consult one of my colleagues. And at once I imagine how my colleague, after listening to me, would walk away to the window without speaking, would think a moment, then would turn round to me and, trying to prevent my reading the truth in his face, would say in a careless tone: 'So far I see nothing serious, but at the same time, *collega*, I advise you to lay aside your work . . .' And that would deprive me of my last hope.

Who is without hope? Now that I am diagnosing my illness and prescribing for myself, from time to time I hope that I am deceived by my own illness, that I am mistaken about the albumen and the sugar I find, and about both my heart, and the swellings I have twice noticed in the mornings; when, with the fervour of the hypochondriac, I look through the therapy textbooks and take a different medicine every day, I keep fancying that I shall hit upon something comforting. All that is petty.

Whether the sky is covered with clouds or the moon and the stars are shining, I turn my eye towards it every evening and think that death will take me soon. One would think that my thoughts at such times ought to be deep as the sky, brilliant, striking . . . But no! I think about myself, about my wife, about Liza, Gnekker, the students, people in general; my thoughts are evil, petty, I am insincere with myself, and at such times my theory of life may be expressed in the words the celebrated Arakcheev* said in one of his intimate letters: 'Nothing good can exist in the world without evil, and there is more evil than good.' That is, everything is disgusting; there is nothing to live for, and the sixty-two years I have already lived must be reckoned as wasted. I catch myself in these thoughts, and try to persuade myself that they are accidental, temporary, and not deeply rooted in me, but at once I think:

'If so, then what lures you every evening to those two toads?'

And I vow to myself that I will never go to Katia's again, though I know I shall go next evening.

Ringing the bell at the door and going upstairs, I feel that I have no family now and no desire to bring it back again. It is clear that the new Arakcheev thoughts are not casual, temporary visitors, but have possession of my whole being. With my conscience ill at ease, dejected, languid, hardly able to move my limbs, feeling as though tons were added to my weight, I get into bed and quickly drop asleep.

And then – insomnia . . .

IV

Summer comes on and life is changed.

One fine morning Liza comes to me and says in a jesting tone:

'Come, your Excellency! Everything's ready.'

My Excellency is conducted into the street, and seated in a cab. As I go along, having nothing to do, I read the signboards from right to left. The word 'Traktir' reads 'Ritkart': that would make a good baronial surname: Baroness Ritkart. Further on I drive through fields, by the graveyard, which makes absolutely no impression on me, though I shall soon lie in it; then I drive by forests and again by fields. There is nothing of interest. After two hours of driving, my Excellency is conducted into the lower storey of a summer villa and installed in a small, very cheerful room with light blue wallpaper.

At night there is sleeplessness as before, but in the morning I do not put a good face upon it nor listen to my wife, but lie in bed. I do not sleep, but lie in the drowsy, half-conscious state in which you know you are not asleep, but dreaming. At midday I get up and from habit sit down at my desk, but I do not work now; I amuse myself with French books in yellow covers, sent to me by Katia. Of course, it would be more patriotic to read Russian authors, but I must confess I have no particular liking for them. With the exception of two or three of the older writers, all our literature of today strikes me as not being literature, but a special sort of cottage industry, which exists simply to be encouraged, though people are reluctant to use its products. The very best of these home products cannot be called remarkable and cannot be sincerely praised without *buts*. I must say the same of all the literary novelties I have read during the last ten or fifteen years. Not one of them is remarkable, and not one of them can be praised without a *but*. Cleverness, decency, but no talent; talent, decency, but no cleverness; or talent, cleverness, but no decency.

I don't say the French books have talent, cleverness, and decency.

They don't satisfy me, either. But they are not so tedious as the Russian, and it is not unusual to find in them the chief element of artistic creation – the feeling of personal freedom which is lacking in Russian authors. I don't remember one new book in which the author does not try from the first page to entangle himself in all sorts of conditions and contracts with his conscience. One is afraid to speak of the naked body; another ties himself up hand and foot in psychological analysis; a third must have a 'warm attitude to man'; a fourth purposely scrawls whole decriptions of nature that he may not be suspected of writing tendentiously . . . One is bent upon being middle-class in his work, another must be a nobleman, and so on. There is tendentiousness, circumspection, and self-will, but they have neither the independence nor the courage to write as they like, and therefore there is no creativity.

All this applies to what is called belles-lettres.

As for serious treatises in Russian on sociology, for instance, on art, and so on, I do not read them simply from timidity. In my childhood and early youth I had for some reason a terror of doorkeepers and attendants at the theatre, and that terror has remained with me to this day. I am afraid of them even now. It is said that we are only afraid of what we do not understand. And, indeed, it is very difficult to understand why doorkeepers and theatre attendants are so dignified, haughty, and majestically rude. I feel exactly the same terror when I read serious articles. Their extraordinary dignity, their bantering lordly tone, their familiarity with foreign authors, their ability to split hairs with dignity – all that is beyond my understanding; it is intimidating and utterly unlike the quiet, gentlemanly tone to which I am accustomed when I read the works of our medical writers and natural scientists. It oppresses me to read not only the articles written by serious Russians, but even works translated or edited by them. The pretentious, edifying tone of the preface; the redundancy of remarks made by the translator, which prevent me from concentrating my attention; the question marks and *sic* in parentheses scattered all over the book or article by the liberal translator, are to my mind an outrage on the author and on my independence as a reader.

Once I was summoned as an expert to a circuit court; in an interval one of my fellow experts drew my attention to the rudeness of the public prosecutor to the defendants, among whom there were two ladies of good education. I believe I did not exaggerate at all when I told him that the prosecutor's manner was no ruder than that of the authors of serious articles to one another. Their manners are, indeed, so rude that I cannot speak of them without distaste. They treat one another and the writers they criticise either with superfluous respect, at the sacrifice of their own dignity, or, on the contrary, with far more ruthlessness than I have shown in my notes and my thoughts in regard to my future son-in-law Gnekker. Accusations of insanity, of impure intentions, and, indeed, of every sort of crime, form an habitual ornament of serious articles. And that, as young medical men are fond of saying in their monographs, is the *ultima ratio*! Such ways must infallibly have an effect on the morals of the younger generation of writers, and so I am not at all surprised that in the new works with which our literature has been enriched during the last ten or fifteen years the heroes drink too much vodka and the heroines are not very chaste.

I read French books, and I look out of the window which is open; I can see the spikes of my garden fence, two or three scraggy trees, and beyond the fence the road, the fields, and beyond them a broad stretch of pine wood. Often I admire a boy and girl, both flaxen-headed and ragged, who clamber on the fence and laugh at my baldness. In their shining little eyes I read, like Elisha, 'Go up thou baldhead!' They are almost the only people who care nothing for my celebrity or my rank.

Visitors do not come to me every day now. I will only mention the visits of Nikolai and Piotr. Nikolai usually comes to me on holidays, on some pretext of business, though really to see me. He arrives very tipsy, a thing which never occurs to him in the winter.

'What have you to tell me?' I ask, going out to him in the hall.

'Your Excellency!' he says, pressing his hand to his heart and looking at me with the ecstasy of a lover – 'your Excellency! God be my witness! Strike me dead on the spot! *Gaudeamus igitur juvenes*!'

And he avidly kisses me on the shoulder, on the sleeve, and on the buttons.

'Is everything going well?' I ask him.

'Your Excellency! So help me God! . . .'

He persists in grovelling before me for no sort of reason, and soon bores me, so I send him away to the kitchen, where they give him dinner. Piotr comes to see me on holidays, too, with the special object of seeing me and sharing his thoughts with me. He usually sits down near my table, modest, neat, and reasonable, and does not venture to cross his legs or put his elbows on the table. All the time, in a soft, even, little voice, in rounded bookish phrases, he tells me various, to his mind, very interesting and piquant items of news which he has read in the magazines and journals. They are all alike and may be reduced to this type: 'A Frenchman has made a discovery; someone else, a German, has denounced him, proving that the discovery was made in 1870 by some American; while a third person, also a German, trumps them both by proving they both had made fools of themselves, mistaking bubbles of air for dark pigment under the microscope.' Even when he wants to amuse me, Piotr tells me things in the same lengthy, circumstantial manner as though he were defending a thesis, enumerating in detail the literary sources he has used, doing his utmost to be accurate as to the date and number of the journals and the name of everyone concerned, invariably in full – Jean-Jacques Petit,* never simply Petit. Sometimes he stays to dinner with us, and then during the whole of dinner-time he goes on telling me the same sort of piquant anecdotes, reducing everyone at the table to depression. If Gnekker and Liza begin talking before him of fugues and counterpoint, Brahms and Bach, he drops his eyes modestly, and is overcome with embarrassment; he is ashamed that such banalities should be discussed before such people as him and me.

In my present state of mind five minutes of him is enough to sicken me as though I had been seeing and hearing him for an eternity. I hate the poor fellow. His soft, smooth voice and bookish language exhaust me, and his stories stupefy me . . . He cherishes the best of feelings for me, and talks to me simply in order to give me pleasure, and I repay him by looking at him as though I wanted to hypnotise him, and think, 'Go, go, go! . . .' But he is not amenable to thought suggestion, and sits on and on and on . . .

While he is with me I can never shake off the thought, 'It's possible when I die he will be appointed to succeed me,' and my poor lecture-hall presents itself to me as an oasis in which the stream has dried up; and I am ungracious, silent, and surly with Piotr, as though he were to blame for such thoughts, and not I myself. When he begins, as usual, praising up the German savants, instead of making fun of him good-humouredly, as I used to do, I mutter sullenly:

'Asses, your Germans! . . .'

That is like the late Professor Nikita Krylov,* who once, when he was bathing with Pirogov at Revel and vexed at the water being very cold, burst out with, 'Scoundrels, these Germans!' I behave badly with Piotr, and only when he is going away, and from the window I catch a glimpse of his grey hat behind the garden fence, I want to call out and say, 'Forgive me, dear fellow!'

Dinner is ever drearier than in the winter. Gnekker, whom now I hate and despise, dines with us almost every day. I used to endure his presence in silence, now I aim biting remarks at him which make my wife and daughter blush. Carried away by evil feeling, I often say things that are simply stupid, and I don't know why I say them. So on one occasion it happened that I stared a long time at Gnekker, and, apropos of nothing, I fired off:

'An eagle may perchance swoop down beneath a hen,*
But never will the fowl soar upwards to the clouds . . .'

And the most vexatious thing is that the fowl Gnekker shows himself much cleverer than the eagle professor. Knowing that my wife and daughter are on his side, he takes up the line of meeting my gibes with condescending silence, as though to say: 'The old chap is in his dotage; what's the use of talking to him?' Or he makes fun of me good-naturedly. It is wonderful how petty a man may become! I am capable of dreaming all dinner-time that Gnekker will turn out to be an intriguer, that my wife and Liza will come to see their mistake, and that I will taunt them – and such absurd thoughts at the time when I have one foot in the grave!

There are now, too, misunderstandings of which in the old days I had no idea except from hearsay. Though I am ashamed of it, I will describe one that occurred the other day after dinner.

I was sitting in my room smoking a pipe; my wife came in as usual, sat down, and began saying what a good time it would be for me to go to Kharkov now while it is warm and I have free time, and there find out what sort of person our Gnekker is.

'Very good; I will go . . .' I assented.

My wife, pleased with me, got up and was going to the door, but turned back and said:

'By the way, I have another favour to ask of you. I know you will be angry, but it is my duty to warn you . . . Forgive my saying it, Nikolai, but all our neighbours and acquaintances have begun talking about your being so often at Katia's. She is clever and well educated; I don't deny that her company may be agreeable; but at your age and with your social position it seems strange that you should find pleasure in her society . . . Besides, she has such a reputation that . . .'

All the blood suddenly rushed to my brain, my eyes flashed fire, I leaped up and, clutching at my head and stamping my feet, shouted in an alien voice:

'Let me alone! let me alone! let me alone!'

Probably my face was terrible, my voice was strange, for my wife suddenly turned pale and began shrieking aloud in a despairing voice that was equally alien. Liza, Gnekker, then Yegor, came running in at our shouts . . .

'Let me alone!' I cried; 'let me alone! Out!'

My legs turned numb as though they had vanished; I felt myself falling into someone's arms; for a little while I still heard weeping, then sank into a faint which lasted two or three hours.

Now about Katia; she comes to see me every day towards evening, and of course neither the neighbours nor our acquaintances can avoid noticing it. She comes in for a minute and takes me off for a drive with her. She has her own horse and a new chaise bought this summer. Altogether she lives in an expensive style; she has taken a big detached villa with a large garden and has brought all her town retinue with her – two maids, a coachman . . . I often ask her:

'Katia, what will you live on when you have spent your father's money?'

'Then we shall see,' she answers.

'That money, my dear, deserves to be treated more seriously. It was earned by a good man, by honest labour.'

'You have told me that already. I know it.'

At first we drive through the open country, then through the conifer wood which is visible from my window. Nature seems to me as beautiful as it always has been, though some evil spirt whispers to me that these pines and fir trees, birds and white clouds in the sky will not notice my absence when in three or four months I am dead. Katia loves driving, and she is pleased that it is fine weather and that I am sitting beside her. She is in good spirits and does not say harsh things.

'You are a very good man, Nikolai,' she says. 'You are a rare specimen, and there isn't an actor who would understand how to play you. Me or Mikhail, for instance, even a mediocre actor could do, but not you. And I envy you, I envy you horribly! Do you know what I am? What?'

She ponders for a minute, and then asks me:

'Nikolai, I am a negative phenomenon! Yes?'

'Yes,' I answer.

'H'm! what am I to do?'

What answer was I to make her? It is easy to say 'work', or 'give your possessions to the poor', or 'know thyself', and because it is so easy to say that, I don't know what to answer.

My colleagues when they teach therapeutics advise 'the individual study of each separate case'. One has but to obey this advice to gain the conviction that the methods recommended in the textbooks as the best and as providing a safe basis for treatment turn out to be quite unsuitable in individual cases. It is just the same in moral ailments.

But I must make some answer, and I say:

'You have too much free time, my dear; you absolutely must take up some occupation. After all, why shouldn't you be an actress again if it is your vocation?'

'I cannot!'

'Your tone and manner suggest that you are a victim. I don't like that, my dear; it is your own fault. Remember, you began with falling out with people and methods, but you have done nothing to make either better. You did not struggle with evil, but were cast down by it, and you are not the victim of the struggle, but of your own impotence. Well, of course you were young and inexperienced then; now it may all be different. Yes, really, go on the stage. You will work, you will serve a sacred art.'

'Don't be devious, Nikolai,' Katia interrupts me. 'Let us make a pact once and for all; we will talk about actors, actresses, and authors, but we will let art alone. You are a splendid and rare person, but you don't know enough about art sincerely to think it sacred. You have no instinct or feeling for art. You have been hard at work all your life, and have not had time to acquire that feeling. Anyway . . . I don't like to talk about art,' she goes on nervously. 'I don't like it! And how they have vulgarised it, thank you very much!'

'Who has vulgarised it?'

'Some have vulgarised it by drunkenness, the newspapers by familiarity, clever people by philosophy.'

'Philosophy has nothing to do with it.'

'Yes, it has. If anyone philosophises about it, it shows he does not understand.'

To avoid bitterness I hasten to change the subject, and then sit a long time silent. Only when we are driving out of the wood and turning towards Katia's villa I go back to my former question, and say:

'You have still not answered me, why you don't want to go on the stage.'

'Nikolai, this is cruel!' she cries, and suddenly flushes all over. 'You want me to tell you the truth aloud! Very well, if . . . if you like it! I have no talent! No talent and . . . and a great deal of vanity! So there!'

After making this confession she turns her face away from me and to hide the trembling of her hands tugs violently at the reins.

As we are driving towards her villa we see Mikhail walking near the gate, impatiently awaiting us.

'That Mikhail again!' says Katia with vexation. 'Do rid me of him, please! I am sick and tired of him . . . to hell with him!'

Mikhail ought to have gone abroad long ago, but he puts off going from week to week. Of late there have been certain changes in him. He looks, as it were, sunken, has taken to drinking until he is tipsy, a thing which never used to happen to him, and his black eyebrows are beginning to turn grey. When our chaise stops at the gate he does not conceal his joy and his impatience. He fussily helps me and Katia out, hurriedly asks questions, laughs, rubs his hands, and that gentle, imploring, pure expression, which I used to notice only in his eyes, is now diffused all over his face. He is glad and at the same time he is ashamed of his gladness, ashamed of his habit of spending every evening with Katia. And he thinks it necessary to explain his visit by some transparent absurdity such as: 'I was driving by on business, and I thought I'd look in for a minute.'

We all three go indoors; first we drink tea, then the familiar two packs of cards, the big piece of cheese, fruit, and the bottle of Crimean champagne are put upon the table. The subjects of our conversation are not new; they are just the same as in winter. We have it in for the university, the students, and literature and the theatre; the air grows thick and stifling with calumny, and is poisoned by the breath, not of two toads as in the winter, but of three. Besides the velvety baritone laugh and the giggle like the gasp of a concertina, the maid who waits upon us hears an unpleasant cracked 'He, he!', the chuckle of a general in a vaudeville.

V

There are terrible nights with thunder, lightning, rain, and wind, such as are called among the people 'sparrow nights'. I have had one such night in my personal life . . .

I woke up after midnight and leapt suddenly out of bed. It seemed to me for some reason that I was about to die at any moment. Why did I think so? I had no sensation in my body that suggested my imminent end, but my soul was oppressed with terror, as though I had suddenly seen a vast menacing glow of fire.

I rapidly struck a light, drank some water straight out of the decanter, then hurried to the open window. The weather outside was magnificent. There was a smell of hay and some other very sweet scent. I could see the spikes of the fence, the gaunt, drowsy trees by the window, the road, the dark streak of woodland; there was a serene, very bright moon in the sky and not a single cloud. Perfect stillness, not a leaf stirring. I felt that everything was looking at me and listening, waiting for me to die . . .

It was awesome. I closed the window and ran to my bed. I felt for my pulse, and not finding it in my wrist, tried to find it in my temple, then in my chin, and again in my wrist, and everything I touched was cold and clammy with sweat. My breathing came more and more rapidly, my body was shivering, all my inside was in commotion; I had a sensation on my face and on my bald head as though a spider's web had fallen on them.

What should I do? Call my family? No; it would be of no use. I could not imagine what my wife and Liza would do when they came in to me.

I hid my head under the pillow, closed my eyes, and waited and waited . . . My spine was cold; it seemed to be drawn inwards, and I felt as though death were coming upon me stealthily from behind . . .

'Kee-vee! kee-vee!' I heard a sudden shriek in the night's stillness, and did not know where it was – in my chest or outside. 'Kee-vee! kee-vee!'

'My God, how frightening!' I would have drunk some more water, but by then I was afraid to open my eyes and I feared raising my head. I was possessed by unaccountable animal terror, and I cannot understand why I was so frightened: was it that I wanted to live, or that some new unknown pain was in store for me?

Upstairs, overhead, someone moaned or laughed . . . I listened. Soon afterwards there was a sound of footsteps on the stairs. Someone came hurriedly down, then went up again. A minute later there was a sound of steps downstairs again; someone stopped near my door and listened.

'Who is there?' I cried.

The door opened. I boldly opened my eyes, and saw my wife. Her face was pale and her eyes were tear-stained.

'You are not asleep, Nikolai?' she asked.

'What is it?'

'For God's sake, go and have a look at Liza; something's wrong with her . . .'

'Very good, with pleasure,' I muttered, greatly relieved at not being alone. 'Very good . . . this minute.'

I followed my wife, listened to what she said to me, and was too agitated to understand a word. Patches of light from her candle danced about the stairs, our long shadows trembled. My feet caught in the skirts of my dressing gown; I gasped for breath, and felt as though something were pursuing me and trying to catch me from behind.

'I shall die on the spot, here on the staircase,' I thought. 'On the spot . . .' But we passed the staircase, the dark corridor with the Italian windows, and went into Liza's room. She was sitting on her bed in her night-dress, with her bare feet hanging down, and she was moaning.

'Oh, my God! Oh, my God!' she was muttering, screwing up her eyes at our candle. 'I can't bear it.'

'Liza, my child,' I said, 'what is it?'

Seeing me, she began crying out, and flung herself on my neck.

'My kind papa! . . .' she sobbed – 'my dear, good papa . . . my darling, my pet, I don't know what is the matter with me . . . I am miserable!'

She hugged me, kissed me, and babbled fond words I used to hear from her when she was a child.

'Calm yourself, my child, come on now,' I said. 'There is no need to cry. I am miserable, too.'

I tried to tuck her in; my wife gave her water, and we awkwardly stumbled by her bedside; my shoulder jostled against her shoulder, and meanwhile I was thinking how we used to give our children their bath together.

'Help her! help her!' my wife implored me. 'Do something!'

What could I do? I could do nothing. There was some load on the girl's heart; but I did not understand, I knew nothing about it, and could only mutter:

'It's nothing, it's nothing . . . It will pass . . . Sleep, sleep!'

To make things worse, there was a sudden sound of dogs howling, at first subdued and uncertain, then loud, two dogs howling together. I have never attached significance to such omens as the howling of dogs or the shrieking of owls, but on that occasion it sent a pang to my heart, and I hastened to explain the howl to myself.

'It's nonsense,' I thought, 'the influence of one organism on another. The intensely strained condition of my nerves has infected my wife, Liza, the dog – that is all . . . Such transmission explains presentiments, forebodings . . .'

When a little later I went back to my room to write a prescription for Liza, I no longer thought I should die at once; I just had such a weight, such a feeling of oppression in my soul that I felt actually sorry that I had not died on the spot. For a long time I stood motionless in the middle of the room, pondering what to prescribe for Liza. But the moans overhead ceased, and I decided to prescribe nothing, and yet I went on standing there . . .

There was a deathly stillness, such a stillness, as some author has expressed it, that 'it rang in one's ears'. Time passed slowly; the streaks of moonlight on the window-sill did not shift their position, but seemed as though frozen . . . It was still some time before dawn.

But the gate in the fence creaked, someone stole in and, breaking a twig from one of those scraggy trees, cautiously tapped on the window with it.

'Nikolai,' I heard a whisper. 'Nikolai.'

I opened the window, and fancied I was dreaming: under the window, huddled against the wall, stood a woman in a black dress, with the moonlight bright upon her, looking at me with great eyes. Her face was pale, stern, and weird-looking in the moonlight, like marble, her chin was quivering.

'It is me,' she said – 'I . . . Katia.'

In the moonlight all women's eyes look big and black, all people look taller and paler, and that was probably why I had not recognised her straight away.

'What is it?'

'Forgive me!' she said. 'I suddenly felt unbearably miserable . . . I couldn't stand it, so came here. There was a light in your window and . . . and I decided to knock . . . I beg your pardon . . . Ah! if you knew how miserable I am! What are you doing just now?'

'Nothing . . . I can't sleep.'

'I had a feeling that there was something wrong. Anyway, what nonsense.'

Her brows were lifted, her eyes shone with tears, and her whole face was lighted up with the familiar look of trustfulness which I had not seen for so long.

'Nikolai,' she said imploringly, stretching out both hands to me, 'my precious friend, I beg you, I implore you . . . If you don't despise my affection and respect for you, consent to what I ask of you.'

'What is it?'

'Take my money from me!'

'Come! what an idea! What do I want with your money?'

'You'll go away somewhere for your health . . . You ought to go for your health. Will you take it? Yes? Nikolai, darling, yes?'

She looked greedily into my face and repeated: 'Yes? Will you take it?'

'No, my dear, I won't take it . . . ' I said. 'Thank you.'

She turned her back upon me and hung her head. Probably I refused her in a tone which made further conversation about money impossible.

'Go home to bed,' I said. 'We will see each other tomorrow.'

'So you don't consider me your friend?' she asked dejectedly.

'I don't say that. But your money would be of no use to me now.'

'I beg your pardon . . .' she said, dropping her voice a whole octave. 'I understand you . . . to borrow from somebody like me . . . a retired actress . . . But, good-bye . . .'

And she went away so quickly that I had not time even to say good-bye.

VI

I am in Kharkov.

As it would be useless to contend against my present mood and, indeed, beyond my power, I have made up my mind that the last days of my life shall at least be irreproachable externally. If I am unjust in regard to my wife and daughter, which I fully recognise, I will try and do as she wishes; since she wants me to go to Kharkov, I go to Kharkov. Besides, I have become of late so indifferent to everything that it is really all the same to me where I go, to Kharkov, or to Paris, or to Berdichev.

I arrived here at midday, and have put up at the hotel not far from the cathedral. The train was jolting, there were draughts and now I am sitting on my bed, holding my head and expecting *tic douloureux*. I ought to have gone today to see some professors of my acquaintance, but I have neither the strength nor inclination.

The old corridor attendant comes in and asks whether I have brought my own bed-linen. I detain him for about five minutes, and put several questions to him about Gnekker, on whose account I have come here. The attendant turns out to be a native of Kharkov; he knows the town like the fingers of his hand, but does not remember any household of the surname of Gnekker. I question him about the estate – the same answer.

The clock in the corridor strikes one, then two, then three . . . These last months in which I am waiting for death seem much longer than the whole of my life. And I have never before been so ready to resign myself to the slowness of time as now. In the old days, when one sat in the station and waited for a train, or presided in an examination room, a quarter of an hour would seem an eternity. Now I can sit all night on my bed without moving, and quite unconcernedly reflect that tomorrow will be followed by another night as long and colourless, and the day after tomorrow.

In the corridor it strikes, five, six, seven . . . It grows dark.

There is a dull pain in my cheek, the tic beginning. To occupy myself with thoughts, I go back to my old point of view, when I was not so indifferent, and ask myself why I, a distinguished man, a privy councillor, am sitting in this little hotel room, on this bed with the unfamiliar grey quilt. Why am I looking at that cheap tin wash-stand and listening to the whir of the wretched clock in the corridor? Is all this in keeping with my fame and my lofty position? And I answer these questions with a jeer. I am amused by the naïveté with which I used in my youth to exaggerate the value of renown and of the exceptional position which celebrities are supposed to enjoy. I am famous, my name is pronounced with reverence, my portrait has been both in the *Cornfield* and in the *Universal Illustrated*; I have read my biography even in a German magazine. And what of all that? Here I am sitting utterly alone in a strange town, on a strange bed, rubbing my aching cheek with my hand . . . Domestic worries, the hard-heartedness of creditors, the rudeness of the railway servants, the inconveniences of the passport system, the expensive and unwholesome food in the refreshment rooms, the general rudeness and coarseness in social intercourse – all this, and a great deal more which would take too long to reckon up, affects me as much as any humble householder who is famous only in his alley. In what way does my exceptional position find expression? Let's suppose that I am celebrated a thousand times over, that I am a hero of whom my country is proud. They publish bulletins of my illness in every paper, letters of sympathy come to me by post from my colleagues, my pupils, the general public; but none of that stops me from dying in a strange bed, in misery, in utter loneliness . . . Of course, no one is to blame for that; but I, however deplorably, dislike my popularity. I feel as though it had cheated me.

At ten o'clock I fall asleep, and in spite of the tic I sleep soundly, and should have gone on sleeping if I had not been awakened. Soon after one came a sudden knock at the door.

'Who is there?'

'A telegram.'

'You might have waited till tomorrow,' I say angrily, taking the telegram from the attendant. 'Now I shall not get to sleep again.'

'I am sorry. Your light was burning, so I thought you were not asleep.'

I tear open the telegram and look first at the signature. From my wife.

'What does she want?'

'Gnekker was secretly married to Liza yesterday. Return.'

I read the telegram, and my dismay does not last long. I am dismayed, not by what Liza and Gnekker have done, but by the indifference with which I hear of their marriage. They say philosophers and the truly wise are indifferent. Wrong: indifference is the paralysis of the soul; it is premature death.

I go to bed again, and begin trying to think of something to occupy my mind. What am I to think about? I feel as though everything had been thought over already and there is nothing which could hold my attention now.

When daylight comes I sit up in bed with my arms round my knees, and to pass the time I try to know myself. 'Know thyself' is excellent and useful advice; it is only a pity that the ancients never thought to indicate a way of using this precept.

When I have wanted to understand somebody or myself, I have considered, not the actions, in which everything is relative, but the desires.

'Tell me what you want, and I will tell you who you are.'

And now I examine myself: what do I want?

I want our wives, our children, our friends, our pupils, to love in us, not our fame, not the brand and not the label, but to love us as ordinary men. Anything else? I should like to have had helpers and successors. Anything else? I should like to wake up in a hundred years' time and to have just a peep out of one eye at what is happening in science. I should have liked to have lived another ten years . . . What further?

Nothing further. I think and think for a long time, and can think of nothing more. And however much I might think, and however far my thoughts might travel, it is clear to me that there is nothing vital, nothing of great importance in my desires. In my passion for science, in my desire to live, in this sitting on a strange bed, and in this striving to know myself – in all the thoughts, feelings, and ideas I form about everything, there is no common bond to bind it all into one whole. Every feeling and every thought exists apart in me; and in all my criticisms of science, the theatre, literature, my pupils, and in all the pictures my imagination draws, even the most skilful analyst could not find what is called a general idea, or a god by which a man could live.

And if that is missing, then there is nothing.

In such impoverishment a serious ailment, the fear of death, the influences of circumstance and men were enough to turn upside down and scatter in fragments all that I had once looked upon as my theory of life, and in which I had seen the meaning and joy of my existence. So there is nothing surprising in the fact that I have overshadowed the last months of my life with thoughts and feelings only worthy of a slave and barbarian, and that now I am indifferent and take no heed of the dawn. When a man lacks what is loftier and mightier than all external impressions, a bad cold is really enough to upset his equilibrium and make him begin to see an owl in every bird, to hear a dog howling in every sound. And all his pessimism or optimism with his thoughts great and small are then significant as symptoms and nothing more.

I am vanquished. If it is so, it is pointless to go on thinking or talking. I will sit and wait in silence for what is to come.

In the morning the corridor attendant brings me tea and a copy of the local newspaper. Mechanically I read the advertisements on the first page, the leading article, the extracts from the newspapers and journals, the chronicle of events . . . In the latter I find, among other things, the following paragraph: 'Our distinguished savant, Professor Nikolai So-and-so, arrived yesterday in Kharkov, and is staying in the So-and-so Hotel.'

Apparently, illustrious names are created to live on their own account, apart from those that bear them. Now my name is promenading tranquilly about Kharkov; in another three months, printed in gold letters on my monument, it will shine bright as the sun itself, while I shall be already under the moss.

A light tap at the door. Somebody wants me.

'Who is there? Come in.'

The door opens, and I step back surprised and hurriedly wrap my dressing-gown round me. Before me stands Katia.

'How do you do?' she says, breathless with running upstairs. 'You didn't expect me? I have come here, too . . . I have come, too!'

She sits down and goes on, hesitating and not looking at me.

'Why don't you speak to me? I have come, too . . . today . . . I found out that you were in this hotel, and have come to you.'

'Very glad to see you,' I say, shrugging my shoulders, 'but I am surprised. You seem to have dropped from the skies. What have you come for?'

'Oh . . . I've simply come.'

Silence. Suddenly she jumps up impulsively and comes to me.

'Nikolai,' she says, turning pale and pressing her hands on her breast – 'Nikolai, I cannot go on living like this! I cannot! For God's sake, tell me quickly, this minute, what am I to do! Tell me, what am I to do?'

'What can I tell you?' I ask in perplexity. 'I can do nothing.'

'Tell me, I beseech you,' she goes on, breathing hard and trembling all over. 'I swear that I cannot go on living like this. It's too much for me!'

She sinks on a chair and begins sobbing. She flings her head back, wrings her hands, stamps with her feet; her hat falls off and hangs bobbing on its elastic; her hair is dishevelled.

'Help me! help me!' she implores me. 'I cannot go on!'

She takes her handkerchief out of her travelling bag, and with it pulls out several letters, which fall from her lap to the floor. I pick them up, and on one of them I recognise the handwriting of Mikhail and accidentally read a bit of a word 'passiona . . .'

'There is nothing I can tell you, Katia,' I say.

'Help me!' she sobs, clutching at my hand and kissing it. 'You are my father, you know, my only friend! You are clever, educated; you have lived so long; you have been a teacher! Tell me, what am I to do?'

'Upon my word, Katia, I don't know . . .'

I am utterly at a loss and confused, touched by her sobs, and hardly able to stand.

'Let us have lunch, Katia,' I say, with a forced smile. 'Give over crying.'

And at once I add in a sinking voice:

'I shall soon be gone, Katia . . .'

'Only one word, only one word!' she weeps, stretching out her hands to me. 'What am I to do?'

'You're an odd girl, really . . .' I mutter. 'I don't understand it! So sensible, and all at once . . . crying your eyes out . . .'

A silence follows. Katia straightens her hair, puts on her hat, then crumples up the letters and stuffs them in her bag – and all this deliberately, in silence. Her face, her breast, and her gloves are wet with tears, but her expression now is cold and forbidding . . . I look at her, and feel ashamed that I am happier than she. The absence of what my philosophic colleagues call a general idea I have detected in myself only just before death, in the decline of my days, while the soul of this poor girl has known and will know no refuge all her life, all her life!

'Let us have lunch, Katia,' I say.

'No, thank you,' she answers coldly.

Another minute passes in silence.

'I don't like Kharkov,' I say; 'it's so grey here – such a grey town.'

'Yes, perhaps . . . It's ugly. I am here not for long, passing through. I am going on today.'

'Where?'

'To the Crimea . . . that is, to the Caucasus.'

'Oh! For long?'

'I don't know.'

Katia gets up, and, with a cold smile, holds out her hand without looking at me.

I want to ask her, 'Then, you won't be at my funeral?' but she does not look at me; her hand is cold and, as it were, strange. I escort her to the door in silence. She goes out, walks along the long corridor without looking back; she knows that I am looking after her, and most likely she will look back at the turn.

No, she did not look back. I've seen her black dress for the last time: her steps have died away . . . Farewell, my treasure!

1889

The Duel

I

It was eight o'clock in the morning – the time when the officers, the local officials, and the visitors usually took their morning dip in the sea after the hot, stifling night, and then went into the pavilion to drink tea or coffee. Ivan Andreich Laevsky, a thin, fair young man of about twenty-eight, wearing the cap of an employee in the Ministry of Finance and with slippers on his feet, coming down to bathe, found a number of acquaintances on the beach, and among them his friend Samoilenko, the army doctor.

With his big cropped head, short neck, his red face, his big nose, his shaggy black eyebrows and grey whiskers, his stout puffy figure and his hoarse military bass, this Samoilenko made on every newcomer the unpleasant impression of a gruff bully; but two or three days after making his acquaintance, one began to think his face extraordinarily good-natured, kind, and even handsome. In spite of his clumsiness and rough manner, he was a peaceable man, of infinite kindliness and goodness of heart, always ready to be of use. He was on familiar terms with everyone in the town, lent everyone money, doctored everyone, made matches, patched up quarrels, arranged picnics at which he cooked *shashlik* and an awfully good soup of grey mullets. He was always looking after other people's affairs and trying to interest someone on their behalf, and was always delighted about something. The general opinion about him was that he was without faults of character. He had only two weaknesses: he was ashamed of his own good nature, and tried to disguise it by a surly expression and an assumed gruffness; and he liked his assistants and his soldiers to call him 'Your Excellency', although he was only a civil councillor.

'Answer one question for me, Alexandr,' Laevsky began, when both he and Samoilenko were in the water up to their shoulders. 'Suppose you had loved a woman, got on intimate terms with her and had been living with her for two or three years, and then stopped caring for her, as one does, and began to feel that you had nothing in common with her. How would you behave in that case?'

'It's very simple. "You go where you please, madam" – and that would be the end of it.'

'It's easy to say that! But if she has nowhere to go? A woman with no friends or relations, without a kopeck, who can't work . . .'

'Well? Five hundred roubles down or an allowance of twenty-five roubles a month – and nothing more. It's very simple.'

'Even supposing you have five hundred roubles and can pay twenty-five roubles a month, the woman I am speaking of is an educated woman and proud. Could you really bring yourself to offer her money? And how would you do it?'

Samoilenko was going to answer, but at that moment a big wave covered them both, then broke on the beach and rolled back noisily over the shingle. The friends got out and began dressing.

'Of course, it is difficult to live with a woman if you don't love her,' said Samoilenko, shaking the sand out of his boots. 'But one must look at the thing humanely, Vania. If it were my case, I'd never show a sign that I didn't love her, and I should go on living with her till I died.'

He was at once ashamed of his own words; he pulled himself up and said:

'But for all I care, women might as well not exist. Let them go to the devil!'

The friends dressed and went into the pavilion. There Samoilenko was quite at home, and even had a special cup and saucer. Every morning they brought him on a tray a cup of coffee, a tall cut glass of iced water, and a tiny glass of brandy. He would first drink the brandy, then the hot coffee, then the iced water, and this must have been very nice, for after drinking it his eyes looked moist with pleasure, he would stroke his whiskers with both hands, and say, looking at the sea:

'A wonderfully magnificent view!'

After a long night spent in cheerless, unprofitable thoughts which prevented him from sleeping, and seemed to intensify the darkness and sultriness of the night, Laevsky felt listless and shattered. He felt no better for the bathe and the coffee.

'Let us go on with our talk, Alexandr,' he said. 'I won't make a secret of it; I'll speak to you openly as to a friend. Things are in a bad way with Nadezhda and me . . . a very bad way! Forgive me for forcing my private affairs upon you, but I must get it out.'

Samoilenko, who sensed what the matter was, dropped his eyes and drummed his fingers on the table.

'I've lived with her for two years and have ceased to love her,' Laevsky went on; 'or, rather, I realised that I never had felt any love for her . . . These two years have been a mistake.'

It was Laevsky's habit as he talked to gaze attentively at the pink palms of his hands, to bite his nails, or to crumple his cuffs with his fingers. And he did so now.

'I know very well you can't help me,' he said. 'But I tell you, because failures and superfluous people like me find their salvation in talking. I have to generalise about everything I do. I'm bound to look for an explanation and justification of my absurd existence in somebody else's theories, in literary types – in the idea that we, upper-class Russians, are degenerating, for instance, and so on. Last night, for example, I comforted myself by thinking all the time: "Ah, how true Tolstoy is, how mercilessly true!" And that did me good. Yes, really, brother, he is a great writer, say what you like!'

Samoilenko, who had never read Tolstoy and was intending to do so every day of his life, was a little embarrassed, and said:

'Yes, all other authors write from imagination, but he writes straight from nature.'

'My God!' sighed Laevsky; 'how distorted we all are by civilisation! I fell in love with a married woman and she with me . . . To begin with, we had kisses, and calm evenings, and vows, and Herbert Spencer,* and ideals, and interests in common . . . What a deception! We really ran away from her husband, but we lied to ourselves and made out that we ran away from the emptiness of the life of the educated class. We pictured our future like this: to begin with, in the Caucasus, while we were getting to know the people and the place, I would put on the government uniform and enter the service; then at our leisure we would get a plot of ground, would toil in the sweat of our brow, would have a vineyard and a field, and so on. If you were in my place, or that zoologist of yours, Von Koren, you might live with Nadezhda for thirty years, perhaps, and might leave your heirs a rich vineyard and three thousand acres of maize; but I felt like a bankrupt from the first day. In the town you have insufferable heat, boredom, and no society; if you go out into the country, you fancy poisonous spiders, scorpions, or snakes lurking behind every bush, and beyond the fields – mountains and wilderness. Alien people, an alien country, a wretched form of civilisation – all that is not so easy, brother, as walking down the Nevsky Prospect in your fur coat, arm in arm with Nadezhda, dreaming of the sunny south. Here you have a life and death struggle, and I'm not a fighting man. A wretched neurotic, an idle gentleman . . . From the first day I knew that my dreams of a life of labour and of a vineyard were worthless. As for love, I ought to tell you that living with a woman who has read Spencer and has followed you to the ends of the earth is no more interesting than living with Anfisa, Akulina or any other servant-girl. There's the same smell of ironing, of powder, and of medicines, the same curl-papers every morning, the same self-deception.'

'You can't do without an iron in the house,' said Samoilenko, blushing at Laevsky's speaking to him so openly of a lady he knew. 'You are out of humour today, Vania, I notice. Nadezhda is a splendid woman, highly educated, and you are a man of the highest intellect. Of course, you are not married,' Samoilenko went on, glancing round at the adjacent tables, 'but that's not your fault; and besides . . . one ought to be above conventional prejudices and rise to the level of modern ideas. I believe in common-law marriage myself, yes . . . But to my thinking, once you are living together, you ought to go on together all your life.'

'Without love?'

'I'll tell you now,' said Samoilenko. 'Eight years ago there was an old fellow, an agent, here – a man of very great intelligence. Well, he used to say that the great thing in married life was patience. Do you hear, Vania? Not love, but patience. Love cannot last long. You have lived two years in love, and now evidently your married life has reached the period when, in order to preserve equilibrium, so to speak, you ought to exercise all your patience . . .'

'You believe your old agent; to me his words are meaningless. Your old man might be a hypocrite; he might praise the virtue of patience, and, as he did so, look upon a person he did not love as an object indispensable for his moral exercises; but I have not yet fallen so low. If I want to practise patience, I will buy dumb-bells or a frisky horse, but I'll leave human beings alone.'

Samoilenko asked for some iced white wine. When they had drunk a glass each, Laevsky suddenly asked:

'Tell me, please, what is the meaning of softening of the brain?'

'How can I explain it to you? . . . It's a disease in which the brain becomes softer . . . as it were, liquefies.'

'Is it curable?'

'Yes, if the disease in not neglected. Cold douches, blisters . . . Something internal, too.'

'Oh! . . . Well, you see my position; I can't live with her: it is more than I can do. While I'm with you I can be philosophical about it and smile, but at home, I lose heart completely; I am so utterly miserable, that if I were told, for instance, that I should have to live another month with her, I should blow out my brains. At the same time, parting with her is out of the question. She has no friends or relations; she cannot work, and neither she nor I have any money . . . What could become of her? To whom could she go? There is nothing one can think of . . . Come, tell me, what am I to do?'

'H'm! . . .' growled Samoilenko, not knowing what to answer. 'Does she love you?'

'Yes, she loves me in so far as at her age and with her temperament she wants a man. It would be as difficult for her to do without me as to do without her powder or her curling papers. I am for her an indispensable, integral part of her boudoir.'

Samoilenko was embarrassed.

'You are out of humour today, Vania,' he said. 'You must have had a bad night.'

'Yes, I slept badly . . . Altogether, I feel bad, brother. My head feels empty; my heart is sinking, a weakness . . . I must run away.'

'Run where?'

'Home, to the north. To the pines and the mushrooms, to people and ideas . . . I'd give half my life to bathe now in some little stream in the province of Moscow or Tula; to feel chilly, you know, and then to stroll for three hours even with the most pathetic student, and to talk and talk endlessly . . . And the scent of hay! Do you remember it? And in the evening, when one walks in the garden, sounds of the piano float from the house; one hears the train passing . . .'

Laevsky laughed with pleasure; tears came into his eyes, and to cover them, without getting up, he stretched across the next table for the matches.

'I haven't been in Russia for eighteen years,' said Samoilenko. 'I've forgotten what it is like. To my mind, there is no country more splendid than the Caucasus.'

'Vereshchagin* has a picture in which some men condemned to death are languishing at the bottom of a very deep well. Your magnificent Caucasus strikes me as just like that well. If I were offered the choice of a chimney-sweep in Petersburg or a prince in the Caucasus, I should choose the job of chimney-sweep.'

Laevsky grew pensive. Looking at his stooping figure, at his eyes fixed dreamily on one spot, at his pale, perspiring face and sunken temples, at his bitten nails, at the slipper which had dropped off his heel, displaying a badly darned sock, Samoilenko was moved to pity, and probably because Laevsky reminded him of a helpless child, he asked:

'Is your mother alive?'

'Yes, but we are on bad terms. She could not forgive me for this affair.'

Samoilenko was fond of his friend. He looked upon Laevsky as a good-natured fellow, a student, a man with no nonsense about him, with whom one could drink, and laugh, and talk without reserve. What he understood in him he disliked extremely. Laevsky drank a great deal and at the wrong time; he played cards, despised his work, lived beyond his means, frequently used obscene expressions in conversation, walked about the streets in his slippers, and squabbled with Nadezhda in public – and Samoilenko did not like this. But the fact that Laevsky had once been a student in the faculty of arts, subscribed to two fat reviews, often talked so cleverly that only a few people understood him, was living with a well-educated woman – all this Samoilenko did not understand, and he liked this and respected Laevsky, thinking him superior to himself.

'There is another point,' said Laevsky, shaking his head. 'Only it is between ourselves. I'm concealing it from Nadezhda for the time being. Don't let it out in her hearing . . . I got a letter the day before yesterday, telling me that her husband has died from softening of the brain.'

'May he rest in peace!' sighed Samoilenko. 'Why are you concealing it from her?'

'To show her that letter would be equivalent to "Come to church to be married". But first we have to sort out our differences. When she understands that we can't go on living together, I will show her the letter. Then there will be no danger in it.'

'Do you know what, Vania,' said Samoilenko, and a sad and imploring expression came into his face, as though he were going to ask him about something very touching and were afraid of being refused, 'Marry her, my dear boy!'

'Why?'

'Do your duty to that fine woman! Her husband is dead, and so Providence itself shows you what to do!'

'But do understand, you odd fellow, that it is impossible. To marry without love is as base and unworthy of a man as to perform mass without believing in it.'

'But it's your duty to.'

'Why is it my duty?' Laevsky asked irritably.

'Because you took her away from her husband and made yourself responsible for her.'

'But now I tell you in plain Russian, I don't love her!'

'Well, if you've no love, show her proper respect, indulge her . . '

'Show her proper respect, indulge her . . .' Laevsky mimicked him. 'As though she were some mother superior! . . . You are a poor psychologist and physiologist if you think that living with a woman one can get off with nothing but respect and consideration. For women the bedroom comes first.'

'Vania, Vania!' said Samoilenko.

'You are an elderly child, a theorist, while I am an old man in spite of my years, and practical, and we shall never understand one another. We had better drop this conversation. Mustafa!' Laevsky shouted to the waiter. 'What do we owe you?'

'No, no . . .' the doctor cried in dismay, clutching Laevsky's arm. 'I'll pay. I ordered it. Chalk it up to me,' he cried to Mustafa.

The friends got up and walked in silence along the sea-front. When they reached the boulevard, they stopped and shook hands at parting.

'You gentry are awfully spoilt!' Samoilenko sighed. 'Fate has sent you a young, beautiful, cultured woman, and you refuse the gift; if God were to give me only a crooked old woman, how pleased I should be if only she were kind and affectionate! I would live with her in my vineyard and . . .'

Samoilenko caught himself up and said:

'And let her put the samovar on for me there, the old hag.'

After parting with Laevsky he walked along the boulevard. When, bulky and majestic, with a stern expression on his face, he walked along the boulevard in his snow-white tunic and superbly polished boots, squaring his chest, decorated with the Vladimir Cross on a ribbon, he was very pleased with himself, and it seemed as though the whole world were looking at him with pleasure. Without turning his head, he looked to each side and thought that the boulevard was extremely well laid out; that the young cypress trees, the eucalyptuses, and the ugly, anaemic palm trees were very handsome and would in time give abundant shade; that the Circassians were an honest and hospitable people. 'It's strange that Laevsky does not like the Caucasus,' he thought, 'very strange.' Five soldiers, carrying rifles, met him and saluted him. On the right side of the boulevard the wife of a local official was walking along the pavement with her son, a schoolboy.

'Good morning, Maria,' Samoilenko shouted to her with a pleasant smile. 'Have you been to bathe? Ha, ha, ha! . . . My respects to Nikodim!'

And he went on, still smiling pleasantly, but seeing an orderly from the military hospital coming towards him, he suddenly frowned, stopped him, and asked:

'Is there anyone in the hospital?'

'No one, your Excellency.'

'What?'

'No one, your Excellency.'

'Very well, run along . . .'

Swaying majestically, he made for the lemonade stall, where sat a full-bosomed old Jewess, who claimed to be a Georgian, and said to her loudly as though he were giving a command to a regiment:

'Be so good as to give me some soda water!'

II

Laevsky's not loving Nadezhda showed itself chiefly in the fact that everything she said or did seemed to him a lie, or equivalent to a lie, and everything he read against woman and love seemed to him to apply perfectly to himself, to Nadezhda and her husband. When he returned home, she was sitting at the window, dressed and with her hair done, and with a preoccupied face was drinking coffee and turning over the leaves of a thick magazine; and he thought the drinking of coffee was not such a remarkable event that she need put on a preoccupied expression over it, and that she had been wasting her time doing her hair in a fashionable style, as there was no one here to attract and no need to be attractive. And in the magazine he saw nothing but falsity. He thought she had dressed and done her hair so as to look handsomer, and was reading in order to seem clever.

'Will it be all right for me to go to bathe today?' she said.

'Why? There won't be an earthquake whether you go or not, I suppose . . .'

'No, I only ask in case the doctor should be vexed.'

'Well, ask the doctor, then; I'm not a doctor.'

On this occasion what displeased Laevsky most in Nadezhda was her white open neck and the little curls at the back of the head. And he remembered that when Anna Karenina got tired of her husband, what she disliked most of all was his ears, and thought; 'How true it is, how true!' Feeling weak and empty-headed, he went into the study, lay down on the sofa, and covered his face with a handkerchief to avoid being bothered by flies. Despondent and oppressive thoughts always about the same thing trailed slowly across his brain like a string of wagons on a gloomy autumn evening, and he sank into a state of drowsy oppression. It seemed to him that he had wronged Nadezhda and her husband, and that it was through his fault that her husband had died. It seemed to him that he had sinned against his own life, which he had ruined, against the world of lofty ideas, of learning, and of work, and he conceived that wonderful world as real and possible, not on this sea-front with hungry Turks and lazy mountain tribesmen sauntering on it, but there in the north, where there were operas, theatres, newspapers, and all kinds of intellectual activity. One could only there – not here – be honest, intelligent, lofty, and pure. He accused himself of having no ideal, no guiding principle in life, though he had only dimly understood now what it meant. Two years before, when he fell in love with Nadezhda, it seemed to him that he had only to go with her as his wife to the Caucasus, and he would be saved from vulgarity and emptiness; in the same way now, he was convinced that he had only to part from Nadezhda and to go to Petersburg, and he would get everything he wanted.

'Run away!' he muttered to himself, sitting up and biting his nails. 'Run away!'

He pictured in his imagination boarding the steamer and then having lunch, drinking cold beer, talking on deck with ladies, then getting into the train at Sevastopol and setting off. Hallo, freedom! One station after another would flash by, the air would keep growing colder and keener, then the birches and the fir trees, then Kursk, Moscow . . . Cabbage soup, mutton with kasha, sturgeon, beer in the buffets, no more Asiatic squalor, but Russia, real Russia. The passengers in the train would talk about trade, new singers, the Franco-Russian *entente*; on all sides there would be the feeling of keen, cultured, intellectual, eager life . . . Quickly, quickly! At last Nevsky Prospect, and Great Morskaia Street, and then Kovno Lane, where he used to live at one time when he was a student, the dear grey sky, the drizzling rain, the drenched cabmen . . .

'Mr Laevsky!' someone called from the next room. 'Are you at home?'

'I'm here,' Laevsky responded. 'What do you want?'

'Papers.'

Laevsky got up languidly, feeling giddy, walked into the other room, yawning and shuffling with his slippers. There, at the open window that looked into the street, stood one of his young colleagues, laying out some government documents on the window-sill.

'One minute, my dear fellow,' Laevsky said softly, and he went to look for the ink; returning to the window, he signed the papers without looking at them, and said: 'It's hot!'

'Yes. Are you coming in today?'

'I don't think so . . . I'm not quite well. Tell Sheshkovsky, old boy, that I will come and see him after dinner.'

The civil servant went away. Laevsky lay down on his sofa again and began thinking:

'And so I must weigh all the circumstances and reflect on them. Before I go away from here I ought to pay my debts. I owe about two thousand roubles. I have no money . . . Of course, that's not important; I shall pay part now, somehow, and I shall send the rest, later, from Petersburg. The chief point is Nadezhda . . . First of all we must sort out our differences . . . Yes.'

A little later he was considering whether it would not be better to go to Samoilenko for advice.

'I could go,' he thought, 'but what use would it be? I shall only say something out of place about boudoirs, about women, about what is right or wrong. What the hell is the use of talking about right and wrong, if I must hurry and save my life, if I am suffocating in this cursed slavery and am killing myself? . . . After all, it must be understood that to go on leading the life I do is so base and so cruel that everything else seems petty and trivial beside it. To run away,' he muttered, sitting down, 'run away!'

The deserted seashore, the unquenchable heat, and the monotony of the smoky violet mountains, ever the same and silent, everlastingly solitary, overwhelmed him with depression, and, as it were, made him drowsy and sapped his energy. He was perhaps very clever, talented, remarkably honest; perhaps if the sea and the mountains had not closed him in on all sides, he might have become an excellent district council leader, a statesman, an orator, a political writer, a saint. Who knows? If so, was it not stupid to argue whether it were right or wrong when a gifted and useful man – an artist or musician, for instance – to escape from prison, breaks a wall and deceives his jailors? Anything is right when a man is in such a position.

At two o'clock Laevsky and Nadezhda sat down to dinner. When the cook gave them rice and tomato soup, Laevsky said:

'The same thing every day. Why not have cabbage soup?'

'There are no cabbages.'

'It's strange. Samoilenko has cabbage soup and Maria has cabbage soup, and only I have to eat this sugary mess. We can't go on like this, darling.'

As happens with the vast majority of husbands and wives, not a single dinner had in earlier days passed without absurd behaviour and scenes between Nadezhda and Laevsky; but ever since Laevsky had made up his mind that he no longer loved her, he had tried to give way to Nadezhda in everything, spoke to her gently and politely, smiled, and called her 'darling'.

'This soup tastes like liquorice,' he said, smiling; he made an effort to control himself and seem amiable, but could not refrain from saying: 'Nobody looks after the housekeeping . . . If you are too ill or busy with reading, let me look after the cooking.'

In earlier days she would have said to him, 'Do by all means,' or, 'I see you want to turn me into a cook'; but now she only looked at him timidly and flushed.

'Well, how do you feel today?' he asked kindly.

'I am all right today. Just a slight weakness.'

'You must take care of yourself, darling. I am awfully anxious about you.'

Nadezhda had some illness or other. Samoilenko said she had intermittent fever, and gave her quinine; the other doctor, Ustimovich, a tall, lean, unsociable man, who used to sit at home in the daytime, and in the evenings walk slowly up and down on the sea-front coughing, with his hands folded behind him and a cane stretched along his back, was of the opinion that she had a gynaecological illness, and prescribed warm compresses. Once, when

Laevsky loved her, Nadezhda's illness had excited his pity and terror; now he saw lies even in her illness. Her yellow, sleepy face, her jaded eyes and the yawning that always followed her attacks of fever, and the fact that during them she lay under a travelling rug and looked more like a boy than a woman, and that her stuffy room smelt bad – all this, in his opinion, destroyed the illusion and was a protest against love and marriage.

The next dish given him was spinach with hard-boiled eggs, while Nadezhda, as an invalid, had blancmange and milk. When with a preoccupied face she touched the blancmange with her spoon and then began languidly eating it, washing it down with milk, and he heard her swallowing, he was possessed by such an overwhelming hatred that it made his head tingle. He recognised that such a feeling would be an insult even to a dog, but he was angry, not with himself but with Nadezhda, for arousing such a feeling, and he understood why lovers sometimes murder their mistresses. He would not murder her, of course, but if he had been on a jury now, he would have acquitted the murderer.

'*Merci*, darling,' he said after dinner, and kissed Nadezhda on the forehead.

Going back to his study, he spent five minutes walking to and fro, looking at his boots; then he sat down on his sofa and muttered:

'Run away, run away! I must have it out and run away!'

He lay down on the sofa and recalled again that Nadezhda's husband had died, perhaps, because of him.

'To blame a man for loving a woman, or ceasing to love a woman, is stupid,' he tried to persuade himself, lying down and raising his legs in order to put on his boots. 'Love and hatred are beyond our control. As for her husband, maybe I was in an indirect way one of the causes of his death; but again, is it my fault that I fell in love with his wife and she with me?'

Then he got up, and finding his cap, set off to the lodgings of his colleague, Sheshkovsky, where the officials met every day to play whist and drink cold beer.

'My indecision reminds me of Hamlet,' thought Laevsky on the way. 'How truly Shakespeare caught it! Ah, how truly!'

III

To make life more interesting and to mitigate the hard plight of newcomers without families, who, as there was no hotel in the town, had nowhere to dine, Dr Samoilenko kept a sort of *table d'hôte*. At this time there were only two men who habitually dined with him: a young zoologist called Von Koren, who had come for the summer to the Black Sea to study the embryology of jellyfish, and a deacon called Pobedov, who had only just left the seminary and been sent to the town to do the job of the old deacon who had gone away for a cure. Each of them paid twelve roubles a month for their dinner and supper, and Samoilenko made them promise to turn up at two o'clock punctually.

Von Koren was usually the first to appear. He sat down in the drawing-room in silence, and taking an album from the table, began attentively scrutinising the faded photographs of unknown men in full trousers and top hats, and ladies in crinolines and caps. Samoilenko only remembered a few of them by name, and of those whom he had forgotten he said with a sigh: 'A very fine fellow, remarkably intelligent!' When he had finished with the album, Von Koren took a pistol from the whatnot, and screwing up his left eye, took deliberate aim at the portrait of Prince Vorontsov,* or stood still at the looking glass and gazed a long time at his swarthy face, his big forehead, and his black hair, which curled like a negro's, and his shirt of dull-coloured cotton with big flowers on it like a Persian rug, and the broad leather belt he wore instead of a waistcoat. The contemplation of his own image seemed to afford him almost more satisfaction than looking at photographs or playing with the pistols. He was very well pleased with his face, and his becomingly clipped beard, and the broad shoulders, which were unmistakable evidence of his excellent health and physical strength. He was pleased, too, with his stylish get-up, from the cravat, which matched the colour of his shirt, down to his brown boots.

While he was looking at the album and standing before the glass, at that moment, in the kitchen and in the passage near, Samoilenko, without his coat and waistcoat, bare-chested, excited and bathed in perspiration, was bustling about the tables, mixing the salad, or making some sauce, or preparing meat, cucumbers, and onion for the cold soup, while he glanced fiercely at the orderly who was helping him, and brandished first a knife and then a spoon at him.

'Give me the vinegar!' he said. 'That's not the vinegar – it's the salad oil!' he shouted, stamping. 'Where are you off to, you brute?'

'To get the butter, your Excellency,' answered the flustered orderly in a cracked voice.

'Make haste; it's in the cupboard! And tell Daria to put some fennel in the jar with the cucumbers! Fennel! Cover the cream up, you gawping idiot, or the flies will get into it!'

And the whole house seemed to resound with his shouts. When it was ten or fifteen minutes to two the deacon would come in; he was a lanky young man of twenty-two, with long hair, with no beard and a hardly perceptible moustache. Going into the drawing-room, he crossed himself before the icon, smiled, and held out his hand to Von Koren.

'Good morning,' the zoologist said coldly. 'Where have you been?'

'I've been catching sea gudgeon in the harbour.'

'Oh, of course . . . Evidently, deacon, you will never get on with real work.'

'Why not? Work is not a bear; it won't run off to the woods,' said the deacon, smiling and thrusting his hands into the very deep pockets of his white cassock.

'You need a good beating!' sighed the zoologist.

Another fifteen or twenty minutes passed and they were not called to dinner, and they could still hear the orderly running into the kitchen and back again, noisily stamping with his boots, and Samoilenko shouting:

'Put it on the table! Where are your wits? Wash it first!'

The deacon and Von Koren, both famished, began tapping their heels on the floor, expressing in this way their impatience like the audience in the gods at the theatre. At last the door opened and the harassed orderly announced that dinner was ready! In the dining-room they were met by Samoilenko, crimson in the face, wrathful, perspiring from the heat of the kitchen; he looked at them furiously, and with an expression of horror, took the lid off the soup tureen and helped each of them to a plateful; and only when he was convinced that they were eating it with relish and liked it, he gave a sigh of relief and settled himself in his deep arm-chair. His face looked languid and his eyes grew moist . . . He deliberately poured himself out a glass of vodka and said:

'To the health of the younger generation.'

After his conversation with Laevksy, from early morning till dinner Samoilenko had been conscious of a load on his heart, although he was in the best of humours; he felt sorry for Laevsky and wanted to help him. After drinking a glass of vodka before the soup, he heaved a sigh and said:

'I saw Vania Laevsky today. He is having a hard time of it, poor fellow! The material side of life is not encouraging for him, and the main thing is his psyche – it's got him down. I'm sorry for the boy.'

'Well, that is a person I am not sorry for,' said Von Koren. 'If that charming individual were drowning, I would push him under with a stick and say, "Drown, brother, drown away." . . .'

'That's untrue. You wouldn't do that.'

'Why do you think that?' The zoologist shrugged his shoulders. 'I'm just as capable of good deeds as you are.'

'Is drowning a man a good deed?' asked the deacon, laughing.

'Laevsky? Yes.'

'I think there is something missing in the soup...' said Samoilenko, anxious to change the subject.

'Laevsky is definitely pernicious and is as dangerous to society as the cholera microbe,' Von Koren went on. 'To drown him would be a service.'

'It does you no credit to talk like that about your neighbour. Tell us: why do you hate him?'

'Don't talk nonsense, doctor. To hate and despise a microbe is stupid, but to look upon everybody one meets without distinction as one's neighbour, whatever happens – thanks very much, that is equivalent to giving up criticism, renouncing a straightforward attitude to people, washing one's hands of responsibility, in fact! I consider your Laevsky a blackguard; I do not conceal it, and I am perfectly conscientious in treating him as such. Well, you look upon him as your neighbour – and you may kiss him if you like: you look upon him as your neighbour, and that means that your attitude to him is the same as to me and to the deacon; that is no attitude at all. You are equally indifferent to all.'

'To call a man a blackguard,' muttered Samoilenko, frowning with distaste – 'that is so wrong that I can't find words for it!'

'People are judged by their actions,' Von Koren continued. 'Now you decide, deacon... I am going to talk to you, deacon. Mr Laevsky's career lies open before you, like a long Chinese scroll, and you can read it from beginning to end. What has he been doing the two years that he has been living here? Let's add up his doings on our fingers. First, he has taught the inhabitants of the town to play whist; two years ago that game was unknown here; now they all play it from morning till late at night, even the women and the boys. Secondly, he has taught the residents to drink beer, which was not known here either; the inhabitants are indebted to him for the knowledge of various sorts of spirits, so that now they can distinguish Kosheliov's vodka from Smirnov's No. 21 blindfolded. Thirdly, people here used to live with other men's wives in secret, for the same reasons as thieves steal in secret and not openly; adultery was considered something they were ashamed to make a public display of. Laevsky was a pioneer in that line; he lives with another man's wife openly... Fourthly...'

Von Koren hurriedly ate up his soup and gave his plate to the orderly.

'I understood Laevsky the first month of our acquaintance,' he went on, addressing the deacon. 'We arrived here at the same time.

Men like him are very fond of friendship, intimacy, solidarity, and all the rest of it, because they always want company for whist, drinking, and eating; besides, they are talkative and must have listeners. We made friends – that is, he turned up every day, stopped me working, and told me intimate things about his kept woman. From the first he struck me by his exceptional untruthfulness, which simply made me want to vomit. As a friend I pitched into him, asking him why he drank too much, why he lived beyond his means and got into debt, why he did nothing and read nothing, why he had so little culture and so little knowledge; and in answer to all my questions he used to smile bitterly, sigh, and say: "I am a failure, a superfluous man," or: "What do you expect, my dear fellow, from us, the debris of the serf-owning class?" or: "We are degenerating . . ." Or he would begin with a long rigmarole about Onegin, Pechorin, Byron's Cain, and Bazarov,* of whom he would say: "They are our fathers in flesh and in spirit." So we are to understand that it was not his fault that government envelopes lay unopened in his office for weeks together, and that he drank and taught others to drink, but Onegin, Pechorin, and Turgenev, who had invented the failure and the superfluous man, were responsible for it. The cause of his extreme dissoluteness and unseemliness lies, do you see, not in himself, but somewhere outside in space. And so – an ingenious idea! – it is not only he who is dissolute, false, and disgusting, but we . . . "we men of the eighties", "we, the jaded, highly strung offspring of the serf-owning class"; "civilisation has crippled us" . . . in fact, we are to understand that such a great man as Laevsky is great even in his fall: that his dissoluteness, his ignorance and turpitude are a phenomenon of natural history, sanctified by inevitability; that the causes of it are world-wide, elemental; and that we ought to put Laevsky on a pedestal, since he is the fated victim of the age, of influences, of heredity, and so on. All the officials and their ladies were in ecstasies when they listened to him, and I could not make out for a long time what sort of man I had to deal with, a cynic or a clever rogue. Such types as he, on the surface intellectual with a smattering of education and a great deal of talk about their own nobility, are very clever in posing as exceptionally complex natures.

'Hold your tongue!' Samoilenko flared up. 'I will not allow a splendid fellow to be spoken ill of in my presence!'

'Don't interrupt, Alexandr,' said Von Koren coldly; 'I am just finishing. Laevsky is by no means a complex organism. Here is his moral skeleton: in the morning, slippers, a bathe, and coffee; then till dinner-time, slippers, a constitutional, and conversation; at two o'clock slippers, dinner, and wine; at five o'clock a bathe, tea and wine, then whist and lying; at ten o'clock supper and wine; and after midnight sleep and *la femme*. His existence is confined within this narrow programme like an egg within its shell. Whether he walks or sits, is angry, writes, rejoices, it may all be reduced to wine, cards, slippers, and women. Woman plays a fatal, overwhelming part in his life. He tells us himself that at thirteen he was in love; that when he was a student in his first year he was living with a lady who had a good influence over him, and to whom he was indebted for his musical education. In his second year he bought a prostitute out from a brothel and raised her to his level – that is, took her as his kept mistress, and she lived with him for six months and then ran away back to the brothel-keeper, and her flight caused him much spiritual suffering. Alas! his sufferings were so great that he had to leave the university and spend two years at home doing nothing. But this was all for the best. At home he made friends with a widow who advised him to leave the faculty of jurisprudence and go into the faculty of arts. And so he did. When he had taken his degree, he fell passionately in love with his present . . . what's her name? . . . married woman, and had to flee with her here to the Caucasus for the sake of his ideals, he would have us believe . . . Any day now he will tire of her and flee back to Petersburg, and that, too, will be for the sake of his ideals.'

'How do you know?' growled Samoilenko, looking angrily at the zoologist. 'Just eat, will you?'

The next course consisted of boiled mullet with Polish sauce. Samoilenko helped each of his companions to a whole mullet and poured out the sauce with his own hand. About two minutes passed in silence.

'Woman plays an essential part in the life of every man,' said the deacon. 'You can't help that.'

'Yes, but to what degree? For each of us woman means mother, sister, wife, friend. To Laevsky she is everything, and at the same time nothing but a mistress. She – that is, cohabitation with her – is the happiness and object of his life; he is cheerful, sad, bored, disenchanted – on account of woman; if he is fed up with life – woman is to blame; the dawn of a new life begins to glow, ideals turn up – and again look for the woman . . . He only derives enjoyment from books and pictures in which there is woman. Our age is, to his thinking, poor and inferior to the forties and the sixties only because we do not know how to abandon ourselves obliviously to the passion and ecstasy of love. These voluptuaries must have in their brains a special growth like a sarcoma, which stifles the brain and directs their whole psyche. Watch Laevsky when he is sitting anywhere in company. You notice: when one raises any general question in his presence, for instance, about the cell or instinct, he sits apart, and neither speaks nor listens; he looks languid and disillusioned; nothing has any interest for him, everything is vulgar and trivial. But as soon as you speak of male and female – for instance, of the fact that the female spider, after fertilisation, devours the male – his eyes glow with curiosity, his face brightens, and the man revives, in fact. All his thoughts, however noble, lofty, or neutral they may be, they all have one point of resemblance. You walk along the street with him and meet a donkey, for instance ... "Tell me, please," he asks, "what would happen if you crossed a donkey with a camel?" And his dreams! Has he told you of his dreams? It is magnificent! First, he dreams that he is married to the moon, then that he is summoned before the police and ordered to live with a guitar ...'

The deacon burst into resounding laughter; Samoilenko frowned and wrinkled up his face angrily so as not to laugh, but could not restrain himself, and laughed.

'And he talks nothing but nonsense!' he said, wiping his tears. 'Yes, by Jove, nonsense!'

IV

The deacon was very easily amused, and laughed at every trifle till he got a stitch in his side, till he was helpless. It seemed as though he only liked to be in people's company because there was a ridiculous side to them, and because they might be given ridiculous nicknames. He had nicknamed Samoilenko 'the tarantula', his orderly 'the drake', and was in ecstasies when on one occasion Von Koren spoke of Laevsky and Nadezhda as 'rhesus monkeys'. He watched people's faces greedily, listened without blinking, and it could be seen that his eyes filled with laughter and his face was tense with expectation of the moment when he could let himself go and burst into laughter.

'He is a corrupt and depraved type,' the zoologist continued, while the deacon kept his eyes riveted on his face, waiting for something funny. 'It is not often one can meet with such a nonentity. In body he is inert, feeble and old, while in intellect he differs in no respect from a fat shopkeeper's wife who does nothing but eat, drink, and sleep on a feather bed, and who keeps her coachman as a lover.'

The deacon began guffawing again.

'Don't laugh, deacon,' said Von Koren. 'It's stupid, really. I should not have paid attention to his insignificance,' he went on, after waiting for the deacon to stop laughing; 'I should have passed him by if he were not so noxious and dangerous. He is noxious mainly because he has great success with women, and so threatens to leave descendants – that is, to present the world with a dozen Laevskys as feeble and as depraved as himself. Secondly, he is in the highest degree contaminating. I have told you already about the whist and beer. In another year or two he will conquer the whole Caucasian coast. You know how the mass, especially its middle stratum, believe in intellectuality, in a university education, in gentlemanly manners, and in literary language. Whatever filthy thing he did, they would all believe that it was right, since he is an intellectual, a liberal with a university education. What is more, he is a failure, a superfluous man, a neurotic, a victim of the age, and that means he can do anything. He is a charming fellow, a regular good sort, he is so genuinely indulgent to human weaknesses; he is compliant, accommodating, easy, and not proud; one can drink with him and gossip and slander people . . . The masses, always inclined to anthropomorphism in religion and morals, like best of all the little gods who have the same weaknesses as themselves. Only think what a wide field he has for contamination! Besides, he is not a bad actor and is a clever hypocrite, and knows very well how to twist things round. Only take his little shifts and dodges, his attitude to civilisation, for instance. He has never had a whiff of civilisation, yet: "Ah, how we have been crippled by civilisation! Ah, how I envy those savages, those children of nature, who know nothing of civilisation!" We are to understand, you see, that once, in ancient days, he was devoted to civilisation with his whole soul, served it, sounded it to its depths, but it has exhausted him, disillusioned him, deceived him; he is a Faust, do you see? – a second Tolstoy . . . As for Schopenhauer and Herbert Spencer, he treats them like small boys and pats them on the shoulder in a fatherly way: "Well, how are things, Spencer old boy?" He has not read Spencer, of course, but how charming he is when with light, careless irony he says of his lady friend: "She has read Spencer!" And they all listen to him, and refuse to understand that this charlatan has not the right to kiss the sole of Spencer's foot, let alone speak about him in that tone! Sapping the foundations of civilisation, of authority, of other people's altars, spattering them with filth, winking like a clown at them only to justify and conceal one's own rottenness and moral poverty is only possible for a very vain, base, and nasty creature.'

'I don't know what it is you expect of him, Kolia,' said Samoilenko, looking at the zoologist, not with anger now, but with a guilty air. 'He is a man the same as everyone else. Of course, he has his weaknesses, but he is abreast of modern ideas, he works, is of use to his country. Ten years ago there was an old fellow serving as agent here, a man of the greatest intelligence . . . and he used to say . . .'

'Stop, stop!' the zoologist interrupted. 'You say he works. But how? Do you mean to tell me that things have been done better because he is here, and the officials are more punctual, honest, and civil? On the contrary, he has only sanctioned their slackness by his prestige as an intellectual university man. He is only punctual on the twentieth of the month, when he gets his salary; on the other days he lounges about at home in slippers and tries to look as if he were doing the government a great service by living in the Caucasus. No, Alexandr, don't stick up for him. You are insincere from beginning to end. If you really loved him and considered him your neighbour, you would above all not be indifferent to his weaknesses, you would not be indulgent to him, but for his own sake would try to render him harmless.'

'That is?'

'Harmless. Since he is incorrigible, he can only be rendered harmless in one way . . .' Von Koren ran his finger round his throat. 'Or he might be drowned . . .' he added. 'In the interests of humanity and in their own interests, such people ought to be destroyed. Absolutely.'

'What are you saying?' muttered Samoilenko, getting up and looking with amazement at the zoologist's calm, cold face. 'Deacon, what is he saying? Why – are you out of your mind?'

'I don't insist on the death penalty,' said Von Koren. 'If it is proved that it is pernicious, devise something else. If we can't destroy Laevsky, why then, isolate him, take away his individual rights, make him do community labour.'

'What are you saying?' said Samoilenko in horror. 'With pepper, with pepper,' he cried in a voice of despair, seeing that the deacon was eating stuffed courgettes without pepper. 'You with your great intellect, what are you saying! Send our friend, a proud intellectual man, to community labour!'

'Well, if he is too proud and starts to resist, put him in fetters!'

Samoilenko could not utter a word, and only twiddled his fingers; the deacon looked at his flabbergasted and really absurd face, and laughed.'

'Let's stop talking about it,' said the zoologist. 'Only remember one thing, Alexandr: primitive man was preserved from such as Laevsky by the struggle for existence and by natural selection; now our civilisation has considerably weakened the struggle and the selection, and we have to see to the destruction of the rotten and worthless for ourselves; otherwise, when the Laevskys multiply, civilisation will perish and mankind will degenerate utterly. It will be our fault.'

'If it depends on drowning and hanging,' said Samoilenko, 'to hell with your civilisation, to hell with humanity! To hell with them! I tell you what: you are a very learned and intelligent man and the pride of your country, but the Germans have ruined you. Yes, the Germans! The Germans!'

Since Samoilenko had left Dorpat, where he had studied medicine, he had rarely seen a German and had not read a single German book, but, in his opinion, every harmful idea in politics or science was due to the Germans. Where he had got this notion he could not have said himself, but he held it firmly.

'Yes, the Germans!' he repeated once more. 'Come and have some tea.'

All three stood up, and putting on their hats, went out into the little garden, and sat there under the shade of the light green maples, the pear trees, and a chestnut tree. The zoologist and the deacon sat on a bench by the table, while Samoilenko sank into a deep wicker chair with a sloping back. The orderly handed them tea, jam, and a bottle of syrup.

It was very hot, about ninety in the shade. The sultry air was stagnant and motionless, and a long spider's web, stretching from the chestnut tree to the ground, hung limply and did not stir.

The deacon picked up the guitar, which always lay on the ground near the table, tuned it, and began singing softly in a thin voice: 'Gathered round the tavern were the seminary lads,' but instantly subsided, overcome by the heat, mopped his brow and glanced upwards at the blazing blue sky. Samoilenko grew drowsy; the sultry heat, the stillness and the delicious after-dinner languor, which quickly pervaded all his limbs, made him feel heavy and sleepy; his arms hung limply, his eyes grew small, his head sank on his breast. He looked with almost tearful tenderness at Von Koren and the deacon, and muttered:

'The younger generation . . . A scientific star and a luminary of the Church . . . I shouldn't wonder if the long-skirted alleluia ends up a bishop; you never know, I might have to kiss his hand . . . Well . . . God grant . . .'

Soon a snore was heard. Von Koren and the deacon finished their tea and went out into the street.'

'Are you going to the harbour again to catch sea-gudgeon?' asked the zoologist.

'No, it's a bit hot.'

'Come and see me. You can pack up a parcel and copy a few things for me. By the way, we must have a talk about what you are to do. You must work, deacon. You can't go on like this.'

'Your words are just and logical,' said the deacon. 'But my laziness finds an excuse in the circumstances of my present life. You know yourself that an uncertain position has a great tendency to make people apathetic. God only knows whether I have been sent here for a time or permanently. I am living here in uncertainty, while my wife is vegetating at her father's and is missing me. And I must confess my brain is melting with the heat.'

'That's all nonsense,' said the zoologist. 'You can get used to the heat, and you can get used to being without the deaconess. You mustn't be slack; you must pull yourself together.'

V

Nadezhda went to bathe in the morning, and her cook, Olga, followed her with a jug, a copper basin, towels, and a sponge. In the bay stood two unknown steamers with dirty white funnels, obviously foreign cargo vessels. Some men dressed in white and wearing white shoes were walking along the harbour, shouting loudly in French, and were answered from the steamers. The bells were ringing briskly in the little church of the town.

'Today is Sunday!' Nadezhda remembered with pleasure.

She felt perfectly well, and was in a cheerful holiday mood. In a new loose-fitting dress of coarse thick tussore silk, and a big wide-brimmed straw hat which was bent down over her ears, so that her face seemed to be boxed in, she fancied she looked very charming. She thought that in the whole town there was only one young, pretty, intellectual woman, and that was herself, and that she was the only one who knew how to dress herself cheaply, elegantly, and with taste; that dress, for example, cost only twenty-two roubles, and yet how charming it was! In the whole town she was the only one who could attract men; there were a lot of men, so they must all, like it or not, envy Laevsky.

She was glad that of late Laevsky had been cold to her, reserved and polite, and at times even harsh and rude; in the past she had met all his outbursts, all his contemptuous, cold or strange incomprehensible glances, with tears, reproaches, and threats to leave him or to starve herself to death; now she only blushed, looked guiltily at him, and was glad he was not affectionate to her. If he had abused her, or threatened her, it would have been better and pleasanter, since she felt hopelessly guilty towards him. She felt she was to blame, in the first place, for not sympathising with the dreams of a life of hard work, for the sake of which he had given up Petersburg and had come here to the Caucasus, and she was convinced that he had been angry with her of late for precisely that. When she was travelling to the

Caucasus, it seemed that she would find here on the first day a cosy nook by the sea, a snug little garden with shade, with birds, with little brooks, where she could grow flowers and vegetables, rear ducks and hens, entertain her neighbours, doctor poor peasants and distribute little books amongst them. It had turned out that the Caucasus was nothing but bare mountains, forests, and huge valleys, where it took a long time and a great deal of effort to find anything and settle down; that there were no neighbours of any sort; that it was very hot and one might be robbed. Laevsky had been in no hurry to obtain a piece of land; she was glad of it, and they seemed to be in a tacit compact never to allude to a life of hard work. He was silent about it, she thought, because he was angry with her for being silent about it.

In the second place, she had without his knowledge during those two years bought about three hundred roubles' worth of various trifles at Achmianov's shop. She had bought the things by degrees, at one time materials, at another time silk or a parasol, and the debt had piled up imperceptibly.

'I will tell him about it today . . .' she decided, but at once reflected that in Laevsky's present mood it would hardly be easy to talk to him of debts.

Thirdly, she had on two occasions in Laevsky's absence received a visit from Kirilin, the police captain: once in the morning when Laevsky had gone to bathe, and another time at midnight when he was playing cards. Remembering this, Nadezhda flushed crimson, and looked round at the cook as though she might overhear her thoughts. The long, insufferably hot, wearisome days, beautiful languorous evenings and stifling nights, and the whole manner of living, when from morning to night one is at a loss to fill up the useless hours, and the persistent thought that she was the prettiest young woman in the town, and that her youth was passing and being wasted, and Laevsky himself, though honest and idealistic, always the same, always lounging about in his slippers, biting his nails, and wearying her with his caprices, led by degrees to her becoming possessed by desire, and as though she were mad, she thought of nothing else day and night. Breathing, looking, walking, she felt nothing but desire. The sound of the sea told her she must love; the darkness of the evening – the same; the mountains – the same . . . And when Kirilin began courting her, she had neither the power nor the wish to resist, and surrendered to him . . .

Now the foreign steamers and the men in white reminded her for some reason of a huge hall; together with the shouts of French she heard the strains of a waltz, and her chest heaved with unaccountable delight. She longed to dance and talk French.

She reflected joyfully that there was nothing terrible about her infidelity. Her soul had no part in her infidelity; she still loved Laevsky, and that was proved by the fact that she was jealous of him, was sorry for him, and missed him when he was away. Kirilin had turned out to be very mediocre, rather coarse, though handsome; everything had broken off with him and there would be nothing more. What had happened was over; it had nothing to do with anyone, and if Laevsky found it out he would not believe it.

There was a bathing-house only for ladies on the sea-front; men bathed under the open sky. Going into the bathing-house, Nadezhda found there a middle-aged lady, Maria Konstantinovna Bitiugova, and her daughter Katia, a schoolgirl of fifteen; both of them were sitting on a bench undressing. Maria was a good-natured, enthusiastic, and genteel person, who talked in a drawling and pathetic voice. She had been a governess until she was thirty-two, and then had married Bitiugov, a government official – a bald little man with his hair combed on to his temples and very meek. She was still in love with him, was jealous, blushed at the word 'love', and told everybody she was very happy.

'My dear!' she cried enthusiastically, on seeing Nadezhda, assuming an expression which all her acquaintances called 'saccharine'. 'My dear, how delightful that you have come! We'll bathe together – that's enchanting!'

Olga flung off her dress and chemise, and began undressing her mistress.

'It's not quite so hot today as yesterday, is it?' said Nadezhda, shrinking at the coarse touch of the naked cook. 'Yesterday I almost died of the heat.'

'Oh yes, my dear; I could hardly breathe myself. Would you believe it? I bathed yesterday three times! Just imagine, my dear, three times! Even Nikodim was worried.'

'How can anyone be so ugly?' thought Nadezhda, looking at Olga and the official's wife; she glanced at Katia and thought: 'The girl's not bad-looking.'

'Your Nikodim is very charming!' she said. 'I'm simply in love with him.'

'Ha, ha, ha!' cried Maria, with a forced laugh; 'That's quite enchanting.'

Free from her clothes, Nadezhda felt a desire to fly. And it seemed to her that if she were to wave her hands she would fly upwards. When she was undressed, she noticed that Olga looked scornfully at her white body. Olga, a young soldier's wife, was living with her lawful husband, and so considered herself superior to her mistress. Nadezhda also sensed that Maria and Katia were afraid of her, and did not respect her. This was disagreeable, and to raise herself in their opinion, Nadezhda said:

'At home, in Petersburg, summer villa life is at its height now. My husband and I have so many friends! We ought to go and see them.'

'I believe your husband is an engineer?' said Maria timidly.

'I am speaking of Laevsky. He has a great many acquaintances. But unfortunately his mother is a proud aristocrat, not very intelligent . . .'

Nadezhda threw herself into the water without finishing; Maria and Katia made their way in after her.

'There are so many conventional ideas in the world,' Nadezhda went on, 'and life is not so easy as it seems.'

Maria, who had been a governess in aristocratic families and who was an authority on social matters, said:

'Oh yes! Would you believe me, my dear, at the Garatynskys' I was expected to dress for lunch as well as for dinner, so that, like an actress, I received a special allowance for my wardrobe in addition to my salary.'

She stood between Nadezhda and Katia as though to screen her daughter from the water that washed the former.

Through the open doors looking out to the sea they could see someone swimming a hundred paces from their bathing place.

'Mother, it's our Kostia,' said Katia.

'Oh, no!' Maria cackled in her dismay. 'Oh, Kostia!' she shouted, 'Come back! Kostia, come back!'

Kostia, a boy of fourteen, to show off his prowess before his mother and sister, dived and swam further, but began to be exhausted and hurried back, and from his strained and serious face it could be seen that he could not trust his own strength.

'The trouble one has with these boys, my dear!' said Maria, growing calmer. 'You never know, he could break his neck. Ah, my dear, how sweet it is, and yet at the same time how difficult, to be a mother! One's afraid of everything.'

Nadezhda put on her straw hat and dashed out into the open sea. She swam some thirty feet and then turned on her back. She could see the sea to the horizon, the steamers, the people on the sea-front, the town; and all this, together with the sultry heat and the soft, transparent waves, excited her and whispered that she must live, live . . . A sailing boat darted by her rapidly and vigorously, cleaving the waves and the air; the man sitting at the helm looked at her, and she liked being looked at . . .

After bathing, the ladies dressed and went away together.

'I have a fever every other day, and yet I don't get thin,' said Nadezhda, licking her lips, which were salty from the bathe, and responding with a smile to the bows of her acquaintances. 'I've always been plump, and now I believe I'm plumper than ever.'

'That, my dear, is constitutional. If, like me, you have no predisposition to stoutness, food won't help . . . But you've got your hat wet, my dear.'

'It doesn't matter; it will dry.'

Nadezhda saw again the men in white who were walking on the sea-front and talking French; and again felt a sudden thrill of joy, and had a vague memory of some big hall in which she had once danced, or of which, perhaps, she had once dreamed. And something at the bottom of her soul dimly and obscurely whispered to her that she was a petty, common, miserable, worthless woman . . .

Maria stopped at her gate and asked her to come in and sit down.

'Come in, my dear,' she said, in an imploring voice, and at the same time she looked at Nadezhda with anxiety and hope: perhaps she would refuse and not come in!

'With pleasure,' said Nadezhda, accepting. 'You know how I love visiting you!'

And she went into the house. Maria sat her down and gave her coffee, regaled her with milk rolls, then showed her photographs of her former pupils, the Garatynskys, who were by now married. She showed her, too, the examination reports of Kostia and Katia. The reports were very good, but to make them seem even better, she complained, with a sigh, how difficult the lessons at school were now . . . She made much of her visitor, and was sorry for her, though at the same time she was pained by the thought that Nadezhda's presence might contaminate the morals of Kostia and Katia, and was glad that her Nikodim was not at home. Seeing that in her opinion all men are fond of 'women like that', Nadezhda might have a bad effect on Nikodim too.

As she talked to her visitor, Maria kept remembering that they were to have a picnic that evening, and that Von Koren had particularly begged her to say nothing about it to the 'rhesus monkeys' – that is, Laevsky and Nadezhda; but she dropped a word about it unawares, crimsoned, and said in confusion:

'I hope you will come too!'

VI

It was agreed to drive five miles out of town on the road to the south, to stop near a native inn at the junction of two streams – the Black

River and the Yellow River – and to make a fish soup. They started out soon after five. The party was led by Samoilenko and Laevsky in a charabanc; they were followed by Maria, Nadezhda, Katia and Kostia, in a coach with three horses, carrying with them the crockery and a basket with provisions. In the next carriage came the police captain, Kirilin, and the young Achmianov, the son of the shopkeeper to whom Nadezhda owed three hundred roubles; opposite them, huddled up on the little seat with his feet tucked under him, sat Nikodim, a neat little man with hair combed to his temples. Last of all came Von Koren and the deacon; at the deacon's feet stood a basket of fish.

'Keep to the r-r-right!' Samoilenko shouted at the top of his voice when he met a cart or an Abkhaz riding on a donkey.

'In two years' time, when I shall have the means and the people ready, I shall set off on an expedition,' Von Koren was telling the deacon. 'I shall go by the sea coast from Vladivostok to the Bering Straits, and then from the straits to the mouth of the Yenisei. We shall map the coast, study the fauna and the flora, and make detailed geological, anthropological, and ethnographic researches. It's up to you whether you go with me or not.'

'It's impossible,' said the deacon.

'Why?'

'I am a man with ties and a family.'

'Your wife will let you go; we will provide for her. Better still if you were to persuade her for the public benefit to go into a nunnery; that would make it possible for you to become a monk, too, and join the expedition as a priest. I can arrange it for you.'

The deacon was silent.

'Do you know your theology well?' asked the zoologist.

'No, rather badly.'

'H'm! . . . I can't give you any advice on that score, because I don't know much about theology myself. You give me a short list of books you need, and I will send them to you from Petersburg in the winter. It will be necessary for you to read the notes of missionaries, too; among them are some good ethnologists and Oriental scholars. When you are familiar with their approach, it will be easier for you to set to work. And you needn't waste your time till you get the books; come to me, and we will study the compass and go through a course of meteorology. All that's indispensable.'

'To be sure . . .' muttered the deacon, and he laughed. 'I was trying to get a place in Central Russia, and my uncle, the archpriest, promised to help me. If I go with you I shall have troubled them for nothing.'

'I don't understand your hesitation. If you go on being an ordinary deacon, who has to hold a service only on holidays, and on the other days can rest, you will be exactly the same as you are now in ten years' time, and will have gained nothing but a beard and moustache; while on returning from this expedition in ten years' time you will be a different man, you will be enriched by knowing that something has been done by you.'

From the ladies' carriage came shrieks of terror and delight. The carriages were driving along a road cut into a completely perpendicular coastal rock, and it seemed to everyone that they were galloping along a shelf on a steep wall, and that in a moment the carriages would drop into the abyss. On the right stretched the sea; on the left was a rough brown wall with black blotches and red veins and with climbing roots; while on the summit stood shaggy fir trees bent over, as though looking down in terror and curiosity. A minute later there were shrieks and laughter again: they had to drive under a huge overhanging rock.

'I don't know why the devil I'm coming with you,' said Laevsky. 'How stupid and vulgar it is! I want to go to the north, to run away, to escape; but here I am, for some reason, going to this stupid picnic.'

'But look, what a view!' said Samoilenko as the horses turned to the left, and the valley of the Yellow River came into sight and the stream itself gleamed in the sunlight, yellow, turbid, frantic.

'I see nothing fine in that, Sasha,' answered Laevsky. 'To be in continual ecstasies over nature shows poverty of imagination. In comparison with what my imagination can give me, all these streams and rocks are trash, and nothing else.'

The carriages were now following the bank of the stream. The high mountain banks gradually grew closer, the valley narrowed and ended in a gorge; the rocky mountain round which they were driving had been piled together by nature out of huge rocks, pressing upon each other with such terrible weight that Samoilenko could not help gasping every time he looked at them. The dark and beautiful mountain was cleft in places by narrow fissures and gorges from which came a breath of dewy moisture and mystery; through the gorges could be seen other mountains, brown, pink, violet, smoky, or bathed in vivid sunlight. From time to time as they passed a gorge they caught the sound of water falling from the heights and splashing on the stones.

'Ugh, the damned mountains!' sighed Laevsky. 'How sick I am of them!'

At the place where the Black River falls into the Yellow, and the water black as ink stains the yellow and fights it, stood the Tatar

Kerbalai's native inn with the Russian flag on the roof and with an inscription written in chalk: 'The Pleasant Inn'. Near it was a little garden, enclosed in a hurdle fence, with tables and chairs set out in it, and in the midst of a thicket of wretched thorn bushes stood a single solitary cypress, dark and beautiful.

Kerbalai, a nimble little Tatar in a blue shirt and a white apron, was standing in the road, and, holding his stomach, he bowed low to welcome the carriages, and smiled, showing his glistening white teeth.

'Hallo, Kerbalai,' shouted Samoilenko. 'We are driving on a little further; you bring along the samovar and chairs! Look sharp!'

Kerbalai nodded his shaven head and muttered something, and only those sitting in the last carriage could hear: 'We've got trout, your Excellency.'

'Bring them, bring them!' Von Koren told him.

Five hundred paces from the inn the carriages stopped. Samoilenko selected a small meadow round which there were scattered stones good for sitting on, and a fallen tree blown down by the storm with roots overgrown by moss and dry yellow needles. Here there was a fragile wooden bridge over the stream and just opposite on the other bank there was a little barn for drying maize, standing on four low piles, and looking like the hut on hen's legs in the fairy tale; a little ladder sloped from its door.

The first impression in all was a feeling that they would never get out of that place again. On all sides, wherever they looked, the mountains rose up and towered above them, and the shadows of evening were stealing rapidly, rapidly from the inn and dark cypress, making the narrow winding valley of the Black River narrower and the mountains higher. They could hear the river murmuring and the unceasing chirrup of the grasshoppers.

'Enchanting!' said Maria, heaving deep sighs of ecstasy. 'Children, look how fine! What peace!'

'Yes, it really is fine,' assented Laevsky, who liked the view, and for some reason felt sad as he looked at the sky and then at the blue smoke rising from the chimney of the inn. 'Yes, it is fine,' he repeated.

'Mr Laevsky, describe this view,' Maria said mawkishly.

'Why?' asked Laevsky. 'The impression is better than any description. The wealth of sights and sounds which everyone receives from nature by direct impression is ranted about by authors in a hideous and unrecognisable way.'

'Really?' Von Koren asked coldly, choosing the biggest stone by the side of the water, and trying to clamber up and sit upon it. 'Really?' he repeated, looking directly at Laevsky. 'What of *Romeo and Juliet*? Or, for instance, Pushkin's *Ukrainian Night*? Nature ought to come and bow down at their feet.'

'Perhaps,' said Laevsky, who was too lazy to think and oppose him. 'Though what is *Romeo and Juliet* after all?' he added after a short pause. 'The beauty of poetry and holiness of love are simply the roses under which they try to hide its rottenness. Romeo is just the same sort of animal as all the rest of us.'

'Whatever one talks to you about, you always bring it round to . . .' Von Koren glanced round at Katia and broke off.

'What do I bring it round to?' asked Laevsky.

'One tells you, for instance, how beautiful a bunch of grapes is, and you answer: "Yes, but how ugly it is when it is chewed and digested in one's stomach!" Why say that? It's not new, and . . . anyway it's a strange manner.'

Laevsky knew that Von Koren did not like him, and so was afraid of him, and felt in his presence as though everyone were constrained and someone were standing behind his back. He made no answer and walked away, regretting that he had come.

'Gentlemen, quick march for brushwood for the fire!' commanded Samoilenko.

They all wandered off in different directions, and no one was left but Kirilin, Achmianov, and Nikodim. Kerbalai brought chairs, spread a rug on the ground, and set a few bottles of wine.

The police captain, Kirilin, a tall, good-looking man, who in all weathers wore his greatcoat over his tunic, with his haughty deportment, stately carriage, and thick, rather hoarse voice, looked like a young provincial chief of police; his expression was mournful and sleepy, as though he had just been woken against his will.

'What have you brought this for, you brute?' he asked Kerbalai, deliberately articulating each word. 'I ordered you to give us Qvareli wine and what have you brought, you ugly Tatar? Eh? What?'

'We have plenty of wine of our own, Captain Kirilin,' Nikodim observed, timidly and politely.

'What? But I want us to have my wine, too; I'm taking part in the picnic and I imagine I have full right to contribute my share. I im-ma-gine so! Bring ten bottles of Qvareli!'

'Why so many?' asked Nikodim, in wonder, knowing Kirilin had no money.

'Twenty bottles! Thirty!' shouted Kirilin.

'Never mind, let him,' Achmianov whispered to Nikodim, 'I'll pay.'

Nadezhda was in a light-hearted, mischievous mood; she wanted to skip and jump, to laugh, to shout, to tease, to flirt. In her cheap cotton dress with blue pansies on it, in her red shoes and the same straw hat, she seemed to herself little, simple, light, ethereal as a butterfly. She ran over the rickety bridge and looked for a minute into the water, in order to feel giddy; then, shrieking and laughing, ran to the other side to the drying-shed, and she fancied that all the men were admiring her, even Kerbalai. When in the rapidly falling darkness the trees began to melt into the mountains and the horses into the carriages, and a light gleamed in the windows of the inn, she climbed up the mountain by the little path which zigzagged between stones and thorn bushes and sat on a stone. Down below, the camp fire was burning. Near the fire, with his sleeves rolled up, the deacon was moving to and fro, and his long black shadow kept describing a circle round it; he put on wood, and with a spoon tied to a long stick he stirred the cauldron. Samoilenko, with a copper-red face, was fussing round the fire just as though he were in his own kitchen, shouting furiously:

'Where's the salt, gentlemen? I bet you've forgotten it. Why are you all sitting about like lords while I do all the work?'

Laevsky and Nikodim were sitting side by side on the fallen tree looking pensively at the fire. Maria, Katia, and Kostia were taking the cups, saucers, and plates out of the baskets. Von Koren, with his arms folded and one foot on a stone, was standing on a bank at the very edge of the water, thinking about something. Patches of red light from the fire moved together with the shadows over the ground near the dark human figures, and quivered on the mountain, on the trees, on the bridge, on the drying-shed; on the other side the steep, scooped-out bank was all lighted up and glimmering in the stream, and the rushing turbid water broke its reflection into little bits.

The deacon went to fetch the fish which Kerbalai was cleaning and washing on the bank, but he stood still halfway and looked about him.

'My God, how fine it is!' he thought. 'People, rocks, the fire, the twilight, a monstrous tree – nothing more, and yet how fine it is!'

On the further bank some unknown persons appeared near the drying-shed. The flickering light and the smoke from the camp fire puffing in that direction made it impossible to get a full view of them all at once, but glimpses were caught now of a shaggy hat and a grey beard, now of a blue shirt, now of a figure, ragged from shoulder to knee, with a dagger across the belly; then a swarthy young face with black eyebrows, as thick and bold as though they had been drawn in charcoal. Five of them sat in a circle on the ground, and the other five went into the drying-shed. One was standing at the door with his back to the fire, and with his hands behind his back was telling a

story, which must have been very interesting, for when Samoilenko
threw on twigs and the fire flared up, and scattered sparks and threw
a glaring light on the shed, two calm countenances with an expression
on them of deep attention could be seen, looking out of the door,
while those who were sitting in a circle turned round and began
listening to the story. Soon after, those sitting in a circle began softly
singing something slow and melodious, that sounded like Lenten
church music . . . Listening to them, the deacon imagined how it
would be with him in ten years' time, when he would come back from
the expedition: he would be a young missionary priest, an author
with a name and a splendid past; he would be consecrated an
archimandrite, then a bishop; and he would serve mass in the
cathedral; in a golden mitre he would come out into the body of the
church with the icon on his breast, and blessing the mass of the people
with the two- and three-branched candlesticks, would proclaim:
'Look down from heaven, O God, behold and visit this vineyard
which Thy Hand has planted,' and the children with their angel
voices would sing in response: 'Holy God . . .'

'Deacon, where is that fish?' he heard Samoilenko's voice.

As he went back to the fire, the deacon imagined the church
procession going along a dusty road on a hot July day; in front the
peasants carrying the banners and the women and children the icons,
then the boy choristers and the sacristan with his face bandaged and
straw in his hair, then in due order himself, the deacon, and behind
him the priest wearing his skullcap and carrying a cross, and behind
them, tramping in the dust, a crowd of peasants – men, women, and
children; in the crowd his wife and the priest's wife with kerchiefs on
their heads. The choristers sing, the babies cry, the quails call, the lark
bursts into song . . . Then they stop and sprinkle the herd with holy
water . . . They go on again, and then kneel and pray for rain. Then
lunch and talk . . .

'And that's fine too . . .' thought the deacon.

VII

Kirilin and Achmianov climbed up the mountain by the path.
Achmianov dropped behind and stopped, while Kirilin went up to
Nadezhda.

'Good evening,' he said, touching his cap.

'Good evening.'

'Well?' said Kirilin, looking at the sky and pondering.

'Why "well"?' asked Nadezhda after a brief pause, noticing that
Achmianov was watching them both.

'And so it seems,' said the officer, slowly, 'that our love has withered before it had blossomed, so to speak. How am I supposed to understand it? Is it a sort of coquetry on your part, or do you look upon me as a nonentity who can be treated as you choose?'

'It was a mistake! Leave me alone!' Nadezhda said sharply, on that beautiful, marvellous evening, looking at him with terror and asking herself with bewilderment, could there really have been a moment when she had found the man an attractive intimate?

'So that's it!' said Kirilin; he thought in silence for a few minutes and said: 'Well, I'll wait till you are in a better humour, and meanwhile let me assure you I am a gentleman, and I don't allow anyone to doubt it. Adieu!'

He touched his cap and walked off, making his way between the bushes. After a short interval Achmianov approached hesitatingly.

'What a fine evening!' he said with a slight Armenian accent.

He was nice-looking, fashionably dressed, and behaved unaffectedly like a well-bred youth, but Nadezhda did not like him because she owed his father three hundred roubles; it was displeasing to her, too, that a shopkeeper had been asked to the picnic, and she was vexed at his coming up to her that evening when her heart felt so pure.

'The picnic is a success on the whole,' he said, after a pause.

'Yes,' she agreed, and as though suddenly remembering her debt, she said carelessly: 'Oh, tell them in your shop that Mr Laevsky will come round in a day or two and will pay three hundred roubles . . . I don't remember how much.'

'I'd give another three hundred roubles if you would not mention that debt every day. Why be prosaic?'

Nadezhda laughed; the amusing idea occurred to her that if she had been willing and sufficiently immoral she might in one minute get out of debt. If she, for instance, were to turn the head of this handsome young fool! How amusing, absurd, wild it would be really! And she suddenly felt a longing to make him love her, to plunder him, throw him over, and then see what would come of it.

'Allow me to give you one piece of advice,' Achmianov said timidly. 'I beg you to beware of Kirilin. He says horrible things about you everywhere.'

'It doesn't interest me to know what every fool says of me,' Nadezhda said coldly, and the amusing thought of playing with handsome young Achmianov suddenly lost its charm.

'We must go down,' she said; 'they're calling us.'

The fish soup was ready by now. They were ladling it out by the plateful, and eating it with the religious solemnity unique to picnics; and everyone thought the fish soup very good, and thought that at home they had never eaten anything so nice. As is always the case at picnics, in the mass of napkins, parcels, useless greasy papers fluttering in the wind, no one knew where his glass or his bread were. They poured wine on the carpet and on their own knees, spilt the salt, while it was dark all round them and the fire burnt more dimly, and everyone was too lazy to get up and put kindling on. They all drank wine, and even gave Kostia and Katia half a glass each. Nadezhda drank one glass and then another, got a little drunk and forgot about Kirilin.

'A splendid picnic, an enchanting evening,' said Laevsky, growing lively with the wine. 'But I should prefer a fine winter to all this. "His beaver collar has turned silver with the powdery frost." '

'Everyone to his taste,' observed Von Koren.

Laevsky felt uncomfortable; the heat of the camp fire was beating upon his back, and the hatred of Von Koren upon his breast and face: this hatred on the part of a decent, clever man, a feeling which probably concealed a good reason, humiliated him and enervated him, and unable to stand up against it, he said in an ingratiating tone:

'I am passionately fond of nature, and I regret that I'm not a naturalist. I envy you.'

'Well, I don't envy you, and don't regret it,' said Nadezhda. 'I don't understand how anyone can seriously interest himself in beetles and bugs while the people are suffering.'

Laevsky shared her opinion. He was absolutely ignorant of natural science, and so could never reconcile himself to the authoritative tone and the learned and profound air of the people who devoted themselves to ants' antennae and cockroaches' feet, and he always felt vexed that these people, relying on these antennae, feet, and something they called protoplasm (he always imagined it in the form of an oyster), should undertake to decide questions involving the origin and life of man. But in Nadezhda's words he felt the falsity, and simply to contradict her he said:

'The point is not the bugs, but the conclusions!'

VIII

It was late, getting on for eleven, when they began to get into their carriages to go home. Everyone was seated: the only ones missing were Nadezhda and Achmianov, who were chasing each other, laughing, on the other side of the stream.

'Hurry up, ladies and gentlemen,' shouted Samoilenko.

'You ought not to have given wine to the ladies,' said Von Koren quietly.

Laevsky, exhausted by the picnic, by Von Koren's hatred, and by his own thoughts, went to meet Nadezhda, and when, cheerful and happy, feeling light as a feather, breathless and laughing, she took him by both hands and laid her head on his breast, he stepped back and said dryly:

'You are behaving like a . . . slut.'

It sounded so horribly coarse that he even felt sorry for her. On his angry, exhausted face she read hatred, pity and vexation with himself, and her heart sank at once. She realised instantly that she had gone too far, had been too free and easy in her behaviour, and overcome with misery, feeling herself heavy, stout, coarse and drunk, she got into the first empty carriage together with Achmianov. Laevsky got in with Kirilin, the zoologist with Samoilenko, the deacon with the ladies, and the party set off.

'You see what the rhesus monkeys are like,' Von Koren began, rolling himself up in his cloak and shutting his eyes. 'You heard she wouldn't like to study beetles and bugs because the people are suffering. That's how all the rhesus monkeys look upon people like us. They're a slavish, cunning race, cowed by the whip and the fist for ten generations; they tremble and burn incense only before violence; but let the monkey into a free state where there's no one to take it by the collar, and it relaxes at once and shows itself in its true colours. Look how bold they are in picture galleries, in museums, in theatres, or when they talk of science: they puff themselves out and get excited, they are abusive and critical . . . They are bound to criticise – it's the sign of the slave. You listen carefully: men of the liberal professions are more often sworn at than pickpockets – that's because three-quarters of society are made up of slaves, of rhesus monkeys. It never happens that a slave holds out his hand to you and sincerely says, "Thank you" to you for your work.'

I don't know what you are getting at,' said Samoilenko, yawning; 'the poor thing, in the simplicity of her heart, wanted an intelligent conversation with you, and you draw a conclusion from that. You're cross with him for something or other, and with her, too, to keep him company. She's a fine woman.'

'Ah, nonsense! An ordinary kept woman, depraved and vulgar. Listen, Alexandr; when you meet a simple peasant woman, who is living with a man not her husband, who does nothing but giggle, you tell her to go and work. Why are you timid in this case and afraid to tell the truth? Just because Nadezhda is kept, not by a sailor, but by an official.'

'What am I do with her?' said Samoilenko, getting angry. 'Beat her or what?'

'Not pander to vice. We curse vice only behind its back, and that's cowardly. I am a zoologist or a sociologist, which is the same thing; you are a doctor; society believes in us; we ought to point out the terrible harm which threatens it and the next generation from the existence of ladies like Nadezhda Ivanovna.'

'Fiodorovna,' Samoilenko corrected. 'But what ought society to do?'

'Society? That's its affair. To my thinking the surest and most direct method is – force. *Manu militari* she ought to be returned to her husband; and if her husband won't take her in, then she ought to be sent to penal servitude or some house of correction.'

'Ugh!' sighed Samoilenko. He paused and asked quietly: 'You said the other day that people like Laevsky ought to be destroyed . . . Tell me, if you . . . if the state or society commissioned you to destroy him, could you . . . bring yourself to do it?'

'Without the slightest qualm.'

IX

When they got home, Laevsky and Nadezhda went into their dark, stuffy, dull rooms. Both were silent. Laevsky lit a candle, while Nadezhda sat down, and without taking off her cloak and hat, lifted her melancholy, guilty eyes to him.

He knew that she expected him to have it out with her, but this would be wearisome, useless and exhausting, and his heart was heavy because he had lost control and been rude to her. He chanced to feel in his pocket the letter which he had been intending every day to read to her, and thought if he were to show that letter now, it would turn her thoughts in another direction.

'It is time to have it out,' he thought. 'I will give it her; what is to be will be.'

He took out the letter and gave it her.

'Read it. It concerns you.'

Saying this, he went into his own room and lay down on the sofa in the dark without a pillow. Nadezhda read the letter, and it seemed to her as though the ceiling had collapsed and the walls had closed in on her. It seemed suddenly dark and shut in and terrible. She crossed herself quickly three times and said:

'Give him peace, O Lord . . . give him peace . . .'

And she began crying.

'Vania,' she called. 'Ivan!'

There was no answer. Thinking that Laevsky had come in and was standing behind her chair, she sobbed like a child, and said:

'Why didn't you tell me before that he'd died? I wouldn't have gone to the picnic; I shouldn't have laughed so horribly . . Men said vile things to me. What a sin, what a sin! Save me, Vania, save me . . . I have been mad . . . I am lost . . .'

Laevsky heard her sobs. He felt stifled and his heart was beating violently. In his misery he got up, stood in the middle of the room, groped his way in the dark to the arm-chair by the table, and sat down.

'This is a prison . . .' he thought. 'I must get away . . . I can't bear it.'

It was too late to go and play cards; there were no restaurants in the town. He lay down again and covered his ears that he might not hear her sobbing, and he suddenly remembered that he could go to Samoilenko. To avoid going near Nadezhda, he got out of the window into the garden, climbed over the garden fence, and went along the street. It was dark. A steamer, judging by its lights, a big passenger one, had just come in . . . The anchor chain clanked. A red light was moving rapidly from the shore in the direction of the steamer: it was the Customs boat going out to it.

'The passengers are asleep in their cabins . . .' thought Laevsky, and he envied other people's peace of mind.

The windows in Samoilenko's house were open. Laevsky looked in at one of them, then in at another; it was dark and still in the rooms.

'Alexandr, are you asleep?' he called. 'Alexandr!'

He heard a cough and an uneasy shout:

'Who's there? What the devil?'

'It's me, Alexandr; I'm sorry.'

A little later the door opened; there was a glow of soft light from the lamp, and Samoilenko's huge figure appeared, all in white, with a white night-cap on his head.

'What do you want?' he asked, half-asleep, scratching himself and breathing hard. 'Wait a minute; I'll unlock the door.'

'Don't bother; I'll use the window . . .'

Laevsky climbed through the little window, and when he reached Samoilenko, seized him by the hand.

'Alexandr,' he said in a shaking voice, 'save me! I beseech you, I implore you. Understand me! My position is agonising. If it goes on for another two days I shall strangle myself like . . . like a dog.'

'Wait a bit . . . What are you on about, actually?'

'Light a candle.'

'Oh . . . oh! . . ' sighed Samoilenko, lighting a candle. 'My God! My God! . . . Why, it's past one, brother.'

'Excuse me, but I can't stay at home,' said Laevsky, feeling great comfort from the light and the presence of Samoilenko. 'You are my best, my only friend, Alexandr . . . You are my only hope. For God's sake, come to my rescue, like it or not. I must get away from here, come what may! . . . Lend me the money!'

'Oh, my God, my God! . . .' sighed Samoilenko, scratching himself. 'I was dropping asleep and I hear the whistle of the steamer, and now you . . . Do you want much?'

'Three hundred roubles at least. I must leave her a hundred, and I need two hundred for the journey . . . I owe you about four hundred already, but I will send it you all . . . all.'

Samoilenko took hold of both his whiskers in one hand, and standing with his legs wide apart, pondered.

'Yes . . .' he muttered, musing. 'Three hundred . . . Yes . . . But I haven't got that much. I shall have to borrow it from someone.'

'Borrow it, for God's sake!' said Laevsky, seeing from Samoilenko's face that he wanted to lend him the money and certainly would lend it. 'Borrow it, and I'll be sure to pay you back. I will send it from Petersburg as soon as I get there. You can set your mind at rest about that. I'll tell you what, Sasha,' he said, growing more animated; 'let's have some wine.'

'Yes . . . we can have some wine, too.'

They both went into the dining-room.

'And how about Nadezhda?' asked Samoilenko, setting three bottles and a plate of peaches on the table. 'Surely she's not staying?'

'I will arrange it all, I will arrange it all,' said Laevsky, feeling an unexpected rush of joy. 'I will send her the money afterwards and she will join me . . . Then we will sort things out. To your health, friend.'

'Wait a bit,' said Samoilenko. 'Drink this first . . . This is from my vineyard. This bottle is from Navaridze's vineyard and this one is from Akhatulov's . . . Try all three kinds and tell me candidly . . . There seems a little acidity about mine. Eh? Don't you taste it?'

'Yes. You have comforted me, Alexandr. Thank you . . . I feel better.'

'Is there any acidity?'

'Goodness only knows, I don't know. But you are a splendid, wonderful man!'

Looking at his pale, excited, good-natured face, Samoilenko remembered Von Koren's view that men like that ought to be destroyed, and Laevsky seemed to him a weak, defenceless child, whom any one could injure and destroy.

'And when you go, make it up with your mother,' he said. 'It's not right.'

'Yes, yes; I certainly shall.'

They were silent for a while. When they had emptied the first bottle, Samoilenko said:

'You ought to make it up with Von Koren too. You are both such very fine, clever fellows, and you glare at each other like wolves.'

'Yes, he's a fine, very intelligent fellow,' Laevsky assented, ready now to praise and forgive everyone. 'He's a remarkable man, but it's impossible for me to get on with him. No! Our natures are too different. I'm of an indolent, weak, submissive nature. Perhaps in a good minute I might hold out my hand to him, but he would turn away from me . . . with contempt.'

Laevsky took a sip of wine, walked from corner to corner and went on, standing in the middle of the room:

'I understand Von Koren very well. His is a resolute, strong, despotic nature. You have heard him continually talking of "the expedition" and it's not mere talk. He wants the wilderness, the moonlit night: all around in little tents, under the open sky, his sick and hungry Cossacks lie sleeping, guides, porters, doctor, priest, all exhausted with their weary marches, while only he is awake, sitting like Stanley* on a camp-stool, feeling himself the monarch of the desert and the master of these men. He goes on and on and on, his men groan and die, one after another, and he goes on and on, and in the end perishes himself, but still is monarch and ruler of the desert, since the cross upon his tomb can be seen by the caravans for thirty or forty miles over the desert. I am sorry the man is not in the army. He would have made a splendid military genius. He would not have hesitated to drown his cavalry in the river and make a bridge out of dead bodies. And in war such boldness is more necessary than any kind of fortifications or strategy. Oh, I understand him perfectly! Tell me: why is he wasting his time here? What does he want here?'

'He is studying the marine fauna.'

'No, no, brother, no!' Laevsky sighed. 'A scientist who was on the steamer told me the Black Sea was poor in animal life, and that in its depths, thanks to the abundance of sulphuretted hydrogen, organic life was impossible. All the serious zoologists work at the biological station at Naples or Villefranche. But Von Koren is independent and obstinate: he works on the Black Sea because nobody else is working there; he is at loggerheads with the university, does not care to know his comrades and other scientists because he is first of all a despot and only secondly a zoologist. And you'll see he'll do something. He is already dreaming that when he comes back from his expedition he will purify our universities from intrigue and mediocrity, and will make the scientists knuckle under. Despotism is just as strong in science as in the army. And he is spending his second summer in this stinking little town because he would rather be first in a village than second in a town. Here he is a king and an eagle; he keeps all the inhabitants under his thumb and oppresses them with his authority. He has enlisted everyone, he meddles in other people's affairs; he wants everything, and everyone is afraid of him. I am slipping out of his clutches, he feels that and hates me. Hasn't he told you that I ought to be destroyed or sent to community labour?'

'Yes,' laughed Samoilenko.

Laevsky laughed too, and drank some wine.

'His ideals are despotic too,' he said, laughing, and washing the wine down with a peach. 'Ordinary mortals think of their neighbour – me, you, humanity – if they work for the common weal. To Von Koren men are puppets and nonentities, too trivial to be the object of his life. He works, will go for his expedition and break his neck there, not for the sake of love of his neighbour, but for such abstractions as humanity, future generations, an ideal race of men. He exerts himself for the improvement of the human race, and we are in his eyes only slaves, cannon fodder, beasts of burden; some he would destroy or stow away in Siberia, others he would break by discipline, would, like Arakcheev,* force them to get up and go to bed to the sound of the drum; would appoint eunuchs to preserve our chastity and morality, would order them to fire at anyone who steps out of the circle of our narrow conservative morality; and all this in the name of the improvement of the human race . . . And what is the human race? Illusion, mirage . . . Despots have always been illusionists. I understand him very well, brother. I appreciate him and don't deny his importance; the world rests on men like him, and if the world were left only to such men as us, for all our good nature and good intentions, we should make as great a mess of it as the flies have of that picture. Yes.'

Laevsky sat down beside Samoilenko, and said with genuine feeling: 'I'm a foolish, worthless, depraved man. The air I breathe, this wine, love, life in fact – for all that, I have given nothing in exchange so far but lying, idleness, and cowardice. Till now I have deceived myself and other people; I have been miserable about it, and my misery was cheap and common. I bow my back humbly before Von Koren's hatred because at times I hate and despise myself.'

Laevsky began again pacing from one end of the room to the other in excitement, and said:

'I'm glad I see my faults clearly and am conscious of them. That will help me to reform and become a different man. My dear fellow, if only you knew how passionately, with what anguish, I long for such a change. And I swear to you I'll be a man! I will ! I don't know whether it is the wine that is speaking in me, or whether it really is so, but it seems to me that it's a long time since I have spent such pure and lucid moments as I have just now with you.'

'It's time to sleep, brother,' said Samoilenko.

'Yes, yes . . . Excuse me; I'll go in a minute.'

Laevsky moved hurriedly about the furniture and windows, looking for his cap.

'Thank you,' he muttered, sighing. 'Thank you . . . Kind and friendly words are better than charity. You have given me new life.'

He found his cap, stopped, and looked guiltily at Samoilenko.

'Alexandr,' he said in an imploring voice.

'What is it?'

'Let me stay the night with you, my dear fellow!'

'Certainly . . . Why not?'

Laevsky lay down on the sofa, and went on talking to the doctor for a long time.

X

Three days after the picnic, Maria unexpectedly called on Nadezhda, and without greeting her or taking off her hat, seized her by both hands, pressed them to her breast and said in great excitement:

'My dear, I am deeply touched and moved: our dear kind-hearted doctor told my Nikodim yesterday that your husband was dead. Tell me, my dear . . . tell me, is it true?'

'Yes, it's true; he is dead,' answered Nadezhda.

'That is awful, awful, my dear! But there's no evil without some compensation; your husband was no doubt a noble, wonderful, holy man, and such are more needed in heaven than on earth.'

Every line and feature in Maria's face began quivering as though little needles were jumping up and down under her skirt; she gave a saccharine smile and said, breathlessly, enthusiastically:

'And so you are free, my dear. You can hold your head up high now, and look people boldly in the face. Henceforth God and man will bless your union with Ivan Laevsky. It's enchanting. I am trembling with joy, I can find no words. My dear, I will give you away . . . Nikodim and I are so fond of you, you will allow us to give our blessing to your pure, lawful union. When, when do you think of getting married?'

'I haven't thought of it,' said Nadezhda, freeing her hands.

'That's impossible, my dear. You have thought of it, you have.'

'Upon my word, I haven't,' said Nadezhda, laughing. 'Why should we be married? I see no necessity for it. We'll go on living as we have lived.'

'What are you saying!' cried Maria in horror. 'For God's sake, what are you saying!'

'Our getting married won't make things any better. On the contrary, it will make them even worse. We shall lose our freedom.'

'My dear, my dear, what are you saying!' exclaimed Maria, stepping back and flinging up her hands. 'You are talking wildly! Think what you are saying. You must settle down!'

' "Settle down." How do you mean? I haven't lived yet, and you tell me to settle down.'

Nadezhda reflected that she really had not lived. She had finished her studies in a boarding-school and had been married to a man she did not love; then she had thrown in her lot with Laevsky, and had spent all her time with him on this empty, desolate coast, always expecting something better. Was that life?

'I ought to be married though,' she thought, but remembering Kirilin and Achmianov she flushed and said:

'No, it's impossible. Even if Laevsky begged me on his knees – even then I would refuse.'

Maria sat on the sofa for a minute in silence, grave and mournful, gazing fixedly into space; then she got up and said coldly:

'Good-bye, my dear! Forgive me for having troubled you. Though it's not easy for me, it's my duty to tell you that from this day all is over between us, and, in spite of my profound respect for Mr Laevsky, the door of my house is closed to you.'

She uttered these words with great solemnity and was herself overwhelmed by her solemn tone. Her face began quivering again; it assumed a soft, saccharine expression. She held out both hands to Nadezhda, who was overcome with alarm and confusion, and said in an imploring voice:

'My dear, allow me if only for a moment to be a mother or an elder sister to you! I will be as frank with you as a mother.'

Nadezhda felt in her breast warmth, gladness, and pity for herself, as though her own mother had really risen up and were standing before her. She impulsively embraced Maria and pressed her face to her shoulder. Both of them shed tears. They sat down on the sofa and for a few minutes sobbed without looking at one another or being able to utter a word.

'My dear child,' began Maria, 'I will tell you some harsh truths, without sparing you.'

'For God's sake, for God's sake, do!'

'Trust me, my dear. You remember of all the ladies here, I was the only one to receive you. You horrified me from the very first day, but I had not the heart to treat you with disdain like all the rest. I grieved over dear, good Laevsky as though he were my son – a young man in a strange place, inexperienced, weak, with no mother; and I was worried, dreadfully worried . . . My husband was opposed to our making his acquaintance, but I talked him round . . . persuaded him . . . We began receiving Laevsky, and with him, of course, you. If we had not, he would have been insulted. I have a daughter and a son . . . You understand the tender mind, the pure heart of childhood . . . "Whosoever offendeth one of these little ones" . . . I received you into my house and trembled for my children. Oh, when you become a mother, you will understand my fears. And everyone was surprised at my receiving you, excuse my saying so, as a respectable woman, and hinted to me . . . well, of course, slanders, suppositions . . . At the bottom of my heart I blamed you, but you were unhappy, flighty, to be pitied, and my heart was wrung with pity for you.'

'But why, why?' asked Nadezhda, trembling all over. 'What harm have I done anyone?'

'You are a terrible sinner. You broke the vow you made your husband at the altar. You seduced a fine young man, who perhaps had he not met you might have taken a lawful partner for life from a good family in his own circle, and would have been like everyone else now. You have ruined his youth. Don't speak, don't speak, my dear! I never believe that man is to blame for our sins. It is always the woman's fault. Men are frivolous in domestic life; they are guided by their minds, and not by their hearts. There's a great deal they don't understand; woman understands it all. Everything depends on her. To her much is given and from her much will be required. Oh, my dear, if she had been more foolish or weaker than man in that respect, God would not have entrusted her with the education of boys and girls. And then, my dear, you entered on the path of vice, forgetting all modesty; any other woman in your place would have hidden herself from people, would have sat shut up at home, and would only have been seen in the temple of God, pale, dressed all in black and weeping, and everyone would have said in genuine compassion: "Oh Lord, this erring angel is coming back again to Thee . . ." But you, my dear, have forgotten all discretion; have lived openly, extravagantly, have seemed to be proud of your sin; you have been gay and laughing, and I, looking at you, shuddered with horror, and have been afraid that thunder from heaven would strike our house while you were sitting with us. My dear, don't speak, don't speak,' cried Maria, noticing that Nadezhda meant to speak. 'Trust me, I will not deceive you, I will not hide one truth from the eyes of your soul. Listen to me, my dear . . .

God marks great sinners, and you have been marked out: only think –
your costumes have always been appalling.'

Nadezhda, who had always had the highest opinion of her
costumes, left off crying and looked at her with surprise.

'Yes, appalling,' Maria went on. 'Anyone could judge of your
behaviour from the fancy gaudiness of your attire. People laughed
and shrugged their shoulders as they looked at you, and I grieved, I
grieved . . . And forgive me, my dear; you are not nice in your person!
When we met in the bathing-place, you made me tremble. Your outer
clothing was decent enough, but your petticoat, your chemise . . . My
dear, I blushed! Poor Laevsky! No one ever ties his cravat properly,
and from his linen and his boots, poor fellow! one can see he has no
one at home to look after him. And he is always hungry, my darling,
and of course, if there is no one home to think of the samovar and the
coffee, one is forced to spend half one's salary at the pavilion. And it's
simply awful, awful in your home! No one else in town has flies, but
there's no getting rid of them in your rooms: all the plates and dishes
are black with them. If you look at the windows and the chairs,
there's nothing but dust, dead flies, and glasses . . . What do you want
glasses standing about for? And, my dear, the table's not cleared till
this time in the day. And one's ashamed to go into your
bedroom: underclothes flung about everywhere, rubber tubes hanging on the walls, pails and basins standing about . . . My dear! A
husband ought to know nothing, and his wife ought to be as neat as a
little angel in his presence. I wake up every morning before it is light,
and wash my face with cold water that my Nikodim doesn't see me
looking drowsy.'

'That's not important,' Nadezhda sobbed. 'If only I were happy,
but I am so unhappy!'

'Yes, yes; you are very unhappy!' Maria sighed, hardly able to
restrain herself from weeping. 'And there's terrible grief in store for
you in the future! A solitary old age, ill health; and then you will have
to answer at the Last Judgment . . . It's awful, awful. Now fate itself
holds out to you a helping hand, and you madly thrust it from you.
Get married, make haste and get married!'

'Yes, we must, we must,' said Nadezhda; 'but it's impossible!'

'Why?'

'It's impossible. Oh, if only you knew!'

Nadezhda had an impulse to tell her about Kirilin, and how the
evening before she had met handsome young Achmianov at the
harbour, and how the mad, ridiculous idea had occurred to her of
cancelling her debt for three hundred; it had amused her very much,
and she returned home late in the evening feeling that she had sold

herself and was irrevocably lost. She did not know herself how it had happened. And she longed to swear to Maria that she would certainly pay that debt, but sobs and shame prevented her from speaking.

'I am going away,' she said. 'Laevsky may stay, but I am going.'

'Where?'

'To Russia.'

'But how will you live there? Why, you have nothing.'

'I will do translations, or . . . or I will open a library . . .'

'Don't fantasise, my dear. You need money for a library. Well, I will leave you now, and you calm yourself and think things over, and tomorrow come and see me, bright and happy. That will be enchanting! Well, good-bye, my angel. Let me kiss you.'

Maria kissed Nadezhda on the forehead, made the sign of the cross over her, and softly withdrew. It was getting dark, and Olga lit a light in the kitchen. Still crying, Nadezhda went into the bedroom and lay on the bed. She began to be very feverish. She undressed without getting up, crumpled up her clothes at her feet, and curled herself up under the bedclothes. She was thirsty, but there was no one to give her a drink.

'I'll pay it back!' she said to herself, and it seemed to her in delirium that she was sitting beside some sick woman, and recognised her as herself. 'I'll pay it back. It would be stupid to imagine that for money I . . . I will go away and send him the money from Petersburg. First a hundred . . . then another hundred . . . and then the third hundred . . .'

It was late at night when Laevsky came in.

'First a hundred . . .' Nadezhda said to him, 'then another hundred . . .'

'You ought to take some quinine,' he said, and thought, 'Tomorrow is Wednesday; the steamer is going and I'm not. So I shall have to stay here till Saturday.'

Nadezhda knelt up in bed.

'I didn't say anything just now, did I?' she asked, smiling and screwing up her eyes at the light.

'No, nothing. We shall have to send for the doctor tomorrow morning. Sleep.'

He took a pillow and went to the door. Ever since he had finally made up his mind to go away and leave Nadezhda, she had begun to rouse in him pity and a sense of guilt; he felt a little ashamed in her presence, as though in the presence of a sick or old horse whom one has decided to kill. He stopped in the doorway and looked round at her.

'I was bad-tempered at the picnic and was rude to you. Forgive me, for God's sake!'

Saying this, he went off to his study, lay down, and for a long while could not get to sleep.

Next morning when Samoilenko, attired, as it was a holiday, in full dress uniform with epaulettes on his shoulders and decorations on his breast, came out of the bedroom after feeling Nadezhda's pulse and looking at her tongue. Laevsky, who was standing in the doorway, asked him anxiously, 'Well? Well?'

There was an expression of terror, of extreme uneasiness, and of hope on his face.

'Don't worry yourself; there's nothing dangerous,' said Samoilenko; 'it's the usual fever.'

'I don't mean that,' Laevsky frowned impatiently. 'Have you got the money?'

'My dear soul, forgive me,' he whispered, looking round at the door with embarrassment. 'For God's sake, forgive me! No one has anything to spare, and I've only been able to collect in five and ten-rouble notes . . . Only a hundred and ten in all. Today I'll speak to someone else. Have patience.'

'But Saturday is the latest date,' whispered Laevsky, trembling with impatience. 'By all that's sacred, get it by Saturday! If I don't get away by Saturday, nothing's any use, nothing! I can't understand how a doctor can be without money!'

'Lord have mercy on us!' Samoilenko whispered rapidly and intensely, and there was positively a breaking note in his throat. 'I've been stripped of everything; I am owed seven thousand, and I'm in debt all round. Is it my fault?'

'Then you'll get it by Saturday? Yes?'

'I'll try.'

'I implore you, my dear fellow. So as the money is in my hands on Friday morning!'

Samoilenko sat down and prescribed solution of quinine, kalii bromati, tincture of rhubarb, tincturae gentianae, aquae foeniculi – all in one mixture, added some rose-hip syrup to sweeten it, and went away.

XI

'You look as though you were coming to arrest me,' said Von Koren, seeing Samoilenko coming in, in full dress uniform.

'I was passing by and thought: "Let's go in and see how zoology is doing," ' said Samoilenko, sitting down at the big table, knocked together by the zoologist himself out of plain boards. 'Hello, holy father,' he said to the deacon, who was sitting in the window, copying something. 'I'll stay a minute and then run home to see to dinner. It's time . . . I'm not in your way?'

'Not in the least,' answered the zoologist, laying out over the table slips of paper covered with small writing. 'We are busy copying.'

'Ah! . . . Oh, my God! my God! . . .' sighed Samoilenko. He cautiously took up from the table a dusty book on which there was lying a dead dried spider, and said: 'Only fancy, though; some little green beetle is going about its business, when suddenly a monster like this swoops down upon it. Horrible, I imagine.'

'Yes, I suppose so.'

'Is the poison to protect it from its enemies?'

'Yes, for protection and for attack.'

'To be sure, to be sure . . . And everything in nature, my dear fellows, is consistent and can be explained,' sighed Samoilenko; 'only I tell you what I don't understand. You're a man of great intellect, so explain it to me, please. There are, you know, little beasts no bigger than rats, rather handsome to look at, but nasty and immoral in the extreme, let me tell you. Suppose this little animal is running in the woods. He sees a bird; he catches it and devours it. He goes on and sees in the grass a nest of eggs; he does not want to eat them – he is not hungry, but yet he tastes one egg and scatters the others out of the nest with his paw. Then he meets a frog and begins to play with it; when he has tormented the frog he goes on licking himself and meets a beetle; he crushes the beetle with his paw . . . And he spoils and destroys everything on his way . . . He creeps into other animals' holes, tears up anthills for nothing, bites a snail in two. If he meets a rat, he fights with it; if he meets a snake or a mouse, he must strangle it; and so the whole day long. Come, tell me: what is the use of an animal like that? Why was he created?'

'I don't know what animal you are talking of,' said Von Koren; 'most likely one of the insectivores. Well, he got the bird because it was careless; he broke into the nest of eggs because the bird was inept, had made the nest badly and couldn't conceal it. The frog probably had some defect in its colouring or he would not have seen it, and so on. Your little beast only destroys the weak, the inept, the careless – in fact, those who have defects which nature does not think fit to hand on to posterity. Only the cleverer, the stronger, the more careful and developed survive; and so your little beast, without suspecting it, is serving the great ends of perfecting creation.'

'Yes, yes, yes . . . By the way, brother,' said Samoilenko casually, 'lend me a hundred roubles.'

'Very good. There are some very interesting types among the

insectivores. For instance, the mole is said to be useful because he devours noxious insects. There is a story that some German sent Wilhelm I a fur coat of moleskins, and the Emperor ordered him to be reprimanded for destroying so great a number of useful animals. And yet the mole is no less cruel than your little beast; and is very mischievous, besides, as he spoils meadows terribly.'

Von Koren opened a box and took out a hundred-rouble note.

'The mole has a powerful thorax, just like the bat,' he went on, shutting the box; 'the bones and muscles are tremendously developed, the mouth is extraordinarily powerfully furnished. If it had the proportions of an elephant, it would be an all-destructive, invincible animal. It is interesting when two moles meet underground; they begin at once as though by agreement digging a little platform; they need the platform to make combat easier. When they have made the platform they begin a ferocious struggle and fight till the weaker one falls. Take the hundred roubles,' said Von Koren, dropping his voice, 'but only on condition that you're not borrowing it for Laevsky.'

'And if it were for Laevsky,' cried Samoilenko, flaring up, 'what is that to you?'

'I can't give it to you for Laevsky. I know you like lending people money. You would give it to Kerim, the brigand, if he were to ask you; but, excuse me, I can't assist you in that direction.'

'Yes, it is for Laevsky I am asking it,' said Samoilenko, standing up and waving his right arm. 'Yes! For Laevsky! And no fiend or devil has a right to dictate to me how to dispose of my own money. You prefer not to lend it to me? No?'

The deacon began laughing.

'Don't get excited, but be reasonable,' said the zoologist. 'To give Mr Laevsky charity is, to my thinking, as senseless as to water weeds or to feed locusts.'

'To my thinking, it is our duty to help our neighbours!' cried Samoilenko.

'In that case, help that hungry Turk who is lying under the fence! He is a workman and more useful and better than your Laevsky. Give him that hundred-rouble note! Or subscribe a hundred roubles to my expedition!'

'Will you give me the money or not? I ask you!'

'Tell me openly: what does he want money for?'

'It's not a secret; he wants to go to Petersburg on Saturday.'

'So that is it!' Von Koren drawled out. 'Aha! . . . We understand. And is she going with him or how is it to be?'

'She's staying here for the time. He'll sort out his affairs in Petersburg and send her the money, and then she'll go.'

'That's neat!' said the zoologist, and he gave a short tenor laugh. 'Neat, well planned.'

He went rapidly up to Samoilenko, and standing face to face, looking him in the eyes, asked: 'Tell me now honestly: is he tired of her? Yes? Tell me: is he tired of her? Yes?'

'Yes,' Samoilenko articulated, and burst into a sweat.

'How repulsive it is!' said Von Koren, and from his face it could be seen that he felt revulsion. 'One of two things, Alexandr: either you are in the plot with him, or, excuse my saying so, you are a simpleton. Surely you must see that he is taking you in like a child in the most shameless way? Why, it's as clear as day that he wants to get rid of her and abandon her here. She'll be left round your neck. It's as clear as day that you will have to send her to Petersburg at your own expense. Surely your fine friend can't have so blinded you by his dazzling qualities that you can't see the simplest thing?'

'That's all supposition,' said Samoilenko, sitting down.

'Supposition? But why is he going alone instead of taking her with him? And ask him why he doesn't send her off first. The rogue!'

Overcome with sudden doubts and suspicions about his friend, Samoilenko weakened and took a humbler tone.

'But it's impossible,' he said, recalling the night Laevsky had spent at his house. 'He is so unhappy!'

'What of that? Thieves and arsonists are unhappy too!'

'Even supposing you are right . . .' said Samoilenko, hesitating. 'Let's suppose . . . He's a young man in a strange place . . . a student. We have been students, too, and there is no one but us to support him.'

'To help him to do abominable things, because he and you at different times have been at university, and neither of you did anything there! What nonsense!'

'Stop; let us talk it over coolly. I imagine it will be possible to make some arrangement . . .' Samoilenko reflected, twiddling his fingers. 'I'll give him the money, you see, but make him promise on his honour that within a week he'll send Nadezhda the money for the journey.'

'And he'll give you his word of honour – in fact, he'll shed tears and believe in it himself; but what's his word of honour worth? He won't keep it, and when in a year or two you meet him on the Nevsky Prospect with a new mistress on his arm, he'll excuse himself on the ground that he has been crippled by civilisation, and that he is made in the mould of Rudin.* Drop him, for God's sake! Keep away from the filth; don't get both hands in it!'

Samoilenko thought for a minute and said resolutely:

'But I shall give him the money all the same. As you please. I can't bring myself to refuse a man simply on an assumption.'

'Excellent. You can kiss him if you like.'

'Give me the hundred roubles then,' Samoilenko asked timidly.

'I won't.'

A silence ensued. Samoilenko was quite crushed; his face wore a guilty, abashed, and ingratiating expression, and it was strange to see this pitiful, childish, shamefaced countenance on a huge man wearing epaulettes and orders of merit.

'The bishop here goes the round of his diocese on horseback instead of in a carriage,' said the deacon, laying down his pen. 'It's extremely touching to see him sit on his horse. His simplicity and humility are full of Biblical grandeur.'

'Is he a good man?' asked Von Koren, who was glad to change the subject.

'Of course! If he hadn't been a good man, do you suppose he would have been consecrated a bishop?'

'Among bishops you often find good and gifted men,' said Von Koren. 'The only drawback is that some of them have the weakness to imagine themselves statesmen. One busies himself with Russification, another criticises the sciences. That's not their business. They had much better look into their consistory a little.'

'A layman cannot judge of bishops.'

'Why so, deacon? A bishop is a man just the same as you or I.'

'The same, but not the same.' The deacon was offended and took up his pen. 'If you had been the same, Divine Grace would have rested upon you, and you would have been bishop yourself; and since you are not a bishop, it follows you are not the same.'

'Don't talk nonsense, deacon,' said Samoilenko dejectedly. 'Listen to what I suggest,' he said, turning to Von Koren. 'Don't give me that hundred roubles. You'll be having your dinners with me for three months before the winter, so let me have the money beforehand for three months.'

'I won't.'

Samoilenko blinked and turned crimson; he mechanically drew towards him the book with the spider on it and looked at him, then he got up and took his hat.

Von Koren felt sorry for him.

'What it is to have to live and do with people like this,' said the zoologist, and he kicked a paper into the corner with indignation. 'You must understand that this is not kindness, it is not love, but cowardice, slackness, poison! What's gained by reason is lost by your flabby good-for-nothing hearts! When I was ill with typhoid as a schoolboy, my aunt in her sympathy gave me pickled mushrooms to eat, and I very nearly died. You, and my aunt too, must understand that love for man is not to be found in the heart or the stomach or the bowels, but here!'

Von Koren slapped himself on the forehead.

'Take it,' he said, and flung out a hundred-rouble note.

'You've no need to be angry, Kolia,' said Samoilenko mildly, folding up the note. 'I quite understand you, but . . . you must put yourself in my place.'

'You are an old woman, that's what you are.'

The deacon burst out laughing.

'Hear my last request, Alexandr,' said Von Koren hotly. 'When you give that scoundrel the money, make it a condition that he takes his lady with him, or sends her on ahead, and don't give it him without. There's no need to stand on ceremony with him. Tell him so, or, if you don't, I give you my word I'll go to his office and kick him downstairs, and I'll break off all acquaintance with you. So now you know.'

'Why not? To go with her or send her on ahead will be better for him,' said Samoilenko. 'He'll be delighted indeed. Well, good-bye.'

He said good-bye affectionately and went out, but before shutting the door after him, he looked round at Von Koren and, with a ferocious face, said:

'It's the Germans who have ruined you, brother! Yes! The Germans!'

XII

Next day, Thursday, Maria was celebrating the birthday of her Kostia. All were invited to come at midday and eat pies, and in the evening to drink chocolate. When Laevsky and Nadezhda arrived in the evening, the zoologist, who was already sitting in the drawing-room, drinking chocolate, asked Samoilenko:

'Have you talked to him?'

'Not yet.'

'Mind now, don't stand on ceremony. I can't understand the insolence of these people! Why, they know perfectly well the view in this family of their cohabitation, and yet they force themselves in here.'

'If you paid attention to every prejudice,' said Samoilenko, 'there'd be nowhere to go.'

'Do you mean to say that the repugnance felt by the masses for extramarital love and moral laxity is a prejudice?'

'Of course it is. It's prejudice and hate. When the soldiers see a girl of light behaviour, they laugh and whistle; but just ask them what they are themselves.'

'They whistle for good reason. The fact that girls strangle their illegitimate children and go to prison for it, and that Anna Karenina flung herself under a train, and in the villages they smear the gates with tar, and that you and I, without knowing why, like Katia to be pure, and that every one of us feels a vague craving for pure love, though he knows there is no such love – is all that prejudice? That's the one thing, brother, which has survived intact from natural selection, and, if it were not for that obscure force regulating sexual relations, the Laevskys would have it all their own way, and mankind would degenerate in two years.'

Laevsky came into the drawing-room, greeted everyone, and shaking hands with Von Koren, smiled ingratiatingly. He waited for a favourable moment and said to Samoilenko:

'Excuse me, Alexandr, I must say two words to you.'

Samoilenko got up, put his arm round Laevsky's waist, and both of them went into Nikodim's study.

'Tomorrow's Friday,' said Laevsky, biting his nails. 'Have you got what you promised?'

'I got only two hundred. I'll get the rest today or tomorrow. Don't worry.'

'Thank God . . .' sighed Laevsky, and his hands began trembling with joy. 'You are saving me, Alexandr, and I swear to you by God, by my happiness and anything you like, I'll send you the money as soon as I arrive. And I'll pay you my old debt too.'

'Look here, Vania . . .' said Samoilenko, turning crimson and taking him by the button. 'You must forgive my meddling in your private affairs, but . . . why shouldn't you take Nadezhda with you?'

'You are odd. How can I? One of us must stay, or our creditors will raise an outcry. You see, I owe seven hundred or more to the shops. Only wait, and I will send them the money. I'll stop their mouths, and then she can come away.'

'I see . . . But why shouldn't you send her on first?'

'My goodness, how could I?' Laevsky was horrified. 'Why, she's a woman; what would she do there alone? What does she know? That would only be a loss of time and a waste of money.'

'Reasonable . . .' thought Samoilenko, but remembering his conversation with Von Koren, he looked down and said sullenly: 'I can't agree with you. Either go with her or send her first; otherwise . . . otherwise I won't give you the money. That's my final word . . .'

He staggered back, lurched backwards against the door, and went into the drawing-room, crimson, and terribly embarrassed.

'Friday . . . Friday,' thought Laevsky, returning to the drawing-room. 'Friday . . .'

He was handed a cup of chocolate; he burnt his lips and tongue with the scalding chocolate and thought: 'Friday . . . Friday . . .'

For some reason he could not get the word 'Friday' out of his head; he could think of nothing but Friday, and the only thing that was clear to him, not in his brain but somewhere in his heart, was that he would not get off on Saturday. Before him stood Nikodim, very neat, with his hair combed over his temples, saying:

'Please take something to eat . . .'

Maria showed the visitors Katia's school report and said, drawling:

'It's very, very difficult to do well at school nowadays! So much is expected . . .'

'Mama!' groaned Katia, not knowing where to hide from the embarrassment and the praise.

Laevsky, too, looked at the report and praised it. Scripture, Russian language, conduct, 'excellent' and 'good', danced before his eyes, and all this, mixed with the haunting refrain of 'Friday', with Nikodim's carefully combed locks and Katia's red cheek, gave him a sensation of such immense overwhelming anguish that he almost shrieked with despair and asked himself: 'Will I, will I really not get away?'

Two card tables were put side by side: they sat down to a game of post. Laevsky sat down too.

'Friday . . . Friday . . .' he kept thinking, as he smiled and took a pencil out of his pocket. 'Friday . . .'

He wanted to think over his position, and was afraid to think. It was terrible to him to realise that the doctor had detected him in the deception which he had so long and carefully concealed from himself. Every time he thought of his future he would not let his thoughts have full rein. He would get into the train and set off, and thereby the problem of his life would be solved, and he did not let his thoughts go further. Like a far-away dim light in the fields, the thought sometimes flickered in his mind that in one of the side-streets of Petersburg, in the remote future, he would have to have recourse to a tiny lie in order to get rid of Nadezhda and pay his debts; he would tell a lie only once, and then a completely new life would begin. And that was right: at the price of a small lie he would win so much truth.

Now when the doctor's blunt refusal had crudely hinted at his deception, he began to understand that he would need deception not only in the remote future, but today, and tomorrow, and in a month's time, and perhaps to the very end of his life. In fact, in order to get away he would have to lie to Nadezhda, to his creditors, and to his superiors in the service; then, in order to get money in Petersburg, he would have to lie to his mother, to tell her that he had already broken with Nadezhda; and his mother would not give him more than five hundred roubles, so he had already deceived the doctor, as he would not be in a position to pay him back the money for some time. Afterwards, when Nadezhda came to Petersburg, he would have to resort to a regular series of deceptions, little and big, in order to get free of her; and again there would be tears, unhappiness, a disgusting existence, remorse, and so there would be no new life.

Deception and nothing more. A whole mountain of lies rose before Laevsky's imagination. To leap over it at one bound and not to do his lying piecemeal, he would have to bring himself to stern, uncompromising action; for instance, to getting up without saying a word, putting on his hat, and at once setting off without money and without explanation. But Laevsky felt that was impossible for him.

'Friday, Friday . . .' he thought. 'Friday . . .'

They wrote little notes, folded them in two, and put them in Nikodim's old top hat. When there were a sufficient heap of notes, Kostia, who acted the part of postman, walked round the table and delivered them. The deacon, Katia and Kostia, who received amusing notes and tried to write as funnily as they could, were highly delighted.

'We must have a little talk,' Nadezhda read in a little note; she caught Maria's eye; Maria gave her a saccharine smile and nodded.

'Talk of what?' thought Nadezhda. 'If one can't say everything, it's no use talking.'

Before going out for the evening she had tied Laevsky's cravat for him, and that simple action filled her soul with tenderness and sorrow. The anxiety in his face, his absent-minded looks, his pallor, and the incomprehensible change that had taken place in him of late, and the fact that she had a terrible, revolting secret from him, and the fact that her hands trembled when she tied his cravat – all this seemed to tell her that they had not long left to be together. She looked at him as though he were an icon, with terror and penitence, and thought: 'Forgive, forgive.'

Opposite her sat Achmianov, and he never took his black, love-sick eyes off her. She was stirred by passion; she was ashamed of herself, and afraid that even her misery and sorrow would not prevent her from yielding to impure desire tomorrow, if not today – and that, like a hopeless drunkard, she would not have the strength to stop herself.

She made up her mind to go away that she might not continue this life, shameful for herself, and humiliating for Laevsky. She would beseech him with tears to let her go; and if he opposed her, she would go away secretly. She would not tell him what had happened; let him keep a pure memory of her.

'I love you, I love you, I love you,' she read. It was from Achmianov.

She would live in some far remote place, would work and send Laevsky money, embroidered shirts, and tobacco 'from a well-wisher', and would return to him only in old age or if he were dangerously ill and needed a nurse. When in his old age he learned why she had left him and refused to be his wife, he would appreciate her sacrifice and forgive.

'You've got a long nose.' That must be from the deacon or Kostia.

Nadezhda imagined how, parting from Laevsky, she would embrace him warmly, would kiss his hand, and would swear to love him all her life, all her life, and then, living in obscurity among strangers, she would every day think that somewhere she had a friend, someone she loved – a pure, noble, lofty man who kept a pure memory of her.

'If you don't give me a rendezvous today, I shall take measures, I assure you on my word of honour. You can't treat decent people like this; you must understand that.' That was from Kirilin.

XIII

Laevsky received two notes; he opened one and read: 'Don't go away, my darling.'

'Who could have written that?' he thought. 'Not Samoilenko, of course. And not the deacon, for he doesn't know I want to go away. Von Koren, perhaps?'

The zoologist bent over the table, drawing a pyramid. Laevsky fancied that his eyes were smiling.

'Most likely Samoilenko has been gossiping . . .' thought Laevsky.

In the other note, in the same disguised angular handwriting with long tails to the letters, was written: 'Somebody won't go away on Saturday.'

'A stupid gibe,' thought Laevsky. 'Friday, Friday . . .'

Something rose in his throat. He touched his collar and coughed, but instead of a cough a laugh broke from his throat.

'Ha-ha-ha!' he laughed. 'Ha-ha-ha! What am I laughing at?' he thought. 'Ha-ha-ha!'

He tried to restrain himself, covered his mouth with his hand, but the laugh choked his chest and throat, and his hand could not cover his mouth.

'How stupid it is!' he thought, rolling with laughter. 'Have I gone mad?'

The laugh grew shriller and shriller, and became something like the bark of a lap-dog. Laevsky tried to get up from the table, but his legs would not obey him and his right hand was strangely, against his will, dancing on the table, convulsively clutching and crumpling up the bits of paper. He saw looks of amazement, Samoilenko's grave, frightened face, and the eyes of the zoologist full of cold irony and disgust, and realised that he was in hysterics.

'How hideous, how shameful!' he thought, feeling the warmth of tears on his face . . . 'Oh, oh, what a disgrace! This has never happened to me . . .'

They took him under his arms, and supporting his head from behind, led him away; a glass gleamed before his eyes and knocked against his teeth, and the water was spilt on his chest; he was in a little room, with two beds in the middle, side by side, covered by two snow-white quilts. He collapsed on to one of the beds and sobbed.

'It's nothing, it's nothing,' Samoilenko kept saying; 'it does happen . . . it does happen . . .'

Chill with horror, trembling all over and dreading something awful, Nadezhda stood by the bedside and kept asking:

'What is it? What is it? For God's sake, tell me.'

'Can Kirilin have written him something?' she thought.

'It's nothing,' said Laevsky, laughing and crying; 'go away, darling.'

His face expressed neither hatred nor revulsion: so he knew nothing; Nadezhda was somewhat reassured, and she went into the drawing-room.

'Don't agitate yourself, my dear!' said Maria, sitting down beside her and taking her hand. 'It will pass. Men are just as weak as we poor sinners. You are both going through a crisis . . . One can so well understand it! Well, my dear, I am waiting for an answer. Let us have a little talk.'

'No, we are not going to talk,' said Nadezhda, listening to Laevsky's sobs. 'I feel miserable . . . Let me go home.'

'What do mean, what do you mean, my dear?' cried Maria in alarm. 'Do you think I could let you go without supper? We will have something to eat, and then you may go with my blessing.'

'I feel miserable . . .' whispered Nadezhda, and she caught at the arm of the chair with both hands to avoid falling.

'He's having a tantrum,' said Von Koren gaily, coming into the drawing-room, but seeing Nadezhda, he was taken aback and retreated.

When the attack was over, Laevsky sat on the strange bed and thought:

'Disgraceful! I've been howling like some wretched girl! I must have been absurd and disgusting. I will go away by the back stairs . . . But that would seem as though I took my hysterics too seriously. I ought to make a joke of it . . .'

He looked in the looking-glass, sat there for some time, and went back into the drawing-room.

'Here I am,' he said, smiling; he felt agonisingly ashamed, and he felt others were ashamed in his presence. 'Fancy such a thing happening,' he said, sitting down. 'I was sitting here, and all of a sudden, do you know, I felt a terrible piercing pain in my side . . . unendurable, my nerves could not stand it, and . . . and it led to this silly performance. Ours is the age of nerves; there's nothing one can do.'

At supper he drank some wine, and, from time to time, with an abrupt sigh rubbed his side as though to suggest that he still felt the pain. And no one, except Nadezhda, believed him, and he saw that.

After nine o'clock they went for a walk on the boulevard. Nadezhda, afraid that Kirilin would speak to her, did her best to keep all the time beside Maria and the children. She felt weak with fear and misery, and felt she was going to be feverish; she was exhausted and her legs would hardly move, but she did not go home, because she felt sure that she would be followed by Kirilin or Achmianov or both at once. Kirilin walked behind her with Nikodim, and kept humming in an undertone:

'I don't le-et people pla-ay with me! I don't le-et them.'

From the boulevard they went back to the pavilion and walked along the beach, and looked for a long time at the phosphorescence on the water. Von Koren began telling them why it was phosphorescent.

XIV

'It's time I went to my whist . . . They're expecting me,' said Laevsky. 'Good-bye, my friends.'

'I'll come with you; wait a minute,' said Nadezhda, and she took his arm.

They said good-bye to the company and went away. Kirilin took his leave too, and saying that he was going the same way, went alongside them.

'What will be, will be,' thought Nadezhda. 'So be it . . .'

And it seemed to her that all the evil moments had left her head and were walking beside her in the darkness, breathing heavily, while she, like a fly that had fallen into the ink pot, was crawling painfully along the pavement and besmirching Laevsky's side and arm with blackness. If Kirilin should do anything horrid, she thought, it would be she who was to blame. There was a time when no man would have talked to her as Kirilin had done, and she had broken that time like a thread and destroyed it irrevocably – who was to blame for it? Intoxicated by her passions she had smiled at a complete stranger, probably just because he was a fine, tall figure. After two meetings she was weary of him, had thrown him over: did not that, she thought now, give him the right to treat her as he chose?

'Here I'll say good-bye to you, darling,' said Laevsky. 'Captain Kirilin will see you home.'

He nodded to Kirilin, and, quickly crossing the boulevard, walked along the street to Sheshkovsky's, where there were lights in the windows, and then they heard the gate bang as he went in.

'Allow me to have it out with you,' said Kirilin. 'I'm not a boy, not some Achkasov or Lachkasov, Zachkasov . . . I demand proper consideration.'

Nadezhda's heart began beating violently. She made no reply.

'The abrupt change in your behaviour to me I put down at first to coquetry,' Kirilin went on; 'now I see that you don't know how to behave with decent people. You simply wanted to play with me, as you are playing with that wretched Armenian boy; but I'm a gentleman and I insist on being treated like a gentleman. And so I am at your service . . .'

'I'm miserable . . .' said Nadezhda, beginning to cry, and to hide her tears she turned away.

'I'm miserable too,' said Kirilin, 'but so what?'

Kirilin was silent for a space, then he said distinctly and emphatically:

'I repeat, madam, that if you do not give me a rendezvous this evening, I'll make a scene this evening.'

'Let me off this evening,' said Nadezhda, and she did not recognise her own voice, it was so weak and pitiful.

'I must give you a lesson . . . Excuse my rough tone, but I must give you a lesson. Yes, I regret to say I must give you a lesson. I insist on two meetings – today and tomorrow. After tomorrow you are perfectly free and can go wherever you like with anyone you choose. Today and tomorrow.'

Nadezhda went up to her gate and stopped.

'Let me go,' she murmured, trembling all over and seeing nothing before her in the darkness but his white tunic. 'You're right: I'm a horrible woman . . . I'm to blame, but let me go . . . I beg you.' She touched his cold hand and shuddered. 'I beseech you . . .'

'Alas!' sighed Kirilin, 'alas! it's not part of my plan to let you go; I only mean to give you a lesson and make you realise. And what's more, madam, I've very little faith in women.'

'I'm miserable . . .'

Nadezhda listened to the even splash of the sea, looked at the sky studded with stars, and longed to make haste and end it all, and get away from the cursed sensation of life, with its sea, stars, men, fever.

'Only not in my home,' she said coldly. 'Take me somewhere else.'

'Come to Miuridov's. That's the best.'

'Where's that?'

'Near the old wall.'

She walked quickly along the street and then turned into the side-street that led towards the mountains. It was dark. There were pale streaks of light here and there on the pavement, from the lighted windows, and it seemed to her that, like a fly, she kept falling into the ink and crawling out into the light again. At one point he stumbled, almost fell down and burst out laughing.

'He's drunk,' thought Nadezhda. 'Never mind . . . Never mind . . . So be it.'

Achmianov had also left the party early; he followed Nadezhda to ask her to go for a boat ride. He went to her house and looked over the fence: the windows were wide open, there were no lights.

'Nadezhda!' he called.

A moment passed, he called again.

'Who's there?' he heard Olga's voice.

'Is Nadezhda at home?'

'No, she has not come in yet.'

'Strange . . . very strange,' thought Achmianov, feeling very uneasy. 'She went home . . .'

He walked along the boulevard, then along the street, and glanced in at the windows of Sheshkovsky's. Laevsky was sitting at the table in his shirt-sleeves, looking attentively at his cards.

'Strange, strange,' muttered Achmianov, and remembering Laevsky's hysterics, he felt ashamed. 'If she is not at home, where is she?'

He went to Nadezhda's lodgings again, and looked at the dark windows.

'It's a trick, a trick . . .' he thought, remembering that, meeting him at midday at Maria's, she had promised to go on a boat ride with him that evening.

The windows of the house where Kirilin lived were dark, and there was a policeman sitting asleep on a little bench at the gate. Everything was clear to Achmianov when he looked at the windows and the policeman. He made up his mind to go home, and set off in that direction, but somehow found himself near Nadezhda's lodgings again. He sat down on the bench near the gate and took off his hat, feeling that his head was burning with jealousy and resentment.

The clock in the town church only struck twice in the twenty-four hours – at midday and midnight. Soon after it struck midnight he heard hurried footsteps.

'Tomorrow evening, then, again at Miuridov's,' Achmianov heard, and he recognised Kirilin's voice. 'At eight o'clock; good-bye!'

Nadezhda made her appearance near the garden. Without noticing that Achmianov was sitting on the bench, she passed him like a shadow, opened the gate, and leaving it open, went into the house. In her own room she lit a candle and quickly undressed, but instead of getting into bed, she sank on her knees before a chair, flung her arms round it, and rested her head on it.

It was past two when Laevsky came home.

XV

Having made up his mind to lie, not all at once but piecemeal, Laevsky went soon after one o'clock next day to Samoilenko to ask for the money so as to be sure of leaving on Saturday. After yesterday's hysteria, which had added an acute feeling of shame to his depressed state of mind, it was unthinkable to remain in the town. If Samoilenko should insist on his conditions, he thought he could agree to them and take the money, and next day, just as he was starting, to say that Nadezhda refused to go. He would be able to persuade her that evening that the whole arrangement would be for her benefit. If Samoilenko, who was obviously under the influence of Von Koren, should refuse the money altogether or make fresh conditions, then he, Laevsky, would go off that very evening in a cargo vessel, or even in a sailing boat, to Novy Afon or Novorossiisk, would send from there a humiliating telegram, and would stay there till his mother sent him the fare.

When he went into Samoilenko's, he found Von Koren in the drawing-room. The zoologist had just arrived for dinner, and, as usual, was turning over the album and scrutinising the gentlemen in top hats and the ladies in bonnets. 'How very unlucky!' thought Laevsky, seeing him. 'He may interfere. Good morning.'

'Good morning,' answered Von Koren, without looking at him.

'Is Alexandr at home?'

'Yes, in the kitchen.'

Laevsky went into the kitchen, but seeing from the door that Samoilenko was busy with the salad, he went back into the drawing-room and sat down. He always had a feeling of awkwardness in the zoologist's presence, and now he was afraid they would talk about hysterics. There was more than a minute of silence. Von Koren suddenly raised his eyes to Laevsky and asked:

'How do you feel after yesterday?'

'Very well indeed,' said Laevsky, flushing. 'It really was nothing much . . .'

'Until yesterday I thought it was only ladies who had hysterics, and so at first I thought you had St Vitus's dance.'

Laevsky smiled ingratiatingly, and thought:

'How tactless of him! He knows very well that I am suffering . . .'

'Yes, it was a ridiculous performance,' he said, still smiling. 'I've been laughing over it the whole morning. What's so curious in an attack of hysterics is that you know it is absurd, and are laughing at it in your heart, and at the same time you sob. In our neurotic age we are slaves of our nerves; they are our masters and do as they like with us. Civilisation has done us a bad turn in that way . . .'

As Laevsky talked, he disliked Von Koren listening to him gravely, looking at him steadily and attentively as though studying him; and he was vexed with himself that in spite of his dislike of Von Koren, he could not banish the ingratiating smile from his face.

'I must admit, though,' he added, 'that there were immediate causes for the attack, and quite strong ones too. My health has been terribly shaky of late. To which one must add boredom, constantly being hard up . . . the absence of people and general interests . . . My position is worse than the governor's.'

'Yes, your position is hopeless,' said Von Koren.

These calm, cold words, implying something between a jeer and an uninvited prediction, offended Laevsky. He recalled the zoologist's eyes the evening before, full of mockery and disgust. He was silent for a space and then asked, no longer smiling:

'How do you know about my position?'

'You were only just speaking of it yourself. Besides, your friends take such a warm interest in you, that I hear only about you all day long.'

'What friends? Samoilenko, I suppose?'

'Yes, he too.'

'I would ask Alexandr and my friends in general not to bother so much about me.'

'Here is Samoilenko; you had better ask him not to bother so much about you.'

'I don't understand your tone,' Laevsky muttered, suddenly feeling as though he had only just realised that the zoologist hated and despised him, and was jeering at him, and was his bitterest and most inveterate enemy. 'Keep that tone for someone else,' he said softly, unable to speak aloud for the hatred with which his chest and throat were choking, as they had been the night before with laughter.

Samoilenko came in his shirt-sleeves, crimson and sweaty from the stifling kitchen.

'Ah, you here?' he said. 'Good morning, my dear boy. Have you had dinner? Don't stand on ceremony. Have you had dinner?'

'Alexandr,' said Laevsky, standing up, 'though I did appeal to you to help me in a private matter, it did not follow that I released you from the obligation of discretion and respect for other people's private affairs.'

'What's this?' asked Samoilenko, in astonishment.

'If you have no money,' Laevsky went on, raising his voice and shifting from one foot to the other in his excitement, 'don't give it; refuse it. But why spread abroad in every back street that my position is hopeless, and all the rest of it? I can't endure such benevolence and friend's assistance, when it's all talk and no action! You can boast of your benevolence as much as you please, but no one has given you the right to gossip about my private affairs.'

'What private affairs?' asked Samoilenko, puzzled and beginning to be angry. 'If you've come here to be abusive, you had better clear out. You can come back later!'

He remembered the rule that when you are angry with your neighbour, you must begin to count a hundred and will grow calm again; and he began rapidly counting.

'I beg you not to trouble yourself about me,' Laevsky went on. 'Don't pay any attention to me, and whose business is it what I do and how I live? Yes, I want to go away. Yes, I get into debt, I drink, I am living with another man's wife, I'm hysterical, I'm ordinary. I am not so profound as some people, but whose business is that? Respect the individual.'

'I'm sorry, brother,' said Samoilenko, who had counted up to thirty-five, 'but . . .'

'Respect the individual!' interrupted Laevsky. 'This continual gossip about other people's affairs, this sighing and groaning and everlasting prying, this eavesdropping, this friendly sympathy . . .

damn it all! I'm lent money and given conditions as though I were a schoolboy! I am treated as the devil knows what! I don't want anything,' shouted Laevsky, staggering with excitement and afraid that it might end in another attack of hysterics. 'I shan't get away on Saturday, then,' flashed through his mind. 'I want nothing. All I ask of you is to spare me your patronage. I'm not a boy, and I'm not mad, and I beg you to stop this supervision.'

The deacon came in, and seeing Laevsky pale and gesticulating, addressing his strange speech to the portrait of Prince Vorontsov, stood still by the door as though petrified.

'This continual prying into my soul,' Laevsky went on, 'is insulting to my human dignity, and I beg these amateur detectives to stop prying! Enough!'

'What's that . . . what did you say?' said Samoilenko, who had counted up to a hundred. He turned crimson and went up to Laevsky.

'It's enough,' said Laevsky, breathing hard and snatching his cap.

'I'm a Russian doctor, a nobleman by birth, and a civil councillor,' said Samoilenko emphatically. 'I've never been a spy, and I allow no one to insult me!' he shouted in a shattering voice, emphasising 'insult'. 'Shut up!'

The deacon, who had never seen the doctor so majestic, so swelling with dignity, so crimson and so ferocious, shut his mouth, ran out into the entry and there exploded with laughter.

As though through a fog, Laevsky saw Von Koren get up and, putting his hands in his trouser-pockets, stand still in an attitude of expectancy, as though to see what would happen. This calm attitude struck Laevsky as insolent and insulting to the last degree.

'Kindly take back your words,' shouted Samoilenko.

Laevsky, who no longer remembered what words, answered:

'Leave me alone! I ask for nothing. All I ask is for you and Jewish German upstarts to leave me alone! Or I shall take steps! I shall fight you!'

'Now we understand,' said Von Koren, coming from behind the table. 'Mr Laevsky wants to amuse himself with a duel before he goes away. I can give him that pleasure. Mr Laesvky, I accept your challenge.'

'A challenge,' said Laevsky in a low voice, going up to the zoologist and looking with hatred at his swarthy brow and curly hair. 'A challenge? By all means! I hate you! I hate you!'

'Delighted. Tomorrow morning early near Kerbalai's, with all details to your taste. And now, clear out!'

'I hate you,' Laevsky said softly, breathing hard. 'I have hated you a long while! A duel! Yes!'

'Get rid of him, Alexandr, or else I'm off,' said Von Koren. 'He might bite me.'

Von Koren's cool tone calmed the doctor; he seemed suddenly to come to himself, to recover his reason; he put both arms round Laevsky's waist, and, leading him away from the zoologist, muttered in a friendly voice that shook with emotion.

'My friends . . . dear, good . . . you've lost your tempers and that's enough . . . and that's enough, my friends.'

Hearing his soft, friendly voice, Laevsky felt that something unheard of, monstrous, had just happened to him, as though he had been nearly run over by a train; he almost burst into tears, waved his arm, and ran out of the room.

'To feel hatred, to expose oneself before the man who hates you, in the most pitiful, contemptible, helpless state. My God, how wretched it makes me!' he thought a little while afterwards, as he sat in the pavilion, feeling the hatred he had just experienced like rust on his body. 'How crude, my God!'

Cold water with brandy in it revived him. He vividly pictured Von Koren's calm, haughty face; his eyes the day before, his shirt like a rug, his voice, his white hand; and heavy, passionate, hungry hatred rankled in his breast and clamoured for satisfaction. In his thoughts he felled Von Koren to the ground, and trampled him underfoot. He remembered to the minutest detail all that had happened, and wondered how he could have smiled ingratiatingly to that nonentity, and how he could care for the opinion of wretched petty people whom nobody knew, living in a contemptible little town which was not, it seemed, even on the map, and of which not one decent person in Petersburg had heard. If this wretched little town suddenly fell into ruins or caught fire, the telegram with the news would be read in Russia with no more interest than an advertisement for the sale of second-hand furniture. Whether he killed Von Koren next day or left him alive, it would be just the same, equally useless and uninteresting. Better to shoot him in the leg or arm, wound him, then laugh at him, and let him, like an insect with a broken leg lost in the grass – let him be lost with his obscure sufferings in the crowd of nonentities like himself.

Laevsky went to Sheshkovsky, told him all about it, and asked him to be his second; then they both sent to the superintendent of the postal telegraph department, and asked him, too, to be a second, and stayed to dinner with him. At dinner there was a great deal of joking and laughing. Laevsky made jests at his own expense, saying he hardly knew how to fire off a pistol, calling himself a royal sharpshooter and William Tell.

'We must give this gentleman a lesson . . .' he said.

After dinner they sat down to cards. Laevsky played, drank wine, and thought the duelling was stupid and senseless, as it did not decide the question but only complicated it, but that it was sometimes impossible to get by without it. In the present case, for instance, one could not, of course, bring an action against Von Koren. And this duel was good because it made it impossible for Laevsky to remain in the town afterwards. He got a little drunk and was carried away by the cards, and felt at ease.

But when the sun had set and it grew dark, he was possessed by a feeling of unease. It was not fear at the thought of death because, while he was dining and playing cards, he had for some reason a confident belief that the duel would end in nothing; it was dread at the thought of something unknown which was to happen next morning for the first time in his life, and dread of the coming night . . . He knew that the night would be long and sleepless, and that he would have to think not only of Von Koren and his hatred, but also of the mountains of lies which he had to get through, and which he had not strength or ability to dispense with. It was as though he had been taken suddenly ill; all at once he lost all interest in the cards and in people, grew restless, and began asking them to let him go home. He was eager to get to bed, to lie motionless, and to collect his thoughts for the night. Sheshkovsky and the postal superintendent saw him home and went on to Von Koren's to arrange the duel.

Near his lodgings Laevsky met Achmianov. The young man was breathless and excited.

'I've been looking for you, Mr Laevsky,' he said. 'I beg you to come quickly . . .'

'Where?'

'Someone wants to see you, someone you don't know, about very important business; he earnestly begs you to come for a minute. He wants to speak to you of something . . . For him it's a question of life and death . . .'

In his excitement Achmianov spoke in a strong Armenian accent.

'Who is it?' asked Laevsky.

'He asked me not to tell you his name.'

'Tell him I'm busy; tomorrow, if he likes . . .'

'How can you?' Achmianov was aghast. 'He wants to tell you something very important for you . . . very important! If you don't come, something dreadful will happen.'

'Strange . . .' muttered Laevsky, unable to understand why Achmianov was so excited and what mysteries there could be in this dull, useless little town.

'Strange,' he repeated in hesitation. 'Let's go, anyway; I don't care.'

Achmianov walked rapidly on ahead and Laevsky followed him. They walked down a street, then turned into an alley.

'What a bore this is!' said Laevsky.

'Just a minute, just a minute . . . it's near.'

Near the old rampart they went down a narrow alley between two empty enclosures, then they came into a sort of large yard and went towards a small house.

'That's Miuridov's, isn't it?' asked Laevsky.

'Yes.'

'But why have we come by the back yards, I don't understand. We could have come by the street; it's quicker . . .'

'Never mind, never mind . . .'

It struck Laevsky as strange, too, that Achmianov led him to a back entrance, and motioned him as though bidding him to go quietly and hold his tongue.

'This way, this way . . .' said Achmianov, cautiously opening the door and going into the passage on tiptoe. 'Quietly, quietly, I beg you . . . they may hear.'

He listened, drew a deep breath and said in a whisper:

'Open that door, and go in . . . don't be afraid.'

Laevsky, puzzled, opened the door and went into a room with a low ceiling and curtained windows.

There was a candle on the table.

'Who do you want?' asked someone in the next room. 'Is it you, Miuridov?'

Laevsky turned into that room and saw Kirilin, and beside him Nadezhda.

He didn't hear what was said to him; he staggered back, and did not know how he found himself in the street. His hatred for Von Koren and his unease – all had vanished from his soul. As he went home he waved his right arm awkwardly and looked carefully at the ground under his feet, trying to step where it was smooth. At home in his study he walked backwards and forwards, rubbing his hands, and awkwardly shrugging his shoulders and neck, as though his jacket and shirt were too tight; then he lit a candle and sat at the table . . .

XVI

'The "humanities" of which you speak will only satisfy human thought when, as they advance, they meet the exact sciences and progress side by side with them. Whether they will meet under a microscope, or in the monologues of a new Hamlet, or in a new region, I do not know, but I expect the earth will be covered with a crust of ice before it comes to pass. Of all humane knowledge the most durable and living is, of course, the teaching of Christ; but look how differently even that is interpreted! Some teach that we must love all our neighbours but make an exception for soldiers, criminals, and lunatics. They allow the first to be killed in war, the second to be isolated or executed, and the third they forbid to marry. Other interpreters teach that we must love all our neighbours without exception, with no plusses or minuses. According to their teaching, if a consumptive or murderer or an epileptic asks your daughter in marriage, you must let him have her. If cretins go to war against the physically and mentally healthy, don't defend yourselves. This advocacy of love for love's sake, like art for art's sake, if it came into force, would bring mankind in the long run to complete extinction, and so would become the biggest crime that has ever been committed upon earth. There are very many interpretations, and since there are many of them, serious thought is not satisfied by any one of them, and hastens to add its own individual interpretation to the mass. For that reason you should never put a question on a philosophical or so-called Christian basis; by so doing you are only further from solving the question.'

The deacon heard the zoologist out attentively, thought a little, and asked:

'Have the philosophers invented the moral law which is innate in every man, or did God create it together with the body?'

'I don't know. But that law is so universal among all peoples and ages that I fancy we ought to recognise it as organically connected with man. It is not invented, but exists and will exist. I don't tell you that one day it will be seen under the microscope, but its organic connection is shown, indeed, by evidence: serious pathological conditions of the brain and all so-called mental diseases, to the best of my belief, show themselves first of all in the perversion of the moral law.'

'Good. So then, just as our stomach bids us eat, our moral sense bids us love our neighbours. Is that it? But our natural man through self-love opposes the voice of conscience and reason, and this gives rise to many questions to rack your brains with. To whom ought we to turn to solve these questions if you forbid us to put them on a philosophical basis.'

'Turn to what little exact science we have. Trust in data and the logic of facts. True, it is but little, but, on the other hand, it is less fluid and shifting than philosophy. The moral law, let us suppose, demands that you love your neighbour. Well? Love ought to show itself in the removal of everything which in one way or another is injurious to men and threatens them with danger in the present or in the future. Our knowledge and the evidence tells us that the morally and physically abnormal are a menace to humanity. If so you must struggle against the abnormal; if you are not able to raise them to the normal standard, you must have strength and ability to render them harmless – that is, to destroy them.'

'So love consists in the strong overcoming the weak.'

'Undoubtedly.'

'But you know the strong crucified our Lord Jesus Christ,' said the deacon hotly.

'The fact is that those who crucified Him were not the strong but the weak. Human culture weakens and strives to nullify the struggle for existence and natural selection; hence the rapid advancement of the weak and their predominance over the strong. Imagine that you succeeded in instilling into bees humanitarian ideas in their crude and elementary form. What would come of it? The drones who ought to be killed would remain alive, would devour the honey, would corrupt and stifle the worker bees, resulting in the predominance of the weak over the strong, and the degeneration of the latter. The same process is taking place now with humanity; the weak are oppressing the strong. Among savages untouched by civilisation the strongest, cleverest, and most moral takes the lead; he is the chief and the master. But we civilised men have crucified Christ, and we go on crucifying Him, so there is something lacking in us . . . And that something one ought to restore in ourselves, or there will be no end to these mistakes.'

'But what criterion have you to distinguish the strong from the weak?'

'Knowledge and evidence. The tubercular and the scrofulous are recognised by their diseases, and the insane and the immoral by their actions.'

'But mistakes may be made!'

'Yes, but it's no use to be afraid of getting your feet wet when you are threatened with the deluge!'

'That's philosophy,' laughed the deacon.

'Not a bit of it. You are so corrupted by your seminary philosophy that you want to see nothing but fog in everything. The abstract studies with which your youthful head is stuffed are called abstract because they abstract your minds from what is obvious. Look the devil straight in the eye, and if he's the devil, tell him he's the devil, and don't go calling to Kant or Hegel for explanations.'

The zoologist paused and went on:

'Twice two's four, and a stone's a stone. Here tomorrow we have a duel. You and I will say it's stupid and absurd, that the duel is outmoded, that there is no real difference between an aristocratic duel and a drunken brawl in a tavern, and yet we shall not stop, we shall go there and fight. So there is some force stronger than our reasoning. We shout that war is plunder, robbery, atrocity, fratricide; we cannot look upon blood without fainting; but the French or the Germans have only to insult us for us to feel at once an exaltation of spirit; in the most genuine way we shout "Hurrah!" and rush at the foe. You will invoke the blessing of God on our weapons, and our valour will arouse universal and general enthusiasm. Again it follows that there is no force, if not higher, at any rate stronger, than us and our philosophy. We can no more stop it than that cloud which is moving upwards over the sea. Don't be hypocritical, don't make a long nose of it on the sly; and don't say, "Ah, old-fashioned, stupid! Ah, it's inconsistent with Scripture!", but look it straight in the face, recognise its rational lawfulness, and when, for instance, it wants to destroy a rotten, scrofulous, corrupt race, don't hinder it with your pills and misunderstood quotations from the gospel. Leskov has a story of a conscientious Danila who found a leper outside the town, and fed and warmed him in the name of love and of Christ. If that Danila had really loved humanity, he would have dragged the leper as far as possible from the town, and would have flung him in a pit, and would have gone to save the healthy. Christ, I hope, taught us a rational, intelligent, practical love.'

'What a fellow you are!' laughed the deacon. 'You don't believe in Christ. Why do you mention His name so often?'

'Yes, I do believe in Him. Only, of course, in my own way, not in yours. Oh, deacon, deacon!' laughed the zoologist; he put his arm round the deacon's waist, and said gaily: 'Well? Are you coming with us to the duel tomorrow?'

'My orders don't allow it, or else I should come.'

'What do you mean by "orders"?'

'I have been consecrated. I am in a state of grace.'

'Oh, deacon, deacon,' repeated Von Koren, laughing. 'I love talking to you.'

'You say you have faith,' said the deacon. 'What sort of faith is it? Why, I have an uncle, a priest, and he believes so firmly that when in a drought he goes out into the fields to pray for rain, he takes his umbrella and leather overcoat for fear of getting soaked on his way home. That's faith! When he speaks of Christ, his face is full of radiance, and all the peasants, men and women, weep floods of tears. He would stop that cloud and put all those forces you talk about to flight. Yes . . . Faith moves mountains.'

The deacon laughed and slapped the zoologist on the shoulder.

'Yes . . .' he went on; 'here you are teaching all the time, fathoming the depths of the ocean, dividing the weak and the strong, writing books and challenging people to duels – and everything remains as it is; but, behold! some feeble old man will mutter just one word with a holy spirit, or a new Mohammed, with a sword, will gallop from Arabia, and everything will be upside down, and in Europe not one stone will be left standing upon another.'

'Well, deacon, that's all fantasy.'

'Faith without works is dead, but works without faith are worse still – mere waste of time and nothing more.'

The doctor came into sight on the sea-front. He saw the deacon and the zoologist, and went up to them.

'I believe everything is ready,' he said, breathing hard. 'Govorovsky and Boiko will be the seconds. They will start at five o'clock in the morning. How it has clouded over,' he said, looking at the sky. 'One can see nothing; there will be rain directly.'

'I hope you are coming with us?' said the zoologist.

'No, God preserve me; I've been through enough as it is. Ustimovich is going instead of me. I've spoken to him already.'

Far over the sea came a flash of lightning, followed by a hollow roll of thunder.

'How stifling it is before a storm!' said Von Koren. 'I bet you've been to Laevsky already and have been weeping on his chest.'

'Why would I go to him?' answered the doctor in confusion. 'Whatever next?'

Before sunset he had walked several times along the boulevard and the street in the hope of meeting Laevsky. He was ashamed of his hastiness and the sudden outburst of friendliness which had followed it. He wanted to apologise to Laevsky in a joking tone, to give him a good talking to, to soothe him and to tell him that the duel was a relic of medieval barbarism, but that Providence itself had brought them to the duel as a means of reconciliation; that the next day, both being splendid and highly intellectual people, they would, after exchanging shots, appreciate each other's noble qualities and would become friends. But he had not met Laevsky.

'What should I go and see him for?' repeated Samoilenko. 'I did not insult him; he insulted me. Tell me, please, why he attacked me. What harm had I done him? I go into the drawing-room, and, all of a sudden, without the least provocation: "Spy!" There's a nice thing! Tell me, how did it begin? What did you say to him?'

'I told him his position was hopeless. And I was right. It is only honest men or scoundrels who can find an escape from any position, but one who wants to be at the same time an honest man and a scoundrel – it is a hopeless position. But it's eleven o'clock, gentlemen, and we have to be up early tomorrow.'

There was a sudden gust of wind; it blew up the dust on the sea-front, whirled it round in eddies, with a howl that drowned the roar of the sea.

'A squall,' said the deacon. 'We must go in, our eyes are getting full of dust.'

As they went, Samoilenko sighed and, holding his hat, said: 'I don't suppose I shall sleep tonight.'

'Don't worry,' laughed the zoologist. 'You can set your mind at rest; the duel will end in nothing. Laevsky will magnanimously fire into the air – he can do nothing else; and I dare say I shall not fire at all. To be arrested and waste time on Laevsky's account – the game's not worth the candle. By the way, what is the penalty for duelling?'

'Arrest, and if your opponent dies a maximum of three years' imprisonment.'

'In the Petropavlovsk prison?'

'No, in a military prison, I believe.'

'Even so, this fine gentleman ought to have a lesson!'

Behind them on the sea, there was a flash of lightning, which for an instant lit up the roofs of the houses and the mountains. The friends parted near the boulevard. When the doctor had disappeared in the darkness and his steps had died away, Von Koren shouted to him:

'I only hope the weather won't stop us tomorrow!'

'Who knows? Please God it may!'

'Good night!'

'What about the night? What did you say?'

In the roar of the wind and the sea and the crashes of thunder, it was difficult to hear.

'It's nothing,' shouted the zoologist, and hurried home.

XVII

Upon my mind, weighed down with woe,
Crowd thoughts, a heavy multitude:
In silence memory unfolds
Her long, long scroll before my eyes.
Loathing and shuddering I curse
And bitterly lament in vain,
And bitter though the tears I weep
I do not wash those lines away.

Pushkin

Whether they killed him next morning, or mocked him – that is, spared him his life – he was ruined, anyway. Whether this disgraced woman killed herself in her shame and despair, or dragged on her pitiful existence, she was ruined anyway . . .

So thought Laevsky as he sat at the table late in the evening, still rubbing his hands. The windows suddenly blew open with a bang; a violent gust of wind burst into the room, and the papers fluttered from the table. Laevsky closed the windows and bent down to pick up the papers. He was aware of something new in his body, a sort of awkwardness he had not felt before, and his movements were strange to him. He moved timidly, jerking with his elbows and shrugging his shoulders; and when he sat down to the table again, he began again rubbing his hands. His body had lost its suppleness.

On the eve of death one ought to write to one's nearest relation. Laevsky recalled this. He took a pen and wrote with a tremulous hand:

'Mama!'

He wanted to write to beg his mother, for the sake of merciful God in whom she believed, to give shelter and bring a little warmth and kindness into the life of the unhappy woman who, by his doing, had been disgraced and was in solitude, poverty, and weakness, to forgive and forget everything, everything, everything, and by her sacrifice atone to some extent for her son's terrible sin. But he remembered his mother, a stout, heavily built old woman in a lace cap, going into the garden in the morning, followed by her companion with the lap-dog; her shouting in a peremptory way at the gardener and the servants, and her proud and haughty face – he remembered all this and crossed out the word he had written.

There was a vivid flash of lightning at all three windows, and it was followed by a prolonged, deafening roll of thunder, beginning with a hollow rumble and ending with a crash so violent that all the window-panes rattled. Laevsky got up, went to the window, and pressed his forehead against the pane. There was a fierce, magnificent storm. On the horizon lightning flashes were flung in white streams from the storm clouds into the sea, lighting up the high, dark waves over the far-away expanse. And to right and to left, and, no doubt, over the house too, the lightning flashed.

'The storm!' whispered Laevsky; he had a longing to pray to someone or to something, if only to the lightning or the storm clouds. 'Dear storm!'

He remembered as a boy running bare-headed into the garden when there was a storm, and two fair-haired girls with blue eyes chasing him, and them getting soaked with the rain; they laughed with delight, but when there was a peal of thunder, the girls used to nestle up to the boy confidingly, while he crossed himself and made haste to repeat: 'Holy, holy, holy . . .' Oh, where had you vanished to! In what sea did you drown, those dawning days of pure, fair life? He had no fear of the storm, no love of nature now; he had no God. All the confiding girls he had ever known had by now been ruined by him and his ilk. All his life he had not planted a single tree, nor grown a blade of grass; and living among the living, he had not saved one fly; he had done nothing but destroy and ruin, and lie, lie . . .

'What in my past was not vice?' he asked himself, trying to clutch at some bright memory as a man falling down a precipice clutches at the bushes.

School? The university? But that was a sham. He had neglected his work and forgotten what he had learnt. The service of his country? That, too, was a sham, for he did nothing in the service, took a salary for doing nothing, and it was an abominable swindling of the state for which one was not prosecuted.

He had no use for the truth, and had not sought it; spellbound by vice and lying, his conscience had slept or been silent. Like a stranger, like an alien from another planet, he had taken no part in the common life of men, had been indifferent to their sufferings, their ideas, their religions, their sciences, their strivings, and their struggles. He had not said one good word, not written one line that was not useless and vulgar; he had not done his fellows one kopeck's worth of service: he had eaten their bread, drunk their wine, abducted their wives, lived on their thoughts, and to justify his contemptible, parasitic life in their eyes and in his own, he had always tried to assume an air of being higher and better than they. Lies, lies, lies . . .

He vividly remembered what he had seen that evening at Miuridov's, and he was in an insufferable anguish of loathing and misery. Kirilin and Achmianov were loathsome, but they were only continuing what he had begun; they were his accomplices and his disciples. This young weak woman had trusted him more than a brother, and he had deprived her of her husband, of her friends and of her country, and had brought her here – to the heat, to fever, and to boredom; and from day to day she was bound to reflect, like a mirror, his idleness, his viciousness and falsity – and that was all she had had to fill her weak, listless, pitiable life. Then he had grown sick of her, had begun to hate her, but had not had the pluck to abandon her, and he had tried to entangle her more and more closely in a web of lies . . . These men had finished the job.

Laevsky sat at the table, then got up and went to the window; at one minute he put out the candle and then he lit it again. He cursed himself aloud, wept and wailed, and asked forgiveness; several times he ran to the table in despair, and wrote:

'Mama!'

Except his mother, he had no relations or near friends; but how could his mother help him? And where was she? He had an impulse to run to Nadezhda, to fall at her feet, to kiss her hands and feet, to beg her forgiveness; but she was his victim, and he was afraid of her as though she were dead.

'My life is ruined,' he repeated, rubbing his hands. 'Why am I still alive, my God! . . .'

He had cast out of heaven his dim star; it had fallen, and its track was lost in the darkness of night. It would never return to the sky again, because life was given only once and never came a second time. If he could have turned back the days and years of the past, he would have replaced the lies with truth, the idleness with work, the misery with happiness; he would have given back purity to those whom he had robbed of it. He would have found God and justice, but that was as impossible as to put back the fallen star into the sky, and because it was impossible he was in despair.

When the storm was over, he sat by the open window and thought calmly of what was before him. Von Koren would most likely kill him. The man's clear, cold theory of life justified the destruction of the rotten and the useless; if it changed at the crucial moment, it would be the hatred and the repugnance that Laevsky inspired in him that would save him. If he missed his aim or, in mockery of his hated opponent, only wounded him, or fired in the air, what could he do then? Where could he go?

'Go to Petersburg?' Laevsky asked himself. But that would mean beginning over again the old life which he cursed. And the man who seeks salvation in change of place like a migrating bird would find nothing anywhere, for all the world is alike to him. Seek salvation in men? In whom and how? Samoilenko's kindness and generosity could no more save him than the deacon's laughter or Von Koren's hatred. He must look for salvation in himself alone, and if it was not to be found, why waste time? He must kill himself, that was all . . .

He heard the sound of a carriage. It was getting light. The carriage passed by, turned, and crunching on the wet sand, stopped near the house. There were two men in the carriage.

'Wait a minute; I'm just coming,' Laevsky said to them out of the window. 'I'm not asleep. Is it already time?'

'Yes, it's four o'clock. By the time we get there . . .'

Laevsky put on his overcoat and cap, put some cigarettes in his pocket, and stood still hesitating. He felt as though there was something else he must do. In the streets the seconds talked in low voices and the horses snorted, and this sound in the damp, early morning, when everybody was asleep and light was hardly dawning in the sky, filled Laevsky's soul with a disconsolate feeling which was like a presentiment of evil. He stood for a little, hesitating, and went into the bedroom.

Nadezhda was lying stretched out on the bed, wrapped from head to foot in a rug. She did not stir, and her whole appearance, especially her head, suggested an Egyptian mummy. Looking at her in silence, Laevsky mentally asked her forgiveness, and thought that if the heavens were not empty and there really were a God, then He would save her; if there were no God, then she had better perish – there was nothing for her to live for.

All at once she jumped up, and sat up in bed. Lifting her pale face and looking with horror at Laevsky, she asked:

'Is it you? Is the storm over?'

'Yes.'

She remembered; put both her hands to her head and shuddered all over.

'How miserable I am!' she said. 'If only you knew how miserable I am! I expected,' she went on, half closing her eyes, 'you to kill me or turn me out of the house into the rain and storm, but you are holding back . . . holding back . . .'

Warmly and impulsively he put his arms round her and covered her knees and hands with kisses. Then when she muttered something and shuddered with the thought of the past, he stroked her hair, and looking into her face, realised that this unhappy, sinful woman was the one creature close, dear, to him, irreplaceable.

When he left the house and got into the carriage he wanted to return home alive.

XVIII

The deacon got up, dressed, took his thick gnarled stick and slipped quietly out of the house. It was dark, and for the first minute when he went into the street, he could not even see his white stick. There was not a single star in the sky, and it looked as though there would be rain again. There was a smell of wet sand and sea.

'Let's hope the Chechens* don't attack us,' thought the deacon, hearing the tap of the stick on the pavement, and noticing how loud and lonely the tapping sounded in the stillness of the night.

When he got out of town, he began to see both the road and his stick. Here and there in the black sky there were dark cloudy patches, and soon a star peeped out and timidly blinked its one eye. The deacon walked along the high rocky coast and did not see the sea; it was slumbering below, and its unseen waves broke languidly and heavily on the shore, as though sighing 'Oof!', and how slowly! One wave broke – the deacon had time to count eight steps; then another broke, and six steps; later a third. As before, nothing could be seen, and in the darkness one could hear the languid, drowsy drone of the sea. One could sense the infinitely far-away, inconceivable time when God moved above chaos.

The deacon felt awe. He hoped God would not punish him for keeping company with unbelievers, and even going to look at their duels. The duel would be nonsensical, bloodless, absurd, but however that might be, it was a heathen spectacle, and it was altogether unseemly for a cleric to be present at it. He stopped and wondered – should he go back? But an intense, restless curiosity triumphed over his doubts, and he went on.

'Though they are unbelievers, they are good people, and will be saved,' he reassured himself. 'They are sure to be saved,' he said aloud, lighting a cigarette.

By what standard must one measure men's qualities, to judge rightly of them? The deacon remembered his enemy, the theological college inspector, who believed in God, lived in chastity, and did not fight duels; but he used to feed the deacon on bread with sand in it, and on one occasion almost pulled off the deacon's ear. If human life was so poorly constructed that everyone respected this cruel and dishonest inspector who stole the government flour, and his health and salvation were prayed for in the schools, was it just to shun such men as Von Koren and Laevsky, simply because they were un-believers? The deacon was weighing this question, but he recalled how absurd Samoilenko had looked yesterday, and that broke the thread of his ideas. What fun they would have next day! The deacon imagined how he would sit under a bush and look on, and when Von Koren began boasting next day at dinner, he, the deacon, would begin laughing and telling him all the details of the duel.

'How do you know all about it?' the zoologist would ask.

'Well, there you are! I stayed at home, but I know all about it.'

It would be nice to write a comic description of the duel. His father-in-law would read it and laugh. A good story, spoken or written, was more than meat and drink to his father-in-law.

The valley of the Yellow River opened before him. The stream was broader and fiercer for the rain, and instead of murmuring as before, it was raging. It began to get light. The grey, dingy morning, and the clouds racing towards the west to overtake the storm clouds, the mountains girt with mist, and the wet trees, all struck the deacon as ugly and sinister. He washed at the brook, repeated his morning prayer, and felt a longing for tea and hot rolls, with sour cream, which was served every morning at his father-in-law's. He remembered his wife and the 'Days past Recall', which she played on the piano. What sort of woman was she? His wife had been introduced, betrothed, and married to him all in one week: he had lived with her less than a month when he was ordered here, so that he had not had time to find out what she was like. All the same, he rather missed her.

'I must write her a nice letter . . .' he thought.

The flag on the inn hung limp, soaked by the rain, and the inn with its wet roof seemed darker and squatter than it used to be. Near the door was standing a cart; Kerbalai, with two mountaineers and a young Tatar woman in trousers – no doubt Kerbalai's wife or daughter – were bringing sacks of something out of the inn, and putting them on maize straw in the cart. Near the cart stood a pair of asses hanging their heads. When they had loaded all the sacks, the Abkhaz and the Tatar woman began covering them over with straw, while Kerbalai began hurriedly harnessing the asses.

'Smuggling, perhaps,' thought the deacon.

Here was the fallen tree with the dried pine-needles, here was the blackened patch from the fire. He remembered the picnic and all its incidents, the fire, the singing of the Abkhaz, his sweet dreams of becoming a bishop, and of the church procession . . . The Black River had grown blacker and broader with the rain. The deacon walked cautiously over the rickety bridge, which by now was reached by the topmost crests of the dirty water, and went up to the ladder to the drying-shed.

'A splendid head,' he thought, stretching himself on the straw, and thinking of Von Koren. 'A fine head – God grant him health; only there is cruelty in him . . .'

Why did he hate Laevsky and Laevsky hate him? Why were they going to fight a duel? If from their childhood they had known poverty as the deacon had; if they had been brought up among ignorant, hard-hearted, gasping, coarse and ill-mannered people who grudged you a crust of bread, who spat on the floor and hiccoughed at dinner and at prayers; if they had not been spoilt from childhood by the pleasant surroundings and the select circle of friends they lived in – how they would have rushed at each other, how readily they would have overlooked each other's shortcomings and would have prized each other's strong points! Why, how few even outwardly decent people there were in the world! It was true that Laevsky was flighty, dissipated, odd, but he did not steal, did not spit loudly on the floor; he did not abuse his wife and say, 'You eat till you burst, but you won't work'; he would not beat a child with reins, or give his servants stinking salted meat to eat – surely this was reason enough to be indulgent to him? Besides, he was the chief sufferer from his failings, like a sick man from his sores. Instead of being led by boredom and some sort of misunderstanding to look for degeneracy, extinction, heredity, and other such incomprehensible things in each other, would they not do better to stoop a little lower and turn their hatred and anger where whole streets resounded with moans from coarse ignorance, greed, scolding, filth, swearing, the shrieks of women . . .

The sound of the carriage interrupted the deacon's thoughts. He glanced out of the door and saw a carriage and in it three persons: Laevsky, Sheshkovsky, and the superintendent of the post office.

'Stop!' said Sheshkovsky.

All three got out of the carriage and looked at one another.

'They are not here yet,' said Sheshkovsky, shaking the mud off. 'Well? Till the show begins, let us go and find a suitable spot; there's not room to turn round here.'

They went further up the river and soon vanished from sight. The Tatar driver sat in the carriage with his head resting on his shoulder and fell asleep. After waiting ten minutes the deacon came out of the drying-shed, and taking off his black hat that he might not be noticed, he began threading his way among the bushes and the strips of maize along the bank, crouching and looking about him. The grass and maize were wet, and big drops fell on his head from the trees and bushes. 'Disgraceful!' he muttered, picking up his wet and muddy hems. 'If I'd known, I wouldn't have come.'

Soon he heard voices and caught sight of them. Laevsky was walking rapidly to and fro in the small glade with bowed back and hands thrust in his sleeves; his seconds were standing at the water's edge, rolling cigarettes.

'Strange,' thought the deacon, not recognising Laevsky's walk; 'like an old man . . .'

'How impolite of them!' said the superintendent of the post office, looking at his watch. 'It may be learned manners to be late, but to my thinking it's despicable.'

Sheshkovsky, a stout man with a black beard, listened and said:

'They're coming!'

XIX

'It's the first time in my life I've seen it! How glorious!' said Von Koren, pointing to the glade and stretching his hands to the east. 'Look: green rays!'

In the east behind the mountains rose two green streaks of light, and it really was beautiful. The sun was rising.

'Good morning!' the zoologist went on, nodding to Laevsky's seconds. 'I'm not late, am I?'

He was followed by his seconds, Boiko and Govorovsky, two very young officers of the same height, wearing white tunics, and Ustimovich, the thin, unsociable doctor; in one hand he had something in a bundle, and in the other hand, as usual, a cane which he held behind him. Laying the bundle on the ground and greeting no one, he put the other hand, too, behind his back and began pacing up and down the glade.

Laevsky felt the exhaustion and awkwardness of a man who is soon perhaps to die, and is for that reason an object of general attention. He wanted to be killed as soon as possible or taken home. He saw the sunrise now for the first time in his life; the early morning, the green rays of light, the dampness, and the men in wet boots, seemed to him to have nothing to do with his life, to be superfluous and intimidating. All this had no connection with the night he had been through, with his thoughts and his feeling of guilt, and so he would have gladly gone away without waiting for the duel.

Von Koren was noticeably excited and tried to conceal it, pretending that he was more interested in the green light than anything. The seconds were embarrassed, and looked at one another as though wondering why they were here and what they were to do.

'I imagine, gentlemen, there is no need for us to go further,' said Sheshkovsky. 'This place will do.'

'Yes, of course,' Von Koren agreed.

A silence followed. Ustimovich, pacing to and fro, suddenly turned sharply to Laevsky and said in a low voice, breathing into his face:

'They have very likely not told you my terms yet. Each side is to pay me fifteen roubles, and in the case of death of one party, the survivor is to pay thirty.'

Laevsky was already acquainted with the man, but now for the first time he had a distinct view of his lacklustre eyes, his stiff moustaches, and wasted, consumptive neck; he was a money grubber, not a doctor; his breath had an unpleasant smell of beef.

'What people there are in the world!' thought Laevsky, and answered: 'Good.'

The doctor nodded and began pacing to and fro again, and it was evident he did not need the money at all, but simply asked for it from hatred. Everyone felt it was time to begin, or to end what had been begun, but instead of beginning or ending, they stood about, moved to and fro and smoked. The young officers, who were present at a duel for the first time in their lives, and even now hardly believed in this civilian and to their thinking, unnecessary duel, looked critically at their tunics and stroked their sleeves. Sheshkovsky went up to them and said softly: 'Gentlemen, we must use every effort to prevent this duel; they ought to be reconciled.'

He flushed crimson and added:

'Kirilin was at my rooms last night complaining that Laevsky had found him with Nadezhda, and all that sort of thing.'

'Yes, we know that too,' said Boiko.

'Well, you see, then . . . Laevsky's hands are trembling and all that sort of thing . . . He can scarcely hold a pistol now. To fight with him is as inhumane as to fight a man who is drunk or who has typhoid. If a reconciliation cannot be arranged, we ought to put off the duel, gentlemen, or something . . . It's such a sickening business, I can't bear to see it.'

'Talk to Von Koren.'

'I don't know the rules of duelling, to hell with them, and I don't want to either; perhaps he'll imagine Laevsky's lost his nerve and has sent me to him, but he can think what he likes – I'll speak to him.'

Sheshkovsky hesitatingly walked up to Von Koren with a slight limp, as though his leg had gone to sleep; and as he went towards him, clearing his throat, his whole figure was a picture of indolence.

'There's something I must say to you, sir,' he began, carefully scrutinising the flowers on the zoologist's shirt. 'It's confidential . . . I don't know the rules of duelling, to hell with them, and I don't want to, and I look on the matter not as a second and that sort of thing, but as a man, and that's all about it.'

'Yes. Well?'

'When seconds suggest reconciliation they are usually not listened to; it is looked upon as a formality. *Amour propre* and all that. But I humbly beg you to look carefully at Mr Laevsky. He's not in a normal state, so to speak, today – not in his right mind, and a pitiable object. He has had a misfortune. I can't endure gossip,' Sheshkovsky flushed crimson and looked round. 'But in view of the duel, I think I must inform you, Laevsky found his madam last night at Miuridov's with . . . a certain gentleman.'

'How disgusting!' muttered the zoologist; he turned pale, frowned, and spat loudly. 'Ugh!'

His lower lip quivered, he walked away from Sheshkovsky, unwilling to hear more, and as though he had accidentally tasted something bitter, spat loudly again, and for the first time that morning looked with hatred at Laevsky. His excitement and awkwardness passed off; he tossed his head and said aloud:

'Gentlemen, what are we waiting for, I should like to know? Why don't we begin?'

Sheshkovsky glanced at the officers and shrugged his shoulders.

'Gentlemen,' he said aloud, addressing no one in particular. 'Gentlemen, we propose that you should be reconciled.'

'Let us make haste and get the formalities over,' said Von Koren. 'Reconciliation has been discussed already. What is the next formality? Make haste, gentlemen, time won't wait for us.'

'But we insist on reconciliation all the same,' said Sheshkovsky, in a guilty voice, as a man compelled to interfere in another man's business; he flushed, laid his hand on his heart, and went on: 'Gentlemen, we see no grounds for linking the offence with a duel. There's nothing in common between duelling and offences against one another which we sometimes commit through human weakness. You are university men and men of culture, and no doubt you see in the duel nothing but a foolish and out-of-date formality, and all that sort of thing. That's how we look at it ourselves, or we shouldn't have come, for we cannot allow that in our presence men should fire at one another, and all that.' Sheshkovsky wiped the sweat off his face and went on: 'Make an end of your misunderstanding, gentlemen; shake hands, and let us go home and drink to peace. Upon my honour, gentlemen!'

Von Koren did not speak. Laevsky, seeing that they were looking at him, said:

'I have nothing against Mr Von Koren; if he considers I'm to blame, I'm ready to apologise to him.'

Von Koren was offended.

'It is evident, gentlemen,' he said, 'you want Mr Laevsky to return home a magnanimous and chivalrous figure, but I cannot give you or him that satisfaction. And there was no need to get up early and drive five miles out of town simply to drink to peace, to have breakfast, and to explain to me that the duel is an out-of-date formality. A duel is a duel, and there is no need to make it more false and stupid than it is in reality. I want to fight!'

A silence followed. Boiko took a pair of pistols out of a box; one was given to Von Koren and one to Laevsky, and then there followed a difficulty which afforded a brief amusement to the zoologist and the seconds. It appeared that none of the people present had ever in his life been at a duel, and no one knew precisely how they ought to stand, and what the seconds ought to say and do. But then Boiko remembered and began, with a smile, to explain.

'Gentlemen, who remembers the description in Lermontov?' asked Von Koren, laughing. 'In Turgenev, too, Bazarov had a duel with someone . . .'

'There's no need to remember,' said Ustimovich impatiently. 'Measure the distance, that's all.'

And he took three steps as though to show how to measure it. Boiko counted out the steps while his companion drew his sabre and scratched the earth at the extreme points to mark the barrier. In complete silence the opponents took their places.

'Moles,' the deacon thought, sitting in the bushes.

Sheshkovsky said something, Boiko explained something again, but Laevsky did not hear – or rather heard, but did not understand. He cocked his pistol when the time came to do so, and raised the cold, heavy weapon with the barrel upwards. He forgot to unbutton his overcoat, and it felt very tight over his shoulder and under his arm, and his arm rose as awkwardly as though the sleeve had been cut out of tin. He remembered the hatred he had felt the night before for the swarthy brow and curly hair, and felt that even yesterday at the moment of intense hatred and anger he could not have shot a man. Fearing that the bullet might somehow hit Von Koren by accident, he raised his pistol higher and higher, and felt that this too obvious magnanimity was tactless and anything but magnanimous, but he did not know what else to do and could do nothing else. Looking at the pale, ironically smiling face of Von Koren, who evidently had been convinced from the beginning that his opponent would fire in the air, Laevsky thought that, thank God, everything would be over directly, and all that he had to do was to press the trigger rather hard . . .

He felt a violent shock on the shoulder; there was a sound of a shot and an answering echo in the mountains: ping-ting!

Von Koren cocked his pistol and looked at Ustimovich, who was pacing as before with his hands behind his back, taking no notice of anyone.

'Doctor,' said the zoologist, 'be so good as not to move to and fro like a pendulum. You make me dizzy.'

The doctor stood still. Von Koren began to take aim at Laevsky.

'It's all over!' thought Laevsky.

The barrel of the pistol aimed straight at his face, the expression of hatred and contempt in Von Koren's attitude and whole figure, and the murder just about to be committed by a decent man in broad daylight, in the presence of decent men, and the stillness and the

unknown force that compelled Laevsky to stand still and not to run –
how mysterious it all was, how incomprehensible and terrible!

The moment while Von Koren was taking aim seemed to Laevsky
longer than a night: he glanced imploringly at the seconds; they were
pale and did not stir.

'Make haste and fire,' thought Laevsky, and felt that his pale,
quivering, and pitiful face must arouse even greater hatred in Von
Koren.

'I'm going to kill him,' thought Von Koren, aiming at his forehead,
with his finger already on the catch. 'Yes, of course I'll kill him . . .'

'He'll kill him!' A despairing shout was suddenly heard somewhere
very close at hand.

A shot rang out at once. Seeing that Laevsky remained standing
where he was and did not fall, they all looked in the direction from
which the shout had come, and saw the deacon. With pale face and
wet hair sticking to his forehead and cheeks, soaked and muddy, he
was standing in the maize on the further bank, smiling rather oddly
and waving his wet hat. Sheshkovsky laughed with joy, burst into
tears, and stood back . . .

XX

A little while afterwards Von Koren and the deacon met near the little
bridge. The deacon was worked up; he breathed hard, and avoided
looking people in the face. He felt ashamed both of his terror and his
muddy, wet garments.

'I thought you meant to kill him . . .' he muttered. 'How contrary
to human nature it is! How utterly unnatural it is!'

'But how did you come here?' asked the zoologist.

'Don't ask,' said the deacon, waving his hand. 'The evil one
tempted me, saying: "Go, go . . ." So I went and almost died of fright
in the maize. But now, thank God, thank God . . . I am pleased with
all of you,' muttered the deacon. 'Old Granddad Tarantula will be
glad . . . It's funny, it's too funny! Only I beg of you most earnestly
don't tell anybody I was there, or I may get into hot water with the
authorities. They will say: "The deacon was a second." '

'Gentlemen,' said Von Koren, 'the deacon asks you not to tell
anyone you've seen him here. He might get into trouble.'

'How contrary to human nature it is!' sighed the deacon. 'Excuse
my saying so, but your face was so dreadful that I thought you were
going to kill him.'

'I was very much tempted to put an end to that scoundrel,' said Von
Koren, 'but you shouted close by, and I missed my aim. The whole

procedure is revolting to anyone who is not used to it, and it has exhausted me, deacon. I feel awfully tired. Come along . . .'

'No, you must let me walk back. I must get dry, for I am wet and cold.'

'Well, as you like,' said the zoologist, in a weary tone, feeling dispirited, and, getting into the carriage, he closed his eyes. 'As you like . . .'

While they were moving about the carriages and taking their seats, Kerbalai stood in the road, and, laying his hands on his stomach, he bowed low, showing his teeth; he imagined that the gentry had come to enjoy the beauties of nature and drink tea, and could not understand why they were getting into the carriages. The party set off in complete silence and only the deacon was left by the inn.

'Come in, drink tea,' he said to Kerbalai. 'Me want eat.'

Kerbalai spoke good Russian, but the deacon imagined that the Tatar would understand him better if he talked to him in broken Russian. 'Cook omelette, give cheese . . .'

'Come, come, Father,' said Kerbalai, bowing. 'I'll give you everything . . . I've cheese and wine . . . Eat what you like.'

'What is "God" in Tatar?' asked the deacon, going into the inn.

'Your God and my God are the same,' said Kerbalai, not understanding him. 'God is the same for all men, only men are different. Some are Russian, some are Turks, some are English – there are many sorts of men, but God is one.'

'Very good. If all men worship the same God, why do you Mohammedans look upon Christians as your everlasting enemies?'

'Why are you so angry?' said Kerbalai, laying both hands on his stomach. 'You are a priest; I am a Moslem: you say, "I want to eat" – I give it you . . . Only the rich man distinguishes your God from my God; for the poor man it is all the same. If you please, it is ready.'

While this theological conversation was taking place at the inn, Laevsky was driving home thinking how dreadful it had been driving there at daybreak, when the roads, the rocks, and the mountains were wet and dark, and the uncertain future seemed like a terrible abyss, of which one could not see the bottom; while now the raindrops hanging on the grass and on the stones were sparkling in the sun like diamonds, nature was smiling joyfully, and the terrible future was left behind. He looked at Sheshkovsky's sullen, tear-stained face, and at the two carriages ahead of them in which Von Koren, his seconds, and the doctor were sitting, and it seemed to him as though they were all coming back from a graveyard in which a wearisome, insufferable man who was a burden to others had just been buried.

'Everything is over,' he thought of his past, cautiously stroking the neck with his fingers.

On the right side of his neck was a small swelling, of the length and breadth of his little finger, and he felt a pain, as though someone had passed a hot iron over his neck. The bullet had grazed it.

Afterwards, when he got home, a strange, long, sweet day began for him, misty as forgetfulness. Like a man released from prison or from hospital, he stared at the long-familiar objects and wondered that the tables, the windows, the chairs, the light, and the sea stirred in him a keen, childish delight such as he had not known for long, long years. Nadezhda, pale and haggard, could not understand his gentle voice and strange movements; she made haste to tell him everything that had happened to her . . . It seemed to her that very likely he couldn't hear properly and did not understand her, and that if he did know everything he would curse her and kill her, but he listened to her, stroked her face and hair, looked into her eyes and said:

'I have nobody but you . . .'

Then they sat a long while in the garden, huddled close together, saying nothing, or dreaming aloud of their happy life in the future, in brief, broken sentences, while it seemed to him that he had never spoken at such length or so eloquently.

XXI

More than three months had passed.

The day came that Von Koren had fixed for his departure. A cold, heavy rain had been falling from early morning, a north-east wind was blowing, and the waves were high on the sea. It was said to be unlikely that the steamer would be able to come into the harbour in such weather. By the timetable it should have arrived at ten o'clock in the morning, but Von Koren, who had gone on to the sea-front at midday and again after dinner, could see nothing through the field-glass but grey waves and rain covering the horizon.

Towards the end of the day the rain ceased and the wind began to drop perceptibly. Von Koren had already made up his mind that he would not be able to get off that day, and had settled down to play chess with Samoilenko; but after dark the orderly announced that there were lights on the sea and that a flare had been seen.

Von Koren made haste. He put his satchel over his shoulder, and kissed Samoilenko and the deacon. Though there was not the slightest necessity, he went through the rooms again, said good-bye to the orderly and the cook, and went out into the street, feeling that he had left something behind, either at the doctor's or his lodging. In the street he walked beside Samoilenko, behind them came the deacon with a box, and last of all the orderly with two portmanteaus. Only Samoilenko and the orderly could distinguish the dim lights on the sea. The others gazed into the darkness and saw nothing. The steamer had stopped a long way from the coast.

'Make haste, make haste,' Von Koren hurried them. 'I am afraid it will set off.'

As they passed the little house with three windows, into which Laevsky had moved soon after the duel, Von Koren could not resist peeping in at the window. Laevsky was sitting, writing, bent over the table, with his back to the window.

'I'm amazed!' said the zoologist softly. 'He really has pulled his socks up!'

'Yes, one may well wonder,' said Samoilenko. 'He sits from morning till night, he's always at work. He works to pay off his debts. And he lives, brother, worse than a beggar!'

Half a minute of silence followed. The zoologist, the doctor, and the deacon stood at the window and went on looking at Laevsky.

'So he didn't get away from here, poor fellow,' said Samoilenko. 'Do you remember how hard he tried?'

'Yes, he has pulled his socks up,' Von Koren repeated. 'His marriage, the way he works all day long for his daily bread, a new expression in his face, and even in his walk – it's all so extraordinary that I don't know what to call it.'

The zoologist took Samoilenko's sleeve and went on with emotion in his voice: 'You tell him and his wife that when I went away I was full of admiration for them and wished them all happiness . . . and I beg him, if he can, not to think badly of me. He knows me. He knows that if I could have foreseen this change, then I might have become his best friend.'

'Go in and say good-bye to him.'

'No, that wouldn't do.'

'Why? God knows, perhaps you'll never see him again.'

The zoologist reflected, and said:

'That's true.'

Samoilenko tapped softly with one finger at the window. Laevsky started and looked round.

'Vania, Von Koren wants to say good-bye to you,' said Samoilenko. 'He is just leaving.'

Laevsky got up from the table, and went into the passage to open the door. Samoilenko, the zoologist, and the deacon went into the house.

'I've only come for a minute,' began the zoologist, taking off his galoshes in the passage, and already wishing he had not given way to his feelings and come in, uninvited. 'It is as though I were forcing myself on him,' he thought, 'and that's stupid.'

'Forgive me for disturbing you,' he said as he went into the room with Laevsky, 'but I'm just going away, and I had an impulse to see you. God knows whether we shall ever meet again.'

'I am very glad to see you ... Please come in,' said Laevsky, and he awkwardly set chairs for his visitors as though he wanted to bar their way, and stood in the middle of the room, rubbing his hands.

'I should have done better to have left the witnesses in the street,' thought Von Koren, and he said firmly: 'Don't think badly of me, Laevsky. To forget the past is, of course, impossible – it's too painful, and I've not come here to apologise or declare that I was not to blame. I acted sincerely, and I have not changed my conviction since then ... It is true that I see, to my great delight, that I was mistaken in regard to you, but it's human to err, and, in fact, it's the natural human lot: if one is not mistaken in the main, one is mistaken in the details. Nobody knows the real truth.'

'No, no one knows the truth,' said Laevsky.

'Well, good-bye ... God give you all the best.'

Von Koren gave Laevsky his hand; the latter took it and bowed.

'Don't think badly of me,' said Von Koren. 'Give my regards to your wife, and say I am very sorry not to say good-bye to her.'

'She is at home.'

Laevsky went to the door of the next room, and said:

'Nadezhda, Mr Von Koren wants to say good-bye to you.'

Nadezhda came in; she stopped in the doorway and looked shyly at the visitors. There was a look of guilt and dismay on her face, and she held her hands like a schoolgirl receiving a scolding.

'I'm just leaving, Mrs Laevsky,' said Von Koren, 'and have come to say good-bye.'

She held out her hand uncertainly while Laevsky bowed.

'What pitiful figures they are, though!' thought Von Koren. 'The life they are living does not come easy to them.' 'I shall be in Moscow and Petersburg; can I send you anything?' he asked.

'Oh!' said Nadezhda, and she looked anxiously at her husband. 'I don't think there's anything ...'

'No, nothing ...' said Laevsky, rubbing his hands. 'Our greetings ...'

Von Koren did not know what he could or ought to say, though as he went in he had thought he would say a very great deal that would be warm and good and important. He shook hands with

Laevsky and his wife in silence, and left them with a depressed feeling.

'What people!' said the deacon in a low voice, as he walked behind them. 'My God, what people! Of a truth, the right hand of God has planted this vine! Lord! Lord! One man vanquishes thousands and another tens of thousands. Von Koren,' he said ecstatically, 'let me tell you that today you have conquered the greatest of man's enemies – pride.'

'That's enough, deacon! Fine conquerors we are! Conquerors ought to look like eagles, while he's a pitiful figure, timid, crushed; he bows like a nodding doll, and I, I am sad . . .'

They heard steps behind them. It was Laevsky, hurrying after them to see him off. The orderly was standing on the quay with the two portmanteaus, and at a little distance stood four boatmen.

'There is a wind, though . . . Brrr!' said Samoilenko. 'There must be a pretty stiff storm on the sea now! You are not going off at a nice time, Kolia.'

'I'm not afraid of seasickness.'

'That's not the point . . . I only hope these fools won't tip your boat over. You ought to have crossed in the agent's sloop. Where's the agent's sloop?' he shouted to the boatmen.

'It has gone, your Excellency.'

'And the Customs boat?'

'That's gone, too.'

'Why didn't you let us know?' said Samoilenko angrily. 'You dolts!'

'It's all the same, don't worry yourself . . .' said Von Koren. 'Well, good-bye. God keep you.'

Samoilenko embraced Von Koren and made the sign of the cross over him three times.

'Don't forget us, Kolia . . . Write . . . We shall look out for you next spring.'

'Good-bye, deacon,' said Von Koren, shaking hands with the deacon. 'Thank you for your company and for your pleasant conversation. Think about the expedition.'

'Oh Lord, yes! to the ends of the earth,' laughed the deacon. 'I've nothing against it.'

Von Koren recognised Laevsky in the darkness, and held out his hand without speaking. The boatmen were by now below, holding the boat, which was beating against the piles, though the breakwater screened it from the great swell. Von Koren went down the ladder, jumped into the boat, and sat at the helm.

'Write!' Samoilenko shouted to him. 'Take care of yourself.'

'No one knows the real truth,' thought Laevsky, turning up

the collar of his coat and thrusting his hands into his sleeves.

The boat turned briskly out of the harbour into the open sea. It vanished in the waves, but at once from a deep hollow glided up on to a high breaker, so that they could distinguish the men and even the oars. The boat moved three fathoms forward and was sucked two fathoms back.

'Write!' shouted Samoilenko; 'It's devilish weather for you to go in.'

'Yes, no one knows the real truth . . .' thought Laevsky looking with yearning at the dark, restless sea.

'It flings the boat back,' he thought; 'it takes two steps forward and one step back; but the boatmen are stubborn, they work the oars unceasingly, and are not afraid of the high waves. The boat goes on and on. Now she is out of sight, but in half an hour the boatmen will see the steamer lights distinctly, and within an hour they will be by the steamer ladder. So it is in life . . . In the search for the truth man takes two steps forward and one step back. Suffering, mistakes, and the dreariness of life thrust them back, but the thirst for truth and stubborn will drive them on and on. And who knows? Perhaps they will reach the real truth at last.'

'Good-by-y-ye,' shouted Samoilenko.

'There's no sight or sound of them,' said the deacon. 'Farewell!'

It began to spot with rain.

1891

Ward No. 6

I

In the hospital yard there stands a small lodge surrounded by a perfect forest of burdocks, nettles, and wild hemp. Its roof is rusty, the chimney is tumbling down, the steps at the front door are rotting away and overgrown with grass, and there are only traces left of the stucco. The front of the lodge faces the hospital; at the back it looks out into the open country, from which it is separated by the grey hospital fence with nails on it. These nails, with their points upwards, and the fence, and the lodge itself, have that peculiar, desolate, godforsaken look which is only found in our hospital and prison buildings.

If you are not afraid of being stung by the nettles, let's take the narrow footpath that leads to the lodge and look at what is going on inside. Opening the first door, we walk into the lobby. Here along the walls and by the stove every sort of hospital rubbish lies littered about. Mattresses, old tattered dressing-gowns, trousers, blue striped shirts, worn-out footwear no good for anything – all these remnants are piled up in heaps, mixed up and crumpled, mouldering and giving out a stifling smell.

The porter, Nikita, an old soldier wearing rusty good-conduct stripes, is always lying on the pile of junk with a pipe between his teeth. He has a grim, surly, battered-looking face, overhanging eyebrows which give him the expression of a sheep-dog of the steppes, and a red nose; he is short and looks thin and scraggy, but he has an imposing stance and his fists are very solid. He belongs to the class of simple-hearted, dependable, and dull-witted people, who like discipline better than anything in the world, and so are convinced that it is their duty to beat *them*. He showers blows on the face, on the chest, on the back, on whatever comes first, and is convinced that there would be no order in the place if he did not.

Next you come into a big, spacious room which fills up the whole lodge except for the lobby. Here the walls are painted a dirty blue, the ceiling is as sooty as in a hut without a chimney – it is evident that in the winter the stove smokes and the room is full of fumes. The windows are disfigured by iron gratings on the inside. The wooden floor is grey and full of splinters. There is a stench of sour cabbage, of smouldering wicks, of bugs, and of ammonia, and for the first time this stench gives you the impression of having walked into a menagerie . . .

There are bedsteads screwed to the floor. Men in blue hospital dressing-gowns, and wearing night-caps in the old style, are sitting and lying on them. These are the lunatics.

There are just five of them in all here. Only one is of the upper class, the rest are all ordinary townspeople. The one nearest the door – a tall, lean workman with shining red whiskers and tear-stained eyes – sits with his head propped on his hand, staring at the same point. Day and night he grieves, shaking his head, sighing and smiling bitterly. He rarely takes a part in conversation and usually makes no answer to questions; he eats and drinks mechanically when food is offered him. To judge by his agonising, throbbing cough, his thinness, and the flush on his cheeks, he is in the first stage of consumption.

Next to him is a little, alert, very lively old man, with a pointed beard and curly black hair like a negro's. By day he walks up and down the ward from window to window, or sits on his bed, cross-legged like a Turk, and, ceaselessly as a bullfinch whistles, softly sings and titters. He shows his childish gaiety and lively character at night also when he gets up to say his prayers – that is, to beat himself on the chest with his fists, and to scratch with his fingers at the door. This is the Jew Moiseika, an imbecile, who went mad twenty years ago when his hat workshop was burnt down.

And of all the inhabitants of Ward No. 6, only he is allowed to leave the lodge, and even the yard, to go into the street. He has enjoyed this privilege for years, probably because he is an old inhabitant of the hospital – a quiet, harmless imbecile, the buffoon of the town, where people are used to seeing him surrounded by boys and dogs. In his wretched gown, in his absurd night-cap, and in slippers, sometimes with bare legs and even without trousers, he walks about the streets, stopping at the gates and little shops, and begging for a kopeck. In one place they will give him some kvas, in another some bread, in another a kopeck, so that he generally goes back to the ward rich and well-fed. Everything that he brings back Nikita takes from him for his own benefit. The soldier does this roughly, angrily turning the Jew's pockets inside out, and calling God to witness that he will not let him go into the street again, and that a breach of the regulations is to him the worst thing in the world.

Moiseika likes to make himself useful. He gives his companions water, and covers them up when they are asleep; he promises each of them to bring him back a kopeck, and to make him a new hat; he feeds with a spoon his neighbour on the left, who is paralysed. He acts in this way, not from compassion nor from any considerations of a humane kind, but because he imitates and automatically submits to Gromov, his neighbour on the right.

Gromov, a man of thirty-three, who is a gentleman by birth, and has been a bailiff and provincial secretary, suffers from persecution mania. He either lies curled up in bed or walks from corner to corner as though for exercise; he very rarely sits down. He is always excited, agitated, and overwrought by a sort of vague, undefined expectation. The faintest rustle in the entry or shout in the yard is enough to make him raise his head and begin listening: is it he they are coming to get, is it he they are looking for? And at such times his face expresses the utmost uneasiness and revulsion.

I like his broad face with its high cheek bones, always pale and unhappy, and reflecting, as though in a mirror, a soul tormented by conflict and continuous terror. His grimaces are strange and abnormal, but the delicate lines traced on his face by profound, genuine suffering show intellect and sense, and there is a warm and healthy light in his eyes. I like the man himself courteous, anxious to be of use, and extraordinarily gentle to everyone except Nikita. When anyone drops a button or a spoon, he jumps from his bed quickly and picks it up; every day he says good morning to his companions, and when he goes to bed he wishes them good night.

Besides his continually overwrought condition and his grimaces, his madness shows itself in another way. Sometimes in the evenings he wraps himself in his dressing-gown, and, trembling all over, with his teeth chattering, begins walking rapidly from corner to corner and between the bedsteads. It seems as though he is in a violent fever. From the way he suddenly stops and glances at his companions, it can be seen that he is longing to say something very important, but, apparently reflecting that they would not listen or would not understand him, he shakes his head impatiently and goes on pacing up and down. But soon the desire to speak gets the upper hand of every consideration, and he will let himself go and speak fervently and passionately. His talk is disordered and feverish like delirium, disconnected, and not always intelligible, but, on the other hand, something extremely fine may be felt in it, both in the words and the voice. When he talks you recognise in him the lunatic and the human being. It is difficult to reproduce on paper his insane talk. He speaks of the baseness of mankind, of violence trampling on justice, of the glorious life which will one day be upon earth, of the window gratings, which remind him every minute of the stupidity and cruelty of oppressors. It makes a disorderly, incoherent potpourri of songs old but still singable.

II

Some twelve or fifteen years ago an official called Gromov, a highly respectable and prosperous person, was living in his own house in the principal street of the town. He had two sons, Sergei and Ivan. When Sergei was a student in his fourth year he was taken ill with galloping consumption and died, and his death was, as it were, the first of a whole series of calamities which suddenly showered on the Gromov family. Within a week of Sergei's funeral the old father was put on trial for fraud and misappropriation, and he died of typhus in the prison hospital soon afterwards. The house, with all their belongings, was sold by auction, and Gromov and his mother were left entirely without means.

Hitherto, in his father's lifetime, Ivan Gromov, who was studying in the University of Petersburg had received an allowance of sixty or seventy roubles a month, and had had no conception of poverty; now he had to make an abrupt change in his life. He had to spend his time from morning to night giving lessons for next to nothing, to work at copying, and with all that to go hungry, as all his earnings were sent to keep his mother. Ivan Gromov could not stand such a life; he lost heart and strength, and, giving up the university, went home. Here, in this little town, through connections, he found the post of teacher in the district school, but could not get on with his colleagues, was not liked by the boys, and soon gave up the post. His mother died. He was for six months without work, living on nothing but bread and water; then he became a bailiff. He kept this post until he was dismissed because of illness.

He had never even in his young student days given the impression of being perfectly healthy. He had always been pale, thin, and given to catching cold; he ate little and slept badly. A single glass of wine went to his head and made him hysterical. He always had a craving for society, but, owing to his irritable temperament and suspiciousness, he never became very intimate with anyone, and had no friends. He always spoke with contempt of his fellow townsmen, saying that their coarse ignorance and sleepy animal existence seemed to him loathsome and horrible. He spoke in a loud tenor, with heat, and invariably either with scorn and indignation, or with wonder and enthusiasm, and always with perfect sincerity. Whatever one talked to him about he always brought it round to the same subject: that life was dull and stifling in the town; that the townspeople had no lofty interests, but lived a dingy, meaningless life, diversified by violence, coarse profligacy, and hypocrisy; that scoundrels were well fed and clothed, while honest men lived from hand to mouth; that they needed schools, a progressive local paper, a theatre, public lectures, solidarity among the intelligentsia; that society must see its failings and be horrified. In his criticisms of people he laid on the colours thick, using only black and white, and no fine shades; mankind was divided for him into honest men and scoundrels: there was nothing in between. He always spoke with passion and enthusiasm of women and of love, but he had never been in love.

In town, despite the severity of his judgments and his nervousness; he was liked, and behind his back was spoken of affectionately as Vania. His innate refinement and readiness to be of service, his good breeding, his moral purity, and his shabby coat, his frail appearance and family misfortunes, aroused a kind, warm, sorrowful feeling. Moreover, he was well educated and well read; according to the townspeople's notions, he knew everything, and was in their eyes something like a walking encyclopaedia.

He had read a great deal. He would sit at the club, nervously pulling at his beard and looking through the magazines and books; and from his face one could see that he was not reading, but devouring the pages without giving himself time to digest what he read. It must be supposed that reading was one of his morbid habits, as he fell upon anything that came into his hands with equal avidity, even last year's newspapers and calendars. At home he always read lying down.

III

One autumn morning Ivan Gromov, turning up the collar of his greatcoat and splashing through the mud, made his way by side-streets and back lanes to see some artisan, and to collect some payment that was owing. He was in a gloomy mood, as he always was in the morning. In one of the side-streets he was met by two convicts in fetters and an escort of four soldiers with rifles. Gromov had very often met convicts before, and they had always excited feelings of compassion and discomfort in him; but now this meeting made a peculiar, strange impression on him. It suddenly seemed to him for some reason that he, too, might be put into fetters and led through the mud to prison like that. After visiting the artisan, on the way home he met near the post office a police superintendent of his acquaintance, who greeted him and walked a few paces along the street with him, and for some reason this seemed to him suspicious. At home he could not get the convicts or the soldiers with their rifles out of his head all day, and an unaccountable inward agitation prevented him from reading or concentrating his mind. In the evening he did not light his lamp, and at night he could not sleep, but kept thinking that he might be arrested, put into fetters, and thrown into prison. He did not know of any harm he had done, and could be certain that he would never be guilty of murder, arson, or theft in the future either; but was it not easy to commit a crime by accident, unconsciously, and was not false witness always possible, and, indeed, miscarriage of justice? It was not without good reason that the age-old experience of the simple people teaches that beggary and prison are ills none can be safe from. A miscarriage of justice is very possible given the way legal proceedings are conducted nowadays, and there is nothing extraordinary about it. People who have an official, professional relation to other men's sufferings — for instance, judges, police officers, doctors — in course of time, through habit, grow so callous that they cannot, even if they wished it, take any but a formal attitude to their clients; in this respect they are no different from the peasant who slaughters sheep and calves in the back yard, and does not notice the blood. With this formal, soulless attitude to human personality the judge needs but one thing in order to deprive an innocent man of all rights of property, and to condemn him to penal servitude: time. Only the time spent on performing certain formalities for which the judge is paid his salary, and then — it is all over. Then you may look in vain for justice and protection in this dirty wretched little town a hundred and twenty miles from a railway. And, indeed, is it not absurd even to think of justice when every kind of vice is accepted by society as a rational and consistent necessity, and every act of mercy — for instance, a verdict of acquittal — calls forth a whole outburst of dissatisfied vindictiveness?

In the morning Gromov got up from his bed in a state of horror, with cold sweat on his forehead, completely convinced that he might be arrested any minute. Since his gloomy thoughts of yesterday had haunted him so long, he thought, it must be that there was some truth in them. They could not, indeed, have come into his mind without any grounds whatever.

A policeman walking slowly passed by the windows: that was significant. Here were two men standing still and silent near the house. Why were they silent?

And agonising days and nights followed for Gromov. Everyone who passed by the windows or came into the yard seemed to him a spy or a detective. At midday the chief of the police usually drove down the street with a pair of horses; he was coming from his country estate to the police department; but Gromov fancied every time that he was driving especially quickly, and that he had a peculiar expression: it was evident that he was in haste to announce that there was a very important criminal in the town. Gromov started at every ring at the bell and knock at the gate, and was agitated whenever he came upon anyone new at his landlady's; when he met police officers and gendarmes he smiled and began whistling so as to seem unconcerned. He could not sleep for whole nights in succession expecting to be arrested, but he snored loudly and sighed as though in deep sleep, that his landlady might think he was asleep; for if he could not sleep it meant that he was tormented by the stings of conscience – what a clue! Facts and common sense persuaded him that all these terrors were nonsense and morbidity, that if one looked at the matter more broadly there was nothing really terrible in arrest and imprisonment – so long as the conscience is at ease; but the more sensibly and logically he reasoned, the more acute and agonising his mental distress became. It might be compared with the story of a hermit who tried to cut a dwelling-place for himself in a virgin forest: the more zealously he worked with his axe, the thicker the forest grew. In the end Gromov, seeing it was useless, gave up reasoning altogether, and abandoned himself entirely to despair and terror.

He began to avoid people and to seek solitude. His work had been distasteful to him before: now it became unbearable to him. He was afraid they would somehow get him into trouble, would put a bribe in his pocket unnoticed and then denounce him, or that he would accidentally make a mistake in official papers that would be as good as fraud, or would lose other people's money. It is strange that his imagination had never at other times been so agile and inventive as now when every day he thought of thousands of different reasons for being seriously anxious over his freedom and honour; but, on the other hand, his interest in the outer world, in books in particular, grew noticeably fainter, and his memory began to fail him.

In the spring when the snow melted there were found in the ravine near the cemetery two half decomposed corpses – the bodies of an old woman and a boy bearing the traces of death by violence. Nothing was talked of but these bodies and their unknown murderers. That people might not think he had been guilty of the crime, Gromov walked about the streets, smiling, and when he met acquaintances he turned pale, flushed, and began declaring that there was no greater crime than the murder of the weak and defenceless. But this duplicity soon exhausted him, and after some reflection he decided that in his position the best thing to do was to hide in his landlady's cellar. He sat in the cellar all day and then all night, then another day, was fearfully cold, and waiting till dusk, stole secretly like a thief back to his room. He stood in the middle of the room till daybreak, listening without stirring. Very early in the morning, before sunrise, some workmen came into the house. Gromov knew perfectly well that they had come to mend the stove in the kitchen, but terror suggested to him that they were police officers disguised as workmen. He slipped steadily out of the flat, and, overcome by terror, ran along the street without his hat and coat. Dogs raced after him barking, a peasant shouted somewhere behind him, the wind whistled in his ears, and it seemed to Gromov that the force and violence of the whole world were massed together behind his back and were chasing him.

He was stopped and brought home, and his landlady sent for a doctor. Doctor Andrei Efimych Ragin, of whom we shall have more to say hereafter, prescribed cold compresses on his head and laudanum drops, shook his head, and went away, telling the landlady he would not come again, as one should not interfere with people who are going out of their minds. As he had not the means to live at home and be nursed, Gromov was soon sent to the hospital, and was there put into the ward for venereal patients. He could not sleep at night, misbehaved, and disturbed the patients, and was soon afterwards, by Dr Ragin's orders, transferred to Ward No. 6.

Within a year Gromov was completely forgotten in the town, and his books, heaped up by his landlady in a sledge in the shed, were pilfered by boys.

IV

Gromov's neighbour on the left is, as I have said already, the Jew Moiseika; his neighbour on the right hand is a peasant so rolling in fat that he is almost spherical, with a blankly stupid face, utterly devoid of thought. This is a motionless, gluttonous, unclean animal who has long ago lost all powers of thought or feeling. An acrid, stifling stench always comes from him.

Nikita, who has to clean up after him, beats him terribly with all his might, not sparing his fists; and what is dreadful is not being beaten – that one can get used to – but the fact that this stupefied creature does not respond to the blows with a sound or a movement, nor by a look in the eyes, but only sways a little like a heavy barrel.

The fifth and last inhabitant of Ward No. 6 is a man of the artisan class who has once been a sorter in the post office, a thinnish, fair little man with a good-natured but rather sly face. To judge from the clear, cheerful look in his calm and intelligent eyes, he has some pleasant idea in his mind, and has some very important and agreeable secret. He has under his pillow and under his mattress something that he never shows anyone, not from fear of its being confiscated or stolen, but from modesty. Sometimes he goes to the window, and turning his back to his companions, puts something on his breast, and bending his head, looks at it; if you go up to him at such a moment, he is embarrassed and snatches something off his breast. But it is not difficult to guess his secret.

'Congratulate me,' he often says to Gromov; 'I have been presented with the Stanislav order of the second degree with the star. The second degree with the star is only given to foreigners, but for some reason they want to make an exception for me,' he says with a smile, shrugging his shoulders in perplexity. 'That I must confess I did not expect.'

'I don't understand anything about that,' Gromov replies morosely.

'But do you know what I shall get sooner or later?' the former sorter persists, screwing up his eyes slyly. 'I shall certainly get the Swedish "Polar Star". That's an order worth working for, a white cross with a black ribbon. It's very beautiful.'

Probably in no other place is life so monotonous as in this ward. In the morning the patients, except the paralytic and the fat peasant, wash in the entry at a big tub and wipe themselves with the skirts of their dressing-gowns; after that they drink tea out of pewter mugs which Nikita brings them out of the main building. Everyone is allowed one mugful. At midday they have soup made out of sour cabbage and boiled grain, in the evening their supper consists of grain left from dinner. In the intervals they lie down, sleep, look out the window, and walk from one corner to the other. And so every day. Even the former sorter always talks of the same orders.

Fresh faces are rarely seen in Ward No. 6. The doctor has not taken in any new lunatics for a long time, and the people who are fond of visiting lunatic asylums are few in this world. Once every two months Semion Lazarich, the barber, appears in the ward. How he cuts the patients' hair, and how Nikita helps him to do it, and what a trepidation the lunatics are always thrown into by the arrival of the drunken, smiling barber, we will not describe.

No one even looks into the ward except the barber. The patients are condemned to see day after day no one but Nikita.

A rather strange rumour has, however, been circulating in the hospital of late.

It is rumoured that the doctor has begun to visit Ward No. 6.

v

A strange rumour!

Dr Andrei Yefimich Ragin is a strange man in his way. They say that when he was young he was very religious, and prepared himself for a clerical career, and that when he had finished his studies at the high school in 1863 he intended to enter a theological academy, but that his father, a surgeon and doctor of medicine, jeered at him and declared point-blank that he would disown him if he became a priest. How far this is true I don't know, but Dr Ragin himself has more than once confessed that he has never had a natural bent for medicine or science in general.

However that may have been, when he finished his studies in the medical faculty he did not enter the priesthood. He showed no special devoutness, and was no more like a priest at the beginning of his medical career than he is now.

His exterior is heavy, coarse like a peasant's, his face, his beard, his flat hair, and his coarse, clumsy figure, suggest an overfed, intemperate, and harsh innkeeper on the highroad. His face is surly looking and covered with blue veins, his eyes are small and his nose is red. With his height and broad shoulders he has huge hands and feet; one would think that a blow from his fist would knock the life out of anyone, but his step is soft, and his walk cautious and insinuating; when he meets anyone in a narrow passage he is always the first to stop and make way, and to say, not in a bass, as one would expect, but in a high, soft tenor: 'I beg your pardon!' He has a little swelling on his neck which prevents him from wearing stiff starched collars, and so he always goes about in soft linen or cotton shirts. Altogether he does not dress like a doctor. He wears the same suit for ten years, and the new clothes, which he usually buys at a Jewish shop, look as shabby and crumpled on him as his old ones; he sees patients and dines and pays visits all in the same coat; but this is not due to niggardliness, but to complete carelessness about his appearance.

When Dr Ragin came to the town to take up his duties the 'pious institution' was in a terrible condition. One could hardly breathe for the stench in the wards, in the passages, and in the courtyards of the hospital. The hospital servants, the nurses, and their children slept in the wards together with the patients. They complained that cockroaches, bedbugs, and mice made life unbearable. The surgical wards were never free from erysipelas. There were only two scalpels and not one thermometer in the whole hospital; potatoes were kept in the baths. The superintendent, the housekeeper, and the medical assistant robbed the patients; and of the old doctor, Ragin's predecessor, people declared that he secretly sold the hospital alcohol, and that he kept a regular harem of nurses and female patients. These disorderly proceedings were perfectly well known in the town, and were even exaggerated, but people took them calmly; some justified them on the ground that there were only patients and working men in the hospital, who could not be dissatisfied, since they were much worse off at home than in the hospital – they couldn't be fed on woodcocks! Others said in excuse that the town alone, without help from the rural district council, the *zemstvo*,* was not equal to maintaining a good hospital; thank God for having one at all, even a poor one. And the newly formed rural council did not open infirmaries either in the town or the neighbourhood, relying on the fact that the town already had its hospital.

After looking over the hospital Dr Ragin came to the conclusion that it was an immoral institution and extremely prejudicial to the health of the townspeople. In his opinion the most sensible thing that could be done was to let out the patients and close the hospital. But he reflected that his will alone was not enough to do this and that it would be useless; if physical and moral impurity were driven out of one place, they would only move to another; one must wait for it to wither away of itself. Besides, if people open a hospital and put up with having it, it must be because they need it; superstition and all the nastiness and abominations of daily life were necessary, since in process of time they worked out to something sensible, just as manure turns into black earth. There was nothing on earth so good that it had not something nasty about its first origin.

When Dr Ragin undertook his duties he was apparently not greatly concerned about the irregularities at the hospital. He only asked the attendants and nurses not to sleep in the wards, and had two cupboards of instruments put up; the superintendent, the house-keeper, the medical assistant, and the erysipelas remained un-changed.

Dr Ragin loved intelligence and honesty intensely, but he had no strength of will nor belief in his right to organise an intelligent and honest life about him. He was absolutely unable to give orders, to forbid things, and to insist. It seemed as though he had taken a vow never to raise his voice and never to make use of the imperative. It was difficult for him to say 'Fetch' or 'Bring'; when he wanted his meals he would cough hesitatingly and say to the cook: 'How about tea? . . .' or 'How about dinner? . . .' To dismiss the superintendent or to tell him to stop stealing, or to abolish the unnecessary parasitic post altogether, was absolutely beyond his powers. When Dr Ragin was deceived or flattered, or accounts he knew to be crooked were brought him to sign, he would turn as red as a crab and feel guilty, but yet he would sign the accounts. When the patients complained to him of being hungry or of the roughness of the nurses, he would be embarrassed and mutter guiltily: 'Very well, very well, I'll sort it out later . . . Probably it's a misunderstanding . . .'

At first Dr Ragin worked very zealously. He saw patients every day from morning till dinner-time, performed operations, and even acted as obstetrician. The ladies said of him that he had a good bedside manner and was an excellent diagnostician, especially of women's and children's diseases. But as time passed the work's monotony and obvious uselessness clearly wearied him. Today you see thirty patients, and tomorrow you find they have shot up to thirty-five, the next day forty, and so on from day to day, from year to year, while the mortality of the town did not decrease and the patients did not stop coming. To be any real help to forty patients between morning and dinner was not physically possible, so it could lead only to deception. If twelve thousand patients were seen in a year it meant, if one looked at it simply, that twelve thousand people were deceived. To put those who were seriously ill into wards, and to treat them according to the principles of science, was impossible, too, because though there were principles there was no science; if he were to put aside philosophy and pedantically follow the rules as other doctors did, the things above all necessary were cleanliness and ventilation instead of dirt, wholesome nourishment instead of broth made of stinking, sour cabbage, and good assistants instead of thieves.

And, indeed, why hinder people dying if death is the normal and legitimate end of everyone? What is gained if some shopkeeper or clerk lives an extra five or ten years? If the aim of medicine is by drugs to alleviate suffering, the question forces itself on one: why alleviate it? In the first place, they say that suffering leads man to perfection; and in the second, if mankind really learns to alleviate its sufferings with pills and drops, it will completely abandon religion and philosophy, in which it has hitherto found not merely protection from all sorts of trouble, but even happiness. Pushkin suffered terrible agonies before his death, poor Heine lay paralysed for several years; why, then, should not some Dr Ragin or peasant woman Matriona suffer illness, since their lives had nothing of importance in them, and would have been entirely empty and like the life of an amoeba except for suffering?

Oppressed by such reflections, Dr Ragin relaxed his efforts and gave up visiting the hospital every day.

VI

This is how his life passes. As a rule he gets up at eight o'clock in the morning, dresses, and drinks his tea. Then he sits down in his study to read, or goes to the hospital. At the hospital the outpatients are sitting in the dark, narrow little corridor waiting to be seen by the doctor. The nurses and the attendants, tramping with their boots over the brick floors, run by them; gaunt-looking patients in dressing-gowns pass; dead bodies and vessels full of filth are carried by, the children are crying, and there is a cold draught. Dr Ragin knows that such surroundings are torture to feverish, consumptive, and impressionable patients; but what can be done? In the consulting-room he is met by his assistant, Sergei Sergeich – a fat little man with a plump, well-washed, shaven face, with soft, smooth manners, wearing a new loosely cut suit and looking more like a senator than a medical assistant. He has an immense practice in the town, wears a white tie, and considers himself more proficient than the doctor, who has no practice. In the corner of the consulting-room there stands a huge icon in a shrine with a heavy lamp in front of it, and near it a candle-stand with a white cover on it. On the walls hang portraits of bishops, a view of the Monastery of Sviatye Gory,* and wreaths of dried cornflowers. Sergei is religious, and likes solemnity and decorum. The icon has been put up at his expense; on his instructions one of the patients reads the hymns of praise in the consulting-room on Sundays, and after the reading Sergei himself goes through the ward with a censor and burns incense.

There were a great many patients, but the time was short, and so the work was confined to the asking of a few brief questions and the administration of some drugs, such as castor oil or volatile ointment. Dr Ragin would sit with his head resting in his hand, lost in thought and asking questions mechanically. Sergei sat down too, rubbing his hands, and from time to time putting in his word.

'We suffer pain and poverty,' he would say, 'because we do not pray to merciful God as we should. Yes!'

Dr Ragin never performed any operations in surgery; he had long ago given up doing so, and the sight of blood upset him. When he had to open a child's mouth in order to look at its throat, and the child cried and tried to defend itself with its little hands, the noise in his ears made his head go round and brought tears into his eyes. He would make haste to prescribe a drug, and motion to the woman to take the child away.

He was soon wearied by the timidity of the patients and their incoherence, by the proximity of the pious Sergei, by the portraits on the walls, and by his own questions which he had asked over and over again for twenty years. And he would go away after seeing five or six patients. The rest would be seen by his assistant in his absence.

With the agreeable thought that, thank God, he had no private practice now, and that no one would interrupt him, Dr Ragin sat down to the table immediately on reaching home and took up a book. He read a great deal and always with enjoyment. Half his salary went on buying books and of the six rooms that made up his abode three were heaped up with books and old magazines. He liked best of all works on history and philosophy, the only medical publication to which he subscribed was *The Doctor*,* of which he always read the last pages first. He would always go on reading for several hours without a break and without being weary. He did not read as rapidly and impulsively as Gromov had done in the past, but slowly and with concentration, often pausing over a passage which he liked or did not find intelligible. Near the books there always stood a decanter of vodka, and a pickled gherkin or a bottled apple lay beside it, not on a plate, but on the baize table-cloth. Every half-hour he would pour himself out a glass of vodka and drink it without taking his eyes off the book. Then without looking at it he would feel for the gherkin and bite off a bit.

At three o'clock he would go cautiously to the kitchen door, cough, and say: 'Dariushka, what about dinner? . . .'

After his dinner – a rather poor and untidily served one – Dr Ragin would walk up and down his rooms with his arms folded, thinking. The clock would strike four, then five, and still he would be walking up and down thinking. Occasionally the kitchen door would creak, and the red and sleepy face of Dariushka would appear.

'Dr Ragin, isn't it time for you to have your beer?' she would ask anxiously.

'No, it is not time yet . . .' he would answer. 'I'll wait a little . . . I'll wait a little . . .'

Towards the evening the postmaster, Mikhail Averianych, the only man in the town whose society did not weary Dr Ragin, would come in. Mikhail had once been a very rich landowner, and had served in the cavalry, but had come to ruin, and was forced late in life by poverty to take a job in the post office. He had a hale and hearty appearance, luxuriant grey whiskers, the manners of a well-bred man, and a loud, pleasant voice. He was good-natured and emotional, but hot-tempered. When anyone in the post office made a protest, expressed disagreement, or even began to argue, Mikhail would turn scarlet, shake all over, and shout in a voice of thunder, 'Hold your tongue!' so that the post office had long enjoyed the reputation of an institution frightening to visit. Mikhail liked and respected Dr Ragin for his culture and the loftiness of his soul; he treated the other inhabitants of the town superciliously, as though they were his subordinates.

'Here I am,' he would say, going in to Dr Ragin. 'Good evening, my dear fellow! I'll be bound, you are getting sick of me, aren't you?'

'On the contrary, I am delighted,' said the doctor. 'I am always glad to see you.'

The friends would sit down on the sofa in the study and for some time would smoke in silence.

'Dariushka, what about the beer?' Dr Ragin would say.

They would drink their first bottle still in silence the doctor brooding and Mikhail with a gay and animated face, like a man who has something very interesting to tell. The doctor was always the one to begin the conversation.

'What a pity,' he would say quietly and slowly, not looking his friend in the face (he never looked anyone in the face) – 'what a great pity it is that there are no people in our town who are capable of carrying on intelligent and interesting conversation, or care to do so. It is an immense privation for us. Even the educated class do not rise above vulgarity; the level of their development, I assure you, is not a bit higher than that of the lower orders.'

'Perfectly true. I agree.'

'You know, of course,' the doctor went on quietly and deliberately, 'that everything in this world is insignificant and uninteresting except the higher spiritual manifestations of the human mind. Intellect draws a sharp line between the animals and man, suggests the divinity of the latter, and to some extent even takes the place of immortality, which does not exist. Consequently the intellect is the only possible source of enjoyment. We see and hear of no trace of intellect about us, so we are deprived of enjoyment. We have books, it is true, but that is not at all the same as living talk and conversation. If you will allow me to make a not quite apt comparison: books are the printed score, while talk is the singing.'

'Perfectly true.'

A silence would follow. Dariushka would come out of the kitchen and with an expression of blank dejection would stand in the doorway to listen, with her face propped on her fist.

'Eh!' Mikhail would sigh. 'To expect intelligence of this generation!'

And he would describe how wholesome, entertaining, and interesting life had been in the past. How intelligent the educated class in Russia used to be, and what lofty ideas it had of honour and friendship, how they used to lend money without an IOU, and how it was thought a disgrace not to give a helping hand to a comrade in need; and what campaigns, what adventures, what skirmishes, what comrades, what women! And the Caucasus, what a marvellous country! The wife of a battalion commander, an odd woman, used to put on an officer's uniform and drive off into the mountains in the evening, alone, without a guide. It was said that she had a love affair with some princeling in a native village.

'Queen of Heaven, Holy Mother . . .' Dariushka would sigh.

'And how we drank! And how we ate! And what desperate liberals we were!'

Dr Ragin would listen without hearing; he was musing as he sipped his beer.

'I often dream of intellectual people and conversation with them,' he said suddenly, interrupting Mikhail. 'My father gave me an excellent education, but under the influence of the ideas of the sixties made me become a doctor. I believe if I had not obeyed him then, by now I should have been in the very centre of the intellectual movement. Most likely I should have become a member of some university. Of course, intellect, too, is transient and not eternal but you know why I cherish a partiality for it. Life is a vexatious trap; when a thinking man reaches maturity and attains to full conscious-ness he cannot help feeling that he is in a trap from which there is no escape. Indeed, he is summoned without his choice by fortuitous circumstances from non-existence into life . . . What for? He tries to find out the meaning and object of his existence; he is told nothing, or he is told absurdities; he knocks and it is not opened to him; death comes to him – also against his will. And so just as in prison men held together by common misfortune feel more at ease when they are together, so one does not notice the trap in life when people with a bent for analysis and generalisation meet together and pass their time in the interchange of proud and free ideas. In that sense the intellect is the source of an enjoyment nothing can replace.'

'Perfectly true.'

Not looking his friend in the face, Dr Ragin would go on, quietly and with pauses, talking about intellectual people and conversation with them, and Mikhail would listen attentively and agree: 'Perfectly true.'

'And you do not believe in the immortality of the soul?' the postmaster would ask suddenly.

'No, honoured Mikhail; I do not believe in it, and have no grounds for believing in it.'

'I must own I doubt it, too. And yet I have a feeling that I shall never die. "Oh," I think to myself, "you old sod, it is time you were dead!" But there is a little voice in my soul that says: "Don't believe it; you won't die." '

Soon after nine o'clock Mikhail would go away. As he put on his fur coat in the entry he would say with a sigh:

'What a wilderness fate has carried us to, though, really! What's most vexatious of all is to have to die here. Eh! . . .'

VII

After seeing his friend out Dr Ragin would sit down at the table and begin reading again. The stillness of the evening, and afterwards of the night, was not broken by a single sound, and it seemed as though time were standing still and brooding with the doctor over the book, and as though there were nothing in existence but the books and the lamp with the green shade. The doctor's coarse peasant-like face was gradually lit up by a smile of delight and wonderment over the progress of the human intellect. 'Oh, why is not man immortal?' he thought. What is the good of the brain centres and convolutions, what is the good of sight, speech, self-consciousness, genius, if it is all destined to depart into the soil, and in the end to grow cold together with the earth's crust, and then for millions of years to fly with the earth round the sun with no meaning or no object? To do that there was no need at all to draw man with his lofty, almost god-like intellect out of non-existence, and then, as though in mockery, to turn him into clay.

The transmutation of matter! But what cowardice to comfort oneself with that cheap substitute for immortality. The unconscious processes that take place in nature are lower even that the stupidity of man, since in stupidity there is, anyway, consciousness and will, while in those processes there is absolutely nothing. Only the coward who has more fear of death than dignity can comfort himself with the fact that his body will in time live again in the grass, in the stones, in the toad. To find one's immortality in the transmutation of matter is as strange as to prophesy a brilliant future for the case after a precious violin has been broken and become useless.

When the clock struck, Dr Ragin would sink back into his chair and close his eyes to think a little. And under the influence of the fine ideas of which he had been reading he would at random recall his past and his present. The past was hateful – better not to think of it. And it was the same in the present as in the past. He knew that at the very time when his thoughts were floating together with the cooling earth round the sun, in the main building beside his abode people were suffering in sickness and physical filth: someone perhaps could not sleep and was making war upon the insects, someone was being infected by erysipelas, or moaning over too tight a bandage; perhaps the patients were playing cards with the nurses and drinking vodka. According to the yearly return, twelve thousand people had been deceived; the whole hospital rested, as it had done twenty years ago, on thieving, squabbles, gossip, nepotism, on gross quackery, and, as before, it was an immoral institution extremely injurious to the health of the inhabitants. He knew that Nikita knocked the patients about behind the barred windows of Ward No. 6, and that Moiseika went about the town every day begging for alms.

On the other hand, he knew very well that a magical change had taken place in medicine during the last twenty-five years. When he was studying at the university he had fancied that medicine would soon be overtaken by the fate of alchemy and metaphysics; but now when he was reading at night the science of medicine touched him and excited his wonder, and even enthusiasm. What unexpected brilliance, what a revolution! Thanks to the antiseptics, operations were performed such as the great Pirogov* had considered impossible theoretically, or *in spe*, as they used to say. Ordinary rural council doctors were venturing to perform the resection of the kneecap; of abdominal operations only one per cent was fatal; while kidney stones were considered such a trifle that they did not even write about it. A radical treatment for syphilis had been discovered. And the theory of heredity, hypnotism, the discoveries of Pasteur and of Koch,* hygiene based on statistics, and the work of our rural council doctors!

Psychiatry with its modern classification of mental diseases, methods of diagnosis and treatment, was a perfect Mt Everest in comparison with what it had been in the past. They no longer poured cold water on the heads of lunatics nor put straitjackets on them; they treated them with humanity, and even, so it was stated in the papers, got up balls and entertainments for them. Dr Ragin knew that with modern tastes and views such an abomination as Ward No. 6 was possible only a hundred and twenty miles from a railway in a little town where the mayor and all the town council were semi-literate tradesmen who looked upon the doctor as an oracle who must be believed without any criticism even if he poured molten lead into their mouths; in any other place the public and newspapers would long ago have torn this little Bastille to pieces.

'But, after all, what of it?' Dr Ragin would ask himself, opening his eyes. 'There are antiseptics, there is Koch, there is Pasteur, but the essential reality is not altered a bit, ill health and mortality are still the same. They get up balls and entertainments for the mad, but still they don't let them go free; so it's all nonsense and vanity, and there is no difference in reality between the best Vienna clinic and my hospital.'

But depression and a feeling akin to envy prevented him from feeling indifferent; it must have been exhaustion. His heavy head sank on to the book, he put his hands under his face to make it softer, and thought: 'I serve in a pernicious institution and receive a salary from people whom I am deceiving. I am not honest, but then, I of

myself am nothing, I am only part of an inevitable social evil: all local
officials are pernicious and receive their salary for doing nothing . . .
And so for my dishonesty it is not I who am to blame, but the
times . . . If I had been born two hundred years later I should have
been different . . .'

When it struck three he would put out his lamp and go into his
bedroom; he was not sleepy.

VIII

Two years before, the rural council in a liberal mood had decided to
allow three hundred roubles a year to pay for additional medical
service in the town until the council hospital was opened, and the
district doctor, Yevgeni Fiodorych Khobotov, was invited to the
town to assist Dr Ragin. He was a very young man – not yet thirty –
tall and dark, with broad cheek bones and little eyes; his forefathers
had probably come from one of the many alien races of Russia. He
arrived in the town without a kopeck to his name, with a small
portmanteau, and a plain young woman whom he called his cook.
This woman had a baby at the breast. Khobotov used to go about in a
peaked cap and high boots, and in the winter wore a short fur coat.
He made great friends with Sergei, the medical assistant, and with the
treasurer, but held aloof from the other officials, and for some reason
called them aristocrats. He had only one book in his lodgings, *The
Latest Prescriptions of the Vienna Clinic for 1881*. When he visited a
patient he always took this book with him. He played billiards in the
evening at the club; he did not like cards. He was very fond of using in
conversation such expressions as 'maundering', 'canting soft soap',
'stop pulling the wool over my eyes . . .'

He visited the hospital twice a week, did the round of the wards,
and saw outpatients. The complete absence of antiseptics and the
cupping roused his indignation, but he did not introduce any new
system, being afraid of offending Dr Ragin. He regarded his colleague
as a sly old rascal, suspected him of being a man of means, and
secretly envied him. He would have been very glad to have his post.

IX

On a spring evening towards the end of March when there was no
snow left on the ground and the starlings were singing in the
hospital garden, the doctor went out to see his friend the postmaster
as far as the gate. At that very moment the Jew Moiseika, returning
with his booty, came into the yard. He had no hat on, and his bare

feet were thrust into galoshes; in his hand he had a little bag of alms.

'Give me a kopeck!' he said to the doctor, smiling, and shivering with cold. Dr Ragin, who could never refuse anyone anything, gave him a ten-kopeck piece.

'How bad that is!' he thought, looking at the Jew's bare feet with their thin red ankles. 'Why, it's wet.'

And stirred by a feeling akin both to pity and disgust, he went into the lodge behind the Jew, looking now at his bald head, now at his ankles. As the doctor went in, Nikita jumped up from his heap of junk and stood to attention.

'Good day, Nikita,' Dr Ragin said mildly. 'That Jew should be provided with boots or something, he will catch cold.'

'Certainly, your Honour. I'll inform the superintendent.'

'Please do; ask him in my name. Tell him that I asked.'

The door into the ward was open. Gromov, lying propped on his elbow on the bed, listened in alarm to the unfamiliar voice, and suddenly recognised the doctor. He trembled all over with anger, jumped up, and with a red and spiteful face, with his eyes starting out of his head, ran out into the middle of the road.

'The doctor has come!' he shouted, and broke into a laugh. 'At last! Gentlemen, I congratulate you. The doctor is honouring us with a visit. Cursed reptile!' he shrieked, and stamped in a frenzy such as had never been seen in the ward before. 'Kill the reptile! No, killing's too good. Drown him in the latrine!'

Dr Ragin, hearing this, looked into the ward from the entry and asked gently: 'What for?'

'What for?' shouted Gromov, going up to him with a menacing air and convulsively wrapping himself in his dressing-gown. 'What for? Thief!' he said with a look of revulsion, moving his lips as though he would spit at him. 'Quack! hangman!'

'Calm yourself,' said Dr Ragin, smiling guiltily. 'I assure you I have never stolen anything; and as to the rest, most likely you greatly exaggerate. I see you are angry with me. Calm yourself, please, if you can, and tell me coolly, why are you angry?'

'Why are you keeping me here?'

'Because you are ill.'

'Yes I am. But you know dozens, hundreds of madmen are walking about in freedom because your ignorance is incapable of distinguishing them from the sane. Why am I and these poor wretches to be shut up here like scapegoats for all the rest? You, your assistant, the superintendent, and all your hospital swine, are immeasurably inferior to every one of us morally; why then are we locked up and not you? Where's the logic?'

'Morality and logic don't come in to it, it all depends on chance. If anyone is locked up he has to stay, and if anyone is not locked up he can walk about, that's all. There is neither morality nor logic in my being a doctor and your being a mental patient, there is nothing but idle chance.'

'That twaddle I don't understand . . .' Gromov uttered in a hollow voice and sat down on his bed.

Moiseika, whom Nikita did not venture to search in the presence of the doctor, laid out on his bed pieces of bread, bits of paper, and little bones, and, still shivering with cold, began rapidly in a singsong voice saying something in Yiddish. He probably imagined that he had opened a shop.

'Let me out,' said Gromov, and his voice quivered.

'I cannot.'

'But why, why?'

'Because it is not in my power. Think, what use will it be to you if I do let you out? Go. The townspeople or the police will detain you and bring you back.'

'Yes, yes, that's true,' said Gromov, and he rubbed his forehead. 'It's awful! But what am I to do, what?'

Dr Ragin liked Gromov's voice and his intelligent young face with its grimaces. He longed to be kind to the young man and soothe him; he sat down on the bed beside him, thought, and said:

'You ask me what to do. The very best thing in your position would be to run away. But, unfortunately, that is useless. You would be detained. When society protects itself from the criminal, mentally deranged, or just inconvenient people, it is invincible. There is only one thing left for you: to resign yourself to the thought that your presence here is inevitable.'

'It is no use to anyone.'

'So long as prisons and madhouses exist someone must be shut up in them. If not you, I. If not I, some third person. Wait till in the distant future prisons and madhouses no longer exist, and there will be neither bars on the windows nor hospital gowns. Of course, that time will come sooner or later.'

Gromov smiled ironically.

'You are jesting,' he said, screwing up his eyes. 'Such gentlemen as you and your assistant Nikita have nothing to do with the future, but you may be sure, sir, better days will come! I may express myself in a vulgar way, you may laugh, but the dawn of a new life is at hand; truth and justice will triumph, and – our turn will come! I shall not live to see it, I shall perish, but some people's great-grandsons will see it. I greet them with all my heart and rejoice, rejoice with them! Onward! God be your help, friends!'

With shining eyes Gromov got up, and stretching his hands towards the window, went on with emotion in his voice:

'From behind these bars I bless you! Hurrah for truth and justice! I rejoice!'

'I see no particular reason to rejoice,' said Dr Ragin, who thought Gromov's gestures theatrical, though he was delighted by them. 'Prisons and madhouses will disappear and truth, as you have just expressed it, will triumph; but the reality of things, after all, will not change, the laws of nature will still remain the same. People will suffer pain, grow old, and die just as they do now. However magnificent a dawn lit up your life, you would still in the end be nailed up in a coffin and thrown into a hole.'

'And immortality?'

'Oh, come, now!'

'You don't believe in it, but I do. Somebody in Dostoevsky or Voltaire said that if there had not been a God man would have invented him. And I firmly believe that if there is no immortality the great intellect of man will sooner or later invent it.'

'Well said,' observed Dr Ragin, smiling with pleasure; 'it's a good thing you have faith. With such faith some may live very nicely even incarcerated behind walls. You have had an education, I presume?'

'Yes, I have been to university, but did not finish.'

'You are a reflective and a thoughtful man. In any surroundings you can find tranquillity in yourself. Free and deep thinking which strives to make sense of life, and complete contempt for the foolish bustle of the world – those are two blessings beyond any that man has ever known. And you can possess them even though you lived behind threefold bars. Diogenes lived in a tub, yet he was happier than all the kings of the earth.'

'Your Diogenes was a blockhead,' said Gromov morosely. 'Why do you talk to me about Diogenes and some foolish rationalisation of life?' he cried, growing suddenly angry and leaping up. 'I love life; I love it passionately. I have a persecution mania, a continual agonising terror; but I have moments when I am overwhelmed by the thirst for life, and then I am afraid of going mad. I want dreadfully to live, dreadfully!'

He walked up and down the ward in agitation, and said, dropping his voice:

'When I dream I am haunted by phantoms. People visit me, I hear voices and music, and I fancy I am walking through woods or by the seashore, and I long so passionately for bustle, for interests ... Come, tell me, what news is there?' asked Gromov; 'What's happening?'

'Do you wish to know about the town or in general?'

'Well, tell me first about the town, and then in general.'

'Well, in the town it is appallingly dull . . . There's no one to say a word to, no one to listen to. There are no new people. A young doctor called Khobotov has come here recently.'

'He came in my time. A lout, isn't he?'

'Yes, he is a coarse man. It's strange, you know . . . Judging by every sign, there is no intellectual stagnation in our capital cities; there is a change – so there must be real people there too; but for some reason they always send us people that I would rather not see. It's an unlucky town!'

'Yes, it is an unlucky town,' sighed Gromov, and he laughed. 'And how are things in general? What are they writing in the papers and reviews?'

It was by now dark in the ward. The doctor got up, and, standing, began to describe what was being written abroad and in Russia, and the trends in thought that now existed. Gromov listened attentively and put questions, but suddenly, as though recalling something terrible, clutched at his head and lay down on the bed with his back to the doctor.

'What is the matter?' asked Dr Ragin.

'You will not hear another word from me,' said Gromov rudely. 'Leave me alone.'

'Why?'

'I tell you, leave me alone. Why the devil?'

Dr Ragin shrugged his shoulders, heaved a sigh, and went out. As he crossed the entry he said:

'You might clear up here, Nikita . . . there's an awfully stuffy smell.'

'Certainly, your Honour.'

'Whar an agreeable young man!' thought Dr Ragin, going back to his flat. 'In all the years I have been living here I do believe he is the first I have met with whom one can talk. He is capable of reasoning and is interested in just the right things.'

While he was reading, and afterwards, while he was going to bed, he kept thinking about Gromov, and when he woke next morning he remembered that he had the day before made the acquaintance of an intelligent and interesting man, and decided to visit him again as soon as possible.

X

Gromov was lying in the same position as on the previous day, with his head clutched in both hands and his legs drawn up. His face was not visible.

'Good day, my friend,' said Dr Ragin. 'You are not asleep, are you?'

'In the first place, I am not your friend,' Gromov articulated into the pillow; 'and in the second, your efforts are useless, you will not get one word out of me.'

'Strange,' muttered Dr Ragin in confusion. 'Yesterday we talked peacefully, but suddenly for no reason you took offence and broke off all at once . . . Probably I expressed myself awkwardly, or perhaps gave utterance to some idea which did not fit in with your convictions . . .'

'Yes, a likely idea!' said Gromov, sitting up and looking at the doctor with irony and uneasiness. His eyes were red. 'You can go and spy and probe somewhere else, it's no use your doing it here. I knew yesterday what you had come for.'

'A strange fancy,' laughed the doctor. 'So you suppose me to be a spy?'

'Yes, I do . . . A spy or a doctor who has been charged to test me – it's all the same.'

'Oh, I'm sorry, what an odd fellow you are really!'

The doctor sat down on the stool near the bed and shook his head reproachfully.

'But let us suppose you are right,' he said, 'let us suppose that I am treacherously trying to trap you into saying something so as to betray you to the police. You would be arrested and then tried. But would you be any worse off being tried and in prison than you are here? If you are banished to a settlement, or even sent to penal servitude, would it be worse than being shut up in this ward? I imagine it would be no worse . . . What, then, are you afraid of?'

These words evidently had an effect on Gromov. He sat down quietly.

It was between four and five in the afternoon – the time when Dr Ragin usually walked up and down his rooms, and Dariushka asked whether it was time for his beer. It was a still, bright day.

'I came out for a walk after dinner, and here I am, as you see,' said the doctor. 'It really is spring.'

'What month is it? March?' asked Gromov.

'Yes, the end of March.'

'Is it very muddy?'

'No, not very. There are already paths in the garden.'

'It would be nice now to drive in an open carriage somewhere into the country,' said Gromov, rubbing his red eyes as though he were just awake, 'then to come home to a warm, snug study, and . . . and to have a decent doctor to cure your headache . . . It's so long since I have lived like a human being. It's foul here! Insufferably foul!'

After his excitement the previous day he was exhausted and listless, and spoke unwillingly. His fingers twitched, and his face showed that he had a splitting headache.

'There is no real difference between a warm snug study and this ward,' said Dr Ragin. 'A man's peace and contentment do not lie outside a man, but in himself.'

'What do you mean?'

'The ordinary man looks for good and evil in external things – that is, carriages, in studies – but a thinking man looks for it in himself.'

'You should go and preach that philosophy in Greece, where it's warm and fragrant with the scent of pomegranates, but here it doesn't suit the climate. With whom was it I was talking of Diogenes? Was it with you?'

'Yes, with me yesterday.'

'Diogenes did not need a study or warm accommodation; it's hot there without. You can lie in your tub and eat oranges and olives. But bring him to Russia to live: he'd be begging to be let indoors in May, let alone in December. He'd be doubled up with the cold.'

'No. One can be insensible to cold as to every other pain. Marcus Aurelius says: "A pain is a vivid idea of pain; make an effort of will to change that idea, dismiss it, cease to complain, and the pain will disappear." That is true. The wise man, or simply the reflecting, thoughtful man, is distinguished precisely by his contempt for suffering; he is always contented and surprised at nothing.'

'Then I am an idiot, since I suffer and am discontented and astounded at human baseness.'

'You are wrong there; if you reflect more on the subject you will understand how insignificant is all the external world that upsets us. We must strive to make sense of life, and in that is true happiness.'

'Rationalisation,' repeated Gromov, frowning. 'External, internal . . . I'm sorry, but I don't understand it. I only know,' he said, getting up and looking angrily at the doctor, 'I only know that God has created me of warm blood and nerves, yes, indeed! If organic tissue is capable of life it must react to every stimulus. And I do! To pain I respond with tears and outcries, to baseness with indignation, to filth with loathing. To my mind, that is just what is called life. The lower the organism, the less sensitive it is, and the more feebly it reacts to stimuli; and the higher it is, the more responsively and vigorously it reacts to reality. How is it you don't know that? A doctor, and not know such trifles! To despise suffering, to be always contented, and to be surprised at nothing, one must reach this condition' – and Gromov pointed to the peasant who was a mass of fat – 'or to harden oneself by suffering to such a point that one loses all sensibility to it, that is, in other words, to cease to live. You must excuse me, I am not a sage or a philosopher,' Gromov continued with irritation, 'and I don't understand anything about it. I am not capable of reasoning.'

'On the contrary, your reasoning is excellent.'

'The Stoics, whom you are parodying, were remarkable people, but their doctrine crystallised two thousand years ago and has not advanced and will not advance an inch forward, since it isn't practical or alive. It had a success only with a minority which spends its life in savouring all sorts of theories and ruminating over them; the majority did not understand it. A doctrine which advocates indifference to wealth and to the comforts of life, and a contempt for suffering and death, is quite unintelligible to the vast majority of men, since that majority has never known wealth or the comforts of life; and to despise suffering would mean despising life itself, since the whole existence of man is made up of the sensations of hunger, cold, injury, loss, and a Hamlet-like dread of death. The whole of life lies in these sensations; one may be oppressed by it, one may hate it, but one cannot despise it. And so I repeat, the doctrine of the Stoics can never have a future; from the beginning of time up to today you see continually increasing the struggle, the sensibility to pain, the capacity of responding to stimuli.'

Gromov suddenly lost the thread of his thoughts, stopped, and rubbed his forehead with vexation.

'I meant to say something important, but I was side-tracked,' he said. 'What was I saying? Oh yes! This is what I mean: one of the Stoics sold himself into slavery to redeem his neighbour, so, you see, even a Stoic did react to a stimulus, since, for such a generous act as the destruction of oneself for the sake of one's neighbour, he must have had a soul capable of pity and indignation. Here in prison I have forgotten everything I learned, or else I could have recalled something else. Take Christ, for instance: Christ responded to reality by sleeping, smiling, being sorrowful and moved to wrath, even overcome by misery. He did not go to meet His sufferings with a smile, He did not despise death, but prayed in the Garden of Gethsemane that this cup might pass Him by.'

Gromov laughed and sat down.

'Granted that a man's peace and contentment lie not outside but in himself,' he said, 'granted that one must despise suffering and not be surprised at anything, but on what ground do you preach this? Are you a sage? A philosopher?'

'No, I am not a philosopher, but everyone ought to preach it because it is reasonable.'

'No, I want to know how it is that you consider yourself competent to judge of rationalisation, of contempt for suffering, and so on. Have you ever suffered? Have you any idea of suffering? Allow me to ask you, were you thrashed as a child?'

'No, my parents had an aversion for corporal punishment.'

'My father used to flog me cruelly; my father was a harsh government clerk with haemorrhoids, a long nose and a yellow neck. But let's talk of you. No one has laid a finger on you all your life, no one has scared you or battered you; you are as strong as a bull. You grew up under your father's wing and studied at his expense, and then you dropped at once into a sinecure. For more than twenty years you have lived rent free with heating, lighting, and service all provided, and had the right to work how you pleased and as much as you pleased, even to do nothing. You were naturally a flabby, lazy man, and so you have tried to arrange your life so that nothing should disturb you or make you move. You have handed over your work to the assistant and the rest of the swine while you sit in peace and warmth, accumulate money, read, amuse yourself with reflections, with all sorts of lofty nonsense, and' (Gromov looked at the doctor's red nose) 'with boozing; in fact, you have seen nothing of life, you know absolutely nothing of it, and are only theoretically acquainted with reality; you despise suffering and are surprised at nothing for a very simple reason: vanity of vanities, the external and the internal, contempt for life, for suffering and for death, rationalisation, true happiness – that's the philosophy that suits the Russian sluggard best. You see a peasant beating his wife for instance. Why interfere? Let him beat her, they will both die sooner or later, anyway – and, besides, the man's blows injure not the person he is beating, but himself. To get drunk is stupid and unseemly, but if you drink you die, and if you don't drink you die. A peasant woman comes in with a toothache . . . well, what of it? Pain is the idea of pain, and besides "you can't live in this world without illness, we shall all die, and so, go away, woman, don't hinder me from thinking and drinking vodka." A young man asks advice, what he is to do, how he is to live; anyone else would think before answering, but you have got the answer ready: strive for rationalisation or for true good. And what is this "true good"? There's no answer, of course. We are kept here behind barred windows, tortured, left to rot; but there is no difference at all between this ward and a warm, snug study. A convenient philosophy. You can do nothing, and your conscience is clear, and you feel you are wise . . . No, sir, it is not philosophy, it's not thinking, it's not breadth of vision, but laziness, fakirism, drowsy stupefaction. Yes,' cried Gromov, getting angry again, 'you despise suffering, but I'll bet if you pinch your finger in the door you will howl at the top of your voice.'

'And perhaps I shouldn't howl,' said Dr Ragin, with a meek smile.

'Oh, I dare say! Well if you were struck down with paralysis, or supposing some fool or bully took advantage of his position and rank to insult you in public, and if you knew he could do it with impunity, then you would understand what it means to fob people off with rationalisation and "true good".'

'That's original,' said Dr Ragin, laughing with pleasure and rubbing his hands. 'I am agreeably struck by your tendency to generalise, and the sketch of my character you have just drawn is simply brilliant. I must confess that talking to you gives me great pleasure. Well, I've listened to you, and now kindly listen to me.'

XI

The conversation went on for about an hour longer, and apparently made a deep impression on Dr Ragin. He began going to the ward every day. He went there in the mornings and after dinner, and often the dusk of evening found him in conversation with Gromov. At first Gromov shunned him, suspected him of evil designs, and openly expressed his hostility. But afterwards he got used to him, and his abrupt manner changed to one of condescending irony.

Soon it was all over the hospital that Dr Ragin had taken to visiting Ward No. 6. No one – neither Sergei, nor Nikita, nor the nurses – could conceive why he went there, why he stayed there for hours on end, what he was talking about, and why he did not write prescriptions. His actions seemed strange. Often Mikhail could not find him at home, which had never happened in the past, and Dariushka was greatly perturbed, for the doctor drank his beer now at no definite time, and sometimes was even late for dinner.

One day – it was at the end of June – Dr Khobotov went to see Dr Ragin about something. Not finding him at home, he proceeded to look for him in the yard; there he was told that the old doctor had gone to see the mental patients. Going into the lodge and stopping in the entry, Khobotov heard the following conversation:

'We shall never agree, and you will not succeed in converting me to your faith,' Gromov was saying irritably; 'you are utterly ignorant of reality, and you have never known suffering, but have only like a leech fed on the sufferings of others, while I have been in continual suffering from the day of my birth to this day. For that reason, I tell you frankly, I consider myself superior to you and more competent in every respect. It's not for you to teach me.'

'I have absolutely no ambition to convert you to my faith,' said Dr Ragin gently, and with regret that the other wouldn't understand him. 'And that's not the point, my friend; what matters is not that you have suffered and I have not. Joy and suffering are passing; let us leave them, never mind them. What matters is that you and I think we see in each other people who are capable of thinking and reasoning, and that is a common bond between us however different our views. If you knew, my friend, how sick I am of universal senselessness, ineptitude, stupidity, and with what delight I always talk with you! You are an intelligent man, and I enjoy your company.'

Khobotov opened the door an inch and glanced into the ward; Gromov in his night-cap and Dr Ragin were sitting side by side on the bed. The madman was grimacing, twitching, and convulsively wrapping himself in his gown, while the doctor sat motionless with bowed head, and his face was red and looked helpless and sorrowful. Khobotov shrugged his shoulders, grinned, and caught Nikita's eye. Nikita shrugged his shoulders too.

Next day Khobotov went to the lodge, accompanied by the assistant. Both stood in the lobby and listened.

'I suspect our old man has gone clean off his head!' said Khobotov as he came out of the lodge.

'Lord have mercy upon us sinners!' sighed the decorous Sergei, scrupulously avoiding the puddles so as not to muddy his polished boots. 'I must own, honoured Dr Khobotov, I have been expecting it for a long time.'

<h2 style="text-align:center">XII</h2>

After this Dr Ragin began to notice an air of mystery all around him. The attendants, the nurses, and the patients looked at him inquisitively when they met him, and then whispered together. The superintendent's little daughter Masha, whom he liked to meet in the hospital garden, for some reason ran away from him now when he went up with a smile to pat her head. The postmaster no longer said, 'Perfectly true,' as he listened to him, but in unaccountable embarrassment muttered, 'Yes, yes, yes . . .' and looked at him with a grieved and thoughtful expression; for some reason he took to advising his friend to give up vodka and beer, but as a man of tact he did not say this directly, but hinted it, telling him first about the commanding officer of his battalion, an excellent man, or about the regimental chaplain, a capital fellow, both of whom drank and fell ill, but on giving up drink completely regained their health. On two or three occasions Dr Ragin was visited by his colleague Khobotov, who also advised him to give up spirits, and for no apparent reason recommended him to take potassium bromide.

In August Dr Ragin got a letter from the mayor of the town asking him to attend on very important business. On arriving at the town hall at the fixed time, Dr Ragin found there the military commander, the superintendent of the district school, a member of the town council, Khobotov, and a plump, fair gentleman who was introduced to him as a doctor. This doctor, with a Polish surname difficult to pronounce, lived at a thoroughbred horse stud twenty miles away, and was now passing through the town.

'There's a report that concerns you,' said the member of the town council, addressing Dr Ragin after they had all greeted one another and sat down at the table. 'Here Dr Khobotov says that there is no room for the dispensary in the main building, and that it ought to be moved to one of the lodges. That's of no consequence – of course it can be moved, but the point is that the lodge wants rebuilding.'

'Yes, it would have to be rebuilt,' said Dr Ragin after a moment's thought. 'If the corner lodge, for instance, were fitted up as a dispensary, I imagine it would cost at least five hundred roubles. An unproductive expenditure!'

Everyone was silent for a space.

'I had the honour of submitting to you ten years ago,' Dr Ragin went on in a low voice, 'that the hospital in its present form is a luxury for the town, beyond its means. It was built in the forties, but things were different then. The town spends too much on unnecessary buildings and superfluous staff. I believe with a different system two model hospitals might be maintained for the same money.'

'Well, let us have a different system, then!' the member of the town council said briskly.

'I have already had the honour of submitting to you that the medical department should be transferred to the supervision of the rural council.'

'Yes: transfer the money to the rural council and they will steal it,' laughed the fair-haired doctor.

'That's what it always comes to,' the member of the council agreed, and he too laughed.

Dr Ragin looked with apathetic, lustreless eyes at the fair-haired doctor and said: 'One must be just.'

Again there was silence. Tea was brought in. The military commmander, for some reason much embarrassed, touched Dr Ragin's hand across the table and said: 'You have quite forgotten us, doctor. But of course you are a hermit: you don't play cards and don't like women. You're bored with fellows like us.'

They all began saying how boring it was for a decent person to live in such a town. No theatre, no music, and at the last dance at the club there had been about twenty ladies and only two gentlemen. The young men did not dance, but spent all their time crowding round the refreshment bar or playing cards.

Not looking at anyone and speaking slowly in a low voice, Dr Ragin began saying what a pity, what a terrible pity it was that the townspeople should waste their vital energy, their hearts, and their minds on cards and gossip, and should have neither the power nor the inclination to spend their time in interesting conversation and reading, and should refuse to take advantage of the enjoyments of the mind. The mind alone was interesting and worthy of attention, everything else was low and petty. Khobotov listened to his colleague attentively and suddenly asked:

'Andrei, what day of the month is it?'

Having received an answer, the fair-haired doctor and he, in the tone of examiners conscious of ineptitude, began asking Dr Ragin what day of the week it was, how many days there were in the year, and whether it was true that there was a remarkable prophet living in Ward No. 6.

In response to the last question Dr Ragin blushed and said: 'Yes, he is mentally ill, but he is an interesting young man.'

They asked him no other questions.

When he was putting on his overcoat in the hall, the military commander laid a hand on his shoulder and said with a sigh:

'It's time we old fellows took a rest!'

As he came out of the hall, Dr Ragin understood that it had been a committee appointed to inquire into his mental condition. He recalled the questions he had been asked, flushed crimson, and for some reason, for the first time in his life, felt bitterly grieved for medical science.

'My God . . .' he thought, remembering how these doctors had just examined him; 'why, they have attended psychiatry lectures so recently; they have taken examinations – why this crass ignorance? They have no conception of psychiatry.'

And for the first time in his life he felt insulted and angered.

In the evening of the same day Mikhail came to see him. The postmaster went up to him without waiting to greet him, took him by both hands, and said in an agitated voice:

'My dear fellow, my dear friend, show me that you believe in my genuine affection and look on me as your friend!' And preventing Dr Ragin from speaking, he went on, growing excited: 'I love you for your culture and nobility of soul. Listen to me, my dear fellow. Professional codes compel the doctors to conceal the truth from you, but I blurt out the plain truth like a soldier. You are not well! I'm sorry, my dear fellow, but it is the truth; everyone around you has been noticing for a long time. Doctor Khobotov has just told me that it is essential for you to rest and distract your mind for the sake of your health. Perfectly true! Excellent! In a day or two I am taking a holiday and am going away to sniff a different atmosphere. Show that you are a friend to me, let's go together! Let's go for a jaunt as in the good old days.'

'I feel perfectly well,' said Dr Ragin after a moment's thought. 'I can't go away. Allow me to prove my friendship some other way.'

To go somewhere for no reason, with no books, no Dariushka, no beer, to break abruptly from the routine of life established for twenty years – the idea for the first minute struck him as wild and fantastic, but he remembered the conversation at the office of the town administration and the depressed mood in which he had returned home, and the thought of a brief absence from the town, in which stupid people looked on him as a madman, seemed pleasant to him.

'And where actually do you intend to go?'

'To Moscow, to Petersburg, to Warsaw . . . I spent the five happiest years of my life in Warsaw. What a marvellous town! Let's go there, my dear fellow!'

XIII

A week later it was suggested to Dr Ragin that he should have a rest – that is, take retirement – a suggestion he received with indifference, and a week later still, Mikhail and he were sitting in a mail coach driving to the nearest railway station. The days were cool and bright, with a blue sky and a clear view of the distant horizon. They were two days driving the hundred and twenty miles to the railway station, and stayed two nights on the way. When at the posting station the glasses for their tea had not been properly washed, or the horses were harnessed too slowly, Mikhail would turn crimson, and quivering all over would shout:

'Hold your tongue! Don't argue!'

And in the carriage he talked without ceasing for a moment, describing his campaigns in the Caucasus and in Poland. What adventures he had had, what encounters! He talked loudly and opened his eyes so wide with wonder that he might well be thought to be lying. Moreover, as he talked he breathed in Dr Ragin's face and laughed into his ear. This got on the doctor's nerves and prevented him from thinking and concentrating.

In the train they travelled, for economy, third-class in a non-smoking compartment. Only half the passengers were decent. Mikhail soon made friends with everyone, and moving from one seat to another, kept saying loudly that they ought not to travel by these appalling lines. It was a regular swindle! A very different thing riding on a good horse: one could do over seventy miles a day and feel fresh and well after it. And our bad harvests were due to the draining of the Pinsk marshes; altogether, dreadful incompetence. He got excited, talked loudly, and would not let others speak. This endless chatter to the accompaniment of loud laughter and expressive gestures wearied Dr Ragin.

'Which of us is the madman?' he thought with vexation. 'I, who try not to disturb my fellow passengers in any way, or this egotist who thinks that he is cleverer and more interesting than anyone here, and so will leave no one in peace?'

In Moscow Mikhail put on a military coat without epaulettes and trousers with red braid. He wore a cap and overcoat in the street, and soldiers saluted him. It seemed to Dr Ragin, now, that his companion was a man who had squandered all that was good and kept only what was bad of the country gentleman that he had once been. He liked to be waited on even when it was quite unnecessary. The matches would be lying before him on the table, and he would see them and shout to the waiter to give him the matches; he did not hesitate to appear before a maid-servant in nothing but his underclothes; he used the familiar mode of address to all footmen indiscriminately, even old men, and when he was angry called them fools and blockheads. This, Dr Ragin thought, was lordly, but vile.

First of all Mikhail led his friend to the icon of the Iberian Madonna. He prayed fervently, shedding tears and bowing down to the earth, and when he had finished, heaved a deep sigh and said:

'Even though you don't believe it makes you somehow feel when you pray. Kiss the icon, my dear fellow.'

Dr Ragin was embarrassed and he kissed the icon, while Mikhail pursed his lips and prayed in a whisper, and again tears came into his eyes. Then they went to the Kremlin and looked there at the Tsar-cannon and the Tsar-bell, and even touched them with their fingers, admired the view over the river, visited St Saviour's and the Rumiantsev Museum.*

They dined at Testov's. Mikhail looked a long time at the menu, stroking his whiskers, and said in a tone of a gourmet accustomed to dine in restaurants:

'Let's see what you give us to eat today, my angel!'

XIV

The doctor walked about, looked at things, ate and drank, but he had one constant feeling: annoyance with Mikhail. He longed to have a rest from his friend, to get away from him, to hide himself, while the friend thought it was his duty not to let the doctor move a step away from him, and to provide him with as many distractions as possible. When there was nothing to look at, he entertained him with conversation. For two days Dr Ragin put up with it, but on the third day he announced to his friend that he was ill and wanted to stay at home for the whole day; his friend replied that in that case he would stay too – that really he needed a rest, for he was run off his legs already. Dr Ragin lay on the sofa, with his face to the back, and clenching his teeth, listened to his friend, who assured him with heat that sooner or later France would certainly thrash Germany, that there were a great many scoundrels in Moscow, and that it was impossible to judge of a horse's quality by its outward appearance. The doctor began to feel a buzzing in his ears and palpitations of the heart, but tact stopped him from begging his friend to go away or hold his tongue. Fortunately Mikhail grew bored of sitting in the hotel room, and after dinner he went out for a walk.

As soon as he was alone Dr Ragin abandoned himself to a feeling of relief. How pleasant to lie motionless on the sofa and to know that you are alone in the room! Real happiness is impossible without solitude. The fallen angel betrayed God probably because he longed for solitude, of which the angels know nothing. Dr Ragin wanted to think about what he had seen and heard during the last few days, but he could not get Mikhail out of his head.

'Why, he has taken a holiday and come with me out of friendship, out of generosity,' thought the doctor with vexation; 'nothing could be worse than this friendly supervision. I suppose he is good-natured and generous and a lively fellow, but he is a bore. An insufferable bore. In the same way there are people who say only clever and good things, yet you feel that they are dull-witted people.'

For the following days Dr Ragin declared himself ill and would not leave the hotel room, he lay with his face to the back of the sofa and languished when his friend entertained him with conversation, or rested when his friend was absent. He was vexed with himself for having come, and with his friend, who grew every day more talkative and more free and easy; he could not succeed in attuning his thoughts to a serious and lofty level.

'This is what I get from the real life Gromov talked about,' he thought, angry at his own pettiness. 'It's of no consequence, though . . . I shall go home, and everything will go on as before . . .'

It was the same thing in Petersburg too; for whole days on end he did not leave the hotel room, but lay on the sofa and only got up to drink beer.

Mikhail was all haste to get to Warsaw.

'My dear man, why should I go there?' said Dr Ragin in an imploring voice. 'You go alone and let me go home! I beg you!'

'Certainly not,' protested Mikhail. 'It's a marvellous city. I spent five of the happiest years of my life there!'

Dr Ragin was too weak-willed to insist on his own way, and, gritting his teeth, went to Warsaw. There he stayed in the hotel room, and lay on the sofa, furious with himself, with his friend, and with the waiters, who obstinately refused to understand Russian; while Mikhail, healthy, hearty, and full of spirits as usual, went around town from morning to night, looking up his old acquaintances. Several times he did not return home at night. After one night spent in some unknown haunt he returned home early in the morning, in a violently excited condition, red and dishevelled. For a long time he paced the room from corner to corner muttering something to himself, then stopped and said:

'Honour comes first.'

After walking up and down a little longer he clutched his head in both hands and pronounced in a tragic voice: 'Yes, honour comes first! I curse the moment when the idea first entered my head to visit this Babylon! Old chap,' he added, addressing the doctor, 'you may despise me, I have lost at gambling; lend me five hundred roubles!'

Dr Ragin counted out five hundred roubles and gave them to his friend without a word. The latter, still crimson with shame and anger, incoherently articulated some pointless vow, put on his cap, and went out. Returning two hours later he flopped into an arm-chair, heaved a loud sigh, and said:

'My honour is saved. Let's go, my friend; I do not care to remain another hour in this damned town. Scoundrels! Austrian spies!'

By the time the friends were back in their own town it was November, and deep snow was lying in the streets. Dr Khobotov had Dr Ragin's post; he was still living in his old lodgings, waiting for Dr Ragin to arrive and clear out of the hospital apartments. The plain woman whom he called his cook was already established in one of the lodges.

Fresh scandals about the hospital were going round the town. It was said that the plain woman had quarrelled with the super-intendent, and that the latter had crawled on his knees to her begging forgiveness. On the very first day he arrived Dr Ragin had to look for lodgings.

'My friend,' the postmaster said to him timidly, 'excuse an indiscreet question: what means have you at your disposal?'

Dr Ragin, without a word, counted out his money and said: 'Eighty-six roubles.'

'I don't mean that,' Mikhail said, embarrassed and misunderstanding him. 'I mean, what have you got to live on?'

'I tell you, eighty-six roubles . . . That's all I have.'

Mikhail regarded the doctor as an honest, honourable man, yet he suspected that he had accumulated a fortune of at least twenty thousand. Now, learning that Dr Ragin was destitute, that he had nothing to live on, he was for some reason suddenly moved to tears and embraced his friend.

XV

Dr Ragin now lodged with a Mrs Belova in a little house with three windows. There were only three rooms besides the kitchen in the little house. The doctor lived in two of the them which looked into the street, while Dariushka and the landlady with her three children lived in the third room and the kitchen. Sometimes the landlady's lover, a drunken peasant who was rowdy and reduced the children and Dariushka to terror, would come for the night. When he arrived and established himself in the kitchen and demanded vodka, they all felt very uncomfortable, and the doctor would be moved by pity to take the children into his room and put them to bed on his floor, and this gave him great satisfaction.

He got up as before at eight o'clock, and after his morning tea sat down to read his old books and magazines: he had no money for new ones. Either because the books were old, or perhaps because of the changed surroundings, reading exhausted him, and did not grip his attention as before. So as not to idle his time away he made a detailed catalogue of his books and gummed little labels on their backs, and this mechanical, tedious work seemed to him more interesting than reading. The monotonous, tedious work lulled his thoughts to sleep in some unaccountable way, and time passed quickly while he thought of nothing. Even sitting in the kitchen, peeling potatoes with Dariushka or picking over the buckwheat grain, seemed to him interesting. On Saturdays and Sundays he went to church. Standing near the wall and half closing his eyes, he listened to the singing and thought of his father, of his mother, of the university, of the religions of the world; he felt calm and melancholy, and as he went out of the church afterwards he regretted that the service had ended so quickly. He went twice to the hospital to talk to Gromov. But on both occasions Gromov was unusually excited and spiteful; he asked the doctor to leave him in peace, as he had long been sick of empty chatter, and declared, to make up for all his sufferings, he asked from the damned scoundrels only one favour – solitary confinement. Surely they would not refuse him even that? On both occasions when Dr Ragin was taking leave of him and wishing him good night, he snarled:

'Go to hell!'

And Dr Ragin did not know now whether to visit him a third time or not. But he wanted to go.

Once Dr Ragin used to walk about his rooms and think in the interval after dinner, but now from dinner-time till evening tea he lay on the sofa with his face to the back and gave himself up to trivial thoughts which he could not repress. He was mortified that after more than twenty years of service he had been given neither a pension nor any assistance. It is true that he had not done his work honestly, but, then, anyone in the service gets a pension without distinction, honest or not. Modern justice consists of bestowing promotions, honours and pensions, not for moral qualities or capacities, but for service regardless of merit. Why was he alone to be an exception? He had no money at all. He was ashamed to pass by the shop and look at the woman who owned it. He owed thirty-two roubles for beer already. There was money owing to the landlady also. Dariushka sold old clothes and books on the sly, and told lies to the landlady, saying that the doctor was about to receive a large sum of money.

He was angry with himself for having wasted on travelling the thousand roubles he had saved up. How useful that thousand roubles would be now! He was vexed that people would not leave him in peace. Khobotov thought it was his duty to look in on his sick colleague from time to time. Everything in Khobotov revolted Dr Ragin – his well-fed face and vulgar, condescending tone, his use of the word 'colleague', and his high top-boots; the most revolting thing was that he thought it was his duty to treat Dr Ragin, and thought that he really was treating him. On every visit he brought a phial of bromide and rhubarb pills.

Mikhail, too, thought it his duty to visit his friend and entertain him. Every time he went in to Dr Ragin, pretending to be relaxed, with forced laughter, and began assuring him that he was looking very well today, and that, thank God, he was on the highroad to recovery: from this you could tell that he looked on his friend's condition as hopeless. He had not yet repaid his Warsaw debt, and was overwhelmed by shame; he was tense, and so tried to laugh louder and talk more amusingly. His anecdotes and descriptions seemed endless now, and were an agony both to Dr Ragin and himself.

In his presence Dr Ragin usually lay on the sofa with his face to the wall, and listened with his teeth clenched; his soul was oppressed with rankling disgust, and after every visit from his friend he felt as though this disgust had risen higher, and was literally rising to his throat.

To stifle petty thoughts he made haste to reflect that he himself, and Khobotov, and Mikhail, would all sooner or later perish, leaving not a trace on nature. If one imagined some spirit flying by the earthly globe in space in a million years, it would see nothing but clay and bare rocks. Everything – culture and the moral law – would pass away and not even a burdock would be growing. Of what consequence was shame because of a shopkeeper, of what consequence was the insignificant Khobotov or Mikhail's wearisome friendship? It was all trivial and nonsensical.

But such reflections did not help him now. Scarcely had he imagined the earthly globe in a million years, when Khobotov in his high top-boots or Mikhail with his forced laugh would appear from behind a bare rock, and he even heard the shamefaced whisper: 'The Warsaw debt . . . I will repay it in a day or two, old chap . . . Without fail.'

XVI

One day Mikhail came after dinner when Dr Ragin was lying on the sofa. It so happened that Khobotov arrived at the same time with his bromide. Dr Ragin got up heavily and sat down, propping both arms on the sofa.

'Your face is a much better colour today than yesterday, my dear man,' began Mikhail. 'Yes, you look fine. Upon my soul, you do!'

'It's high time you recovered, colleague,' said Khobotov, yawning. 'I'm sure you are sick of this maundering.'

'And we shall recover,' said Mikhail cheerfully. 'We shall live another hundred years! To be sure!'

'If not a hundred at least another twenty,' Khobotov said reassuringly. 'It's all right, all right, colleague; don't lose heart . . . Stop pulling the wool over my eyes.'

'We'll show 'em,' laughed Mikhail, and he slapped his friend on the knee. 'We'll show 'em! Next summer, God willing, we shall be off to the Caucasus, and we will ride all over it on horseback – trot, trot, trot! And when we are back from the Caucasus I shouldn't wonder if we don't end up dancing at a wedding.' Mikhail gave a sly wink. 'We'll make a fine bridegroom of you . . . we will . . .'

Dr Ragin felt suddenly the rising disgust reaching his throat, his heart began beating violently.

'That's coarse,' he said, getting up quickly and walking away to the window. 'Don't you understand that you are talking vulgar nonsense?' He meant to go on softly and politely, but against his will he suddenly clenched his fists and raised them above his head.

'Leave me alone,' he shouted in a voice unlike his own, flushing scarlet and shaking all over. 'Go away, both of you!'

Mikhail and Khobotov got up and stared at him with amazement and then with alarm.

'Out, both of you!' Dr Ragin went on shouting. 'Stupid people! Foolish people! I don't want either your friendship or your medicines, stupid man! Vulgarity! Vileness!'

Khobotov and Mikhail, looking at each other in bewilderment, staggered to the door and went out. Dr Ragin snatched up the phial of bromide and flung it after them; the phial smashed loudly on the threshold.

'Go to hell!' he shouted in a tearful voice, running out into the passage. 'To hell with you!'

When his guests had gone Dr Ragin lay down on the sofa, trembling as though in a fever, and went on for a long while repeating: 'Stupid people! Foolish people!'

When he was calmer, what occurred to him first of all was the thought that poor Mikhail must be feeling fearfully ashamed and depressed now, and that it was all dreadful. Nothing like this had ever happened to him before. Where were his intellect and his tact? Where were his rationalisation of things and his philosophical equanimity?

The doctor could not sleep all night for shame and vexation with himself, and at ten o'clock next morning he went to the post office and apologised to the postmaster.

'We won't think again of what has happened,' Mikhail, greatly touched, said with a sigh, warmly pressing his hand. 'Let bygones be bygones. Liubavkin,' he suddenly shouted so loud that all the postal workers and customers started, 'give me a chair; and you wait,' he shouted to a peasant woman who was stretching out a registered letter to him through the grating. 'Can't you see I am busy? We will forget the past,' he went on, affectionately addressing Dr Ragin; 'sit down, I beg you, old chap.'

For a minute he stroked his knees in silence, and then said:

'I have never even thought of taking offence. Illness is no joke, I understand. Your attack frightened the doctor and me yesterday, and we had a long talk about you afterwards. My dear friend, why won't you treat your illness seriously? You can't go on like this . . . Excuse me for speaking openly as a friend,' whispered Mikhail. 'You live in the most deplorable surroundings, crowded, unclean, no one to look after you, no money for proper treatment . . . My dear friend, the doctor and I implore you with all our hearts, listen to our advice: go into the hospital! There you will have wholesome food and attendance and treatment. Though, between ourselves, Khobotov is not one of us, he does understand his work, you can fully rely upon him. He has promised me he will look after you.'

Dr Ragin was touched by the postmaster's genuine sympathy and the tears which suddenly glittered on his cheeks.

'My dear man, don't believe them!' he whispered, laying his hand on his heart; 'don't believe them. It's a sham. My illness is only that in twenty years I have only found one intelligent man in the whole town, and he is mad. I am not ill at all, it's simply that I have got into a vicious circle which there is no getting out of. I don't care; I am ready for anything.'

'Go into the hospital, my dear fellow.'

'I don't care if it were a pit.'

'Give me your word, old chap, that you will obey Khobotov to the letter.'

'All right, I give you my word. But I repeat, my friend, I am in a vicious circle. Now everything, even the genuine sympathy of my friends, leads to the same thing – to my perdition. I am perishing and I have the courage to admit it.'

'My dear fellow, you will recover.'

'What's the use of saying that?' said Dr Ragin, with irritation. 'There are few men who at the end of their lives do not experience what I am experiencing now. When you are told that you have something such as bad kidneys or an enlarged heart, and you begin treatment for it, or are told you are mad or a criminal – that is, in fact, when people suddenly pay attention to you – you may be sure you have got into a vicious circle from which you will not escape. If you try to escape you make things worse. Give in, because no human efforts can save you now. That's what I think.'

Meanwhile the public was crowding at the grating. To let them get on, Dr Ragin rose and began to take leave. Mikhail made him promise on his honour once more, and escorted him to the street door.

Towards evening on the same day Khobotov, in his sheepskin and his high top-boots, suddenly made his appearance, and said to Dr Ragin in a tone as though nothing had happened the day before:

'I have come on business, colleague. I have come to ask you whether you would join me in a consultation. Eh?'

Thinking that Khobotov wanted to distract him with an outing, or perhaps really to enable him to earn something, Dr Ragin put on his coat and hat, and went out with him into the street. He was glad of the opportunity to make up for yesterday and to make his peace, and in his heart thanked Khobotov, who did not even allude to yesterday's scene and was evidently sparing him. One would never have expected such tact from this coarse man.

'Where is your patient?' asked Dr Ragin.

'In the hospital . . . I have meant to show him to you for some time . . . A very interesting case.'

They went into the hospital yard, and going round the main building, turned towards the lodge where the mental cases were kept, and all this, for some reason, in silence. When they went into the lodge Nikita as usual leapt up and stood to attention.

'One of the patients here has a lung complication,' Khobotov said in an undertone, going into the ward with Dr Ragin. 'You wait here. I'll be back directly. I'll just fetch a stethoscope.'

And he walked out.

XVII

Dusk was falling. Gromov was lying on his bed with his face thrust into his pillow; the paralytic was sitting motionless, crying quietly and moving his lips. The fat peasant and the former sorter were asleep. It was quiet.

Dr Ragin sat down on Gromov's bed and waited. But half an hour passed, and not Khobotov, but Nikita came into the ward with a dressing-gown, someone's linen, and a pair of slippers piled on his arm.

'Please change your things, your Honour,' he said softly. 'Here is your bed; come this way,' he added, pointing to an empty bedstead which had obviously just been brought into the ward. 'It's all right; God willing, you'll get better.'

Dr Ragin understood it all. Without a word he crossed to the bed to which Nikita pointed and sat down; seeing that Nikita was standing waiting, he stripped naked and he felt ashamed. Then he put on the hospital clothes – the drawers were too short, the shirt too long, and the dressing-gown smelt of smoked fish.

'God willing, you'll get better,' repeated Nikita.

He gathered up an armful of Dr Ragin's clothes, went out, and shut the door after him.

'No matter . . .' thought Dr Ragin, bashfully wrapping himself in his dressing-gown and feeling that he looked like a convict in his new costume. 'It's no matter . . . It does not matter whether it's a dress coat or a uniform or this dressing-gown . . .'

But how about his watch? And the notebook that had been in the side pocket? And his cigarettes? Where had Nikita taken his clothes? Now perhaps to the day of his death he would not put on trousers, a waistcoat, or high boots. It was all somehow strange and even incomprehensible at first. Dr Ragin was still convinced that there was no difference between Mrs Belova's house and Ward No. 6, that everything in this world was nonsense and vanity of vanities, yet his hands were trembling, his feet were cold, and he was filled with dread at the thought that soon Gromov would get up and see that he was wearing a dressing-gown. He got up and walked across the room and sat down again.

He had sat half an hour, an hour and he was miserably sick of it: was it really possible to live here a day, a week, and even years like these people? Why, he had been sitting here, had walked about and sat down again; he could get up and look out of the window and walk from corner to corner again, and then what? Just sit all the time, like a statue and think? No, that could not be possible.

Dr Ragin lay down, but at once got up, wiped the cold sweat from his brow with his sleeve, and felt that his whole face smelt of smoked fish. He walked about again.

'It's some misunderstanding . . .' he said, spreading his arms in perplexity. 'I must have it out, there has been a misunder-standing . . .'

Meanwhile Gromov had woken up; he sat up and propped his cheeks on his fists. He spat. Then he glanced lazily at the doctor, and for the first minute seemed not to understand; but soon his sleepy face turned malicious and mocking.

'Aha! so they have put you in here, too, old fellow?' he said in a voice husky with sleep an' ' ¬ ved up one eye. 'Very glad to see you. You've sucked the blood of others, and now they will suck yours. Excellent!'

'It's a misunderstanding . . .' Dr Ragin brought out, frightened by Gromov's words; he shrugged his shoulders and repeated: 'It's some misunderstanding . . .'

Gromov spat again and lay down.

'Damned life,' he grumbled, 'and what's so bitter and hurtful is that this life will not end in compensation for our sufferings, it will not end with apotheosis as it would in an opera, but with death; the porters will come and drag one's dead body by the arms and the legs to the cellar. Ugh! Well, it does not matter . . . We shall have our good time in the other world . . . I shall come here as a ghost from the other world and frighten these reptiles. I'll turn their hair grey.'

Moiseika returned, and, seeing the doctor, held out his hand.

'Give me just a kopeck,' he said.

XVIII

Dr Ragin retreated to the window and looked out into the open country. It was getting dark, and on the horizon to the right a cold crimson moon was rising. Not far from the hospital fence, two hundred yards away, stood a tall white house surrounded by a stone wall. This was the prison.

'So this is real life,' thought Dr Ragin, and he felt frightened.

The moon and the prison, and the nails on the fence, and the far-away flames at the bone-processing factory were equally frightening. Behind him he heard a sigh. Dr Ragin looked round and saw a man with glittering stars and orders on his breast, who was smiling and slyly winking. And this, too, seemed frightening.

Dr Ragin tried to tell himself that there was nothing special about the moon or the prison, that even sane persons wear medals, and that everything in time will decay and turn to earth, but he was suddenly overcome with despair; he clutched at the grating with both hands and shook it with all his might. The strong grating did not yield.

Then, to lessen his fear, he went to Gromov's bed and sat down.

'I have lost heart, my dear fellow,' he muttered, trembling and wiping away the cold sweat, 'I have lost heart.'

'Why not philosophise?' said Gromov sarcastically.

'My God, my God . . . Yes, yes . . . You once said that there was no philosophy in Russia, but that all people, even the paltriest, philosophise. But the philosophising of the paltriest does not harm anyone,' said Dr Ragin as if he were on the verge of tears and laments. 'Why, then, that malignant laugh, my friend, and how can these paltry creatures help philosophising if they are dissatisfied? For an intelligent, educated man made in God's image, proud and freedom-loving, to have no alternative but to be a doctor in a filthy, stupid, wretched little town, and to spend his whole life among bottles, leeches, mustard plasters! Quackery, narrowness, vulgarity! Oh, my God!'

'You are talking rubbish. If you didn't like being a doctor you should have been a statesman.'

'I couldn't, I couldn't do anything. We are weak, my dear friend . . . I used to be above it all, I reasoned boldly and soundly, but life has only to touch me roughly and I have lost heart . . . Prostration . . . We are weak, we are poor creatures . . . and you, too, my dear friend, you are intelligent, generous, you drank in noble urges with your mother's milk, but you had hardly started life when you were exhausted and fell ill . . . Weak, weak!'

As evening drew on, Dr Ragin was constantly tormented by a persistent sensation other than terror and resentment. At last he realised that he wanted to smoke and to drink beer.

'I am going out, my friend,' he said. 'I will tell them to bring a light; I can't put up with this . . I can't take it . . .'

Dr Ragin went to the door and opened it, but at once Nikita jumped up and barred his way.

'Where are you going? You can't, you can't!' he said. 'It's bed-time.'

'But I'm only going out for a minute to stroll about the yard,' said Dr Ragin.

'You can't, you can't; it's forbidden. You know that yourself.'

'But what difference will it make to anyone if I go out?' asked Dr Ragin, shrugging. 'I don't understand. Nikita, I must go out!' he said in a trembling voice. 'I must.'

'Don't break the rules, it's bad,' Nikita admonished him.

'Who the hell does he think he is,' Gromov cried suddenly, and he jumped up. 'What right has he not to let people out? How dare they keep us here? It is clearly laid down in the law, isn't it, that no one can be deprived of freedom without trial! It's an outrage! It's tyranny!'

'Of course it's tyranny,' said Dr Ragin, encouraged by Gromov's outburst. 'I must go out, I want to. He has no right! Let us out, I tell you.'

'Do you hear, you dull-witted brute,' cried Gromov, and he banged on the door with his fist. 'Open the door, or I will break it open. Torturer!'

'Open the door,' cried Dr Ragin, trembling all over; 'I insist!'

'One more word!' Nikita answered through the door, 'Just one more . . .'

'At least go and call Dr Khobotov! Say that I ask him to come for a minute!'

'His honour will come tomorrow anyway.'

'They will never let us out,' Gromov was going on meanwhile. 'They will leave us to rot here! Oh, Lord, can there really be no hell in the next world, and will these wretches be pardoned? Where's the justice? Open the door, you wretch! I am choking!' he cried in a hoarse voice, and flung himself upon the door. 'I'll dash out my brains, you murderers!'

Nikita opened the door quickly, and roughly with both hands and his knee shoved Dr Ragin back, then swung his arm and punched him in the face with his fist. It seemed to Dr Ragin as though a huge salt wave enveloped him from his head downwards and dragged him to the bed; there really was a salt taste in his mouth: most likely the blood was running from his teeth. He waved his arms as though he were trying to swim out and clutched at a bedstead, and at the same moment felt Nikita hit him twice on the back.

Gromov gave a loud scream. He must have been beaten too.

Then all was still, the faint moonlight came through the grating, and a shadow like a net fell on the floor. It was terrible. Dr Ragin lay and held his breath: he was expecting with horror to be struck again. He felt as though someone had taken a sickle, thrust it into him, and turned it round several times in his breast and bowels. He bit the pillow from pain and clenched his teeth, and all at once through the chaos in his brain there flashed the terrible unbearable thought that these people, who seemed now like black shadows in the moonlight, had to endure such pain day by day for years. How could it have happened that for more than twenty years he had not known it and had refused to know it? He knew nothing of pain, had no conception of it, so he was not to blame, but his conscience, as inexorable and as rough as Nikita, made him turn cold from the back of his neck to his heels. He leapt up, tried to cry out with all his might, and to run in haste to kill Nikita, and then Khobotov, the superintendent and the assistant, and then himself; but no sound came from his chest, and his legs would not obey him. Gasping for breath, he tore at the dressing-gown and the shirt on his breast, rent them, and collapsed senseless on to the bed.

XIX

Next morning his head ached, there was a drumming in his ears and a feeling of utter weakness all over. He was not ashamed at recalling his weakness the day before. Yesterday he had been cowardly and even been afraid of the moon, had openly expressed thoughts and feelings such as he had not suspected in himself before; for instance, the thought that the paltry people who philosophised were in fact dissatisfied. But now he did not care.

He neither ate nor drank. He lay motionless and silent.

'I don't care,' he thought when asked questions. 'I am not going to answer . . . I don't care.'

After dinner Mikhail brought him a quarter of a pound of tea and a pound of fruit pastilles. Dariushka came too and stood for a whole hour by the bed with an expression of dull grief on her face. Dr Khobotov visited him. He brought a phial of bromide and told Nikita to fumigate the ward with something.

Towards evening Dr Ragin died of an apoplectic stroke. At first he had a violent shivering fit and a feeling of sickness; something revolting seemed to invade his whole body, even his fingers, stretched from his stomach to his head and flooded his eyes and ears. His eyes saw green. Dr Ragin understood that his end had come, and remembered that Gromov, Mikhail, and millions of people believed in immortality. And what if it really existed? But he did not want immortality, and he thought of it only for an instant. A herd of deer, extraordinarily beautiful and graceful, which he had been reading about the day before, ran by him; then a peasant woman stretched out her hand to him with a registered letter . . . Mikhail said something. Then it all vanished, and Dr Ragin sank into oblivion for ever.

The porters came, took him by his arms and legs, and carried him off to the chapel.

There he lay on the table, with open eyes, and the moon shed its light upon him at night. In the morning Sergei came, prayed piously before the crucifix, and closed his former chief's eyes.

Next day Dr Ragin was buried. Mikhail and Dariushka were the only people at the funeral.

1892

The Black Monk

Andrei Kovrin, a master of arts, had exhausted himself, and had strained his nerves. He did not seek treatment, but casually, over a bottle of wine, he spoke to a friend who was a doctor; the latter advised him to spend the spring and summer in the country. Very opportunely a long letter came from Tania Pesotskaia, who asked him to come and stay with them at Borisovka. And he decided that he really needed a break.

To begin with – that was in April – he went to his own estate, Kovrinka, and there spent three weeks in solitude; then, as soon as the roads were passable, he set off, in a carriage, to visit Pesotsky, his former guardian, who had brought him up, and was a horticulturist well known all over Russia. The distance from Kovrinka to Borisovka was reckoned to be no more than forty-five miles. To drive along a soft road in May in a comfortable carriage with springs was a real pleasure.

Pesotsky had an immense house with columns and lions, off which the stucco was peeling, and he had a footman in swallow-tails at the entrance. The old park, laid out in the English style, gloomy and severe, stretched for almost three-quarters of a mile to the river, and there ended in a steep, precipitous clay bank, where pines grew with bare roots that looked like shaggy paws; the water shone below with an unfriendly gleam, and the pewits flew up with a plaintive cry: there you always felt that you might as well sit down and write a ballad. But near the house itself, in the courtyard and orchard, which together with the nurseries covered eighty acres, it was all life and gaiety even in bad weather. Such marvellous roses, lilies, camellias; such tulips of all possible shades, from glistening white to sooty black – such a wealth of flowers, in fact, Kovrin had never seen anywhere except at Pesotsky's. It was only the beginning of spring, and the real glory of the flower-beds was still hidden away in the hothouses. But even the flowers along the avenues, and here and there in the flower-beds, were enough to make one feel, as one walked about the garden, as though one were in a realm of soft colours, especially in the early morning when the dew was glistening on every petal.

What was the decorative part of the garden, and what Pesotsky contemptuously called insignificant, had at one time in his childhood given Kovrin the impression of fairyland. Every sort of caprice, of elaborate monstrosity and mockery of nature was here. There were espaliers of fruit trees, a pear tree in the shape of a pyramid poplar, spherical oaks and lime trees, an apple tree in the shape of an umbrella, plum trees trained into arches, crests, candelabra, and even into the number *1862* – the year when Pesotsky first took up horticulture. One came across, too, lovely, graceful trees with strong, straight stems like palms, and only by looking closely could you recognise these trees as gooseberries or currants. But what made the orchard most cheerful and gave it a lively air was the continual coming and going in it, from early morning till evening; people with wheelbarrows, shovels, and watering-cans swarmed round the trees and bushes, in the avenues and the flower-beds, like ants . . .

Kovrin arrived at Pesotsky's at ten o'clock in the evening. He found Tania and her father, Yegor, in a state of great alarm. The clear starlit sky and the thermometer foretold a frost towards morning, but Ivan, the gardener, had gone to town, and they had no one to rely upon. At supper they talked of nothing but the morning frost, and it was settled that Tania would not go to bed: between twelve and one she would walk through the orchard, and see that everything was being done properly, and Yegor would get up at three or even earlier.

Kovrin sat with Tania all evening, and after midnight went out with her into the orchard. It was cold. There was already a strong smell of burning in the orchard. In the big orchard, which was called the farm, and which brought Yegor several thousand roubles clear profit, a thick, black, acrid smoke was creeping over the ground and, curling round the trees, was saving those thousands from the frost. Here the trees were arranged like chess pieces, in straight and regular rows like ranks of soldiers, and this severe pedantic regularity, and the fact that all the trees were of the same size, and had tops and trunks all exactly alike, made them look monotonous and even depressing. Kovrin and Tania walked along the rows where fires of dung, straw, and all sorts of refuse were smouldering, and from time to time they came across labourers who wandered in the smoke like shades. The only trees in blossom were the cherries, plums, and certain sorts of apples, but the whole orchard was plunged in smoke, and it was only near the nurseries that Kovrin could breathe freely.

'Even as a child the smoke here used to make me sneeze,' he said, shrugging, 'but to this day I don't understand how smoke can keep off frost.'

'Smoke takes the place of clouds when there are none...' answered Tania.

'And why do you want cloud?'

'In overcast and cloudy weather there is no frost.'

'You don't say so.'

He laughed and took her arm. Her broad, very earnest face, chilled with the frost, with her delicate black eyebrows, the turned-up collar of her coat, which prevented her moving her head freely, and the whole of her thin, graceful figure, with her skirts tucked up on account of the dew, touched him.

'Good heavens! she is grown up,' he said. 'When I went away from here last, five years ago, you were still a child. You were such a thin, long-legged creature, with your hair hanging on your shoulders; you used to wear short frocks, and I used to tease you, calling you a heron ... What time does!'

'Yes, five years!' sighed Tania. 'Much water has flowed since then. Tell me, Andrei, honestly,' she began eagerly, looking him in the face, 'have you grown away from us? But why do I ask you? You are a man, you live your own interesting life, you are somebody ... To grow apart is so natural! But however that may be, Andrei, I want you to think of us as family. We have a right to that.'

'I do, Tania.'

'Honestly?'

'Yes, honestly.'

'You were surprised this evening that we have so many photographs of you. You know my father adores you. Sometimes it seems to me that he loves you more than he does me. He is proud of you. You are a clever, extraordinary man, you have made a brilliant career for yourself, and he is convinced that you have turned out like this because he brought you up. I don't try to stop him thinking so. Let him.'

Dawn was already breaking, and that was especially perceptible from the distinctness with which the coils of smoke and the tops of the trees began to stand out in the air. The nightingales sang and the cries of the quail drifted in from the fields.

'It's bed-time, though,' said Tania, 'and cold, too.' She took his arm. 'Thank you for coming, Andrei. We have uninteresting friends, and not many of them. We have only the orchard, the orchard, the orchard, and nothing else. Standards, half-standards,' she laughed. 'Different sorts of apples – Oporto, rennet, Borovinka, budded stocks, grafted stocks ... All, all our life has gone into the orchard. I never even dream of anything but apples and pears. Of course, it is very nice and useful, but sometimes one longs for something else for variety. I remember that when you used to come to us for the summer holidays, or simply a visit, it always seemed to be fresher and brighter in the house, as though the covers had been taken off the candelabras and the furniture. I was only a little girl then, but I still understood.'

She talked a long while and with great feeling. For some reason the idea came into his head that in the course of the summer he might grow fond of this weak, little, talkative creature, might be carried away and fall in love; in their position it was so possible and natural! This thought touched and amused him; he bent down to her sweet, preoccupied face and hummed softly:

> 'Onegin, I shall not conceal it;
> I love Tatiana wildly, madly . . .'*

By the time they reached the house, Yegor had got up. Kovrin did not feel sleepy; he talked to the old man and went to the orchard with him. Yegor was a tall, broad-shouldered, corpulent man, and he suffered from breathlessness, yet he walked so fast that it was hard work to keep up with him. He had an extremely preoccupied air; he was always hurrying somewhere, with an expression that suggested that if he were one minute late all would be ruined!

'Here is an odd thing, brother . . .' he began, standing still to take a breath. 'The surface of the ground, as you see, is frosted; but if you raise the thermometer on a stick fourteen feet above the ground, it is warm . . . Why is that?'

'I really don't know,' said Kovrin, and he laughed.

'H'm! . . . You can't know everything, of course . . . However large the intellect may be, you can't find room for everything in it. I suppose you still go in chiefly for philosophy?'

'Yes, I lecture in psychology; but I am studying philosophy.'

'And it does not bore you?'

'On the contrary, it's all I live for.'

'Well, God bless you! . . .' said Yegor, meditatively stroking his grey whiskers. 'God bless you! . . . I am delighted for you . . . delighted, my boy . . .'

But suddenly he listened, and, with a terrible face, ran off and quickly disappeared behind the trees in a cloud of smoke.

'Who tied a horse to an apple tree?' Kovrin heard his despairing, heart-rending cry. 'Who is the low scoundrel who has dared to tie a horse to an apple tree? My God, my God! They have ruined everything; they have spoilt everything; they have done everything filthy, horrible, and abominable. The orchard's done for, the orchard's ruined. My God!'

When he came back to Kovrin, his face looked exhausted and mortified.

'What is one to do with these accursed people?' he sai in a tearful voice, flinging up his hands. 'Stiopka was carting dung at night, and tied the horse to an apple tree! He twisted the reins round it, the rascal, as tightly as he could, so that the tree is barked in three places. What do you think of that! I spoke to him and he stands like a dummy and only blinks. Hanging is too good for him.'

Growing calmer, he embraced Kovrin and kissed him on the cheek.

'Well, God bless you! . . . God bless you! . . .' he muttered. 'I am very glad you have come. More than I can say . . . Thank you.'

Then, with the same rapid step and preoccupied face, he made the round of the whole orchard, and showed his former ward all his greenhouses and hothouses, his covered-in garden, and two apiaries which he called the marvel of our century.

While they were walking the sun rose, flooding the garden with brilliant light. It grew warm. Foreseeing a long, bright, cheerful day, Kovrin recollected that it was only the beginning of May, and that he had before him a whole summer as bright, cheerful, and long; and suddenly there stirred in his chest a joyous, youthful feeling, such as he used to experience in his childhood, running about in that garden. And he hugged the old man and kissed him affectionately. Both of them, feeling touched, went indoors and drank tea out of old-fashioned china cups, with cream and rich krendels made with milk and eggs; and these trifles reminded Kovrin again of his childhood and boyhood. The delightful present was blended with the impressions of the past that stirred within him; his heart and soul were overwhelmed, yet he was happy.

He waited for Tania to awake and had coffee with her, went for a walk, then went to his room and sat down to work. He read attentively, making notes, and from time to time raised his eyes to look out at the open windows or at the fresh, still dewy flowers in the vases on the table; and again he dropped his eyes to his book, and it seemed to him as though every vein in his body was quivering and fluttering with pleasure.

II

In the country he led just as tense and restless a life as in town. He read and wrote a great deal, he studied Italian, and when he was out for a walk, thought with pleasure that he would soon get back to work again. He slept so little that everyone wondered at him; if he accidentally dozed for half an hour in the daytime, he would lie awake all night, and, after a sleepless night, would feel cheerful and vigorous as though nothing had happened.

He talked a great deal, drank wine, and smoked expensive cigars. Very often, almost every day, young ladies of neighbouring families would come to the Pesotskys', and would sing and play the piano with Tania; sometimes a young neighbour who was a good violinist would come too. Kovrin listened with eagerness to the music and singing, and was exhausted by it, and this showed itself by his eyelids closing and his head falling to one side.

One day he was sitting on the balcony after evening tea, reading. At the same time, in the drawing-room, Tania taking soprano, one of the young ladies a contralto, and the young man with his violin, were practising Braga's* serenade, *A Wallachian Legend*. Kovrin listened to the words – they were in Russian – but could not understand their meaning. At last, leaving his book and listening attentively, he understood: a maiden, with a morbid imagination, hears one night in her garden mysterious sounds, so strange and lovely which she has to recognise them as a holy harmony which is unintelligible to us mortals, and so flies back to heaven. Kovrin's eyes began to close. He got up, and in exhaustion walked up and down the drawing-room, and then the dining-room. When the singing was over he took Tania's arm, and with her went out on to the balcony.

'All day I have been preoccupied by a legend,' he said. 'I don't remember whether I have read it somewhere or heard it, but it is a strange legend that makes no sense. To begin with, it's not particularly lucid. A thousand years ago a monk, dressed in black, wandered about the desert, somewhere in Syria or Arabia . . . Some miles from where he was, some fishermen saw another black monk, who was moving slowly over the surface of a lake. This second monk was a mirage. Now forget all the laws of optics, which the legend seems not to recognise, and listen to the rest. That mirage cast another mirage, then from that one a third, so that the image of the black monk began to be transmitted endlessly from one layer of the atmosphere to another. So that he was seen at one time in Africa, at another in Spain, then in Italy, then in the Far North . . . Then he passed out of the atmosphere of the earth, and now he is wandering all over the universe, still never coming into conditions in which he might disappear. Possibly he may be seen now in Mars or in some star of the Southern Cross. But, my dear, the crux of the legend is that exactly a thousand years from the day when the monk walked in the desert the mirage will return to the atmosphere of the earth again and will appear to men. And apparently the thousand years is almost up . . . According to the legend, we can expect the black monk any day now.'

'A strange mirage,' said Tania, who did not like the legend.

'But the most astounding thing,' laughed Kovrin, 'is that I simply cannot recall where I got this legend from. Have I read it somewhere? Have I heard it? Or perhaps I dreamed of the black monk. I swear I don't remember. But the legend preoccupies me. I have been thinking about it all day.'

Letting Tania go back to her visitors, he left the house, and, lost in meditation, took a walk by the flower-beds. The sun was already setting. The flowers, having just been watered, gave forth a damp, irritating fragrance. In the house the singing started again, and from afar the violin had the effect of a human voice. Kovrin, racking his brains to remember where he had read or heard the legend, turned slowly towards the park, and did not notice that he had reached the river.

By a little path that ran along the steep bank, between the bare roots, he went down to the water, disturbed the sandpipers there and frightened off two ducks. The last rays of the setting sun still threw light here and there on the gloomy pines, but on the surface of the river it was already evening. Kovrin crossed on the stepping stones to the other side. Before him lay a wide field covered with young rye not yet in flower. There was no human habitation, no living soul in the distance, and it seemed as though the path, if one went along it, would take one to the unknown, mysterious place where the sun had just set, and where the evening glow was flaming, immense and splendid.

'How open, how free, how still it is here!' thought Kovrin, walking along the path. 'And it feels as though all the world were watching me, holding back and waiting for me to understand it . . .'

But then waves began running across the rye, and a light evening breeze softly touched his bare head. A minute later there was another gust of wind, but stronger – the rye began rustling, and he heard behind him the hollow murmur of the pines. Kovrin stood still in amazement. On the horizon there rose up from the earth to the sky, like a whirlwind or a waterspout, a tall black column. Its outline was indistinct, but straight away Kovrin could see that it was not standing still, but moving with fearful rapidity, moving straight towards him, and the nearer it came the smaller and more distinct it was. Kovrin leapt aside into the rye to make way for it, and was only just in time.

A monk dressed in black with a grey head and black eyebrows, his arms crossed over his breast, was borne past him . . . His bare feet did not touch the earth. After he had floated about six yards past him, he looked round at Kovrin, and nodded to him with a friendly but sly smile. But what a pale, fearfully pale, thin face! Beginning to grow larger again, he flew across the river, collided noiselessly with the clay bank and pines, and passing through them, vanished like smoke.

'Well, you see . . .' muttered Kovrin, 'there must be truth in the legend.'

Without trying to account for the strange apparition, glad that he had succeeded in seeing so near and so distinctly, not only the monk's black garments, but even his face and eyes, agreeably excited, he returned to the house.

In the park and in the garden people were moving about quietly, in the house they were playing – so he alone had seen the monk. He had an intense desire to tell Tania and Yegor everything, but he realised that they would certainly think he was raving, and that would frighten them; he had better say nothing. He laughed loudly, sang, and danced the mazurka; he was in high spirits, and all of them, the visitors and Tania, thought he had a peculiar look, radiant and inspired, and that he was very interesting.

III

After supper, when the visitors had gone, he went to his room and lay down on the sofa: he wanted to think about the monk. But a minute later Tania came in.

'Here, Andrei; read father's articles,' she said, giving him a bundle of pamphlets and offprints. 'They are splendid articles. He writes extremely well.'

'Extremely well, indeed!' said Yegor, following her and forcing himself to smile; he was embarrassed. 'Don't listen to her, please; don't read them! Though, if you want to go to sleep, read them by all means; they are a fine soporific.'

'I think they are splendid articles,' said Tania, with deep conviction. 'You read them, Andrei, and persuade father to write a bit more often. He could write a complete manual of horticulture.'

Yegor laughed loud and tensely, blushed, and began uttering the phrases usually heard from embarrassed authors. Finally he began to yield.

'In that case, begin with Gaucher's article and these Russian articles,' he muttered, turning over the pamphlets with a trembling hand, 'or else you won't understand. Before you read my objections, you must know what I am objecting to. But all nonsense . . . tiresome stuff. Besides, I believe it's bed-time.'

Tania went away. Yegor sat down on the sofa by Kovrin and heaved a deep sigh.

'Yes, my boy . . .' he began after a pause. 'That's how it is, my dear

Master of Arts. Here I write articles, and take part in exhibitions, and receive medals . . . Pesotsky, they say, has apples the size of a human head, and Pesotsky, they say, has made his fortune with his orchard. In short, "Kochubei is rich and glorious".* But one asks oneself: what is it all for? The orchard is certainly fine, a model . . . not so much an orchard as a regular institution, which is of the greatest public importance because it marks, so to say, a new era in Russian agriculture and Russian industry. But, what for? What's the point?'

'The business speaks for itself.'

'I do not mean in that sense. I meant to ask: what will happen to the orchard when I die? In the state in which you see it now, it would not last for one month without me. The whole secret of success lies not in its being a big orchard or a great number of labourers being employed in it, but in the fact that I love the work. Do you understand? I love it perhaps more than myself. Look at me; I do everything myself. I work from morning to night: I do all the grafting myself, the pruning myself, the planting myself. I do it all myself: when anyone helps me I am jealous and irritable, even offensive. The whole secret is love – that is, the owner's sharp eye; yes, and in the master's hands, and in the feeling that makes one, when one goes anywhere for an hour's visit, sit, ill at ease, with one's heart far away, afraid that something may go wrong in the orchard. But when I die, who will see to it? Who will work? The gardener? The labourers? Yes? But I tell you, my dear fellow, the worst enemy in the orchard is not a hare, not a cockchafer, and not the frost, but any outsider.'

'And Tania?' asked Kovrin, laughing. 'She can't be more harmful than a hare? She loves the work and understands it.'

'Yes, she loves it and understands it. If after my death the orchard goes to her and she is the mistress, of course that's the best thing that could happen. But if, God forbid, she should marry,' Yegor whispered, giving Kovrin a frightened look, 'that's just it. If she marries and has children, she'll have no time to think about the orchard. What I fear most is: she will marry some fine gentleman, and he will be greedy, and he will let the orchard to market women, and it will all go to the dogs the very first year! In our line females are the scourge of God!'

Yegor sighed and paused for a while.

'Perhaps it is egotism, but I tell you frankly: I don't want Tania to get married. I am afraid of it! There's a dandy who brings his violin and saws away; I know Tania won't marry him, I'm sure; but I can't bear the sight of him! I suppose, my boy, I am very odd. I admit it.'

Yegor got up and walked about the room in excitement, and it was evident that he wanted to say something very important, but could not bring himself to it.

'I am very fond of you, and I am going to speak to you frankly,' he decided at last, thrusting his hands into his pockets. 'I take a plain view of some delicate questions, and say exactly what I think, and I cannot stand so-called hidden thoughts. I'll speak plainly: you are the only man to whom I should not be afraid to marry my daughter. You are a clever man with a good heart, and would not let my beloved work go to ruin; and the chief reason is that I love you as a son, and I am proud of you. If Tania and you were to fall in love then – well! I should be very glad and even happy. I tell you this plainly, without affectation, like an honest man.'

Kovrin laughed. Yegor opened the door to go out, and stood in the doorway.

'If Tania and you had a son, I would make a horticulturist of him,' he said, after a moment's thought. 'However, this is idle dreaming . . . Good night.'

Left alone, Kovrin lay down and made himself comfortable and started at the articles. One was called 'On Intercropping'; another, 'A Few Words on the Remarks of Monsieur Z – concerning the Trenching of the Soil for a New Orchard'; a third, 'More on Grafting with a Dormant Bud'; and all were of the same sort. But what a restless, unbalanced tone! What nervous, almost hysterical obsession! Here was an article, one would have thought, with most peaceable title and neutral contents: it was about the Russian Antonov apple. But Yegor began it with '*Audiatur altera pars*,' and finished it with '*Sapienti sat*.'; and between these two quotations a perfect torrent of venomous phrases directed 'at the learned ignorance of our recognised horticultural authorities, who observe Nature from the height of their university chairs', or at Monsieur Gaucher,* 'whose success has been the work of the vulgar and the dilettanti'. And then followed an inappropriate, affected, and insincere regret that peasants who stole fruit and broke branches could no longer be flogged.

'It is beautiful, charming, healthy work, but it too has strife and passion,' thought Kovrin. 'I suppose that everywhere and in all careers men of ideas are highly strung, and are markedly over-sensitive. Probably, it is inevitable.'

He thought of Tania, who was so pleased with Yegor's articles. Small, pale, and so thin that her collar-bones stuck out, her wide-open eyes, dark and intelligent, stared into the distance, as though looking for something. Like her father's, her gait was fussy and hurried. She talked a great deal and was fond of arguing, accompanying every phrase, however insignificant, with expressive mimicry and gesticulation. No doubt she was extremely highly strung.

Kovrin tried to go on reading, but he understood nothing, and gave it up. The same pleasant excitement with which he had earlier in the evening danced the mazurka and listened to the music was now wearing him down and rousing a multitude of thoughts. He got up and began walking about the room, thinking about the black monk. It occurred to him that if this strange, supernatural monk had appeared only to him, that meant that he was ill and was already suffering from hallucinations. This conclusion frightened him, but not for long.

'But I'm all right, and I'm doing no harm to anyone; so there's no harm in my hallucinations,' he thought; and he felt happy again.

He sat down on the sofa and clasped his hands round his head.

Restraining the unaccountable joy which filled his whole being, he then paced up and down again, and sat down to his work. But the thoughts that he was perusing in a book did not satisfy him. He wanted something gigantic, unfathomable, stupendous. Towards morning he undressed and reluctantly went to bed: he ought to sleep.

When he heard the footsteps of Yegor going out into the garden, Kovrin rang the bell and asked the footman to bring him some wine. He drank several glasses of Lafitte, then buried himself in the bedclothes; his mind grew clouded and he fell asleep.

IV

Yegor and Tania often quarrelled and said nasty things to each other.

One morning they had lost their tempers about something. Tania burst out crying and went to her room. She would not come down to dinner nor to tea. At first Yegor went about looking sulky and dignified, as though to let everyone know that for him the claims of justice and good order were above all else in the world; but he could not keep it up for long, and soon lost spirit. He walked about the park dejectedly, continually sighing: 'Oh, my God! My God!' and at dinner did not eat a morsel. At last, guilty and conscience-stricken, he knocked at the locked door and called timidly:

'Tania! Tania!'

And from behind the door came a faint voice, weak with crying, but still determined:

'Leave me alone, please.'

The depression of the master and mistress affected the whole household, even the labourers working in the orchard. Kovrin was absorbed in his interesting work, but in the end he, too, felt miserable and uncomfortable. To dissipate the general ill humour in some way, he made up his mind to intervene, and towards evening he knocked at Tania's door. He was admitted.

'Really, shame on you!' he began playfully, looking with surprise at Tania's tear-stained, woebegone face, flushed in patches with crying. 'Is it really so serious? Really!'

'But if you knew how he tortures me!' she said, and floods of scalding tears streamed from her big eyes. 'He's worn me out,' she went on, wringing her hands. 'I said nothing to him . . . nothing . . . I only said that there was no need to keep . . . too many labourers . . . if we could hire them by the day when we need to. After all . . . after all the labourers have been doing nothing for a whole week . . . I . . . I . . . only said that, and he shouted and . . . said . . . a lot of hurtful, deeply insulting things to me. Why?'

'There, there,' said Kovrin, smoothing her hair. 'You've quarrelled with each other, you've cried, and that's enough. You must not be angry for long – that's wrong . . . all the more as he loves you beyond everything.'

'He has . . . has spoiled my whole life,' Tania went on, sobbing. 'I hear nothing but abuse and . . . insults. He thinks I am of no use in the house. Well! He is right. I'll leave tomorrow; I shall become a telegraph clerk . . . I don't care . . .'

'Come, come, come . . . You mustn't cry, Tania. You mustn't, dear . . . You are both hot-tempered and irritable, and you are both to blame. Come along; I'll help you make it up.'

Kovrin talked tenderly and persuasively, while she went on crying, twitching her shoulders and wringing her hands, as though some terrible misfortune had really befallen her. He felt all the sorrier for her because her grief was not serious, yet she suffered deeply. What trivial things were enough to make this little creature miserable for a whole day, perhaps for her whole life! Comforting Tania, Kovrin thought that, apart from this girl and her father, he might hunt he world over and would not find people who would love him as one of themselves, as one of their kin. If it had not been for those two he might very likely, having lost his father and mother in early childhood, never to the day of his death have known genuine affection and that naive, uncritical love which is only lavished on very close blood relations; and he felt that the nerves of this weeping, shaking girl responded to his half-sick, overstrained nerves like iron to a magnet. He never could have loved a healthy, strong, rosy-cheeked woman, but pale, weak, unhappy Tania attracted him.

And he liked stroking her hair and her shoulders, pressing her hand and wiping away her tears . . . At last she stopped crying. She went on for a long time complaining of her father and her hard, insufferable life in that house, entreating Kovrin to put himself in her place; then she began, little by little, smiling, and sighing that God had given her such a bad temper. At last, laughing aloud, she called herself a fool, and ran out of the room.

When a little later Kovrin went into the garden, Yegor and Tania were walking side by side along an avenue as though nothing had happened, and both were eating rye bread with salt on it, as both were hungry.

V

Glad that he had been so successful as a peacemaker, Kovrin went into the park. Sitting on a garden seat, thinking, he heard carriages rattling and women laughing – visitors were arriving. When the shades of evening began falling on the garden, then he heard the faint sounds of the violin and singing voices reached him, and that reminded him of the black monk. Where, in what land or in what planet, was that optical absurdity moving now?

Hardly had he recalled the legend and pictured in his imagination the dark apparition he had seen in the rye field, when, from behind a pine tree exactly opposite, there came out noiselessly, without the slightest rustle, a man of medium height with uncovered grey head, all in black, and barefooted like a beggar, and his black eyebrows stood out conspicuously on his pale, death-like face. Nodding his head graciously, this beggar or pilgrim came noiselessly to the seat and sat down, and Kovrin recognised him as the black monk. For a minute they looked at one another, Kovrin with amazement, and the monk with tenderness, and, just as before, a little slyness, with a knowing expression.

'But you are a mirage,' said Kovrin. 'Why are you here and sitting still? That does not fit in with the legend.'

'That does not matter,' the monk answered in a low voice, not immediately turning his face towards him. 'The legend, the mirage, and I are all the products of your excited imagination. I am a phantom.'

'Then you don't exist?' said Kovrin.

'You can think as you like,' said the monk, with a faint smile. 'I exist in your imagination, and your imagination is part of nature, so I exist in nature.'

'You have a very old, wise, and extremely expressive face, as though you really had lived more than a thousand years,' said Kovrin. 'I did not know that my imagination was capable of creating such phenomena. But why do you look at me with such delight? Do you like me?'

'Yes, you are one of those few who are justly called God's chosen.

You serve eternal truth. Your thoughts, your aims, marvellous scholarship, and your whole life, bear a divine, heavenly stamp, since they are dedicated to the rational and the beautiful – that is, to what is eternal.'

'You said "eternal truth" . . . But is eternal truth of use to man and within his reach, if there is no eternal life?'

'There is eternal life,' said the monk.

'Do you believe in the immortality of man?'

'Yes, of course. A grand, brilliant future is in store for you, for humanity. And the more there are like you on earth, the sooner will this future be realised. Without you who serve a higher principle and live in full understanding and freedom, mankind would be of little account; developing in a natural way, it would have to wait a long time for the end of its earthly history. You will lead it some thousands of years earlier into the kingdom of eternal truth – and therein lies your supreme service. You are the incarnation of the blessing of God, which rests upon men.'

'And what is the object of eternal life?' asked Kovrin.

'As in all life – enjoyment. True enjoyment lies in knowledge, and eternal life provides innumerable and inexhaustible sources of knowledge, and in that sense it has been said: "In my Father's house are many mansions." '

'If only you knew how pleasant it is to listen to you!' said Kovrin, rubbing his hands with satisfaction.

'I'm very glad.'

'But I know that when you go away I shall be worried by the question of your reality. You are a phantom, an hallucination. So I am mentally ill, not normal?'

'What if you are? Why trouble yourself? You are ill because you have overworked and exhausted yourself, and that means that you have sacrificed your health to the idea, and the time is near at hand when you will give up life itself to it. What could be better? That is the goal towards which all divinely endowed, noble natures strive.'

'If I know I am mentally ill, can I trust myself?'

'And are you sure that the men of genius, whom all men trust, did not see phantoms, too? The learned say now that genius is allied to madness. My friend, healthy and normal people are only the common herd. Reflections upon the age of neurasthenia, exhaustion and degeneracy, etc., can only seriously worry those who think the aim of life is the present – that is, the common herd.'

'The Romans used to say: *Mens sana in corpore sano*.'

'Not everything the Greeks and the Romans said is true. Exaltation, enthusiasm, ecstasy – all that distinguishes prophets, poets, martyrs for the idea, from the common folk – are repellent to the animal side of man – that is, his physical health. I repeat, if you want to be healthy and normal, join the herd.'

'Strange that you repeat what often comes into my mind,' said Kovrin. 'It is as though you had seen and overheard my secret thoughts. But don't let us talk about me. What do you mean by "eternal truth"?'

The monk did not answer. Kovrin looked at him and could not distinguish his face. His features grew blurred and misty. Then the monk's head and arms disappeared; his body seemed merged into the seat and the evening twilight, and he vanished altogether.

'The hallucination is over,' said Kovrin; and he laughed: 'a pity.'

He went back to the house, light-hearted and happy. The little the monk had said to him had flattered, not his vanity, but his whole soul, his whole being. To be one of the chosen, to serve eternal truth, to stand in the ranks of those who could make mankind worthy of the kingdom of God some thousands of years sooner – that is, to free men from some thousands of years of unnecessary struggle, sin, and suffering; to sacrifice to the idea everything – youth, strength, health; to be ready to die for the common good – what an exalted, what a happy lot! He recalled his past – pure, chaste, industrious; he remembered what he had learned himself and what he had taught to others, and decided that there was no exaggeration in the monk's words.

Tania came to meet him in the park: she was by now wearing a different dress.

'Are you here?' she said. 'And we have been looking and looking for you . . . But what is the matter with you?' she asked in wonder, glancing at his radiant, ecstatic face and eyes full of tears. 'How strange you are, Andrei!'

'I am pleased, Tania,' said Kovrin, laying his hand on her shoulders. 'I am more than pleased: I am happy. Tania, darling Tania, you are an extraordinary, nice creature. Dear Tania, I am so glad, I am so glad!'

He kissed both her hands ardently, and went on:

'I have just experienced exalted, wonderful, unearthly moments. But I can't tell you about it or you would call me mad and not believe me. Let us talk of you. Dear, delightful Tania! I love you, and am used to loving you. To have you near me, to meet you a dozen times a day, has become a vital necessity to me; I don't know how I shall do without you when I go back home.'

'Oh,' laughed Tania, 'you will forget about us in two days. We are humble people and you are a great man.'

'No; let us talk in earnest!' he said. 'I shall take you with me, Tania. Yes? Will you come with me? Will you be mine?'

'Come,' said Tania, and tried to laugh again, but the laugh would not come, and red patches appeared on her face.

She began breathing quickly and walked very quickly, not to the house, but further into the park.

'I hadn't thought of it . . . I hadn't thought!' she said, wringing her hands as though in despair.

Kovrin followed her and went on talking, with the same radiant, enthusiastic face: 'I want a love that will take me over; and that love only you, Tania, can give me. I am happy! I am happy!'

She was overwhelmed, she bent double, shrivelled and immediately seemed ten years older, while he thought her beautiful and expressed his rapture aloud:

'How lovely she is!'

VI

Learning from Kovrin that there was not only mutual love, but even a wedding to come, Yegor spent a long time pacing from one corner of the room to the other, trying to conceal his emotion. His hands began trembling, his neck swelled and turned purple, he ordered his light carriage and drove off somewhere. Tania, seeing how he lashed the horse, and seeing how he pulled his cap over his ears, understood his mood, shut herself up in her room, and cried the whole day.

In the hothouses the peaches and plums were already ripe; packing and despatching these tender and fragile goods to Moscow took a great deal of care, work, and trouble. Because the summer was very hot and dry, it was necessary to water every tree, and a great deal of time and labour was spent on doing it. Numbers of caterpillars made their appearance, which, to Kovrin's disgust, the labourers and even Yegor and Tania squashed with their fingers. In spite of all that, they had already to book autumn orders for fruit and trees, and to carry on a great deal of correspondence. And at the very busiest time, when no one seemed to have a free moment, agricultural work took more than half their labourers out of the orchard. Yegor, deeply tanned, exhausted, ill-humoured, galloped from the fields to the orchard and back again; cried that he was being torn to pieces, and that he would put a bullet through his brains.

Then came the fuss and worry of the trousseau, to which the Pesotskys attached a good deal of importance. Everyone's head was in a whirl from the snipping of the scissors, and the rattle of the sewing machine, the smell of hot irons, and the caprices of the dressmaker, a huffy and highly strung lady. And, as ill luck would have it, visitors came every day: they had to be entertained, fed, and even put up for the night. But all this hard labour passed unnoticed as though in a fog. Tania felt that love and happiness had taken her unawares, though she had, since she was fourteen, for some reason been convinced that Kovrin would marry her and no one else. She was bewildered, could not grasp it, could not believe herself ... At one minute such joy would swoop down upon her that she longed to fly away to the clouds and there pray to God, at another moment she would remember that in August she would have to part from her home and leave her father; or, goodness knows why, the idea would occur to her that she was worthless, insignificant and unworthy of a great man like Kovrin – and she would go to her room, lock herself in, and cry bitterly for several hours. When there were visitors, she would suddenly fancy that Kovrin looked extraordinarily handsome, and that all the women were in love with him and envying her, and her soul was filled with pride and rapture, as though she had vanquished the whole world; but he had only to smile politely at any young lady for her to tremble with jealousy, to retreat to her room – and tears again. These new sensations mastered her completely; she helped her father mechanically, without noticing peaches, caterpillars or labourers, or how rapidly the time was passing.

It was almost the same with Yegor. He worked from morning till night, was always in a hurry, was irritable, and flew into rages, but all of this was in a sort of spellbound dream. It seemed as though there were two men in him: one was the real Yegor, who was moved to indignation, and clutched his head in despair when he heard of any breaches of order from Ivan the gardener; and another – not the real one -- who seemed as though he were half drunk, would interrupt a business conversation at half a word, touch the gardener on the shoulder, and begin muttering:

'Say what you like, there is a great deal in blood. His mother was a wonderful woman, most high-minded and intelligent. It was a pleasure to look at her good, candid, pure face; it was like the face of an angel. She drew splendidly, wrote verse, spoke five foreign languages, sang ... Poor thing! God rest her; she died of consumption.'

The unreal Yegor sighed, and after a pause went on:

'When he was a boy and growing up in my house, he had the same angelic face, good and candid. The way he looks and talks and moves is as soft and elegant as his mother's. And his intellect! We were always struck with his intelligence. To be sure, not for nothing he's a Master of Arts! Not for nothing! And just wait, Ivan, what will he be in ten years' time? He will be far above us!'

But at this point the real Yegor, suddenly coming to himself, would make a terrible face, would clutch his head and cry:

'The devils! They have spoilt everything! They have ruined everything! They have spoilt everything! The orchard's done for, the orchard's ruined!'

Kovrin, meanwhile, worked with the same ardour as before, and did not notice the general commotion. Love only added fuel to the flames. After every meeting with Tania he went to his room, happy and triumphant, took up his book or his manuscript with the same passion with which he had just kissed Tania, and told her of his love. What the black monk had told him of God's chosen, of eternal truth, of the brilliant future of mankind and so on, gave peculiar and extraordinary significance to his work, and filled his soul with pride and an awareness of his own loftiness. Once or twice a week, in the park or in the house, he met the black monk and had long conversations with him, but this did not alarm him, but, on the contrary, delighted him, as he was now firmly persuaded that such apparitions only visited the outstanding few elect who had dedicated themselves to serving an idea.

One day the monk appeared at dinner-time and sat in the dining-room window. Kovrin was delighted, and very adroitly began a conversation with Yegor and Tania of what might be of interest to the monk; the black-robed visitor listened and nodded his head graciously, and Yegor and Tania listened, too, and smiled gaily without suspecting that Kovrin was talking not to them but to his hallucination.

Imperceptibly the fast of the Dormition* was approaching, and soon after came the wedding, which, at Yegor's urgent desire, was celebrated with 'a flourish' – that is, with senseless festivities that lasted for two whole days and nights. Three thousand roubles' worth of food and drink was consumed, but the music of the wretched hired band, the noisy toasts, the scurrying to and fro of the footmen, the uproar and crowding, prevented them from appreciating the taste of the expensive wines and wonderful delicacies ordered from Moscow.

VII

One long winter night Kovrin was lying in bed, reading a French novel. Poor Tania, who had headaches in the evening because she was not used to living in town, had been asleep a long while, and, from time to time, uttered incoherent phrases in her restless state.

The clock struck three. Kovrin put out the light and lay down, lay for a long time with his eyes closed, but could not get to sleep because he fancied the room was very hot and Tania was talking in her sleep. At half-past four he lit the candle again, and this time he saw the black monk sitting in an arm-chair near the bed.

'Good morning,' said the monk, and after a brief pause he asked: 'What are you thinking of now?'

'Of fame,' answered Kovrin. 'In the French novel I have just been reading, there is a description of a young savant, who does silly things and pines away through worrying about fame. I can't understand such anxiety.'

'Because you are wise. Your attitude towards fame is one of indifference; it is a toy which no longer interests you.'

'Yes, that is true.'

'Renown does not allure you now. What is there flattering, amusing, or edifying in their carving your name on a tombstone, then time rubbing off the inscription together with the gilding? Moreover, happily there are too many of you for the weak memory of mankind to be able to retain your names.'

'Of course,' assented Kovrin. 'Besides, why should they be remembered? But let us talk of something else. Of happiness, for instance. What is happiness?'

When the clock struck five, he was sitting on the bed, dangling his feet on the carpet, talking to the monk:

'In ancient times a happy man grew at last frightened of his happiness – it was so great! – and to propitiate the gods he brought as a sacrifice his favourite ring. Do you know, I, too, like Polykrates, am beginning to be uneasy about my happiness. It seems strange to me that from morning to night I feel nothing but joy; it fills my whole being and smothers all other feelings. I don't know what sadness, grief, or boredom are. For instance, I don't sleep; I suffer from sleeplessness, but I am not bored. I mean it; I am beginning to feel perplexed.'

'But why?' the monk asked in wonder. 'Is joy a supernatural feeling? Ought it not to be the normal state of man? The more highly a man is developed on the intellectual and moral side, the freer he is, the more pleasure life gives him. Socrates, Diogenes, and Marcus Aurelius, felt joy, not sorrow. And the apostle tells us: "Rejoice continually." Rejoice and be happy.'

'Suppose the gods get angry?' Kovrin jested; and he laughed. 'If they take from me comfort and make me cold and hungry, I probably shan't like it.'

Meanwhile Tania had woken up; she was looking with amazement and horror at her husband. He was talking, addressing the arm-chair, laughing and gesticulating; his eyes were gleaming, and there was something strange in his laugh.

'Andrei, whom are you talking to?' she asked, clutching the hand he stretched out to the monk. 'Andrei! Whom?'

'Oh! Whom?' said Kovrin in confusion. 'Why, to him . . . He is sitting here,' he said, pointing to the black monk.

'There is no one here . . . no one! Andrei, you are ill!'

Tania put her arm round her husband and held him tight, as though protecting him from the apparition, and put her hand over his eyes.

'You are ill!' she sobbed, trembling all over. 'Forgive me, my precious, my darling, but I noticed a long time ago that something had deranged your mind . . . You are mentally ill, Andrei . . .'

Her trembling infected him, too. He glanced once more at the arm-chair, which was now empty, felt a sudden weakness in his arms and legs, was frightened, and began dressing.

'It's nothing, Tania; nothing,' he muttered, shivering. 'I really am not quite well . . . It's time I admitted it.'

'I have noticed it for a long time . . . and father has noticed it,' she said, trying to suppress her sobs. 'You talk to yourself, smile somehow strangely . . . and can't sleep. Oh, my God, my God, save us!' she said in terror. 'But don't be afraid, Andrei; for God's sake don't be afraid . . .'

She began dressing, too. Only now, looking at her, Kovrin realised the danger of his position – realised the meaning of the black monk and his conversations with him. It was clear to him now that he was mad.

Neither of them knew why they dressed and went into the dining-room: she in front and he following her. There they found Yegor standing in his dressing-gown and with a candle in his hand. He was staying with them, and had been awakened by Tania's sobs.

'Don't be frightened, Andrei,' Tania was saying, shivering as though in a fever; 'don't be frightened . . . Father, it will all pass . . . it will all pass . . .'

Kovrin was too much agitated to speak. He wanted to say to his father-in-law in a playful tone:

'Congratulate me; I believe I've gone mad.' But he could only move his lips and smile bitterly.

At nine in the morning they put on his jacket and fur coat, wrapped him up in a shawl, and took him by carriage to see a doctor. He began treatment.

VIII

Summer had come again, and the doctor ordered them to go to the country. Kovrin had recovered; he had stopped seeing the black monk, and he needed only to restore his physical strength. Staying in the country at his father-in-law's, he drank a great deal of milk, worked for only two hours out of twenty-four, and neither smoked nor drank wine.

On the evening before Elijah's Day* they had an evening service in the house. When the sexton handed the priest the censer, a graveyard smell filled the enormous old hall, and Kovrin felt depressed. He went into the orchard. Without noticing the gorgeous flowers, he walked about the orchard, sat for a while on a bench, then strolled about the park; reaching the river, he went down and then stood lost in thought, looking at the water. The sullen pines with their shaggy roots, which had seen him a year before so young, so joyful and confident, were not whispering now, but standing mute and motionless, as if they did not recognise him. And, indeed, his head was closely cropped, his beautiful long hair was gone, his step was languid, his face was fuller and paler than last summer.

He crossed over the stepping stones to the other side. Where the year before there had been rye there were oats, reaped, and lying in rows. The sun had set and there was a broad stretch of glowing red on the horizon, a sign of windy weather next day. It was still. Looking in the direction from which the year before the black monk had first appeared, Kovrin stood for twenty minutes, till the evening glow had begun to fade . . .

When, listless and dissatisfied, he returned home the service was over. Yegor and Tania were sitting on the steps of the veranda, drinking tea. They were talking of something, but, seeing Kovrin, ceased at once, and he concluded from their faces he had been the subject of the conversation.

'I think it's time you had your milk,' Tania said to her husband.

'No, not yet . . .' he said, sitting down on the very bottom step. 'Drink it yourself; I don't want to.'

Tania exchanged a worried glance with her father, and said in a guilty voice:

'You notice yourself that milk does you good.'

'Yes, a great deal of good!' Kovrin laughed. 'I congratulate you: I have gained a pound in weight since Friday.' He pressed his head tightly in his hands and said miserably: 'Why, why have you cured me? Bromide mixtures, idleness, warm baths, supervision, cowardly fear of every mouthful, at every step – all this will end by reducing me to idiocy. I was going mad, I had megalomania; but I was cheerful, confident, and even happy; I was interesting and original. Now I have become more sensible and stolid, but I am just like everyone else: I am a mediocrity; I am bored with living . . . Oh, how cruelly you have treated me! . . . I was having hallucinations, but what harm did that do to anyone? I ask, what harm did that do anyone?'

'God knows what you are saying!' sighed Yegor. 'It's depressing to listen to.'

'Then don't listen.'

The presence of other people, especially Yegor, irritated Kovrin now; he answered him dryly, coldly, and even rudely, never looked at him but with irony and hatred, while Yegor was overcome with embarrassment and cleared his throat guiltily, though he was not aware of any guilt. Bewildered that their charming and affectionate relations had changed so abruptly, Tania huddled up to her father and looked anxiously into his eyes; she wanted to understand, but could not; she could only see that their relations were growing worse and worse every day, that of late her father had begun to look much older, and her husband had grown irritable, capricious, quarrelsome and uninteresting. She could no longer laugh or sing; at dinner she ate nothing, did not sleep for nights on end, expecting something awful, and was so worn out that on one occasion she lay in a dead faint from dinner-time till evening. During the service she thought her father was crying, and now while the three of them were sitting together on the terrace she made an effort not to think of it.

'How fortunate Buddha, Mohammed, and Shakespeare were that their kind relations and doctors did not try to cure their ecstasy and their inspiration,' said Kovrin. 'If Mohammed had taken bromide for his nerves, had worked only two hours out of the twenty-four, and had drunk milk, that remarkable man would have left no more traces than his dog. Doctors and kind relations will end by stupefying mankind, making mediocrity pass for genius and in ruining civilisation. If only you knew,' Kovrin said with spite, 'how grateful I am to you.'

He felt intense irritation, and to avoid saying too much, he got up quickly and went into the house. It was still, and the fragrance of nicotiana and the marvel of Peru floated in at the open window. The moonlight fell in green patches on the floor and on the piano in the big dark dining-room. Kovrin remembered the raptures of the previous summer when there had been the same scent of the marvel of Peru and the moon had shone in at the window. To bring back the mood of last year he went quickly to his study, lit a strong cigar, and told the footman to bring him some wine. But the cigar left a bitter and disgusting taste in his mouth, and the wine tasted different from the year before. So much for giving up a habit. The cigar and the two gulps of wine made him giddy, and brought on palpitations of the heart, and he was obliged to take potassium bromide.

Before going to bed, Tania said to him:

'Father adores you. You are cross with him for some reason, and it is killing him. Look at him; he is ageing by the hour, not the day. I beg you, Andrei, for God's sake, for the sake of your dead father, for the sake of my peace of mind, be kind to him.'

'I can't, I don't want to.'

'But why?' asked Tania, beginning to tremble all over. 'Explain why.'

'Because I find him unlikeable, that's all,' said Kovrin casually; and he shrugged his shoulders. 'But we won't talk about him: he's your father.'

'I can't understand, I can't,' said Tania, pressing her hands to her temples and staring at a fixed point. 'Something incomprehensible, awful, is going on in the house. You have changed, grown unlike yourself . . . You, a clever, extraordinary man, get irritated by trifles, meddle in paltry nonsense . . . Such trivial things excite you, that sometimes one is simply amazed and can't believe that it is you. Come, come, don't be angry, don't be angry,' she went on, kissing his hands, frightened of her own words. 'You are clever, kind, noble. You will be fair to father. He is so good.'

'He is not good; he is just good-natured. Burlesque old uncles like your father, with well-fed, good-natured faces, extraordinarily hospitable and eccentric, at one time used to touch me and amuse me in novels and in farces and in life; now I dislike them. They are egotists to the marrow of their bones. What disgusts me most of all is their being so well-fed, and that purely bovine, purely hoggish optimism of a full stomach.'

Tania sat down on the bed and laid her head on the pillow.

'This is torture,' she said, and from her voice it was evident that she was utterly exhausted, and that it was hard for her to speak. 'Not one moment of peace since winter . . . Why, it's awful! My God! I am wretched . . .'

'Oh, of course, I am Herod, and you and your father are the innocents. Of course.'

His face seemed to Tania ugly and unpleasant. Hatred and ironical expression did not suit him. And, indeed, she had noticed before that there was something lacking in his face, as though ever since his hair had been cut his face had changed, too. She wanted to say something wounding to him, but immediately she caught herself in this antagonistic feeling, she was frightened and left the bedroom.

IX

Kovrin received a professorship at the university. The inaugural lecture was fixed for the second of December, and a notice to that effect was hung up in the corridor at the university. But on the day appointed he informed the registrar, by telegram, that he was prevented by illness from giving the lecture.

He had a haemorrhage from the throat. He had often spat blood, but every two or three times a month there was a considerable loss of blood, and then he grew extremely weak and sank into a drowsy condition. This illness did not particularly frighten him, as he knew that his mother had lived for ten years or longer suffering from the same disease, and the doctors assured him that there was no danger, and had only advised him to avoid excitement, to lead a regular life, and to speak as little as possible.

In January again his lecture did not take place for the same reason, and in February it was too late to begin the course. It had to be put off to the following year.

By now he was living not with Tania, but with another woman, who was two years older than he was, and who looked after him as though he were a baby. He was in a calm and tranquil state of mind; he readily gave in to her, and when Varvara – that was the name of his friend – decided to take him to the Crimea, he agreed, though he had a presentiment that no good would come of the trip.

They reached Sevastopol in the evening and stopped at an hotel to rest and go on the next day to Yalta.* They were both exhausted by the journey. Varvara had some tea, went to bed and was soon asleep. But Kovrin did not go to bed. An hour before starting for the station, he had received a letter from Tania, and had not brought himself to open it, and now it was lying in his coat pocket, and the thought of it disturbed him disagreeably. At the bottom of his heart he genuinely considered now that his marriage to Tania had been a mistake. He was glad that their separation was final, and the thought of that woman who in the end had turned into a living relic, still walking about, though everything seemed dead in her except her big, staring, intelligent eyes – the thought of her roused in him nothing but pity and annoyance with himself. The handwriting on the envelope reminded him how cruel and unjust he had been two years before, how he had worked off his anger at his spiritual emptiness, his boredom, his loneliness, and his dissatisfaction with life by revenging himself on people in no way to blame. He remembered, also, how he had torn up his dissertation and all the articles he had written during his illness, and how he had thrown them out of the window, and the bits of paper had fluttered in the wind and caught on the trees and flowers. In every line of them he saw strange, utterly groundless pretension, shallow defiance, arrogance, megalomania; and they made him feel as though he were reading a description of his vices. But when the last notebook had been torn up and sent flying out of the window, he felt, for some reason, suddenly bitter and angry; he went to his wife and said a great many unpleasant things to her. My God, how he had tormented her! One day, wanting to cause her pain, he told her that her father had played a very unprepossessing part in their romance, that he had asked him to marry her. Yegor accidentally overheard this, ran into the room, and, in his despair, could not utter a word, could only stamp and make a strange, bellowing sound as though he had lost the power of speech, and Tania, looking at her father, had uttered a heart-rending shriek and fainted. It was hideous.

All this came back to his memory as he looked at the familiar writing. Kovrin went out on to the balcony; it was still warm weather and there was a smell of the sea. The wonderful bay reflected the moonshine and the lights, and was of a colour for which it was hard to find a name. It was a soft and tender blending of dark blue and green; in places the water was like blue vitriol, and in places it seemed as though the moonlight were liquefied and filling the bay instead of water. And what harmony of colours, what an atmosphere of peace, calm, and sublimity!

In the lower storey under the balcony the windows were probably open, for women's voices and laughter could be heard distinctly. Apparently there was a party.

Kovrin made an effort of will, tore open the envelope, and, entering his room, read:

'My father has just died. I owe that to you, for you have killed him. Our orchard is being ruined; strangers are managing it now – that is, the very thing is happening that poor father dreaded. That too I owe to you. I hate you with my whole soul, and I hope you may soon perish. Oh, how wretched I am! Insufferable anguish burning my soul . . . My curses on you. I took you for an extraordinary man, a genius; I loved you, and you turned out to be a madman . . .'

Kovrin could read no more, he tore up the letter and threw it away. He was overcome by an uneasiness that was akin to terror. Varvara was asleep behind the screen, and he could hear her breathing. From the lower storey came the sounds of laughter and women's voices but he felt as though in the whole hotel there were no living soul but him. Because Tania, unhappy, broken by sorrow, had cursed him in her letter and hoped for his perdition, he felt horrified and kept glancing hurriedly at the door, as though he were afraid that the uncomprehended force which two years before had wrought such havoc in his life and in the life of those near him might come into the room and dispose of him once more.

He knew by experience that when his nerves were out of control the best thing for him to do was to work. He must sit down to the table and force himself, at all costs, to concentrate his mind on a single idea. He took from his red portfolio a notebook containing an outline of a short compilatory work, which he had planned in case he should find it dull in the Crimea with nothing to do. He sat down at the table and began working at this plan, and it seemed to him that his calm, peaceful, equanimous mood was coming back. The notebook's outline even led him to meditate on the vanity of the world. He thought how much life exacts for the worthless or very commonplace blessings it can give a man. For instance, to gain, before forty, a university chair, to be an ordinary professor, to expound ordinary and second-hand thoughts in dull, heavy, insipid language – in fact, to gain the position of a mediocre learned man, he, Kovrin, had had to study for fifteen years, to work day and night, to endure terrible mental illness, to experience an unhappy marriage, and to do a great number of stupid and unjust things which it would have been pleasant not to remember. Kovrin recognised clearly, now, that he was a mediocrity, and readily resigned himself to it, as he considered that every man ought to be satisfied with what he is.

The outline of the book would have soothed him completely, but he saw the white sheets of the torn letter on the floor and this prevented him from concentrating. He got up from the table, picked up the pieces of the letter and threw them out of the window, but there was a light wind blowing from the sea, and the bits of paper were scattered on the window-sill. Again he was overcome by unease akin to terror, and he felt as though in the whole hotel there were no living soul but himself . . . He went out on to the balcony. The bay, like a living thing, looked at him with its multitude of light blue, dark blue, turquoise and fiery eyes, and seemed to beckon to him. And it really was hot and oppressive, and it wouldn't have been a bad idea to go for a bathe.

Suddenly in the lower storey under the balcony a violin began playing, and two soft female voices began singing. It was something familiar. The song was about a maiden, with a morbid imagination, who hears one night in her garden mysterious sounds, and decides that this is a holy harmony unintelligible to us mortals . . . Kovrin caught his breath and there was a pang of sadness in his heart, and a thrill of the sweet, exquisite delight he had so long forgotten began to stir in his breast.

A tall black column, like a whirlwind or a waterspout, appeared on the further side of the bay. It moved with fearful rapidity across the bay, towards the hotel, growing smaller and darker as it came, and Kovrin only just had time to get out of the way to let it pass . . . The monk with bare grey head, black eyebrows, barefoot, his arms crossed over his breast, floated by him, and stood in the middle of the room.

'Why did you not believe me?' he asked reproachfully, looking affectionately at Kovrin. 'If you had believed me then, that you were a genius, you would not have spent these two years so gloomily and so wretchedly.'

Kovrin now believed that he was one of God's chosen and a genius; he vividly recalled his conversations with the monk in the past and tried to speak, but the blood flowed from his throat on to his breast, and not knowing what he was doing, he passed his hands over his breast, and his cuffs were soaked with blood. He tried to call Varvara, who was asleep behind the screen, he made an effort and said: 'Tania!'

He fell on the floor, and propping himself on his arms, called again: 'Tania!'

He called Tania, called to the great orchard with the gorgeous flowers sprinkled with dew, called to the park, the pines with their shaggy roots, the rye field, his marvellous learning, his youth, courage, joy – called to life, which was so lovely. He could see on the floor near his face a great pool of blood, and was too weak to utter a word, but an unspeakable, infinite happiness flooded his whole being. Below, under the balcony, they were playing the serenade, and the black monk whispered to him that he was a genius, and that he was dying only because his frail human body had lost its balance and could no longer serve as the mortal garb of genius.

When Varvara woke up and came out from behind the screen, Kovrin was dead, and a blissful smile had congealed on his face.

1894

The Student

At first the weather was fine and still. The thrushes were calling, and in the swamps close by something alive hooted pitifully with a sound like someone blowing into an empty bottle. A snipe flew by, and a shot fired at it boomed out with a gay, resounding note in the spring air. But once it had got dark in the forest a cold, penetrating wind blew unwelcome from the east, and everything sank into silence. Needles of ice stretched across the pools, and the forest became cheerless, remote, and lonely. There was a whiff of winter.

Ivan Velikopolsky, the son of a sacristan, and a student of the clerical academy, returning home from shooting, had been walking all the time by the path in the water-meadow. His fingers were numb and his face was burning with the wind. It seemed to him that the cold that had suddenly come on had destroyed the order and harmony of things, that nature itself felt ill at ease, and that was why the evening darkness was falling more rapidly than usual. All around was deserted and peculiarly gloomy. The only light gleaming was in the widows' gardens near the rivers; the village, over three miles away, and everything in the distance all round was plunged in the cold evening mist. The student remembered that, as he was leaving from the house, his mother had been sitting barefoot on the floor in the entry, cleaning the samovar while his father lay on the stove coughing; as it was Good Friday there had been no cooking, and the student was excruciatingly hungry. And now, shrinking from the cold, he thought that the very same wind had blown in the days of Rurik* and in the time of Ivan the Terrible and Peter, and in their time there had been just the same desperate poverty and hunger, the same thatched roofs with holes in them, ignorance, misery, the same desolation around, the same darkness, the same feeling of oppression – all these had existed, did exist, and would exist, and if a thousand years passed life would become no better. And he did not want to go home.

The gardens were called the widows' because they were kept by two widows, mother and daughter. A bonfire was burning, hot and crackling, lighting up the ploughed earth far around. The widow Vasilisa, a tall, fat old woman in a man's short fur coat, was standing by and looking thoughtfully into the fire; her daughter Lukeria, a

little pock-marked woman with a rather stupid face, was sitting on
the ground, washing a pot and spoons. Apparently they had just had
supper. There was a sound of men's voices; the local labourers were
watering their horses at the river.

'Here's winter back again,' said the student, going up to the
bonfire. 'Good evening.'

Vasilisa started, but at once recognised him and smiled cordially.

'I didn't recognise you; you startled me,' she said. 'I wish you
wealth.'

They talked. Vasilisa, a woman of experience, who had been in
service with the gentry, first as a wet-nurse, afterwards as a children's
nurse, expressed herself with refinement, and a soft, sedate smile
never left her face; her daughter Lukeria, a village peasant woman,
who had been cowed by her violent husband, just screwed up her eyes
at the student and said nothing, and she had an odd expression, like a
deaf mute.

'On a night just like this the Apostle Peter warmed himself at the
fire,' said the student, stretching out his hands to the fire, 'so it must
have been cold then, too. Ah, what a terrible night it must have been,
Granny! An utterly dismal long night!'

He looked round at the darkness, shook his head abruptly and
asked:

'You were at the reading of the Twelve Gospels, I suppose?'

'Yes,' answered Vasilisa.

'If you remember at the Last Supper Peter said to Jesus, "I am ready
to go with Thee into the darkness and unto death." And our Lord
answered him thus: "I say unto thee Peter, before the cock croweth
thou wilt have denied Me thrice." After the supper Jesus suffered
mortal anguish in the garden and prayed, and poor Peter was weary
in spirit and faint, his eyelids were heavy and he could not fight off
sleep. He slept. Then you heard how Judas the same night kissed Jesus
and betrayed Him to His tormentors. They took Him bound to the
high priest and beat Him, while Peter, exhausted, worn out with
misery and alarm, hardly awake, you know, feeling that something
awful was just going to happen on earth, followed behind . . . He
loved Jesus passionately, intensely, and now from afar he saw Him
being beaten . . .'

Lukeria left the spoons and fixed an immovable stare upon the
student.

'They came to the high priest,' he went on; 'they began to question
Jesus, and meantime the labourers made a fire in the yard as it was
cold, and warmed themselves. Peter, too, stood with them near the
fire and warmed himself as I am doing. A woman, seeing him, said:

"He was with Jesus, too" – in other words, he, too, should be taken to be questioned. And all the labourers that were standing near the fire must have looked sourly and suspiciously at him, because he was embarrassed and said: "I don't know Him." A little while after again someone recognised him as one of Jesus's disciples and said: "Thou, too, art one of them," but again he denied it. And for the third time someone turned to him: "Why, did I not see thee with Him in the garden today?" For the third time he denied it. And immediately after that the cock crowed, and Peter, looking from afar off at Jesus remembered what He had said to him in the evening ... He remembered, he came to himself, went out of the yard and wept bitterly – bitterly. In the gospel it is written: "He went out and wept bitterly." I imagine it: the still, still, dark, dark garden, and in the stillness, faintly audible, smothered sobs . . .'

The student sighed and sank into thought. Still smiling, Vasilisa suddenly gave a gulp, big tears flowed freely down her cheeks, and she screened her face from the fire with her sleeve as though ashamed of her tears, and Lukeria, staring immovably at the student, flushed crimson, and her expression became strained and heavy like that of someone repressing intense pain.

The labourers were coming back from the river, and one of them on horseback was near, and the light of the fire quivered upon him. The student said good night to the widows and went on. And again the darkness was about him and his fingers began to go numb. A cruel wind was blowing, winter really had returned and it did not feel as though Easter was the day after tomorrow.

Now the student was thinking about Vasilisa: since she had shed tears all that had happened to Peter the night before the Crucifixion must have some connection to her . . .

He looked round. The solitary light was still gleaming in the darkness and no figures could be seen near it now. The student thought again that if Vasilisa had shed tears, and her daughter had been upset, then clearly what he had just been telling them about, which had happened nineteen centuries ago, was connected to the present – to both women, to the desolate village, to himself, to everyone. The old woman had wept, not because he could tell the story movingly, but because Peter was close to her, because her whole being was involved in what was happening in Peter's soul.

And joy suddenly stirred in his soul, and he even stopped for a minute to take breath. 'The past,' he thought, 'is linked with the present by an unbroken chain of events flowing one out of another.' And it seemed to him that he had just seen both ends of that chain: that when he touched one end the other quivered.

When he crossed the river by the ferry raft and afterwards, mounting the hill, looked at his village and towards the west which the cold purple sunset was covering with a narrow streak of light, he thought that truth and beauty which had guided human life in the Garden of Gethsemane and in the high priest's courtyard had gone on uninterruptedly to this day, and must always have been the chief thing in human life and in all earthly life, indeed; and the feeling of youth, health, vigour – he was only twenty-two – and an inexpressible sweeet expectation of happiness, of unknown mysterious happiness, took possession of him little by little, and life seemed to him enchanting, marvellous, and full of lofty meaning.

1894

Ariadna

On the deck of a steamer sailing from Odessa to Sevastopol, a rather good-looking gentleman, with a little round beard, came up to me for a light, and said:

'Notice those Germans sitting near the shelter? Whenever Germans or Englishmen get together, they talk about crops, the price of wool, or their own business deals. But for some reason or other when we Russians get together we never discuss anything but women and lofty subjects – but mainly women.'

I'd seen this gentleman's face before. We had returned from abroad the evening before in the same train, and at Volochisk,* at the Customs inspetion, I saw him standing with a lady, his travelling companion, before a whole mountain of trunks and baskets filled with ladies' clothes, and I noticed how embarrassed and downcast he was when he had to pay duty on some piece of silk frippery, and his companion protested and threatened to complain. Afterwards, as we travelled to Odessa, I saw him carrying little pies and oranges to the ladies' compartment.

It was rather damp; there was a slight swell, and the ladies had retired to their cabins. The gentleman with the round beard sat down beside me and continued:

'Yes, when Russians come together they discuss nothing but lofty matters and women. We are so intellectual, so solemn, that we utter nothing but truths and can discuss only questions of a higher order. Russian actors don't know how to clown; they act with profundity even in a farce. We're just the same: when we have to talk of trifles we treat them only from an exalted point of view. It comes from a lack of boldness, sincerity, and simplicity. We talk so often about women, I fancy, because we are dissatisfied. We take too ideal a view of women, and make demands out of all proportion with what reality can give us; we get something quite unlike what we want, and the result is dissatisfaction, shattered hopes, and inner suffering, and people wear their hearts on their sleeves. It doesn't bore you to go on with this conversation?'

'No, not in the least.'

'In that case, allow me to introduce myself,' said my companion, rising from his seat a little: 'Ivan Shamokhin, a Moscow landowner of a sort . . . You I know very well.'

He sat down and went on, looking at me with a genuine and friendly expression:

'A mediocre philosopher, like Max Nordau, would explain these incessant conversations about women as erotic madness, or would put it down to our having been serf-owners, and so on; I take quite a different view of it. I repeat, we are dissatisfied because we are idealists. We want the creatures who bear us and our children to be superior to us and to everything in the world. When we are young we adore and poeticise those with whom we are in love: love and happiness with us are synonyms. Here in Russia marriage without love is despised, sensuality is ridiculed and inspires revulsion, and the greatest success is enjoyed by those tales and novels in which women are beautiful, poetical, and exalted; and if the Russian has been for years in ecstasies over Raphael's Madonna, or is eager for the emancipation of women, I assure you he is quite sincere. But the trouble is that after only two or three years' marriage or intimacy with a woman we begin to feel deceived and disillusioned: we pair off with others, and again – disappointment, again – revulsion, and in the long run we become convinced that women are liars, petty, fussy, unfair, primitive, cruel – in fact, far from being superior, immeasurably inferior to us men. And in our dissatisfaction and disappointment all we can do is to grumble and talk off-hand about what has so cruelly disillusioned us.'

While Shamokhin was talking I noticed that speaking Russian and being in Russian surroundings gave him great pleasure. This was probably because he had been very homesick abroad. Though he praised the Russians and ascribed to them a rare idealism, he did not disparage foreigners, and that I put down to his credit. It could be seen, too, that there was some unease in his soul, that he wanted to talk more of himself than of women, and that I was in for a long story like a confession. And when we had ordered a bottle of wine and had each drunk a glass, he began:

'I remember in a novel of Veltman's* somebody says, "So that's the story!" and some one else answers, "No, that's not the story – that's only the introduction to the story." In the same way what I've said so far is only the introduction; what I really want to tell you is my own love story. I'm sorry, I must ask again; it won't bore you to listen?'

I told him it would not, and he went on:

'The action takes place in Moscow province in one of its northern districts. The scenery there, I must tell you, is amazing. Our estate is on the high bank of a rapid stream, where the water roars day and night. Imagine a big old garden, neat flower-beds, beehives, a kitchen garden, and below it a river with leafy willows, which, when there is a heavy dew on them, have a lustreless look as though they had turned grey; and on the other side a meadow, and beyond the meadow on a hill a terrible, dark pine forest. In that forest delicious, red agarics grow in endless profusion, and elk live in its deepest recesses. When I am nailed up in my coffin I believe I shall still dream of those early mornings, you know, when the sun hurts your eyes: or the wonderful spring evenings when the nightingales and the landrails call in the garden and beyond the garden, and sounds of the harmonica float across from the village, while they play the piano indoors and the river roars . . . when there is such music, in fact, that you want to cry and sing aloud. We don't have much arable land, but our pasture keeps us going, and with the forest yields about two thousand roubles a year. I am my father's only son; we are both modest persons, and with my father's pension that sum used to be quite enough for us. The first three years after finishing university I spent in the country, looking after the estate and constantly expecting to be elected to some local assembly; but what was most important, I was very much in love with an extraordinarily beautiful and fascinating girl. She was the sister of our neighbour, Kotlovich, a ruined landowner who had on his estate pineapples, marvellous peaches, lightning conductors, a fountain in the courtyard, and at the same time not a kopeck in his pocket. He did nothing and was incapable of doing anything. He was as flabby as though he had been made of boiled turnip; he treated the peasants homeopathically and went in for spiritualism. He was, however, a man of great tact and mildness, and by no means a fool, but I have no liking for these gentlemen who converse with spirits and cure peasant women by magnetism. In the first place, the ideas of people with captive minds are always in a muddle, and it's extremely difficult to talk to them; and, secondly, they usually love no one, and don't live with women, and this mysteriousness has an unpleasant side effect on sensitive people. I did not care for his appearance either. He was tall, stout, white-skinned, with a little head, little shining eyes, and chubby white fingers. He did not shake your hand, he kneaded it. And he was always apologising. If he asked for anything it was "Sorry"; if he gave you anything it was "Sorry" too. As for his sister, she was quite another matter. I should say that I hadn't known the Kotloviches in my childhood and early youth, for my father had been a professor at N—, and we had for many years lived in the provinces. When I did make their acquaintance the girl was twenty-two, had left school long before, and had spent two or three years in Moscow with a wealthy aunt who brought her out into society. When I was introduced and first had to talk to her, what struck me most of all was her rare and beautiful name – Ariadna. It suited her so wonderfully. She was a brunette, very thin, very slender, supple, elegant, and extremely graceful, with refined and exceedingly noble features. Her eyes were shining, too, but her brother's eyes had a cold sickly shine like sugar-candy, while hers had the glow of youth, proud and beautiful. She conquered me on the first day of our acquaintance, and indeed it was inevitable. My first impression was so overwhelming that to this day I cannot get rid of my illusions; I am still tempted to imagine that nature had some grand, marvellous design when she created that girl. Ariadna's voice, her walk, her hat, even her footprints on the sandy bank where she used to angle for gudgeon, filled me with delight and a passionate hunger for life. I judged of her spiritual being from her lovely face and lovely figure, and every word, every smile of Ariadna's bewitched me, conquered me and made me believe she had an exalted soul. She was friendly, ready to talk, cheerful and behaved naturally. She had a poetic belief in God, made poetic reflections about death, and there was such a wealth of nuances in her temperament that it coloured even her faults with peculiar, charming qualities. Suppose she needed a new horse and had no money – what did that matter? Something could be sold or pawned, or if the steward swore that nothing could possibly be sold or pawned, the iron roofs might be torn off the lodges and taken to the factory, or at the very busiest time the farm horses might be driven to the market and sold there for next to nothing. These unbridled desires reduced the whole household to despair at times, but she expressed them with such elegance that everything was forgiven her; she was allowed all things, like a goddess or Caesar's wife. My love was touching and was soon noticed by every one – my father, the neighbours, and the peasants – and they all sympathised with me. When I used to stand the workmen vodka, they would bow and say:

' "God grant you marry the Kotlovich young lady!"

'And Ariadna herself knew that I loved her. She would often ride over on horseback or drive in the charabanc to see us, and would spend whole days with me and my father. She made great friends with the old man, and he even taught her to bicycle, his favourite amusement. I remember they were going off on a ride one evening and I helped her on to the bicycle, and she looked so lovely that I felt as though I were burning my hands when I touched her. I shuddered with rapture, and when the two of them, my old father and she, both looking so handsome and elegant, set off side by side down the main road, a black horse ridden by the steward dashed aside on meeting them, and it seemed to me that it dashed aside because it was too overcome by her beauty. My love, my worship, touched Ariadna and softened her; she had a passionate longing to be captivated like me and to respond with the same love. It was so poetical!

'But, unlike me, she was incapable of really loving, for she was cold and already somewhat depraved. There was a demon in her, whispering to her day and night that she was enchanting, adorable; and, having no definite idea what she was created for, or why she was alive, she never pictured herself in the future except as very wealthy and distinguished; she had visions of balls, races, liveries, of sumptuous drawing-rooms, of a salon of her own, and of a perfect swarm of counts, princes, ambassadors, celebrated painters and artists, all of them adoring her and in ecstasies over her beauty and her dresses . . . This thirst for personal success, and these constant thoughts all in the same direction, make people cold, and Ariadna was cold – to me, to nature, and to music. Meanwhile time was passing, and still there were no ambassadors on the scene. Ariadna went on living with her brother, the spiritualist; things went from bad to worse, so that she had no money for hats and dresses, and had to resort to all sorts of tricks and dodges to conceal her poverty.

'As luck would have it, a certain Prince Maktuev, a wealthy man, but an utter nonentity, had wooed her when she was living at her aunt's in Moscow. She had refused him outright. But now she was sometimes fretted by the worm of repentance: why had she refused him? Just as a peasant pouts with revulsion at a mug of kvas with cockroaches in it but yet drinks it, so she frowned disdainfully when she recalled the prince, and yet she would say to me:

' "Say what you like, there is something inexplicable, fascinating, in a title . . ."

'She dreamed of a title, of a brilliant position, and at the same time she did not want to let me go. However one may dream of ambassadors, your heart is not a stone, and you feel sorry for your youth. Ariadna tried to fall in love, made a show of being in love, and even swore that she loved me. But I am a highly strung and sensitive man; when I am loved I feel it even at a distance, without vows and assurances; at once I felt a chill in the air, and when she talked to me of love, I felt I was listening to a metal nightingale singing. Ariadna herself sensed that she hadn't got it in her. She was vexed and more than once I saw her cry. Anyway, can you imagine it, all of a sudden she embraced me impulsively and kissed me. It happened in the evening on the river-bank, and I saw by her eyes that she did not love me, but was embracing me from curiosity, to test herself and to see what would come of it. And I felt dreadful. I took her hands and said to her in despair:

' "These caresses without love cause me suffering."

' "You are . . . an odd man!" she said with annoyance, and stepped back.

'After a year or two, in all probability, I should have married her, and so my story would have ended, but fate was pleased to arrange our romance differently. It happened that a new person appeared on our horizon. Ariadna's brother had a visit from an old university friend called Mikhail Lubkov, a charming man of whom coachmen and footmen used to say: "An entertaining gentleman." He was a man of medium height, lanky and bald, with a face like a good-natured bourgeois, not interesting, but pale and presentable, with a stiff, well-kept moustache, with goose-pimples on his neck and a big Adam's apple. He used to wear a pince-nez on a wide black ribbon, lisped, and could not pronounce either *r* or *l*, so that he pronounced "realise" as "weawise". He was always in good spirits, everything amused him. He had made an exceedingly foolish marriage at twenty, and had acquired two houses in Moscow near the Devichii Convent as part of his wife's dowry. He began doing them up and building a bath- house, and went completely broke. Now his wife and four children lodged in the "Oriental Furnished Rooms" in great poverty, and he had to support them – and this amused him. He was thirty-six and his wife was by now forty-two, and that, too, amused him. His mother, a conceited, sulky personage, with aristocratic pretensions, despised his wife and lived apart with a whole horde of cats and dogs, and he had to allow her seventy-five roubles a month also; he was, too, a man of taste, liked lunching at the Slaviansky Bazaar and dining at the Hermitage; he needed a great deal of money, but his uncle only allowed him two thousand roubles a year, which was not enough, and for days on end he would run about Moscow with his tongue out, as the saying is, looking for some one to borrow from – and this, too, amused him. He had come to Kotlovich to rest in the lap of nature, as he said, from family life. At dinner, at supper, and on our walks, he talked about his wife, about his mother, about his creditors, about the bailiffs, and laughed at them; he laughed at himself and assured us that, thanks to his talent for borrowing, he had made a great number of agreeable acquaintances. He laughed without ceasing and we laughed too. Moreover, in his company we spent our time differently. I was more inclined to quiet, so to say idyllic pleasures; I liked fishing, evening walks, gathering mushrooms; Lubkov preferred picnics, fireworks, hunting to hounds. He used to organise picnics three times a week, and Ariadna, with an earnest and inspired face, used to write a list of oysters, champagne, sweets, and used to send me to Moscow to get them, without inquiring, of course, whether I had the money. And at the picnics there were toasts and laughter, and again mirthful descriptions of how old his wife was, what fat lap-dogs his mother had, and what nice people his creditors were . . .

'Lubkov was fond of nature, but he regarded it as something long familiar and at the same time really infinitely beneath himself and created only for his pleasure. He would sometimes stand still before some magnificent landscape and say: "It would be nice to have tea here." One day, seeing Ariadna walking in the distance with a parasol, he nodded in her direction and said:

' "She's thin, and that's what I like; I don't like fat women."

'This made me wince. I asked him not to speak like that about women before me. He looked and me in surprise and said:

' "What's wrong in my liking thin women and disliking fat ones?"

'I made no answer. Afterwards, being in very good spirits and a trifle drunk, he said:

' "I've noticed Ariadna likes you. I can't understand why you don't do something about it."

'His words made me feel uncomfortable, and with some embarrassment I told him my views on love and women.

' "I don't know," he sighed; "to my thinking, a woman's a woman and a man's a man. Ariadna may be poetical and exalted, as you say, but it doesn't follow that she must be above the laws of nature. You see for yourself that she has reached the age when she must have a husband or a lover. I respect women as much as you do, but I don't think certain relations exclude poetry. Poetry's one thing and a lover is another. It's just the same as it is in farming. The beauty of nature is one thing and the income from your forests or fields is quite another."

'When Ariadna and I were fishing. Lubkov would lie on the sand close by and make fun of me, or lecture me on the conduct of life.

' "I wonder, my dear sir, how you can live without a love affair," he would say. "You are young, handsome, interesting – in fact, you're a man not to be sniffed at, yet you live like a monk. Oh, I can't stand these fellows who are old at twenty-eight! I'm nearly ten years older than you are, and yet which of us is the younger? Ariadna, which?"

' "You, of course," Ariadna answered him.

'And when he was bored with our silence and the attention with which we stared at our floats he went home, and she said, looking at me angrily:

' "You're really not a man, but a ninny, God forgive me! A man should let himself go, do mad things, make mistakes, suffer! A woman will forgive you audacity and insolence, but she will never forgive your prudence!'

'She was angry in earnest, and went on:

' "To succeed, a man must be resolute and bold. Lubkov is not as handsome as you are, but he is more interesting and will always succeed with women because he's not like you; he's a man . . ."

'And there was actually a note of exasperation in her voice. One day at supper she began saying, not addressing me, that if she were a man she would not stagnate in the country, but would travel, would spend the winter somewhere abroad – in Italy, for instance. Oh, Italy! At this point my father unconsciously poured oil on the flames; he began telling us at length about Italy, how splendid it was there, the exquisite scenery, the museums. Ariadna suddenly conceived a burning desire to go to Italy. She even slammed her fist on the table and her eyes flashed: "I must go!"

'After that came conversations every day about Italy: how splendid it would be in Italy – ah, Italy! oh, Italy! – and when Ariadna looked at me over her shoulder, from her cold and obstinate expression I saw that in her dreams she had already conquered Italy with all its salons, celebrated foreigners and tourists, and there was no holding her back now. I advised her to wait a little, to put off her tour for a year or two, but she frowned disdainfully and said:

' "You're as prudent as an old woman."

'Lubkov was in favour of the tour. He said it could be done very cheaply, and he, too, would love to go to Italy and rest there from family life. I behaved, I confess, as naively as a schoolboy. Not from jealousy, but from a foreboding of something terrible and extra-ordinary, I tried as far as possible not to leave them alone together, and they made fun of me. For instance, when I came in they would pretend they had just been kissing, and so on.

'But one fine morning, her plump, white-skinned brother, the spiritualist, made his appearance and expressed his desire to speak to me alone. He was a man with no will of his own; in spite of his upbringing and his tact he could never resist reading another person's letter, if it lay before him on the table. And now he admitted that he had by chance read a letter of Lubkov's to Ariadna.

' "From that letter I learned that she is very shortly going abroad. My dear fellow, I am very much upset! Explain it to me for God's sake. I can make nothing of it!"

'As he said this he breathed hard, breathing straight in my face and he smelled of boiled beef.

' "Excuse me for revealing the secret of this letter to you," he continued, "but you are Ariadna's friend, she respects you. Perhaps you know something of it. She wants to go away, but with whom? Mr Lubkov is proposing to go with her. I'm sorry, but this is very strange of Mr Lubkov; he is a married man, he has children, and yet he is

making a declaration of love; he writes to Ariadna, 'darling'. I'm
sorry but it is strange!"

'I turned cold all over; my hands and feet went numb and I felt an
ache in my chest, as if a three-cornered stone had been driven into it.
Kotlovich sank helplessly into an arm-chair, and his arms hung
limply like thongs.

' "What can I do?" I inquired.

' "Persuade her . . . Impress her . . . Just consider, what is Lubkov
to her? Is he a match for her? Oh, good God! How awful it is, how
awful it is!" he went on, clutching his head. "She has had such
splendid offers – Prince Maktuev and . . . and others. The prince
adores her, and only last Wednesday week his late grandfather,
Ilarion, declared positively that Ariadna would be his wife –
positively! His grandfather Ilarion is dead, but he is a wonderfully
intelligent person; we call up his spirit every day."

'After this conversation I lay awake all night and thought of
shooting myself. In the morning I wrote five letters and tore them all
up, then I sobbed in the barn, then I took a sum of money from my
father and set off for the Caucasus without saying good-bye.

'Of course, a woman's a woman and a man's a man, but can all that
be as simple in our day as it was before the Flood, and must I, a
cultivated man endowed with a complex spiritual organisation,
explain the intense attraction I feel towards a woman simply by the fact
that her body has a different shape from mine? Oh, how awful that
would be! I want to believe that in his struggle with nature the spirit of
man has struggled with physical love too, as with an enemy, and that, if
he has not conquered it, he has at least succeeded in tangling it in a
network of illusions of brotherhood and love; and for me, at any rate, it
is no longer a simple instinct of my animal nature as with a dog or a frog,
but is real love, and every embrace is spiritualised by a pure impulse of
the heart and respect for the woman. In reality, a revulsion against
animal instinct has been trained by the ages over hundreds of
generations; I've inherited it in my blood, it is part of my nature, and if I
poeticise love, isn't that as natural and inevitable in our day as my ears
not being able to move and my not being covered with fur? I fancy that's
how the majority of civilised people look at it, so that the absence of a
moral, poetical element in love is treated in these days as a sign of
atavism; they say it is a symptom of degeneracy, of many forms of
insanity. It is true that, in poeticising love, we assume in those we love
qualities that they may not have, and that is a source of continual
mistakes and continual miseries for us. But to my mind, even if so, it is
better; that is, it is better to suffer than to content yourself that women
are women and men are men.

'In Tiflis I received a letter from my father. He wrote that Ariadna
had on such-and-such a date gone abroad, intending to spend the
whole winter away. A month later I returned home. It was now
autumn. Every week Ariadna sent my father extremely interesting
letters on scented paper, written in an excellent literary style. It is my
opinion that every woman can be a writer. Ariadna described in great
detail how hard it had been for her to make it up with her aunt and
induce the latter to give her a thousand roubles for the journey, and
what a long time she had spent in Moscow trying to find an old lady, a
distant relation, in order to persuade her to go with her. The
superfluous details suggested fiction, and I realised, of course, that
she had no chaperon with her. Soon afterwards I, too, had a letter
from her, also scented and literary. She wrote that she had missed me,
missed my beautiful, intelligent, loving eyes. She reproached me in a
friendly way for wasting my youth, for stagnating in the country
when I might, like her, be living in paradise under the palms,
breathing the fragrance of the orange trees. And she signed herself
"Your forsaken Ariadna". Two days later came another letter in the
same style, signed "Your forgotten Ariadna". My mind was in a
whirl. I loved her passionately, I dreamed of her every night, and then
this "your forsaken", "your forgotten" – what did it mean? Why?
What with the dreariness of the country, long evenings, lingering
thoughts about Lubkov ... The uncertainty tortured me, and
poisoned my days and nights; it became unendurable. I could not
bear it and went abroad.

'Ariadna summoned me to Abbazia. I arrived there on a bright
warm day after rain; the raindrops were still hanging on the trees and
glistening on the huge, barrack-like annexe where Ariadna and
Lubkov were living.

'They were not at home. I went into the park, wandered about the
avenues, then sat down. An Austrian general, with his hands behind
him, walked past me, with red stripes on his trousers such as our
generals wear. A baby was wheeled by in a perambulator and the
wheels squeaked on the damp sand. A decrepit old man with jaundice
passed, then a crowd of Englishwomen, a Catholic priest, then the
Austrian general again. A military band, only just arrived from
Fiume, with glittering brass instruments, sauntered by to the band-
stand – they began playing. Have you ever been at Abbazia? It's a
filthy little Slav town with only one street, which stinks, and you can't
walk there after rain without galoshes. I had read so much and always
with such intense feeling about this earthly paradise that when
afterwards, holding up my trousers, I cautiously crossed the narrow
street, and in my ennui bought some hard pears from an old peasant

woman who, recognising me as a Russian, said: "Cheeteery" for *chetyre* [four] – "davadtsat" for *dvadtsat* [twenty], and when I wondered in perplexity where to go and what to do here, and when I inevitably met Russians as disappointed as I was, I began to feel vexed and ashamed. There is a calm bay there full of steamers and boats with coloured sails. From there I could see Fiume and the distant islands covered with lilac mist, and it would have been picturesque if the view over the bay had not been hemmed in by the hotels and their annexes – buildings in an absurd, vulgar style of architecture, with which the whole of that green shore has been covered by greedy speculators, so that for the most part you see nothing in this little paradise but windows, terraces, and little squares with tables and waiters' black coats. There is a park such as you find now in every watering-place abroad. And the dark, motionless, silent foliage of the palms, and the bright yellow sand in the avenue, and the bright green seats, and the glitter of the braying military horns, and the general's red stripes – all this sickens you in ten minutes! And yet for some reason you have to spend ten days, ten weeks there. Dragged reluctantly from one of these watering-places to another, I was more and more struck by the inconvenient and niggardly life led by the wealthy and the well-fed, the dullness and feebleness of their imagination, their unadventurous tastes and desires. And how much happier are those tourists, old and young, who are too poor to stay in hotels and live where they can, admire the view of the sea from the tops of the mountains, lying on green grass, walk instead of riding, see the forests and villages at close quarters, observe the customs of the country, listen to its songs, fall in love with its women . . .

'While I was sitting in the park, it began to get dark, and in the twilight my Ariadna appeared, elegant and dressed like a princess; Lubkov followed her, wearing a new loose-fitting suit, probably bought in Vienna.

' "Why are you angry?" he was saying. "What have I done to you?"

'Seeing me, she uttered a cry of joy, and probably, if we had not been in the park, would have thrown herself on my neck. She pressed my hands warmly and laughed; and I laughed too and almost cried with emotion. Questions followed, about life in the country, my father, whether I had seen her brother, and so on. She insisted on my looking her straight in the eyes, and asked if I remembered the gudgeon, our little quarrels, the picnics . . .

' "How good it all was really!" she sighed. "But we're not having a boring time here either. We have a great many friends, my dear, my dearest! Tomorrow I'll introduce you to a Russian family here, but please buy yourself another hat." She scrutinised me and frowned. "Abbazia is not the country," she said; "here one must be *comme il faut . . .*"

'Then we went to the restaurant. Ariadna was laughing and mischievous all the time; she kept calling me "dear", "good", "clever", and seemed as though she could not believe her eyes that I was with her. We stayed till eleven o'clock, and parted very pleased with the supper and with each other. Next day Ariadna presented me to the Russian family as: "The son of a distinguished professor on the neighbouring estate."

'She talked to this family about nothing but estates and crops, and kept referring to me. She wanted to appear to be a very wealthy landowner, and did so successfully. Her manner was superb, like a real aristocrat's, which indeed she was by birth.

' "My aunt really is too much!" she said suddenly, looking at me with a smile. "We had a slight tiff, and she bolted off to Merano. What about that?"

'Afterwards when we were walking in the park I asked her:

' "What aunt were you talking of just now? What aunt is that?"

' "That was a white lie," laughed Ariadna. "They must not know I have no chaperon." After a moment's silence she came closer to me and said: "My dear, my dear, do be friends with Lubkov. He is so unhappy! His wife and mother are simply awful."

'She spoke formally to Lubkov, and when she was going up to bed she said good night to him exactly as she did to me, "until tomorrow", and their rooms were on different floors. All this led me to hope that it was all nonsense, and that there was no love affair between them, and I felt at ease when I met him. And when one day he asked me to lend him three hundred roubles, I gave it to him with great pleasure.

'Every day we spent enjoying ourselves and only enjoying ourselves; we strolled in the park, we ate, we drank. Every day there were conversations with the Russian family. By degrees I got used to the fact that if I went into the park I should be sure to meet the old man with jaundice, the Catholic priest, and the Austrian general, who always carried a pack of little cards, and wherever it was possible sat down and played patience, nervously twitching his shoulders. And the band played the same thing over and over again. At home in the country I used to feel ashamed to meet the peasants when I was fishing or picnicking on a working day; here too I was ashamed at the sight of the footmen, the coachmen, and the workmen who met us. It always seemed to me that they were looking at me and thinking: "Why are you doing nothing?" And I was conscious of this feeling of shame every day from morning to night. It was a strange, unpleasant, monotonous time; it was only varied by Lubkov's borrowing from me now a hundred, now fifty guldens, and being suddenly revived by the money as a morphine addict is by morphine, beginning to laugh noisily at his wife, at himself, at his creditors.

'In the end it turned rainy and cold. We went to Italy, and I telegraphed my father begging him for God's sake to send me about eight hundred roubles at Rome. We stayed in Venice, in Bologna, in Florence, and in every town invariably put up at an expensive hotel, where we were charged separately for lighting, for service, for heating, for bread at lunch, and for the right to dine by ourselves. We ate enormously. In the morning they gave us *café complet*; at one o'clock, lunch: meat, fish, some sort of omelette, cheese, fruits, and wine. At six o'clock, dinner of eight courses with long intervals, during which we drank beer and wine. At nine o'clock, tea. At midnight, Ariadna would declare she was hungry, and ask for ham and boiled eggs. We would eat to keep her company. In the intervals between meals we used to rush to the museums and exhibitions constantly worried about being late for dinner or lunch. I was anguished at the sight of the pictures; I longed to go home and lie down; I was exhausted, looked about for a chair and hypocritically repeated after other people: "How exquisite, what atmosphere!" Like sated boa-constrictors, we noticed only the most glaring objects. The shop windows hypnotised us; we went into ecstasies over fake brooches and bought a mass of useless junk.

'The same thing happened in Rome, where it rained and there was a cold wind. After a heavy lunch we went to look at St Peter's, and thanks to our replete condition and perhaps the bad weather, it made no impression on us, and detecting each other's indifference to art, we almost quarrelled.

'The money came from my father. I went to get it, I remember, in the morning. Lubkov went with me.

' "The present cannot be full and happy when one has a past," said he. "I have heavy burdens left on me by the past. However, if only I get the money, it's no great matter, but if not, I'm in a fix. Would you believe it, I have only eight francs left, yet I must send my wife a hundred and my mother another. And we must live here too. Ariadna's like a child; she won't compromise, she throws money about like a duchess. Why did she buy a watch yesterday? And, tell me, what point is there in our going on playing at being good children? Why, our hiding our relationship from the servants and our friends costs us from ten to fifteen francs a day, as I have a separate room. What's the point?"

'The sharp stone turned round in my chest. There was no uncertainty now; it was all clear to me. I turned cold all over, and at once made a resolution not to see them, to run away from them, to go home at once . . .

' "To be intimate with a woman is easy enough," Lubkov went on. "You have only to undress her; but afterwards what a bore it is, what a silly business!"

When I counted over the money I received he said:

' "If you don't lend me a thousand francs, I am faced with complete ruin. Your money is my only resource."

'I gave him the money, and he at once revived and began laughing about his uncle, an odd fellow, who could never keep his address secret from his wife. When I reached the hotel I packed and paid my bill. I had still to say good-bye to Ariadna.

'I knocked at the door.

' "*Entrez!*"

'Her room was full of the wreckage of the morning: tea things on the table, an unfinished roll, an eggshell; a strong overpowering reek of scent. The bed had not been made, and it was obvious that two had slept in it.

'Ariadna herself had only just got up and had put on a flannel dressing-jacket. Her hair was undone.

'I said good morning to her, and then sat in silence for a minute while she tried to tidy her hair, and then I asked her, trembling all over:

' "Why . . . why . . . did you send for me here?"

'Evidently she guessed what I was thinking about; she took me by the hand and said:

' "I want you to be here, you are so pure."

'I felt ashamed of my emotion, my trembling. And I was afraid I might begin sobbing too; I went out without saying another word, and within an hour I was sitting in the train. All the journey, for some reason, I imagined Ariadna pregnant, and she seemed disgusting to me, and all the women I saw in the trains and at the stations looked to me, for some reason, as if they were pregnant, and they too seemed disgusting and pitiable. I was in the position of a greedy, passionate miser who suddenly discovers that all his gold coins are false. The pure, gracious images which my imagination, warmed by love, had cherished for so long, my plans, my hopes, my memories, my ideas of love and of woman – all now were jeering and putting out their tongues at me. "Ariadna," I kept asking with horror, "that young, intellectual, extraordinarily beautiful girl, the daughter of a senator, carrying on an affair with such an ordinary, uninteresting vulgarian?

But why should she not love Lubkov?" I answered myself. "How is he inferior to me? Oh, let her love any one she likes, but why lie to me? But why is she bound to be open with me?" And so I went on over and over again till I was stupefied. It was cold in the train; I was travelling first class, but even so there were three on a side, there were no double glazing, the outer door opened straight into the compartment, and I felt as though I were in the stocks, cramped, abandoned, pitiful, and my legs were fearfully numb, and at the same time I kept recalling how seductive she had been that morning in her dressing-jacket and with her hair down, and I was suddenly overcome by such acute jealousy that I leapt up in anguish, so that my neighbours stared at me in wonder and even fear.

'At home I found deep snow and twenty degrees below zero. I'm fond of the winter; I'm fond of it because at that time, even in the hardest frosts, it's particularly snug at home. It's pleasant to put on one's fur jacket and felt overboots on a clear frosty day, to do something in the garden or in the yard, or to read in a well warmed room, to sit in my father's study before the open fire, to wash in my country bath-house . . . Only if there is no mother in the house, no sister and no children, it is somehow awful on winter evenings, and they seem extraordinarily long and quiet. And the warmer and snugger it is, the more acutely is this lack felt. In the winter when I came back from abroad, the evenings were endlessly long, I was intensely depressed, so depressed that I could not even read; by day I still moved about, clearing away the snow in the garden or feeding the chickens and the calves, but in the evenings I was fit to perish.

'I had never cared for visitors before, but now I was glad of them, for I knew there was sure to be talk of Ariadna: Kotlovich, the spiritualist, would often come to talk about his sister, and sometimes he brought with him his friend Prince Maktuev, who was as much in love with Ariadna as I was. To sit in Ariadna's room, to finger the keys of her piano, to look at her music was a necessity for the prince – he could not live without it; and the spirit of his grandfather Ilarion was still predicting that sooner or later she would be his wife. The prince usually stayed a long time with us, from lunch to midnight, saying nothing all the time; in silence he would drink two or three bottles of beer, and from time to time, to show that he too was taking part in the conversation, he would laugh an abrupt, melancholy, foolish laugh. Before going home he would always take me aside and ask me in an undertone: "When did you see Ariadna last? Is she well? I suppose she's not bored there?"

'Spring came. There was the harrowing to do and then the sowing of spring corn and clover. I was sad, but in a spring-like way. One longed to accept the inevitable. Working in the fields and listening to the larks, I asked myself: "Shouldn't I settle this question of personal happiness once and for all? Couldn't I simply marry an ordinary peasant girl?"

'Suddenly, when we were at our very busiest, I got a letter with an Italian stamp, and the clover and the beehives and the calves and the peasant girl all vanished like smoke. This time Ariadna wrote that she was profoundly, infinitely unhappy. She reproached me for not holding out a helping hand to her, for looking down upon her from the heights of my virtue and deserting her at the moment of danger. All this was written in a large, highly strung handwriting with blots and smudges, and you could see that she wrote in haste and distress. In conclusion she begged me to come and save her.

'Again I broke my anchor and was carried away. Ariadna was in Rome. I arrived late in the evening, and when she saw me, she sobbed and threw herself on my neck. She had not changed at all that winter, and was just as young and charming. We had supper together and afterwards drove about Rome until dawn, and all the time she kept telling me about her doings. I asked where Lubkov was.

' "Don't remind me of that creature!" she shouted. "I loathe him, he's vile."

' "But I thought you loved him," I said.

' "Never," she said. "At first he struck me as original and aroused my pity, that was all. He is insolent and takes a woman by storm, and that's attractive. But we won't talk about him. That is a sad page in my life. He has gone to Russia to get money. Serve him right! I told him not to dare to come back."

'She was living then, not at an hotel, but in a private lodging of two rooms which she had decorated in her own taste, frigidly and luxuriously. After Lubkov had gone away she had borrowed from her acquaintants about five thousand francs, and my arrival certainly was salvation for her. I had reckoned on taking her back to the country, but I did not succeed. She was homesick for her native place, but her recollections of the poverty she had been through there, of privations, of the rusty roof on her brother's house, roused a shudder of disgust, and when I suggested going home to her, she squeezed my hands convulsively and said:

' "No, no, I shall die of boredom there!"

'Then my love entered upon its final phase, its last quarter.

' "Be the darling that you used to be; love me a little," said Ariadna, leaning towards me. "You're sullen and prudent, you're afraid to yield to impulse, and keep thinking of consequences, and that's dull. Come, I beg you, I beseech you, be nice to me! . . . My pure one, my holy one, my dear one, I love you so . . ."

'I became her lover. For a month anyway I was like a madman, conscious of nothing but rapture. To hold in your arms a young and lovely body, with bliss to feel her warmth every time you woke up from sleep, and to remember that she was there – she, my Ariadna! – oh, it was not easy to get used to that. But yet I did get used to it, and by degrees became capable of reflecting on my new position. First of all, I realised, as before, that Ariadna did not love me. But she wanted to be really in love, she was afraid of solitude, and, above all, I was healthy, young, vigorous; she was sensual, like all cold people, as a rule – and we pretended to be drawn together by a passionate, mutual love. Afterwards I realised a few other things.

'We stayed in Rome, in Naples, in Florence; we went to Paris, but there we thought it cold and went back to Italy. We introduced ourselves everywhere as husband and wife, wealthy landowners. People readily made our acquaintance and Ariadna had great social success everywhere. As she took lessons in painting, she was called an artist, and, imagine, that quite suited her, though she had not the slightest trace of talent.

'She would sleep every day till two or three o'clock; she had her coffee and lunch in bed. At dinner she would eat soup, lobster, fish, meat, asparagus, game, and after she had gone to bed I used to bring up something, for instance roast beef, and she would eat with a melancholy, careworn expression, and if she woke in the night she would eat apples and oranges.

'The chief, so to say fundamental, characteristic of the woman was an amazing duplicity. She was continually deceitful every minute, apparently quite unnecessarily, as it were by instinct, by an impulse such as makes the sparrow chirrup and the cockroach waggle its antennae. She was deceitful with me, with the footman, with the porter, with the tradesmen in the shops, with her acquaintances; not one conversation, not one meeting, took place without affectation and pretence. A man had only to come into our room – whoever it might be, a waiter, or a baron – for her eyes, her expression, her voice to change, even the contours of her figure changed. At the very first glance at her then, you would have said there were no more wealthy and fashionable people in Italy than us. She never met an artist or a musician without telling him all sorts of lies about his remarkable talent.

' "You have such talent!" she would say, in honeyed cadences, "I'm really afraid of you. I think you must see right through people."

'And all this simply in order to please, to be successful, to be fascinating! She woke up every morning with the one thought of "attracting". It was the aim and object of her life. If I had told her that in such a house, in such a street, there lived a man who was not attracted to her, it would have caused her real suffering. She wanted every day to enchant, to captivate, to drive men crazy. The fact that I was in her power and reduced to a complete nonentity by her charms gave her the same sort of satisfaction that victors used to feel in tournaments. As though she had not degraded me enough, at nights, stretched out like a tigress, uncovered – she was always too hot – she would read letters sent her by Lubkov; he begged her to return to Russia, vowing if she did not he would rob or murder someone to get the money to come to her. She hated him, but his passionate, slavish letters excited her. She had an extraordinary opinion of her own charms; she imagined that if somewhere, in some great assembly, men could have seen how beautifully she was made and the colour of her skin, she would have vanquished all Italy, the whole world. Her talk of her figure, of her skin, offended me, and observing this, she would, when she was angry, to vex me, say all sorts of vulgar things, taunting me. One day when we were at the summer villa of a lady we knew, and she lost her temper, she even went so far as to say: "If you don't leave off boring me with your sermons, I'll undress this minute and lie naked here on these flowers."

'Often looking at her asleep, or eating, or trying to assume a naive expression, I wondered why that extraordinary beauty, grace, and intelligence had been given her by God. Could it simply be for lolling in bed, eating and telling lies, endless lies? And was she even intelligent? She was afraid of three candles in a row, of the number thirteen, was terrified of spells and bad dreams. She argued about free love and freedom in general like a bigoted old woman, declared that Boleslav Markevich was a better writer than Turgenev. But she was diabolically cunning and sharp, and knew how to seem a highly educated, emancipated person in company.

'Even at a good-humoured moment, she could always insult a servant or kill an insect without a pang; she liked bull-fights, liked to read about murders, and was angry when prisoners were acquitted.

'For the life Ariadna and I were leading, we had to have a great deal of money. My poor father sent me his pension, all the little sums he received, borrowed for me wherever he could, and when one day he answered me: "*Non habeo*", I sent him a desperate telegram in which I begged him to mortgage the estate. A little later I begged him to get money somehow on a second mortgage. He did this too without a murmur and sent me every kopeck. Ariadna despised the practical side of life; all this was no concern of hers, and when flinging away thousands of francs to satisfy her mad desires I groaned like an old tree, she would be singing "Addio bella Napoli" with a light heart.

Little by little I grew cold to her and began to be ashamed of our affair. I am not fond of pregnancy and childbirth but now I sometimes dreamed of a child who would have been at least a formal justification of our life. So that I could still stand myself, I began reading and visiting museums and galleries, gave up drinking and took to eating very little. If you keep yourself well in hand from morning to night, your heart seems lighter.

'Ariadna was fed up with me, too. Actually, the people with whom she won her triumphs were mediocre; there were still no ambassadors or salon, the money did not run to it, and this mortified her and made her sob, and she announced to me at last that, all right, she would not be against our returning to Russia. And here we are on our way. For the last few months she has been zealously corresponding with her brother; she evidently has some secret projects, but what they are – God knows! I am sick of trying to fathom her schemes. But we're going, not to the country, but to Yalta and afterwards to the Caucasus. She can only exist now at spas, and if you knew how I hate these spas, how suffocated and ashamed I am in them. I'd like to go to the country now! I'd like to work now, earning my bread by the sweat of my brow, atoning for my follies. I feel I have superabundant energy and I believe that if I were to put that energy to work I could redeem my estate in five years. But now, as you see, there is a complication. Here we're not abroad, but in Mother Russia; we shall have to think of lawful wedlock. Of course, all attraction is over; there is no trace left of my old love, but, all the same, I am bound in honour to marry her.'

Shamokhin, excited by his story, came with me below deck, and we continued talking about women. It was late. It turned out that he and I were in the same cabin.

'So far it is only in the village that woman has not fallen behind man,' said Shamokhin. 'There she thinks and feels just as man does, and struggles with nature in the name of culture as zealously as he. In the towns the woman of the bourgeois or intellectual class has long since fallen behind, and is returning to her primitive condition. She is half a human beast already, and, thanks to her, a great deal of what had been won by the human spirit has been lost again; the woman gradually disappears and in her place is the primitive female. This backwardness on the part of the educated woman is a real danger to culture; in her retrograde movement she tries to drag man after her and prevents him from moving forward. That is incontestable.'

I asked: 'Why generalise? Why judge all women by Ariadna alone? The very struggle of women for education and sexual equality, which

I look upon as a struggle for justice, precludes any hypothesis of a retrograde movement.' But Shamokhin scarcely listened to me and he smiled distrustfully. He was a passionate, convinced misogynist, and it was impossible to alter his convictions.

'Oh, nonsense!' he interrupted. 'When once a woman sees in me, not a man, not an equal, but a male, and her one anxiety all her life is to attract me – that is, to take possession of me – how can one talk of their rights? Oh, don't you believe them; they are very, very cunning! We men make a great stir about their emancipation, but they don't care about their emancipation at all, they only pretend to care about it; they are horribly cunning things, horribly cunning!'

I began to feel sleepy and bored with arguing. I turned my face to the wall.

'Yes,' I heard as I fell asleep – 'yes, and it's our education that's at fault, sir. In our towns, the whole education and bringing up of women is basically reduced to developing her into a human beast – that is, to make her attractive to the male and able to vanquish him. Yes, sir,' – Shamokhin sighed – 'little girls ought to be taught and brought up with boys, so that they might be always together. A woman ought to be trained, like a man, to recognise when she's wrong, or else she always thinks she's in the right. Instil into a little girl from her cradle that a man is not first and foremost a bridegroom or a lover, but her neighbour, her equal in everything. Train her to think logically, to generalise, and do not tell her that her brain weighs less than a man's and that therefore she can ignore sciences, arts, the tasks of culture in general. The apprentice cobbler or house painter has a smaller brain than the adult male, yet he works, suffers, takes his part in the general struggle for existence. We must also stop using physiology as an excuse – pregnancy and childbirth – seeing that in the first place women don't have babies every month; secondly, not all women have babies; and, thirdly, a normal countrywoman works in the fields up to the day she gives birth and it does her no harm. Then there ought to be absolute equality in everyday life. If a man gives a lady a chair or picks up the handkerchief she has dropped, let her repay him in the same way. I have no objection if a girl of good family helps me to put on my coat or hands me a glass of water . . .'

I heard no more, for I fell asleep. Next morning when we were approaching Sevastopol, it was damp, unpleasant weather; the ship rocked. Shamokhin sat on deck with me, brooding and silent. When the bell rang for tea, men with their coat-collars turned up and ladies with pale, sleepy faces began going below; a young and very beautiful lady, the one who had been so angry with the Customs officers at Volochisk, stopped before Shamokhin and said with the expression of a naughty, fretful child:

'*Jean*, your birdie's been seasick.'

Afterwards when I was at Yalta I saw the same beautiful lady dashing about on horseback with a couple of officers hardly able to keep up with her. And one morning I saw her in an overall and a Phrygian cap, sketching on the sea-front with a great crowd admiring her a little way off. I too was introduced to her. She pressed my hand with great warmth, and looking at me ecstatically, thanked me in honeyed cadences for the pleasure I had given her by my writings.

'Don't you believe her,' Shamokhin whispered to me, 'she has never read a word of them.'

When I was walking on the sea-front in the early evening Shamokhin met me with his arms full of big parcels of fruits and dainties.

'Prince Maktuev is here!' he said joyfully. 'He came yesterday with her brother, the spiritualist! Now I understand what she was writing to him about! Oh, Lord!' he went on, gazing up to heaven, and pressing his parcels to his bosom. 'If she hits it off with the prince, it means freedom, then I can go back to the country to my father!'

And he ran ahead.

'I begin to believe in spirits,' he called to me, looking back. 'The spirit of grandfather Ilarion seems to have prophesied the truth! Oh, if only!'

The day after this meeting I left Yalta and how Shamokhin's love affair ended I don't know.

1895

The House with
the Mezzanine
(An Artist's Story)

I

This happened six or seven years ago when I was living in one of the districts of the province of T—, on the estate of a young landowner called Belokurov, who used to get up very early, wear a peasant tunic, drink beer in the evenings, and continually complain to me that he never had any sympathy from anyone. He lived in the lodge in the garden, and I in the old manor house, in a big room with columns, where there was no furniture except a wide sofa on which I used to sleep, and a table on which I used to set out patience. There was always, even in still weather, a droning noise in the old Ammosov stoves,* and thunderstorms made the whole house shake and, it seemed, crack into pieces; and it was rather terrifying, especially at night, when all the ten big windows were suddenly lit up by lightning.

Fated to be perpetually idle, I did absolutely nothing. For hours together I gazed out of the window at the sky, at the birds, at the avenue, read everything that the post brought me, slept. Sometimes I went out of the house and wandered about till late in the evening.

One day as I was returning home, I accidentally strayed into an estate I did not know. The sun was already sinking, and the shades of evening lay across the flowering rye. Two rows of old, closely planted, very tall fir trees stood like two dense walls forming a handsome, gloomy avenue. I easily climbed over the fence and walked along the avenue, slipping over the fir needles which lay two inches deep on the ground. It was still and dark, and only here and there on the high tree-tops the vivid golden light quivered and made rainbows in the spiders' webs. There was a strong, almost stifling smell of resin. Then I turned into a long avenue of limes. Here, too, all was abandonment and age; last year's leaves rustled mournfully under my feet and in the twilight shadows lurked between the trees. From the old orchard on the right came the weak, reluctant note of a golden oriole, who must have been old too. But then the limes ended. I walked by an old white house with a terrace and a mezzanine, and there suddenly opened before me a view of a courtyard, a large pond with a bathing-house, a group of green willows, and a village on the further bank, with a high, narrow belfry on which there glittered a cross reflecting the setting sun. For a moment I felt the fascination of something near and very familiar waft over me, as though I had seen that landscape at some time in my childhood.

At the white stone gates which led from the yard to the fields, old-fashioned solid gates with lions on them, were standing two girls. One of them, the elder, a slim, pale, very handsome girl with a perfect haystack of chestnut hair and a little obstinate mouth, had a severe expression and paid hardly any attention to me, while the other, who was still very young, not more than seventeen or eighteen, and was also slim and pale, with a large mouth and large eyes, looked at me with astonishment as I passed by, said something in English, and was overcome with embarrassment. And I felt that these two charming faces, too, had long been familiar to me. And I returned home feeling as though I had had a pleasant dream.

One morning soon afterwards, as Belokurov and I were walking near the house, a carriage drove unexpectedly into the yard, rustling over the grass, and in it was one of those girls. It was the elder one. She had come collecting contributions for some villagers whose houses had been burnt down. Speaking with great earnestness and in some detail, and not looking at us, she told us how many houses at the village of Siyanovo had been burnt, how many men, women, and children were left homeless, and what steps were proposed, to begin with, by the relief committee, of which she was now a member. After handing us the subscription list for our signatures, she put it away and immediately began to take leave of us.

'You have quite forgotten us, Piotr,' she said to Belokurov as she shook hands with him. 'Do come, and if Mr N— (she mentioned my name) cares to make the acquaintance of admirers of his work, and will come and see us, mother and I will be delighted.

I bowed.

When she had gone Belokurov began to tell me about her. The girl was, he said, of good family, and her name was Lidia Volchaninova, and the estate on which she lived with her mother and sister, like the village on the other side of the pond, was called Shelkovka. Her father had once held an important position in Moscow, and had died with the rank of privy councillor. Although they had ample means, the Volchaninovs lived on their estate summer and winter without going away. Lidia was a teacher in the rural district council school in her own village, and received a salary of twenty-five roubles a month. She spent nothing on herself but her salary, and was proud of earning her own living.

'An interesting family,' said Belokurov. 'Let's go over one day. They will be delighted to see you.'

One afternoon on a holiday we thought of the Volchaninovs, and went to Shelkovka to see them. They – the mother and two daughters – were at home. The mother, Ekaterina, who at one time had been handsome, but now, asthmatic, depressed, vague, and too fleshy for her years, tried to entertain me with a conversation about painting. Having heard from her daughter that I might come to Shelkovka, she had hurriedly recalled two or three of my landscapes which she had seen in exhibitions in Moscow, and now asked what I meant to express by them. Lidia, or, as they called her, Lida, talked more to Belokurov than to me. Earnest and unsmiling, she asked him why he was not on the rural council, and why he had not attended any of its meetings.

'It's not right, Piotr,' she said reproachfully. 'It's not right. It's too bad.'

'That's true, Lida – that's true,' the mother assented. 'It isn't right.'

'Our whole district is in the hands of Balagin,' Lida went on, addressing me. 'He is the chairman of the council administration, and he has distributed all the posts in the district among his nephews and sons-in-law; and he does as he likes. He ought to be opposed. The young men ought to make a strong party, but you see what the young men among us are like. It's a shame, Piotr!'

The younger sister, Zhenia, was silent while they were talking of the council. She took no part in serious conversation. She was not looked upon as quite grown up by her family, and, like a child, was always called by the nickname of Misius, because that was what she had called her English governess when she was a child. She was all the time looking at me with curiosity, and when I glanced at the photographs in the album, she explained to me: 'That's uncle . . . that's godfather,' moving her finger across the photograph. As she did so she touched me with her shoulder like a child, and I had a close view of her delicate, undeveloped chest, her slender shoulders, her plait, and her thin little body tightly drawn in by her sash.

We played croquet and lawn tennis, we walked about the garden, drank tea, and then sat a long time over supper. After the huge empty room with columns, I felt, as it were, at home in this small snug house where there were no oleographs on the walls and where the servants were spoken to with civility, and everything seemed to me young and pure, thanks to the presence of Lida and Misius, and there was an atmosphere of refinement over everything. At supper Lida talked to Belokurov again about the council, Balagin, and school libraries. She was an energetic, genuine girl, with convictions, and it was interesting to listen to her, though she talked a great deal and in a loud voice – perhaps because she was accustomed to talking at school. On the other hand, Belokurov, who had retained from his student days the habit of reducing every conversation to an argument, was tedious, flat, long-winded, and unmistakably anxious to appear clever and advanced. Gesticulating, he upset a sauce-boat with his sleeve, making a huge pool on the table-cloth, but no one except me appeared to notice it.

It was dark and still as we went home.

'Good breeding is shown, not by not upsetting the sauce, but by not noticing when somebody else does,' said Belokurov, with a sigh. 'Yes, a splendid, intellectual family! I'm out of touch with decent people; it's dreadful how out of touch! It's all work, work, work!'

He talked of how hard one had to work if one wanted to be a model landowner. And I thought what a tedious, lazy fellow he was! Whenever he talked of anything serious he articulated 'Er-er' with intense effort, and worked just as he talked – slowly, always late and missing deadlines. I had little faith in his business capacity since he carried the letters I gave him to post in his pocket for weeks on end.

'The hardest thing of all,' he muttered as he walked beside me – 'the hardest thing of all is that, work as you may, you get no sympathy from anyone. No sympathy!'

II

I took to visiting the Volchaninovs. As a rule I sat on the lower step of the terrace; I fretted with dissatisfaction at myself; I regretted my life passing so rapidly and uninterestingly, and felt as though I would like to tear out of my breast the heart which had grown so heavy. And meanwhile I heard talk on the terrace, the rustling of dresses, the pages of a book being turned. I soon grew used to Lida's days spent receiving patients, issuing books, and often going to the village bare-headed with a parasol, and the evenings full of loud talk about the council and schools. This slim, handsome, invariably austere girl, with her small well-cut mouth, always said dryly when the conversation turned to serious subjects:

'That's of no interest to you.'

She did not like me. She disliked me because I was a landscape painter and did not in my pictures portray the privations of the peasants, and because, as she fancied, I was indifferent to what she put such faith in. I remember when I was travelling on the banks of Lake Baikal, I met a Buriat* girl on horseback, wearing a shirt and trousers of blue Chinese canvas; I asked her if she would sell me her pipe. While we talked she looked contemptuously at my European face and hat, and in a moment she was bored with talking to me; she shouted to her horse and galloped on. And in just the same way Lida despised me as an alien. She never outwardly expressed her dislike for me, but I felt it, and sitting on the lower step of the terrace, I felt irritated, and said that doctoring peasants when one was not a doctor was deceiving them, and that it was easy to be benevolent when one had six thousand acres.

Her sister Misius had no cares, and spent her life in complete idleness just as I did. When she got up in the morning she immediately took up a book and sat down to read on the terrace in a deep arm-chair, with her feet hardly touching the ground, or hid herself with her book in the lime avenue, or walked out into the fields. She spent the whole day reading, poring greedily over her book, and only from the tired, dazed look in her eyes and the extreme paleness of her face could one sense that this continual reading was tiring her brain. When I arrived she would flush a little, leave her book, and looking into my face with her big eyes, would tell me eagerly of anything that had happened – for instance, that there had been a chimney-fire in the servants' hall, or that one of the men had caught a huge fish in the pond. On ordinary days she usually went about in a light blouse and a dark blue skirt. We went for walks together, picked cherries for making jam, went out in the boat. When she jumped up to reach a cherry or worked at the oars, her thin, weak arms showed through her transparent sleeves. Or I sketched a study, and she stood beside me watching rapturously.

One Sunday at the end of July I came to the Vochaninovs' at about nine in the morning. I walked about the park, keeping as far as I could from the house, looking for white mushrooms, of which there was a great number that summer, and putting markers down so as to pick them afterwards with Zhenia. There was a warm breeze. I saw Zhenia and her mother, both in light festive dresses, coming home from church, Zhenia holding her hat in the wind. Afterwards I heard them having tea on the terrace.

For a carefree person like me, trying to find justification for my perpetual idleness, those Sunday mornings in our country houses in the summer have always had a particular charm. When the green garden, still wet with dew, is all sparkling in the sun and looks radiant with happiness, when there is a scent of mignonette and oleander near the house, when the young people have just come back from church and are having breakfast in the garden, all so charmingly dressed and gay, and one knows that all these healthy, well-fed, handsome people are going to do nothing the whole long day, one wishes that all life were like that. Now, too, I had the same thought, and walked about the garden prepared to walk about like that, aimless and unoccupied, the whole day, the whole summer.

Zhenia came out with a basket; she had a look in her face as though she knew she would find me in the garden, or had a presentiment of it. We gathered mushrooms and talked, and when she asked a question she walked a little ahead so as to see my face.

'A miracle happened in the village yesterday,' she said. 'The lame woman Pelageia has been ill the whole year. Doctors or medicines did her no good; but yesterday an old woman came and whispered something over her, and her illness passed away.'

'That's nothing much,' I said. 'You mustn't look for miracles only among sick people and old women. Isn't health a miracle? And life itself? Whatever is beyond understanding is a miracle.'

'And aren't you afraid of what is beyond understanding?'

'No. Phenomena I don't understand I face boldly, and am not overwhelmed by them. I am above them. Man ought to recognise himself as superior to lions, tigers, stars, superior to everything in nature, even what seems miraculous and is beyond his understanding, or else he is not a man, but a mouse afraid of everything.'

Zhenia believed that as an artist I knew a very great deal, and could instinctively divine what I did not know. She longed for me to initiate her into the domain of the Eternal and the Beautiful, into that higher world in which, as she imagined, I was quite at home. And she talked to me of God, of eternal life, of the miraculous. And I, who could never admit that my self and my imagination would be lost for ever after death, answered: 'Yes, people are immortal.' 'Yes, eternal life awaits us.' And she listened, believed, and did not ask for proof.

As we were going home she stopped suddenly and said:

'Our Lida is a remarkable person – isn't she? I love her very dearly, and would give my life for her any minute. But tell me,' – Zhenia touched my sleeve with her finger – 'tell me, why do you always argue with her? Why are you irritated?'

'Because she is wrong.'

Zhenia shook her head and tears came into her eyes.

'How incomprehensible that is!' she said.

Lida had just then returned from somewhere, and standing by the porch with a whip in her hand, a slim, beautiful figure in the sunlight, she was giving orders to one of the men. Talking loudly, she hurriedly received two or three sick villagers; then with a busy and anxious face she walked about the rooms, opening one cupboard after another, and went upstairs to the mezzanine. For a long time she was searched for and called to dinner: she came in when we had finished our soup. All these tiny details I remember with tenderness, and that whole day I remember vividly, although nothing special happened. After dinner Zhenia lay in a deep arm-chair reading, while I sat on the bottom step of the terrace. We were silent. The whole sky was overcast with clouds, and it began to spot with fine rain. It was hot; the wind had dropped, and it seemed as though the day would never end. Ekaterina came out on the terrace, looking drowsy and carrying a fan.

'Oh, Mother,' said Zhenia, kissing her hand, 'it's not good for you to sleep in the day.'

They adored each other. When one went into the garden, the other would stand on the terrace, and, looking towards the trees, call 'Aa-oo, Zhenia!' or 'Mother, where are you?' They always said their prayers together, and had the same faith; and they understood each other perfectly even when they did not speak. And their attitude to people was the same. Ekaterina, too, quickly got used to me and fond of me, and when I did not come for two or three days, sent to ask if I were well. She, too, gazed at my sketches with enthusiasm, and with the same openness and readiness to chatter as Misius, she told me what had happened, and confided to me her domestic secrets.

She was in awe of her elder daughter. Lida did not care for endearments, she talked only of serious matters; she lived her life apart, and to her mother and sister was as sacred and enigmatic a person as an admiral, always sitting in his cabin, is to the sailors.

'Our Lida is a remarkable person,' the mother would often say. 'Isn't she?'

Now, while it was drizzling with rain, we talked of Lida.

'She is a remarkable girl,' said her mother, and added in an undertone, like a conspirator, looking about her timidly: 'People like her are rare; only, do you know, I am beginning to be a little uneasy. The school, the dispensary, books – all that's very good, but why go to extremes? She is twenty-three, you know; it's time for her to think seriously about herself. With her books and her dispensary in no time she will find life has slipped by . . . She must get married.'

Zhenia, pale from reading, with her hair disarranged, raised her head and said as it were to herself, looking at her mother:

'Mother, everything is in God's hands.'

And again she buried herself in her book.

Belokurov came in his tunic and embroidered shirt. We played croquet and tennis, then, when it got dark, sat a long time over supper and talked again about schools, and about Balagin, who had the whole district under his thumb. As I left the Volchaninovs' that evening, I took away with me the impression of a long, long idle day, with a melancholy consciousness that everything ends in this world, however long it may be. Zhenia saw us out to the gate, and perhaps because she had been with me all day, from morning till night, I felt somehow listless without her, and that all that charming family was dear to me, and for the first time that summer I had a yearning to paint.

'Tell me, why do you lead such a dreary, colourless life?' I asked Belokurov as I went home. 'My life is dreary, difficult, and monotonous because I am an artist, a strange person. From my earliest days I've been wrung by envy, self-dissatisfaction, distrust in my work. I'm always poor, I'm a wanderer, but you – you're a healthy, normal man, a landowner, and a gentleman. Why do you live in such an uninteresting way? Why do you get so little out of life? Why haven't you, for instance, fallen in love with Lida or Zhenia?'

'You forget that I love another woman,' answered Belokurov.

He was referring to Liubov, the lady who shared the lodge with him. Every day I saw this lady, very plump, rotund, and dignified, not unlike a fat goose, walking about the garden, in the Russian national dress and beads, always carrying a parasol; and the servant was continually calling her in to dinner or to tea. Three years before she had taken one of the lodges for a summer holiday, and had settled down at Belokurov's apparently for ever. She was ten years older than he was, and kept him on a short lead, so much so that he had to ask her permission to leave the house. She often sobbed in a deep masculine note, and then I used to send word to her that if she did not stop, I would move out; and she stopped.

When we got home Belokurov sat down on the sofa and frowned thoughtfully, and I began walking up and down the room, conscious of a soft emotion as though I were in love. I wanted to talk about the Volchaninovs.

'Lida could only fall in love with a member of the council, as devoted to schools and hospitals as she is,' I said. 'Oh, for the sake of a girl like that one might not only join the council, but even wear out iron shoes, like the girl in the fairy tale. And Misius? What a sweet creature she is, that Misius!'

Belokurov, drawling out 'Er-er,' began a long-winded disquisition on the malady of the age – pessimism. He talked assertively, in a tone that suggested that I was opposing him. Hundreds of miles of desolate, monotonous, burnt-up steppe cannot induce such deep depression as one man when he sits and talks, and nobody knows when he will go away.

'It's not a question of pessimism or optimism,' I said irritably; 'it's simply that ninety-nine people out of a hundred have no sense.'

Belokurov took this as aimed at himself, was offended, and went away.

III

'The prince is staying at Maloziomovo, and he asks to be remembered to you,' said Lida to her mother. She had just come in, and was taking off her gloves. 'He gave me a great deal of interesting news . . . He promised to raise the question of a medical relief centre at Maloziomovo again at the provincial assembly, but he says there is very little hope of it.' And turning to me, she said: 'Excuse me, I always forget that this cannot be interesting to you.'

I felt irritated.

'Why not interesting to me?' I said, shrugging my shoulders. 'You do not care to know my opinion, but I assure you the question has great interest for me.'

'Yes?'

'Yes. In my opinion a medical relief centre at Maloziomovo is quite unnecessary.'

My irritation infected her; she looked at me, screwing up her eyes, and asked:

'What is necessary? Landscapes?'

'Nor are landscapes. Nothing is.'

She finished taking off her gloves, and opened the newspaper, which had just been brought from the post. A minute later she said quietly, evidently restraining herself:

'Last week Anna died in childbirth, and if there had been a medical emergency centre near, she would have lived. And I think even landscape painters ought to have some convictions on the subject.'

'I have a very definite conviction on that subject, I assure you,' I answered; and she screened herself with the newspaper, as though unwilling to listen to me. 'To my mind, all these schools, dispensaries, libraries, medical emergency centres, under present conditions, only serve to aggravate the bondage of the people. The peasants are fettered by a great chain, and you do not break the chain, but only add fresh links to it – that's my conviction.'

She raised her eyes to me and smiled ironically, and I went on trying to formulate my leading idea.

'What matters is not that Anna died in childbirth, but that all these Annas, Mavras, Pelageias, toil from early morning till dark, fall ill from work too hard for them, all their lives they tremble for their sick and hungry children, all their lives they are being doctored, and in dread of death and disease, fade and grow old early, and die in filth and stench. Their children begin the same story over again as soon as they grow up, and so it goes on for hundreds of years and billions of men live worse than beasts – in continual terror, for a mere crust of bread. The whole horror of their position lies in their never having time to think of their souls, of their divine image. Cold, hunger, animal terror, a burden of toil, like avalanches of snow, block for them every way to spiritual activity – that is, to what distinguishes man from the brutes and what is the only thing which makes life worth living. You go to their help with hospitals and schools, but you don't free them from their fetters; on the contrary, you bind them in closer bonds, as, by introducing new prejudices, you increase the number of their wants, to say nothing of the fact that they've got to pay the council for plasters and books, and so toil harder than ever.'

'I am not going to argue with you,' said Lida, putting down the paper. 'I've heard all that before. I will only say one thing: one cannot sit with one's hands in one's lap. It's true that we are not saving humanity, and perhaps we make a great many mistakes; but we do what we can, and we are right. The highest and holiest task for a civilised person is to serve his neighbours, and we try to serve them as best we can. You don't like it, but one can't please everyone.'

'That's true, Lida,' said her mother – 'that's true.'

In Lida's presence she was always a little timid, and looked at her nervously as she talked, afraid of saying something superfluous or inopportune. And she never contradicted her, but always assented: 'That's true, Lida – that's true.'

'Teaching the peasants to read and write, books of wretched precepts and rhymes, and medical relief centres, cannot diminish either ignorance or the death rate, just as the light from your windows cannot light up this huge garden,' said I. 'You give nothing. By meddling in these people's lives you only create new wants in them, and new demands on their labour.'

'Oh, my God! But one must do something!' said Lida with vexation, and from her tone one could see that she thought my arguments worthless and despised them.

'The people must be freed from hard physical labour,' said I. 'We must lighten their yoke, let them have time to breathe, not to spend all their lives at the stove, at the wash-tub, and in the fields, but to have time also to think of their souls, of God – to develop their spiritual capacities. The highest vocation of man is spiritual activity – the perpetual search for truth and the meaning of life. Make rough animal labour unnecessary for them, let them feel themselves free, and then you will see what a mockery these dispensaries and books are. Once a man recognises his true vocation, he can only be satisfied by religion, science, and art, and not by these trifles.'

'Free them from labour?' laughed Lida. 'But is that possible?'

'Yes. Take upon yourself a share of their labour. If all of us, townspeople and country people, all without exception, would agree to divide between us the labour which mankind spends on the satisfaction of their physical needs, each of us would perhaps need to work only for two or three hours a day. Imagine that we all, rich and poor, work only for three hours a day, and the rest of our time is free. Imagine further that in order to depend even less upon our bodies and to labour less, we invent machines to replace our work, we try to cut down our needs to the minimum. We would train ourselves and our children not to fear hunger and cold, and we shouldn't be continually trembling for their health like Anna, Mavra, and Pelageia. Imagine that we don't doctor ourselves, don't keep dispensaries, tobacco factories, distilleries – what a lot of free time we would have over, after all! All of us together would devote our leisure to science and art. Just as the peasants sometimes work communally, mending the roads, so all of us, as a community, would search for truth and the meaning of life, and I am convinced that the truth would be discovered very quickly; man would escape from this continual, agonising, oppressive dread of death, and even from death itself.'

'You contradict yourself, though,' said Lida. 'You talk about science, and are yourself opposed to literacy.'

'Literacy when a man has nothing to read but the signs on public houses and sometimes books which he cannot understand – that we have had ever since the times of Rurik; Gogol's Petrushka has been reading for a long time, yet as the village was in the days of Rurik, so it has remained. What is needed is not literacy, but freedom to develop spiritual capacities on a wide scale. What is wanted is not schools, but universities.'

'You are opposed to medicine, too?'

'Yes. It would be necessary only for the study of diseases as natural phenomena, and not for the cure of them. If one must cure, it should not be diseases, but the causes of them. Remove the principal cause – physical labour, and then there will be no disease. I don't believe in a science that cures disease,' I went on excitedly. 'When science and art are real, they aim not at temporary, private ends, but at the eternal and the universal – they seek for truth and the meaning of life, they seek for God, for the soul, and when they are tied down to the needs and evils of the day, to dispensaries and libraries, they only complicate and hamper life. We have plenty of doctors, chemists, lawyers, plenty of people can read and write, but we are quite without biologists, mathematicians, philosophers, poets. The whole of our intelligence, the whole of our spiritual energy, is spent on satisfying temporary, passing needs . . . Scientists, writers, artists, are hard at work; thanks to them, the conveniences of life are multiplied from day to day. Our physical demands increase, yet truth is still a long way off, and man still remains the most rapacious and dirty animal; everything tends to the degeneration of the majority of mankind, and the loss for ever of all fitness for life. In such conditions an artist's work has no meaning, and the more talented he is, the stranger and the more unintelligible his position, as when one looks into it, it is evident that he is working for the amusement of a rapacious and unclean animal, and is supporting the existing order. And I don't want to work and I shan't . . . Nothing is any use; let the earth sink to perdition!'

'Misius, leave the room!' said Lida to her sister, apparently thinking my words harmful to such a young girl.

Zhenia looked mournfully at her mother and sister, and left the room.

'These are the charming things people say when they want to justify their indifference,' said Lida. 'It is easier to disapprove of schools and hospitals than to teach or heal.'

'That's true, Lida – that's true,' the mother assented.

'You threaten to give up working,' said Lida. 'You evidently set a high value on your work. Let us give up arguing; we shall never agree, since I put the most imperfect dispensary or library of which you have just spoken so contemptuously on a higher level than any landscape.' And turning at once to her mother, she began speaking in quite a different tone: 'The prince is very much changed, and much thinner than when he was with us last. He is being sent to Vichy.'

She was telling her mother about the prince in order to avoid talking to me. Her face glowed, and to hide her emotion she bent low over the table as though she were short-sighted, and made a show of reading the newspaper. My presence was disagreeable to her. I said good-bye and went home.

IV

It was quite still outside; the village on the further side of the pond was already asleep; there was not a light to be seen, and only the stars were faintly reflected in the pond. At the gate with the lions Zhenia was standing motionless, waiting to see me off.

'Everyone is asleep in the village,' I said to her, trying to make out her face in the darkness, and I saw her mournful dark eyes fixed upon me. 'The innkeeper and the horse-stealers are asleep, while we, well-bred people, argue and irritate each other.'

It was a melancholy August night – melancholy because there was already a feeling of autumn: the moon was rising behind a purple

cloud, and it shed a faint light upon the road and on the dark fields of
winter corn by the sides. From time to time a star fell. Zhenia walked
beside me along the road, and tried not to look at the sky, that she
might not see the falling stars, which for some reason frightened her.

'I believe you are right,' she said, shivering with the damp night air.
'If people, all together, could devote themselves to spiritual ends, they
would soon know everything.'

'Of course. We are higher beings, and if we were really to recognise
the whole force of human spirit and lived only for higher ends, we
should in the end become like gods. But that will never be – mankind
will degenerate and no traces of its spirit will remain.'

When the gates were out of sight, Zhenia stopped and shook hands
with me.

'Good night,' she said, shivering; she had nothing but her blouse
over her shoulders and was huddled up with cold. 'Come tomorrow.'

I felt horrified at the thought of being left alone, irritated and
dissatisfied with myself and other people; and I, too, tried not to look
at the falling stars.

'Stay with me another minute,' I said to her, 'please.'

I loved Zhenia. I must have loved her because she met me when I
came and saw me off when I went away; because she looked at me
tenderly and enthusiastically. How touchingly beautiful were her
pale face, slender neck, slender arms, her weakness, her idleness, her
reading. And intelligence? I suspected she had exceptional intelligence. I was fascinated by the breadth of her views, perhaps because
they were different from those of the stern, handsome Lida, who
disliked me. Zhenia liked me because I was an artist. I had conquered
her heart by my talent, and had a passionate desire to paint for her
sake alone; and I dreamed of her as of my little queen who with me
would possess those trees, those fields, the mists, the dawn, the
exquisite and beautiful scenery in the midst of which I had felt myself
hopelessly solitary and useless.

'Stay another minute,' I begged her. 'I beg you.'

I took off my overcoat and put it over her frozen shoulders. Afraid
of looking ugly and absurd in a man's overcoat, she laughed, threw it
off, and at that instant I put my arms round her and covered her face,
shoulders, and hands with kisses.

'Till tomorrow,' she whispered, and softly, as though afraid of
breaking upon the silence of the night, she embraced me. 'We have no
secrets from one another. I must tell my mother and my sister at once
. . . It's so dreadful! Mother is all right; mother likes you – but Lida!'

She ran to the gates.

'Good-bye!' she called.

And then for about two minutes I heard her running. I did not want to go home, and I had nothing to go for. I stood still for a little time hesitating, and made my way slowly back, to look once more at the house in which she lived, the sweet, simple old house, whose windows, like eyes, seemed to be watching me from the mezzanine, understanding all about it. I walked by the terrace, sat on the seat by the tennis court, in the dark under the old elm tree, and looked from there at the house. In the windows of the top storey where Misius slept there appeared a bright light, which changed to a soft green – they had covered the lamp with the shade. Shadows began to move . . . I was full of tenderness, peace, and satisfaction with myself – satisfaction at having been able to be carried away by my feelings and having fallen in love, and at the same time I felt uncomfortable at the thought that only a few steps away from me, in one of the rooms of that house, there was Lida, who disliked and perhaps hated me. I went on sitting there wondering whether Zhenia would come out; I listened and fancied I heard voices talking in the mezzanine.

About an hour passed. The green light went out, and the shadows were no longer visible. The moon was standing high above the house, and lighting up the sleeping garden and the paths; the dahlias and the roses in front of the house could be seen distinctly, and looked all the same colour. It was getting very cold. I left the garden, picked up my coat on the way, and slowly wandered home.

When next day after dinner I went to the Volchaninovs', the glass door into the garden was wide open. I sat for a while on the terrace, expecting Zhenia every minute to appear from behind the flower-beds on the lawn, or from one of the avenues, or that I should hear her voice from the house. Then I walked into the drawing-room, the dining-room. There was not a soul to be seen. From the dining-room I walked down the long corridor to the hall and back. In this corridor there were several doors, and through one of them I heard the voice of Lida:

' "God . . . sent . . . a crow," ' she said in a loud, emphatic voice, probably dictating – ' "God sent a crow a piece of cheese . . . A crow . . . A piece of cheese . . ." Who's there?' she called suddenly, hearing my steps.

'It's I.'

'Ah! I'm sorry, I can't come out to you at the moment; I'm giving Dasha her lesson.'

'Is your mother in the garden?'

'No, she went away with my sister this morning to our aunt in the province of Penza. And in the winter they will probably go abroad,' she added after a pause. ' "God sent . . . the crow . . . a piece . . . of cheese . . ." Have you written it?'

I went into the hall, and stared vacantly at the pond and the village, and the sound reached me of 'A piece of cheese . . . God sent the crow a piece of cheese.'

And I went back by the way I had come here the first time – first from the yard into the garden past the house, then into the avenue of lime trees . . . At this point I was overtaken by a small boy who gave me a note:

'I told my sister everything and she demands that we part,' I read. 'I could not hurt her by disobeying. God will give you happiness, forgive me. If only you knew how bitterly my mother and I are crying!'

Then there was the dark fir avenue, the broken-down fence . . . On the field where the rye used to be in flower and the corncrakes were calling, cows and hobbled horses were now roaming. On the slopes there were bright green patches of winter corn. A sober workaday feeling came over me and I felt ashamed of all I had said at the Volchaninovs', and life became as dreary as before. When I got home, I packed and set off that evening for Petersburg.

I never saw the Volchaninovs again. Not long ago, on my way to the Crimea, I met Belokurov in the train. As before, he was wearing a jerkin and an embroidered shirt, and when I asked how he was, he replied that, God be praised, he was well. We began talking. He had sold his old estate and bought another smaller one, in Liubov's name. He could tell me little about the Volchaninovs. Lida, he said, was still living in Shelkovka and teaching in the school; she had by degrees succeeded in gathering round her a circle of people sympathetic to her who made a strong party, and at the last election had turned out Balagin, who had till then had the whole district under his thumb. About Zhenia he only told me that she did not live at home, and that he did not know where she was.

I am beginning to forget the old house, and only sometimes when I am painting or reading I suddenly, apropos of nothing, remember the green light in the window, the sound of my footsteps as I walked home through the fields in the night, with my heart full of love, rubbing my hands in the cold. And still more rarely, at moments when I am sad and depressed by loneliness, I have dim memories, and little by little I begin to feel that I have not been forgotten, either – that she is waiting for me, and that we shall meet . . .

Misius, where are you?

1896

My Life
(The Story of a Provincial)

I

The office manager said to me: 'I only keep you out of respect for your father, who is highly regarded; otherwise you would have been sent flying long ago.' I replied to him: 'You flatter me too much, your Excellency, if you assume that I can fly.' And then I heard him say: 'Take that gentleman away; he gets on my nerves.'

Two days later I was dismissed. And in this way I have, during the years I have been regarded as an adult, lost nine situations, to the great mortification of my father, the town architect. I have served in various departments, but all these nine jobs have been as alike as peas in a pod: I had to sit, write, and listen to rude or stupid reprimands, and wait to be dismissed.

When I came in to my father he was sitting deep in an arm-chair with his eyes closed. His dry, emaciated face, blue-coloured where it was shaved (he looked like an old Catholic organist), expressed meekness and resignation. Without responding to my greeting or opening his eyes, he said:

'If my dear wife and your mother were living, your life would have been a source of continual distress to her. I see Divine Providence in her premature death. You wretch,' he continued, opening his eyes, 'please tell me: what am I to do with you?'

In the past when I was bit younger my friends and relations had known what to do with me: some advised me to volunteer for the army, others to get a job in a pharmacy, and others in the telegraph department; now that I am over twenty-five, and grey hairs are even beginning to show on my temples, and I have been a volunteer, and in a pharmacy, and in the telegraph department, it would seem that all earthly possibilities have been exhausted, and people have given up advising me, and merely sigh or shake their heads.

'Who do you think you are?' my father went on. 'By the time they are your age, young men have a secure social position, while look at you: you are a proletarian, a beggar, a burden on your father!'

And as usual he proceeded to declare that the young people of today were on the road to perdition through unbelief, materialism, and self-conceit, and that amateur theatricals ought to be prohibited, because they seduced young people from religion and their duties.

'Tomorrow we shall go together, and you shall apologise to the office manager, and promise him to work conscientiously,' he concluded. 'You must not remain one day without a regular position in society.'

'I beg you to listen to me,' I said sullenly, expecting nothing good from this conversation. 'What you call a position in society is the privilege of capital and education. Those who have neither wealth nor education earn their daily bread by manual labour, and I see no grounds for my being an exception.'

'When you begin talking about manual labour it is always stupid and vulgar!' said my father with irritation. 'Understand, you dense fellow, understand, you brainless idiot, that besides coarse physical strength you have the divine spirit, a spark of the holy fire, which utterly distinguishes you from the ass or the reptile, and brings you nearer to the Deity! This fire is the fruit of the efforts of the best of mankind during thousands of years. Your great-grandfather Poloznev, the general, fought at Borodino; your grandfather was a poet, an actor, and a Marshal of the Nobility; your uncle is a schoolmaster; and lastly, I, your father, am an architect! All the Poloznevs have guarded the sacred fire simply for you to put it out!'

'One must be just,' I said. 'Millions of people do manual labour.'

'And let them do it! They don't know how to do anything else! Anybody, even the most abject fool or criminal, is capable of manual labour; it is the distinguishing mark of the slave and the barbarian, while the holy fire is vouchsafed only to a few!'

It was pointless to persist with this conversation. My father worshipped himself, and nothing was convincing to him but what he said himself. Besides, I knew perfectly well that the disdain with which he talked of physical toil was founded not so much on reverence for the sacred fire as on a secret dread that I should become a workman, and should set the whole town talking about me; what was worse, all my contemporaries had long ago taken their degrees and were doing well, and the son of the manager of the State Bank was already a collegiate assessor, while I, his only son, was nothing! To continue the conversation was pointless and unpleasant, but I still sat on and feebly retorted, hoping that I might at last be understood. The whole question, of course, was clear and simple, and only concerned with the means of my earning my living; but the simplicity passed unnoticed, and I was talked to in sickly rounded phrases of Borodino, of the sacred fire, of my uncle a forgotten poet, who had once written poor and artificial verses; I was rudely called brainless and dense. And how I longed to be understood! In spite of everything, I loved my father and my sister and it had been my habit from childhood to consult them – a habit so deeply rooted that I doubt whether I shall ever get rid of it; whether I am in the right or the wrong, I am in constant dread of wounding them, constantly afraid that the excitement would turn my father's thin neck crimson and that he would have a stroke.

'To sit in a stuffy room,' I began, 'to copy, to compete with a typewriter, is shameful and humiliating for a man of my age. What can the sacred fire have to do with it?'

'It's intellectual work, anyway,' said my father. 'But that's enough; let us cut short this conversation, and in any case I warn you: if you don't go back to work again, but follow your contemptible propensities, then my daughter and I will banish you from our hearts. I shall strike you out of my will, I swear by the living God!'

With perfect sincerity, to prove the purity of the motives by which I wanted to be guided in all my doings, I said:

'The question of inheritance does not seem important to me. I renounce it all beforehand.'

For some reason or other, quite to my surprise, these words hurt my father deeply. He went scarlet.

'Don't dare to talk to me like that, fool!' he shouted in a thin, shrill voice, 'wastrel!' And with a rapid, skilful, and habitual movement he slapped me twice in the face. 'You are forgetting yourself.'

When my father beat me as a child I had to stand up straight, with my hands held stiffly against my trouser seams, and look him straight in the face. And now when he hit me I was utterly overwhelmed, and, as though I were still a child, drew myself up and tried to look him in the face. My father was old and very thin, but his thin muscles must have been as strong as leather, for his blows hurt a good deal.

I staggered back into the passage, and there he snatched up his umbrella, and hit me several times on the head and shoulders; at that moment my sister opened the drawing-room door to see what the noise was, but at once turned away with a look of horror and pity without uttering a word in my defence.

My determination not to return to the government office, but to begin a new life of manual work, was not to be shaken. I had only to choose the kind of work – and there was no particular difficulty about that, as it seemed to me that I was very strong and fitted for the very heaviest labour. I was faced with a monotonous life of toil in the midst of hunger, coarseness, and stench, continually preoccupied with earning my daily bread. And – who knows? – as I returned from my work along Great Dvorianskaia Street, I might very likely frequently envy Dolzhikov the engineer, who lived by intellectual work; but, at the moment, thinking over all my future hardships made me lighthearted. At times I had dreamed of spiritual activity, imagining myself a teacher, a doctor, or a writer, but these dreams remained dreams. The taste for intellectual pleasures – for the theatre, for instance, and for reading – was a passion with me, but whether I had any ability for intellectual work I don't know. At school I had had an unconquerable aversion for Greek, so that I was only in the fourth class when they had to remove me from school. For a long time private teachers coached me for the fifth class. Then I served in various government offices, spending most of the day in complete idleness, and I was told that this was intellectual work. My activity in the scholastic and official sphere had required neither mental application nor talent, nor special qualifications, nor creative impulse; it was mechanical. Such intellectual work I put on a lower level than physical toil; I despise it, and I don't think that for one moment it could serve as a justification for an idle, careless life, as it is indeed nothing but a sham, one of the forms of that same idleness. Real intellectual work I have in all probability never known.

Evening came. We lived in Great Dvorianskaia* Street; it was the principal street in the town, and in the absence of decent public gardens our beau monde used it as a promenade in the evenings. This charming street did to some extent take the place of a public garden, as on each side of it there was a row of poplars which smelt sweet, particularly after rain, and acacias, tall bushes of lilac, wild cherries and apple trees hung over the fences and palings. The May twilight, the tender young greenery with its shifting shades, the scent of the lilac, the buzzing of the insects, the stillness, the warmth – how fresh and marvellous it all is, though spring is repeated every year! I stood at the garden gate and watched the passers-by. With most of them I had grown up and at one time played pranks; now they might have been disconcerted by my being near them, for I was poorly and unfashionably dressed, and they used to say of my very narrow trousers and huge, clumsy boots that they were like sticks of macaroni stuck in boats. Besides, I had a bad reputation in the town because I had no decent social position, and often played billiards in cheap inns, and also, perhaps, because I had on two occasions been hauled up before a police officer, though I had done nothing to deserve it.

In the big house opposite, at Dolzhikov's, someone was playing the piano. It was beginning to get dark, and stars were twinkling in the sky. Here my father, in an old top hat with a wide upturned brim, walked slowly by with my sister on his arm, bowing in response to greetings.

'Look up,' he said to my sister, pointing to the sky with the same umbrella with which he had beaten me that afternoon. 'Look up at the sky! Even the tiniest stars are all worlds! How insignificant is man in comparison with the universe!'

And he said this in a tone that suggested that it was particularly agreeable and flattering to him that he was so insignificant. What a mediocrity! Sad to say, he was the only architect in the town, and in the fifteen to twenty years that I could remember not one single decent house had been built in it. When any one asked him to plan a house, he usually drew first the reception hall and drawing-room; just as in old days the boarding-school misses always started from the stove when they danced, so his artistic ideas could only begin and develop from the hall and drawing-room. To them he tacked on a dining-room, a nursery, a study, linking the rooms together with doors, and so they all inevitably turned into passages, and every one of them had two or even three unnecessary doors. His imagination must have been unclear, extremely muddled, curtailed. As though feeling that something was lacking, he invariably resorted to all sorts of outbuildings, planting one beside another; and I can see now the narrow entries, the poky little passages, the crooked staircases leading to half-landings where one could not stand upright, and where, instead of a floor, there were three huge steps like the shelves of a bath-house; and the kitchen was invariably in the basement with a brick floor and vaulted ceilings. The front of the house had a harsh, stubborn expression; its lines were stiff and timid; the roof was low-pitched and squat; and the chimneys, plump as buns, were invariably crowned by wire caps with squeaking black cowls. And for some reason all these houses, built by my father exactly like one another, vaguely reminded me of his top hat and the back of his head, stiff and stubborn-looking. In the course of years they have grown used in the town to my father's mediocrity. It has taken root and become our style.

This same style my father had brought into my sister's life also, beginning with christening her Kleopatra (just as he had named me Misail).* When she was a little girl he scared her by mentioning the stars, sages of ancient times, our ancestors, and discoursed at length on the nature of life and duty; and now, when she was twenty-six, he kept up the same habits, allowing her to walk arm in arm with no one but himself, and imagining for some reason that sooner or later a suitable young man would be sure to appear, and to desire to enter into matrimony with her out of respect for his personal qualities. She adored my father, feared him, and believed in his exceptional intelligence.

It was quite dark, and gradually the street grew empty. The music had ceased in the house opposite; the gate was thrown wide open, and a troika's three horses trotted frolicking along our street with a soft tinkle of little bells. That was the engineer off for a drive with his daughter. It was time for bed!

I had my own room in the house, but I lived in a shed in the yard, under the same roof as a brick barn which had been built some time or other, probably to keep harness in; great spikes were driven into the wall. It was now surplus, and for the last thirty years my father had stowed away in it his newspapers, which for some reason he had bound in half-yearly volumes and allowed nobody to touch. Living here, I was less liable to be seen by my father and his visitors, and I fancied that if I did not live in a real room, and did not go into the house every day to dinner, my father's words that I was a burden upon him somehow did not sound so offensive.

My sister was waiting for me. Unseen by my father, she had brought me some supper: a small slice of cold veal and a piece of bread. In our house such sayings as: 'A penny saved is a penny gained,' and 'Take care of the pence and the pounds will take care of themselves,' and so on, were frequently repeated, and my sister, weighed down by these vulgar maxims, did her utmost to cut down the expenses, and so we ate badly. Putting the plate on the table, she sat down on my bed and began to cry.

'Misail,' she said, 'what are you doing to us?'

She did not cover her face; her tears dropped on her chest and arms, and there was a look of distress on her face. She fell back on the pillow, and abandoned herself to her tears, sobbing and quivering all over.

'You have left your job again . . .' she said. 'Oh, how awful it is!'

'But do understand, sister, do understand . . .' I said, and I was overcome with despair because she was crying.

As ill luck would have it, the paraffin in my little lamp had run out; it began to smoke and was on the point of going out, and the old spikes on the walls looked down sullenly, and their shadows flickered.

'Have mercy on us,' said my sister, sitting up. 'Father is in terrible distress and I am ill; I shall go out of my mind. What will become of you?' she said, sobbing and stetching out her arms to me. 'I beg you, I implore you, for our dear mother's sake, I beg you to go back to the office!'

'I can't, Kleopatra!' I said, feeling that a little more and I should give way. 'I cannot!'

'Why not?' my sister went on. 'Why not? Well, if you can't get on with the head, look out for another post. Why shouldn't you get a job on the railway, for instance? I have just been talking to Aniuta Blagovo; she is sure they would take you on the railway, and even promised to put in a word for you. For God's sake, Misail, think! Think, I beg you.'

We talked a little longer and I gave in. I said that I had never thought of a job on the railway that was being built, and that, all right, I was ready to try it.

She smiled joyfully through her tears and squeezed my hand, and then went on crying because she could not stop, while I went to the kitchen to fetch paraffin.

II

Among the devoted supporters of amateur theatricals, concerts, and *tableaux vivants* for charity, the Azhogins, who lived in their own house in Great Dvorianskaia Street, took a foremost place; they always provided the hall, and took on all the troublesome arrangements and the expenses. They were a family of wealthy landowners who had a luxurious estate of some eight thousand acres in the district, but they did not like the country, and lived all year round in town. The family consisted of the mother, a tall, spare, refined lady, with short hair, a short jacket, and a skirt without a bustle in the English fashion, and three daughters who, when they were spoken of, were called not by their names but simply: the eldest, the middle, and the youngest. They all had ugly sharp chins, and were short-sighted and round-shouldered. They were dressed like their mother, they lisped disagreeably, and yet, in spite of that, had to have a part in every performance and were always doing something for charity – acting, reciting, singing. They were very serious and never smiled, and even in a musical comedy they played without the faintest trace of gaiety, with a businesslike air, as though they were engaged in book-keeping.

I loved our theatricals, especially the numerous, noisy, and rather incoherent rehearsals, after which we were always given supper. In the choice of plays and distribution of parts I had no hand at all. I was responsible for the off-stage part. I painted scenery, copied out parts, prompted, did the make-up; and I was entrusted, too, with various stage effects such as thunder, nightingale song, and so on. Since I had no proper social position and no decent clothes, at the rehearsals I stood aside from the rest in the shadows of the wings and maintained a shy silence.

I painted the scenery at the Azhogins' either in the barn or in the yard. I was assisted by Andrei Ivanov, a house painter, or, as he called himself, a contractor for all kinds of house decoration, a tall, very thin, pale man of about fifty, with a hollow chest, with sunken temples, with blue rings round his eyes, a little bit frightening to look at in fact. He had some wasting disease, and every autumn and spring people said that he was on his last legs, but after being laid up for a while he would get up and say afterwards with surprise: 'I didn't die again.'

In the town he was called Radish, and it was said that this was his real name. He was as fond of the theatre as I was, and as soon as rumours reached him that a performance was being got up he threw aside all his work and went to the Azhogins' to paint scenery.

The day after my talk with my sister, I was working at the Azhogins' from morning till night. The rehearsal was fixed for seven o'clock in the evening, and an hour before it began all the amateurs were gathered together in the hall, and the eldest, the middle, and the youngest Azhogin were pacing about the stage, reading from exercise books. Radish, in a long reddish overcoat and a scarf muffled round his neck, already stood with his head leaning against the wall, gazing with a devout expression at the stage. Mrs Azhogina went up first to one and then to another guest, saying something agreeable to each. She had a way of gazing into your face, and speaking softly as though telling a secret.

'It must be difficult to paint scenery,' she said softly, coming up to me. 'I was just talking to Madame Mufke about superstitions when I saw you come in. My goodness, my whole life I have been waging war against superstitions! To convince the servants what nonsense all their fears are, I always light three candles, and begin all my important undertakings on the thirteenth of the month.'

Dolzhikov's daughter came in, a plump, fair beauty, dressed, as people said, as Parisian as you can get. She did not act, but a chair was set for her on the stage at the rehearsals, and the performances never began till she had appeared in the front row, dazzling and astounding everyone with her fine clothes. As a city sophisticate she was allowed to make remarks during the rehearsals; and she did so with a sweet indulgent smile, and one could see that she looked upon our performance as a childish amusement. It was said she had studied singing at the Petersburg Conservatoire, and even sang for a whole winter in a private opera. I thought her very charming, and I usually watched her through the rehearsals and performances without taking my eyes off her.

I had just picked up the notebook to begin prompting when my sister suddenly made her appearance. Without taking off her cloak or hat, she came up to me and said:

'Come along, I beg you.'

I went with her. Aniuta Blagovo, also in her hat and wearing a dark veil, was standing behind the scenes at the door. She was the daughter of the assistant chairman of the court, who had held that office in our town almost ever since the establishment of the circuit court. Since she was tall and had a good figure, she was considered indispensable for *tableaux vivants*, and when she represented a fairy or something like Glory her face burned with shame; but she took no part in dramatic performances, and came to the rehearsals only for a moment on some special errand, and did not enter the hall. Now, too, it was evident that she had only looked in for a minute.

'My father mentioned you,' she said dryly, blushing and not looking at me. 'Dolzhikov has promised you a post on the railway line. Apply to him tomorrow; he will be at home.'

I bowed and thanked her for the trouble she had taken.

'And you can give up this,' she said, indicating the notebook.

My sister and she went up to Mrs Azhogina and for two minutes they were whispering with her looking towards me; they were consulting about something.

'Yes, indeed,' said Mrs Azhogina, softly coming up to me and looking intently into my face. 'Yes, indeed, if this distracts you from serious pursuits' – she took the manuscript book from my hands – 'you can hand it over to someone else; don't distress yourself, my friend, go home, and good luck to you.'

I said good-bye to her, and went away overcome with confusion. As I went down the stairs I saw my sister and Aniuta Blagovo going away; they were hastening along, talking eagerly about something, probably about my going to work on the railway. My sister had never been to a rehearsal before, and now she was most likely conscience-stricken, and afraid our father might find out that, without his permission, she had been to the Azhogins'!

I went to Dolzhikov's next day after twelve. The footman showed me into a very beautiful room, which was the engineer's drawing-room and, at the same time, his office. Everything here was soft and elegant, and, for a man so unaccustomed to luxury as I was, it seemed strange. There were costly rugs, huge arm-chairs, bronzes, pictures, gold and plush frames; among the photographs scattered about the walls there were very beautiful women, clever, lovely faces, relaxed attitudes; from the drawing-room there was a door leading straight into the garden on to a veranda: one could see lilac trees; one could see a table laid for lunch, a number of bottles, a bouquet of roses; there was a smell of spring and expensive cigars, a smell of happiness – and everything seemed to indicate: 'Here is a man who has lived and

laboured, and has attained at last the happiness possible on earth.'
The engineer's daughter was sitting at the desk, reading a newspaper.

'You have come to see my father?' she asked. 'He is having a
shower; he will be here shortly. Please sit down and wait.'

I sat down.

'I believe you live opposite?' she questioned me, after a brief
silence.

'Yes.'

'I am so bored that I watch you every day out of the window; you
must excuse me,' she went on, looking at the newspaper, 'and I often
see your sister; she always has such a look of kindness and
concentration.'

Dolzhikov come in. He was rubbing his neck with a towel.

'Papa, Mr Poloznev,' said his daughter.

'Yes, yes, Blagovo was telling me,' he turned briskly to me without
giving me his hand. 'But listen, what can I give you? What jobs have I
got? You gentleman are odd people!' he went on aloud in a tone as if
he were lecturing me. 'A score of you keep coming to me every day;
you imagine I'm the head of a government department! I'm building a
line, my friends; I have real hard labour: I need mechanics, smiths,
navvies, carpenters, well-sinkers, and none of you can do anything
but sit and write. You're all clerks.'

And he seemed to me to have the same air of happiness as his rugs
and easy-chairs. He was stout and healthy, ruddy-cheeked and
broad-chested, scrubbed, in a print cotton shirt and full trousers like
a toy china coachman. He had a curly round beard – and not a single
grey hair – a hooked nose, and clear, dark, guileless eyes.

'What can you do?' he went on. 'There is nothing you can do! I am
an engineer, there's always work for me, but before they gave me a
railway line I had a hard grind for years; I was an engine-driver. For
two years I worked in Belgium as an ordinary greaser. Judge for
yourself, my dear fellow, what kind of work can I offer you?'

'Of course that is so . . .' I muttered, very embarrassed, unable to
face his clear, guileless eyes.

'Can you work the telegraph, anyway?' he asked, after a moment's
thought.

'Yes, I have been a telegraph clerk.'

'H'm! Well, we will see, then. Meanwhile, go to Dubechnia. I have
got a man there, but he is awful rubbish.'

'And what will my duties consist of?' I asked.

'We shall see. Go there; meanwhile I will make arrangements. Only
please don't get drunk, and don't bother me with any requests. I'll
sack you.'

He turned away from me without even a nod.

I bowed to him and his daughter who was reading a newspaper, and went away. My heart felt so heavy that when my sister began asking me how the engineer had received me I could not utter a single word.

I got up early in the morning, at sunrise, to go to Dubechnia. There was not a soul in our Great Dvorianskaia Street; everyone was asleep, and my footsteps rang out with a solitary, hollow sound. The poplars, covered with dew, filled the air with soft fragrance. I was sad, and did not want to leave town. I was fond of my native town. It seemed to be so beautiful and so snug! I loved the fresh greenery, the still, sunny morning, the chiming of our bells; but I found the people with whom I lived in this town boring, alien, sometimes even vile. I did not like them nor understand them.

I did not understand what these sixty-five thousand people lived for and by. I knew that Kimry lived by boots, that Tula made samovars and guns, that Odessa was a seaport, but what our town was, and what it did, I did not know. Great Dvorianskaia Street and the two other smarter streets lived on capital, or on salaries received by officials from the public treasury; but what the other eight streets, which ran parallel for over two miles and vanished beyond the hills, lived on, was always an insoluble riddle to me. And the way these people lived one is ashamed to describe! No garden, no theatre, no decent band; the public library and the club library were only visited by Jewish youths,* so that the magazines and new books lay for months uncut; rich and well-educated people slept in close, stuffy bedrooms, on wooden bedsteads infested with bugs; their children were kept in revoltingly dirty rooms called nurseries, and the servants, even the old and respected ones, slept on the floor in the kitchen, covered with rags. On ordinary days the houses smelt of beetroot soup, and on fast days of sturgeon cooked in sunflower oil. They ate badly, and drank insanitary water. In the town council, at the governor's, at the head priest's, on all sides in private houses, people had been saying for years and years that our town had no good, cheap water-supply, and that two hundred thousand must be borrowed from the treasury to lay on water; very rich people, of whom there were at least three dozen in our town, and who at times lost whole estates at cards, drank the polluted water too, and talked all their lives with great excitement of a loan for the water-supply – and I did not understand that; it seemed to me it would have been simpler just to take the two hundred thousand out of their own pockets.

I did not know one honest man in the town. My father took bribes, and imagined that they were given him out of respect for his moral qualities; at the high school, in order to be moved up rapidly from class to class, the boys boarded with their teachers, who charged them exorbitant sums; the wife of the military commander took bribes from the recruits when they were called up before the board and even deigned to let them buy her drink, and on one occasion could not get up from her knees in church because she was drunk; the doctors took bribes, too, when the recruits came up for examination, and the town doctor and the veterinary surgeon levied a regular tax on the butchers' shops, and restaurants; at the district school they did a trade in certificates, qualifying for partial exemption from military service; the higher clergy took bribes from the humbler priests and from the Church elders; at the municipal, the artisans', and all the other boards every petitioner was pursued by a shout: 'What about a thank-you?' and the petitioner would turn back to give thirty or forty kopecks. And those who did not take bribes, such as the higher officials of the Department of Justice, were haughty, offered two fingers instead of shaking hands, were distinguished by the frigidity and narrowness of their judgments, spent a great deal of time over cards, drank to excess, married heiresses, and undoubtedly had a pernicious corrupting influence on those around them. It was only the girls who had still the fresh fragrance of moral purity; most of them had noble impulses, pure and honest hearts; but they had no understanding of life, and believed that bribes were given out of respect for moral qualities, and after they were married grew old quickly, let themselves go completely, and sank hopelessly in the mire of vulgar, petty bourgeois existence.

III

The railway line was being built in our neighbourhood. On the eve of feast days the streets were thronged with ragged fellows whom the townspeople called 'navvies' and of whom they were afraid. And more than once I had seen one of these ruffians with a bloodstained countenance being led to the police station, while a samovar or some linen, wet from the wash, was carried behind by way of material evidence. The navvies usually congregated about the taverns and the market place; they drank, ate, and used bad language, and pursued with shrill whistles every slut who passed by. To entertain this hungry rabble our shopkeepers made cats and dogs drunk with vodka, or tied an old paraffin can to a dog's tail; a hue and cry was raised, and the dog dashed along the street, jingling the can, squealing with terror; it thought a monster was close upon its heels; it would run far out of the town into the open country and there sink exhausted. There were in the town several dogs who went about trembling, with their tails between their legs; and people said the fun had been too much for them and had driven them mad.

A station was being built three miles from the town. It was said that the engineers asked for a bribe of fifty thousand roubles for bringing the line right up to the town, but the town council would only consent to give forty thousand; they could not come to an agreement over the difference, and now the townspeople regretted it, as they had to make a road to the station and that, it was reckoned, would cost more. The sleepers and rails had been laid along the whole length of the line, and trains ran up and down it, bringing building materials and labourers, and further progress was only delayed on account of the bridges which Dolzhikov was building, and some of the stations were not yet finished.

Dubechnia, as our first station was called, was ten miles from the town. I walked. The cornfields, bathed in the morning sunshine, were bright green. It was a flat, cheerful country, and in the distance there were the distinct outlines of the station, of ancient barrows, and far-away manor houses . . . How nice it was in the open country! And how I longed to be filled with the sense of freedom, if only for that one morning, that I might not think of my needs, not feel hungry! Nothing has so marred my existence as an acute feeling of hunger, which made images of buckwheat porridge, rissoles, and baked fish mingle strangely with my best thoughts. Here I was standing alone in the open country, gazing upward at a lark which hovered in the air at the same spot, trilling as though in hysterics, and meanwhile I was thinking: 'How nice it would be to eat a piece of bread and butter!' Or I would sit down by the roadside to rest, and shut my eyes to listen to the delicious sounds of May, and I would recall the smell of hot potatoes. Though I was tall and strongly built, I rarely had much to eat, and so the predominant sensation throughout the day was hunger, and perhaps that was why I knew so well how it is that such multitudes of people toil merely for their daily bread, and can talk only about food.

At Dubechnia they were plastering the inside of the station, and building a wooden upper storey to the pumping shed. It was hot; there was a smell of lime, and the workmen sauntered listlessly between the heaps of shavings and mortar rubble. The signal man lay asleep near his box, and the sun was blazing full on his face. There was not a single tree. The telegraph wire hummed faintly and hawks were perching on it here and there. I, wandering, too, among the heaps of rubbish, and not knowing what to do, recalled how the engineer, in answer to my question what my duties would consist in, had said: 'We shall see when you are there'; but what could one see in that wilderness? The plasterers spoke of the foreman, and of a certain Fedot Vasiliev. I did not understand, and gradually I was overcome by depression – the physical depression in which you are conscious of your arms and legs and huge body, and do not know what to do with them or where to put them.

After I had been walking about for at least a couple of hours, I noticed that there were telegraph poles running off to the right from the station, and that they ended a mile or a mile and a half away at a white stone wall. The workmen told me the office was there, and at last I reflected that that was where I ought to go.

It was a very old manor house, deserted long ago. The wall round it, of porous white stone, was mouldering and had fallen away in places, and the lodge, the blank wall of which looked out on the open country, had a rusty roof with patches of tin-plate gleaming here and there on it. Within the gates could be seen a spacious courtyard overgrown with rough weeds, and an old manor house with sun blinds on the windows, and a high roof red with rust. Two wings, exactly alike, stood one on each side of the house to right and to left: one had its windows nailed up with boards; near the other, of which the windows were open, there was washing on the line, and there were calves wandering about. The last of the telegraph poles stood in the courtyard, and the wire from it ran to the window of the lodge, whose blank wall faced the open country. The door was open; I went in. By the telegraph apparatus a gentleman with a curly dark head, wearing a reefer coat made of sailcloth, was sitting at a table; he glanced at me morosely from under his brows, but immediately smiled and said:

'Hullo, Better-than-nothing!'*

It was Ivan Cheprakov, an old school fellow of mine, who had been expelled from the second class for smoking. We used at one time, during autumn, to catch goldfinches, finches, and linnets together, and to sell them in the market early in the morning, while our parents were still in bed. We ambushed flocks of migrating starlings and shot at them with small shot, then we picked up the wounded, and some of them died in terrible agonies (I remember to this day how they moaned in cages at my home at night); those that recovered we sold, and brazenly swore that they were all cocks. On one occasion at the market I had only one starling left, which I had offered to purchasers in vain, till at last I sold it for a kopeck. 'Anyway, it's better than nothing,' I said to comfort myself, as I put the kopeck in my pocket, and from that day the street urchins and the schoolboys called after

me: 'Better-than-nothing', and to this day the street boys and the
shopkeepers mock me with the nickname, though no one remembers
how it came about.

Cheprakov was frail: he was narrow-chested, round-shouldered,
and long-legged. He wore a silk cord for a tie, had no trace of a
waistcoat, and his boots were worse than mine, with the heels worn
down on one side. He stared, hardly even blinking, with a fixed
expression, as though he were just going to catch something, and he
kept fussing.

'You wait a minute,' he would say fussily. 'You listen. Whatever
was I talking about?'

We got into conversation. I learned that the estate on which I now
was had until recently been the property of the Cheprakovs, and had
only the autumn before passed into the possession of Dolzhikov, who
considered it more profitable to put his money into land than to keep
it in notes, and had already bought up three decent mortgaged estates
in our neighbourhood. At the sale Cheprakov's mother had reserved
for herself the right to live for the next two years in one of the side
wings, and had wheedled a job for her son in the office.

'He can afford it!' Cheprakov said of the engineer. 'See what he
fleeces out of the contractors alone! He fleeces everyone!'

Then he took me to dinner, deciding fussily that I should live with
him in the wing, and have my meals from his mother.

'She's stingy,' he said, 'but she won't charge you much.'

It was very cramped in the little rooms in which his mother lived;
they were all, even the passage and the entry, piled up with furniture
which had been brought from the big house after the sale; and the
furniture was all old-fashioned mahogany. Mrs Cheprakova, a very
stout middle-aged lady with slanting Chinese eyes, was sitting in a big
arm-chair by the window, knitting a stocking. She received me
ceremoniously.

'This is Poloznev, Mama,' Cheprakov introduced me. 'He is going
to work here.'

'Are you a nobleman?' she asked in a strange, disagreeable voice: it
seemed to me to sound as though fat were bubbling in her throat.

'Yes,' I answered.

'Sit down.'

Dinner was bad. Nothing was served but pies filled with bitter
curd, and milk soup. Elena Cheprakova, my landlady, kept blinking
in a queer way, first with one eye and then with the other. She talked,
she ate, but yet there was something deathly about her whole figure,
and one almost fancied the faint smell of a corpse. There was only a
glimmer of life in her, a glimmer of consciousness that she had been a

lady who had once had her own serfs, that she was the widow of a general whom the servants had to address as 'your Excellency', and when these pathetic relics of life flared up in her for an instant she would tell her son:

'*Jean*, you are not holding your knife properly!'

Or she would say to me, breathing heavily, with the mincing air of a hostess trying to entertain a visitor:

'You know, we have sold our estate. Of course, it is a pity, we are used to the place, but Dolzhikov has promised to make *Jean* stationmaster of Dubechnia, so we shall not have to go away; we shall live here at the station, and that is just the same as being on our own property! The engineer is so nice! Don't you think he is very handsome?'

Until recently the Cheprakovs had lived in a wealthy style, but since the death of the general everything had been changed. Mrs Cheprakova had taken to quarrelling with the neighbours, to going to law, and to not paying her bailiffs or her labourers; she was in constant terror of being robbed, and in some ten years Dubechnia had become unrecognisable.

Behind the great house was an old garden which had already run wild, and was overgrown with rough weeds and bushes. I walked up and down the veranda, which was still solid and beautiful; through the glass doors one could see a room with a parquet floor, probably the drawing-room; an old-fashioned piano and pictures in wide mahogany frames – and nothing else. In the old flower-beds all that remained were peonies and poppies, which lifted their white and bright red heads above the grass. Young maples and elms, already nibbled by the cows, grew beside the paths, drawn up and hindering each other's growth. It was dense, and the garden seemed impassable, but this was only near the house where there stood poplars, fir trees, and old lime trees, all of the same age, relics of the former avenues. Further on, beyond them the garden had been turned into a hayfield, and here it was not moist and stuffy, and spiders' webs did not get in one's mouth and eyes. A light breeze was blowing. The further one went the more open it was, and here in the open space were cherries, plums, and spreading apple trees, disfigured by props and by canker; and pear trees so tall that one could not believe they were pear trees. This part of the garden was let to some shopkeepers of the town, and it was protected from thieves and starlings by a feeble-minded peasant who lived in a shack.

The garden, growing more and more open, till it became a real meadow, sloped down to the river, which was overgrown with green reeds and osiers. Near the mill dam was the millpond, deep and full of fish; a little mill with a thatched roof was working away with a wrathful sound, and frogs croaked furiously. Circles passed from time to time over the smooth, mirror-like water, and the water-lilies trembled, stirred by the lively fish. On the further side of the river was the little village of Dubechnia. The still, blue millpond was alluring with its promise of coolness and peace. And now all this – the millpond and the mill and the welcoming banks – belonged to the engineer!

And so my new job began. I received and forwarded telegrams, wrote various reports, and made fair copies of the invoices, the complaints, and the reports sent to the office by the illiterate foremen and workmen. But for the greater part of the day I did nothing but walk about the room waiting for telegrams, or made a boy sit in the lodge while I went for a walk in the garden, until the boy ran to tell me that there was a tapping at the operating machine. I had dinner at Mrs Cheprakova's. We were very seldom served meat: our dishes were all made of milk, and Wednesdays and Fridays were fast days, and on those days we had pink plates which were called Lenten plates. Mrs Cheprakova was continually blinking – it was her invariable habit, and I always felt ill at ease in her presence.

As there was not enough work in the wing even for one, Cheprakov did nothing, but simply dozed, or went with his gun to shoot ducks on the millpond. In the evenings he drank too much in the village or the station, and before going to bed stared in the looking-glass and said: 'Hullo, Ivan Cheprakov.'

When he was drunk he was very pale, and kept rubbing his hands and laughing with a sound like a neigh: 'hee-hee-hee!' By way of bravado he used to strip and run about the country naked. He ate flies and said they were rather sour.

IV

One day, after dinner, he ran breathless into the lodge and said: 'Go along, your sister has come.'

I went out, and there I found a hired brake from the town standing before the entrance of the great house. My sister had come in it with Aniuta Blagovo and a gentleman in a military tunic. Going up closer I recognised the latter: it was Aniuta Blagovo's brother, the army doctor.

'We have come to have a picnic with you,' he said; 'is that all right?'

My sister and Aniuta wanted to ask how I was getting on here, but both were silent, and simply gazed at me. I was silent too. They saw that I did not like the place, and tears came into my sister's eyes, while Aniuta Blagovo blushed.

We went into the garden. The doctor walked ahead of us all and said enthusiastically:

'What air! Holy Mother, what air!'

In appearance he was still a student. And he walked and talked like a student, and the expression of his grey eyes was as keen, honest, and frank as a good student's. Beside his tall and handsome sister he looked frail and thin; and his beard was thin too, and his voice, too, was a thin but rather agreeable tenor. He was serving in a regiment somewhere, and had come home to his people for a holiday, and said he was going in the autumn to Petersburg to take his examination as a doctor of medicine. He was already a family man, with a wife and three children; he had married very young, in his second year at the university, and now people in the town said he was unhappy in his family life and was not living with his wife.

'What time is it?' my sister asked uneasily. 'We must get back in good time. Papa let me come to see my brother on condition I was back at six.'

'Oh, bother your papa!' sighed the doctor.

I lit the samovar. We put down a carpet before the veranda of the great house and had our tea there, and the doctor knelt down, drank out of his saucer, and declared that he now knew what bliss was. Then Cheprakov went to fetch the key and opened the glass door, and we all went into the house. There it was twilit and mysterious, and smelt of fungus, and our footsteps made a hollow sound as though there were cellars under the floor. The doctor stopped and touched the keys of the piano, and it responded faintly with a husky, quivering, but still tuneful chord; he tried his voice and sang a song, frowning and tapping impatiently with his foot when a key was mute. My sister was no longer anxious to get home, but walked about the rooms and kept saying:

'I feel cheerful! I feel very, very cheerful!'

There was a note of astonishment in her voice, as though it seemed to her incredible that she, too, could feel light-hearted. It was the first time in my life I had seen her so happy. She actually looked prettier. In profile she was ugly; her nose and mouth somehow stuck out and gave her a pouting expression, but she had beautiful dark eyes, a pale, very delicate complexion, and a touching expression of goodness and melancholy, and when she talked she seemed good-looking and even beautiful. We both, she and I, took after our mother, were broad-shouldered, strongly built, and capable of endurance, but her pallor was a sign of ill health; she often had a cough, and I sometimes caught in her face that look one sees in people who are seriously ill, but for some reason conceal it. There was something naive and childish in her gaiety now, as though the joy that had been suppressed and smothered in our childhood by harsh education had now suddenly awakened in her soul and broken free.

But when evening came on and the horses were brought round, my sister sank into silence and looked thin and shrunken, and she got into the brake as though she were going into the dock.

Now they had all gone, and the sound had died away ... I remembered that Aniuta Blagovo had not said a word to me all day.

'She is a wonderful girl!' I thought. 'Wonderful girl!'

St Peter's fast came, and we had nothing but Lenten dishes every day. I was weighed down by physical depression due to idleness and my unsettled position, and dissatisfied with myself, listless and hungry. I lounged about the garden and only waited until I was in the mood to go away.

Towards evening one day, when Radish was sitting in the wing with us, Dolzhikov, very sunburnt and grey with dust, walked in unexpectedly. He had been spending three days on his site, and had come now to Dubechnia by locomotive, and walked to see us from the station. While waiting for the carriage, which was to come for him from the town, he walked round the grounds with his bailiff, giving orders in a loud voice, then sat for a whole hour in our wing, writing letters. While he was there telegrams came for him, and he himself tapped off the answers. We three stood in silence at attention.

'What a muddle!' he said, glancing contemptuously at a record book. 'In a fortnight I am transferring the office to the station, and I don't know what I am to do with you, my friends.'

'I do my best, your Honour,' said Cheprakov.

'To be sure, I see how you do your best. The only thing you can do is to take your salary,' the engineer went on, looking at me; 'you keep relying on patronage to *faire la carrière* as quickly and as easily as possible. Well, I don't care for patronage. No one took any trouble on my behalf. Before they gave me a railway I was an engine-driver and worked in Belgium as an ordinary greaser. And you, Pantelei, what are you doing here?' he asked, turning to Radish. 'Drinking with them?'

He, for some reason, always called humble people Pantelei, and people like me and Cheprakov he despised, and called us drunkards, beasts, and rabble to our face. Altogether he was cruel to humble subordinates, and used to fine them and dismiss them coldly without explanations.

At last the horses came for him. As he said good-bye he promised to turn us all off in a fortnight; he called his bailiff a blockhead; and then, lolling at ease in his carriage, drove back to the town.

'Andrei,' I said to Radish, 'take me on as a workman.'

'Oh, all right!'

And we set off together in the direction of the town. When the station and the big house with its buildings were left behind I asked: 'Andrei, why did you come to Dubechnia this evening?'

'In the first place my fellows are working on the line, and in the second place I came to pay the general's lady my interest. Last year I borrowed fifty roubles from her, and I pay her now a rouble a month interest.'

The painter stopped and took me by the button.

'Misail, angel,' he went on. 'The way I look at it is that if any man, gentle or simple, charges even the lowest interest, he is an evil-doer. There cannot be truth in such a man.'

Radish, lean, pale, dreadful-looking, shut his eyes, shook his head, and, in the tone of a philosopher, pronounced:

'Lice eat grass, rust eats iron, and lies eat the soul. Lord, save us sinners.'

v

Radish was not practical, and was not at all good at estimating; he took on more work than he could get through, and when calculating he was agitated, lost his head, and so was almost always out of pocket over his jobs. He undertook painting, glazing, paper-hanging, and even tiling roofs, and I can remember his running about for three days to find tilers for the sake of a paltry job. He was a first-rate workman; he sometimes earned as much as ten roubles a day; and if it had not been for the desire at all costs to be a master, and to be called a contractor, he would probably have had plenty of money.

He was paid by the job, but he paid me and the other workmen by the day, from seventy kopecks to a rouble a day. When it was fine and dry we did all kinds of outside work, chiefly painting roofs. When I was new to the work my feet burned as though I were walking on a red-hot stove, and when I put on felt boots my feet could not breathe. But this was only at first; later on I got used to it, and everything went smoothly. I was living now among people to whom labour was obligatory, inevitable, and who worked like cart-horses, often with no idea of the moral significance of labour, and, indeed, never using the word 'labour' in conversation at all. Beside them I, too, felt like a cart-horse, growing more and more imbued with the feeling of the obligatory and inevitable character of what I was doing, and this made my life easier, setting me free from all doubts.

At first everything interested me, everything was new, as though I had been born again. I could sleep on the ground and go about barefoot, and that was extremely pleasant; I could stand in a crowd of the common people and not bother anyone, and when a cab horse fell down in the street I ran to help it up without being afraid of getting my clothes dirty. And the best of it all was, I was living on my own account and was no burden to anyone!

Painting roofs, especially with our own oil and colours, was regarded as a particularly profitable job, and so this rough, dull work was not disdained, even by such good workmen as Radish. In short breeches, and wasted, purple-looking legs, he used to go about the roofs, looking like a stork, and I used to hear him, as he plied his brush, breathing heavily and saying: 'Woe, woe to us sinners!'

He walked about the roofs as freely as though he were upon the ground. In spite of his being ill and pale as a corpse, his agility was extraordinary: he used to paint the domes and cupolas of the churches without scaffolding, like a young man, with only the help of a ladder and a rope, and it was rather horrible, when standing high above the earth, he would draw himself up erect, and for some unknown reason pronounce:

'Lice eat grass, rust eats iron, and lies eat the soul!'

Or, thinking about something, he would answer his thoughts aloud:

'Anything may happen! Anything may happen!'

When I went home from work, all the people who were sitting on benches by the gates, all the shopmen and boys and their employers, made sneering and spiteful remarks after me, and this upset me at first and seemed to be simply monstrous.

'Better-than-nothing!' I heard on all sides. 'Painter! Yellow ochre!'

And none behaved so ungraciously to me as those who had only lately been humble people themselves, and had earned their bread by hard manual labour. In the streets full of shops I was once passing an ironmonger's when water was thrown over me as though by accident, and on one occasion someone darted out with a stick at me, while a fishmonger, a grey-headed old man, barred my way and said, looking at me angrily:

'I am not sorry for you, you fool! It's your father I am sorry for.'

And my acquaintances were for some reason overcome with embarrassment when they met me. Some of them looked upon me as an oddity and clown; others were sorry for me; others did not know what to make of me, and it was difficult to understand them. One day I met Aniuta Blagovo in a side-street near Great Dvorianskaia Street. I was going to work, and was carrying two long brushes and a pail of paint. Recognising me, Aniuta flushed crimson.

'Please don't greet me in the street,' she said nervously, harshly, and in a shaking voice, without offering me her hand, and tears suddenly gleamed in her eyes. 'If you think you have to do all this, so be it . . . so be it, but I beg you, don't try and meet me!'

I no longer lived in Great Dvorianskaia Street, but in Makarikha, a suburb, with my old nurse Karpovna, a good-natured but gloomy old woman, who always had bad premonitions, was afraid of all dreams, and even in the bees and wasps that flew into her room saw omens of evil; and the fact that I had become a workman, to her thinking, boded nothing good.

'You are doomed,' she would say, mournfully shaking her head, 'doomed.'

Her adopted son Prokofi, a huge, uncouth, red-headed fellow of about thirty, with bristling moustaches, a butcher by trade, lived in the little house with her. When he met me in the passage he would make way for me in respectful silence, and if he was drunk he would salute me with all five fingers at once. He used to have supper in the evening, and through the partition wall of boards I could hear him clear his throat and sigh as he drank glass after glass of vodka.

'Mama,' he would call in an undertone.

'Well,' Karpovna, who was passionately devoted to her adopted son, would respond: 'What is it, son?'

'I can show you a testimony of my affection, Mama. All this earthly life I will cherish you in your declining years in this vale of tears, and when you die I will bury you at my expense; I have said it, and I mean it.'

I got up every morning before sunrise, and went to bed early. We house painters ate a great deal and slept soundly; the only thing amiss was that my heart used to beat violently at night. I did not quarrel with my mates. Violent abuse, desperate oaths, and wishes such as, 'Blast your eyes,' or 'Cholera take you,' never ceased all day, but nevertheless we lived on very friendly terms. The other fellows suspected me of being some sort of religious sectarian, and made good-natured jokes at my expense, saying that even my own father had disowned me, and thereupon would add that they rarely looked into church themselves, and that many of them had not been to confession for ten years. They justified this laxity on their part by saying that a painter among men was like a jackdaw among birds.

The men had a good opinion of me, and treated me with respect; it was evident that my not drinking, not smoking, but leading a quiet, steady life pleased them very much. It was only an unpleasant shock to them that I took no hand in stealing oil, and did not go with them to ask for tips from people on whose property we were working.

Stealing oil and paints from those who employed them was a house painter's custom, and was not regarded as theft, and it was remarkable that even so upright a man as Radish would always carry away a little white lead and oil as he went home from work. And even the most respectable old fellows, who owned the houses in which they lived in Makarikha, were not ashamed to ask for a tip, and it made me feel vexed and ashamed to see the men go in a body to congratulate some nonentity on the start or the completion of the job, and thank him with degrading servility when they had received a few kopecks.

With customers they behaved like wily courtiers, and almost every day I was reminded of Shakespeare's Polonius.

'I fancy it is going to rain,' the man whose house was being painted would say, looking at the sky.

'It is, there is not a doubt it is,' the painters would agree.

'I don't think it is a rain cloud, though. Perhaps it won't rain after all.'

'No, it won't, your Honour! I'm sure it won't.'

But their attitude to their patrons behind their backs was usually one of irony, and when they saw, for instance, a gentleman sitting on the veranda reading a newspaper, they would observe:

'He reads the paper, but I bet he has nothing to eat.'

I never went home to see my own people. When I came back from work I often found waiting for me little notes, brief and anxious, in which my sister wrote to me about my father; that he had been particularly preoccupied at dinner and had eaten nothing, or that he had been giddy and staggering, or that he had locked himself in his room and had not come out for a long time. Such items of news troubled me; I could not sleep, and at times even walked up and down Great Dvorianskaia Street at night by our house, looking in at the dark windows and trying to guess if everything was well at home. On Sundays my sister came to see me, but came in secret, as though to see not me but our nurse. And if she came in to see me she was very pale, with tear-stained eyes, and she began crying at once.

'Our father won't survive this,' she would say. 'If anything should happen to him – God forbid – your conscience will torment you all your life. It's awful, Misail; for our mother's sake I beg you: mend your ways.'

'My darling sister,' I would say, 'how can I mend my ways if I am convinced that I am acting by my conscience? Do understand!'

'I know you are acting by conscience, but perhaps it could be done differently, somehow, so as not to hurt anybody.'

'Ah, holy Saints!' the old woman sighed through the door. 'You're doomed! There will be trouble, my dears, there will be trouble!'

VI

One Sunday Dr Blagovo turned up unexpectedly. He was wearing a military tunic over a silk shirt and high boots of patent leather.

'I have come to see you,' he began, shaking my hand heartily like a student. 'I hear about you every day, and I have been meaning to come and have a heart-to-heart, as they say. The boredom in the town is awful, there is not a living soul, no one to talk to. It's hot, Holy Mother,' he went on, taking off his tunic and sitting in his silk shirt. 'Old chap, let me talk to you.'

I was bored myself, and had for a long time been craving for company of someone other than a house painter. I was genuinely glad to see him.

'I'll begin by saying,' he said, sitting down on my bed, 'that I sympathise with you from the bottom of my heart, and deeply respect the life you are leading. They don't understand you here in the town, and, indeed, there is no one to understand, seeing that, as you know, they are all, with very few exceptions, regular Gogolian pig faces here. But I saw what you were at once that time at the picnic. You are a noble soul, an honest, high-minded man! I respect you, and feel it a great honour to shake your hand!' he went on enthusiastically. 'To change your life so sharply and thoroughly, as you have done, you must have passed through a complex mental process, and to continue this manner of life now, and to live up to your convictions continually, must be a strain on your mind and heart from day to day. Now to begin our talk, tell me, don't you consider that if you had spent your strength of will, these efforts, all these powers on something else, for instance, on eventually becoming a great scientist, or artist, your life would have been broader and deeper and would have been more productive in every way?'

We talked, and when we got on to manual labour I expressed this idea: the strong must not enslave the weak, the minority must not be a parasite, a pump for ever sucking the vital sap from the majority; that is, all, without exception, strong and weak, rich and poor, should take part equally in the struggle for existence, each one for himself, and that for this there was no better leveller than manual labour, in the form of universal compulsory service.

'So you think everyone without exception ought to do manual labour?' asked the doctor.

'Yes.'

'And don't you think that if everyone, including the best men, the thinkers and great scientists, taking part in the struggle for existence, each for himself, is to waste their time breaking stones and painting roofs, might not that jeopardise progress?'

'Where is the danger?' I asked. 'Why, progress is acting out of love, fulfilling the moral law; if you don't enslave anyone, if you don't oppress anyone, what further progress do you want?'

'But surely,' Blagovo suddenly fired up and rose to his feet, 'but surely, if a snail in its shell goes in for self-perfection and muddles about with the moral law, do you call that progress?'

'Why muddles?' I said, offended. 'If you don't force your neighbours to feed and clothe you, to transport you from place to place and defend you from enemies, since our life entirely rests on slavery, that is progress, isn't it? To my mind it is the most real progress, and perhaps the only one possible and necessary for man.'

'The limits of universal world progress are in infinity, and to talk of some 'possible' progress limited by our needs and temporary theories is, I'm sorry, quite strange.'

'If the limits of progress are in infinity as you say, it follows that its aims are not definite,' I said. 'To live without knowing definitely what you are living for!'

'So be it! But that "not knowing" is not so dull as your "knowing". I am climbing a ladder called progress, civilisation, culture; I climb and climb without knowing definitely where I am going, but really it is worth living for the sake of that wonderful ladder; while you know what you are living for – that people may not enslave others, that the artist and the man who grinds his paints may dine equally well. But you know that's the petty bourgeois, kitchen-sink, grey side of life, and surely it is revolting to live for that alone? If one lot of insects enslaves others, to hell with them, let them devour each other! It's not them we should be thinking about – after all they will die and decay just the same, however zealously you rescue them from slavery. We must think of that great X which awaits all mankind in the remote future.'

Blagovo argued heatedly with me, but at the same time one could see he was troubled by some secondary idea.

'I suppose your sister isn't coming?' he said, looking at his watch. 'She was with me and friends yesterday, and said she would be seeing you today. You keep saying slavery, slavery . . .' he went on, 'but you know that is an individual question, and all those questions are solved by humanity gradually, automatically.'

We began talking about gradualness. I said that everyone decides himself the question of doing good or evil, without waiting for humanity to settle it by gradual development. Moreover, gradualness is a two-edged sword. Side by side with the gradual development of human ideas we can see the gradual growth of another kind of idea.

Serfdom is no more, but capitalism is growing. And in the very heyday of emancipating ideas, just as in the days of the Mongol Khans, the majority feeds, clothes, and defends the minority while remaining hungry, in rags, and defenceless. This situation fits very nicely with any tendencies and currents of thought you like, because the art of enslaving is also gradually being cultivated. We no longer flog our servants in the stable, but we invent refined forms of slavery, at least, we can find a justification for it in each particular case. Our ideas are one thing, but if now, at the end of the nineteenth century, it were possible to add the burden of our nastiest physiological functions on to the working class, we should certainly do so, and afterwards, of course, justify ourselves by saying that if the best people, the thinkers and great scientists, were to waste their precious time on these functions, progress might be jeopardised.'

Here my sister arrived. Seeing the doctor she was flustered and troubled, and began saying immediately that it was time she went home to father.

'Kleopatra,' said Blagovo earnestly, pressing both hands to his heart, 'what will happen to your father if you spend half an hour or so with your brother and me?'

He was simple-hearted, and could communicate his liveliness to others. After a moment's thought, my sister laughed, and suddenly cheered up, instantly, as she had at the picnic. We went out into the fields, and lying in the grass continued our talk, and looked towards the town where all the windows facing west seemed bright gold because the sun was setting.

After that, whenever my sister came to me Blagovo turned up too, and they always greeted each other as though meeting in my room was accidental. My sister listened while the doctor and I argued, and at such times her expression was joyfully enthusiastic, full of tenderness and curiosity, and it seemed to me that a new world she had never dreamed of before, and which she was now striving to fathom, was gradually opening up before her eyes. When the doctor was not there she was quiet and sad, and now if she sometimes shed tears as she sat on my bed it was for reasons of which she did not speak.

In August Radish ordered us to get ready to go to the railway line. Two days before we were 'banished' from town my father came to see me. He sat down and in a leisurely way, without looking at me, wiped his red face, then took out of his pocket our town *Messenger*, and deliberately, with emphasis on each word, read out the news that the son of the branch manager of the state bank, a young man of my age, had been appointed head of a department in the treasury.

'And now look at you,' he said, folding up the newspaper, 'a beggar, in rags, scoundrel! Even the lower middle class and peasants get an education in order to make something of themselves, while you, a Poloznev, with ancestors of rank and distinction, aspire to the gutter! But I have not come here to talk to you; I have washed my hands of you,' he added in a strangled voice, getting up. 'I have come to find out where your sister is, you scoundrel. She left home after dinner, and now it is nearly eight and she is not back. She has taken to going out frequently, without telling me; she is less respectful – and I see your evil vile influence here. Where is she?'

In his hand he had the umbrella I knew so well, and I was already flustered and drew myself up like a schoolboy, expecting my father to begin hitting me, but he noticed my glance at the umbrella and most likely that restrained him.

'Live as you please!' he said. 'I withdraw my blessing from you.'

'Holy Saints!' my nurse muttered behind the door. 'You poor, unlucky child! Ah, my heart senses evil, it does.'

I worked on the railway line. It rained without stopping all August; it was damp and cold; they had not carted the corn from the fields, and on big farms where the wheat was reaped by machine it lay not in sheaves but in heaps, and I remember how those luckless heaps of wheat turned blacker every day and the grain was sprouting in them. It was hard to work; the pouring rain spoiled everything we managed to do. We were not allowed to live or to sleep in the railway buildings, and we took refuge in the damp and filthy mud huts in which the navvies had lived during the summer, and I could not sleep at night for the cold and the wood lice crawling on my face and hands. And when we worked near the bridges the navvies used to come in the evenings in a gang, simply in order to beat the painters – it was a form of sport to them. They used to beat us, to steal our brushes. And to annoy us and make us fight they used to spoil our work; they would, for instance, smear the signal boxes with green paint. The last straw was that Radish took to paying us very irregularly. All the painting work on the line was given out to a contractor; he gave it out to another; and this subcontractor gave it to Radish after subtracting twenty per cent for himself. The job was unprofitable in itself, and the rain made it worse; time was wasted; we could not work, while Radish was obliged to pay his men by the day. The hungry painters came close to beating him, called him a cheat, a blood-sucker, a Judas, while he, poor fellow, sighed, lifted up his hand to heaven in despair, and was continually going to Mrs Cheprakova for money.

VII

Autumn came on, rainy, dark, and muddy. I was unemployed, and I used to sit at home doing nothing for three days at a stretch, or did various little jobs, not in the painting line. For instance, I barrowed topsoil for embankments, earning twenty kopecks a day. Dr Blagovo had gone away to Petersburg. My sister stayed away. Radish was laid up at home ill, expecting death any day.

And my mood was autumnal too. Perhaps because becoming a workman made me see only the seamy side of our town life, almost every day I made discoveries which reduced me simply to despair. Those of my fellow citizens, about whom I had no opinion before, or who had externally appeared perfectly decent, turned out now to be base, cruel people, capable of every dirty trick. We common people were deceived, cheated, and kept waiting for hours together in cold lobbies or kitchens; we were insulted and treated with the utmost rudeness. In the autumn I papered the reading-room and two other rooms at the club; I was paid at seven kopecks a roll, but had to sign a receipt for twelve kopecks, and when I refused to do so, a respectable-looking gentleman in gold rimmed spectacles, who must have been one of the club committee, told me:

'If you argue, you blackguard, I'll smash your face in!'

And when the flunkey whispered to him that I was the son of Poloznev the architect, he became embarrassed, turned crimson, but immediately recovered himself and said:

'To hell with him.'

In the shops they palmed off on us workmen putrid meat, musty flour, and tea-leaves that had been used and dried again; the police jostled us in church, the assistants and nurses in the hospital plundered us, and if we were too poor to give them a bribe they revenged themselves by feeding us in dirty crockery. In the post office the pettiest official considered he had a right to treat us like animals, and to shout with coarse insolence: 'Wait! Where do you think you're going?' Even the yard dogs were unfriendly to us, and attacked us with special viciousness. But the thing that struck me most of all in my new position was the complete lack of justice, what is defined by the peasants in the words: 'They've forgotten God.' Rarely did a day pass without swindling. The merchants who sold us oil, the contractors and the workmen and the people who employed us were all swindlers. Obviously, there could never be a question of our rights, and we always had to ask for our earnings as though they were alms, and to stand at the back door, cap in hand.

I was papering a room at the club next to the reading-room; in the evening, when I was just getting ready to go, the daughter of Dolzhikov, the engineer, walked into the room with a bundle of books under her arm.

I bowed to her.

'Oh, how do you do?' she said, recognising me at once, and holding out her hand. 'Very glad to see you.'

She smiled and looked with curiosity and wonder at my smock, my pail of paste, the paper stretched on the floor; I was embarrassed, and she, too, felt awkward.

'You must excuse my looking at you like this,' she said. 'I have been told so much about you. Especially by Dr Blagovo; he is simply in love with you. And I have got to know your sister too; a sweet, dear girl, but I can never persuade her that there is nothing awful about your adopting the simple life. On the contrary, you have become the most interesting man in the town.'

She looked again at the pail of paste and the wallpaper, and went on:

'I asked Dr Blagovo to help me get to know you, but apparently he forgot, or hasn't had time. Anyway, we do know each other, and if you'd drop in and see me I should be extremely obliged to you. I so long to have a talk. I am a simple person,' she added, holding out her hand to me, 'and I hope that you will feel at home with me. My father isn't here, he is in Petersburg.'

She went off into the reading-room, rustling her skirts, while I went home, and for a long time could not get to sleep.

That cheerless autumn some kind soul, evidently wishing to alleviate my existence, occasionally sent me tea and lemons, or biscuits, or roast game. Karpovna told me that they were always brought by a soldier, and from whom they came she did not know; and the soldier used to inquire whether I was well, and whether I dined every day, and whether I had warm clothing. When the frosts began I was presented in the same way, in my absence, with a soft knitted scarf brought by the soldier. There was a faint elusive smell of scent about it, and I guessed who my good fairy was. The scarf smelt of lilies of the valley, Aniuta Blagovo's favourite scent.

Towards winter there was more work and it was more cheerful. Radish recovered, and we worked together in the cemetery church, where we were putting the ground-work on the iconostas before gilding. It was a clean, quiet job, and, as our fellows used to say, profitable. One could get through a lot of work in a day, and the time passed quickly, imperceptibly. There was no swearing, no laughter, no loud talk. The place itself compelled us to be quiet and behave decently, and inclined us to quiet, serious thoughts. Absorbed in our work we stood or sat motionless like statues; there was a deathly silence in keeping with the cemetery, so that if a tool fell, or a flame spluttered in the lamp, the noise of such sounds rang out abrupt and resonant, and made us look round. After a long silence we would hear a buzzing like the swarming of bees: it was a requiem for a baby being chanted slowly in subdued voices in the porch; or an artist, painting a dove with stars round it on a cupola, would begin softly whistling, and pulling himself up would at once fall silent; or Radish, answering his thoughts, would say with a sigh: 'Anything is possible! Anything is possible!' or a slow disconsolate bell would begin ringing over our heads, and the painters would observe that the funeral must be for someone rich . . .

My days I spent in this stillness in the twilight of the church, and in the long evenings I played billiards or went to the theatre in the gallery wearing the new woollen suit I had bought out of my own earnings. Concerts and performances had already begun at the Azhogins'; Radish used to paint the scenes alone now. He used to tell me the plot of the plays and describe the *tableaux vivants* which he witnessed. I listened to him with envy. I felt greatly drawn to the rehearsals, but I could not bring myself to go to the Azhogins'.

A week before Christmas Dr Blagovo arrived. And again we argued and played billiards in the evenings. When he played he used to take off his coat and unbutton his shirt to his chest, and for some reason tried altogether to assume the air of a desperate rake. He drank little, but noisily, and managed to run through twenty roubles in an evening at a poor cheap tavern like the Volga.

My sister began visiting me again; they both expressed surprise every time they saw each other, but from the joyful, guilty face it was evident that these meetings were not accidental. One evening, when we were playing billiards, the doctor said to me:

'I say, why don't you go and see Miss Dolzhikova? You don't know Masha; she is a clever creature, a charmer, a simple, good-natured soul.'

I described how her father had received me in the spring.

'Nonsense!' laughed the doctor, 'the engineer's one thing and she's another. Really, my dear fellow, you mustn't be nasty to her; go and see her sometimes. For instance, let's go and see her tomorrow evening. What do you say?'

He persuaded me. The next evening I put on my new woollen suit, and in some agitation I set off to Miss Dolzhikova's. The footman did not seem so haughty and terrible, nor the furniture so gorgeous, as on the morning I had come to ask a favour. Masha was expecting me, and she received me like an old acquaintance, shaking hands with me in a friendly way. She was wearing a grey cloth dress with full sleeves, and had her hair done in the style which we used to call 'dogs' ears', when it came into fashion in the town a year before. The hair was combed down over the ears, and this made Masha's face look broader, and she seemed to me this time very much like her father, whose face was broad and red, with something in its expression like a coach-driver. She was handsome and elegant, but not youthful looking; she looked thirty, though in reality she was no more than twenty-five.

'Dear doctor, how grateful I am to him,' she said, making me sit down. 'If it hadn't been for him you wouldn't have come to see me. I am bored to death! My father has gone away and left me alone, and I don't know what to do with myself in this town.'

Then she began asking me where I was working now, how much I earned, where I lived.

'You spend on yourself only what you earn?' she asked.

'Yes.'

'Happy man!' she sighed. 'All the evil in life, it seems to me, comes from idleness, boredom, and spiritual emptiness, and all that is inevitable when you're used to living at other people's expense. Don't think I am showing off, I tell you honestly: it is boring and unpleasant to be rich. "Make to yourselves friends of the mammon of unrighteousness" is said because there isn't and can't be a mammon that's righteous.'

She looked round at the furniture with a grave, cold expression, as though about to make an inventory, and went on:

'Comfort and luxury have a magical power; little by little they draw into their clutches even strong-willed people. At one time father and I lived modestly and simply, but now look! It is something monstrous,' she said, shrugging her shoulders; 'we spend up to twenty thousand a year! In the provinces!'

'You have to see comfort and luxury as the unavoidable privilege of capital and education,' I said, 'but it seems to me that the comforts of life may be combined with any sort of labour, even the hardest and dirtiest. Your father is rich, and yet he says himself that he has been an engine-driver and a greaser.'

She smiled and shook her head doubtfully: 'My father sometimes eats bread dipped in kvas,' she said. 'It's a fancy, a whim!'

At that moment there was a ring and she got up.

'The rich and well educated ought to work like everyone else,' she said, 'and if there is comfort it should be the same for everybody. There should be no privileges. But that's enough philosophising. Tell me something amusing. Tell me about the painters. What are they like? Funny?'

The doctor came in; I began telling them about the painters, but, being unused to talking, I was inhibited, and described them like an ethnologist, gravely and tediously. The doctor, too, told us some anecdotes of working men: he staggered about, shed tears, dropped on his knees, and even, mimicking a drunkard, lay on the floor; it was as good as a play, and Masha laughed till she cried as she looked at him. Then he played on the piano and sang in his thin, pleasant tenor, while Masha stood by and chose songs for him to sing, and corrected him when he made a mistake.

'I hear that you sing, too?' I asked.

'Sing, too!' cried the doctor in horror. 'She's a wonderful singer, a professional, and you say "you sing too"! How could you?'

'I did study seriously at one time,' she said, answering my question, 'but now I have given it up.'

Sitting on a low stool she told us of her life in Petersburg, and mimicked some celebrated singers, imitating their voice and manner of singing. She made a sketch of the doctor in her album, then of me; she did not draw well, but both portraits looked like us. She laughed, and was full of mischief and charming grimaces, and this suited her better than talking about the mammon of unrighteousness, and it seemed to me that she had been talking just before about wealth and luxury, not in earnest, but in imitation of someone. She was a superb comic actress. I mentally compared her with our young ladies, and even the handsome, dignified Aniuta Blagovo could not stand comparison with her; the difference was immense, like the difference between a beautiful, cultivated rose and a wild briar.

We had supper, just the three of us. The doctor and Masha drank red wine, champagne, and coffee with brandy; they clinked glasses and drank to friendship, to enlightenment, to progress, to liberty, and they did not get drunk but only flushed, and were continually, for no reason, laughing till they cried. So as not to seem tiresome I too drank red wine.

'Talented, richly endowed natures,' said Miss Dolzhikova, 'know how to live, and go their own way; mediocre people, like myself for instance, know nothing and can do nothing by themselves; there is nothing left for them but to find a deep social current, and to drift wherever it takes them.'

'How can you find what doesn't exist?' asked the doctor.

'They exist but we can't see them.'

'Really? Social currents have been invented by modern literature. We don't have any.'

An argument began.

'There are no deep social currents among us and never have been,' the doctor declared loudly. 'Modern literature has invented all sorts of things. It has invented intellectual workers in the country, and you may search through all our villages and find at the most some yokel in a jacket or a black frock-coat who will make four spelling mistakes in a three-letter word. Cultured life has not yet begun among us. There's the same savagery, the same uniform boorishness, the same triviality, as five hundred years ago. Movements, currents there have been, but it has all been petty, paltry, tied to vulgar and mercenary interests – and you can't see anything serious in them, can you? If you think you have found a deep social current, and by following it you devote yourself to tasks in the modern taste, such as the emancipation of insects from slavery or abstinence from beef rissoles, I congratulate you, Miss. We must study, and study, and study, and we must wait a bit for our deep, social currents; we are not mature enough for them yet; and to tell the truth, we don't understand anything about them.'

'You may not, but I do,' said Masha. 'God knows how tiresome you are today!'

'Our duty is to study and to study, to try to accumulate as much knowledge as possible, for genuine social currents arise where there is knowledge; and the happiness of mankind in the future lies only in knowledge. I drink to science!'

'One thing is certain: we must arrange our life somehow differently,' said Masha, after a moment's silence and thought. 'Life, as it has been so far, is worthless. Let's not talk about it.'

As we came away from her the cathedral clock struck two.

'Did you like her?' asked the doctor; 'she's lovely, isn't she?'

On Christmas Day we dined with Masha, and all through the holidays we went to see her almost every day. There was never anyone there but us, and she was right when she said that she had no friends in the town but the doctor and me. We spent our time for the most part in conversation; sometimes the doctor brought a book or magazine and read aloud to us. In reality he was the first well-educated man I had met in my life: I cannot judge whether he knew a great deal, but he constantly displayed his knowledge as though he wanted other people to share it. When he talked about anything relating to medicine he was not like any one of the doctors in our town, but made a fresh, special impression upon me, and I thought that he might have become a real man of science, had he wanted to. And he was perhaps the only person who had a real influence upon me at that time. Seeing him, and reading the books he gave me, I began little by little to feel a thirst for knowledge which would give my cheerless labour meaning and spirit. It seemed strange to me, for instance, that I had not known till then that the whole world was made up of sixty elements, I had not known what oil was, what paints were, and that I could have got on without knowing. My friendship with the doctor elevated me morally, too. I was continually arguing with him and, though I usually stuck to my own opinion, yet, thanks to him, I began to perceive that not everything was clear to me, and I began trying to work out my convictions as clearly as I could, so that the dictates of conscience might be definite, and that there might be nothing vague in my mind. Yet, though he was the most cultivated and best man in the town, he was far from perfect. In his manners, in his habit of turning every conversation into an argument, in his pleasant tenor, even in his friendliness, there was something coarse, like a seminary student, and when he took off his coat and sat in his silk shirt, or flung a tip to a waiter in the restaurant, I always fancied that culture might be all very well, but the Tatar was fermenting in him still.

At Epiphany he went back to Petersburg. He went off in the morning, and after dinner my sister came in. Without taking off her fur coat and her hat she sat down in silence, very pale, and kept her eyes fixed on the same spot. She had caught a chill and one could see that she was fighting it hard.

'You must have caught cold,' I said.

Her eyes filled with tears; she got up and went out to Karpovna without saying a word to me, as though I had hurt her feelings. And a little later I heard her saying, in a tone of bitter reproach:

'Nanny, what have I been living for till now? What? Tell me, haven't I wasted my youth? All the best years of my life to know nothing but keeping accounts, pouring out tea, counting the kopecks, entertaining visitors, and thinking there was nothing better in the world! Nanny, try to understand, I have human needs and I want to live, and they have turned me into a housekeeper. It's horrible, horrible!'

She flung her keys at the door, and they fell with a jingle into my room. They were the keys to the sideboard, the kitchen cupboard, the cellar, and the tea-caddie, the keys which my mother used to carry.

'Oh, Merciful Heavens!' cried the old woman in horror. 'Holy Saints above!'

Before going home my sister came into my room to pick up the keys, and said:

'You must forgive me. Something odd has been happening to me lately.'

VIII

On returning home late one evening from Masha's I found waiting in my room a young police officer in a new uniform; he was sitting at my table, leafing through my books.

'At last,' he said, getting up and stretching himself. 'This is the third time I've called on you. The governor orders you to come and see him at nine o'clock tomorrow morning. Without fail.'

He took from me a signed statement that I would obey his Excellency's command to the letter, and went away. This visit late in the evening from the police and unexpected invitation to the governor's had a most oppressive effect upon me. From my earliest childhood I have felt terror-stricken in the presence of gendarmes, policemen, and law court officials, and now I was uneasy and worried, as though I really had done something wrong. And I could not get to sleep. Nanny and Prokofi were also upset and could not sleep. Nanny had earache too; she moaned and several times began crying with pain. Hearing that I was awake, Prokofi came into my room with a lamp and sat down by the table.

'You ought to have some pepper vodka,' he said, after a moment's thought. 'If you have a drink in this vale of tears it does no harm. And if Mama were to pour a little pepper vodka in her ear it would do her a lot of good.'

Between two and three he was off to the slaughter-house to fetch the meat. I knew I should not sleep till morning now, and to get through the time till nine, I went with him. We carried a lantern, while his boy Nikolka, aged about thirteen, with blue patches of frostbite on his cheeks, a complete rogue to judge by his expression, drove after us in the sledge, urging on the horse in a husky voice.

'I suppose they will punish you at the governor's,' Prokofi said to me on the way. 'There are rules for governors, and rules for the higher clergy, and rules for officers, and rules for doctors, and every class has its rules. But you haven't kept to your rules, and that can't be allowed.'

The slaughter-house was behind the cemetery; till then I had only seen it in the distance. It consisted of three gloomy sheds, surrounded by a grey fence, and when the wind blew from that quarter on hot days in summer, it brought a stifling stench from them. Now going into the yard in the dark I could not see the sheds; I kept coming across horses and sledges, some empty, some loaded up with meat. Men were walking about with lanterns, swearing in a disgusting way. Prokofi and Nikolka swore just as revoltingly, and the air was in a continual uproar with swearing, coughing, and the neighing of horses.

There was a smell of corpses and of dung. It was thawing, the snow was changing into mud; and in the darkness it seemed to me that I was walking through pools of blood.

After loading the sledge full of meat we set off to the butcher's shop in the market. It began to get light. Cooks with baskets and elderly ladies in mantles came along one after another. Prokofi, with a chopper in his hand, in a white apron spattered with blood, swore fearful oaths, crossed himself at the church, shouted aloud for the whole market to hear that he was giving away the meat at cost price and even at a loss to himself. He gave short weight and short change, the cooks saw that, but, deafened by his shouts, did not protest, and only called him a hangman. Brandishing and bringing down his terrible chopper he threw himself into picturesque attitudes, and each time uttered the sound 'Heck' with a ferocious expression, and I was afraid he really would chop off somebody's head or hand.

I spent all morning in the butcher's shop, and when at last I went to the governor's, my fur coat smelt of meat and blood. My state of mind was as though I had been sent to fight a bear with a catapult. I remember the tall staircase with a striped carpet, and the young official, with light-coloured buttons, who mutely motioned me to the door with both hands, and ran to announce me. I went into a hall luxuriously but frigidly and tastelessly furnished, and the high, narrow mirrors in the spaces between the walls, and the bright yellow window curtains, struck the eye particularly unpleasantly. One could see that the governors changed, but the furniture remained the same. Again the young official motioned me with both hands to the door, and I went up to a big green table at which a military general, with the Order of Vladimir round his neck, was standing.

'Mr Poloznev, I have asked you to come,' he began, holding a letter in his hand, and opening his mouth wide like a round O, 'I have asked you to come here to inform you of this. Your highly respected father has appealed by letter and by word of mouth to the Marshal of the Nobility begging him to summon you, and to lay before you the inconsistency of your behaviour with the rank of the nobility to which you have the honour to belong. His Excellency Alexandr Pavlovich, rightly supposing that your conduct might corrupt others, and considering that mere persuasion on his part would not be sufficient, but that official intervention in earnest was essential, presents me here in this letter with his views about you, which I share.'

He said this quietly, respectfully, standing erect, as though I were his superior officer and looking at me with no trace of severity. His face looked worn and wizened, and was all wrinkles; there were bags under his eyes; his hair was dyed; and it was impossible to tell from his appearance how old he was – forty or sixty.

'I trust,' he went on, 'that you appreciate the tact of our honoured Alexandr Pavlovich, who contacted me not officially, but privately. I, too, have asked you to come here unofficially, and I am speaking to you, not as a governor, but out of sincere respect for your father. And so I beg you either to alter your behaviour and return to duties in keeping with your rank, or to avoid setting a bad example, move to another district where you are not known, and where you can follow any occupation you please. Otherwise, I shall be forced to take extreme measures.'

He stood for half a minute in silence, looking at me with his mouth open.

'Are you a vegetarian?' he asked.

'No, your Excellency, I eat meat.'

He sat down and drew some papers towards him. I bowed and went out.

It was not worth while now to go to work before dinner. I went home to sleep, but an unpleasant, sick feeling, induced by the slaughter-house and my conversation with the governor, stopped me sleeping, and when evening came I went, gloomy and out of sorts, to Masha. I told her how I had been to the governor's, while she stared at me in perplexity as though she did not believe it, then suddenly began laughing gaily, loudly, mischievously, as only good-natured, laughter-loving people can.

'If only one could tell that in Petersburg!' she said, almost falling over with laughter, and bending down to the table. 'If I told that story in Petersburg!'

IX

Now we met often, sometimes twice a day. She used to come to the cemetery almost every day after dinner, and read the epitaphs on the crosses and tombstones while she waited for me. Sometimes she would come into the church, and, standing by me, would look on while I worked. The stillness, the naive work of the painters and gilders, Radish's sage reflections, and the fact that I was no different externally from the other workmen, and worked just as they did in waistcoat and worn shoes, and that I was addressed familiarly by them – all this was new to her and touched her. One day a workman, who was painting a dove on the ceiling, called out to me in her presence:

'Misail, pass me the white paint.'

I took him the white paint, and afterwards, when I was climbing down the frail scaffolding, she looked at me, touched to tears and smiling.

'What a dear you are!' she said.

I remembered from my childhood how a green parrot, belonging to one of the rich men of the town, had escaped from its cage, and how for quite a month afterwards the beautiful bird had wandered the town, flying from garden to garden, homeless and solitary. Masha reminded me of that bird.

'There is positively nowhere for me to go now but the cemetery,' she said to me with a laugh. 'The town has become disgustingly dull. At the Azhogins' they are still reciting, singing, lisping. I can't stand them nowadays; your sister is an unsociable creature; Miss Blagovo hates me for some reason. I don't like the theatre. Tell me, where am I to go?'

When I went to see her I smelt of paint and turpentine, and my hands were stained – and she liked that; she wanted me to come to her in my ordinary working clothes; but in her drawing-room those clothes made me feel awkward. I felt embarrassed, as though I were in uniform, so I always put on my new woollen suit when I went to her. And she did not like that.

'Admit it, you are not quite at home in your new role,' she said to me one day. 'Your work clothes don't feel natural to you; you are awkward in them. Tell me, isn't that because you're not sure, and are not satisfied? Can the kind of work you have chosen – your painting – possibly satisfy you?' she asked, laughing. 'I know paint makes things look nicer and last longer, but those things belong to rich people who live in towns, and after all they are luxuries. Besides, you have often said yourself that everybody ought to earn his bread with his own hands, yet you get money and not bread. Why shouldn't you keep to the literal sense of your words? You ought to be getting bread, that is, you ought to be ploughing, sowing, reaping, threshing, or doing something which has a direct connection with agriculture, for instance, looking after cows, digging, building log huts . . .'

She opened a pretty cupboard by her desk, and said:

'I am saying all this to you because I want to let you into my secret. Voilà! This is my agricultural library. Here I have fields, kitchen garden and orchard, and cattle yard and beehives. I read them greedily, and have already learnt all the theory to the tiniest detail. My ideal, my sweet daydream, is to go to our Dubechnia as soon as March is here. It's marvellous there, exquisite, isn't it? The first year I shall have a look round and get the hang of things, and the year after I shall begin to work properly myself, putting my back into it as they say. My father has promised to give me Dubechnia, and I shall do exactly what I like with it.'

Flushed, excited to tears, and laughing, she dreamed aloud how she would live at Dubechnia, and what an interesting life it would be! I envied her. March was near, the days were growing longer and longer, and on bright sunny days water dripped from the roofs at midday, and there was a fragrance of spring; I, too, longed for the country.

And when she said that she should move to Dubechnia, I realised vividly that I should remain in the town alone, and I felt that I was jealous of her cupboard of books and her agriculture. I knew nothing of work on the land, and did not like it, and I should have liked to have told her that work on the land was slavish toil, but I remembered that something similar had been said more than once by my father, and I held my tongue.

Lent began. Dolzhikov, whose existence I had begun to forget, arrived from Petersburg. He arrived unexpectedly, without even a telegram to say he was coming. When I went in, as usual, in the evening, he was walking about the drawing-room, telling some story, with his face freshly washed and shaven, looking ten years younger; his daughter was kneeling on the floor, taking out of his trunks boxes, bottles, and books, and handing them to Pavel the footman. I involuntarily drew back a step when I saw the engineer, but he held out both hands to me and said, smiling, showing his strong white teeth that looked like a coach-driver's:

'Here he is, here he is! Very glad to see you, Mr House Painter! Masha has told me all about it; she has been singing your praises. I quite understand and approve,' he went on, taking my arm. 'To be a good workman is much more honest and more sensible than wasting government paper and wearing a cockade on your head. I myself worked in Belgium with these very hands and then spent two years as an engine-driver . . .'

He was wearing a short jacket and indoor slippers; he walked like a man with gout, rolling slightly from side to side and rubbing his hands. Humming something he softly purred and hugged himself with satisfaction at being at home again at last, and able to take his beloved shower.

'There is no doubt,' he said to me at supper, 'no dispute you are all nice and charming people, but for some reason, as soon as you take to manual labour, or go in for saving the peasants, in the long run it all comes to no more than being a sectarian crank. Aren't you a dissenter? You don't drink vodka, do you? So you're a dissenter, aren't you?'

To satisfy him I drank vodka. I drank some wine, too. We tasted the cheese, the sausage, the patés, the pickles, and the savouries of all sorts that the engineer had brought with him, and the wine that had come in his absence from abroad. The wines were first-rate. For some reason the engineer got wine and cigars from abroad duty-free; the caviar and the dried sturgeon someone sent him for nothing; he did not pay rent for his flat as the owner of the house supplied paraffin for the line; and altogether he and his daughter gave me the impression that they had all the best in the world at their service, and for nothing.

I went on visiting them, but not so eagerly now. The engineer made me feel inhibited, and in his presence I felt tied. I could not face his clear, guileless eyes, his reflections wearied and repelled me; I was bothered, too, by the memory that so recently I had been in the employment of this red-faced, well-fed man, that he had been brutally rude to me. It is true that he put his arm round my waist, slapped me on the shoulder in a friendly way, approved of my life, but I felt that, as before, he despised my insignificance, and only put up with me to please his daughter, and I couldn't now laugh and talk as I liked, and I behaved unsociably and kept expecting that in another minute he would call me Pantelei as he did his footman Pavel. How my provincial petty burgeois pride protested! I, a proletarian, a house painter, went every day to rich people who were alien to me, and whom the whole town regarded as foreigners, and every day I drank expensive wines with them and ate unusual dainties – my conscience wouldn't accept it! On my way to the house I sullenly avoided meeting people, and frowned at them as though I really were a dissenter, and when I left the engineer's for home I was ashamed of my satedness.

Above all I was afraid of falling in love. Whether I was walking along the street, or working, or talking to the men, I was all the time thinking of one thing only, of going in the evening to see Masha and was picturing her voice, her laugh, her gait. When I was getting ready to go to her I always spent a long time before nanny's warped looking-glass, as I put on my tie; my woollen suit seemed detestable, and I suffered, and at the same time despised myself for being so petty. When she called to me from the other room that she was not dressed and asked me to wait, I listened to her dressing; it agitated me, I felt as though the ground were giving way under my feet. And when I saw a woman's figure in the street, even at a distance, I invariably compared it. It seemed to me that all our girls and women were vulgar, that they were absurdly dressed, and did not know how to hold themselves; and these comparisons aroused a feeling of pride in me: Masha was better than any of them! And at night I dreamed of her and myself.

One evening at supper with the engineer we ate a whole lobster. As I was going home afterwards I remembered that the engineer had twice called me 'My dear fellow' at supper, and I reflected that they treated me very kindly in that house, as they might an unfortunate hound who had been kicked out by its owners, that they were amusing themselves with me, and that when they were tired of me they would turn me out like a cur. I felt ashamed and wounded, wounded to the point of tears as though I had been insulted, and looking up at the sky I took a vow to put an end to all this.

The next day I did not go to the Dolzhikovs'. Late in the evening, when it was quite dark and raining, I walked along Great Dvorianskaia Street, looking up at the windows. Everyone was asleep at the Azhogins' and the only light was in one of the furthest windows. It was Mrs Azhogina in her own room, sewing by the light of three candles, imagining that she was combating superstition. Our house was in darkness, but at the Dolzhikovs', on the contrary, the windows were lit up, but you couldn't distinguish anything behind the flowers and the curtains. I kept walking up and down the street; the cold March rain drenched me. I heard my father come home from the club; he knocked at the gate. A minute later a light appeared at the window, and I saw my sister hastening down with a lamp, while with the other hand she was tidying her thick hair as she went. Then my father walked about the drawing-room, talking and rubbing his hands, while my sister sat in a low chair, thinking and not listening to what he said.

But then they left; the light went out ... I glanced round at the engineer's, and there, too, all was darkness now. In the dark and the rain I felt hopelessly alone, abandoned to the whims of destiny; I felt that all my doings, my desires, and everything I had thought and said till then were trivial in comparison with my loneliness, in comparison with my present suffering, and the suffering that lay before me in the future. Alas, the thoughts and doings of living creatures are not nearly so significant as their griefs! And without thinking what I was doing, I pulled at the bell of the Dolzhikovs' gate, broke it, and ran along the street like some naughty boy, with a feeling of terror in my heart, expecting every moment that they would come out and recognise me. When I stopped at the end of the street to draw breath I could hear nothing but the sound of the rain, and somewhere in the distance a watchman striking a sheet of iron.

For a whole week I did not go to the Dolzhikovs'. My woollen suit had been sold. There was no painting work. I knew the pangs of hunger again, and earned from ten to twenty kopecks a day, anywhere, by heavy and unpleasant work. Struggling up to my knees in cold mud, straining my chest, I tried to stifle my memories, and, as it were, to punish myself for the cheeses and preserves with which I had been regaled at the engineer's. But all the same, as soon as I lay in bed, wet and hungry, my sinful imagination immediately began to paint exquisite, seductive pictures, and with amazement I acknowledged to myself that I was in love, passionately in love, and I fell into a sound, heavy sleep, feeling that this penal servitude only made my body stronger and younger.

One evening it snowed unseasonably, and the wind blew from the north as though winter had come back again. When I returned from work that evening I found Masha in my room. She was sitting in her fur coat, and had both hands in her muff.

'Why won't you come to see me?' she asked, raising her clear, clever eyes, and I was utterly confused with delight and stood stiffly upright before her, as I used to stand facing my father when he was going to beat me; she looked into my face and I could see from her eyes that she understood why I was embarrassed.

'Why won't you come to see me?' she repeated. 'If you won't visit me, you see, I've come to you.'

She got up and moved close to me.

'Don't desert me,' she said, and her eyes filled with tears. 'I am alone, utterly alone.'

She began crying; and, hiding her face in her muff, said:

'Alone! My life is hard, very hard, and in all the world I have no one but you. Don't desert me!'

Looking for a handkerchief to wipe her tears she smiled; we were silent for some time, then I put my arms round her and kissed her, and so scratched my cheek on her hat pin, so that it bled.

And we began talking as though we had been intimate friends for ages.

X

About two days later she sent me to Dubechnia and I was unutterably delighted to go. As I walked towards the station, and afterwards in the train, I kept laughing for no reason, and people looked at me as though I were drunk. Snow was falling, and there were still frosts in the mornings, but the roads were already dark-coloured and rooks hovered over them, cawing.

At first I had intended to make accommodation for us two, Masha and me, in the wing at the side opposite Mrs Cheprakova's wing, but it turned out that doves and ducks had been living there for a long time, and it was impossible to clear them out without destroying a great number of nests. There was nothing for it but to live in the comfortless rooms of the big house with the shutters. The peasants called the house 'the palace'; it had more than twenty rooms, and the only furniture was a piano and a child's arm-chair lying in the attic. And if Masha had brought all her furniture from the town we should still not have managed to get rid of the impression of sullen emptiness and cold. I picked out three small rooms with windows looking into the garden, and worked from early morning till night, setting them to rights, putting in new panes, papering the walls, filling up the holes and chinks in the floors. It was easy, pleasant work. I was continually running to the river to see if the ice was moving; I kept fancying that the starlings had come. And at night, thinking of Masha, I listened with an unutterably sweet feeling, with spasms of joy, to the rats scurrying and the wind droning and banging above the ceiling. It seemed as though some old house spirit were coughing in the attic.

The snow was deep; a great deal had fallen even at the end of March, but it melted quickly, as though by magic, and the spring floods passed in a tumultuous rush, so that by the beginning of April the starlings were already chattering, and yellow butterflies were flying in the garden. It was wonderful weather. Every day, towards evening, I used to walk to town to meet Masha, and what a delight it was to walk with bare feet along the road which was drying out and still soft. Half-way I used to sit down and look towards town, reluctant to approach it. The sight of it troubled me. I kept wondering how the people I knew would behave to me when they heard of my love. What would my father say? What troubled me particularly was the thought that my life was more complicated, and that I had completely lost all power to set it right, and that, like a balloon, it was bearing me away, God knows where. I no longer worried about earning my daily bread, how to live, but thought – I really don't know what about.

Masha used to come in a carriage; I used to get in with her, and we drove to Dubechnia, feeling light-hearted and free. Or, after waiting till sunset, I would go back dissatisfied and depressed, wondering why Masha had not come; at the gate or in the garden I would be met by a sweet, unexpected apparition – it was she! It would turn out that she had come by rail, and had walked from the station. What a celebration we had! In a simple woollen dress with a kerchief on her head, with a modest sunshade, but laced in, slender, in expensive foreign boots – she was a talented actress playing the part of a simple town girl. We looked round our domain and decided which should be her room, and which mine, where we would have our tree-lined walks, our kitchen garden, our beehives. We already had hens, ducks, and geese, which we loved because they were ours. We had, all ready for sowing, oats, clover, timothy grass, buckwheat, and vegetable seeds, and we always looked at all these stores and discussed at length the crop we might get; and everything Masha said to me seemed extraordinarily clever and fine. This was the happiest time of my life.

Soon after St Thomas's week we were married at our parish church in the village of Kurilovka, two miles from Dubechnia. Masha wanted everything to be done quietly; at her wish our best men were peasant lads, the sacristan sang alone, and we came back from the church in a small, jolting chaise which she drove herself. Our only guest from the town was my sister Kleopatra, to whom Masha sent a note three days before the wedding. My sister came in a white dress and wore gloves. During the wedding she cried quietly from joy and tenderness. Her expression was motherly and infinitely kind. She was intoxicated with our happiness, and smiled as though she were breathing in sweet fumes, and, looking at her during our wedding, I realised that for her there was nothing in the world higher than love, earthly love, and that she was dreaming of it secretly, timidly, but continually and passionately. She embraced and kissed Masha, and, not knowing how to express her rapture, said to her of me: 'He's kind! He's very good!'

Before she left us she changed into her everyday dress, and drew me into the garden to talk to me alone.

'Father is very much hurt,' she said, 'that you didn't write to him. You ought to have asked for his blessing. But actually he is very pleased. He says that this marriage will raise you in the eyes of all society, and that under the influence of Masha you will begin to take a more serious view of life. We talk of nothing but you in the evenings now, and yesterday he actually used the expression "Our Misail". That pleased me. It seems as if he has something in mind, and I fancy he wants to set you an example of magnanimity and be the first to speak of reconciliation. It is very possible he may come here to see you in a day or two.'

She hurriedly made the sign of the cross over me several times and said:

'Well, God be with you. Be happy. Aniuta Blagovo is a very clever girl; she says about your marriage that God is sending you a fresh ordeal. Well? Married life brings not only joy but suffering. That's bound to be so.'

Masha and I walked a couple of miles to see her off; we walked back slowly and in silence, as though we were resting. Masha held my hand, my heart felt light, and I had no inclination to talk about love;

we had become closer and more akin now that we were married, and we felt that nothing now could separate us.

'Your sister is a nice creature,' said Masha, 'but it seems as though she had been tormented for years. Your father must be a horrible man.'

I began telling her how my sister and I had been brought up, and what a senseless torture our childhood had really been. When she heard how my father had so recently beaten me, she shuddered and drew closer to me.

'Don't tell me any more,' she said, 'It's frightening!'

Now she never left me. We lived together in the three rooms in the big house, and in the evenings we bolted the door which led to the empty part of the house, as though someone unknown and fearful were living there. I got up early, at dawn, and immediately set to work of some sort. I mended carts, made paths in the garden, dug flower-beds, painted the roof. When the time came to sow oats, I tried to plough the ground over again, to harrow and to sow, and I did it all conscientiously, keeping up with our labourer; I was worn out, the rain and the cold wind made my face and feet burn for hours afterwards. I dreamed of ploughed land at night. But field labour did not attract me. I did not understand farming, and I did not care for it; it was perhaps because my forefathers had not been tillers of the soil, and the blood that flowed in my veins was purely urban. I loved nature tenderly; I loved the fields and meadows and kitchen gardens, but the peasant who turned the soil with his plough and urged on his pitiful horse, wet and tattered, with its neck straining, was to me the expression of coarse, savage, ugly force, and every time I looked at his uncouth movements I involuntarily began thinking of the legendary life of the remote past, before men knew the use of fire. The fierce bull that ran with the peasants' herd, and the horses, when they dashed about the village, stamping their hoofs, moved me to fear, and everything rather big, strong, and angry, whether it was the ram with its horns, the gander, or the yard-dog, seemed to me the expression of the same coarse, savage force. This prejudice affected me particularly in bad weather, when heavy clouds were hanging over the black ploughed land. Above all, when I was ploughing or sowing, and two or three people stood looking at me doing it, I had no feeling that this work was inevitable and obligatory, and it seemed to me that I was amusing myself. I preferred doing something in the yard, and there was nothing I liked so much as painting the roof.

I used to walk through the garden and the meadow to our mill. It was let to a peasant of Kurilovka called Stepan, a handsome, dark fellow with a thick black beard, who looked very strong. He did not like milling, and looked upon it as dreary and unprofitable, and only lived at the mill in order not to live at home. He was a leather-worker, and was always surrounded by a pleasant smell of pitch and leather. He was not fond of talking, he was listless and sluggish, and was always sitting in the doorway or on the river-bank, humming 'oo-loo-loo'. His wife and mother-in-law, both white-faced, languid, and meek, used sometimes to come from Kurilovka to see him; they made low bows to him and addressed him formally, 'Stepan Petrovich', while he went on sitting on the river-bank, softly humming 'oo-loo-loo', without responding by word or movement to their bows. One hour and then another would pass in silence. His mother-in-law and wife, after exchanging whispers, would get up and gaze at him for some time, expecting him to look round; then they would make a low bow, and in sugary, chanting voices, say:

'Good-bye, Stepan Petrovich!'

And they would go away. After that Stepan, picking up the parcel they had left, containing bagels or a shirt, would heave a sigh and say, winking in their direction:

'The female sex!'

The mill with two sets of millstones worked day and night. I used to help Stepan; I liked the work, and when he went off I was glad to stay and take his place.

XI

After bright warm weather came a wet spell; all May it rained and was cold. The sound of the mill-wheels and of the rain made one lazy and drowsy. The floor shook, there was a smell of flour, and that, too, induced drowsiness. My wife in a short fur-lined jacket, and in men's high galoshes, would turn up twice a day, and she always said the same thing:

'And this is supposed to be summer! Worse than October!'

We used to have tea and make porridge together, or we would sit for hours at a stretch without speaking, waiting for the rain to stop. Once, when Stepan had gone off to the fair, Masha stayed all night at the mill. When we got up we could not tell what time it was, as rain-clouds covered the whole sky; but sleepy cocks were crowing at Dubechnia, and landrails were calling in the meadows; it was still very, very early . . . My wife and I went down to the millpond and drew out the net which Stepan had thrown in overnight in our presence. A big perch was thrashing about, and a furious crayfish was clawing upwards with its pincers.

'Let them go,' said Masha. 'Let them be happy too.'

Because we got up so early and afterwards did nothing, that day seemed very long, the longest day in my life. Towards evening Stepan came back and I went home.

'Your father came today,' said Masha.

'Where is he?' I asked.

'He's left. I refused to see him.'

Seeing me stand there silently sorry for my father, she said:

'One must be consistent. I refused to see him, and sent word to him not to trouble to come and see us again.'

A minute later I was past the gate, walking to town to explain things to my father. It was muddy, slippery, cold. For the first time since marriage I felt suddenly sad, and in my brain, exhausted by that long grey day, there was stirring the thought that perhaps I was not living as I ought. I was worn out; little by little I was overcome by despondency and indolence, I did not want to move or think, and after going on a little I gave it up with a wave of my arm and turned back.

The engineer in a leather overcoat with a hood was standing in the middle of the yard.

'Where's the furniture? There used to be lovely Empire style furniture; there used be pictures, there used to be vases, while now you could play ball in it! I bought the place with the furniture. The devil take her!'

Moisei, a thin pock-marked fellow of twenty-five, with insolent little eyes, who was in the service of the general's widow, stood near him crumpling his cap in his hands; one of his cheeks was bigger than the other, as though he had lain too long on it.

'Your Honour bought the place without the furniture,' he brought out irresolutely, 'I remember.'

'Shut up!' shouted the engineer; he turned crimson and shook with anger, and the echo in the garden loudly repeated his shout.

XII

When I was doing anything in the garden or the yard, Moisei would stand beside me, and folding his arms behind his back he would stand lazily and impudently stare at me with his little eyes. And this irritated me to such a degree that I abandoned work and went away.

From Stepan we heard that Moisei was Mrs Cheprakova's lover. I noticed that when people came to her to borrow money they addressed themselves first to Moisei, and once I saw a peasant, black from head to foot – he must have been a coalman – bow down at Moisei's feet. Sometimes, after a little whispering, he gave out money himself, without telling his mistress, from which I concluded that he occasionally did a little business on his own account.

He shot in our garden under our windows, stole food from our cellar, borrowed our horses without asking, and we were indignant and began to feel Dubechnia was not ours, and Masha would say, turning pale:

'Do we really have to go on living with these reptiles another eighteen months?'

Mrs Cheprakova's son, Ivan, was serving as a guard on our railway. He had grown much thinner and feebler during the winter, so that a single glass was enough to make him drunk, and he shivered out of the sunshine. He wore the guard's uniform with aversion and was ashamed of it, but considered his post a good one as he could steal candles and sell them. My new position excited in him a mixed feeling of wonder, envy, and a vague hope that something of the same sort might happen to him. He used to watch Masha with ecstatic eyes, ask me what I had for dinner now, and his lean and ugly face wore a sad and sweetish expression, and he moved his fingers as though he were feeling my happiness with them.

'Listen, Better-than-nothing,' he said fussily, relighting his cigarette at every instant; there was always a mess where he stood, for he used dozens of matches to light one cigarette. 'Listen, my life now is the vilest possible. The worst of it is any subaltern can shout: "Hey guard!" I have overheard all sorts of things in the train, my boy, and do you know, I have learned that life's beastly! My mother has been and ruined me! A doctor in the train told me that if parents are debauched, the children are drunkards or criminals. So that's it!'

Once he came into the yard, staggering; his eyes roamed about senselessly, his breathing was laboured; he laughed and cried and babbled as though in delirium, and the only words I could catch in his muddled talk were, 'My mother! Where's my mother?' which he uttered with a wail like a child who has lost his mother in a crowd. I led him into our garden and laid him down under a tree, and Masha and I took turns to sit by him all that day and all night. He was very sick, and Masha looked with aversion at his pale, wet face, and said:

'Will these reptiles really go on living another year and a half in our farm? It's awful! It's awful!'

And how much distress the peasants caused us! How many bitter disappointments in those early days in the spring months, when we so longed to be happy. My wife wanted to build a school. I drew a plan of a school for sixty boys, and the rural council administration approved of it, but advised us to build the school at Kurilovka, the big village which was only two miles from us. Moreover, the school at

Kurilovka in which children from four villages, our Dubechnia being one of them, were taught, was old and too small, and the rotten floor was frightening to walk upon. At the end of March, at Masha's wish, she was appointed guardian of the Kurilovka school, and at the beginning of April we three times summoned the village assembly, and tried to persuade the peasants that their school was old and over-crowded, and that it was essential to build a new one. A member of the administration and the Inspector of Peasant Schools came, and they, too, tried to persuade them. After each meeting the peasants surrounded us, begging for a bucket of vodka; we were hot in the crowd; we were soon exhausted, and returned home dissatisfied and a little ill at ease. In the end the peasants set apart a plot of ground for the school, and were obliged to bring all the building material from the town with their own horses. And the very first Sunday after the spring corn was sown carts set off from Kurilovka and Dubechnia to fetch bricks for the foundations. They set off at daybreak, and came back late in the evening; the peasants were drunk, and said that they were worn out.

As ill luck would have it, the rain and the cold persisted all through May. The road was unusable: it turned to mud. The carts usually drove into our yard when they came back from the town – and what a horrible ordeal it was. A pot-bellied horse would appear at the gate, its front legs wide apart; it would stumble forward before coming into the yard; a beam, nine yards long, wet and slimy-looking, crept in on a low wagon. Beside it, muffled up against the rain, strode a peasant with the skirts of his coat tucked up in his belt, not looking where he was going, but stepping through the puddles. Another cart would appear with boards, then a third with a beam, a fourth . . . and the space before our house was gradually crowded up with horses, beams, and planks. Men and women, with their heads muffled and their skirts tucked up, would stare angrily at our windows, make an uproar, and clamour for the mistress to come out to them; you could hear coarse swearwords. Meanwhile Moisei stood aside, and we fancied he was enjoying our discomfiture.

'We are not going to cart any more,' the peasants would shout. 'We are worn out! Let her go and cart it herself.'

Masha, pale and flustered, expecting them any minute to break into the house, would send them out a half-pail of vodka; after that the noise would subside and the long beams, one after another, would crawl slowly out of the yard.

When I was setting off to the building site my wife was worried and said:

'The peasants are resentful, I only hope they don't do you a mischief. No, wait, I'll come with you.'

We drove to Kurilovka together, and there the carpenter asked us for a tip. The framework of the house was ready. It was time to lay the foundations, but the masons did not come; this caused a delay, and the carpenters complained. And when at last the masons did come, it appeared that there was no sand; somehow they had forgotten that it would be needed. Taking advantage of our helpless position, the peasants demanded thirty kopecks for each cart-load, though the distance from the building to the river where they got the sand was less than a quarter of a mile, and more than five hundred cart-loads were needed. There was no end to the misunderstandings, swearing, and importunity; my wife was indignant, and the masons' contractor, Tit Petrov, an old man of seventy, took her by the arm, and said:

'You look here! You look here! You just bring me the sand; I'll put ten men on at once, and in two days it will be done! You look here!'

But they brought the sand and two days passed, and four, and a week, and instead of the promised foundations there was still a yawning hole.

'It's enough to drive one mad,' said my wife, in distress. 'What people! What people!'

In the midst of this chaos the engineer arrived; he brought with him parcels of wine and savouries, and after a prolonged meal lay down for a nap on the veranda and snored so loudly that the labourers shook their heads and said:

'Really!'

Masha was not pleased at his coming, she did not trust him, but still consulted him. When, after a long sleep after dinner, he got up in a bad humour and said unpleasant things about our management of the place, or expressed regret that he had bought Dubechnia, which had already made him a loss, the misery showed on poor Masha's face. She would complain to him, and he would yawn and say that the peasants ought to be flogged.

He called our marriage and our life a farce, and said it was a caprice, a whim.

'She has done something of the sort before,' he said about Masha. 'She once fancied herself a great opera singer and left me; I spent two months looking for her, and, sonny, I spent a thousand roubles on telegrams alone.'

He no longer called me a sectarian or Mr Painter, and did not as in the past express approval of my living like a workman, but said:

'You are a strange person! You are not a normal person! I won't prophesy, but you will come to a bad end, sir!'

And Masha slept badly at night, and was always sitting at our bedroom window thinking. There was no laughter at supper now, no charming grimaces. I was wretched and, when it rained, every drop that fell seemed to pierce my heart, like small shot, and I felt ready to fall on my knees before Masha and apologise for the weather. When the peasants shouted in the yard I also felt guilty. For hours on end I sat in the same place, thinking only what a splendid person Masha was, what a wonderful person. I loved her passionately, and I was delighted by everything she did, everything she said. She had a bent for quiet studious pursuits; she was fond of reading for hours, of studying. Knowing farming only from books, she surprised us all by what she knew; and every piece of advice she gave was of value; not one was wasted in the household. Moreover, what nobility, what taste, what graciousness, that graciousness which is only found in well brought-up people.

To this woman, with her sound, positive mind, the disorderly surroundings with petty cares and squabbles in which we were living now were an agony; I saw that and could not sleep at night; my brain worked feverishly and I had a lump in my throat. I rushed about not knowing what to do.

I galloped to the town and brought Masha books, newspapers, sweets, flowers; with Stepan I caught fish, wading for hours up to my neck in the cold water in the rain to catch turbot to vary our fare; I humbly begged the peasants not to make a noise; I plied them with vodka, bought them off, made all sorts of promises. And how many other foolish things I did!

At last the rain ceased, the earth dried out. You could get up at four o'clock in the morning; you could go out into the garden – where there was dew sparkling on the flowers, the twitter of birds, the hum of insects, not one cloud in the sky; and the garden, the meadows, and the river were so lovely, but the memories of the peasants, of their carts, of the engineer! Masha and I drove out together in the racing chaise to the fields to look at the oats. She drove, I sat behind; her shoulders were raised and the wind played with her hair.

'Keep to the right!' she shouted to anyone in the way.

'You're like a coach-driver,' I said to her one day.

'Maybe! Why, my grandfather, the engineer's father, was a coach-driver. Didn't you know that?' she asked, turning to me, and there and then she mimicked the way coach-drivers shout and sing.

'And thank God for that,' I thought as I listened to her. 'Thank God.'

And again the memories of the peasants, of the carts, of the engineer . . .

XIII

Dr Blagovo arrived on a bicycle. My sister began visiting often. Again there were conversations about manual labour, about progress, about a mysterious X awaiting mankind in the remote future. The doctor did not like our farm work, because it interfered with arguments, and said that ploughing, reaping, keeping calves were unworthy of a free man, and all these coarse forms of the struggle for existence men would in time relegate to animals and machines, while they would devote themselves exclusively to scientific investigation. My sister kept begging them to let her go home earlier, and if she stayed on till late in the evening, or spent the night with us, there would be no end to the agitation.

'My God, what a child you are still!' said Masha reproachfully. 'It's ridiculous, actually.'

'Yes, it is,' my sister agreed, 'I know it's ridiculous; but what is to be done if I haven't the strength to force myself? I keep feeling I am acting badly.'

At hay making I ached all over because I wasn't used to it; in the evening, sitting on the veranda and talking with the others, I would suddenly fall asleep, and they laughed aloud at me. They woke me up and made me sit down to supper; I was overpowered with slumber, and I saw the lights, the faces, and the plates as it were in a dream, heard the voices, but did not understand them. And getting up early in the morning, I took up the scythe at once, or went to the site and worked hard all day.

When I stayed home on holidays I noticed that my sister and Masha were hiding something from me, and even seemed to be avoiding me. My wife was tender to me as before, but she had thoughts of her own, which she did not share with me. There was no doubt that her exasperation with the peasants was growing, the life was becoming more and more distasteful to her, and yet she no longer complained to me. She talked to the doctor now more readily than she did to me, and I did not understand why it was so.

It was the custom in our province at hay making and harvest time for labourers to come to the manor house in the evening and be treated to vodka; even young girls drank a glass. We did not keep up this practice; the reapers and the peasant women stood about in our yard till late in the evening expecting vodka, and then departed abusing us. And all the time Masha frowned grimly and said nothing, or murmured to the doctor with exasperation: 'Savages! Pechenegs!'*

In the country newcomers are met ungraciously, almost with hostility, as they are at school. And so were we. At first we were looked upon as slightly simple fools, who had bought an estate simply because we did not know what to do with our money. We were laughed at. The peasants grazed their cattle in our wood and even in our garden; they drove our cows and horses off to the village, and then demanded money for the damage done by them. They came in whole companies into our yard, and loudly clamoured that at hay making we had scythed the edge of Bicheevka or Semenikha, some piece of land that did not belong to us; and as we did not yet know the boundaries of our estate very accurately, we took their word for it and paid damages. Afterwards it turned out that we had mowed only what was ours. They barked the lime trees in our wood. One of the Dubechnia peasants, a regular shark, who did a trade in vodka without a licence, bribed our labourers, and in collaboration with them cheated us in a most treacherous way. They took the new wheels off our cart and replaced them with old ones, stole our ploughing harness and actually sold them to us, and so on. But what was most mortifying of all was what happened on site: the peasant women stole by night boards, bricks, tiles, pieces of iron. The village elder with witnesses made a search in their huts; the village meeting fined them two roubles each, and afterwards this money was spent on drink by the whole commune.

When Masha heard about this, she would say to the doctor or my sister, indignantly:

'What beasts! It's horrible! horrible!'

And I heard her more than once express regret that she had undertaken to build the school.

'You must understand,' the doctor tried to persuade her, 'that if you build this school and do good in general, it's not for the sake of the peasants, but in the name of culture, in the name of the future; and the worse the peasants are, all the more reason to build the school. Understand that!'

But there was a lack of conviction in his voice, and it seemed to me that both he and Masha hated the peasants.

Masha often went to the mill, taking my sister with her, and they both said, laughing, that they went to have a look at Stepan, he was so handsome. Stepan, it appeared, was torpid and taciturn only with men; in female company his manners were free and easy, and he talked incessantly. One day, going down to the river to bathe, I accidentally overheard them talking. Masha and Kleopatra, both in white dresses, were sitting on the bank in the spreading shade of a willow, and Stepan was standing by them with his hands behind his back and was saying:

'Are peasants human? They're not human, but, I'm sorry, wild beasts, impostors. What is a peasant's life? Nothing but eating and drinking; all he cares for is food and drink to be cheaper and swilling liquor at the tavern like a fool; and there's no conversation, no manners, no formality, nothing but ignorance! He lives in filth, his wife lives in filth, and his children live in filth. What he stands up in, he lies down to sleep in; he picks the potatoes out of the soup with his fingers; he drinks kvas with a cockroach in it, and doesn't bother to blow it away!'

'Poverty, of course,' my sister put in.

'Poverty? There is want, to be sure, there's different sorts of want, Miss. If a man is in prison, or let us say blind or legless, that really is trouble I wouldn't wish on anyone, but if a man's free and has his senses, if he has his eyes and his hands and his strength and God, what more does he want? Self-indulgence, Miss, and ignorance, not poverty. If you, let us suppose, good gentlefolk, with your education, wish out of kindness to help him he will drink away your money in his vile way; or, what's worse, he will open a drink-shop, and with your money start robbing the people. You say poverty, but does the rich peasant live better? He, too, asking your pardon, lives like a swine: coarse, loudmouthed, wooden-headed, broader than he is long, with his fat, red-faced, mug; I'd like to swing my fist and send him flying, the scoundrel. There's Larion, another rich one at Dubechnia, and I bet he strips the bark off your trees as much as any poor one; and he's a foul-mouthed fellow; his children are the same, and when he has a drop too much he'll topple with his nose in a puddle and sleep there. They're all a worthless lot, Miss. If you live in the village with them it's hell. It has stuck in my teeth, that village has, and thank the Lord, the King of Heaven, I've plenty to eat and clothes to wear, I served out my time in the dragoons, I was village elder for three years, and now I am a free Cossack, I live where I like. I don't want to live in the village, and no one has the right to force me. They say I have a wife. They say you have to live in your house with your wife. But why? I am not her hired man.'

'Tell me, Stepan, did you marry for love?' asked Masha.

'Love among us in the village!' answered Stepan, and he gave a laugh. 'Properly speaking, Ma'am, if you care to know, this is my second marriage. I am not a Kurilovka man, I am from Zalegoshche, but afterwards I was taken to Kurilovka when I married. You see my father did not want to divide the land among us. There were five of us brothers. I took my leave and went to another village to live with my wife's family, but my first wife died when she was young.'

'What did she die of?'

'Of foolishness. She used to cry and cry and cry for no reason, and so she pined away. She was always drinking some sort of herbs to make her better looking, and I suppose she damaged her innards. And my second wife is a Kurilovka woman too, what has she got? She's a village woman, a peasant woman, and nothing more. I was taken in when they plighted me to her. I thought she was young and fair-skinned, and that they lived in a clean way. Her mother was just like a Flagellant and she drank coffee, and the chief thing, to be sure, they were clean in their ways. So I married her, and next day we sat down to dinner; I asked my mother-in-law to give me a spoon, and she gives me a spoon, and I see her wipe it with her finger. So much for you, thought I; nice sort of cleanliness yours is. I lived a year with them and then I left. I might have married a girl from the town,' he went on after a pause. 'They say a wife is a helpmate to her husband. What do I want with a helpmate? I help myself; I'd rather she talked to me, and not clack, clack, clack, but properly, sensitively. What is life without good conversation?'

Stepan suddenly paused, and at once there was the sound of his dreary, monotonous 'oo-loo-loo-loo'. This meant that he had seen me.

Masha used often to go to the mill, and evidently got pleasure from her conversations with Stepan. Stepan abused the peasants with such sincerity and conviction, and she was drawn to him. Every time she came back from the mill the feebleminded peasant who looked after the garden, shouted at her:

'Wench Palashka! Hullo, wench Palashka!' and he would bark at her like a dog: 'Woof! Woof!'

And she would stop and look at him closely, as though in that idiot's barking she found an answer to her thoughts, and probably she was drawn to him in the same way as to Stepan's abuse. At home she could expect such news as, for instance, that the geese from the village had ruined our cabbages in the garden, or that Larion had stolen the reins; and, shrugging her shoulders, she would say with a laugh:

'What do you expect of these people?'

She was indignant, and rancour seethed in her heart, but meanwhile I was growing used to the peasants, and I felt more and more drawn to them. For the most part they were highly strung, irritable, downtrodden people; they were people whose imagination had been stifled, ignorant, with a poor, dim outlook on life, whose thoughts were ever the same: of grey earth, of grey days, of black bread; people who cheated, but like birds hiding just their heads behind a tree – people who could not count. They would not come to mow for us for twenty roubles, but they came for a half a pail of vodka, though for twenty roubles they could have bought four pails. There really was filth and drunkenness and foolishness and deceit, but with all that one yet felt that the life of the peasants revolved on a firm, sound pivot. However uncouth a beast the peasant following the plough seemed, and however he might stupefy himself with vodka, still, looking at him more closely, one felt that there was in him something essential and very important, which was lacking in Masha and in the doctor, for instance, and that was that he believed the chief thing on earth was truth and justice, and that his salvation, and that of the whole people, was only to be found in truth and justice, and so more than anything in the world he loved fairness. I told my wife she saw the spots on the glass, but not the glass itself; she said nothing in reply, or hummed like Stepan 'oo-loo-loo-loo'. When this good-hearted and clever woman turned pale with indignation, and with a quiver in her voice spoke to the doctor of the drunkenness and dishonesty, it perplexed me, and I was puzzled by her poor memory. How could she forget that her father the engineer drank too, and drank heavily, and that the money with which Dubechnia had been bought had been acquired by a whole series of brazen, shameless frauds? How could she forget it?

XIV

My sister, too, was leading a life of her own which she carefully hid from me. She was often whispering with Masha. When I went up to her she seemed to shrink into herself, and there was a guilty, imploring look in her eyes; evidently there was something going on in her heart of which she was afraid or ashamed. To avoid meeting me in the garden, or being left alone with me, she always kept close to Masha, and I rarely had a chance to talk to her except at dinner.

One evening I was walking quietly through the garden on my way back from the site. It was beginning to get dark. Without noticing me, or hearing my step, my sister was walking near a spreading old apple tree, absolutely noiselessly as though she were a phantom. She was dressed in black, and was walking rapidly backwards and forwards on the same track, looking at the ground. An apple fell from the tree; she started at the sound, stood still and pressed her hands to her temples. At that moment I went up to her.

In a rush of tender affection which suddenly flooded my heart, with tears in my eyes, suddenly remembering my mother and our childhood, I put my arm round her shoulders and kissed her.

'What is the matter?' I asked her. 'You're suffering; I've seen it for a long time. Tell me what's wrong?'

'I am frightened . . .' she said, trembling.

'What is it?' I insisted. 'For God's sake, be open!'

'I will, I will be open; I'll tell you the whole truth. To hide it from you is so wretched, so agonising. Misail, I love . . .' she went on in a whisper, 'I love him . . . I love him . . . I am happy, but why am I so frightened?'

We heard footsteps; between the trees appeared Dr Blagovo in his silk shirt with his high top-boots. Evidently they had arranged to meet near the apple tree. Seeing him, she rushed impulsively towards him with a cry of pain, as though he were being taken from her.

'Vladimir! Vladimir!'

She clung to him and looked hungrily into his face, and only then I noticed how pale and thin she had become recently. It was all the more noticeable because her lace collar, which I had known for so long, now hung more loosely than ever before about her thin, long neck. The doctor was disconcerted, but at once recovered himself, and, stroking her hair said:

'There, there . . . Why so upset? You see, I've come.'

We were silent, shyly looking at each other, then the three of us walked on together, and I heard the doctor saying to me:

'Civilised life has not yet begun among us. Old men console themselves by making out that if there is nothing now, there was something in the forties or the sixties; that's the old, you and I are young, our brains have not yet been touched by *marasmus senilis*; we cannot comfort ourselves with such illusions. The beginning of Russia was in 862, but the beginning of civilised Russia, as I understand it, has not come yet.'

But I couldn't follow these reflections. It was somehow strange, I could not believe it, that my sister was in love, that she was walking and holding the arm of a stranger and looking tenderly at him. My sister, this nervous, frightened, crushed, fettered creature, loved a man who was married and had children! I felt sorry for something, but what exactly I don't know; the presence of the doctor was for some reason distasteful to me now, and I could not imagine what would come of this love of theirs.

XV

Masha and I drove to Kurilovka to the dedication of the school. 'Autumn, autumn, autumn . . .' said Masha softly, looking away. 'Summer is over. There are no birds and only the willows are green.'

Yes, summer was over. There were fine, warm days, but it was fresh in the morning, and the shepherds went out in their sheepskins already; and in our garden the dew did not dry on the daisies all day long. There were plaintive sounds all the time, and you could not make out whether they came from the shutters creaking on their rusty hinges, or from the flying cranes – and your heart felt light, and one was eager for life.

'The summer is over,' said Masha. 'Now you and I can sum up. We have done a lot of work, a lot of thinking; we are the better for it – all honour and glory to us – we have succeeded in self-improvement; but have our successes had any perceptible influence on the life around us, have they brought any benefit to anyone whatever? No. Ignorance, physical filth, drunkenness, appallingly high infant mortality, everything remains as it was, and no one is the better for your having ploughed and sown, and my having spent money and read books. Obviously we have been working only for ourselves and been thinking freely only for ourselves.'

Such reasoning perplexed me, and I did not know what to think.

'We have been sincere throughout,' I said, 'and anyone sincere is right.'

'Who's arguing? We were right, but we applied the right ideas the wrong way. To begin with, our outward tactics – aren't they mistaken? You want to be of use to people, but just by buying an estate, from the very start you cut yourself off from any possibility of doing anything useful for them. Then if you work, dress, eat like a peasant you legitimise, as it were, by your authority, their heavy, clumsy dress, their horrible huts, their stupid beards . . . On the other hand, all right, you work for a long, long time, your whole life, so that in the end some practical results are obtained, yet what are they, your results, what can they do against such elemental forces as wholesale ignorance, hunger, cold, degeneracy? A drop in the ocean! Other methods of struggle are needed, strong, bold, rapid! If you really want to be of use you must get out of the narrow circle of ordinary activity, and try to act directly upon the mass! Loud, energetic propaganda is the first requirement. Why is it that art, music, for instance, is so alive, so popular, and in fact so powerful? Because the musician or the singer affects thousands at once. Precious, precious art!' she went on, looking dreamily at the sky. 'Art gives us wings and carries us far, far away! Anyone who is sick of filth, of petty, mercenary interests, anyone who is revolted, wounded, and indignant, can find peace and satisfaction only in the beautiful.'

As we approached Kurilovka the weather was bright and joyous. Here and there they were threshing; there was a smell of rye straw. Behind the hurdle fences was a bright red rowan tree, and all the trees wherever we looked were ruddy or golden. Bells were ringing, icons were being carried to the school, and we could hear them sing: 'Holy Mother, our Defender,' and how limpid the air was, and how high the doves were flying.

The service was held in the classroom. Then the peasants of Kurilovka presented Masha with an icon, and the peasants of Dubechnia offered her a big loaf and a gilt salt cellar. And Masha broke into sobs.

'If we said anything wrong or did anything not to your liking, forgive us,' said an old man, and he bowed to her and to me.

As we drove home Masha kept looking round at the school; the green roof, which I had painted, and which was glistening in the sun, stayed in view for a long while. And I felt that the looks Masha gave it now were farewells.

XVI

In the evening she packed to go to the town.

Lately she had taken to going to town often and staying the night there. In her absence I could not work, my hands felt weak and limp; our huge courtyard seemed a dreary, repulsive, empty hole. The garden was full of angry noises, and without her the house, the trees, the horses were no longer 'ours'.

I did not leave the house, but stayed sitting at her table beside her cupboard with books on agriculture, once favoured, now unwanted and looking at me so shamefacedly. For hours on end, while the clock struck seven, eight, nine, while the autumn night, black as soot, fell outside, I kept examining her old glove, or the pen with which she always wrote, or her little scissors. I did nothing, and realised clearly that all I had done before, ploughing, mowing, chopping, was done only because she wished it. And if she had sent me to clean a deep well, where I had to stand up to my waist in deep water, I should have crawled into the well without considering whether it was necessary or not. And now when she was not near, Dubechnia, with its ruins, its untidiness, its banging shutters, with its thieves by day and by night, seemed to me a chaos in which any work would be useless. Besides, what had I to work for here, why worry or think about the future, if I felt that the earth was giving way under my feet, that I had played my part in Dubechnia, and that I would share the fate of the books on farming? Oh, what misery it was at night, in hours of solitude, when I was listening every minute in alarm, as though I were expecting someone to shout that it was time for me to leave! I did not grieve for Dubechnia. I grieved for my love, whose autumn had apparently also come. What an immense happiness it is to love and be loved, and how horrible to feel that you are beginning to tumble from that high tower!

Masha returned from town towards the evening of the next day. She was annoyed with something, but she hid it, and only asked, why was it all the double glazing had been put in for the winter, it was enough to suffocate one. I took out two frames. We were not hungry, but we sat down to supper.

'Go and wash your hands,' said my wife; 'you smell of putty.'

She had brought some new illustrated magazines from town, and we looked at them together after supper. There were supplements with fashion plates and patterns. Masha looked through them casually, and was putting them aside to examine them properly later on; but one dress, with a smooth skirt as full as a bell and large sleeves, interested her, and she looked at it for a minute gravely and attentively.

'That's not bad,' she said.

'Yes, that dress would suit you beautifully,' I said, 'beautifully.'

And looking with fond emotion at the dress, admiring that patch of grey simply because she liked it, I went on tenderly:

'A charming, wonderful dress! Splendid, beautiful Masha! My darling Masha!'

And tears dropped on the fashion plate.

'Splendid Masha . . .'

She went off to bed, while I sat another hour looking at the illustrations.

'You shouldn't have removed the double glazing,' she said from the bedroom, 'I am afraid it will be cold. For heaven's sake, what a draught there is!'

I read a few things in the 'Miscellany', a recipe for making cheap ink, and the story of the biggest diamond in the world. Again I found the fashion plate of the dress she liked, and I imagined her at a ball, with a fan, with bare shoulders, brilliant, voluptuous, knowing her way around painting, music, literature, and how small and how brief my role seemed!

Our meeting, our conjugal life, had been only one of the episodes of which there would be many more in the life of this vital, richly gifted woman. All the best in the world, as I said before, was at her service, and she had it for absolutely nothing, and even ideas and a fashionable intellectual movement served simply for her recreation, giving variety to her life, and I was only the coach-driver who drove her from one entertainment to another. Now she did not need me. She would take flight, and I should be left alone.

And as though in response to my thought, there came a despairing scream from the garden.

'He-e-elp!'

It was a shrill, womanish voice, and as though to mimic it the wind whistled in the chimney on the same shrill note. About half a minute passed, and again through the noise of the wind, but coming, it seemed, from the other end of the yard:

'He-e-elp!'

'Misail, can you hear?' my wife asked me softly. 'Can you hear?'

She came out from the bedroom in her night-gown, with her hair down, and listened, looking at the dark window.

'Someone is being strangled,' she said. 'That is the last straw.'

I took my gun and went out. It was very dark outside, the wind was high, and it was difficult to stand. I went to the gate and listened, the trees roared, the wind whistled, and probably at the feeble-minded peasant's, a dog howled lazily. Outside the gates the darkness was absolute, not a light on the railway. And near the wing, which a year before had been the office, suddenly sounded a smothered scream:

'He-e-elp!'

'Who's there?' I called.

Two people were fighting. One was pushing the other out, while the other was resisting, and both were breathing heavily.

'Let go,' said one, and I recognised Ivan Cheprakov; it was him shrieking in a shrill, womanish voice: 'Let go, you damned brute, or I'll bite your hands all over.'

The other I recognised as Moisei. I pulled them apart, and as I did could not resist hitting Moisei twice in the face. He fell down, then got up again, and I hit him once more.

'He tried to kill me,' he muttered. 'He was trying to get at his mama's chest of drawers . . . I want to lock him up in the wing for security.'

Cheprakov was drunk and did not recognise me; he kept sighing as if drawing breath in order to shout 'help' again.

I left them and went back to the house; my wife was lying on her bed; she had dressed. I told her what had happened in the yard, and did not even conceal the fact that I had hit Moisei.

'Living in the country is frightful,' she said. 'And what a long night, God, if only it were over!'

'He-e-elp!' we heard again, a little later.

'I'll go and stop them,' I said.

'No, let them cut each other's throats,' she said with an expression of disgust.

She was looking up at the ceiling, listening, while I sat beside her, not daring to speak to her, feeling as though I were to blame for the shouts of 'help' in the yard and for the night being so long.

We were silent, and I waited impatiently for a gleam of light at the window, and Masha looked all the time as though she had awakened from a trance and now was marvelling how she, so clever, and well brought-up, so neat, had come to this pitiful, provincial, empty hole among a crew of petty nonentities, and how she could have so far forgotten herself as even to fall in love with one of these people, and to be his wife for more than six months. It seemed to me that at that moment it did not matter to her whether it was me, Moisei, or Cheprakov; everything for her was merged in that savage drunken 'help' – I, our marriage, our work together, and the mud and slush of autumn, and when she sighed or moved into a more comfortable position I read in her face: 'Oh when will it be morning?'

In the morning she left.

I spent three days more at Dubechnia waiting for her, then I packed up all our things in one room, locked it, and walked to town. It was evening when I rang at the engineer's, and the street lamps were burning in Great Dvorianskaia Street. Pavel told me there was no one at home; Dolzhikov had gone to Petersburg, and Masha was probably at a rehearsal at the Azhogins'. I remember with what emotion I went on to the Azhogins', how my heart throbbed and fainted as I mounted the stairs, and stood waiting a long while on the landing, not daring to enter that temple of the muses! In the big room there were lighted candles everywhere, on a little table, on the piano, and on the stage, everywhere in threes; and the first performance was fixed for the thirteenth, and now the first rehearsal was on a Monday, a bad day. The war against superstition! All the devotees of the stage were gathered together; the eldest, the middle, and the youngest sisters were walking about the stage, reading their parts from exercise books. Apart from all the rest stood Radish, motionless, his temple pressed to the wall as he gazed with adoration at the stage, waiting for the rehearsal to begin. Everything as it used to be.

I made for my hostess – I had to pay my respects to her, but suddenly everyone hissed and waved at me not to bang my heels. There was a silence. The lid of the piano was raised; a lady sat down at it screwing up her short-sighted eyes at the music, and my Masha walked up to the piano, in a low-necked dress, looking beautiful, but with a special, new sort of beauty not in the least like Masha who used to come and meet me in the spring at the mill. She sang:

'Why do I love you, radiant night?'

It was the first time in all the time we had known each other that I had heard her sing. She had a fine, fruity, powerful voice, and while she sang I felt as though I were eating a ripe, sweet, fragrant melon. She ended, the audience applauded, and she smiled, very much pleased, making play with her eyes, turning over the music, smoothing her dress, like a bird that has at last broken out of its cage and preens its wings in freedom. Her hair was combed over her ears, and her face had a mischievous expression that boded ill, as though she wanted to throw down a challenge to us all, or to shout to us as she did to her horses: 'Hey, my beauties!'

And she must at that moment have been very like her grandfather the coach-driver.

'You here too?' she said, giving me her hand. 'Did you hear me sing? Well, what did you think of it?' and without waiting for my answer she went on: 'It's a very good thing you are here. I am going tonight to Petersburg for a short time. You'll let me go, won't you?'

At midnight I saw her off to the station. She embraced me affectionately, probably out of gratitude to me for not asking unnecessary questions, and she promised to write to me, and I held her hands a long time, and kissed them, hardly able to restrain my tears and not uttering a word.

And when she had gone I stood watching the retreating lights, caressing her in imagination and softly saying:

'My darling Masha, glorious Masha . . .'

I spent the night in Makarikha at Karpovna's; next morning I was at work with Radish, upholstering the furniture of a rich merchant who was marrying his daughter to a doctor.

XVII

My sister came after dinner on Sunday and had tea with me. 'I read a great deal now,' she said, showing me the books which she had borrowed from the public library on her way to me. 'Thanks to your wife and to Vladimir, my consciousness has been woken. They have been my salvation; they have made me feel human. Before I used to lie awake at night with various worries: "Oh how much sugar we've got through this week. Oh I mustn't over-salt the cucumbers." I still lie awake at night, but I have different thoughts. I am distressed that half my life has been passed in such a foolish, cowardly way. I despise my past; I am ashamed of it, and I look upon our father now as my enemy. Oh, how grateful I am to your wife? And Vladimir! He is such a wonderful person! They have opened my eyes!'

'It's bad that you don't sleep at night,' I said.

'Do you think I am ill? Not at all. Vladimir examined my chest, and said I was perfectly well. But health is not what matters, it is not so important . . . Tell me: am I right?'

She needed moral support, that was obvious. Masha had gone

away. Dr Blagovo was in Petersburg, and there was no one left in the town but me to tell her she was right. She looked intently into my face, trying to read my secret thoughts, and if I were absorbed or silent in her presence she thought this was on her account, and was grieved. I always had to be on my guard, and when she asked me whether she was right I hastened to assure her that she was right, and that I had a deep respect for her.

'Do you know they have given me a part at the Azhogins'?' she went on. 'I want to act, I want to live – in fact, I mean to drain the full cup. I have no talent, none, and the part is only ten lines, but still this is immeasurably finer and loftier than pouring out tea five times a day, and looking to see if the cook has eaten too much. Above all, let father see I am capable of protest.'

After tea she lay down on my bed, and lay for a little while with her eyes closed, looking very pale.

'What weakness,' she said, getting up. 'Vladimir says all city-bred women and girls are anaemic from doing nothing. What a clever man Vladimir is! He is right, absolutely right. We must work!'

Two days later she came to the Azhogins' with her exercise-book for the rehearsal. She was wearing a black dress with a string of coral round her neck, and a brooch that in the distance was like a pastry puff, and ear-rings each with a sparkling diamond. When I looked at her I felt uncomfortable: I was struck by the poor taste. That she had inopportunely put on ear-rings and diamonds, and that she was strangely dressed, was noticed by other people too; I saw smiles on people's faces, and heard someone say with a laugh: 'Cleopatra of Egypt.'

She was trying to be sophisticated, natural, and at her ease, and so seemed artificial and strange. She had lost simplicity and sweetness.

'I told father just now that I was going to the rehearsal,' she began, as she came up to me, 'and he shouted that he was withdrawing blessing, and actually almost struck me. Only fancy, I don't know my part,' she said, looking at her exercise-book. 'I'm sure to get it wrong. So be it, the die is cast,' she went on in intense excitement. 'The die is cast . . .'

She thought that everyone was looking at her, and that all were amazed at the momentous step she had taken, that everyone was expecting something special of her, and it was impossible to convince her that no one pays attention to people so petty and insignificant as she and I.

She had nothing to do till the third act, and her part, that of a visitor, a provincial crony, consisted only in standing at the door as though listening, and then delivering a brief monologue. In the interval before her appearance, an hour and a half at least, while they were moving about on the stage reading their parts, drinking tea and arguing, she did not leave my side, and was all the time muttering her part and nervously crumpling up the exercise-book. And imagining that everyone was looking at her and waiting for her to come on, with a trembling hand she smoothed back her hair and said to me:

'I shall get it wrong . . . What a load on my heart, if only you knew! I feel as frightened as if I were being led to execution.'

At last her turn came.

'Kleopatra, you're on!' said the stage manager.

She came forward into the middle of the stage with an expression of horror on her face, looking ugly and angular, and for half a minute stood as though in a trance, perfectly motionless, and only her big ear-rings swung beneath her ears.

'The first time you can read it,' said someone.

It was clear to me that she was trembling, and trembling so much that she could not speak, and could not open her book, and that she was preoccupied with something else; I was already on the point of going up to her and saying something, when she suddenly dropped on her knees in the middle of the stage and broke into loud sobs.

All was commotion and hubbub. I alone stood still, leaning against the wings, overwhelmed by what had happened, not understanding and not knowing what to do. I saw them lift her up and lead her away. I saw Aniuta Blagovo come up to me; I had not seen her in the room before, and she seemed to have sprung out of the earth. She was wearing her hat and veil, and, as always, had an air of having come only for a moment.

'I told her not to act,' she said angrily, uttering each word abruptly and turning crimson. 'It's insanity! You ought to have stopped her!'

Mrs Azhogina, in a short jacket with short sleeves, with cigarette ash on her breast, looking thin and flat, came rapidly towards me.

'My dear, this is terrible,' she said, wringing her hands, and, as was her habit, looking intently into my face. 'This is terrible! Your sister is in a condition . . . She is pregnant. Take her away, please . . .'

She was breathing heavily with agitation, while on one side stood her three daughters, exactly like her, thin and flat, scared, huddling together. They were alarmed, overwhelmed, as though an escaped convict had been caught in their house. What a disgrace, how dreadful! And yet this respected family had spent its life waging war on superstition; evidently they imagined that all humanity's superstition and errors were limited to three candles, the thirteenth of the month, and to Monday being a bad day!

'Please . . . would you,' repeated Mrs Azhogina, pursing up her lips
in the shape of a heart on the syllable 'you'. 'Please would you take
her home.'

XVIII

A little later my sister and I were walking along the street. I covered
her with the skirts of my coat; we hastened, choosing back streets
where there were no street lamps, avoiding passers-by; it was as
though we were running away. She was no longer crying, but looked
at me with dry eyes. To Karpovna's, where I took her, it was only
twenty minutes' walk, and, strange to say, in that short time we
succeeded in thinking of our whole life; we discussed everything,
reviewed our position, reflected . . .

   We decided we could not go on living in this town, and that when I
had earned a little money we would move to some other place. In
some houses everyone was asleep, in others they were playing cards;
we hated these houses; we were afraid of them, and talked of the
fanaticism, the coarseness of feeling, the insignificance of these
respectable families, these drama-lovers whom we had so alarmed,
and I kept asking in what way these stupid, cruel, lazy, and dishonest
people were superior to the drunken and superstitious peasants of
Kurilovka, or in what way they were better than animals, who panic
in the same way when some incident disturbs the monotony of their
life limited by instinct. What would happen to my sister now if she
were left to live at home? What moral agonies would she have
undergone, talking to my father, meeting acquaintances every day? I
imagined all this, and at once I recalled people, all people I knew,
who had been slowly driven to their death by their nearest relations.
I remembered the tortured dogs driven mad, the live sparrows
plucked naked by boys and flung into the water, and a long, long
series of obscure lingering miseries which I had looked on continually from early childhood in that town; and I could not understand
what these sixty thousand people lived for, why they read the
gospels, why they prayed, why they read books and magazines.
What good had they gained from all that had been said and written
hitherto if they were still possessed by the same spiritual darkness
and hatred of liberty as they were a hundred and three hundred
years ago? A master carpenter spends his whole life building houses
in the town, and always, to the day of his death, calls a gallery a
'galdery'. So these sixty thousand people have been reading and
hearing of truth, of justice, of mercy, of freedom for generations, and
yet from morning till night, till the day of their death, they tell lies

from morning to night, torment each other, and fear liberty and hate it like a deadly foe.

'And so my fate is decided,' said my sister, as we arrived home. 'After what has happened I cannot go back *there*. Heavens, how good that is! My heart feels lighter.'

She went to bed at once. Tears were glittering on her eyelashes, but her expression was happy; she fell into a sound sweet sleep, and one could see that her heart was lighter and that she was resting. It was a long, long time since she had slept like that.

And so we began our life together. She was always singing and saying that her life was very happy, and the books I brought her from the public library I took back unread, as she could no longer read; she wanted to do nothing but dream and talk of the future, while she mended my linen, or helped Karpovna at the stove; she was always singing, or talking of her Vladimir, of his cleverness, of his charming manners, of his kindness, of his extraordinary learning, and I assented to all she said, though I no longer liked her doctor. She wanted to work, to lead an independent life on her own account, and she used to say that she would become a school-teacher or a doctor's assistant as soon as her health permitted, and would do her own scrubbing and washing. Already she was passionately devoted to her child; he was not yet born, but she knew already the colour of his eyes, what his hands would be like, and how he would laugh. She was fond of talking about education, and as her Vladimir was the best man in the world, all her discussion of education could be summed up in the question how to make the boy as fascinating as his father. There was no end to her talk, and everything she said made her alive with joy. Sometimes I was joyful, too, not knowing why.

I suppose her dreaminess infected me. I, too, gave up reading, and did nothing but dream. In the evenings, in spite of my fatigue, I walked up and down the room, with my hands in my pockets, talking of Masha.

'What do you think?' I would ask of my sister. 'When will she come back? I think she'll come back at Christmas, not later. What can she do there?'

'As she doesn't write to you it's clear she will come back very soon.'

'That's true,' I agreed, though I knew perfectly well that Masha had no reason to return to our town.

I missed her fearfully, and could no longer deceive myself, and tried to get other people to deceive me. My sister was expecting her doctor, and I – Masha; and both of us talked incessantly, laughed, and did not notice that we were preventing Karpovna from sleeping. She lay on the stove and kept muttering:

'The samovar hummed this morning, it did hum! Oh, it bodes no good, my dears, it bodes no good!'

No one ever came to see us but the postman, who brought my sister letters from the doctor, and Prokofi, who sometimes came in to see us in the evening, and after looking at my sister without speaking went away, and when he was in the kitchen said:

'Every class ought to remember its rules, and anyone who is too proud to understand that will find it a vale of tears.'

He was very fond of the phrase 'a vale of tears'. One day – it was in Christmas week, when I was walking by the bazaar – he called me into the butcher's shop, and not shaking hands with me, announced that he had to speak to me about something very important. His face was red from the frost and vodka; near him, behind the counter, stood Nikolka, with the expression of a brigand, holding a bloody knife in his hand.

'I wish to express my words to you,' Prokofi began. 'This incident cannot exist, because, as you understand yourself that in such a vale of tears, people will say nothing good of you or of us. Mama, through pity of course, cannot say anything unpleasant to you, that your sister should move to another lodgings on account of her condition, but I won't have it any more, because I can't approve of her behaviour.'

I understood him, and I left the shop. The same day my sister and I moved to Radish's. We had no money for a cab, and we walked on foot; I carried a parcel of our belongings on my back; my sister had nothing in her hands, but she gasped for breath and coughed, and kept asking if we should get there soon.

XIX

At last a letter came from Masha.

'Dear, good M.' (she wrote), 'kind, gentle "you, our angel" as the old painter calls you, farewell; I am going with my father to America for the exhibition. In a few days I shall see the ocean so far from Dubechnia, it's dreadful to think! It's as far and unfathomable as the sky, and I long to be there in freedom. I am triumphant, I am raving, and you see how incoherent my letter is. Dear, good one, give me my freedom, make haste to break the thread which still holds, binding you and me together. My meeting and knowing you was a ray from heaven that lit up my existence; but my becoming your wife was a mistake, you understand that, and being aware of that mistake is now a burden to me, and I beg you, on my knees, my generous friend, quickly, quickly, before I start for the ocean, telegraph that you consent to our common mistake being put right, to remove this one stone from my wings, and my father, who will undertake all the arrangements, promises me not to bother you too much with formalities. And so I am free to fly where I will? Yes?

'Be happy, and God bless you; forgive me my sins.

'I am well, I am throwing money about, doing lots of silly things, and I thank God every minute that a bad woman like me has no children. I sing and have success, but it's not an infatuation; no, it's my haven, my cell where I retreat for peace. King David had a ring with an inscription on it: "All things pass." When you're sad those words make you cheerful, and when you're cheerful they make you sad. I have had a ring made like that with Hebrew letters on it, and this talisman keeps me from getting carried away. All things pass, life will pass, you need nothing. Or you need only the feeling of freedom, for when someone is free, he needs nothing, nothing, nothing. Do break the thread. A warm hug to you and your sister. Forgive and forget your M.'

My sister was in bed in one room, and Radish, who had been ill again and was now better, in another. Just at the moment when I received this letter my sister went softly into the painter's room, sat down beside him and began reading aloud. She read to him every day Ostrovsky or Gogol, and he listened, staring at one point, not laughing, but shaking his head and muttering to himself from time to time:

'Anything can happen! Anything can happen!'

If anything ugly or unseemly were depicted in the play he would say, almost vindictively thrusting his finger into the book:

'That's lies for you! That's what they do, lies!'

The plays fascinated him, both their subjects and their moral, and their skilled complex construction, and he marvelled at *him*, never calling the author by name:

'How neatly *he* has put it all together!'

This time my sister read softly only one page, and could read no more: her voice would not hold out. Radish took her hand and, moving his parched lips, said, barely audibly, in a husky voice:

'The soul of a righteous man is white and smooth as chalk but the soul of a sinful man is like pumice stone. The soul of a righteous man is like clear oil, but the soul of a sinful man is coal tar. We must labour, we must sorrow, we must suffer sickness,' he went on, 'and he who does not labour and sorrow will not gain the Kingdom of Heaven. Woe, woe to the well fed, woe to the mighty, woe to the rich, woe to the moneylenders! Not for them is the Kingdom of Heaven. Lice eat grass, rust eats iron . . .'

'And lies eat the soul,' my sister added laughing.

I read the letter through once more. Then into the kitchen walked a soldier who twice a week had been bringing us parcels of tea, French rolls and game, which smelt of scent, from some unknown giver. I had no work. I had to sit at home idle for days on end, and probably whoever sent us these rolls knew that we were in want.

I heard my sister talking to the soldier and laughing merrily. Then, lying down, she ate a roll and said to me:

'When you refused to go into the service, but became a house painter, Aniuta Blagovo and I knew from the start that you were right, but we were frightened to say so aloud. Tell me what force hinders us from saying what we think? Take Aniuta Blagovo now, for instance. She loves you, she adores you, she knows you are right, she loves me too, like a sister, and knows I am right, and I dare say in her soul envies me, but some force prevents her from coming to see us, she avoids us, she is afraid.'

My sister crossed her arms over her breast, and said passionately:

'How she loves you, if only you knew! She has confessed her love to no one but me, and then very secretly in the dark. She led me into a dark avenue in the garden, and began whispering how precious you were to her. You will see, she'll never marry, because she loves you. Are you sorry for her?'

'Yes.'

'It's she who's sent the rolls. She is absurd really, why be so secretive? I used to be absurd and foolish, but now I have left and I'm afraid of nobody. I think and say aloud what I like, and I'm happy. When I lived at home I had no idea of what happiness was, and now I wouldn't change places with a queen.'

Dr Blagovo arrived. He had taken his doctorate, and was now staying in our town with his father; he was taking a rest, and said that he would soon go back to Petersburg again. He wanted to study vaccinations for typhus, and, I believe, cholera; he wanted to go abroad to finish his training, and then to become a professor. He had already left the army, and wore generously cut Cheviot jackets, very wide trousers, and magnificent neckties. My sister was in ecstasies over his tie-pins, his studs, and the red silk handkerchief which he wore, I suppose from foppishness, sticking out of the breast pocket of his jacket. One day, having nothing to do, she and I counted up all the suits we remembered him wearing, and decided that he had at least ten. It was clear that he still loved my sister as before, but he never once even in jest spoke of taking her with him to Petersburg or abroad, and I could not picture to myself clearly what would become of her if she remained alive and what would become of her child. She did nothing but dream endlessly, and never thought seriously of the future; she said he might go where he liked, and might abandon her even, so long as he was happy himself; that what had been was enough for her.

As a rule he used to examine her chest very carefully on his arrival, and used to insist on her taking milk and drops in his presence. It was the same now. He examined her and made her drink a glass of milk, and there was a smell of creosote in our room afterwards.

'There's a good girl,' he said, taking the glass from her. 'You mustn't talk too much now; you've taken to chattering like a magpie of late. Please hold your tongue.'

She laughed. Then he came into Radish's room where I was sitting and affectionately slapped me on the shoulder.

'Well, how goes it, old man?' he said, bending down to the invalid.

'Your Honour,' said Radish, moving his lips slowly, 'your Honour, I venture to report . . . Man proposes, God disposes, we all have to die . . . Let me tell you the truth . . . Your Honour, the Kingdom of Heaven will not be for you!'

'There's nothing for it,' the doctor joked; 'somebody's got to go to hell.'

And all at once something happened to my mind; as though I were in a dream, as though I were standing on a winter night in the slaughter-house yard, and Prokofi beside me, smelling of pepper vodka; I exerted all my willpower, and rubbed my eyes, and straight away I imagined that I was going to see the governor for an interview. Nothing of the sort has happened to me before or since, and these strange memories, that were like dreams, I ascribed to nervous exhaustion. I was reliving the scene at the slaughter-house, and the interview with the governor, and yet was dimly aware that they were not real.

When I came to myself I saw that I was no longer in the house, but in the street, and was standing with the doctor near a lamp-post.

'It's sad, it's sad,' he was saying, and tears were trickling down his cheeks. 'She's in good spirits, she's always laughing and hopeful, but her position is hopeless, dear boy. Your Radish hates me, and is always trying to make me feel that I have treated her badly. He is right from his standpoint, but I have my point of view too; and I shall never regret all that has happened. One must love; we ought all to love – oughtn't we? There would be no life without love; anyone who fears and avoids love is not free.'

Little by little he passed to other subjects, began talking of science, of his dissertation which had gone down well in Petersburg. He was carried away by his subject, and no longer thought of my sister, nor of his grief, nor of me. Life was of absorbing interest to him. She has

America and her ring with the inscription, I thought, while this fellow has his doctorate and a professorship to look forward to, and only my sister and I are left as we were.

When I said good-bye to him, I went up to the lamp-post and read the letter once more. And I remembered, I remembered vividly how that spring morning she had come to me at the mill, lain down and covered herself with her jacket – she wanted to be like a simple peasant woman. And how, another time – it was in the morning also – we drew the net out of the water, and heavy drops of rain fell upon us from the willows on the bank, and we laughed . . .

Our house in Great Dvorianskaia Street was dark. I climbed over the fence and, as I used to do in the old days, went by the back way to the kitchen to borrow a lantern. There was no one in the kitchen. The samovar hissed near the stove, waiting for my father. 'Who pours out father's tea now?' I thought. Taking the lantern I went out to the shed, built myself a bed of old newspapers and lay down. The spikes on the walls looked as forbidding as ever, and their shadows flickered. It was cold. I felt that my sister would come in a minute, and bring me supper, but at once I remembered that she was ill and was lying at Radish's, and it seemed to me strange that I should have climbed over the fence and be lying here in this unheated shed. My mind was bewildered, and I saw all sorts of absurd things.

There was a ring. A ring familiar from childhood: first the wire rustled against the wall, then a short plaintive ring in the kitchen. It was my father back from the club. I got up and went into the kitchen. Aksinia the cook clasped her hands on seeing me, and for some reason burst into tears.

'My own!' she said softly. 'My precious! O Lord!'

And she began crumpling up her apron in her agitation. In the window there were demijohn jars of berries and vodka. I poured myself out a tea-cupful and greedily drank it off, for I was extremely thirsty. Aksinia had quite recently scrubbed the table and benches, and there was that smell in the kitchen which is found in bright, snug kitchens kept by tidy cooks. And that smell and the chirp of the cricket used to lure us as children into the kitchen, and put us in the mood for hearing fairy tales and playing a card-game called 'Kings' . . .

'Where's Kleopatra?' Aksinia asked softly, flustered, holding her breath; 'and where is your hat, my dear? They say your wife has gone to Petersburg?'

She had been our servant in our mother's time, and used once to give Kleopatra and me our baths, and to her we were still children who had to be told off. For a quarter of an hour or so she set out before me all the reflections which she had, with the sagacity of an old servant, been accumulating in the stillness of that kitchen all the time since we had last seen each other. She said that the doctor could be forced to marry Kleopatra; he only needed to be given a fright; and that if an appeal were promptly written the bishop would annul the first marriage; that it would be a good thing for me to sell Dubechnia without my wife's knowing, and put the money in the bank in my own name; that if my sister and I were to bow down at my father's feet and ask him properly, he might perhaps forgive us; that we ought to have a service sung to the Queen of Heaven . . .

'Come, go along, my dear, and speak to him,' she said, when she heard my father's cough. 'Go along, speak to him; bow down, your head won't drop off.'

I went in. My father was sitting at the table sketching a plan of a summer villa, with Gothic windows, and with a fat turret like a fireman's watch tower – something peculiarly stiff and tasteless. Going into the study I stood still where I could see this drawing. I did not know why I had gone in to my father, but I remember that when I saw his scraggy face, his red neck, and his shadow on the wall, I wanted to throw myself on his neck, and as Aksinia had told me, bow down at his feet; but the sight of the summer villa with the Gothic windows and the fat turret restrained me.

'Good evening,' I said.

He glanced at me, and at once dropped his eyes on his drawing.

'What do you want?' he asked, after waiting a little.

'I have come to tell you my sister's very ill. She'll die soon,' I added in a hollow voice.

'Well,' sighed my father, taking off his spectacles, and laying them on the table. 'What thou sowest that shalt thou reap. What thou sowest,' he repeated, getting up from the table, 'that shalt thou reap. Kindly remember how you came to me two years ago, and on this very spot I begged you, I besought you to give up your errors; I reminded you of your duty, of your honour, of what you owed to your forefathers whose traditions we ought to preserve as sacred. Did you obey me? You scorned my counsels, and obstinately persisted in clinging to your false ideas; worse still you drew your sister into the path of error with you, and led her to abandon morality and shame. Now you are both in a bad way. Well, as thou sowest, so shalt thou reap.'

As he said this he walked up and down the room. He probably imagined that I had come to him to confess my wrong-doing, and he probably expected that I should begin begging him on behalf of my sister and myself. I was cold, I was shivering as though I were in a fever, and spoke with difficulty in a hoarse voice.

'And I ask you, too, to remember,' I said, 'on this very spot I begged you to understand me, to reflect, to decide with me how and for what we should live, and in answer you began talking about our forefathers, about my grandfather who wrote poems. You're told now that your only daughter is hopelessly ill, and you go on again about your forefathers, your traditions . . . And such frivolity in your old age, when death is close at hand and you haven't more than five or ten years left!'

'What have you come here for?' my father asked sternly, evidently offended at my reproaching him for his frivolity.

'I don't know. I love you, I am unutterably sorry that we are so far apart – so you see I have come. I love you still, but my sister has broken with you completely. She does not forgive you, and will never forgive you now. Your very name arouses her aversion for the past, for life.'

'And who is to blame for it?' cried my father. 'It's your fault, you scoundrel!'

'Well, suppose it is my fault,' I said. 'I admit I have been to blame in many things, but why is it that this life of yours, which you think binding on us, too – why is it so dreary, so barren? How is it that in not one of these houses you have been building for the last thirty years has there been anyone from whom I might have learnt how to live, so as not to be guilty? There is not one honest man in the whole town! These houses of yours are nests of damnation, where mothers and daughters are made away with, where children are tortured . . . My poor mother!' I went on in despair. 'My poor sister! You'd have to stupefy yourself with vodka, with cards, with scandal; you'd have to become a scoundrel, a hypocrite, or go on drawing plans for years and years, so as not to notice all the horrors that lie hidden in these houses. Our town has existed for hundreds of years, and all that time it has not produced one man of service to our country – not one. You have stifled in the womb everything the least bit alive and bright. It's a town of shopkeepers, innkeepers, counting-house clerks, canting hypocrites; it's a useless, unnecessary town, which not one soul would mourn if it suddenly sank through the earth.'

'I don't want to listen to you, you scoundrel!' said my father, and he picked up his ruler from the table. 'You are drunk. Don't dare come and see your father in such a state! I tell you for the last time – and you can repeat it to your depraved sister – that you'll get nothing from me, either of you. I have torn my disobedient children out of my heart, and if they suffer for their disobedience and obstinacy I do not pity them. You can go whence you came. It has pleased God to punish me with you, but I will bear the trial with resignation, and, like Job, I will find consolation in my sufferings and in unremitting labour. You must not cross my threshold till you have mended your ways. I am a just man, all I tell you is for your benefit, and if you desire your own good you ought to remember all your life what I say and have said to you . . .'

I waved my arm in despair and left. I don't remember what happened afterwards, that night and next day.

I am told that I walked about the streets bare-headed, staggering, and singing aloud, while a crowd of boys ran after me, shouting: 'Better-than-nothing! Better-than-nothing!'

XX

If I felt like ordering a ring for myself, the inscription I should choose would be: 'Nothing passes.' I believe that nothing passes without a trace, and that every step we take, however small, has significance for our present and our future existence.

What I have been through has not been for nothing. My great troubles, my patience, have touched people's hearts, and now they don't call me 'Better-than-nothing', they don't laugh at me, and when I walk by the shops they don't throw water over me. They have grown used to my being a workman, and see nothing strange in my carrying a pail of paint and putting in windows, though I am of noble rank; on the contrary, people are glad to give me orders, and I am now considered a first-rate workman, and the best foreman after Radish, who, though he has regained his health, and though, as before, he paints the cupola on the belfry without scaffolding, no longer has the strength to control the workmen; instead of him I now run about the town looking for work, I engage the workmen and pay them, borrow money at a high rate of interest, and now that I myself am a contractor, I understand how one may have to waste three days racing about the town in search of tilers on account of some ten-kopeck job. People are civil to me, they address me politely, and in the houses where I work, they offer me tea, and send to inquire if I'd like dinner. Children and young girls often come and look back at me with curiosity and sadness.

One day I was working in the governor's garden, painting a gazebo there to look like marble. The governor, walking in the garden, came up to the gazebo and, having nothing to do, started a conversation with me, and I reminded him how he had once summoned me to an interview with him. He looked into my face intently for a minute, then made his mouth like a round O, flung his arms apart, and said: 'I don't remember!'

I have grown older, have become silent, stern, and austere, I rarely laugh, and I am told that I have grown like Radish, and that like him I bore the workmen with my pointless exhortations.

Masha, my former wife, is living now abroad, while her father is constructing a railway somewhere in the eastern provinces, and is buying estates there. Dr Blagovo is also abroad. Dubechnia has passed again into the possession of Mrs Cheprakova, who has bought it after forcing the engineer to knock the price down twenty per cent. Moisei goes about now in a bowler hat; he often drives into the town in a racing chaise on business of some sort, and stops near the bank. They say he has already bought up a mortgaged estate, and is constantly making inquiries at the bank about Dubechnia, which he means to buy too. Poor Ivan Cheprakov was for a long while out of work, staggering about the town and drinking. I tried to get him a job with us, and for a time he painted roofs and put in window-panes with us, and even got to like it, and stole oil, asked for tips, and drank like a regular painter. But he soon got sick of the work, and went back to Dubechnia, and afterwards the workmen confessed to me that he had tried to persuade them to join him one night and murder Moisei and rob Mrs Cheprakova.

My father has greatly aged; he is very bent, and in the evenings walks up and down near his house. I never go to see him.

During an epidemic of cholera Prokofi doctored some of the shopkeepers with pepper vodka and pitch, and took money for doing so, and, as I learned from the newspapers, was flogged for slandering the doctors as he sat in his shop. His shop-boy Nikolka died of cholera. Karpovna is still alive and, as always, she loves and fears her Prokofi. When she sees me, she always shakes her head mournfully, and says with a sigh: 'Your life is ruined.'

On work days I am busy from morning till night. On holidays, in fine weather, I take my tiny niece (my sister reckoned on a boy, but the child is a girl) and walk in a leisurely way to the cemetery. There I stand or sit down, and stay a long time gazing at the grave that is so dear to me, and tell the little girl that her mother lies here.

Sometimes, by the graveside, I find Aniuta Blagovo. We greet each other and stand in silence, or talk of Kleopatra, of her child, of how sad life is in this world; then, leaving the cemetery, we walk along in silence and she slackens her pace on purpose to walk beside me a little longer. The little girl, joyous and happy, pulls at her hand, laughing and screwing up her eyes in the bright sunlight, and we stand still and join in caressing the dear child.

When we reach the town, Aniuta Blagovo, agitated and blushing, says good-bye to me and walks on alone, austere and respectable.

And no one who met her could, looking at her, imagine that she had just been walking beside me and even caressing the child.

1896

Peasants

I

Nikolai Chikildeyev, a waiter in the Moscow hotel, the Slaviansky Bazaar, fell ill. His legs went numb and his gait was affected, so that on one occasion, as he was going along the corridor, he stumbled and fell down with a tray full of ham and peas. He had to leave his job. All his own savings and his wife's were spent on doctors and medicines; they had nothing left to live upon. He felt bored with nothing to do, and he decided he must go home to the village. It is better to be ill at home, and living there is cheaper: the proverbial 'there's no place like home' is true.

He reached his Zhukovo towards evening. In childhood memories he had pictured his home as bright, snug, comfortable. Now going into the hut he was frightened; it was so dark, so crowded, so filthy. His wife Olga and his daughter Sasha, who had come with him, kept looking in bewilderment at the big untidy stove, which took up almost half the hut and was black with soot and flies. What a lot of flies! The stove was crooked, the beams lay askew on the walls, and the hut looked as if it might collapse any moment. In the corner, facing the door, under the icons, bottle labels and newspaper cuttings were stuck on the walls instead of pictures. The poverty, the poverty! No adults were at home; they were all reaping. On the stove sat a white-headed girl of about eight, unwashed and apathetic; she did not even glance at them as they came in. On the floor a white cat was rubbing itself against the oven irons.

'Puss, puss!' Sasha called to her. 'Puss!'

'She can't hear,' said the little girl, 'she has gone deaf.'

'Why?'

'No reason. Someone hit her.'

Nikolai and Olga realised from the first glance what life was like here, but said nothing to one another; in silence they put down their bundles, and went out into the village street. Their hut was the third from the end, and seemed the very poorest and oldest-looking; the second was not much better; but the last one had an iron roof and curtains in the windows. That hut stood apart, not enclosed; it was a tavern. The huts were in a single row, and the whole of the little village – quiet and dreamy, with willows, elders and rowan trees peeping out from the yards – had an attractive look.

Beyond the peasants' smallholdings the land sloped down to the river, so steeply and precipitously that huge stones jutted out, bare here and there through the clay. Down the slope, among the stones and holes dug by the potters, ran winding paths; bits of broken pottery, some brown, some red, lay piled up in heaps, and below there stretched a broad, level, bright green meadow, where the hay had been already carted, and the peasants' cattle had been turned out. The river, with beautiful leafy banks, meandered half a mile from the village; on the other side was another broad meadow, a herd of cattle, long strings of white geese; then, just as on this side, a steep climb, and on the top of the hill a hamlet, and a five-domed church, and a little further a manor house.

'It's lovely here!' said Olga, crossing herself at the sight of the church. 'What space, oh Lord!'

Just at that moment the bell began ringing for service (it was Saturday evening). Two little girls, down below, who were dragging up a pail of water, looked round at the church to listen to the bell.

'At this time they are serving dinner at the Slaviansky Bazaar,' said Nikolai dreamily.

Sitting on the edge of the slope, Nikolai and Olga watched the sun setting, watched the gold and crimson sky reflected in the river, in the church windows, and in the whole air, which was soft, still and inexpressibly pure as it never was in Moscow. And when the sun had set the flocks and herds passed, bleating and lowing; geese flew across from the further side of the river, and all sank into silence; the soft light died away in the air, and the evening darkness quickly began looming.

Meanwhile Nikolai's father and mother, two gaunt, bent, toothless old people, identical in height, came back. The women – the sisters-in-law Maria and Fiokla – who had been working on the landowner's estate beyond the river, arrived home, too. Maria, the wife of Nikolai's brother Kiriak, had six children, and Fiokla the wife of Nikolai's brother Denis, who had gone into the army, had two; and when Nikolai entered the hut, saw all the family, all those bodies big and little moving about on bunks, on hanging cradles and in every corner and when he saw the greed with which the old father and the women ate black bread, dipping it in water, he realised he shouldn't have come here, sick, penniless, and with a family, too – a big mistake!

'And where's Kiriak?' he asked after they had exchanged greetings.

'He works for a merchant,' answered his father, 'a keeper in the woods. He'd be all right, if he didn't knock back the drink.'

'He's no earner!' said the old woman tearfully. 'Our men are useless; they bring nothing into the house, but take plenty out. Kiriak drinks, and so does the old man; it is no use hiding a sin; he knows his way to the tavern. The Queen of Heaven is angry.'

As they had visitors they brought out the samovar. The tea smelt of fish; the sugar was grey and had been nibbled at; cockroaches scurried over the bread and the crockery. It was disgusting to drink and the conversation was disgusting, too – about nothing but poverty and illnesses. But hardly had they drunk a cup each, than there came a loud, prolonged, drunken shout from the yard:

'Ma-aria!'

'Sounds as if Kiriak's coming,' said the old man. 'Talk of the devil.'

Everyone fell silent. And shortly afterwards, the same shout, coarse and drawn-out as though subterranean:

'Ma-aria!'

Maria, the elder sister-in-law, turned pale and clung to the stove, and it was strange to see a scared look on the face of this strong, broad-shouldered, ugly woman. Her daughter, the child who had been sitting on the stove and looked so apathetic, suddenly broke into loud weeping.

'Why are you howling, you plague?' Fiokla, a handsome woman, also strong and broad-shouldered, shouted to her. 'He's not going to kill her.'

From his old father Nikolai learned that Maria was afraid to live in the forest with Kiriak, and that when he was drunk he always came for her, rowed and beat her mercilessly.

'Ma-aria,' the shout resounded right by the door.

'Protect me, for Christ's sake, good people!' faltered Maria, breathing as though she had been plunged into very cold water. 'Protect me, kind people . . .'

All the children in the hut began crying, and looking at them, Sasha, too, began to cry. They heard a drunken cough, and a tall, black-bearded peasant wearing a winter hat came into the hut and was the more terrible because his face could not be seen in the dim light of the little lamp. It was Kiriak. Going up to his wife, he swung his arm and punched her in the face with his fist. Stunned by the blow, she did not utter a sound but sat down, and her nose instantly began bleeding.

'What a disgrace! What a disgrace!' muttered the old man, clambering on to the stove. 'Before visitors, too! What a sin!'

The old mother sat silent, bowed, lost in thought; Fiokla rocked the cradle . . . Evidently conscious of inspiring fear, and pleased at doing so, Kiriak seized Maria by the arm, dragged her towards the door, and bellowed like an animal in order to seem still more terrible, but at that moment he suddenly caught sight of the visitors and stopped.

'Oh, they've come . . .' he said, letting his wife go; 'my brother and his family . . .'

Staggering, opening wide his red, drunken eyes, he prayed to the icon and went on:

'My brother and his family have come to the parental home . . . from Moscow, I suppose. The great capital Moscow, to be sure, the mother of cities . . . I'm sorry . . .'

He sank down on the bench near the samovar and began drinking tea, sipping it loudly from the saucer in the midst of general silence . . . He drank a dozen cups, then reclined on the bench and began snoring.

They started going to bed. Nikolai, as an invalid, was put on the stove with his old father: Sasha lay down on the floor, while Olga went with the women into the barn.

'Aye, aye, dearie,' she said, lying down on the hay beside Maria; 'you won't mend your trouble with tears. Bear it in patience, that is all. It is written in the Scriptures: "If anyone smite thee on the right cheek, offer him the left one also . . ." Aye, aye, dearie!'

Then in a low singsong murmur she told them about Moscow, about her own life, how she had been a chambermaid in furnished lodgings.

'And in Moscow the houses are big, built of brick,' she said, 'and there are ever so many churches, forty times forty, dearie; and they are all gentry in the houses, so handsome and so proper!'

Maria told her that she had never been to her own district town, let alone to Moscow; she could not read or write, and knew no prayers, not even 'Our Father'. Both she and Fiokla, the other sister-in-law, who was sitting a little way off listening, were extremely ignorant and could understand nothing. They both disliked their husbands; Maria was afraid of Kiriak, and whenever he stayed with her she was shaking with fear, and always got a headache from the fumes of vodka and tobacco he reeked of. And in answer to the question whether she did not miss her husband, Fiokla answered with vexation:

'Sod him!'

They talked a little and sank into silence . . .

It was cool, and a cock crowed at the top of his voice near the barn, making it hard to sleep. When the bluish morning light was already peeping through all the crevices, Fiokla got up stealthily and went out, and then they heard the sound of her bare feet running off somewhere.

II

Olga went to church, and took Maria with her. As they went down the path towards the meadow both were in good spirits. Olga liked the wide view, and Maria felt that in her sister-in-law she had someone near and akin. The sun was rising. Low down over the meadow floated a drowsy hawk. The river looked gloomy, there was a haze hovering over it here and there, but on the further bank a streak of light already stretched across the hill. The church was gleaming and in the gentry's garden the rooks were cawing furiously.

'The old man is all right,' Maria told her, 'but Granny is strict; she is continually nagging. Our own grain lasted till Lent. We buy flour now at the tavern. She is angry about it; she says we eat too much.'

'Aye, aye, dearie! Bear it in patience, that is all. It is written: "Come unto Me, all ye that labour and are heavy laden."' Olga spoke sedately, rhythmically, and she walked like a pilgrim woman, with a rapid, fussy step. Every day she read the gospel, read it aloud like a deacon; a great deal of it she did not understand, but the words of the gospel moved her to tears, and words like 'forasmuch as' and 'verily' she pronounced with a sweet flutter at her heart. She believed in God, in the Holy Mother, in the saints; she believed she must not hurt anyone in the world – not simple folks, nor Germans, nor gypsies, nor Jews – and woe even to those who have no compassion for the beasts. She believed this was written in the holy Scriptures, and so, when she pronounced phrases from Holy Writ, even though she did not understand them, her face grew softened, compassionate, and radiant.

'What parts do you come from?' Maria asked.

'I am from Vladimir. Only I was taken to Moscow long ago, when I was eight years old.'

They reached the river. On the far bank a woman was standing at the water's edge, undressing.

'It's our Fiokla,' said Maria, recognising her. 'She's been over the river to the manor yard. To the stewards. She is a shameless hussy and foul-mouthed – terribly!'

Fiokla, young and vigorous as a girl with her black eyebrows and her loose hair, jumped off the bank and began splashing the water with her feet, and waves ran in all directions from her.

'Shameless – terribly!' repeated Maria.

The river was crossed by a rickety little log bridge, and right below it in the clear limpid water was a shoal of broad-headed chub. The dew was glistening on the green bushes that looked into the water. There was a feeling of warmth; it was comforting! What a lovely morning! And how lovely life would have been in this world in all likelihood, if it were not for poverty, horrible, hopeless poverty, from which there is no refuge! One had only to look round at the village to remember vividly all that had happened the day before – and the illusion of happiness which they sensed around them vanished instantly.

They reached the church. Maria stood at the entrance, and did not dare to go further. She did not dare to sit down either. Though they only began ringing for mass after eight, she remained standing the whole time.

While the gospel was being read the crowd suddenly parted to make way for the family from the great house. Two young girls in white frocks and wide-brimmed hats walked in; with them a chubby, rosy boy in a sailor suit. Their appearance touched Olga; she made up her mind from the first glance that they were refined, well-educated, handsome people. Maria looked at them from under her brows, sullenly, dejectedly, as though they were not human beings coming in, but monsters who might crush her if she did not make way for them.

And every time the deacon boomed out something in his bass voice she fancied she heard 'Ma-aria!' and she shuddered.

III

The arrival of the visitors was already known in the village, and directly after mass a number of people gathered together in the hut. The Leonychevs and Matveichevs and the Ilyichovs came to inquire about their relations who were in service in Moscow. All the lads of Zhukovo who could read and write were packed off to Moscow and hired out as butlers or waiters (while from the village on the other side of the river the boys all became bakers), and that had been the custom from the days of serfdom long ago when a certain Luka Ivanych, a peasant from Zhukovo, now a legendary figure, who had been a waiter in one of the Moscow clubs, would take none but his fellow villagers into his service, and found jobs for them in taverns and restaurants; and from that time the village of Zhukovo was always called among the inhabitants of the surrounding districts Khamskaia (Boors' Town) or Kholuevka (Lackeys' Town). Nikolai had been taken to Moscow when he was eleven, and Ivan Makarych, one of the Matveichevs, at that time a head-waiter in the Hermitage garden, had found him a job. And now, addressing the Matveichevs, Nikolai said emphatically:

'Ivan Makarych was my benefactor, and I am duty-bound to pray for him day and night, as thanks to him I have made something of myself.'

'Upon my soul!' a tall old woman, the sister of Ivan Makarych, said tearfully, 'there's not been a sign of life from him, poor dear.'

'In the winter he was in service at Aumont's* and this season there was a rumour he was somewhere out of town, in the pleasure-gardens . . . He has aged! In the old days he would bring home as much as ten roubles a day in the summer time, but now things are very quiet everywhere, the old man's having a hard time.'

The women looked at Nikolai's feet, shod in felt boots, and at his pale face, and said mournfully:

'You're no earner, Nikolai; you're no earner! How could you be?'

And everyone fussed over Sasha. She was ten years old, but she was little and very thin, and might have been taken for no more than seven. Among the other little girls, with their sunburnt faces and roughly cropped hair, dressed in long faded smocks, she, so white, with big dark eyes, with a red ribbon in her hair, looked funny, as though she were some little wild creature that had been caught and brought into the hut.

'She can read, too,' Olga boasted, looking tenderly at her daughter. 'Read a little, child!' she said, taking the gospel from her bundle. 'You read, and the good Christian people will listen.'

The testament was an old and heavy one, dog-eared, bound in leather, and it smelt as though monks had come into the hut. Sasha raised her eyebrows and began in a loud rhythmic chant:

'And the angel of the Lord . . . appeared unto Joseph, saying unto him: "Rise up, and take the Babe and His mother."'

'The Babe and His mother,' Olga repeated, and flushed all over with emotion.

'And flee into Egypt . . . and tarry there until such time as . . .'

At the word 'tarry' Olga could not hold back her tears. Looking at her, Maria began to whimper, and after her Ivan Makarych's sister. The old father cleared his throat, and fussed in search of a treat to give his grand-daughter, but, finding nothing, gave up with a wave of his hand. And when the reading was over the neighbours dispersed to their homes, feeling touched and very pleased with Olga and Sasha.

As it was a holiday, the family spent the whole day at home. The old woman, whom her husband, her daughters-in-law, her grand-children all called Granny, tried to do everything herself; she stoked the stove and lit the samovar with her own hands, even brought the labourers their midday meal, and then complained that she was worn out with work. And all the time she was worried that someone might eat more than they should, or that her husband and daughters-in-law might sit idle. She would hear the innkeeper's geese going round the back to her kitchen garden, and she would run out of the hut with a long stick and spend half an hour screaming shrilly by her cabbages, which were as gaunt and scraggy as herself; at another time she fancied that a crow was stalking her chickens, and she rushed to attack it with loud words of abuse. She was cross and grumbling from morning till night. And often she raised such an outcry that passers-by stopped in the street.

She was harsh to her old man, reviling him as a lazy-bones and a plague. He was an irresponsible, unreliable man, and perhaps if she had not nagged him continually he would not have worked at all, but would have simply sat on the stove and talked. He talked to his son at great length about certain enemies of his, complained of the hurts he said he had to put up with every day from the neighbours, and it was tedious to listen to him.

'Yes,' he would say, standing with his arms akimbo, 'yes . . . A week after the Exaltation of the Cross* I was happy to sell my hay at thirty kopecks a bale . . . Well and good . . . So you see I was taking the hay in the morning with a good will; I wasn't bothering anyone. Then, bad luck, but I see the village elder, Antip Sedelnikov, leaving the inn. "Where are you taking it, you so-and-so?" says he, and punches my ear.'

Kiriak had a fearful headache after his drinking bout, and was ashamed to face his brother.

'What vodka does! Ah, my God!' he muttered, shaking his aching head. 'For Christ's sake, forgive me, brother and sister; I'm paying for it.'

As it was a holiday, they bought a herring at the tavern and made a soup of the herring's head. At midday they all sat down to drink tea, and went on drinking it for a long time, till they were all sweating; they looked swollen with tea, and only then began sipping the soup, eating straight from the pot. But Granny had hidden the herring.

In the evening a potter began firing pots in the ravine. In the meadow below the girls got up a choral dance and sang songs. They played the concertina. And on the other side of the river a kiln for baking pots was lighted, too, and the girls sang songs, and in the distance the singing sounded soft and musical. The peasants were rowdy in and outside the inn. They were singing with drunken voices, all out of tune, and swearing so much that Olga could only shudder and say:

'Oh, holy Saints!'

She was amazed that the abuse never stopped, and the loudest and most persistent in this foul language were the old men so near their end. But the girls and children heard the swearing, and were not in the least bothered by it, and clearly they were used to it from the cradle.

It was past midnight, the kilns on both sides of the river had gone out, but in the meadow below and in the inn the merrymaking still went on. The old father and Kiriak, both drunk, walking arm in arm and jostling each other's shoulders went to the shed where Olga and Maria were lying.

'Let her alone,' the old man persuaded him; 'let her alone . . . She is a harmless woman . . . It's a sin . . .'

'Ma-aria,' shouted Kiriak.

'Let her be . . . It's a sin . . . She is not a bad woman.'

Both stopped by the barn and went on.

'I lo-ove the flowers of the fi-ield,' the old man began singing suddenly in a high, piercing tenor. 'I lo-ove to pick them in the meadows!'

Then he spat, and with a filthy oath went into the hut

IV

Granny put Sasha by her kitchen-garden and told her to stop the geese getting in. It was a hot August day. The innkeeper's geese could get to the kitchen-garden by the backs of the huts, but now they were busy pecking up oats by the inn, peacefully chattering, and only the gander craned his head high as though trying to see if the old woman were coming with her stick. The other geese might come up from below, but they were now grazing far away on the other side of the river, stretched out in a long white garland about the meadow. Sasha stood about a little, got bored, and, seeing that the geese were not coming, went away to the ravine.

There she saw Maria's eldest daughter Motka, who was standing motionless on a gigantic stone, staring at the church. Maria had given birth thirteen times, but only six children survived, all girls, not one boy, and the eldest was eight. Motka in a long smock was standing barefoot in the full glare of the sun; the sun burnt her head, but she did not notice, and seemed as though turned to stone. Sasha stood beside her and said, looking at the church:

'God lives in the church. Men have lamps and candles, but God has little green and red and blue lamps like little eyes. At night God walks about the church, and with Him the Holy Mother of God and Saint Nikolai, thud, thud, thud! . . . And the watchman is terrified, terrified! Aye, aye, dearie!' she added, imitating her mother. 'And when the end of the world comes all the churches will be carried up to heaven.'

'With the-ir be-ells?' Motka asked in her deep voice, drawling every syllable.

'With their bells. And when the end of the world comes the good will go to heaven, but the angry will burn in fire eternal and unquenchable, dearie. To my mother as well as to Maria God will say: "You never hurt anyone, and for that go to the right to heaven"; but to Kiriak and to Granny He will say: "You go to the left into the fire." And anyone who has eaten meat in Lent will go into the fire, too.'

She looked upwards at the sky, opening wide her eyes, and said:

'Look at the sky without winking, you'll see angels.'

Motka began looking at the sky, too, and a minute passed in silence.

'Can you see them?' asked Sasha.

'I can't,' said Motka in her deep voice.

'But I can. Little angels are flying about the sky and flap, flap their little wings like mosquitoes.'

Motka thought for a little, with her eyes on the ground, and asked:

'Will Granny burn?'

'She will, dearie.'

From the stone an even, gentle slope ran down to the bottom, covered with soft green grass which you longed to lie down on or to touch with your hands. Sasha lay down and rolled to the bottom. Motka with a grave, severe face, taking a deep breath, lay down, too, and rolled to the bottom, tearing her smock from hem to shoulder.

'What fun that was!' said Sasha, delighted.

They walked up to the top to roll down again but then they heard a shrill, familiar voice. Oh, how awful it was! Granny, a toothless, bony, hunchbacked figure, with short grey hair fluttering in the wind, was driving the geese out of the kitchen garden with a long stick, shouting:

'They have trampled all the cabbages, the damned brutes! I'd cut your throats, thrice accursed plagues! Hanging's too good for you!'

She saw the little girls, flung down the stick and picked up a switch, and, seizing Sasha by the neck with her fingers, thin and hard as the gnarled branches, began whipping her. Sasha cried with pain and terror, while the gander waddling and stretching his neck, went up to the old woman and hissed at her, and when he went back to his flock all the geese greeted him approvingly 'Ga-ga-ga!' Then Granny began to whip Motka, and Motka's smock was torn again. In despair, crying loudly, Sasha went to the hut to complain. Motka followed her; she, too, was crying on a deeper note, without wiping her tears, and her face was as wet as if it had been dipped in water.

'Holy Saints!' cried Olga, aghast, as the two came into the hut. 'Queen of Heaven!'

Sasha began her story, while Granny walked in with a storm of shrill cries and abuse; then Fiokla flew into a rage, and there was uproar in the hut.

'Never mind, never mind!' Olga, pale and upset, tried to comfort them, stroking Sasha's head. 'She is your grandmother; it's a sin to be angry with her. Never mind, my child.'

Nikolai, who was worn out already by the everlasting shouting, hunger, stifling fumes, filth, who now hated and despised the poverty, who was ashamed for his wife and daughter to see his father and mother, swung his legs off the stove and said in an irritable, tearful voice, addressing his mother:

'You must not beat her! You have no right to beat her!'

'You're kicking the bucket on the stove, wretch!' Fiokla shouted at him spitefully. 'The devil brought you all on us, eating us out of house and home.'

Sasha and Motka and all the little girls in the hut huddled on the stove in the corner behind Nikolai's back, and there listened in silent terror, and their little hearts could be heard beating. When someone in a family has long been hopelessly ill, there are painful moments when all timidly, secretly, at the bottom of their hearts long for his death; and only children fear the death of someone near them, and always feel horror at the thought of it. And now the children, with bated breath, with a mournful look on their faces, gazed at Nikolai and thought about his dying soon; and they wanted to cry and say something friendly and compassionate to him.

He pressed close to Olga, as though seeking protection, and said to her softly in a quavering voice:

'Olga darling, I can't stay here longer. I can't bear it. For God's sake, for Christ's sake, write to your sister Klavdia. Let her sell and pawn everything she has and send us money. We'll leave. Oh, Lord,' he went on miserably, 'to have just a look at Moscow! If I could see it in a dream, Mother Moscow!'

And when the evening came, and it was dark in the hut, it was so dismal that it was hard to utter a word. Granny, ill-tempered, soaked some crusts of rye bread in a cup, and was a long time, a whole hour, sucking at them. Maria, after milking the cow, brought a pail of milk and put it on a bench; then Granny poured it from the pail into jugs just as slowly and deliberately, evidently pleased that it was now the Fast of the Assumption, so that no one would drink milk and it would be untouched. And she only poured out a tiny bit in a saucer for Fiokla's baby. When Maria and she carried the jug down to the cellar

Motka suddenly stirred, climbed off the stove, went to the bench on which stood the wooden bowl full of crusts, and splashed milk from the saucer over it.

Granny, coming back into the hut, sat down to her soaked crusts again, while Sasha and Motka, sitting on the stove, gazed at her, and they were glad that she had broken her fast and now would go to hell. They were comforted and lay down to sleep, and Sasha as she dozed off to sleep imagined the Day of Judgment: a huge stove was burning, like a potter's kiln, and a demon, with horns like a cow's, and black all over, was driving Granny into the fire with a long stick, just as Granny had driven the geese.

v

On the day of the Feast of the Assumption, after ten in the evening, the girls and lads who were merrymaking in the meadow suddenly raised a clamour and outcry, and ran towards the village; and those who were above on the edge of the ravine could not for the first moment make out what was the matter.

'Fire! Fire!' they heard desperate shouts from below. 'We're on fire!'

Those who were sitting above looked round, and a terrible and extraordinary spectacle met their eyes. On the thatched roof of one of the end cottages stood a column of flame, seven feet high, which curled round and scattered sparks in all directions as though it were a fountain. And all at once the whole roof burst into bright flame and you could hear the crackling of the fire.

The light of the moon was dimmed, and the whole village was by now bathed in a red quivering glow: black shadows moved over the ground, there was a smell of burning, and those who ran up from below were all gasping, unable to speak for trembling; they jostled each other, fell down, and could hardly see or recognise each other in the unaccustomed bright light. It was terrible. What was especially dreadful was that doves were flying over the fire in the smoke; and in the inn, where they did not yet know of the fire, there was still singing and a concertina playing, as if nothing was the matter.

'Uncle Semion's on fire,' shouted a loud harsh voice.

Maria was rushing around her hut, weeping and wringing her hands, her teeth chattering, although the fire was a long way off at the other end of the village. Nikolai came out in high felt boots, the children ran out in their little smocks. Near the village constable's hut an iron sheet was struck. 'Boom, boom, boom! . . .' floated through the air, and this repeated, relentless sound was chilling and sent a pang to the heart. The old women stood with the holy icons. Sheep, calves, cows were driven out of the back yards into the street; boxes, sheepskins, tubs were carried out. A black stallion, who was kept apart from the drove of horses because he kicked and injured them, once set free, ran once or twice up and down the village, neighing and pawing the ground; then suddenly stopped short near a cart and began kicking it with his hind legs.

They began ringing the church bells on the other side of the river.

Near the burning hut it was hot and so light that one could distinctly see every blade of grass. Semion, a red-haired peasant with a long nose, wearing a jacket and a cap pulled down right over his ears, sat on one of the boxes which they had managed to drag out: his wife was lying on her face, moaning, semi-conscious. A little old man of eighty, with a big beard, who looked like a gnome – not one of the villagers, though obviously connected in some way with the fire – walked about bare-headed, with a white bundle in his arms. The glare was reflected on his bald head. The village elder, Antip Sedelnikov, as swarthy and black-haired as a gypsy, went up to the hut with an axe, and hacked out the windows one after another – no one knew why – then began chopping up the roof.

'Women, water!' he shouted. 'Bring the engine! Look sharp!'

The peasants, who had been drinking in the inn just before, dragged the engine up. They were all drunk; they kept stumbling and falling down, and all had a helpless expression and tears in their eyes.

'Wenches, water!' shouted the elder, who was drunk, too. 'Look sharp, wenches!'

The women and the girls ran downhill to where there was a spring, and kept hauling pails and buckets of water up the hill, and, pouring it into the engine, ran down again. Olga, Maria, Sasha, and Motka all hauled water. The women and the boys pumped the water, the pipe hissed, and the elder, directing it now at the door, now at the windows, held back the stream with his finger, which made it hiss more sharply still.

'Bravo, Antip!' voices shouted approvingly. 'Keep it up!'

Antip went inside the hut into the fire and shouted from within:

'Pump! Move yourselves, good Christian folk, in such a terrible mischance!'

The peasants stood round in a crowd, doing nothing but stare at the fire. No one knew what to do, no one had the sense to do anything though there were stacks of wheat, hay, sheds and piles of faggots standing around. Kiriak and old Osip, his father, both tipsy, were standing there, too. And as though to justify his idleness, old Osip said, addressing the woman who lay on the ground:

'Why thrash about, old girl? The hut's insured – why bother?'

Semion, turning first to one person and then to another, told them how the fire had started.

'That old man, the one with the bundle, a house-serf of General Zhukov's . . . He was cook at our general's, God rest his soul! He came over this evening: "Let me stay the night," says he . . . Well, we had a glass, to be sure . . . The wife got the samovar – she was going to give the old fellow tea, and, bad luck, she put the samovar in the entrance. The sparks from the pipe must have blown straight up to the thatch; that's how it was. We were almost burnt ourselves. And the old fellow's hat has been burnt: what a shame!'

And the sheet of iron was struck tirelessly, and the bells kept ringing in the church the other side of the river. In the glow of the fire Olga, breathless, looking with horror at the red sheep and the pink doves flying in the smoke, kept running down the hill and up again. It seemed to her that the ringing went to her heart with a sharp stab, that the fire would never be over, that Sasha was lost . . . And when the ceiling of the hut fell in with a crash, the thought that now the whole village would be burnt made her weak and faint, and she could not go on fetching water, but sat down on the edge of the ravine, putting the pail down near her; beside her and below her, the peasant women sat wailing as though at a wake.

Then the foremen and labourers from the estate the other side of the river arrived in two carts, bringing with them a fire-engine. A very young student in an unbuttoned white tunic came on horseback. There was a thud of axes, they put a ladder to the burning framework of the house, and five men ran up it at once. Ahead of them all was the student, who was red in the face and shouting in a harsh, hoarse voice and as though putting out fires was a thing he was used to. They pulled the house to pieces, a beam at a time; they dragged away the corn, the hurdles, and the nearest haystacks.

'Don't let them break it up!' cried stern voices in the crowd. 'Don't let them.'

Kiriak made his way up to the hut with a resolute air, as though he meant to prevent the newcomers from breaking up the hut, but one of the workmen turned him back with a blow in his neck. There was the sound of laughter, the workmen dealt him another blow, Kiriak fell down, and crawled back into the crowd on all fours.

Two handsome girls in hats, probably the student's sisters, came from the other side of the river. They stood a little way off, looking at the fire. The beams that had been dragged off were no longer burning, but were smoking vigorously; the student, who was working the hose, turned the water, first on the beams, then on the peasants, then on the women who were bringing the water.

'George!' the girls called to him reproachfully in anxiety, 'George!'

The fire was over. And only when they began to disperse they noticed that day was breaking, that everyone was pale and rather dark in the face, as it always seems in the early morning when the last stars are going out. As they went home, the peasants laughed and made jokes about General Zhukov's cook and his burnt hat; they now wanted to make a joke of the fire, and even seemed sorry that it was over so soon.

'How well you put out the fire, Sir!' said Olga to the student. 'You ought to come to us in Moscow: there we have a fire every day.'

'Why, do you come from Moscow?' asked one of the young ladies.

'Yes, Miss. My husband was a waiter at the Slaviansky Bazaar. And this is my daughter,' she said, pointing to Sasha, who was cold and huddling up to her. 'She's a Moscow girl, too.'

The two young ladies said something in French to the student, and he gave Sasha a twenty kopeck piece.

Old Osip saw this, and there was a gleam of hope in his face.

'We must thank God, your Honour, there was no wind,' he said, addressing the student, 'or else we should have been all burnt up together. Your Honour, kind gentlefolk,' he added in embarrassment in a lower tone, 'It's a chilly morning, something to warm me up . . . half a bottle to your Honour's health.'

He got nothing, and clearing his throat he slouched home. Olga stood afterwards at the end of the street and watched the two carts crossing the river by the ford and the gentlefolk walking across the meadow; a carriage was waiting for them the other side of the river. Going into the hut, she told her husband with delight:

'Such good people! And so beautiful! The young ladies were like cherubim.'

'Plague take them!' Fiokla, sleepy, said spitefully.

VI

Maria considered herself unhappy, and said that she wanted very much to die; Fiokla, on the other hand, found all this life to her taste; the poverty, the filth, and the incessant rowing. She ate what she was given without interest; slept anywhere, on whatever came to hand. She would empty the slops right by the porch, would splash them out from the doorway, and then walk barefoot through the puddle. And from the very first day she took a dislike to Olga and Nikolai just because they did not like this life.

'We shall see what you eat here, you Moscow gentry!' she said malevolently. 'We shall see!'

One morning – it was at the beginning of September – Fiokla, vigorous, good-looking, and rosy from the cold, brought up two pails of water; Maria and Olga were sitting at the table drinking tea.

'Tea and sugar,' said Fiokla sarcastically. 'Fine ladies!' she added, setting down the pails. 'You have taken to the fashion of tea every day. You'd better look out that tea doesn't make you burst,' she went on, looking with hatred at Olga. 'That's how you got your fat mug in Moscow, you lump of flesh!' She swung the yoke and hit Olga such a blow on the shoulder that the two sisters-in-law could only clasp their hands and say:

'Oh, holy Saints!'

Then Fiokla went down to the river to wash the clothes, swearing all the time so loudly that she could be heard in the hut.

The day passed. A long autumn evening came. They wound silk in the hut; everyone did it except Fiokla; she had gone over the river. They got the silk from a factory close by, and the whole family working together earned next to nothing, twenty kopecks a week.

'Things were better in the old days under the gentry,' said the old father as he wound silk. 'You worked and ate and slept, everything in its turn. At dinner you had cabbage soup and boiled grain, and at supper the same again. Cucumbers and cabbage in plenty: you could eat to your heart's content, as much as you wanted. And there was more strictness. Everyone knew his place.'

The hut was lit by a single little lamp, which burned dimly and smoked. When someone screened the lamp and a big shadow fell across the window, the bright moonlight could be seen. Old Osip, speaking slowly, told them how they used to live before the emancipation; how in those very parts, where life was now so poor and so dreary, they used to hunt with harriers, greyhounds, with trios of beaters, and when they went out to help the beaters the peasants were given vodka; how whole wagon loads of game used to be sent to Moscow for the young masters; how the bad were beaten with rods or sent away to the Tver estate while the good were rewarded. And Granny told them a few things, too. She remembered everything, positively everything. She talked about her mistress, a kind, God-fearing woman, whose husband was a profligate and a rake, and all of whose daughters made bad marriages: one married a drunkard, another married a townsman, the other eloped secretly (Granny herself, at that time a young girl, helped in the elopement), and all three, like their mother, had died early from grief. And remembering all this Granny actually began to shed tears.

Suddenly someone knocked at the door, and they all started.

'Uncle Osip, let me stay the night.'

The little bald old man, General Zhukov's cook, the one whose hat had been burnt, walked in. He sat down and listened, then he, too, began telling stories of all sorts. Nikolai, sitting on the stove with his legs hanging down, listened and asked questions about the dishes that were prepared in the old days for the gentry. They talked of rissoles, cutlets, various soups and sauces, and the cook, who remembered everything very well, mentioned dishes that are no longer served. There was one, for instance – a dish made of bulls' eyes, which was called 'waking up in the morning'.

'And did you do cutlets *Maréchal*?' asked Nikolai.

'No.'

Nikolai shook his head reproachfully and said:

'Oh, you misery of a cook!'

The little girls sitting and lying on the stove stared down without blinking; it seemed as if they were a great many of them, like cherubim in the clouds. They liked the stories: they were breathless; they shuddered and turned pale with alternate rapture and terror, and they listened breathlessly, afraid to stir, to Granny, whose stories were the most interesting of all.

They lay down to sleep in silence; and the old people, troubled and excited by their reminiscences, thought how precious was youth, of which, whatever it might have been like, nothing was left in the memory but what was alive, joyful, touching, and how terribly cold was death, which was not far off – better not think of it! The lamp died down. And the dusk, and the two little windows sharply defined by the moonlight, and the stillness and the creak of the cradle, reminded them for some reason that life was over, that nothing one could do would bring it back . . . You doze off, you forget yourself, and suddenly someone touches your shoulder or breathes on your cheek – and sleep is gone; your body feels cramped, and thoughts of death keep creeping into your mind. You turn on the other side: death is forgotten, but old dreary, sickening thoughts of poverty, of food, of how dear flour is getting, stray through the mind, and a little later again you remember that life is over and you cannot bring it back . . .

'Oh Lord!' sighed the cook.

Someone gave a soft, soft tap at the window. Fiokla must have come back. Olga got up, and yawning and whispering a prayer, opened the door, then drew the bolt in the outer room, but no one came in; only from the street came a cold draught and a sudden brightness from the moonlight. The street, still and deserted, and the moon itself floating across the sky, could be seen at the open door.

'Who is there?' called Olga.

'Me,' she heard the answer – 'it's me.'

Near the door, crouching against the wall, stood Fiokla, absolutely naked. She was shivering with cold, her teeth were chattering, and in the bright moonlight she looked very pale, strange, and beautiful. The shadows on her, and the bright moonlight on her skin, stood out vividly, and her dark eyebrows and firm, youthful bosom were outlined with peculiar sharpness.

'The ruffians over there stripped me and turned me out like this,' she said. 'I walked home without my clothes . . . naked as a baby. Bring me something to put on.'

'Come inside!' Olga said softly, beginning to shiver, too.

'I don't want the old folks to see.' Granny was, in fact, already stirring and muttering, and the old father asked: 'Who is there?' Olga brought her own smock and skirt, dressed Fiokla, and then both went softly into the hut trying not to bang the door.

'Is that you, you tart?' Granny grumbled angrily, guessing who it was. 'To hell with you, slut! . . . Hanging's too good for you!'

'It's all right, it's all right,' whispered Olga, wrapping Fiokla up; 'it's all right, dearie.'

All was stillness again. They always slept badly; everyone was kept awake by something worrying and persistent: the old man by the pain in his back, Granny by anxiety and anger, Maria by terror, the children by scabies and hunger. Now, too, their sleep was troubled; they kept turning over from one side to the other, talking in their sleep, getting up for a drink.

Fiokla suddenly broke into a loud, coarse howl, but immediately checked herself, and only uttered sobs from time to time, growing softer and on a lower note, until she lapsed into silence. From time to time from the other side of the river there floated the sound of a watchman beating the hours; but the timing was odd – five was struck and then three.

'Oh Lord!' sighed the cook.

Looking at the windows it was difficult to tell whether it was still moonlight or whether the dawn had begun. Maria got up and went out, and she could be heard milking the cow and saying, 'Steady!' Granny went out, too. It was still dark in the hut, but all the objects were now visible.

Nikolai, who had not slept all night, got down from the stove. He took his dress-coat out of a green box, put it on, and going to the window stroked the sleeves and took hold of the coat-tails – and smiled. Then he carefully took off the coat, put it away in his box, and lay down.

Maria came back and began stoking the stove. She was clearly barely awake, and was dropping asleep as she walked. Probably she had dreamt something, or recalled the stories of the night before, as stretching luxuriously before the stove, she said:

'No, freedom is better.'

VII

The master arrived – that was what they called the police inspector. When and why he was coming had been known for a week. There were only forty households in Zhukovo, but over two thousand roubles of arrears of rates and taxes had accumulated.

The police inspector stopped at the tavern. He drank there two glasses of tea, and then went on foot to the village elder's hut, near which a crowd of men in arrears stood waiting. The elder, Antip Sedelnikov, was, in spite of his youth – he was only just over thirty – strict and always on the side of the authorities, though he himself was poor and did not pay his taxes regularly. Evidently he enjoyed being elder and liked the sense of authority, which he could only display by strictness. In the village council the peasants were afraid of him and obeyed him. It would sometimes happen that he would pounce on a drunken man in the street or near the tavern, tie his hands behind him, and put him in the lock-up. On one occasion he even put Granny in the lock-up because, attending the village council instead of Osip, she began swearing, and he kept her there for a whole day and night. He had never lived in a town or read a book, but somewhere or other had picked up various learned expressions and loved to use them in conversation, and for this he was respected, though not always understood.

When Osip came into the village elder's hut with his tax book, the police inspector, a lean old man with a long grey beard, in a grey double-breasted jacket, was sitting at a table in the passage, writing something. It was clean in the hut; all the walls were dotted with pictures cut out of the illustrated papers, and in the most conspicuous place near the icon there was a portrait of Battenberg, the ex-King of Bulgaria. By the table stood Antip Sedelnikov with his arms folded.

'He has one hundred and nineteen roubles outstanding,' he said when it was Osip's turn. 'Before Easter he paid a rouble, and he has not paid a kopeck since.'

The police inspector raised his eyes to Osip and asked:

'Why is this, brother?'

'Show Divine mercy, your Honour,' Osip began, growing agitated. 'Allow me to say, last year the gentleman at Liutoretsk said to me,

"Osip," he said, "sell your hay . . . You sell it," he said. Why? I had about a hundred bales for sale. The women mowed it on the water meadow. Well we agreed a price . . . Everything was fine, agreed . . .'

He complained of the elder, and kept turning round to the peasants as if inviting them to be witnesses; his face was flushed and sweaty and his eyes sharp and angry.

'I don't know why you are saying all this,' said the police inspector. 'I am asking you . . . I am asking you why you don't pay your arrears. None of you pays, and am I to be answerable for you?'

'I can't do it.'

'His words have no sequel, your Honour,' said the elder. 'The Chikildeyevs certainly are of a defective class, but if you ask the others, the root of it all is vodka, and they are bad troublemakers. With no sort of understanding.'

The police inspector wrote something down and said to Osip quietly, in an even tone, as though he were asking him for water:

'Get out.'

Soon he went away; and when he got into his cheap chaise and cleared his throat, it could be seen from the very expression of his long thin back that he was no longer thinking of Osip or of the village elder, nor of the Zhukovo arrears but was thinking of his own affairs. Before he had gone three-quarters of a mile Antip was carrying off the samovar from the Chikildeyevs' hut, followed by Granny, screaming shrilly, straining her chest:

'I won't let you have it, I won't let you have it, you heathen!'

He walked rapidly with long steps, and she pursued him panting, almost falling over, a bent, ferocious figure; her kerchief slipped on to her shoulders, her grey hair, shot with a greenish tint, was blown about in the wind. She suddenly stopped short, and like a real peasant rebel, fell to beating her breast with her fists and shouting louder than ever in a sing-song voice, like sobbing:

'Good Christians and believers! Neighbours, they've done me wrong! Kind friends, they have robbed me! Oh, oh! good people, help me.'

'Old woman, old woman,' said the village elder sternly, 'have some judgment in your head!'

It was hopelessly dreary in the Chikildeyevs' hut with no samovar; there was something degrading in this loss, insulting, as though the hut had lost its honour. Better if the elder had carried off the table, all the benches, all the pots – it would not have seemed so empty. Granny screamed, Maria cried, and the little girls, looking at her, cried, too. The old father, feeling guilty, sat in the corner with bowed head and said nothing. And Nikolai, too, was silent. Granny loved him and was sorry for him, but now, forgetting her pity, she fell upon him with abuse, with reproaches, shaking her fist right in his face. She shouted that it was all his fault; why had he sent them so little when he boasted in his letters that he was getting fifty roubles a month at the Slaviansky Bazaar? Why had he come, and with his family, too? If he died where was the money to come from for his funeral . . . ? And it was pitiful to look at Nikolai, Olga, and Sasha.

The old father cleared his throat, took his hat, and went to see the elder. Antip was soldering something by the stove, puffing out his cheeks; the air was full of fumes. His children, emaciated and unwashed, no better than the Chikildeyevs, were scrambling about the floor; his wife, an ugly, freckled woman with a big belly, was winding silk. They were a poor, unlucky family, and Antip was the only one who looked vigorous and handsome. On a bench there were five samovars standing in a row. The old man said his prayer to Battenberg and said:

'Antip, show Divine mercy. Give me back the samovar, for Christ's sake!'

'Bring three roubles, then you shall have it.'

'I can't do it!'

Antip puffed out his cheeks, the fire roared and hissed, and the glow was reflected in the samovar. The old man kneaded his hat and said after a moment's thought:

'Give it back.'

The swarthy elder looked quite black, and was like a magician, he turned round to Osip and said sternly and rapidly:

'It all depends on the rural captain. On the twenty-sixth instant you can state the grounds for your dissatisfaction before the administrative session, verbally or in writing.'

Osip did not understand a word, but he let it pass and went home.

Ten days later the police inspector came again, stayed an hour and went away. During those days the weather had changed and it had grown cold and windy; the river had been frozen for some time past, but still there was no snow, and people found it difficult to get about. On a holiday evening some neighbours came in to Osip's to sit and have a talk. They talked in the darkness and did not light the lamp as it would have been a sin to work. There was news, rather unpleasant. In two or three households hens had been taken for the arrears, and had been sent to the district police station, and there they had died because no one had fed them; they had taken sheep, and while they were being driven away tied to one another, shifted into another cart at each village, one had died. And now they were deciding who was to blame.

'The rural council,' said Osip. 'Who else?'

'Of course it's the council.'

The council was blamed for everything – for the arrears, and for the oppressions, and for the failure of the crops, though no one of them knew what was meant by the *zemstvo* or rural district council. And this dated from the time when well-to-do peasants who had factories, shops, and inns of their own became councillors,* were dissatisfied with them, and took to cursing the councils in their factories and inns.

They talked of God's not sending the snow; they had to bring in wood for fuel, and there was no driving nor walking in the frozen ruts. In the old days fifteen to twenty years ago conversation was much more interesting in Zhukovo. In those days every old man looked as though he were treasuring some secret; as though he knew something and was expecting something. They used to talk about an edict in golden letters, about the division of lands, about new land, about treasures; they hinted at something. Now the people of Zhukovo had no mystery at all; their whole life was only too clear and bare and they could talk of nothing but poverty, food, of the lack of snow.

There was a pause. Then they recalled the hens, the sheep, and began deciding whose fault it was.

'The council,' said Osip sadly. 'Who else?'

VIII

The parish church was four miles away at Kosogorovo, and the peasants only attended it when they had to for baptisms, weddings, or funerals; for prayers they went to the church across the river. On holidays in fine weather the girls dressed up in their best and went in a crowd together to church, and it was a cheering sight to see them in their red, yellow and green dresses cross the meadow; in bad weather they all stayed at home. They went for the Easter sacrament to the parish church. From each of those who did not manage in Lent to go to confession in readiness for the sacrament the parish priest, going the round of the huts with the cross at Easter, took fifteen kopecks.

The old father did not believe in God, for he hardly ever thought about Him; he recognised the supernatural, but considered it only affected women, and when religion or miracles were discussed before him, or a question were put to him, he would say reluctantly, scratching:

'Who can tell!'

Granny believed, but her faith was somewhat hazy; everything was mixed up in her memory, and she could scarcely begin to think of sins, of death, of the salvation of the soul, before poverty and her daily cares took possession of her mind, and she instantly forgot what she was thinking about. She could not remember the prayers, and usually in the evenings, before lying down to sleep, she would stand before the icons and whisper:

'Holy Mother of Kazan, Holy Mother of Smolensk, Holy Mother of Troeruchitsa . . .'

Maria and Fiokla crossed themselves, fasted, and took the sacrament every year, but understood nothing. The children were taught no prayers, learnt nothing about God, and no moral principles were instilled into them; they were only forbidden to eat meat or milk in Lent. In the other families it was much the same; few believed, few understood. At the same time everyone loved the holy Scripture, loved it with a tender, reverent love; but they had no Bible, there was no one to read it and explain it, and because Olga sometimes read them the gospel, they respected her, and they all addressed her and Sasha formally, as though superiors.

For church holidays and services Olga often went to neighbouring villages, and to the district town, in which there were two monasteries and twenty-seven churches. She was dreamy, and when she was on these pilgrimages she quite forgot her family, and only when she got home again suddenly made the joyful discovery that she had a husband and daughter, and then would say, smiling and radiant:

'God has sent me blessings!'

What went on in the village revolted and tormented her. On Elijah's day they drank, at the Assumption they drank, at the Exaltation of the Cross they drank. The Feast of the Protective Veil* was the parish holiday for Zhukovo, and the peasants used to drink then for three days; they squandered on drink fifty roubles of community money, and then collected more for vodka from all the households. On the first day of the feast the Chikildeyevs killed a sheep and ate mutton morning, noon, and evening; they ate it ravenously, and the children got up at night to eat more. Kiriak was fearfully drunk for three whole days; he spent everything, even his boots and hat, on drink, and beat Maria so badly that they had to pour water over her. And then they were all ashamed and sick.

However, even in Zhukovo, in this 'Lackeys' Town', there was one outburst of genuine religious enthusiasm. It was in August, when throughout the district they carried from village to village the Holy Mother, the giver of life. It was still and overcast on the day when they expected Her at Zhukovo. The girls set off in the morning to meet the icon, in their bright holiday dresses, and brought Her towards the evening, in procession with the cross and with singing, while the bells pealed in the church across the river. An immense crowd of villagers and strangers flooded the street; there was noise, dust, a great crush . . . And the old father and Granny and Kiriak – all stretched out their hands to the icon, looked eagerly at it and said, weeping:

'Defender! Mother! Defender!'

All seemed suddenly to realise that there was not a void between earth and heaven, that the rich and the powerful had not grabbed everything, that there was still a refuge from injury, from slavish bondage, from crushing, unendurable poverty, from the terrible vodka.

'Defender! Mother!' sobbed Maria. 'Mother!'

But the thanksgiving service ended and the icon was carried away, and everything went on as before; and again coarse drunken voices resounded from the inn.

Only the well-to-do peasants were afraid of death; the richer they were the less they believed in God, and in the redemption of souls, and only through fear of their mortal end offered candles and had services said, to be on the safe side. The poorer peasants were not afraid of death. The old father and Granny were told to their faces that they had lived too long, that it was time they were dead, and they did not mind. They did not mind telling Fiokla in Nikolai's presence that when Nikolai died her husband Denis would get exemption – to come home from the army. And Maria, far from fearing death, regretted that it was so slow in coming, and was glad when her children died.

Death they did not fear, but of every disease they had an exaggerated terror. The merest trifle was enough – a stomach upset, a slight chill, and Granny would be wrapped up on the stove, and would begin moaning loudly and incessantly: 'I am dying!' The old father hurried off for the priest, and Granny received the sacrament and extreme unction. They often talked of colds, of worms, of tumours which move in the stomach and coil round to the heart. Above all, they were afraid of catching cold, and so put on thick clothes even in the summer, and warmed themselves at the stove. Granny was fond of being doctored, and often went to the hospital, where she used to say she was not seventy, but fifty-eight; she supposed that if the doctor knew her real age he would not treat her, but would say it was time she died instead of taking medicine. She usually went to the hospital early in the morning, taking with her two or three of the little girls, and came back in the evening, hungry and ill-tempered – with drops for herself and ointments for the little girls. Once she took Nikolai, who took drops for a fortnight afterwards, and said he felt better.

Granny knew all the doctors and their assistants and the wise men for twenty miles round, and not one of them she liked. At the Intercession when the priest made the round of the huts with the cross, the deacon told her that in the town near the prison lived an old man who had been a medical orderly in the army, and who was very good, and advised her to try him. Granny took his advice. When the first snow fell she drove to the town and fetched an old man with a big beard, a converted Jew, in a long gown, whose face was covered with blue veins. There were journeymen at work in the hut at the time: an old tailor, in terrible spectacles, was making a waistcoat out of rags, and two young men were making felt boots out of wool; Kiriak, who had been dismissed from his place for drunkenness, and now lived at home, was sitting beside the tailor mending a bridle. And it was crowded, stifling, and noisome in the hut. The converted Jew examined Nikolai and said that it was necessary to try cupping.

He put on the cups, and the old tailor, Kiriak, and the little girls stood round and looked on and it seemed to them that they saw the disease being drawn out of Nikolai; and Nikolai, too, watched how the cups suckling at his breast gradually filled with dark blood, and felt as though there really were something coming out of him, and smiled with pleasure.

'It's a good thing,' said the tailor. 'God grant it does you good.'

The Jew put on twelve cups and then another twelve, drank some tea, and went away. Nikolai began shivering; his face looked drawn, and, as the women put it, shrank into a fist; his fingers turned blue. He wrapped himself up in a quilt and in a sheepskin, but got colder and colder. Towards the evening he began to be distressed; asked to be laid on the ground, asked the tailor not to smoke; then he subsided under the sheepskin and towards morning he died.

IX

Oh, what a grim, long winter!

Their own grain ran out before Christmas, and they were buying flour. Kiriak, who lived at home now, was rowdy in the evenings, terrifying everyone; and in the mornings he had agonising headaches and shame; and he was a pitiful sight. In the stall the starving cow bellowed day and night – a heart-rending sound to Granny and Maria. And as ill luck would have it, there was a sharp frost all the winter, the snow drifted in high heaps, and the winter dragged on. At

Annunciation* there was a real blizzard, and there was snow at
Easter.

But in spite of it all the winter did end. At the beginning of April
there came warm days and frosty nights. Winter would not give way,
but one warm day overpowered it at last, and the streams began to
flow and the birds began to sing. The whole meadow and the bushes
near the river were drowned in the spring floods, and all the space
between Zhukovo and the further side was filled up with a vast sheet
of water, from which wild ducks rose up in flocks here and there. The
spring sunset, flaming among gorgeous clouds, gave every evening
something new, extraordinary, incredible – just what one does not
believe in afterwards, when one sees those very colours and those
very clouds in a picture.

The cranes flew very swiftly, with mournful cries, as though they
were calling others to join them. Standing on the edge of the ravine,
Olga looked a long time at the flooded meadow, at the sunshine, at
the bright church, that looked as though it had grown younger; and
her tears flowed and her breath came in gasps from her passionate
longing to leave, to go far away to the edge of the world. It was
already settled that she should go back to Moscow to be a
chambermaid and that Kiriak should set off with her to get a job as a
porter or something. Oh, the quicker the better!

As soon as it dried up and grew warm they got ready to set off. Olga
and Sasha, with satchels on their backs and shoes of plaited bark on
their feet, came out before daybreak; Maria came out, too, to see
them off. Kiriak was not well, and stayed at home for another week.
For the last time Olga prayed at the church and thought of her
husband, and though she did not shed tears, her face puckered up and
looked ugly like an old woman's. During the winter she had grown
thinner and plainer, and her hair had gone a little grey, and instead of
the old look of sweetness and the pleasant smile on her face, she had
the resigned, mournful expression left by the sorrows she had been
through, and there was something blank and still in her eyes, as
though she did not hear what was said. She was sorry to part from the
village and the peasants. She remembered how they had carried out
Nikolai, and how a requiem had been ordered for him at almost every
hut, and all had shed tears in sympathy with her grief. In the course of
the summer and the winter there had been hours and days when it
seemed as though these people lived worse than the beasts, and to live
with them was terrible; they were coarse, dishonest, filthy, and
drunken; they did not live in harmony, but quarrelled continually,
because they distrusted and feared and did not respect one another.
Who keeps the inn and makes the people drunken? A peasant. Who

wastes and spends on drink the community, school, and church funds? A peasant. Who stole from his neighbours, set fire to their property, gave false witness at the court for a bottle of vodka? At the meetings of the council and other local bodies, who was the first to rail against the peasants? A peasant. Yes, to live with them was terrible, but yet they were human, they suffered and wept like human beings, and there was nothing in their lives for which one could not find excuse. Hard labour that made the whole body ache at night, the cruel winters, the scanty harvests, the overcrowding, and no help and no expectation of help. Those who were stronger and better off could be no help, as they were themselves coarse, dishonest, drunken, and abused one another just as revoltingly; the paltriest little clerk or official treated the peasants as though they were tramps, and addressed even the village elders and churchwardens as inferiors, and considered they had a right to do so. And, indeed, can any sort of help or good example be given by mercenary, greedy, depraved, and idle persons who raided the village only to insult, to cheat and to frighten? Olga remembered the pitiful, humiliated look of the old people when in the winter Kiriak had been taken to be flogged . . . And now she felt sorry for all these people, painfully so, and as she walked on she kept looking back at the huts.

After walking two miles with them Maria said good-bye, then kneeling, and falling forward with her face on the earth, she began wailing:

'Again I'm alone. Alas, poor me! poor, unhappy me!'

And she wailed like this for a long time, and for a long way Olga and Sasha could still see her on her knees, bowing down to someone at the side and clutching her head in her hands, while the rooks flew over her head.

The sun rose high; it began to get hot. Zhukovo was left far behind. Walking was pleasant. Olga and Sasha soon forgot both the village and Maria; they were merry and everything entertained them. Now they came upon an ancient barrow, now upon a row of telegraph posts running one after another into the distance and disappearing into the horizon, and the wires hummed mysteriously. Then they saw a homestead, all wreathed in green foliage; there came a scent from it of dampness, of hemp, and it seemed for some reason that happy people lived there. Then they came upon a horse's skeleton whitening in solitude in the open fields. And the larks trilled unceasingly, the quails called to one another, and the landrail cried as though someone were really scraping at an old iron rail.

At midday Olga and Sasha reached a big village. There in the broad street they met the little old man who had been General Zhukov's cook. He was hot, and his red, sweaty bald head shone in the sunshine. Olga and he did not recognise each other, then looked round at the same moment, recognised each other, and went their separate ways without saying a word. Stopping near the hut which looked newest and most prosperous, Olga bowed down before the open windows, and said in a loud, thin, chanting voice:

'Good Christian folk, give alms, for Christ's sake, that God's blessing may be upon you, and that your parents may be in the Kingdom of Heaven in peace eternal.'

'Good Christian folk,' Sasha began chanting, 'give, for Christ's sake, that God's blessing, the Heavenly Kingdom . . .'

X

Olga's sister Klavdia lived in Moscow, in a lane near Patriarch's Ponds, in a two-storey wooden house. The ground floor was a laundry, while the entire upper floor was leased by an old maid, a gentlewoman, quiet and modest, whose income came from renting out rooms. You entered into a dark lobby, with two doors, one to the left and one to the right: one of them led to a little room where Klavdia lived, the other was rented to a typesetter. Then there was a living room, with a divan, arm-chairs, a lamp and lampshade, pictures on the walls – everything proper, except that it smelt of linen and steam that came from the laundry, and all day long you could hear singing. The living room was common to all the tenants and three flats led off it; the landlady's, the flat of the old footman Ivan Makarych from Zhukovo, who had once upon a time found Nikolai his job; a big barn lock was attached by rings to his white, thumb-stained door; the third door led to the flat of a young, lanky, sharp-eyed woman with thick lips who had three children who never stopped crying. A monastery priest visited her on feast days, she walked around all day wearing just a skirt, unwashed, her hair uncombed, but when she was expecting her priest she would put on a fine silk dress and curl her hair.

Klavdia, as they say, didn't have room to swing a cat. She had a bedstead, a chest of drawers, a chair and nothing else – and it was still cramped. Nevertheless, the room was kept tidy and Klavdia called it her boudoir. She was extremely happy with her surroundings, especially with the things on her chest of drawers: a mirror, powder, little bottles, lipstick, little boxes, ceruse, and all the luxuries which she considered essential attributes of her profession and on which she spent almost all her earnings; she also had framed photographs showing her in various poses. There was a picture of her with her husband, a postman, with whom she had lived for only a year before leaving him, since she felt no vocation for family life; she had been photographed, like most women of her kind, with a fringe curled like a lamb's forelock, in a soldier's uniform with a drawn sabre, as a page astride a chair, which made her thighs, clad in tight fitting wool, lie flat across the chair like two thick boiled sausages. There were male portraits too – she called them her visitors and could not put a name to all of them; our Kiriak, as a relative, was among them: he had been photographed full height in a black suit which he had managed to borrow for a short while.

Klavdia had once gone to masked balls and to Filippov's pastry shop and spent whole evenings on Tverskaia Boulevard; as the years passed she gradually became a stay-at-home and now that she was forty-two years old she very rarely had visitors; just a few from old times who went to see her out of loyalty; they too had, alas, aged and visited her more rarely, because there were fewer of them each year. There was only one new visitor, a very young man with no moustaches; he entered the lobby quietly, sullen as a conspirator, turning up the collar of his school coat and trying not to be seen from the living-room, and then, as he went, he left a rouble on the chest of drawers.

Klavdia spent whole days at home doing nothing; sometimes, though, in good weather, she took a walk down Little Bronnaia and Tverskaia, her head raised proudly, feeling a solid, imposing lady; only when she went to the chemist's to ask in a whisper whether they had an ointment for wrinkles or red hands, did she seem to be ashamed. In the evenings she sat in her little room with the lamp unlit waiting for someone to come; some time after ten o'clock – this happened very seldom, once or twice a week – you could hear someone quietly going up- or downstairs, rustling at the door looking for the bell. The door would open, there would be a muttering and a visitor, usually bald, stout, old, ugly, would hesitantly enter the lobby, and Klavdia would hurriedly take him to her room. She adored a good visitor. There was no creature nobler or more worthy; to receive a good visitor, deal with him tactfully, respect and please him was for her a heartfelt need, a duty, happiness and pride; she was incapable of refusing a visitor or not making him welcome, even when she was preparing for Easter communion.

Olga, back from the country, had lodged Sasha with her for the time being, assuming that while the girl was little she wouldn't understand if she saw anything bad. But now Sasha was thirteen the time really had come to find other accommodation for her, but she and her aunt had become attached to one another and it was now hard to separate them; anyway, there was nowhere to take Sasha to, since Olga herself was sheltering in the corridor of a block of furnished rooms and slept on chairs. Sasha spent the day with her mother, or in the street, or downstairs in the laundry, spent her nights on her aunt's floor, between the bedstead and the chest of drawers, and if a visitor came, she went to sleep in the lobby.

She loved in the evening to go where Ivan Makarych worked and look at the dancing from the kitchen. There was always music there, it was bright and noisy, there was a delicious smell of food around the cook and the washers-up, and Granddad Ivan Makarych gave her tea or ice cream and passed her various titbits brought back to the kitchen on plates and dishes . . . Late one autumn evening, returning from Ivan Makarych, she brought a chicken leg, a piece of sturgeon, a slice of cake, all wrapped in paper . . . Her aunt was already in bed . . .

'Auntie dear,' said Sasha sadly, 'I've brought you something to eat.'

They lit the lamp, Klavdia sat up in bed and started to eat. Sasha looked at her curlers, which made her look terrible, at her faded, aged shoulders; Sasha looked long and sadly, as if at a sick woman; and suddenly tears flowed down her cheeks.

'Dear Auntie,' she said with a quivering voice, 'Dear Auntie, this morning in the laundry the girls were saying that you will be begging in the street in your old age or you'll die in hospital. That's not true, Auntie, not true,' Sasha went on, now sobbing, 'I shan't leave you, I'll feed you . . . and I shan't let you go to the hospital.'

Klavdia's chin shook and tears shone in her eyes, but she immediately took hold of herself and said, looking severely at Sasha:

'It's not proper to listen to laundry girls.'

XI

The tenants of the 'Lisbon' furnished rooms gradually quietened down; there was a smell of extinguished lamps and the lanky footman was now stretched out on chairs in the corridor. Olga took off her white beribboned bonnet and her apron, covered her head with a kerchief and went to see her daughter and sister at Patriarch's Ponds. Working at the 'Lisbon' she was busy every day from morning to late evening and could visit her family rarely and only at night; work took all her time, leaving her not a single free minute, so that even since the time she came back from the country she had not been once to church.

She was in a hurry to show Sasha a letter she had received from

Maria in the village. The letter contained only greetings and complaints of poverty, grief, that the old folks were still alive, eating and not working, but for some reason these crooked lines, where every letter was like a cripple, were for Olga full of a special hidden charm and, apart from the greetings and complaints, she also read about the clear warm country days, the fragrant still evening air and heard the hours struck in the church over the river; she could imagine the village cemetery where her husband lay; the green graves breathed peace and calm, you could envy the deceased – and such space, such open expanses! And it was odd: when they had lived in the country, she badly wanted to go to Moscow, while now, on the contrary, she longed for the country.

Olga woke Sasha and, anxious and afraid that the whispering and light might wake others, she read her the letter twice. Then they both went down the dark stinking stairs and left the house. Through the wide open windows you could see the laundry girls ironing; outside the gates two laundresses were smoking. Olga and Sasha quickly went down the street talking about how good it would be to save up two roubles and send them to the village: one rouble for Maria and the other to pay for a requiem on Nikolai's grave.

'Oh, I've had enough worries recently,' Olga was saying, clasping her hands. 'Dinner had only started, dearie, and suddenly Kiriak comes from nowhere – as drunk as a lord. "Olga, give me some money!" And he shouts and stamps his feet – "Just give it to me." But where can I get money? I get no pay, I live on tips the good gentlemen give me, that's all my riches . . . He won't listen – "Give it!" The tenants look out of their rooms, the boss comes – it couldn't be worse, the shame! I begged the students for thirty kopecks and gave them to him. He left . . . And for a whole day I have been walking about whispering, "God, soften his heart!" That's what I've been whispering.'

The streets were quiet; occasionally a night cab drove past, and somewhere far off, presumably in a pleasure garden, music was still playing and you could hear the faint crackle of fireworks.

1897

A Visit to Friends

One morning a letter came.

'Dear Misha, You've quite forgotten us. Come and see us as soon as you can, we want to see you. We both beg on our knees, come today, show us your charming eyes. We can't wait. Ta and Va. Kuzminki, the seventh of June.'

The letter was from Tatiana Loseva, who had been called Ta for short when Podgorin had stayed at Kuzminki ten or twelve years ago. But who was Va?

Podgorin remembered long conversations, merry laughter, singing romances, evening walks and a whole galaxy of girls and young women who had once lived at Kuzminki and near by. Then he remembered a simple, lively, clever face with freckles that suited so well the auburn hair: it was Varvara, Tatiana's friend. Varvara had taken a medical degree and worked at a factory somewhere the other side of Tula. Now she must have come to stay at Kuzminki.

'Lovely Va!' thought Podgorin, surrendering to memories. 'What a fine girl!'

Tatiana, Varvara and he were almost the same age; but he had been a student then, and they were girls old enough to marry and had looked down on him as a boy. Now, although he was a lawyer with greying hair, they still called him Misha and treated him as a junior and said he still had no experience of life.

He was very fond of them – but more, he felt, in his memories than in reality. The present was unfamiliar, closed and strange to him. This short, playful letter was strange, too: it had probably taken time and effort to compose, and when Tatiana was writing it, her husband Sergei may well have been standing behind her . . . The estate of Kuzminki had gone towards her dowry only six years ago, but had now been squandered by this Sergei, and now every time they had to pay the bank or lenders, they consulted Podgorin as a lawyer and, worse, twice asked him for a loan. Clearly they wanted advice or money from him again.

He no longer felt drawn to Kuzminki as he used to. He felt sad there. There was no more laughter, noise, merry, carefree faces, no rendezvous on quiet moonlit nights, above all no youth; and probably all this had been enchanting in memories only . . . Besides Ta and Va there was also a Na: Tatiana's sister Nadezhda, whom both in earnest and in fun they used to call his fiancée; he had watched her grow up, they had counted on him marrying her and at one time he had been in love with her and had intended to propose, but now she was getting on for twenty-four and he was still a bachelor . . .

'Odd how it all turned out, though,' he was thinking now as he re-read the letter in embarrassment. 'I can't refuse to go, they'd be offended . . .'

Not having visited the Losevs yet was a weight on his conscience. After walking round the room, thinking, he forced himself to act and decided to visit them for three days or so and get it over with, so as to be free and at peace at least until next summer. After breakfast, as he got ready to go to the Brest station, he told the servant that he would be back in three days.

Moscow to Kuzminki was a two-hour journey, followed by about twenty minutes by carriage from the station. Tatiana's forest was visible from the station, as were three tall narrow summer cottages which Losev, who had started a number of different projects in the first years of his marriage, had begun to build but never finished. These cottages had also ruined him, as well as various developments on his estate and frequent trips to Moscow, where he lunched at the Slaviansky Bazaar, dined at the Hermitage and rounded off the day with the gypsies on the Little Bronnaia* or the Zhivodiorka (he called this a 'shake-up'). Podgorin himself liked a drink, sometimes a lot, and was not fussy about the women he visited, but he did so in a cold, lazy way, experiencing no pleasure, and he was overcome by a feeling of distaste when in his presence other men indulged in these things with passion, and he could not understand people who felt freer on the Zhivodiorka than at home with decent women, and he disliked such people; he felt that all the dirt stuck to them like burrs. He was not fond of Losev either and found him a bore and had several times experienced this feeling of distaste in his company . . .

As soon as he passed the forest, he was met by Sergei Losev and Nadezhda.

'My dear chap, how could you neglect us so?' said Sergei, kissing him three times and then putting both arms round his waist. 'You don't like us any more, dear friend.'

He had coarse features, a thick nose and a thin reddish beard; he combed his hair down his temples, like a merchant, to seem simple, purely Russian. When he spoke, he breathed straight into your face, and when he stopped speaking he breathed heavily through his nose.

His well-fed and over-indulged body hindered his movements and, so as to move more easily, he puffed out his chest, which gave him a haughty appearance. Next to him Nadezhda, his wife's sister, seemed ethereal. She was a light blonde, pale, with kind gentle eyes, and a slim figure; whether she was beautiful or not, Podgorin couldn't judge, since he had known her since they were children and had got used to her appearance. Now she was wearing an open-necked white dress, and he found the impression made by her long, white, bare neck new and not quite pleasant.

'My sister and I have been expecting you all day,' she said. 'Varia is here and also waiting to see you.'

She took his arm and suddenly laughed for no reason, uttering a light cry of joy, as if a thought had unexpectedly captivated her. The field of flowering rye, motionless in the still air, and the forest, lit up by the sun, were beautiful; and it seemed that Nadezhda noticed them only now that she was walking with Podgorin.

'I've come to stay for three days,' he said. 'I'm sorry I couldn't get away from Moscow earlier.'

'That's not good, not good, you've quite forgotten us,' said Sergei as a good-natured reproach. '*Jamais de ma vie!*' he suddenly said and clicked his fingers.

He had a mannerism of surprising you by pronouncing a phrase, quite irrelevant to the conversation, as an exclamation and clicking his fingers at the same time. He was always imitating somebody; if he rolled his eyes or threw his hair back nonchalantly or put on pathos, it meant he had just been to the theatre or a dinner with speeches. Now he was shuffling with stiff knees, as if he had gout, presumably in imitation of somebody.

'You know, Tatiana didn't believe you would come,' said Nadezhda. 'But Varia and I had a premonition; I somehow knew that you would catch this train.'

'*Jamais de ma vie!*' repeated Sergei.

The ladies were waiting on the garden terrace. Ten years ago Podgorin – then a poor student – had taught Nadezhda mathematics and history in exchange for board and lodging; he gave Varia, who was taking university courses, occasional lessons in Latin. Tania, by then a beautiful grown-up girl, thought of nothing but love and wanted only love and happiness, wanting them passionately and waiting for the bridegroom she dreamt of night and day. And now that she was over thirty, as beautiful, striking as ever in a wide peignoir, with full white arms, she thought only about her husband and two little girls, and her expression suggested that, even if she was talking and smiling, she was aware, on guard for her love and her rights to this love and was ready at any moment to attack the enemy if he tried to take away her husband and children. She loved them strongly and she thought her love was reciprocated, but jealousy and fear for her children constantly tormented her and stopped her being happy.

After a noisy meeting on the terrace they all went to Tatiana's room, except for Sergei. The sun's rays were kept out by the lowered blinds, it was in semi-darkness, so that all the roses in the big bouquet seemed to be the same colour. They made Podgorin sit in the old armchair by the window, Nadezhda sat at his feet on a low stool. He knew that, apart from the gentle reproaches, jokes, the laughter which he was hearing now and which reminded him so strongly of the past, he would have an unpleasant conversation about bills of exchange and mortgage deeds – that was inevitable – and he thought that in fact it would be best to talk about business straight away, without beating about the bush; to get it over and – then go into the garden and the fresh air . . .

'Shouldn't we talk about business first?' he said. 'What's new in Kuzminki? Is something rotten in the state of Denmark?'

'Things are bad in Kuzminki,' Tatiana replied and sighed with melancholy. 'Oh, our affairs are in a bad way, so bad that they couldn't be worse, I suspect,' she said, crossing the room in her emotion. 'Our estate is for sale, the auction is set for the seventh of August, it's been advertised everywhere and buyers are coming here, walking and looking through the rooms . . . Anyone now has the right to come into my room and look. That may be right from a lawyer's point of view, but it humiliates and upsets me deeply. We have no way of paying and nowhere left where we can borrow. In a nutshell, it's horrible, horrible! I swear to you,' she continued, stopping in the middle of the room; her voice was shaking and tears spurted from her eyes, 'I swear to you by all that is holy, by my children's happiness, I can't go on without Kuzminki! I was born here, this is my nest, and if it is taken from me, I shan't survive, I shall die of despair.'

'I think you take too gloomy a view,' said Podgorin. 'It'll all sort itself out. Your husband will get a job, you will find a new routine and live a new life.'

'How can you say that!' shouted Tatiana; now she seemed very beautiful and strong and her readiness to attack any enemy who tried to take her husband, children and nest was expressed especially sharply in her face and her whole figure. 'What do you mean "new life"! Sergei is applying, he's been promised a tax inspector's job somewhere out east in Ufa or Perm provinces, and I'm ready to go anywhere, even to Siberia, I'm ready to live there ten or twenty years, but I must know that sooner or later I shall come back to Kuzminki. I can't go on without Kuzminki. I can't and I won't. I won't!' she shouted and stamped her foot.

'Misha, you're a lawyer,' said Varia. 'You're a fixer and it's your job to advise us what to do.'

There was just one fair and sensible answer: 'There's nothing you can do,' but Podgorin didn't dare say it straight out, and he mumbled hesitantly:

'It needs thinking about . . . I'll think.'

There were two persons in him. As a lawyer he had to deal with hard cases, in court and with clients he kept a haughty distance and gave his opinion straightforwardly and brusquely. He caroused coarsely with his friends; but in his private life, with people he was close to or had known a long time, he showed an unusual tact, was shy and sensitive and couldn't talk directly. One tear, one sideways look, a lie or even an ugly gesture was enough to make him squirm and lose his nerve. Now Nadezhda was sitting at his feet and he did not like her bare neck and this embarrassed him, he even wanted to go home. Once, a year ago, he had encountered Sergei in the house of a certain lady on Little Bronnaia, and now he felt awkward in Tatiana's presence, as if he had connived at this infidelity. The conversation about Kuzminki put him in a very difficult position. He was used to all tricky and unpleasant questions being decided by judges or juries or just by a legal statute, but when a question was put to him personally for a decision he was at a loss.

'Misha, you're our friend, we all love you like a brother,' Tatiana continued. 'I'll tell you frankly: you're our only hope. Tell us, for God's sake, what we are to do. Perhaps we have to send a petition somewhere? Perhaps there's still time to put the estate in Nadezhda's or Varia's name? What are we to do?'

'Get us out of it, Misha, do,' said Varia, lighting a cigarette. 'You always were a clever lad. You've not had much experience of life yet, but you have a head on your shoulders . . . I know you'll help Tatiana.'

'It needs thinking about . . . Perhaps I'll manage to think of something.'

They went off to the garden for a walk, then to the fields. Sergei came with them. He took Podgorin by the arm and kept leading him ahead of the others, apparently intending to have a chat about something, presumably about the bad state of affairs. He kept kissing him, three kisses on each occasion, took his arm, put an arm round his waist, breathed in his face and he seemed to be covered in sickly glue and about to stick to you; the expression in his eyes of wanting something from Podgorin, of being about to ask for something, had a distressing effect, as if he were aiming a revolver at him.

The sun had set and it had begun to get dark. Green and red lights came on along the railway line. Varia stopped and, looking at the lights, began to declaim:

> ' "Straight is the line: narrow embankments,
> Telegraph poles, rails and bridges,
> And along the sides just Russian bones . . .
> How many they are! . . ."*

'How does it go on? Oh, my God, I've forgotten everything!

> "In heat and in cold we have torn our guts,
> Our backs eternally bowed . . ." '

She declaimed in a splendid chesty voice, with feeling, her face flushed a vivacious red and tears welled in her eyes. This was the old Varia, Varia the student, and listening to her Podgorin thought of the past and recalled that he too, as a student, had known a lot of good verse by heart and loved declaiming it.

> ' "He still has not straightened up
> His bowed back: dumb and mute . . ." '

But Varia had forgotten the rest . . . she fell silent and gave a weak, limp smile, while the green and red lights began to seem sad after her recital . . .

'Oh dear, I've forgotten.'

But Podgorin suddenly remembered – by some chance his mind had retained it from student days – and quietly, almost inaudibly recited:

> ' "The Russian people have stood enough,
> They've stood this railway line as well, –
> They can stand anything – and broad and clear
> Is the line that their breasts will lay for themselves . . .
> Only how sad. . ." '

' "How sad," ' Varia interrupted him as she remembered, ' "How sad that neither you nor I will live to see that beautiful future." '

And she laughed and clapped him on the shoulder.

They went back and sat down to supper. Sergei casually tucked the corner of his napkin under his collar, imitating somebody.

'Let's drink,' he said as he poured himself and Podgorin vodka. 'We old students were good at drinking, making speeches and getting things done. I drink to your health, my friend, and you can drink to the health of an old fool of an idealist and hope that he will die just as much an idealist. Leopards don't change their spots.'

During supper Tatiana constantly gave her husband tender looks, jealous and worried lest he ate or drank something bad for him. She felt that he had been spoiled by women and was tired – she liked this side of him, but at the same time she suffered. Varia and Nadezhda were just as tender to him and looked at him anxiously, as if they were afraid that he would suddenly up and leave them. When he was about to pour himself a second glass of vodka, Varia put on an angry expression and said:

'You're poisoning yourself, Sergei. You're a highly strung, impressionable person and you could easily become an alcoholic. Tatiana, have the vodka taken away.'

Sergei had great success with women on the whole. They liked his height and build, his strong facial features, his idleness and his misfortunes. They said that he was a spendthrift because he was very kind; he was impractical because he was an idealist; he had nothing and couldn't find an occupation because he was honest, pure in soul and unable to compromise with people and circumstances. He was deeply trusted, adored and spoilt by their worship, so that he himself began to believe that he was an idealist, impractical, honest, pure in soul and that he was better and a head higher than these women.

'Why haven't you praised my little girls?' Tatiana was saying, looking lovingly at her two healthy, well-fed little girls, who looked like two buns, and serving them bowlfuls of rice. 'Just look at them properly! They say all mothers boast about their children, but I assure you, I'm unbiased, my little girls are extraordinary. Especially the elder.'

Podgorin smiled at her and the girls, but he felt it strange that this healthy, young, intelligent woman, essentially a large complex organism, could spend all her energy, all her vital forces on such simple petty work as making this nest which didn't need any making.

'Perhaps that has to be so,' he thought. 'But it's boring and stupid.'

'Before he'd said "Alas alack",* a bear had sat upon his back,' said Sergei with a click of his fingers.

Supper was over. Tatiana and Varia made Podgorin sit on the drawing-room sofa and started talking to him in a half-whisper about business.

'We must get Sergei out of this mess,' said Varia. 'That's our moral obligation. He has his weaknesses, he's not thrifty, he doesn't think about a rainy day, but that's because he is very kind and generous. He has a childlike soul. If you gave him a million, he'd have nothing left in a month, he'd give it all away.'

'True, true,' said Tatiana, tears flowing down her cheeks. 'I've had a lot to put up with from him, but I must admit he's a wonderful man.'

And neither Tatiana nor Varia could resist a minor cruelty, reproaching Podgorin:

'But your generation, Misha, has lost all that.'

'What have generations got to do with it?' wondered Podgorin. 'Losev is only about six years older than me, no more . . .'

'Life's not easy in this world,' said Varia with a sigh. 'One is constantly threatened with loss. Either they take your estate away, or one of your family is ill and you fear they're going to die – every day brings something. But what can we do, my friends? We must not complain, but submit to a higher will, remember that everything in this world has a purpose, remote goals. Misha, you haven't much experience of life or suffering and you will laugh at me; laugh, but I'll still say it: I have had several moments of clairvoyance during my most anxious, anguished moments, and that has completely changed my heart, and now I know that nothing is accidental, that everything that happens in our life is necessary.'

How different was this Varia, grey-haired, corseted, in a high-sleeved fashionable dress, twisting a cigarette in her long thin fingers, which quivered for some reason, easily lapsing into mysticism, talking in such a flat, monotonous way, from Varia the student, red-haired, merry, rowdy, bold . . .

'Where has all that disappeared to!' thought Podgorin, bored with listening to her.

'Va, sing us a song,' he said to her to stop the talk of clairvoyance. 'You used to sing well.'

'Oh Misha, all that is water under the bridge.'

'Well, recite some Nekrasov.'

'I've forgotten it all. What you heard just now was just an accident.'

Despite the high sleeves and the corset, she was obviously in dire straits, living at starvation level in her factory the other side of Tula. And she was very obviously overworked; heavy, monotonous labour and this constant interference in other people's business, worrying about others had exhausted and aged her, and Podgorin, as he looked at her sad, prematurely faded face, thought that really it was she who was in need of help and not Kuzminki or Sergei, for whom she was pleading.

Higher education and a doctor's career seemed not to have changed her as a woman. Just like Tatiana she loved marriages, births, christenings, long talks about children, she loved frightful novels with happy endings, she read the papers only for news of fire, flood and solemn ceremonies; she very much wanted Podgorin to propose to Nadezhda and, if he did, she would have been moved and burst into tears.

He did not know whether it was by chance or by Varia's contrivance, but he found himself alone with Nadezhda, and just the suspicion that he was under observation and that something was expected of him inhibited and embarrassed him, and he felt, walking side by side with Nadezhda, as if he and she had been put in the same cage.

'Let's go into the garden,' she said.

They did so; he was not pleased, he felt annoyed and did not know what to talk about, while she was joyful, proud of his closeness and seemed to be pleased that he was staying for three days, and perhaps she was full of sweet dreams and hopes. He did not know whether she loved him, but he knew that she had long been used to him and fond of him, and still saw him as her teacher and that what had happened to her sister Tatiana was happening inside her, in other words that she was thinking only of love, only of getting married as soon as possible, to have a husband, children and her own home. She had still preserved the feelings of friendship that are so strong in children, and it was very likely that she only respected Podgorin and was fond of him as a friend and was in love not with him but with her dreams of a husband and children.

'It's getting dark,' he said.

'Yes, the moon rises late now.'

They walked up and down the same avenue near the house. Podgorin was reluctant to go deep into the garden: it was dark there and he would have had to take Nadezhda's arm and be very close to her. Shadows of people were moving on the terrace and he felt that the shadows were Tatiana and Varia keeping watch on him.

'I need your advice,' Nadezhda said and stood still. 'If Kuzminki is sold, then Sergei will go away to work and then our life must change completely. I shan't go with my sister, we'll go our separate ways, because I don't want to be a burden on the family. I must work. I shall get a job in Moscow somewhere and will earn my living, help my sister and her husband. You'll help me with good advice, won't you?'

Knowing absolutely nothing about hard work, she was now inspired with the thought of living and working independently, she was building plans for the future – this was written all over her face – and life, once she was working and helping others, seemed beautiful and poetic. He could see the details of her pale face and dark eyebrows and he recalled what a clever quick-witted pupil she had been, what promise she showed and how pleasant it was to coach her. Now she was probably not just a young lady looking for a husband, but a clever, high-minded girl, of unusual kindness, with a meek soul, as soft as wax, from which you could mould anything you liked and, if she were to get into the right surroundings, she would make an outstanding woman.

'Why not marry her, actually?' thought Podgorin, but the thought immediately frightened him for some reason and he went towards the house.

Tatiana was sitting at the piano in the drawing-room, and her playing vividly brought back the past to him, when in this same drawing-room there was singing and dancing until far into the night, with the windows open, and the birds in the garden and on the river also sang. Podgorin became very light-hearted, started fooling about, danced with both Nadezhda and Varia and then sang. A corn on his foot was inhibiting him and he asked if he might put on Sergei's slippers and, oddly enough, he felt at home in these slippers, one of the family ('Just like a brother-in-law . . .' flashed through his thoughts), and he became even more light-hearted. Everyone came to life at the sight of him, they became merrier as if they had grown younger; everyone's face shone with hope: Kuzminki is saved! It was so easy, wasn't it? Something only had to be found, an obscure legal loophole or marrying Nadezhda to Podgorin . . . And, obviously, things were already going right. Nadezhda, pink, happy, her eyes full of tears, expecting something extraordinary, was swirling as she danced, and her white dress ballooned, and you could see her beautiful little legs in flesh-coloured stockings . . . Varia was very pleased and took Podgorin by the arm, telling him in a whisper, with a meaningful expression:

'Misha, don't run away from happiness. Take it when it's offered on a plate, or else you will have to run after it and it will be too late to catch it.'

Podgorin wanted to make promises, give hope and he himself now believed that Kuzminki was saved and that this was so easy.

'And you-ou will be queen of the wo-orld . . .'* he started to pose and sing, but suddenly remembered that he could do nothing, absolutely nothing, for these people, and he fell silent as if he had done something wrong.

And then he sat in the corner, silent, wearing someone else's slippers, his legs tucked under the chair.

At the sight of him the others realised that there was now nothing to be done, and fell silent. They closed the piano lid. And everyone remarked that it was late and time for bed, and Tatiana put out the big lamp in the drawing-room.

They made up a bed for Podgorin in the lodge he had once lived in. Sergei went with him, holding a candle high over his head, although the moon had risen and it was light. They walked down an avenue of lilac bushes and the gravel crunched under their feet.

'Before he'd said "Alas alack", a bear had sat upon his back,' said Sergei.

And Podgorin felt that he had heard this phrase a thousand times. How fed up he was with it! When they got to the lodge, Sergei pulled a bottle and two glasses from his spacious jacket and placed them on the table.

'Brandy,' he said. 'Number double zero. Varia's in the house and we can't drink while she's there, or she'll start on alcoholism, but we're better off here. The brandy is excellent.'

They sat down. The brandy did in fact turn out to be good.

'Let's have a proper drink today,' Sergei went on, biting a lemon before he swallowed. 'I'm an old student, one of the lads, and I like a good "shake-up" sometimes. It's essential.'

But his eyes had the same expression of wanting something from Podgorin and of being about to ask for something.

'Let's drink, my dear man,' he went on with a sigh; 'life's become far too hard to bear. Eccentrics like me are up against it, we've had it. Idealism is out of fashion now. Now money is king and if you don't want to be pushed into the gutter you've got to bow down to money and worship. But I can't. It goes against the grain.'

'When is the auction?' asked Podgorin, to change the subject.

'The seventh of August. But I don't expect, old man, to save Kuzminki. The arrears have amounted to something enormous and the estate brings in nothing, only losses every year. It isn't worth it . . . Tatiana will miss it, of course, it's her family property, but to be honest, I'm even glad in a way. I am absolutely not a countryman. My field is a big noisy city, my element is struggle!'

He had more to say, but none of it was what he intended and he kept a sharp eye on Podgorin, as if waiting for the right moment. And suddenly Podgorin saw his eyes close up and felt his breath in his face . . .

'My dear chap, save me!' Sergei said, breathing heavily. 'Give me two hundred roubles! I beg you!'

Podgorin meant to say that he was short of money, and thought it would be better to give the money to any poor man or simply to lose it at cards, but he was terribly embarrassed and, feeling himself in this small room with one candle as though in a trap, wishing to get away from this breath, the soft hands which were holding him by the waist and seemed to have stuck there, he began quickly searching his pockets for his notebook where he kept his money.

'Here . . .' he mumbled as he took out a hundred roubles. 'The rest later. That's all I have on me. You see, I don't know how to say no,' he went on with irritation, beginning to get angry. 'I have an unbearable old woman's character. Only, please repay the money later. I'm short myself.'

'Thank you. Thank you, old friend!'

'And for God's sake, stop imagining that you're an idealist. You're as much an idealist as I am a turkey. You are simply a frivolous idler, and nothing else.'

Sergei sighed deeply and sat on the divan.

'My dear man, you're angry,' he said, 'But if you knew how I'm suffering! I'm going through a horrible time at the moment. My dear man, I swear, I'm not sorry for myself, no, I'm sorry for my wife and children. If it weren't for the children and the wife, I'd have killed myself a long time ago.'

And suddenly his shoulders and head began to shake and he started sobbing.

'That's the last straw,' said Podgorin, walking up and down the room with emotion and feeling great annoyance. 'Well, what am I supposed to do with a man who's done a mass of evil and then sobs? Your tears disarm me, I can't say anything to you. You sob, therefore you are right.'

'I have done a mass of evil?' asked Sergei, getting up and looking astounded at Podgorin. 'My dear man, how can you say that? I've done a mass of evil?! Oh how little you know me! How little you understand me!'

'Fine, all right I don't understand you, only, please, don't sob. It's revolting.'

'Oh, how little you know me!' repeated Sergei Losev, completely sincerely. 'How little you know me!'

'Look at yourself in the mirror,' Podgorin continued. 'You're a middle-aged man, soon you'll be old, it's time you came to your senses, to try and realise who and what you are. To do nothing for a lifetime, spending it on idle childish chatter, affectations, dishonesty – doesn't it make your head spin, and aren't you fed up with living like that? You're depressing company! You're stupefyingly boring!'

After saying this, Podgorin left the lodge and slammed the door. Perhaps for the first time in his life he had been sincere and said what he wanted to.

Shortly afterwards he was regretting being so harsh. What was the use of talking seriously or arguing with a habitual liar, a glutton, a heavy drinker, a squanderer of other people's money who is convinced he is an idealist and a martyr for truth? You were dealing with stupidity or long-standing bad habits which had got a grip on his organism, like a disease, and were ineradicable. In any case indignation or harsh criticism were pointless and the best reaction was laughter; one good laugh would have done far more than a dozen sermons.

'It's simpler to pay no attention at all,' thought Podgorin, 'and, the main thing, not to give him money.'

A little later he was no longer thinking about Sergei or his hundred roubles. It was a quiet pensive night, very bright. When Podgorin looked at the sky on moonlit nights, he felt that only he and the moon were awake, that everything else was asleep or drowsy; he did not think of people or money and his mood gradually became quiet, peaceful, he felt alone in this world, and in the nocturnal silence the sound of his own steps seemed so sad to him.

The garden was enclosed by a white stone wall. The side facing the open country had a tower on its right-hand corner; the tower had been built a very long time ago, in the days of serfdom. The lower part was stone, the upper part wood, with a platform, a conical roof and a long spire with a black weathervane on top. There were two doors at the bottom, so that you could leave the garden for the open country, and from the ground to the platform there was a staircase which squeaked when you trod on it. Under the stairs some old broken armchairs had been dumped, and the moonlight, which now came through the door, lit up these arm-chairs, and, with their crooked legs sticking upwards, they seemed to have come alive at night and to be lurking in wait for somebody in the stillness.

Podgorin went up the stairs to the platform and sat down. Right under the wall was a boundary ditch and mound, beyond were the fields, broad and flooded with moonlight. Podgorin knew that straight ahead, just two miles from the manor house, was a forest, and now it seemed to him that he could see the dark streak in the distance. The quails and landrails were calling; occasionally from the forest came the cry of the cuckoo which was just as unable to sleep.

Steps could be heard. Someone was walking round the garden, approaching the tower.

A dog barked.

'Beetle!' a woman's voice called quietly. 'Beetle, come back!'

You could hear them enter the tower below, and a minute later a black dog, an old friend of Podgorin's, appeared on the mound. It stopped and, looking upwards to where Podgorin was sitting, waved its tail in greeting. Then, a little later, a white figure rose from the black ditch and also stood still on the mound. It was Nadezhda.

'What can you see there?' she asked the dog, and started looking upwards.

She could not see Podgorin, but probably sensed his proximity, since she was smiling and her pale face, lit up by the moon, seemed happy. The black shadow of the tower which stretched over the earth far into the fields, the motionless white figure with the blissful smile on its pale face, the black dog, the shadows of both of them – and all of it together was like a dream . . .

'There's somebody there . . .' Nadezhda said quietly.

She stood waiting for him to come down or call her up and finally make a declaration, and they would both be happy on this fine, quiet night. White, pale, thin, very beautiful in the moonlight, she waited for affection; her constant dreams of happiness and love had made her languid, and she could no longer find the strength to conceal her feelings, and her whole figure and the shining eyes and the fixed smile of happiness betrayed her innermost thoughts, and he felt awkward, he shrank, he held his breath, not knowing whether he should speak and turn everything, as usual, into a joke, or be silent, and he felt vexation and thought only that here, on an estate on a moonlight night, near a beautiful infatuated girl in a reverie he was as uninvolved as he was on the Little Bronnaia – the reason being, presumably, that this country poetry had lost its charm for him, just as had the coarse prose of the Little Bronnaia. So had meetings on moonlit nights and white figures with slim waists and mysterious shadows and towers and estates and such 'characters' as Sergei and people like himself, Podgorin, with his cold boredom, constant vexation, with his inability to adapt to real life, inability to take from life what it can give and with a tiresome, nagging thirst for what does not and cannot exist on earth. And now, sitting here on this tower, he would have preferred a good fireworks display or a procession in the moonlight or Varia reciting 'The Railway' again, or another woman who could stand on the mound where Nadezhda was now standing and tell him something interesting, new, which had nothing to do with love or happiness, and if she did speak of love, then let it be a call to new forms of life, lofty and rational, on the eve of which we are perhaps now living and which we sometimes have a premonition of . . .

'There's nobody there,' said Nadezhda.

After standing there for a minute she set off towards the forest, quietly, with her head hanging. The dog ran ahead. And Podgorin could see the white spot for a long time.

'Odd how it has all turned out, though . . .' he repeated to himself as he went back to his lodge.

He could not imagine what he would talk to Sergei or Tatiana about, how he would behave with Nadezhda the next day – or the day after, either, and he anticipated the embarrassment, fear and boredom. How could he fill these three long days which he had promised to spend here? He remembered the conversation about clairvoyance and Sergei's phrase: 'Before he'd said "Alas alack", a bear had sat upon his back,' he recalled that to please Tatiana he would have to smile the next day at her plump, well-fed little girls – and he decided to leave.

At half-past five Sergei appeared on the terrace of the main house wearing an Oriental dressing-gown and a tasselled fez. Podgorin did not waste a minute; he went up to him and started taking his leave.

'I have to be in Moscow by ten o'clock,' he said, not looking at him. 'I completely forgot that I'm expected at the solicitor's. Let me go, please. When your family gets up tell them that I apologise, that I'm terribly sorry . . .'

He did not hear what Sergei said to him; he was in a hurry, constantly looking round at the windows of the main house, afraid that the ladies might have woken up and would detain him. He was ashamed of his anxiety. He felt that he had been to Kuzminki for the last time and would never come again and, as he left, he looked round several times at the lodge where he had spent so many good days, but his soul felt cold and he was not sad . . .

At home on his desk the first thing he saw was the letter he had received the evening before.

'Dear Misha,' he read, 'You've quite forgotten us. Come and see us as soon as you can . . .' And for some reason he remembered Nadezhda swirling as she danced, her dress ballooning, and glimpsing her legs in flesh-coloured stockings . . .

But about ten minutes later he was at his desk working and no longer thought of Kuzminki.

1898

Ionych

When those who arrived in the provincial capital S— complained of the dreariness and monotony of life, the inhabitants of the town, in self-justification, declared that it was very nice in S—, that there was a library, a theatre, a club; that they had balls; and, finally, that there were clever, agreeable, and interesting families whom one could get to know. And they would point to the Turkin family as the most educated and talented.

This family lived in their own house in the principal street, next to the Governor's. Ivan Turkin himself – a stout, handsome, dark man with whiskers – used to get up amateur performances for charity, and used to play elderly generals and cough very amusingly. He knew a lot of anecdotes, charades, proverbs, and was fond of being humorous and witty, and he always wore an expression from which it was impossible to tell whether he were joking or in earnest. His wife, Vera – a thin, nice-looking lady who wore a pince-nez – used to write novels and stories and willingly read them aloud to her visitors. Their young daughter Ekaterina played the piano. In short, every member of the family had a special talent. The Turkins were very hospitable, and good-humouredly displayed their talents in all sincerity. Their stone house was roomy and cool in summer; half of the windows looked into a shady old garden, where nightingales sang in the spring. When there were visitors in the house, there was a clatter of knives in the kitchen and a smell of fried onions in the yard – and that was always a sure sign of a plentiful and savoury supper to follow.

And as soon as Doctor Dmitri Ionych Startsev was appointed by the rural district council, and took up his abode at Dializh, six miles from S—, he, too, was told that as a cultivated man he must make the acquaintance of the Turkins. In the winter he was introduced to Mr Turkin in the street; they talked about the weather, about the theatre, about the cholera; an invitation followed. On a holiday in the spring – it was Ascension Day – after seeing his patients, Startsev set off for town in search of a little recreation and to make some purchases. He walked in a leisurely way (he did not yet own horses), humming all the time:

'Before I'd drunk the tears from life's goblet . . .'*

In town he dined, went for a walk in the gardens, then Mr Turkin's invitation came into his mind, as it were by itself, and he decided to call on the Turkins and see what sort of people they were.

'Hello and welcome,' said Mr Turkin, meeting him on the steps. 'Delighted, delighted to see such an agreeable visitor. Come along; I will introduce you to my better half. I tell him, Verochka,' he went on, as he presented the doctor to his wife, 'I tell him that he has no Roman right to sit at home in a hospital; he ought to devote his leisure to society. Oughtn't he, darling?'

'Sit here,' said Mrs Turkina, making her visitor sit down beside her. 'You can dance attendance on me. My husband is jealous – he is an Othello; but we will try and behave so well that he will notice nothing.'

'Ah, you naughty chicken!' Mr Turkin muttered tenderly, and he kissed her on the forehead. 'You have come just in the nick of time,' he said, addressing the doctor again. 'My better half has written a ginormous novel, and she is going to read it aloud today.'

'*Jean* dear,' said Mrs Turkina to her husband, 'dîtes que l'on nous donne du thé.'

Startsev was introduced to Ekaterina Turkina, a girl of eighteen, very much like her mother, thin and pretty. Her expression was still childish and her waist was soft and slim; and her strong virginal breasts, healthy and beautiful, spoke of spring, real spring. Then they drank tea with jam, honey, and sweetmeats, and with very nice biscuits, which melted in the mouth. As the evening came on, other visitors gradually arrived, and Mr Turkin fixed his laughing eyes on each of them and said:

'Hello and welcome!'

Then they all sat in the drawing-room with very serious faces, and Mrs Turkina read her novel. She began like this: 'The frost was intensifying . . .' The windows were wide open; from the kitchen came the clatter of knives and the smell of fried onions . . . It was comfortable in the soft deep arm-chair; the lights had such a friendly twinkle in the twilight of the drawing-room, and now on a summer evening, when sounds of voices and laughter floated in from the street and whiffs of lilac from the yard, it was difficult to grasp how frost could intensify or the setting sun light with its chilly rays a solitary wayfarer on the snowy plain. Mrs Turkina read about a beautiful young countess founding a school, a hospital, a library, in her village, and falling in love with a wandering artist; she read about what never happens in real life, and yet it was pleasant and cosy to listen to, and such good, serene thoughts kept coming into your head that you did not want to get up.

'Not badsome . . .' Mr Turkin said softly.

And one guest, listening, his thoughts floating far, far away, said hardly audibly:

'Yes . . . really . . .'

One hour passed, then another. In the town gardens close by a band was playing and a choir was singing. When Mrs Turkina shut her manuscript book, the company was silent for five minutes, listening to 'O my torch' being sung by the choir, and the song conveyed what was not in the novel but happens in real life.

'Do you publish your stories in magazines?' Startsev asked Mrs Turkina.

'No,' she answered. 'I never publish. I write and put it away in my cupboard. Why publish?' she explained. 'We have our own means.'

And for some reason everyone sighed.

'And now, Kitten, you play something,' Mr Turkin said to his daughter.

The lid of the piano was raised and the music lying ready was opened. Ekaterina sat down and banged on the piano with both hands, and then banged again with all her might, and then again and again; her shoulders and chest shook. She obstinately banged on the same notes, and it sounded as if she would not leave off until she had hammered the keys into the piano. The drawing-room was filled with the din; everything was rattling, the floor, the ceiling, the furniture . . . Ekaterina was playing a difficult passage, interesting simply on account of its difficulty, long and monotonous, and Startsev, listening, pictured stones falling down a steep hill and going on dropping, and he wished they would stop falling; and at the same time Ekaterina, pink from the violent exercise, strong and vigorous, with a lock of hair falling over her forehead, attracted him very much. After the winter spent at Dializh among patients and peasants, to sit in a drawing-room, to watch this young, elegant and, probably, pure creature, and to listen to these noisy, tedious but still cultured sounds, was so pleasant, so novel . . .

'Well, Kitten, today you have played as never before,' said Mr Turkin, with tears in his eyes, when his daughter had finished and stood up. 'Die, Denis;* you won't write anything better.'

All flocked round her, congratulated her, expressed astonishment, declared that it was ages since they had heard such music, and she listened in silence with a faint smile, and triumph was written all over her.

'Splendid, superb!'

'Splendid,' said Startsev, too, carried away by the general enthusiasm. 'Where have you studied!' he asked Ekaterina Ivanovna. 'At the Conservatoire?'

'No, I am only preparing for the Conservatoire; so far I've been studying with Madame Zawlowska.'

'Have you finished at the high school here?'

'Oh no,' Mrs Turkina answered her. 'We have teachers for her at home; there might be bad influences at the high school or a boarding-school, you know. While a young girl is growing up, she ought to be under no influence but her mother's.'

'All the same, I'm going to the Conservatoire,' said Ekaterina Ivanovna.

'No. Kitten loves her mama. Kitten won't upset papa and mama.'

'No, I shall go, I shall,' said Ekaterina, in a mock tantrum, stamping her foot.

At supper it was Mr Turkin who displayed his talents. Laughing only with his eyes, he told anecdotes, made jokes, asked ridiculous riddles and answered them himself, talking the whole time in his extraordinary language, evolved by prolonged witty exercises and evidently now a habit: 'Badsome', 'Ginormous', 'Thank you most dumbly', and so on.

But that was not all. When the guests, replete and satisfied, trooped into the hall, looking for their coats and sticks, there bustled about them the footman Pavlusha, or, as he was called in the family, Pava – a lad of fourteen with short-cropped head and chubby cheeks.

'Come, Pava, perform!' Mr Turkin said to him.

Pava struck an attitude, flung up his arms, and said in a tragic tone: 'Unhappy woman, die!'

And everyone roared with laughter.

'It's entertaining,' thought Startsev, as he went out into the street.

He went to a restaurant and had a beer, then set off on foot to Dializh. He walked all the way singing:

'Thy voice to me so languid and caressing . . .'

On going to bed, he felt not the slightest fatigue after the six miles' walk. On the contrary, he felt as though he could with pleasure have walked another twenty.

'Not badsome,' he thought, and laughed as he fell asleep.

II

Startsev kept meaning to go to the Turkins' again, but there was a great deal of work in the hospital, and he could not possibly find a free hour. More than a year passed thus in work and solitude; but one day he was handed a letter in a blue envelope from town . . .

Mrs Turkina had long suffered from migraine, but now that Kitten frightened her every day by saying that she was going away to the

Conservatoire, the attacks began to be more frequent. All the doctors of the town had been to the Turkins'; at last it was the district doctor's turn. Mrs Turkina wrote him a touching letter in which she begged him to come and relieve her sufferings. Startsev went, and after that he began visiting the Turkins often, very often . . . He did relieve Mrs Turkina a little and she was now telling all her visitors that he was a wonderful, exceptional doctor. But it was not for the sake of her migraine that he visited the Turkins now . . .

It was a holiday. Ekaterina finished her long, wearisome piano exercises. Then they sat a long time in the dining-room, drinking tea, and Mr Turkin told a funny story. Then there was a ring and he had to go into the hall to welcome a guest; Startsev took advantage of the momentary commotion, and whispered to Ekaterina in great agitation:

'For God's sake, I beg you, don't torment me; let's go into the garden!'

She shrugged her shoulders, as though perplexed and not knowing what he wanted of her, but she got up and went.

'You play the piano for three or four hours,' he said, following her: 'then you sit with your mother, and there is no chance to speak to you. Give me a quarter of an hour at least, I beg you.'

Autumn was approaching, and it was quiet and melancholy in the old garden; the dark leaves lay thick in the walks. It was already beginning to get dark early.

'I haven't seen you for a whole week,' Startsev went on, 'and if you only knew what suffering it is! Let us sit down. Listen to me.'

They had a favourite place in the garden: a seat under an old spreading maple. And now they sat down on this seat.

'What do you want?' said Ekaterina dryly, in a matter-of-fact tone.

'I have not seen you for a whole week; I have not heard you for so long. I long passionately; I thirst for your voice. Speak.'

She fascinated him by her freshness, the naive expression of her eyes and cheeks. Even in the way her dress hung on her he saw something extraordinary charming, touching in its simplicity and naive grace; and at the same time, in spite of this naive quality, she seemed to him very intelligent and developed beyond her years. He could talk with her about literature, about art, about anything he liked; he could complain to her of life, of people, though it sometimes happened that in the middle of a serious conversation she would laugh unexpectedly or run off into the house. Like almost all the girls in S——, she had read a great deal (as a rule, people read very little in S——, and at the town library they said if it were not for the girls and the young Jews, they might as well close the library); this pleased Startsev infinitely; he used to ask her eagerly every time what she had been reading the last few days, and listened enthralled while she told him.

'What have you been reading this week since I saw you last?' he asked now. 'Do please tell me.'

'I have been reading Pisemsky.'*

'What exactly?'

'*A Thousand Souls*,' answered Kitten. 'And what a funny name Pisemsky had – Aleksei Feofilaktovich!'

'Where are you going?' cried Startsev in horror, as she suddenly got up and walked towards the house. 'I must talk to you; I want to explain myself . . . Stay with me just five minutes, I implore you!'

She stopped as though she wanted to say something, then awkwardly thrust a note into his hand, ran home and sat down to the piano again.

'Be in the cemetery,' Startsev read, 'at eleven tonight, near the tomb of Demetti.'

'Well, that's not at all clever,' he thought, coming to his senses. 'Why the cemetery? What for?'

It was clear: Kitten was joking. Who would seriously dream of making an assignation at night in the cemetery far out of town, when it might have been arranged in the street or in the town gardens? And did it become him – a district doctor, an intelligent, staid man – to be sighing, receiving notes, to hang about cemeteries, to do silly things that even schoolboys think ridiculous nowadays? What would this romance lead to? What would his colleagues say when they heard of it? Such were Startsev's reflections as he wandered round the tables at the club, but at half-past ten he suddenly set off for the cemetery.

By now he had his own pair of horses, and a coachman called Panteleimon, in a velvet waistcoat. The moon was shining. It was still warm, warm as it is in autumn. Dogs were howling in the suburb near the slaughter-house. Startsev left his horses in one of the side-streets at the end of the town, and walked on foot to the cemetery.

'We all have our oddities,' he thought. 'Kitten is odd, too; and – who knows? – perhaps she is not joking, perhaps she will come,' and he abandoned himself to this faint, vain hope, and it intoxicated him.

He walked for a third of a mile through a field; the cemetery showed as a dark streak in the distance, like a forest or a big garden. The wall of white stone came into sight, the gates . . . In the moonlight he could read on the gate: 'The hour cometh in which . . .' Startsev went in at the wicker gate, and before anything else he saw the white crosses and monuments on both sides of the broad avenue, and their black shadows and the poplars; and for a long way round it was all white and black, and the slumbering trees bowed their branches over the white stones. It seemed as though it were lighter here than in the fields; the maple leaves stood out sharply like paws on the yellow sand of the avenue and on the stones, and the inscriptions on the tombs could be clearly read. For the first moments Startsev was struck now by what he saw for the first time in his life, and what he would probably never see again: a world not like anything else, a world in which the moonlight was as soft and beautiful, as though slumbering here in its cradle, where there was no life, none whatever; but in every dark poplar, in every grave, there was felt the presence of a mystery that promised a life peaceful, beautiful, eternal. The stones and faded flowers, together with the autumn scent of the leaves, all told of forgiveness, melancholy, and peace.

All was silence around; the stars looked down from the sky in the profound stillness, and Startsev's footsteps sounded loud and out of place, and only when the church clock began striking and he imagined himself dead, buried there for ever, he felt as though someone were looking at him, and for a moment he thought that it was not peace and tranquillity, but stifled despair, the dumb dreariness of non-existence . . .

Demetti's tomb was in the form of a shrine with an angel at the top. The Italian opera had once visited S— and one of the singers had died; she had been buried here, and this monument put up to her. No one in the town remembered her, but the icon lamp at the entrance reflected the moonlight, and looked as though it were burning.

There was no one, and, indeed, who would come here at midnight? But Startsev waited, and as though the moonlight warmed his passion, he waited passionately, and, in imagination, pictured kisses and embraces. He sat near the monument for half an hour, then paced up and down the side avenues, with his hat in his hand, waiting and thinking of the many women and girls buried in these tombs who had been beautiful and fascinating, who had loved, at night burned with passion, yielding themselves to caresses. How wickedly Mother Nature jested at man's expense, after all! How hurtful it was to sense this! These were Startsev's thoughts, and at the same time he wanted to cry out that he wanted love, that he was eager for it at any cost. To his eyes there were no slabs of marble, but fair white bodies in the moonlight; he saw shapes hiding bashfully in the shadows of the trees, felt their warmth, and the languor was oppressive . . .

And as though a curtain were lowered, the moon went behind a cloud, and suddenly all was darkness. Startsev could scarcely find the gate – by now it was as dark as an autumn night. Then he wandered about for an hour and a half, looking for the side-street in which he had left his horses.

'I am tired; I can hardly stand,' he said to Panteleimon.

And getting into his carriage with sweet relief, he thought:

'Ugh! I shouldn't have got so fat!'

III

The following evening he went to the Turkins' to propose. But it turned out to be an inconvenient moment, as Ekaterina was in her room having her hair done. She was getting ready to go to a dance at the club.

He had to sit a long time again in the dining-room drinking tea. Mr Turkin, seeing that his visitor was bored and preoccupied, drew some notes out of his waistcoat pocket, read a funny letter from a German steward, saying that all the ironmongery was ruined and the plasticity was peeling off the walls.

'I expect they'll give a decent dowry,' thought Startsev, listening absent-mindedly.

After a sleepless night, he was in a state of stupefaction, as though he had been given something sweet and soporific to drink; there was fog in his soul, but joy and warmth, and at the same time a cold, heavy bit of his brain was reflecting:

'Stop before it is too late! Is she a match for you? She is spoilt, whimsical, sleeps till two in the afternoon, while you are a sexton's son, a district doctor . . .'

'What of it?' he thought. 'I don't care.'

'Besides, if you marry her,' the bit of his brain went on, 'then her relations will make you give up the district work and live in the town.'

'After all,' he thought, 'if I must, then so be it. They'll give a dowry; we'll set ourselves up properly.'

At last Ekaterina came in, dressed for the ball, with a low neck, looking fresh and pretty; and Startsev admired her so much, and went into such ecstasies, that he could say nothing, but simply stared at her and laughed. She began saying good-bye, and he – with no reason for staying now – got up, saying that it was time for him to go home; his patients were waiting for him.

'Well, there's no help for that,' said Mr Turkin. 'Go, and you might take Kitten to the club on the way.'

It was spotting with rain; it was very dark, and they could only tell where the horses were by Panteleimon's husky cough. The hood of the carriage was put up.

'I stand upright; you lie down right,' said Mr Turkin as he helped his daughter into the carriage. 'He lies all right . . . Go! Hello and welcome.'

They drove off.

'I was at the cemetery yesterday,' Startsev began. 'How mean and cruel it was of you . . .'

'You went to the cemetery?'

'Yes, I went there and waited almost till two o'clock. I suffered . . .'

'Well, suffer, if you cannot take a joke.'

Ekaterina, pleased at having so cleverly taken in a man who was in love with her, and at being the object of such intense love, burst out laughing and suddenly uttered a shriek of terror, for, at that very minute, the horses turned sharply in at the gate of the club, and the carriage tilted on two wheels. Startsev put his arm round Ekaterina's waist; in her fright she clutched him, and he could not restrain himself, and passionately kissed her on the lips and on the chin, and embraced her more tightly.

'That's enough,' she said dryly.

And a minute later she had left the carriage, and a policeman near the lighted entrance of the club shouted in a loathsome voice to Panteleimon:

'What are you stopping for, you crow? Drive on.'

Startsev drove home, but soon afterwards returned. Attired in a borrowed tail-coat and a stiff white tie which made him sore and threatened to slip off his collar, he was sitting at midnight in the club drawing-room, and was saying with enthusiasm to Ekaterina:

'Ah, how little people know who have never loved! It seems to me that no one has ever yet described love truly, and this tender, joyful, agonising feeling is probably indescribable, and anyone who has once experienced it wouldn't put it into words. What use are preliminaries and beating about the bush? What use are unnecessary fine words? My love is immeasurable . . . I am asking, begging you,' Startsev brought out at last, 'be my wife!'

'Dmitri Ionych,' said Ekaterina Ivanovna, with a very grave face, after a moment's thought – 'Dmitri Ionych, I am very grateful to you for the honour. I respect you, but . . .' she got up and continued standing, 'but, I'm sorry, I cannot be your wife. Let us talk seriously. Dmitri Ionych, you know I love art beyond everything in love. I adore music; I love it frantically; I have dedicated my whole life to it. I want to be an artist; I want fame, success, freedom, and you want me to go on living in this town, to go on living this empty, useless life, which has become insufferable to me. To become a wife – oh no, forgive me! We must strive for a lofty, glorious goal, and married life would tie me for ever. Dmitri Ionych' (she faintly smiled as she pronounced Startsev's name; she thought of 'Aleksei Feofilaktovich') – 'Dmitri Ionych, you are a good, clever, honourable man; you are better than anyone . . .' Tears came into her eyes. 'I feel for you with my whole heart, but . . . but you will understand . . .'

And she turned away and left the drawing-room so as not to cry.

Startsev's heart stopped throbbing uneasily. Going out of the club into the street, he first of all tore off the stiff tie and drew a deep breath. He was a little ashamed and his vanity was wounded – he had not expected a refusal – and could not believe that all his dreams, his hopes and yearnings, had led him up to such a stupid end, just as in some little play at an amateur performance, and he was sorry for his feeling, for that love of his, so sorry that he felt as though he could have burst into sobs or have belaboured Panteleimon's broad back with his umbrella with all his might.

For three days he could not get on with work, he neither ate nor slept; but when the news reached him that Ekaterina had gone to Moscow to enter the Conservatoire, he grew calmer and resumed his old life.

Afterwards, remembering sometimes how he had wandered about the cemetery or driven all over the town to get a tail-coat, he stretched lazily and said:

'What a lot of trouble, though!'

IV

Four years passed. Startsev now had a large practice in the town. Every morning he hurriedly saw his patients at Dializh, then he drove in to see his town patients. By now he drove, not a pair, but a team of three with bells, and he returned home late at night. He had grown broader and stouter, and was not very fond of walking, as he suffered from breathlessness. And Panteleimon had grown fat, too, and the broader he grew, the more mournfully he sighed and complained of his bitter lot: he was sick of driving!

Startsev visited various households and met many people, but did not become close friends with anyone. The inhabitants' conversation, views on life, and even appearance irritated him. Experience taught him by degrees that while he played cards or lunched with one of these people, the man was a peaceable, friendly, and even intelligent human being; that as soon as one talked of anything not edible, for instance, of politics or science, he would be completely at a loss, or would expound a philosophy so stupid and vicious that you could only wave your hand in despair and go away. Even when Startsev tried to talk to liberal citizens, saying, for instance, that humanity, thank God, was progressing, and that one day it would be possible to dispense with passports and capital punishment, the citizen would look at him askance and suspiciously and ask him: 'Then anyone could murder anyone he chose in the street?' And when, at tea or supper, Startsev observed in company that people should work, that an idle life was wrong, everyone took this as a reproach, and began to get angry and argue aggressively. Moreover, the inhabitants did nothing, absolutely nothing, and took no interest in anything, and it was quite impossible to think of what to talk to them about. And Startsev avoided conversation, and confined himself to eating and playing whist; and when there was a family festivity in some household and he was invited to a meal, then he sat and ate in silence, looking at his plate. And everything that was said at the time was uninteresting, unjust, and stupid; he felt irritated and disturbed, but held his tongue, and, because he sat glumly silent and looked at his plate, he was nicknamed in the town 'the haughty Pole', though he never had been a Pole.

All such entertainments as theatres and concerts he declined, but he played whist every evening for about three hours with enjoyment. He had another diversion to which he took imperceptibly, little by little: in the evening he would take out of his pockets the banknotes he had gained by his practice, and sometimes there were stuffed in his pockets notes – yellow and green, and smelling of scent and vinegar and fish oil – up to the value of seventy roubles; and when they amounted to some hundreds he took them to the Mutual Credit Bank and deposited the money there to his account.

He was only twice at the Turkins' in the course of the four years after Ekaterina had gone away, on each occasion at the invitation of Mrs Turkina, who was still having treatment for migraine. Every summer Ekaterina came to stay with her parents, but he never saw her; the chance somehow never came.

But now four years had passed. One still, warm morning a letter was brought to the hospital. Mrs Turkina wrote to Mr Startsev, Dmitri Ionych, that she missed him very much, and begged him to come and see them, and to relieve her sufferings; and, by the way, it was her birthday. Below was a postscript: 'I join in mother's request. – E.'

Startsev considered, and in the evening he went to the Turkins'.

'Hello and welcome,' Mr Turkin greeted him, smiling with his eyes only. 'Bongjour.'

Mrs Turkina, white-haired and looking much older, shook Startsev's hand, sighed affectedly, and said:

'You don't care to pay attention to me, doctor. You never come and see us; I am too old for you. But now someone young has come; perhaps she will be more fortunate.'

And Kitten? She had grown thinner, paler, had grown handsomer and more graceful; but now she was Miss Turkina, Ekaterina Ivanovna, not Kitten; she had lost the freshness and look of childish naiveté. And in her eyes and manners there was something new – guilty and diffident, as if she did not feel at home here in the Turkins' house.

'How many summers, how many winters!' she said, giving Startsev her hand, and he could see that her heart was beating with excitement; and looking at him intently and curiously, she went on: 'You have put on weight! You look sunburnt and more mature, but on the whole you have changed very little.'

Now, too, he thought her attractive, very attractive, but there was something missing in her, or else something superfluous – he could not himself have said exactly what it was, but something prevented him from feeling as before. He did not like her pallor, her new expression, her faint smile, her voice, and soon afterwards he disliked her clothes, too, the low chair in which she was sitting; he disliked something in the past when he had almost married her. He thought of his love, of the dreams and the hopes which had troubled him four years before – and he felt awkward.

They had tea and a sweet pie. Then Mrs Turkina read aloud a novel; she read of things that never happen in real life, and Startsev listened, looked at her handsome grey head, and waited for her to finish.

'Stupidity is not being unable to write novels, but being unable to conceal it when you do,' he thought.

'Not badsome,' said Mr Turkin.

Then Ekaterina played long and noisily on the piano, and when she finished she was profusely thanked and warmly praised.

'It's a good thing I didn't marry her,' thought Startsev.

She looked at him, clearly waiting to be asked into the garden, but he remained silent.

'Let's have a talk,' she said, going up to him. 'How are you getting on? What are you doing? How are things? I've been thinking about you all these days,' she went on nervously. 'I wanted to write to you, wanted to come to Dializh to see you. I made up my mind to go, but then thought better of it. God knows what you think of me now; I have been looking forward to seeing you today with such emotion. For God's sake let's go into the garden.'

They went into the garden and sat down on the seat under the old maple, just as they had done four years before. It was dark.

'How are you getting on?' asked Ekaterina Ivanovna.

'Oh, all right; I take life as it comes,' answered Startsev.

And he could think of nothing more. They were silent.

'I feel so stirred up!' said Ekaterina Ivanovna, and she hid her face in her hands. 'But don't pay attention to it. I'm so happy to be at home; I'm so glad to see everyone. I can't get used to it. So many memories! I thought we'd talk without stopping till morning.'

Now he saw her face near, her shining eyes, and in the darkness she looked younger than in the room, and even her old childish expression seemed to have come back. And indeed she was looking at him with naive curiosity, as if she wanted to get a closer view and understanding of the man who had loved her so ardently, with such tenderness and such lack of success; her eyes thanked him for that love. And he recalled all that had been, every minute detail; roaming the cemetery, returning home in the morning exhausted, and he suddenly felt sad and regretted the past. A spark began glowing in his heart.

'Do you remember how I took you to the dance at the club?' he asked. 'It was dark and rainy then.'

A spark in his heart fanned into fire, and he now longed to talk, to complain of life . . .

'Ugh!' he said with a sigh. 'You ask how I am living. How do we live here? We don't. We grow old, we grow stout, we grow slack. Day after day passes; life slips by without colour, without impressions, without thoughts . . . In the daytime working for money, and in the evening the club, the company of card players, alcoholics, wheezy old men whom I can't endure. What's good in it?'

'Well, you have work — a noble object in life. You used to be so fond of talking of your hospital. I was such an odd girl then; I imagined I was a great pianist. Nowadays all young ladies play the piano, and I played, too, like everybody else, and there was nothing special about me. I am as good a pianist as mother is a writer. And of course I didn't understand you then, but afterwards in Moscow I often thought of you. I thought of no one but you. What happiness to be a district doctor; to help the suffering; to be serving the people! What happiness!' Ekaterina repeated with enthusiasm. 'When I thought of you in Moscow, you seemed to me so ideal, so lofty . . .'

Startsev thought of the bank notes he took out of his pockets in the evening with such pleasure, and the spark in his heart went out.

He got up to go into the house. She took his arm.

'You are the best person I've known in my life,' she went on. 'We will see each other and talk, won't we? Promise me. I am not a pianist; I have no illusions about myself now, and I will not play or talk of music when you're there.'

When they had gone into the house, and when Startsev saw her face in the lamp light, and her sad, grateful, searching eyes fixed upon him, he felt uneasy and thought again:

'It's a good thing I did not marry her then.'

He began taking leave.

'You have no Roman right to go before supper,' said Mr Turkin as he saw him off. 'It's extremely perpendicular on your part. Well now, perform!' he added, addressing Pava in the hall.

Pava, no longer a boy, but a young man with moustaches, threw himself into an attitude, flung up his arm, and said in a tragic voice:

'Unhappy woman, die!'

All this irritated Startsev. Getting into his carriage, and looking at the dark house and garden which used to be so precious and so dear, he thought of everything at once – Mrs Turkina's novels and Kitten's noisy playing, and Mr Turkin's jokes and Pava's tragic posturing, and thought if the most talented people in the town were so futile, what must the town be?

Three days later Pava brought a letter from Ekaterina Turkina.

'You don't come and see us – why?' she wrote to him. 'I am afraid that you have changed towards us. I am afraid, and I am terrified at the very thought of it. Reassure me; come and tell me that everything is well.

'I must talk to you. – Your E. T.'

He read this letter, thought a moment, and said to Pava:

'Tell them, my good fellow, that I can't come today; I'm very busy. Say I'll come in three days or so.'

But three days passed, a week passed; he still did not go. Happening once to drive past the Turkins' house, he thought he must go in, if only for a moment, but on second thoughts . . . he drove on.

And he never went to the Turkins' again.

V

Several more years have passed. Startsev has grown stouter still, has grown corpulent, breathes heavily, and now walks with his head thrown back. Stout and red in the face, he drives with his bells and his team of three horses, and Panteleimon, also stout and red in the face with his thick beefy neck, sits on the box, holding his arms stiffly out before him as though they were made of wood, and shouts to those he meets: 'Keep to the ri-i-ight!'; it is an impressive picture – one might think it was not a mortal, but some heathen deity in his chariot. He has an immense practice in the town, no time to breathe, and now owns an estate and two houses in the town, and he is looking out for a third, more profitable one; and when at the Mutual Credit Bank he is told of a house that is for sale, he goes to the house without ceremony, and, marching through all the rooms, regardless of half-dressed women and children who gaze at him in amazement and alarm, he prods at the doors with his stick, and says:

'Is that the study? Is that a bedroom? And what's here?'

And as he does so he breathes heavily and wipes the sweat from his brow.

He has a great deal to do, but still he does not give up his work as district doctor; he is greedy for gain, and he tries to be in all places at once. At Dializh and in the town he is called simply 'Ionych': 'Where is Ionych off to?' or 'Should not we call in Ionych to a consultation?'

Probably because his throat is covered with rolls of fat, his voice has changed; it has become thin and sharp. His temper has changed, too: he has grown bad-tempered and irritable. When he sees his patients he is usually in a bad mood; he impatiently taps the floor with his stick, and shouts in his disagreeable voice:

'Kindly confine yourself to answering my questions! Don't talk!'

He is solitary. He leads a dreary life; nothing interests him.

During all the years he had lived at Dializh his love for Kitten had been his one joy, and probably his last. In the evenings he plays whist at the club, and then sits alone at a big table and has supper. Ivan, the oldest and most respectable of the waiters, serves him, hands him Lafitte No. 17, and everyone at the club – the members of the committee, the cook and waiters – knows what he likes and what he doesn't like, does their very utmost to satisfy him, or else, you never know, he might fly into a rage and bang the floor with his stick.

As he eats his supper, he turns round from time to time and puts in his spoke in some conversation:

'What are you talking about? Eh? Whom?'

And when at a neighbouring table there is talk of the Turkins, he asks:

'What Turkins do you mean? The people whose daughter plays the piano?'

That is all that can be said about him.

And the Turkins? Mr Turkin has grown no older; he is not changed in the least, and still makes jokes and tells anecdotes as of old. Mrs Turkina still reads her novels aloud to her visitors with eagerness and touching simplicity. And Kitten plays the piano for four hours every day. She has grown visibly older, is constantly ailing, and every autumn goes to the Crimea with her mother. When Mr Turkin sees them off at the station, he wipes his tears as the train starts, and shouts:

'Hello and farewell.'

And he waves his handkerchief.

1898

The Little Trilogy

At the far end of the village of Mironositskoe hunters had come late to lodge for the night in the barn of the village elder, Prokofi. There were two of them, the veterinary surgeon Ivan and the schoolmaster Burkin. Ivan had a rather strange double-barrelled surname – Chimsha-Gimalaisky – which did not suit him at all, and he was called just Ivan all over the province. He lived at a horse stud near the town, and had now come out shooting to get a breath of fresh air. Burkin, the high school teacher, stayed every summer with the Count P—, and had been thoroughly at home in this district for years.

They were not asleep. Ivan, a tall, lean old fellow with long moustaches, was sitting outside at the door, smoking a pipe in the moonlight. Burkin was lying inside on the hay, and could not be seen in the darkness.

They were telling each other all sorts of stories. Among other things, they spoke of the fact that the elder's wife, Mavra, a healthy and by no means stupid woman, had never been outside her native village, had never seen a town nor a railway in her life, and had spent the last ten years sitting by the stove, and went out only at night.

'What's so amazing about that?' said Burkin. 'There are plenty of people in the world, solitary by temperament, who try to retreat into their shell like a hermit crab or a snail. Perhaps it is an instance of atavism, a return to the period when man's ancestor was not yet a social animal and lived alone in his den, or perhaps it is only one of the varieties of human character – who knows? I am not a natural scientist, and it is not my business to deal with such questions; I only mean to say that people like Mavra are not uncommon. There is no need to look far; two months ago a man called Belikov, a colleague of mine, the Greek teacher, died in our town. You have heard of him, no doubt. He was remarkable for always wearing galoshes and a warm quilted coat, and carrying an umbrella even in the very best weather. And his umbrella was in a case, and his watch was in a case made of grey chamois leather, and when he took out his penknife to sharpen his pencil, his penknife, too, was in a little case, and his face seemed to be in a case too, because he always hid it in his turned-up collar. He wore dark spectacles and flannel vests, stuffed his ears with cotton wool, and when he got into a cab always told the driver to put up the hood. In short, the man displayed a constant and insurmountable impulse to wrap himself in a membrane, to make, so to speak, a case which would isolate him and protect him from external influences. Reality irritated him, frightened him, kept him in continual agitation, and, perhaps to justify his timidity, his aversion for present reality, he always praised the past and what had never existed; and even the classical languages which he taught were really for him galoshes and umbrellas in which he sheltered from real life.

' "Oh, how sonorous, how beautiful is the Greek language!" he would say, with a saccharine expression; and as though to prove his words he would screw up his eyes and, raising a finger, would pronounce "Anthropos!"

'And Belikov tried to hide his thoughts also in a case. The only things that were clear to his mind were government circulars and newspaper articles in which something was forbidden. When a notice prohibited the boys from going out in the streets after nine in the evening, or some article declared carnal love unlawful, it was to his mind clear and definite: it was forbidden, and that was enough. For him there was always a doubtful element, something vague and not fully expressed, in any authorisation or permit. When a dramatic club or a reading room or a tea-shop was licensed in the town, he would shake his head and say softly:

' "It's all right, of course; it's all very fine but I hope it doesn't lead to anything!"

'Any breach of order, deviation or departure from the rule, depressed him, though you'd have thought it was no business of his. If one of his colleagues was late for church or if rumours reached him of some schoolboy prank, or one of the female class supervisors was seen late in the evening in the company of an officer, he was much disturbed, and said he hoped that it didn't lead to anything. At teachers' meetings he simply oppressed us with his caution, his circumspection, and his wooden-case reflections, for instance, that young people in both male and female high schools behaved badly, that there was too much noise in the classrooms . . . Oh, he hoped it would not reach the ears of the authorities; oh, he hoped it didn't lead to anything, and he thought it would be a very good thing if Petrov were expelled from the second class and Yegorov from the fourth. And, do you know, his sighs, his despondency, the dark glasses on his pale little face, a little face like a ferret's, you know, he crushed us all, and we gave way, lowered Petrov's and Yegorov's marks for conduct, kept them in detention, and in the end expelled them both. He had a strange habit of visiting our lodgings. He would come to see a teacher, would sit down, and remain silent, as though he were carefully inspecting something. He would sit like this in silence for an hour or two and then go away. This he called "maintaining good relations with his colleagues"; and it was obvious that coming to see us and sitting there was tiresome to him, and that he came to see us simply because he considered it his duty as our colleague. We teachers were afraid of him. And even the headmaster was afraid of him. Would you believe it, our teachers were all intellectual, right-minded people, brought up on Turgenev and Shchedrin,* yet this little chap, who always went about in galoshes and an umbrella, had the whole high school under his thumb for fifteen long years! High school, indeed – he had the whole town under his thumb! Our ladies did not organise private theatricals on Saturdays for fear he should hear of it, and the clergy dared not eat meat or play cards in his presence. Under the influence of people like Belikov we have become afraid of everything in our town for the last ten or fifteen years. They are afraid to speak aloud, afraid to make friends, afraid to read books, afraid to help the poor, to teach people to read and write . . .'

Ivan cleared his throat, meaning to say something, but first lit his pipe, gazed at the moon, and then said, pausing between his phrases:

'Yes, decent, thinking people read Shchedrin and Turgenev, Buckle,* and all the rest of them, yet they knuckled under and put up with it . . . That's the point.'

'Belikov lived in the same house as I did,' Burkin went on, 'on the same storey, his door facing mine; we often saw each other, and I knew how he lived when he was at home. And at home it was the same story: dressing-gown, night-cap, blinds, bolts, a whole list of prohibitions and restrictions of all sorts, and – "Oh, I hope it doesn't lead to anything!" Lenten food was bad for him, yet he could not eat meat, as people might perhaps say Belikov did not keep the fasts, yet he ate pike-perch with butter – hard to say whether that was a Lenten dish or not. He did not keep a female servant for fear people might think the worst, but had as cook an old man of sixty, called Afanasi, a half-witted drunkard, who had once been an officer's servant and could cook after a fashion. This Afanasi was usually standing at the door with his arms folded; with a deep sigh, he would mutter always the same thing:

' "There are plenty of *them* about nowadays!"

'Belikov had a little bedroom like a box; his bed had curtains. When he went to bed he buried himself in the bedclothes; it was hot and stuffy; the wind battered on the closed doors; there was a droning noise in the stove and a sound of sighs from the kitchen –

ominous sighs . . . And he was frightened under the bedclothes. He was afraid that something might happen, that Afanasi might cut his throat, that thieves might break in, and so he had troubled dreams all night, and in the morning, when we went together to the high school, he was depressed and pale, and it was clear that the high school full of people excited dread and aversion in his whole being, and that to walk beside me was irksome to a man of his solitary temperament.

' "They make a lot of noise in our classes," he used to say, as though trying to find an explanation for his depression. "It's unbelievable."

'And the Greek teacher, this man in a case – would you believe it? – almost got married.'

Ivan glanced quickly into the barn and said:

'You're joking!'

'Yes, strange as it seems, he almost got married. A new teacher of history and geography, Mikhail Kovalenko, a Ukrainian, was appointed. He came, not alone, but with his sister Varenka. He was a tall, dark young man with huge hands, and one could see from his face that he had a bass voice, and, in fact, he had a voice that seemed to come out of a barrel – "boom boom, boom!" She was not so young, about thirty, but she, too, was tall, with a good figure, with black eyebrows and red cheeks – in fact, she was a regular sugar plum, and so sprightly, so noisy, she was always singing Ukrainian songs and laughing. At the least thing she would go off into a ringing laugh – "Ha-ha-ha!" We first thoroughly got to know the Kovalenkos at the headmaster's name day party. Among the glum and intensely bored teachers who came even to the name day party as a duty we suddenly saw a new Aphrodite risen from the waves, she walked with her arms akimbo, laughed, sang, danced . . . She sang with feeling "The Winds Blow", then another song, and another, and she fascinated us all – all, even Belikov. He sat down by her and said with a honeyed smile:

' "Ukrainian reminds one of ancient Greek in its softness and agreeable resonance."

'That flattered her, and she began telling him with feeling and earnestness that they had a farm in the Gadiach* district, and that her mama lived at the farm, and that they had such pears such melons, such *kabaks*! The Ukrainians call pumpkins *kabaks* (i.e. taverns), while their taverns they call *shinki*, and they make a beetroot soup with tomatoes and aubergines in it, "which is so nice, awfully nice!"

'We listened and listened, and suddenly the same idea dawned upon us all:

' "It would nice to marry them off," the headmaster's wife said to me softly.

'We all for some reason recalled that our friend Belikov was unmarried, and it now seemed to us strange that we had hitherto failed to observe, and had in fact completely lost sight of, such a vital detail of his life. What was his attitude to women? How had he settled this crucial question for himself? This had not interested us in the least till then; perhaps we had not even admitted the idea that a man who went out in all weathers in galoshes and slept under curtains could be in love.

' "He is a good deal over forty and she is thirty," the headmaster's wife went on, developing her idea. "I believe she would marry him."

'All sorts of things are done in the provinces through boredom, all sorts of unnecessary and nonsensical things! And that is because what is necessary is not done at all. Why, for instance, should we make a match for this Belikov, whom you could not even imagine married? The headmaster's wife, the inspector's wife, and all our high school ladies, grew livelier and ever better-looking, as though they had suddenly found a new object in life. The headmaster's wife would take a box at the theatre, and we saw sitting in her box Varenka, with a great big fan, beaming and happy, and beside her Belikov, a little bent figure, looking as though he had been pulled from his house with pincers. I would give an evening party, and the ladies would insist on my inviting Belikov and Varenka. In short, the machinery was set in motion. It appeared that Varenka was not averse to matrimony. She had a fairly cheerless life with her brother, they could do nothing but quarrel and scold one another from morning till night. Here is a scene, for instance. Kovalenko would be coming along the street, a tall, sturdy young lout, in an embroidered shirt, his fringe falling on his forehead under his cap, in one hand a buckle of books, in the other a thick knotted stick, followed by his sister, also with books in her hand.

' "But you haven't read it, Mikhail dear!" she would be arguing loudly. "I tell you, I swear you have not read it at all!"

' "And I tell you I have read it," cries Kovalenko, thumping his stick on the pavement.

' "Oh, my goodness, Mikhail dear, why are you so cross? We are arguing about principles."

' "I tell you that I have read it!" Kovalenko would shout, more loudly than ever.

'And at home, if there was an outsider present, there was sure to be a skirmish. Such a life must have been wearisome, and of course she must have longed for a home of her own. Besides, there was her age to be considered; there was no time left to pick and choose; it was a case of marrying anybody, even a Greek teacher. And, indeed, most of our young ladies don't mind whom they marry, so long as they get married. However that may be, Varenka began to show an unmistakable partiality for Belikov.

'And Belikov? He used to visit Kovalenko just as he did us. He would arrive, sit down, and remain silent. He would sit quiet, and Varenka would sing to him "The Winds Blow", or would look pensively at him with her dark eyes, or would suddenly go off into a peal – "Ha-ha-ha!"

'Suggestion plays a great part in love affairs, and still more in getting married. Everybody – both his colleagues and the ladies – began assuring Belikov that he ought to get married, that there was nothing left for him in life but to get married; we all congratulated him, with solemn countenances uttered various platitudes, such as "Marriage is a serious step." Besides, Varenka was good-looking and interesting; she was the daughter of a state councillor, and had a farm; and what was more, she was the first woman who had been warm and friendly to him. His head was turned, and he decided that he really ought to get married.'

'Well, that was the time to remove his galoshes and umbrella,' said Ivan.

'Only fancy, that turned out to be impossible. He put Varenka's portrait on his table, kept coming to see me and talking about Varenka, and home life, saying marriage was a serious step. He visited the Kovalenkos frequently, but he did not alter his manner of life in the least; on the contrary, indeed, his determination to get married seemed to have a depressing effect on him. He grew thinner and paler, and seemed to retreat further and further into his case.

' "I like Varenka Kovalenko," he used to say to me, with a faint and wry smile, "and I know that everyone ought to get married, but . . . you know all this has happened so suddenly . . . One must think about it."

' "What is there to think about?" I would say to him. "Just get married – that's all."

' "No; marriage is a serious step. One must first weigh the duties before one, the responsibilities . . . so that it doesn't lead to anything. It worries me so much that I don't sleep at night. And I must confess I am afraid: her brother and she have a strange way of thinking; they look at things strangely, you know, and her disposition is very impetuous. One may get married, and then, there is no knowing, one may find oneself in an unpleasant position."

'And he did not propose; he kept putting it off, to the great vexation of the headmaster's wife and all our ladies, he went on weighing his future duties and responsibilities, and meanwhile he

went for a walk with Varenka almost every day – possibly he thought
that this was necessary in his position – and came to see me to talk
about family life. And in all probability in the end he would have
proposed to her, and would have made one of those unnecessary,
stupid marriages such as are made by thousands among us from being
bored and having nothing to do, if it had not been for a *kolossalische
Skandal*. I must mention that Varenka's brother, Kovalenko,
detested Belikov from the first day of their acquaintance, and could
not endure him.

' "I don't understand," he used to say to us, shrugging his
shoulders, "I don't understand how you can put up with that stool
pigeon, that revolting mug. Ugh! how can you live here? The
atmosphere is stifling and unclean! Call yourselves schoolmasters,
teachers? You are paltry government clerks. You keep not a temple of
science, but a department for red tape and loyal behaviour, and it
smells as sour as a police station. No, my friends; I will stay with you
for a while, and then I will go to my farm and there catch crabs and
teach Ukrainian lads. I shall go, and you can stay here with your
Judas – damn his soul!"

'Or he would laugh till he cried, first in a loud bass, then in a shrill,
thin laugh, and ask me, waving his hands:

' "What does he sit here for? What does he want? He sits and
stares."

'He even named Belikov after a Ukrainian comedy *The Man-eating
Spider*.* And it will readily be understood that we avoided talking to
him of his sister's being about to marry "The Man-eating Spider".

'And on one occasion, when his headmaster's wife hinted to him
what a good thing it would be to secure his sister's future with such a
reliable, universally respected man as Belikov, he frowned and
muttered:

' "It's not my business; let her marry a viper if she likes. I don't like
meddling in other people's affairs."

'Now hear what happened next. Some mischievous person drew a
caricature of Belikov walking along with his trousers tucked into his
galoshes, under his umbrella, with Varenka on his arm; below, the
inscription "Anthropos in love". The expression was caught to a
marvel, you know. The artist must have worked for more than one
night, for the teachers of both the boys' and girls' high schools, the
teachers of the seminary, the government officials, all received a copy.
Belikov received one, too. The caricature made a very painful
impression on him.

'We went out together; it was the first of May, a Sunday, and all of
us, the boys and the teachers, had agreed to meet at the high school

and then to go for a walk together to a wood beyond the town. We set off, and he was green in the face and gloomier than a storm cloud.

' "What wicked, evil-minded people there are!" he said, and his lips quivered.

'I felt really sorry for him. We were walking along, and all of a sudden – would you believe it? – Kovalenko came bowling along on a bicycle, and after him, also on a bicycle, Varenka, flushed and exhausted, and joyful and light-hearted.

' "We are going on ahead," she said. "What lovely weather! Awfully lovely!"

'And they both disappeared from our sight. Belikov turned white instead of green, and seemed petrified. He stopped short and stared at me.

' "What is the meaning of it? Tell me, please!" he asked. "Can my eyes have deceived me? Is it proper for high school teachers and ladies to ride bicycles?"

' "What's improper about it?" I said "Let them ride and enjoy themselves."

' "But how can that be?" he cried, amazed at my calm. "What are you saying?"

'And he was so shocked that he refused to come with us, and returned home.

'Next day he was continually twitching and nervously rubbing his hands, and it was evident from his face that he felt unwell. And he left before his work was over, for the first time in his life. And he ate no dinner. Towards evening he wrapped himself up warmly, though it was quite warm weather, and sailed out to the Kovalenkos'. Varenka was out; he found only her brother.

' "Please sit down," Kovalenko said coldly, with a frown. His face looked sleepy; he had just had a nap after dinner, and was in a very bad temper.

'Belikov sat in silence for ten minutes, and then began:

' "I have come to see you to relieve my mind. I am very, very troubled. Some scurrilous fellow has drawn an absurd caricature of me and another person, in whom we are both deeply interested. I regard it as a duty to assure you that I have had no hand in it . . . I have given no sort of ground for such ridicule – on the contrary, I have always behaved in every way like a gentleman."

'Kovalenko sat sulky and silent. Belikov waited a little, and went on slowly in a mournful voice:

' "And I have a few other things to say to you. I have been in service for years while you have only lately entered it, and I consider it my duty as an older colleague to give you a warning. You ride a bicycle, and that pastime is utterly unsuitable for an educator of youth."

' "Why so?" asked Kovalenko in his bass voice.

' "Surely that needs no explanation, Mr Kovalenko, surely you can understand that? If the teacher rides a bicycle, what can you expect the pupils to do? You will have them walking on their heads next! And so long as there is no formal authorisation to do so, it is out of the question. I was horrified yesterday! When I saw your sister I couldn't see straight any more. A woman or a young girl on a bicycle – it's awful!"

' "What is it you want exactly?"

' "All I want is to warn you, Mr Kovalenko. You are a young man, you have a future before you, you must be very, very careful in your behaviour, and you are so careless – oh, so careless! You go about in an embroidered shirt, are constantly seen in the street carrying books and now the bicycle, too. The headmaster will learn that you and your sister ride a bicycle, and then it will reach the higher authorities . . . Will that be a good thing?"

' "It's no business of anybody else if my sister and I do bicycle!" said Kovalenko, and he turned crimson. "And damnation take anyone who meddles in my private affairs!"

Belikov turned pale and got up.

' "If you speak to me in that tone I cannot continue," he said. "And I beg you never to express yourself like that about our superiors in my presence; you ought to be respectful to authority."

' "Was I saying anything against authority?" asked Kovalenko, looking at him wrathfully. "Please leave me alone. I am an honest man, and do not care to talk to a gentleman like you. I don't like stool pigeons."

'Belikov panicked and flustered, and began hurriedly putting on his coat, with an expression of horror on his face. It was the first time in his life he had been spoken to so rudely.

' "You can say what you please," he said, as he went out from the hall to the landing on the staircase. "I ought only to warn you: possibly someone may have overheard us, and that our conversation may not be misunderstood and it doesn't lead to anything, I shall be compelled to inform our headmaster of our conversation . . . in its main features. I am obliged to do so."

' "Inform him? You can go and make your report!"

'Kovalenko seized him from from behind by the collar and gave him a push, and Belikov rolled downstairs, his galoshes banging all the way. The staircase was high and steep, but he rolled to the bottom unhurt, got up, and touched his nose to see whether his glasses were all right. But just as he was falling down the stairs Varenka came in, with two ladies; they stood below staring, and to Belikov this was the most terrible bit. I believe he would rather have broken his neck or both legs than have been an object of ridicule. Why, now the whole town would hear of it; it would come to the headmaster's ears, would reach the higher – oh, it would lead to something. There would be another caricature, and it would all end in his being asked to resign his post . . .

'When he got up, Varenka recognised him, and, looking at his ridiculous face, his crumpled overcoat, and his galoshes, not understanding what had happened and supposing that he had slipped by accident, could not restrain herself, and laughed loud enough to be heard by all the flats:

' "Ha-ha-ha!"

'And this pealing, ringing "Ha-ha-ha!" was the last straw that put an end to everything: to the proposed match and to Belikov's earthly existence. He did not hear what Varenka said to him; he saw nothing. On reaching home, the first thing he did was to remove her portrait from the table; then he went to bed, and he never got up again.

'Three days later Afanasi came to me and asked whether we should not send for the doctor, as there was something wrong with his master. I went in to see Belikov. He lay silent behind the curtain covered with a quilt; if asked a question he said "Yes" or "No" and not another sound. He lay there while Afanasi, gloomy and scowling, hovered about him, sighing heavily, and smelling of vodka, like a tavern.

'A month later Belikov died. We – that is, both the high schools and the seminary – all went to his funeral. Now that he was lying in his coffin his expression was mild, agreeable, even cheerful, as though he were glad that he had at last been put into a case which he would never leave again. Yes, he had attained his ideal! And, as though in his honour, it was dull, rainy weather on the day of his funeral, and we all wore galoshes and took our umbrellas. Varenka too, was at the funeral, and when the coffin was lowered into the grave she burst into tears. I have noticed that Ukrainian woman are always laughing or crying – no intermediate mood.

'I must confess that to bury people like Belikov is a great pleasure. As we were returning from the cemetery we wore discreet Lenten faces; no one wanted to display this feeling of pleasure – a feeling that we had experienced long, long ago as children when our elders had gone and out we ran about the garden for an hour or two, enjoying complete freedom. Ah, freedom, freedom! The merest hint, the faintest hope of its possibility gives wings to the soul, does it not?

'We returned from the cemetery in a good humour. But not more than a week had passed before life went on as in the past, as gloomy, oppressive, and senseless – a life not forbidden by government notices, but not fully permitted either: it was no better. And, indeed, though we had buried Belikov, how many such men in cases were left, how many more of them there will be!'

'That's just how it is,' said Ivan and he lit his pipe.

'How many more of them there will be!' repeated Burkin.

The schoolmaster came out of the barn. He was a short, stout man, completely bald, with a black beard down to his waist. Two dogs came out with him.

'What a moon!' he said, looking upwards.

It was midnight. On the right could be seen the whole village, a long street stretching far away for three miles. All was buried in deep silent slumber; not a movement, not a sound; it was scarcely believable that nature could be so still. When on a moonlit night you see a broad village street, with its cottages, haystacks, and slumbering willows, a feeling of calm comes over the soul; in this peace, wrapped away from care, toil, and sorrow in the darkness of light, it is meek, melancholy, beautiful, and it seems as though the stars look down upon it kindly and with tenderness and as though there were no evil on earth and all were well. On the left the open country began from the end of the village; it could be seen stretching far away to the horizon, and there was no movement, no sound in that whole expanse bathed in moonlight.

'Yes, that's the point,' repeated Ivan; 'and isn't our living in town, airless and crowded, our writing useless papers, our playing whist – isn't that all a sort of case boxing us in? And our spending our whole lives among idle, quarrelsome men and silly, idle women, our talking and our listening to all sorts of nonsense – isn't that another case? If you like, I will tell you a very edifying story.'

'No; it's time we were asleep,' said Burkin. 'Tell it tomorrow.'

They went into the barn and lay down on the hay. And they were both covered up and beginning to doze when they suddenly heard light footsteps – patter, patter . . . Someone was walking not far from the barn, walking a little and stopping, and a minute later – patter, patter again . . . The dogs began growling.

'That's Mavra,' said Burkin.

The footsteps died away.

'You see and hear them telling lies,' said Ivan, turning over on the other side, 'and they call you a fool for putting up with their lying. You endure insult and humiliation, and dare not openly say that you are on the side of the honest and the free, and you lie and smile yourself; and all that for the sake of a crust of bread, for the sake of a warm corner, for the sake of a wretched little worthless rank in the service – no, you can't go on living like this! . . .'

'Well, you are off on another tack now, Ivan,' said the schoolmaster. 'Let's go to sleep!'

And ten minutes later Burkin was asleep. But Ivan kept sighing and turning over from side to side; then he got up, went outside again, and, sitting by the door, lit his pipe.

II GOOSEBERRIES

The whole sky had been overcast with rain clouds since early in the morning; it was a still day, not hot but dreary, as it is in grey dull weather when the clouds have been hanging over the country for a long while, when you expect rain and it does not come. Ivan, the veterinary surgeon, and Burkin, the high school teacher, were already tired from walking, and the fields seemed to them endless. Far ahead of them they could just see the windmills of the village of Mironositskoe; on the right stretched a row of hillocks which disappeared in the distance behind the village, and they both knew that this was the bank of the river, that there were meadows, green willows, homesteads there, and that from one of the hillocks could be seen the same vast plain, telegraph wires, and a train which in the distance looked like a crawling caterpillar, and that in clear weather one could even see the town. Now, in still weather, when all nature seemed mild and dreamy, Ivan and Burkin were filled with love of that countryside, and both thought how great, how beautiful a land it was.

'Last time we were in the elder Prokofi's barn,' said Burkin, 'you were about to tell me a story.'

'Yes. I meant to tell you about my brother.'

Ivan heaved a deep sigh and lit a pipe to begin to tell his story, but just at that moment the rain began. And five minutes later heavy rain came down, without a break in the sky, and it was hard to tell when it would be over. Ivan and Burkin stopped in hesitation; the dogs, already drenched, stood with their tails between their legs, gazing at them fondly.

'We must take shelter somewhere,' said Burkin. 'Let's go to Aliokhin's; it's close by.'

'Come along.'

They turned aside and walked through mown fields, sometimes going straight ahead, sometimes turning to the right, till they came out on to the road. Soon they saw poplars, a garden, then the red roofs of barns; there was a gleam of the river, and the view opened on to a broad expanse of water with a watermill and a white bathing-pool: this was Sofino, where Aliokhin lived.

The watermill was at work, drowning the sound of the rain; the dam was shaking. Here wet horses with drooping heads were standing near their carts, and men were walking about covered with sacks. It was damp, muddy, and desolate; the water looked cold and malignant. Ivan and Burkin were now experiencing wetness, messiness, and discomfort all over, their feet were heavy with mud, and when, crossing the dam, they went up to Aliokhin's barns, they were silent, as though angry with one another.

In one of the barns there was the sound of a winnowing machine, the door was open, and the clouds of dust were coming from it. In the doorway was standing Aliokhin himself, a man of about forty, tall and stout, with long hair, more like a professor or an artist than a landowner. He wore a white shirt that badly needed washing, a cord for a belt, drawers instead of trousers, and his boots, too, were plastered with mud and straw. His eyes and nose were black with dust. He recognised Ivan and Burkin, and was apparently very delighted to see them.

'Go into the house, gentlemen,' he said, smiling; 'I'll come directly, this minute.'

It was a big two-storeyed house. Aliokhin lived in the lower storey, with arched ceilings and little windows, where the farm managers had once lived; here everything was plain, and there was a smell of rye bread, cheap vodka, and harness. He went upstairs into the best rooms only on rare occasions, when visitors came. Ivan and Burkin were met in the house by a maid, a young woman so beautiful that they both stood still and looked at one another.

'You can't imagine how delighted I am to see you, my friends,' said Aliokhin, going into the hall with them. 'It is a surprise! Pelageia,' he said, addressing the girl, 'give our visitors something to change into. And, by the way, I will change too. Only I must first go and clean myself up, for I don't think I've had a bath since spring. Would you like to come into the bathing-pool while they get things ready here?'

Beautiful Pelageia, so tactful and, to look at, so soft, brought them towels and soap, and Aliokhin went to the bathing-pool with his guests.

'Yes, it's a long time since I had a bathe,' he said undressing. 'I've got a nice bathing-pool, as you see; my father built it, but I somehow never have time to bathe.'

He sat down on the steps and soaped his long hair and his neck, and the water round him turned brown.

'Yes, I must say . . .' said Ivan meaningfully, looking at his head.

'It's a long time since I last bathed . . .' said Aliokhin with embarrassment, giving himself a second soaping, and the water near him turned dark blue, like ink.

Ivan went outside, plunged into the water with a loud splash, and swam in the rain, flinging his arms out wide. He stirred the water into waves which set the white lilies bobbing up and down; he swam to the very middle of the millpond and dived, and came up a minute later in another place, and swam on, and kept on diving trying to touch the bottom. 'Oh, my goodness!' he repeated continually, enjoying himself thoroughly. 'Oh, my God!' He swam to the mill, talked to the peasants there about something, then returned and lay on his back in the middle of the pond, turning his face to the rain. Burkin and Aliokhin were dressed and ready to go, but he still went on swimming and diving.

'Oh, my God . . .' he said. 'Oh, Lord have mercy! . . .'

'That's enough!' Burkin shouted to him.

They went back to the house. And only when the lamp was lit in the big drawing-room upstairs, and Burkin and Ivan, attired in silk dressing-gowns and warm slippers, were sitting in arm-chairs; and Aliokhin, washed and combed, in a new coat, was walking about the drawing-room, evidently enjoying the feeling of warmth, cleanliness, dry clothes, and light shoes; and when lovely Pelageia, stepping noiselessly on the carpet and smiling softly, was serving them tea and jam on a tray – only then Ivan began his story, and it seemed as though not only Burkin and Aliokhin were listening, but also the ladies, young and old, and the officers who looked down upon them sternly and calmly from their gold frames.

'There are two of us brothers,' he began, 'me, Ivan, and my brother, Nikolai, two years younger. I went in for a profession and became a veterinary surgeon, while Nikolai sat in a government office from the time he was nineteen. Our father, Chimsha-Gimalaisky, was a serf-soldier* by birth, but he rose to be an officer and left us a little estate and the rank of nobility. After his death the little estate went in debts and legal expenses; but, anyway, we had spent our childhood running wild in the country. Like peasant children, we passed our days and nights in the fields and the woods, looked after horses, stripped lime bark, fished, and so on . . . And, you know, anyone who has once in his life fished for ruff or has seen thrushes migrating in autumn, watched them flock over the village on bright, cool days, will never be a real townsman, and will have a yearning for freedom to the day of his death. My brother was miserable in the government office. Years passed by, and he went on sitting in the same place, went on writing the same papers and thinking of one and the same thing – how to get into the country. And this yearning by degrees passed into a definite desire, into a dream of buying himself a little farm somewhere on the banks of a river or a lake.

'He was a gentle, good-natured fellow, and I was fond of him, but I never sympathised with this desire to shut himself up for the rest of his life in a little farm of his own. It's fashionable to say that a man needs no more than six feet of earth. But six feet are what a corpse needs, not a man.* And they say, too, now, that if our intellectual classes are attracted to the land and yearn for a farm, it's a good thing. But these farms are just the same as six feet of earth. To retreat from town, from the struggle, from the bustle of life, to retreat and bury yourself in your farm – it's not life, it's egotism, laziness, it's monasticism of a sort, but monasticism without good works. A man does not need six feet of earth or a farm, but the entire globe, all nature, where he can have room to display all the qualities and pecularities of his free spirit.

'My brother Nikolai, sitting in his government office, dreamed of eating his own cabbages, which would fill the whole yard with such a savoury smell, of taking his meals on the green grass, sleeping in the sun, sitting for whole hours on the seat by the gate, gazing at the fields and the forest. Gardening books and all those farming tips in calendars were his delight, his favourite spiritual sustenance; he enjoyed reading newspapers, too, but the only things he read in them were the advertisements for so many acres of arable land and a grass meadow with farm houses and buildings, a river, a garden, a mill and millponds for sale. And his imagination pictured the garden paths, flowers, fruit, starling cotes, pond carp, and all that sort of thing, you know. These imaginary pictures were of different kinds according to the advertisements which he came across, but for some reason in every one of them he always had to have gooseberries. He could not imagine a farm house, he could not picture an idyllic nook, without gooseberries.

' "Country life has its conveniences," he would sometimes say. "You sit on the veranda and drink tea, while your ducks swim on the pond; there is a delicious smell everywhere, and ... and the gooseberries are growing."

'He used to draw a map of his property, and on every map there were the same things – (a) a landowner's house; (b) servants' quarters; (c) a kitchen garden; (d) gooseberry bushes. He lived parsimoniously, he starved himself of food and drink, his clothes were beyond description, like a beggar's, but he kept on saving and putting money in the bank. He grew fearfully avaricious. I found it painful to look at him, and I used to give him a few things and send him presents for Christmas and Easter, but he used to save that, too. Once a man is obsessed by an idea, there's nothing you can do.

'Years passed: he was transferred to another province. He was over forty, and he was still reading the advertisements in the papers and saving up. Then I heard he was married. Still with the same object of buying a farm and haaving gooseberries, he married an elderly and ugly widow without a trace of feeling for her, simply because she had a bit of cash. He went on living frugally after marrying her, and kept her short of food, while he put her money in the bank in his name. Her first husband had been a postmaster, and with him she was accustomed to pies and liqueurs, while with her second husband she did not get even black bread in sufficiency; she began to pine away with this sort of life, and three years later she gave up the ghost. And I need hardly say that my brother never for one moment imagined that he was responsible for her death. Money, like vodka, makes a man odd. In our town there was a merchant who, before he died, ordered a plateful of honey and ate up all his money and lottery tickets with the honey, so that no one might get the benefit of it. While I was inspecting cattle at a railway station, a cattle dealer fell under an engine and had his leg cut off. We carried him into the waiting room, the blood was flowing – it was a horrible thing – and he kept asking them to look for his leg and was very much worried about it; there were twenty roubles in the boot on the leg that had been cut off, and he was afraid they would be lost.'

'Well, you are off on another tack now,' said Burkin.

'After his wife's death,' Ivan went on, after thinking for half a minute, 'my brother began looking out for an estate for himself. Of course, you may look about for five years and yet end by making a mistake, and buying something quite different from what you have dreamed of. My brother Nikolai bought through an agent a mortgaged estate of three hundred and thirty acres, with a land-owner's house, with servants' quarters, with a park, but with no orchard, no gooseberry bushes, and no duck pond; there was a river, but the water in it was the colour of coffee because on one side of the estate there was a brickyard and on the other a bone-processing factory. But Nikolai did not grieve much; he ordered twenty gooseberry bushes, planted them, and began living as a country gentleman.

'Last year I went to pay him a visit. I thought I'd go and see what it was like. In his letters my brother called his estate "Chumbaroklova Waste, alias Gimalaiskoe". I reached "alias Gimalaiskoe" in the afternoon. It was hot. Everywhere there were ditches, fences, hedges, fir trees planted in rows, and there was no knowing how to reach the courtyard, where to put your horse. I went up to the house, and was met by a fat red dog that looked like a pig. It tried to bark, but it was too lazy. The cook, a fat, barefooted woman, came out of the kitchen, and she, too, looked like a pig, and said that her master was resting after dinner. I went in to see my brother. He was sitting up in bed with a quilt over his legs; he had grown older, fatter, wrinkled; his cheeks, his nose, and his mouth all stuck out – any moment he might have grunted into the quilt.

'We embraced each other, and shed tears of joy and of sadness at the thought that we had once been young and now were both grey-haired and near the grave. He dressed, and led me out to show me his estate.

' "Well, how are you getting on here?" I asked.

"Oh, all right, thank God; I am getting on very well."

'He was no more a poor timid clerk, but a real landowner, a gentleman. He was already accustomed to it, had grown used to it, and liked it. He ate a great deal, washed in the bath-house, was growing stout, was already suing the village commune and both factories, and was very much offended when the peasants did not call him "Your Honour". And he concerned himself with the salvation of his soul in a substantial, gentlemanly manner, and performed deeds of charity, not simply, but with solemnity. And what deeds of charity! He treated the peasants for every sort of disease with soda and castor oil, and on his name day had a thanksgiving service in the middle of the village, and then treated the peasants to a gallon of vodka – he thought that was the thing to do. Oh, those horrible gallons of vodka! One day the fat landowner hauls the peasants up before the district captain for trespass, and next day, in honour of a holiday, treats them to a gallon of vodka, and they drink and shout "Hurrah!" and when they are drunk bow down to his feet. A change of life for the better, being well-fed, idleness develop in a Russian the most insolent self-conceit. Nikolai, who at one time in the government office was afraid to have any views of his own, now could say nothing that was not gospel truth, and uttered such truths in the tone of a government minister. "Education is essential, but for the peasants it is premature." "Corporal punishment is harmful as a rule, but in some cases it is necessary and there is no substitute."

' "I know the peasants and understand how to treat them," he would say. "The peasants like me . . . I need only to hold up my little finger and the peasants will do anything I like."

'And all this, observe, was uttered with a wise, benevolent smile. He repeated about twenty times over "We the gentry", "I as a member of the gentry"; obviously he did not remember that our grandfather had been a peasant, and our father a soldier. Even our surname Chimsha-Gimalaisky, in reality so incongruous, now seemed to him sonorous, aristocratic, and very agreeable.

'But the point just now is not him, but me. I want to tell you about the change that took place in me during the brief hours I spent at his country place. In the evening, when we were drinking tea, the cook put on the table a plateful of gooseberries. They were not bought, but his own gooseberries, picked for the first time since the bushes were planted. Nikolai laughed and looked for a minute in silence at the gooseberries, with tears in his eyes; he could not speak for excitement. Then he put one gooseberry in his mouth, looked at me with the triumph of a child who has at last received his favourite toy, and said:

' "How delicious!"

'And he ate them greedily, continually repeating, "Ah, how delicious! Do taste them!"

'They were sour and unripe, but, as Pushkin says, "One falsehood that exalts us Is dearer than ten thousand truths."* I was looking at a happy man whose cherished dream had so obviously been fulfilled, who had attained his object in life, who had gained what he wanted, who was satisfied with fate and himself. There is always, for some reason, something sad mixed with my thoughts of human happiness, and, on this occasion, at the sight of a happy man I was overcome by an oppressive feeling that was close to despair. It was particularly oppressive at night. A bed was made up for me in the room next to my brother's bedroom, and I could hear him wake, keep getting up, going to the plate of gooseberries and taking one. I reflected how many satisfied, happy people there really are. What a suffocating force they are! You look at life: the insolence and idleness of the strong, the ignorance and bestiality of the weak, incredible poverty all about us, overcrowding, degeneration, drunkenness, hypocrisy, lying . . . Yet all is calm and stillness in the houses and in the streets; of fifty thousand living in a town, there is not one who would cry out, why would give vent to his indignation aloud. We see people going to market for provisions, eating by day, sleeping by night, talking their silly nonsense, getting married, growing old, serenely escorting their dead to the cemetery; but we do not see and we do not hear those who suffer, and what is terrible in life goes on somewhere behind the scenes. Everything is quiet and peaceful, and only mute statistics protest: so many people gone out of their minds, so many gallons of vodka drunk, so many children dead from malnutrition . . . And this order of things is evidently necessary. Evidently the happy man only feels at ease because the unhappy bear their burdens in silence, and without that silence happiness would be impossible. It's a case of mass hypnotism. There ought to be behind the door of every happy, contented man someone standing with a hammer* continually reminding him with a tap that there are unhappy people; that however happy he may be, life will show him her claws sooner or later, trouble will come for him – disease, poverty, losses – and no one will see or hear, just as now he neither sees nor hears others. But there is no man with a hammer; the happy man lives at his ease, and trivial daily cares faintly agitate him like the wind in the aspen tree – and all seems well.

'That night I realised that I, too, was happy and contented,' Ivan went on, getting up. 'I, too, at dinner and out shooting liked to lay down the law on life and religion, and the way to manage the peasantry. I, too, used to say that science was enlightenment, that culture was essential, but for the simple people reading and writing were enough for the time being. Freedom is a blessing, I used to say, as essential as air, but we must wait a little. Yes, I used to talk like that, and now I ask, "Why are we waiting?" ' inquired Ivan, looking angrily at Burkin. 'Why wait, I ask you? What considerations make us wait? I shall be told, it can't be done all at once; every idea takes shape in life gradually, in due course. But who is saying that? Where is the proof that it's right. You will refer to the natural order of things, the legitimate order of phenomena, but is there order and legitimacy in the fact that I, a living, thinking man, should stand over a chasm and wait for it to close up by itself, or to fill up with mud, when perhaps I might leap over it or build a bridge across it? And again, wait in the name of what? Wait, when we're too weak to live, and yet we must live, and we want to live!

'I left my brother's early in the morning, and ever since then it has been unbearable for me to visit a town. I am oppressed by its peace and quiet, I am afraid to look at the windows, for there is no spectacle more painful to me now than the sight of a happy family sitting round the table drinking tea. I am old and unfit for the struggle; I am not even capable of hatred. I can only grieve inwardly, feel irritated and vexed; but at night my head is hot from the rush of ideas, and I cannot sleep . . . Ah, if only I were young!'

Ivan walked to and fro in excitement, and repeated: 'If only I were young!'

He suddenly went up to Aliokhin and began pressing first one of his hands and then the other.

'Pavel,' he said in an imploring voice, 'don't be calm and contented, don't let yourself be put to sleep! While you are young, strong, confident, don't flag, but go on doing good! There is no happiness, and there mustn't be; but if there is a meaning and an object in life, that meaning and object is not our happiness, but something greater and more rational. Do good!'

And all this Ivan said with a pitiful, imploring smile, as though he were asking him a personal favour.

Then all three sat in arm-chairs at different ends of the drawing-room and were silent. Ivan's story had not satisfied either Burkin or Aliokhin. When the generals and ladies gazed down from their gilt frames, looking in the dusk as if they were alive, it was dreary to listen to the story of the poor clerk who ate gooseberries. They felt inclined, for some reason, to talk about elegant people, about women. And sitting in the drawing-room where everything, the chandelier in its covers, the arm-chairs, and the carpet under their feet, reminded them that these very people who were now looking down from their frames had once moved about, sat, drunk tea in this room, and the lovely Pelageia moving noiselessly about – all this was better than any story.

Aliokhin was fearfully sleepy; he had got up early, before three o'clock in the morning, to do the farm work, and now his eyes kept closing; but he was afraid his visitors might tell some interesting story after he had gone, and he stayed on. He did not go into the question of whether what Ivan had just said was right and true. His visitors did not talk of groats, nor of hay, nor of tar, but of something that had no direct bearing on his life, and he was glad and wanted them to go on . . .

'It's bed-time, though,' said Burkin, getting up. 'Allow me to wish you good night.'

Aliokhin said good night and went downstairs to his own domain, while the visitors remained upstairs. They were both taken for the night to a big room where there stood two old wooden beds decorated with carvings, and in the corner was an ivory crucifix. The big cool beds, which had been made by the lovely Pelageia, smelt agreeably of clean linen.

Ivan undressed in silence and got into bed.

'Lord forgive us sinners,' he said, and buried himself under the bedclothes.

His pipe, which lay on the table, smelt strongly of stale tobacco, and Burkin could not sleep for a long while, and kept wondering where the oppressive smell came from.

The rain was banging on the window-panes all night.

III ABOUT LOVE

At lunch next day they were served very good pies, crayfish, and mutton cutlets; and while they were eating, Nikanor, the cook, came up to ask what the visitors would like for dinner. He was a man of medium height, with a puffy face and little eyes; he was close-shaven, and it looked as though his moustaches had not been shaved, but had been plucked.

Aliokhin explained that the beautiful Pelageia was in love with this cook. As he drank and was of a violent character, she did not want to marry him, but was willing to live with him. He was very devout, and his religious convictions would not allow him to 'live in sin'; he demanded that she marry him, and would consent to nothing else, and when he was drunk he used to abuse her and even beat her. Whenever he got drunk she used to hide upstairs and sob, and on such occasions Aliokhin and the servants stayed in the house to be ready to defend her in case of necessity.

They began talking about love.

'How love is born,' said Aliokhin, 'why Pelageia didn't fall for somebody more like herself in her spiritual and external qualities, and why she fell for Nikanor, that ugly snout – everyone here calls him "The Snout" – how far questions of personal happiness affect love – all that is unknown; you can deal with it as you like. So far only one incontestable truth has been uttered about love: "This is a great mystery." Everything else that has been written or said about love is not a conclusion, but only a statement of questions which have remained unanswered. The explanation which would seem to fit one case does not apply in a dozen others, and the very best thing, to my mind, would be to explain every case individually without trying to generalise. We ought, as the doctors say, to individualise each case.'

'Perfectly true,' Burkin assented.

'We Russians, decent people, have a partiality for questions that remain unanswered. Love is usually poeticised, decorated with roses, nightingales; we Russians decorate our loves with these momentous questions, and select the most uninteresting of them, too. In Moscow, when I was a student, I had a friend who shared my life, a charming lady, and every time I took her my arms she was thinking what I would allow her a month for housekeeping and what was the price of beef a pound. In the same way, when we are in love we are never tired of asking ourselves questions: whether it is honourable or dishonourable, sensible or stupid, what this love is leading to, and so on. Whether it is a good thing or not I don't know, but that it is disturbing, unsatisfactory, and irritating, I do know.'

It looked as though he wanted to tell some story. People who live on their own always have something on their mind which they are eager to talk about. In town bachelors visit the baths and the restaurants on purpose to talk, and sometimes tell bath attendants and waiters most interesting things; in the country, as a rule, they unburden themselves to their guests. Now from the window we could see a a grey sky, trees drenched in the rain; in such weather we could go nowhere, and there was nothing for us to do but to talk and to listen.

'I have lived at Sofino and been farming for a long time,' Aliokhin began, 'ever since I left university. I am sedentary by education, a studious person by disposition; but there was a big debt owing on the estate when I came here, and as my father was in debt partly because he had spent so much on my education, I decided I would stay here and work till I had paid off the debt. That was my decision and I set to work, not, I must confess, without some repugnance. The land here does not yield much, and if you are not to farm at a loss you must employ serfs or hired labourers, which is almost the same thing, or put it on a peasant footing – that is, for you and your family to work the fields. There is no middle way. But in those days I did not go into such subtleties. I did not leave a clod of earth unturned; I gathered together all the peasants, men and women, from the neighbouring villages, the work went on at a tremendous pace. I myself ploughed and sowed and reaped, and was bored doing it, and frowned with disgust, like a village cat driven by hunger to eat cucumbers in the vegetable garden; my body ached, and I slept as I walked. At first it seemed to me that I could easily reconcile this life of toil with my cultured habits; to do so, I thought, I only have to keep up a certain external order in life. I established myself upstairs here in the best rooms, and ordered them to bring me there coffee and liqueur after lunch and dinner, and when I went to bed I read every night the *European Herald.** But one day our priest, Father Ivan, came and drank up all my liqueur at one sitting; and the *European Herald* went to the priest's daughters; as in the summer, especially at the hay making, I never managed to get to bed at all, and slept in the sledge in the barn, or somewhere in the forester's lodge, what chance was there of reading? Little by little I moved downstairs, began dining in the servants' kitchen, and of my former luxury nothing is left but the servants who were in my father's service, and whom it would be painful to dismiss.

'In the first years I was elected here an honorary magistrate. I used to have to go to the town and take part in the assizes and the circuit court, and this was a pleasant change for me. When you live here for two or three months without a break, especially in the winter, you begin at last to pine for a black coat. And in the circuit court there were frock-coats, and uniforms, and dress-coats, too, all lawyers, men who have received a broad education; I had someone to talk to. After sleeping in the sledge and dining in the kitchen, to sit in an arm-chair in clean linen, in town shoes, with a chain on your waistcoast, is such luxury!

'I received a warm welcome in the town. I made friends eagerly. And of all my acquaintances the most intimate and, to tell the truth, the most agreeable to me was my acquaintance with Luganovich, the vice-chairman of the circuit court. You both know him: a most charming personality. It all happened just after a celebrated case of arson; the preliminary investigation lasted two days; we were exhausted. Luganovich looked at me and said:

' "Look here, come round to dinner with me."

'This was unexpected, as I knew Luganovich very little, only officially, and I had never been to his house. I went to my hotel room just for a minute to change and set off to dinner. This was my chance to meet Anna, Luganovich's wife. At that time she was still very young, no more than twenty-two, and her first baby had been born just six months before. It is all in the past, and now I should find it difficult to define what there was so exceptional in her, what it was in her attracted me so much; at the time, at dinner, it was all undeniably clear to me. I saw a lovely young, good, intelligent, fascinating woman, such as I had never met before; and I felt at once that she was close and already familiar, as though that face, those cordial, intelligent eyes, I had seen somewhere in my childhood, in the album which lay on my mother's chest of drawers.

'Four Jews were charged as a gang of arsonists, and, to my mind, quite groundlessly. At dinner I was very stirred up, I was uncomfort-able, and I don't know what I said, but Anna kept shaking her head and saying to her husband:

' "Dmitri, how can this be?"

'Luganovich is a good-natured man, one of those simple-hearted people who firmly maintain the opinion that once a man is on trial he is guilty, and to express doubt of the correctness of a sentence cannot be done except in legal form on paper, but never at dinner or in private conversation.

' "You and I did not set fire to anything," he said softly, "and so we are not on trial or imprisoned."

'And both husband and wife tried to make me eat and drink as much as possible. Trifling details, the way they made coffee together, for instance, and understood each other at a hint, suggested to me that they lived in peace and comfort, and that they were glad of a visitor. After dinner they played a duet on the piano; then it got dark, and I went home. That was at the beginning of spring. After that I spent the whole summer at Sofino without a break, and I had no time to think of town, either, but the memory of the graceful fair-haired woman remained in my mind all those days; I was not thinking of her, but it was as though her light shadow had fallen on my heart.

'In the late autumn there was a theatre performance for some charity in the town. I went into the governor's box (I was invited to go there in the interval); I looked, and there was Anna sitting beside the governor's wife, and again the same irresistible, thrilling impression of beauty and sweet, caressing eyes, and again the same feeling of nearness.

'We sat side by side, then went to the foyer.

' "You've grown thinner," she said; "have you been ill?"

' "Yes, I've had rheumatism in my shoulder, and in rainy weather I can't sleep."

' "You look dispirited. In the spring, when you came to dinner, you were younger, more confident. You enthused and talked a great deal then; you were very interesting, and I really must confess I was a little bit swept off my feet by you. For some reason I often remembered you during the summer, and when I was getting ready for the theatre today I thought I should see you."

'And she laughed.

' "But you look run down today," she repeated; "it makes you seem older."

'The next day I lunched at the Luganoviches'; after lunch they drove out to their summer villa, in order to make arrangements there for the winter, and I went with them. I returned with them to town, and at midnight drank tea with them in quiet domestic surroundings, while the fire glowed, and the young mother kept going to see if her baby girl was asleep. And after that, every time I went to town I never failed to visit the Luganoviches. They grew used to me, and I to them. As a rule I went in unannounced, as though I were one of the family.

' "Who's there?" I would hear from a far-away room, in the drawling voice that seemed to me so lovely.

' "It is Mr Aliokhin," answered the maid or the nurse.

'Anna would come out to me with an anxious face, and would ask every time:

' "Why is it so long since you've been? Has anything happened?"

'Her eyes, the noble, elegant hand she gave me, her indoor dress, the way she did her hair, her voice, her step, always produced the same impression on me of something new and extraordinary in my life, and very important. We talked together for hours, were silent, thinking each our thoughts, or she played the piano to me for hours. If there was no one at home I stayed and waited, talked to the nurse, played with the child or lay on the sofa in the study and read; and when Anna came back I met her in the hall, took all her parcels from her, and for some reason I carried those parcels every time with as much love, with as much solemnity, as a boy.

'There is as proverb that if a peasant woman has no troubles she will buy a pig. The Luganoviches had no troubles, so they made friends with me. If I did not come to town I must be ill or something must have happened to me, and both of them were extremely anxious. They were worried that I, an educated man with a knowledge of languages should, instead of devoting myself to science or literary work, live in the country, rush round like a squirrel in a cage, work hard with never a kopeck to show for it. They fancied that I was unhappy, and that I only talked, laughed, and ate to conceal my sufferings, and even at cheerful moments when I felt happy I was aware of their searching eyes fixed upon me. They were particularly touching when I really was depressed, when I was being harassed by a creditor or had not money enough to pay a debt when it was due. The two of them, husband and wife, would whisper together at the window; then he would come to me and say with a grave face:

' "If you are short of money at the moment, Pavel, my wife and I beg you not to hesitate to borrow from us."

'And he would blush to his ears with emotion. And it would happen that, after whispering in the same way at the window, he would come up to me, with red ears, and say:

' "My wife and I earnestly beg you to accept this present."

'And he would give me cufflinks, a cigar-case, or a lamp, and I would send them game, butter, and flowers from the country. They both, by the way, had considerable means of their own. In the early days I often borrowed money, and was not very fussy – I borrowed wherever I could – but nothing in the world would have induced me to borrow from the Luganoviches. That goes without saying!

'I was unhappy. At home, in the fields, in the barn, I thought of her; I tried to understand the mystery of the beautiful, intelligent young woman marrying someone so uninteresting, almost an old man (her husband was over forty) and having children by him – to understand the mystery of this uninteresting, good, simple-hearted man, who argued with such boring good sense, at balls and evening parties hung about the solid citizens, looking listless and superfluous, with a submissive, uninvolved expression, as if he had been brought there for sale, who yet believed in his right to be happy, to have children by her; and I kept trying to understand why she had met him first and not me, and why such a terrible mistake in our lives need have happened.

'And when I went to the town I saw every time from her eyes that she was expecting me, and she would confess to me herself that she had had a peculiar feeling all that day and had guessed that I should come. We talked a long time and were silent, yet we did not confess our love to each other, but timidly and jealously concealed it. We were afraid of everything that might reveal our secret to ourselves. I loved her tenderly, deeply, but I reflected and kept asking myself what our love could lead to if we had not the strength to fight it. It seemed incredible that my gentle, sad love could at a stroke roughly break the even flow of the life of her husband, her children, and all the household in which I was so loved and trusted. Was that honourable? She would go away with me, but where to? Where could I take her? It would have been a different matter if I had had a beautiful, interesting life – if, for instance, I had been struggling for the liberation of my country, or had been a celebrated scholar, actor or artist; but as it was, it would mean taking her from one everyday humdrum life to another as humdrum or perhaps more so. And how long would our happiness last? What would happen to her if I fell ill, if I died, or if we simply stopped loving one another?

'And she apparently reasoned in the same way. She thought of her husband, her children, and of her mother, who loved Luganovich like a son. If she abandoned herself to her feelings she would have to lie, or else to tell the truth, and in her position either would have been equally frightful and awkward. And she was tormented by the question whether her love would bring me happiness – would she not complicate my life, which, as it was, was hard enough and full of all sorts of trouble? She fancied she was not young enough for me, that she was not hardworking nor energetic enough to begin a new life, and she often talked to her husband of the importance of my marrying a worthy, intelligent girl who would be a good housewife and a help to me – and she would immediately add that it would be difficult to find such a girl in the whole town.

'Meanwhile the years were passing. Anna now had two children. When I arrived at the Luganoviches' the servants smiled cordially, the children shouted that Uncle Pavel had come, and hung around my neck; everyone was overjoyed. They did not understand what was happening deep inside me, and thought that I, too, was happy. Everyone looked on me as a noble being. Grown-ups and children alike felt that a noble being was walking about their rooms, and that gave a peculiar charm to their manner towards me, as though in my presence their life, too, was purer and more beautiful. Anna and I used to go to the theatre together, always walking there; we used to sit next to each other in the stalls, our shoulders touching. I would take the opera-glass from her hands without a word, and feel at that minute that she was near me, that she was mine, that we could not live without each other, but by some strange misunderstanding, when we came out of the theatre, we always said good-bye and parted as though we were strangers. God knows what people were saying about us in the town by now, but there was not a word of truth in any of it!

'In the latter years Anna took to going away for frequent visits to her mother or to her sister; she began to have bad moods, she began to see her life as spoilt and unsatisfied, and at times she did not want to see her husband or children. She was now being treated for nerves.

'We kept silent, and in the presence of outsiders she displayed a strange irritation towards me; whatever I talked about, she disagreed with me, and if I had an argument she sided with my opponent. If I dropped anything, she would say coldly:

' "Congratulations."

'If I forgot to take the opera-glass when we were going to the theatre, she would say afterwards:

' "I knew you'd forget it."

'Luckily or unluckily, there is nothing in our lives that does not end sooner or later. The time came to part, as Luganovich was appointed court chairman in one of the western provinces. They had to sell their furniture, their horses, their summer villa. When they drove out to the villa, and afterwards looked back as they were going away, to look for the last time at the garden, at the green roof, everyone was sad, and I realised that I had to say good-bye not just to the villa. It was arranged that at the end of August we should see Anna off to the Crimea, where the doctors were sending her, and that a little later Luganovich and the children would set off for the western province.

'There was a great crowd of us to see Anna off. When she had said good-bye to her husband and her children and there was only a minute left before the third bell, I ran into her compartment to put a basket, which she had almost forgotten, on the rack, and I had to say good-bye. When our eyes met in the compartment our strength of mind deserted us both; I took her in my arms, she pressed her face to my breast, and tears flowed from her eyes. Kissing her face, her shoulders, her hands wet with tears – oh, how unhappy we were! – I confessed my love for her, and with a burning pain in my heart I realised how unnecessary, how petty, and how deceptive all that had hindered us from loving was. I understood that when you love you must either, in your reasoning about that love, start from what is highest, from what is more important than happiness or unhappiness, sin or virtue in their accepted meaning, or you must not reason at all.

'I kissed her for the last time, pressed her hand, and parted for ever. The train had already started. I went into the next compartment – it was empty – and until I reached the next station I sat there crying. Then I walked home to Sofino.'

While Aliokhin was telling his story, the rain stopped and the sun came out. Burkin and Ivan went out on the balcony, from which there was a beautiful view over the garden and the millpond, which was shining now in the sunshine like a mirror. They admired it, and at the same time they were sorry that this man with the kind, clever eyes, who had told them this story with such genuine feeling, should be rushing round and round this huge estate like a squirrel on a wheel, instead of devoting himself to science or something else which would have made his life more pleasant; and they thought what a sorrowful face the young lady must have had when he said good-bye to her in the railway compartment and kissed her face and shoulders. Both of them had met her in the town, and Burkin had known her and thought her beautiful.

1898

On Official Duty

The acting examining magistrate and the district doctor were going to an inquest in the village of Syrnia. On the road they were overtaken by a snowstorm; they spent a long time going round and round, and arrived, not at midday, as they had intended, but in the evening when it was dark. They put up for the night at a hut belonging to the rural district council, the *zemstvo*. In this very hut the dead body was lying – the corpse of the *zemstvo* insurance agent, Lesnitsky, who had arrived in Syrnia three days before, made himself at home in the hut and, ordering the samovar to be brought, had shot himself, to the great surprise of everyone; and the fact that he had ended his life so strangely, after unpacking his food supplies and laying them out on the table, and with the samovar before him, led many people to suspect that it was a case of murder; an inquest was necessary.

In the outer room the doctor and the examining magistrate shook the snow off their clothes and knocked it off their boots. And meanwhile the old village constable, Ilia Loshadin, stood by, holding a little tin lamp. There was a strong smell of paraffin.

'Who are you?' asked the doctor.

'Conshtable . . .' answered the constable.

He used to spell it 'conshtable' when he signed the receipts at the post office.

'And where are the witnesses?'

'They must have gone to tea, your Honour.'

On the right was the parlour, the travellers' or gentry's room; on the left the room for the lower classes, with a big stove and sleeping-shelves up to the rafters. The doctor and the examining magistrate, followed by the constable, holding the lamp high above his head, went into the parlour. Here a still, long body covered with white linen was lying on the floor close to the table legs. In the dim light of the lamp they could clearly see, besides the white covering, new rubber galoshes, and everything about it was uncanny and sinister: the dark walls, and the silence, and the galoshes, and the stillness of the dead body. On the table stood a samovar, long since cold; and round it parcels, probably the victim's food.

'To shoot oneself in the *zemstvo* hut, how tactless!' said the doctor. 'If you get the urge to put a bullet through your brains, you ought to do it at home in some outhouse.'

He sank on to a bench, just as he was, in his hat, fur coat, and felt overboots; his fellow traveller, the examining magistrate, sat down opposite.

'These hysterical neurotics are great egotists,' the doctor went on hotly. 'If a neurotic sleeps in the same room with you, he rustles his newspaper; when he dines with you, he starts a scene with his wife without letting your presence inhibit him; and when he feels the urge to shoot himself, he does it in a village in a *zemstvo* hut, so as to give the maximum of trouble to everybody. These gentlemen in every circumstance of life think of no one but themselves! That's why the elderly so dislike our "age of nerves".'

'The elderly dislike so many things,' said the examining magistrate, yawning. 'You should point out to the older generation the difference between suicides of the past and suicides of today. In the old days the so-called gentleman shot himself because he had embezzled government money, but nowadays it is because he is sick of life, depressed . . . Which is better?'

'Sick of life, depressed, but you must admit that he might have shot himself somewhere else.'

'Such trouble!' said the constable, 'such trouble! It's a real affliction. The people are very upset, your Honour; they haven't slept for two nights. The children are crying. The cows ought to be milked, but the women won't go to the stall – they are afraid . . . for fear the gentleman haunts them in the darkness. Of course they are silly women, but some of the men are frightened too. As soon as it is dark they won't go by the hut on their own, but only in a flock together. And the witnesses too . . .'

Dr Starchenko, a middle-aged man in spectacles with a dark beard, and the examining magistrate Lyzhin, a fair man, still young, who had only taken his degree two years before and looked more like a student than an official, sat in silence, musing. They were vexed that they were late. Now they had to wait till morning, and to stay here for the night, though it was not yet six o'clock; and they had before them a long evening, a dark night, boredom, uncomfortable beds, cockroaches, and cold in the morning; and listening to the blizzard that howled in the chimney and in the loft, they both thought how unlike all this was the life which they would have chosen for themselves and of which they had once dreamed, and how far away they both were from their contemporaries, who were at that moment walking about the lighted streets in town, not noticing the weather, or were getting ready for the theatre, or sitting in their studies, reading a book. Oh, what they would have given now only to stroll along the Nevsky Prospect, or along Petrovka in Moscow, to listen to decent singing, to sit an hour or so in a restaurant!

'Oo-oo-oo-oo!' sang the storm in the loft, and something outside slammed viciously, probably the signboard on the hut. 'Oo-oo-oo-oo!'

'You can do as you please, but I have no desire to stay here,' said Starchenko, getting up. 'It's not six yet, it's too early to go to bed; I am off. Von Taunitz lives not far from here, only a couple of miles from Syrnia. I shall go and see him and spend the evening there. Constable, run and tell my coachman not to unharness the horses. And what are you going to do?' he asked Lyzhin.

'I don't know; I expect I shall go to sleep.'

The doctor wrapped himself in his fur coat and went out. Lyzhin could hear him talking to the coachman and the bells beginning to quiver on the frozen horses. He drove off.

'It is not nice for you, Sir, to spend the night here,' said the constable; 'come into the other room. It's dirty, but for one night it won't matter. I'll get a samovar from a peasant and put it on, then I'll heap up some hay for you, and then you go to sleep, and God bless you, your Honour.'

A little later the examining magistrate was sitting in the kitchen drinking tea, while Loshadin, the constable, was standing at the door talking. He was an old man, over sixty, short and very thin, bent and white, with a naive smile on his face and watery eyes; and he kept smacking his lips as if he were sucking a boiled sweet. He was wearing a short sheepskin coat and high felt boots, and never let go of his stick. The youth of the examining magistrate aroused his compassion, and that was probably why he addressed him familiarly.

'The elder Fiodor Makarych gave orders that he was to be informed when the police superintendent or the examining magistrate came,' he said, 'so I suppose I must go now . . . It's nearly three miles to the district centre and the blizzard, the snowdrifts, are something terrible – I probably won't get there before midnight. Ugh! how the wind roars!'

'I don't need the elder,' said Lyzhin. 'There is nothing for him to do here.'

He looked at the old man with curiosity, and asked:

'Tell me, grandfather, how many years have you been constable?'

'How many? Why, thirty years. Five years after the emancipation I began work as constable, that's how I reckon it. And from that time I have been going every day since. Other people have holidays, but I am always on the go. When it's Easter and the church bells are ringing and Christ has risen, I still go about with my bag – to the treasury, to the post, to the police superintendent's lodgings, to the rural captain, to the tax inspector, to the municipal office, to the gentry, to the peasants, to all good Christians. I carry parcels, notices, tax papers, letters, forms of different sorts, circulars, and to be sure, kind gentleman, there are all sorts of forms nowadays, so as to note down the numbers – yellow, white, and red – and every gentleman or priest or well-to-do peasant must write down a dozen times in the year how much he has sown and harvested, how many quarters or bushels he has of rye, how many of oats, how many of hay, and what the weather's like, you know, and insects, too, of all sorts. To be sure, you can write what you like, it's only a regulation, but you have to go and give out the notices and then go again and collect them. Here, for instance, there's no need to cut open the gentleman, you know yourself it's a silly thing, it's only dirtying your hands, and here you have been put to trouble, your Honour; you have come because it's the regulation; you can't help it. For thirty years I have been going round according to regulation. In the summer it's all right, it's warm and dry; but in winter and autumn it's uncomfortable. At times I have been almost drowned and almost frozen; all sorts of things have happened – wicked people set on me in the forest and took away my bag; I have been beaten, and I have been on trial.'

'What were you accused of?'

'Of fraud.'

'How do you mean?'

'Why, you see, Khrisanf Grigoriev, the clerk, sold the contractor some boards belonging to someone else – cheated him, in fact. I was mixed up in it. They sent me to the tavern for vodka, well the clerk did not share with me – didn't even offer me a glass; but as through my poverty I was – in appearance, I mean – not a man to be relied upon, not a man of any standing, we were both brought to trial, he was sent to prison, but, praise God! I was acquitted on all counts. They read a notice, you know, in the court. And they were all in uniforms in the court, I mean. I can tell you, your Honour, my duties for anyone not used to them are terrible, absolutely killing; but to me it's nothing. In fact, my feet ache when I am not walking. And at home it is worse for me. At home you have to stoke the stove for the clerk in the district centre office, to fetch water for him, to clean his boots.'

'And what wages do you get?' Lyzhin asked.

'Eighty-four roubles a year.'

'I'll bet you get other little sums coming in. You do, don't you?'

'Other little sums? No, indeed! Gentlemen nowadays don't often give tips. Gentlemen nowadays are strict, they take offence at anything. If you bring then a notice they are offended, if you take off your hat before them they are offended. "You have come to the wrong entrance," they say. "You are a drunkard," they say. "You smell of onion; you are a blockhead; you are a son of a bitch." There are kind-hearted ones, of course; but what do you get from them? They only laugh and call you all sorts of names. Take Mr Altukhin, for instance, he is a good-natured gentleman; and if you look at him he seems sober and in his right mind, but as soon as he sees me he shouts and does not know what he means himself. He called me something really odd. "You," he said, ". . ." The constable uttered some word, but in such a low voice that it was impossible to make out what he had said.

'What?' Lyzhin asked. 'Say it again.'

'Administration,' the constable repeated aloud. 'He has been calling me that for a long while, for the last six years. "Hullo, Administration!" But I don't mind; let him, what do I care? Sometimes a lady will send out a glass of vodka and a bit of pie, and you drink to her health. But peasants give more; peasants are more kind-hearted, they have the fear of God in their hearts: one will give a bit of bread, another a drop of cabbage soup, another will stand you a glass. The village elders treat you to tea in the inn. Now the witnesses have gone to their tea. "Loshadin," they said, "you stay here and keep watch for us," and they gave me a kopeck each. You see, they're frightened, not being used to it, and yesterday they gave me fifteen kopecks and brought me a glass of vodka.'

'But aren't you frightened?'

'I am, Sir; but of course it is my duty, there is no getting away from it. In the summer I was taking a convict to town and he set upon me and gave me such a drubbing! And all around were fields, forest — how could I get away from him? It's just the same here. I remember the gentleman, Mr Lesnitsky, when he was so high, and I knew his father and mother. I am from the village of Nedoshchotova and they, the Lesnitsky family, were no more than three-quarters of a mile from us and less than that, their land is next to ours, and old Mr Lesnitsky had a sister, a God-fearing and tender-hearted lady. Lord remember the soul of Thy servant Yulia, eternal memory to her! She never married, and when she was dying she divided all her property; she left three hundred acres to the monastery, and six hundred to the commune of peasants of Nedoshchotova to commemorate her soul; but her brother hid the will, they say he burnt it in the stove, and took all this land for himself. He thought, to be sure, it was for his benefit; but oh no, you'll see, you won't survive in the world by lies, brother. The gentleman did not go to confession for twenty years after. He kept away from the church, to be sure, and died without being shriven. He burst. He was a very fat man, so he burst lengthways. Then everything was taken from his son the young master, from Seriozha, to pay the debts – everything there was. Well, he had not got very far in his studies, he couldn't do anything, and the president of the district council, his uncle thinks: "I'll take him" – Seriozha, I mean – "for an agent; let him collect insurance, that's not a difficult job." But the gentleman was young and proud, he wanted to have a better life and in better style and with more freedom. To be sure, it was a come-down for him to be jolting about the district in a wretched cart and talking to the peasants; he would walk and keep looking at the ground, looking at the ground and saying nothing; if you called his name right in his ear, "Mr Lesnitsky!" he would look round like this, "Eh?" and look at the ground again, and now you see he has laid hands on himself. There's no sense in it, your Honour, it's not right, and there's no making out what's the meaning of it, merciful Lord! Say your father was rich and you are poor; it is mortifying, there's no doubt about it, but there, you've got to put up with it. I used to live in good style, too; I had two horses, your Honour, three cows, I used to keep twenty head of sheep; but the time has come, and I am left with nothing but a wretched bag, and even that is not mine but government property. And now in our Nedoshchotova, to tell you the truth, my house is the worst of the lot. Mokei had four footmen, and now Mokei is a footman himself. Petrak had four labourers, and now Petrak is a labourer himself.'

'How did you become poor?' asked the examining magistrate.

'My sons hit the vodka terribly. I can't tell you how they drink, you wouldn't believe it.'

Lyzhin listened and thought how he, Lyzhin, would go back sooner or later to Moscow, while this old man would stay here for ever, and would always be talking and walking. And how many times in his life he would come across such battered, unkempt old men, not 'men of any standing', in whose souls fifteen kopecks, glasses of vodka, and a profound belief that you won't survive by lies, were equally firmly rooted.

Then he grew tired of listening, and told the old man to bring him some hay for his bed. There was an iron bedstead with a pillow and a blanket in the traveller's room, and it could be fetched in; but the dead man had been lying by it for nearly three days (and perhaps he had sat on it just before his death), and it would be disagreeable to sleep upon it now . . .

'It's only half-past seven,' thought Lyzhin, glancing at his watch. 'How awful it is!'

He was not sleepy, but he had nothing to do to pass the time, so he lay down and covered himself with a rug. Loshadin went in and out several times, clearing away the tea things; smacking his lips and sighing, he kept tramping round the table; at last he took his little lamp and went out, and, looking at his long, grey headed, bent figure from behind, Lyzhin thought:

'Just like a magician in an opera.'

It was dark. The moon must have been behind the clouds, as the windows and the snow on the window-frames could be seen distinctly.

'Oo-oo-oo-oo!' sang the storm, 'Oo-oo-oo-oo!'

'Ho-o-ly sa-aints!' wailed a woman in the loft, or it sounded like it. 'Ho-o-ly sa-aints!'

'Boo-oof!' something outside banged against the wall. 'Trac!'

The examining magistrate listened: there was no woman up there, it was the wind howling. He felt cold, and he put his fur coat over his rug. As he got warm he thought how remote all this – the storm, the hut, the old man, and the dead body lying in the next room – how remote it all was from the life he wanted for himself, and how alien it all was to him, how petty, how uninteresting. If this man had killed himself in Moscow or somewhere in the neighbourhood, and he had had to hold an inquest on him there, it would have been interesting, important, and perhaps he might even have been afraid to sleep in the next room to the corpse. Here, six hundred miles from Moscow, all this appeared somehow in a different light; it was not life, they were not human beings, but something only existing 'according to the regulation', as Loshadin said; it would leave not the faintest trace in the memory, and would be forgotten as soon as he, Lyzhin, left Syrnia. The motherland, the real Russia, was Moscow, Petersburg; but here he was in the provinces, the colonies; when you dreamed of playing a leading part, of becoming a popular figure, of being, for instance, examining magistrate for especially important cases or prosecutor in a circuit court, of being a society lion, one always thought of Moscow. To live, one must be in Moscow; here there were no wishes, it was easy to resign yourself to your obscure role, and you only expected one thing of life – to get out and away as quickly as you could. And Lyzhin mentally roamed Moscow's streets, went into familiar houses, met his kindred, his comrades, and there was a sweet pang in his heart at the thought that he was only twenty-six, and that if in five or ten years he could break away from here and get to Moscow, even then it would not be too late and he would still have a whole life before him. And as he sank into oblivion, as his thoughts began to blur, he imagined the long corridor of the Moscow courthouse, himself making a speech, his sisters, the orchestra which for some reason kept howling:

'Oo-oo-oo-oo! Oo-oo-oo-oo!'

'Boof! Trac!' it sounded again. 'Boof!'

And he suddenly recalled how one day, when he was talking to the accountant in the little office of the rural council, a thin, pale gentleman with black hair and dark eyes walked in; he had a disagreeable look in his eyes, like someone who has slept too long after dinner, and it spoilt his delicate, intelligent profile; and the high boots he was wearing did not suit him, but looked clumsy. The accountant had introduced him: 'This is our rural insurance agent.'

'So that was Lesnitsky . . . the same man . . .' Lyzhin reflected now.

He recalled Lesnitsky's soft voice, imagined his gait, and it seemed to him that someone was walking beside him now with a step like Lesnitsky's.

All at once he felt frightened, his head turned cold.

'Who's there?' he asked in alarm.

'The conshtable.'

'What do you want here?'

'I have come to ask, your Honour. You said this evening that you did not want the elder, but I'm afraid he may be angry. He told me to go and see him. Shouldn't I go?'

'To hell with you! I've had enough,' said Lyzhin with vexation, and he covered himself up again.

'I don't want him to be angry . . . I'll go, your Honour. God be with you till I come back.'

And Loshadin went out. In the passage there was coughing and subdued voices. The witnesses must have returned.

'We'll let those poor beggars get away early tomorrow . . .' thought the examining magistrate; 'we'll begin the inquest as soon as it is daylight.'

He had begun to sink into oblivion when suddenly there were steps again, not timid this time, but rapid and noisy. A door slammed voices, someone was striking a match . . .

'Are you asleep? Are you asleep?' Dr Starchenko was asking him hurriedly and angrily as he struck one match after another; he was covered with snow, and brought a chill in with him. 'Are you asleep? Get up! Let's go to Von Taunitz's. He's sent his own horses for you. Come along. There, at any rate, you will have supper, and sleep like a human being. Look, I've come for you myself. The horses are splendid, we'll get there in twenty minutes.'

'And what time is it now?'

'A quarter past ten.'

Lyzhin, sleepy and displeased, put on his felt overboots, his fur-lined coat, his hat and balaclava helmet, and went out with the doctor. The frost was not very severe, but a violent and piercing wind was blowing and driving along the street clouds of snow which seemed to be racing away in terror; high drifts were heaped up already under the fences and at the doorways. The doctor and the examining magistrate got into the sledge, and the white coachman bent over them to button up the cover. They were both hot.

'Let's go!'

They drove through the village. 'Cutting a feathery furrow,'* thought the examining magistrate, listlessly watching the action of the trace horse's legs. There were lights in all the huts, as though it was the eve of a great holiday: the peasants had not gone to bed because they were afraid of the dead body. The coachman preserved a sullen silence, probably he had become unhappy while he was waiting by the zemstvo hut, and now he, too, was thinking of the dead man.

'At the Von Taunitz's,' said Starchenko, 'they all went for me when they heard that you were left to spend the night in the hut, and asked me why I had not brought you with me.'

As they drove out of the village, at the turning, the coachman suddenly shouted at the top of his voice: 'Out of the way!'

They caught a glimpse of a man: he was standing up to his knees in the snow, veering off the road and staring at the horses. The examining magistrate saw a stick with a crook, and a beard and a bag on his side, and he fancied that it was Loshadin, and even fancied that he was smiling. He flashed by and disappeared.

The road ran at first along the edge of the forest, then along a broad forest clearing; they caught glimpses of old pines and a young birch copse, and tall, gnarled young oak trees standing isolated in the clearings where the wood had lately been cut; but soon it was all merged in the air, in clouds of snow. The coachman said he could see the forest; but the examining magistrate could see nothing but the trace horse. The wind blew at their backs.

All at once the horses stopped.

'Well, what is it now?' asked Starchenko crossly.

The coachman got down from the box without a word and began running round the sledge, treading on his heels; he made larger and larger circles, getting further and further away from the sledge, and it looked as though he were dancing; at last he came back and began to turn off to the right.

'You've lost the road, eh?' asked Starchenko.

'It's all ri-ight . . .'

Then there was a little village and not a single light in it. Again the forest and the fields. Again they lost the road, and again the coachman got down from the box and danced round the sledge. The sledge flew along a dark avenue, flew swiftly on, and the heated trace horse's hoofs knocked against the sledge. Here there was a fearful roaring sound from the trees, and nothing could be seen, as though they were flying on into space; and all at once the glaring light at the entrance and windows flashed upon their eyes, and they heard the good-natured, prolonged barking of dogs . . . They had arrived.

As they were taking off their fur coats and their felt boots below, 'Un petit verre de Clicquot'* was being played on the piano upstairs, and they could hear children beating time with their feet. As soon as they went in, they were aware of the snug warmth and special smell of the old rooms of a mansion where, whatever the weather outside, life is so warm and clean and comfortable.

'This is wonderful!' said Von Taunitz, a fat man with an incredibly thick neck and with whiskers, as he shook the examining magistrate's hand. 'This is wonderful! You are very welcome, delighted to make your acquaintance. We are colleagues to some extent, you know. At one time I was deputy prosecutor; but not for long, only two years. I came here to look after the estate, and here I have grown old – an old fogey, in fact. You are very welcome,' he went on, evidently controlling his voice so as not to speak too loud; he was going upstairs with his guests. 'I have no wife, she's dead. Wait here, I'll introduce my daughters,' and turning around, he shouted down the stairs in a voice of thunder: 'Tell Ignat to have the sledge ready at eight o'clock tomorrow morning.'

His four daughters, young and pretty girls, all wearing grey dresses and with their hair done in the same style, and their cousin, also young and attractive, with her children, were in the drawing room. Starchenko, who knew them already, began at once to beg them to sing something and two of the young ladies spent a long time declaring they could not sing and that they had no music, then the cousin sat down to the piano, and with trembling voices, they sang a duet from *The Queen of Spades*. Again 'Un petit verre de Clicquot' was played, and the children skipped about, beating time with their feet. And Starchenko pranced about too. Everybody laughed.

Then the children said good night and went off to bed. The examining magistrate laughed, danced a quadrille, flirted, and kept wondering whether it was not all a dream. The kitchen of the *zemstvo* hut, the heap of hay in the corner, the cockroaches rustling, the revolting poverty-stricken surroundings, the witnesses' voices, the wind, the snowstorm, the danger of being lost; and then, out of the blue, this splendid, brightly lit room, the sounds of the piano, the lovely girls, the curly headed children, the gay, happy laughter – such a transformation seemed to him like a fairy tale, and it seemed incredible that such transitions were possible over just two miles and one hour. And dreary thoughts prevented him from enjoying himself, and he kept thinking this was not life here, but bits of life, fragments, that everything here was accidental, that one could draw no conclusions from it, and he even felt sorry for these girls, who were living and would end their lives in the wilds, in a province far away from a cultural centre where nothing is accidental, but everything is in accordance with reason and law, and where, for instance, every suicide is intelligible, so that one can explain why it has happened and what is its significance in the general scheme of things. He imagined that if the life surrounding him here in the wilds were not intelligible to him, and if he did not see it, it meant that it did not exist at all.

At supper the conversation turned on Lesnitsky. 'He has left a wife and child,' said Starchenko. 'I would forbid neurotics and all people whose nervous system is out of order to marry, I would deprive them of the right and possibility of breeding more of their kind. To bring into the world neurotic children is a crime.'

'He was an unhappy young man,' said Von Taunitz sighing gently and shaking his head. 'What a lot you must suffer and think about before you decide to take your own life . . . a young life! Such a misfortune can happen in any family, and that is awful. It is hard to bear such a thing, unbearable . . .'

And all the girls listened in silence with grave face, looking at their father. Lyzhin felt that he, too, must say something, but he couldn't think of anything, and merely said:

'Yes, suicide is an undesirable phenomenon.'

He slept in a warm room, in a soft bed covered with a blanket under which there were fine clean sheets, but for some reason did not feel comfortable: perhaps because the doctor and Von Taunitz were for a long time talking in the adjoining room, and overhead he heard, through the ceiling and in the stove, the wind roaring just as in the *zemstvo* hut, and as plaintively howling, 'Oo-oo-oo-oo!'

Von Taunitz's wife had died two years before, and he was still unable to resign himself to his loss and, whatever he talked about, always mentioned his wife; and there was no trace of the prosecutor left about him now.

'Is it possible that I may some day end up in a state like that?' thought Lyzhin, as he fell asleep, still hearing through the wall his host's subdued, literally bereaved, voice.

The examining magistrate did not sleep soundly. He felt hot and uncomfortable, and it seemed to him in his sleep that he was not at Von Taunitz's, and not in a soft clean bed, but still in the hay at the *zemstvo* hut, hearing the subdued voices of the witnesses; he fancied that Lesnitsky was close by, not fifteen paces away. In his dreams he remembered the insurance agent, black-haired and pale, wearing dusty high boots, coming into the accountant's office. 'This is our insurance agent . . .'

Then he dreamed that Lesnitsky and Loshadin the constable were walking through the open country in the snow, side by side, supporting each other; the snow was whirling about their heads, the wind was blowing on their backs, but they walked on, singing: 'We go on, and on, and on . . .'

The old man was like a magician in an opera and both of them were singing as though they were on the stage:

'We go on, and on, and on! . . . You are in the warmth, in the light and snugness, but we are walking in the frost and the storm, through deep snow . . . We know nothing of ease, we know nothing of joy . . . We bear all the burden of this life, yours and ours . . . Oo-oo-oo. We go on, and on, and on . . .'

Lyzhin woke and sat up in bed. What a troubled, bad dream! And why had he dreamt of the constable and the agent together? What nonsense! And now while Lyzhin's heart was throbbing violently and he was sitting on his bed, holding his head in his hands, it seemed to him that there really was something in common between the lives of the insurance agent and the constable. Don't they really go side by side supporting each other? Some tie, unseen, but significant and essential, existed between them, and even between them and Von Taunitz and between all men, all humanity; in this life, even in the remotest desert, nothing is accidental, everything is filled by a common idea, everything has one soul, one aim, and to understand it thought and reason are not enough, you must have also, it seems, the gift of insight into life, a gift which is clearly not bestowed on everyone. And the unhappy man who had broken down, who had killed himself – the 'neurotic', as the doctor called him – and the old peasant who spent every day of his life going from one man to another, were only accidental, were only fragments of life for one who thought of his own life as accidental, but were parts of one organism – marvellous and rational – for one who thought of his own life as part of that universal whole and understood it. So thought Lyzhin, and it was a thought that had long lain hidden in his soul, and only now it had unfolded broadly and clearly to his conscious mind.

He lay down and began to fall asleep; and again they were going along together, singing: 'We go on, and on, and on . . . We take from life what is hardest and bitterest in it, and we leave you what is easy and joyful; and sitting at supper, you can coldly and sensibly discuss why we suffer and perish, and why we are not as sound and as satisfied as you.'

What they were singing had occurred to him before, but the thought was somewhere in the background behind his other thoughts, and flickered timidly like a far-away light in foggy weather. And he felt that this suicide and the peasant's sufferings lay upon his conscience, too; to accept smugly that these people, submissive to their fate, should take up the burden of what was hardest and gloomiest in life – how awful it was! To accept it, and to want for himself a life full of light and noise among happy and contented people, and to be continually dreaming of such a life, meant dreaming of yet more suicides of men crushed by toil and anxiety, or of the weak and outcasts whom people only talk of sometimes at supper with annoyance or mockery, without doing anything to help them . . . And again:

'We go on, and on, and on . . .' as though someone were hitting his temples with a hammer.

He woke early in the morning with a headache, roused by a noise; in the next room Von Taunitz was saying loudly to the doctor:

'It's impossible for you to go now. Look what it's like outside. Don't argue, you had better ask the coachman; he won't take you in such weather for a million.'

'But it's only two miles,' said the doctor in an imploring voice.

'Well, it makes no difference if it were only half a mile. Just accept that you can't. As soon as you drive out of the gates it is perfect hell, you would be off the road in a minute. Nothing will induce me to let you go, say what you like.'

'It's bound to be quieter towards evening,' said the peasant who was stoking the stove.

And in the next room the doctor began talking of the rigorous climate and its influence on the character of the Russian, of the long winters which, by preventing movement from place to place, hinder the intellectual development of the people; and Lyzhin listened with vexation to these observations and looked out of the window at the snowdrifts which swept up against the fence. He gazed at the white dust which covered the whole visible expanse, at the trees which bowed their heads despairingly to right and then to left, listened to the howling and the banging, and thought gloomily:

'Well, what moral can be drawn from it? It's a blizzard and that's it . . .'

At midday they had lunch, then wandered aimlessly about the house; they went to the windows.

'And Lesnitsky is lying there,' thought Lyzhin watching the

whirling snow, which raced furiously, round and round upon the drifts. 'Lesnitsky is lying there, the witnesses are waiting . . .'

They talked of the weather, saying that the snowstorm usually lasted two days and nights, rarely longer. At six o'clock they had dinner, then they played cards, sang, danced; finally, they had supper; the day was over, they went to bed.

In the night, towards morning, it all subsided. When they got up and looked out of the window, the bare willows with their weakly drooping branches were standing perfectly motionless; it was dull and still, as though nature now were ashamed of its orgy, of its mad nights, and the freedom it had given to its passions. The horses, harnessed in tandem, had been waiting at the front door since five o'clock in the morning. When it was fully daylight the doctor and the examining magistrate put on their fur coats and felt boots, and, saying good-bye to their host, went out.

At the steps beside the coachman stood the familiar figure of the 'conshtable', Ilia Loshadin, with an old leather bag across his shoulder and no hat, covered with snow all over, and his face was red and wet with perspiration. The footman who had come out to help the gentlemen and cover their legs looked at him sternly and said:

'What are you standing here for, you old devil? Get away!'

'Your Honour, the people are anxious,' said Loshadin, smiling naively all over his face, and evidently pleased at seeing at last the people he had waited for so long. 'The people are very unhappy, the children are crying . . . They thought, your Honour, that you had gone back to town again. Show us some heavenly mercy, be our benefactors . . .'

The doctor and the examining magistrate said nothing, got into the sledge, and drove to Syrnia.

1899

The Lady with the Dog

It was said that a new person had appeared on the sea-front: a lady
with a little dog. Dmitri Gurov, who had by then been a fortnight in
Yalta, and so was fairly at home there, had begun to take an interest
in new arrivals. Sitting in Verney's pavilion, he saw, walking on the
sea-front, a fair-haired young lady of medium height, wearing a
beret; a white Pomeranian dog was running behind her.

And afterwards he met her in the public gardens and in the square
several times a day. She was walking alone, always wearing the same
beret, and always with the same white dog; no one knew who she
was, and everyone called her simply 'the lady with the dog'.

'If she is here alone without a husband or friends, it wouldn't be a
bad idea to get to know her,' Gurov reflected.

He was under forty, but he had a daughter already twelve years
old, and two sons at school. He had been married young, when he was
a student in his second year, and by now his wife seemed half as old
again as he. She was a tall, erect woman with dark eyebrows, staid
and dignified, and, as she said of herself, intellectual. She read a great
deal, used phonetic spelling, called her husband not Dmitri, but
Dimitri, and he secretly considered her unintelligent, narrow,
inelegant, was afraid of her, and did not like to be at home. He had
begun being unfaithful to her long ago – had been unfaithful to her
often, and, probably on that account, almost always spoke ill of
women, and when they were talked about in his presence, used to call
them 'the lower race'.

It seemed to him that he had been sufficiently schooled by bitter
experience to call them what he liked, and yet he could not get on for
two days together without 'the lower race'. In the society of men he
was bored and not himself, with them he was cold and uncommuni-
cative; but when he was in the company of women he felt free, and
knew what to say to them and how to behave; and he was at ease with
them even when he was silent. In his appearance, in his character, in
his whole nature, there was something attractive and elusive which
allured women and predisposed them towards him; he knew that,
and some force seemed to draw him, too, to them.

Frequent experience, truly bitter experience, had taught him long ago that with decent people, especially Moscow people, always slow to move and irresolute, every intimacy, which at first so agreeably diversifies life and appears as a light and charming adventure, inevitably grows into a whole problem of extreme intricacy, and in the long run the situation becomes burdensome. But at every fresh meeting with an interesting woman this experience seemed to slip out of his memory, and he was eager for life, and everything seemed simple and amusing.

One evening he was dining in the gardens, and the lady in the beret came up slowly to take the next table. Her expression, her gait, her dress, and the way she did her hair told him that she was a lady, that she was married, that she was in Yalta for the first time and alone, and that she was bored there . . . The stories told of the immorality in such places as Yalta are to a great extent untrue; he despised them, and knew that such stories were for the most part made up by persons who would themselves have been glad to sin if they had been able; but when the lady sat down at the next table three paces from him, he remembered these tales of easy conquests, of trips to the mountains, and the tempting thought of a swift, fleeting love affair, a romance with an unknown woman, whose name he did not know, suddenly took possession of him.

He beckoned coaxingly to the Pomeranian, and when the dog came up to him he shook his finger at it. The Pomeranian growled, Gurov shook his finger at it again.

They lady looked at him and at once dropped her eyes.

'He doesn't bite,' she said, and blushed.

'May I give him a bone?' he asked; and when she nodded he asked courteously, 'Have you been long in Yalta?'

'About five days.'

'And I have already dragged out a fortnight here.'

There was a brief silence.

'Time goes fast, and yet it is so dull here!' she said, not looking at him.

'That's only the fashion to say it is dull here. A provincial will live in Beliov or Zhizdra and not be dull, and when he comes here it's "Oh, the dullness! Oh, the dust!" You'd think he came from Grenada!'

She laughed. Then both continued eating in silence, like strangers, but after dinner they walked side by side; and there sprang up between them the light jesting conversation of people who are free and satisfied, to whom it does not matter where they go or what they talk about. They walked and talked of the strange light on the sea; the water was of a soft warm lilac hue, and there was a golden streak from the moon upon it. They talked of how sultry it was after a hot day. Gurov told her that he came from Moscow, that he had taken his degree in arts, but had a post in a bank; that he owned two houses in Moscow . . . And from her he learnt that she had grown up in Petersburg, but had lived in S— since her marriage two years before, that she was staying another month in Yalta, and that her husband, who needed a holiday too, might perhaps come and fetch her. She was not sure whether her husband had a post in the governor's office or the provincial rural administration – and was amused by her own ignorance. And Gurov learnt, too, that she was called Anna Sergeyevna.

Afterwards he thought about her in his room at the hotel – thought that she would certainly meet him the next day; it would be sure to happen. As he got into bed he thought how recently she had been a girl at school, studying like his own daughter; he recalled the diffidence, the angularity, that was still manifest in her laugh and her manner of talking to a stranger. This must have been the first time in her life she had been alone in surroundings in which she was followed, looked at, and spoken to entirely for a secret motive which she could not fail to guess. He recalled her slender, delicate neck, her lovely grey eyes.

'There's something pitiful about her, though,' he thought, and started to fall asleep.

II

A week had passed since they had met. It was a holiday. It was suffocatingly hot indoors, while in the street the wind whirled the dust round and round, and blew people's hats off. They were thirsty all day, and Gurov often went into the pavilion, and pressed Anna to have syrup and water or an ice. There was no refuge.

In the evening when the wind had dropped a little, they went out on to the pier to see the steamer come in. There were a great many people walking about the harbour; they had gathered to welcome someone, bringing bouquets. And two pecularities of a well-dressed Yalta crowd were very conspicuous: the elderly ladies were dressed like young ones, and there were great numbers of generals.

Owing to the roughness of the sea, the steamer arrived late, after the sun had set, and it was a long time turning about before it reached the pier. Anna looked through her lorgnette at the steamer and the passengers as though looking for acquaintances, and when she turned to Gurov her eyes were shining. She talked a great deal and asked disconnected questions, forgetting next moment what she had asked; then she dropped her lorgnette in the crush.

The festive crowd began to disperse; it was too dark to see people's faces. The wind had completely dropped, but Gurov and Anna still stood as though waiting to see someone else come from the steamer. Anna was silent now, and sniffed flowers without looking at Gurov.

'The weather is a bit better now that it's evening,' he said. 'Where shall we go now? Shall we drive somewhere?'

She made no answer.

Then he looked at her intently, and all at once put his arm round her and kissed her on the lips, and breathed in the moisture and the fragrance of the flowers; and he immediately looked round him, anxiously wondering whether anyone had seen them.

'Let's go to your place . . .' he said softly. And both walked quickly.

The room was close and smelt of the scent she had bought at the Japanese shop. Gurov looked at her and thought: 'What different people one meets in the world!' From the past he preserved memories of careless, good-natured women, who loved him cheerfully and were grateful to him for the happiness he gave them, however brief it might be; and of women like his wife who loved without any genuine feeling, with superfluous phrases, affectedly, hysterically, with an expression that suggested that it was not love nor passion, but something more significant; and of two or three others, very beautiful, cold women, on whose faces he had caught a glimpse of a rapacious expression – an obstinate desire to snatch from life more than it could give, and these were capricious, unreflecting, domineering, unintelligent women not in their first youth, and when Gurov grew cold to them their beauty excited his hatred and the lace on their linen seemed to him like fish scales.

But in this case there was still the diffidence, the angularity of inexperienced youth, an awkward feeling; and there was an impression of consternation as though someone had suddenly knocked at the door. The attitude of Anna – 'the lady with the dog' – to what had happened was somehow peculiar, very grave, as though it were her fall – so it seemed, and it was strange and out of place. Her face drooped and faded, and on both sides of it her long hair hung down mournfully; she mused in a dejected attitude like 'The Scarlet Woman'* in an old-fashioned picture.

'It's wrong,' she said. 'You will be the first not to respect me now.'

There was a water-melon on the table. Gurov cut himself a slice and began eating it without haste. There followed at least half an hour of silence.

Anna was touching; there was about her the purity of a good naive woman who had seen little of life. The solitary candle burning on the table threw a faint light on her face, yet it was clear that she felt unhappy.

'Why should I stop respecting you?' asked Gurov. 'You don't know what you're saying.'

'God forgive me,' she said, and her eyes filled with tears. 'It's awful.'

'You seem to be defending yourself.'

'What defence do I have? No. I am a bad, low woman; I despise myself and don't attempt to justify myself. It's not my husband but myself I have deceived. And not only just now; I have been deceiving myself for a long time. My husband may be a good, honest man, but he is a flunky! I don't know what he does there, what his work is, but I know he is a flunky! I was twenty when I married him. I was tormented by curiosity; I wanted something better. "There must be a different sort of life," I said to myself. I wanted to live! To live, to live! . . . I was fired by curiosity . . . you don't understand it, but, I swear to God, I could not control myself; something happened to me; I could not be restrained. I told my husband I was ill, and came here . . . And here I have been walking about as though I were intoxicated, like a mad creature . . . and now I have become a vulgar, contemptible woman whom anyone may despise.'

Gurov felt bored already with listening to her. He was irritated by the naive tone, by this remorse, so unexpected and inopportune; but for the tears in her eyes, he might have thought she was jesting or playing a part.

'I don't understand,' he said softly. 'What is it you want?'

She hid her face on his breast and pressed close to him.

'Believe me, believe me, I beg you . . .' she said. 'I love a pure, honest life, and sin is loathsome to me. I don't know what I am doing. Simple people say: "The Evil One has beguiled me." And I can say of myself now that the Evil One has beguiled me.'

'Hush, hush . . .' he muttered.

He looked at her fixed scared eyes, kissed her, talked softly and affectionately, and by degrees she was comforted, and her gaiety returned; they both began laughing.

Afterwards when they went out there was not a soul on the seafront. The town with its cypresses had quite a deathly air, but the sea still broke noisily on the shore; a single launch was rocking on the waves, and a lantern was blinking sleepily on it.

They found a cab and drove to Oreanda.*

'I found out your surname in the hall just now; it was written on the board – 'Von Diderits,' said Gurov. 'Is your husband German?'

'No; I believe his grandfather was German, but he is Orthodox Russian himself.'

At Oreanda they sat on a seat not far from the church, looked down at the sea, and were silent. Yalta was hardly visible through the morning mist; white clouds stood motionless on the mountain tops. The leaves did not stir on the trees, cicadas chirruped, and the monotonous hollow sound of the sea, rising up from below, spoke of the peace, of the eternal sleep awaiting us. So it must have sounded before there was a Yalta, an Oreanda here; so it sounds now, and it will sound as indifferently and monotonously when we are no more. And in this constancy, in this complete indifference to the life and death of each of us, there lies hidden, perhaps, a pledge of our eternal salvation, of the unceasing movement of life upon earth, of uninterrupted perfection. Sitting beside a young woman who in the dawn seemed so lovely, tranquil and spellbound in these magical surroundings – the sea, mountains, clouds, the broad sky – Gurov thought how in reality everything is beautiful in this world when one reflects: everything except what we think or do ourselves when we forget the higher aims of our existence and our human dignity.

A man walked up to them – probably a night-watchman – looked at them and walked away. And this detail seemed mysterious and beautiful, too. They saw a steamer come from Feodosia, with its lights out, illuminated by the dawn.

'There's dew on the grass,' said Anna, after a silence.

'Yes. It's time to go home.'

They went back to town.

Then they met every day at twelve o'clock on the sea-front, lunched and dined together, went for walks, admired the sea. She complained that she slept badly, that her heart throbbed violently; asked the same questions, troubled now by jealousy and now by the fear that he did not respect her sufficiently. And often in the square or gardens, when there was no one near them, he suddenly drew her to him and kissed her passionately. Complete idleness, these kisses in broad daylight with circumspection and fear, in case someone saw them, the heat, the smell of the sea, and the continual passing to and fro before him of idle, well-dressed, well-fed people, virtually regenerated him; he told Anna how beautiful she was, how fascinating, he was impatiently passionate, he would not move a step away from her, while she was often pensive and continually urged him to confess that he did not respect her, and did not love her in the least, and thought of her as nothing but a common woman. Rather late almost every evening they drove somewhere out of town, to Oreanda or to the waterfall; and the expedition was always a success, the scenery invariably impressed them as beautiful and majestic.

They were expecting her husband to come, but a letter came from him, saying that there was something wrong with his eyes, and he entreated his wife to come home as quickly as possible. Anna made haste to go.

'It's a good thing I am going away,' she said to Gurov. 'It's fate itself!'

She went by carriage and he went with her. They spent the whole day driving to Sevastopol. There, when she had got into a compartment of the mail train, and when the second bell had rung, she said:

'Let me look at you once more . . . look at you once again. That's right.'

She did not shed tears, but was so sad that she seemed ill, and her face was quivering.

'I shall remember you . . . think of you,' she said. 'God be with you; be happy. Don't think badly of me. We are parting for ever – it must be so, for we ought never to have met. Well, God be with you.'

The train moved off rapidly, its lights soon vanished from sight, and a minute later there was no sound of it, as though everything had conspired together to end as quickly as possible that sweet delirium, that madness. Left alone on the platform, and gazing into the dark distance, Gurov listened to the chirrup of the grasshoppers and the hum of the telegraph wires, feeling as though he had only just woken up. And he reflected that this had been another episode or adventure in his life, and it, too, was at an end, and nothing was left of it but a memory . . . He was much moved, sad, and conscious of a slight penitence, for this young woman whom he would never meet again had not been happy with him; he had been warm and affectionate with her, but yet in his manner, his tone, and his caresses there had been a shade of light irony, the rough-edged condescension of a happy man who was, besides, almost twice her age. All the time she had called him kind, exceptional, lofty; obviously he had seemed to her different from what he really was, so he had unintentionally deceived her . . .

Here at the station there was already a smell of autumn; it was a cool evening.

'It's time I went north, too,' thought Gurov as he left the platform. 'High time!'

III

At home in Moscow everything was in winter routine; the stoves were stoked, and in the morning it was still dark when the children were having breakfast and getting ready for school, and the nurse would light the lamps for a short time. The frosts had begun already.

When the first snow has fallen, on the first day of sledge-driving, it is pleasant to see the white earth, the white roofs, to draw soft delicious breath, and the season brings back the days of your youth. The old limes and birches, white and hoar frost, have a good-natured expression; they are nearer to your heart than cypresses and palms, and near them you no longer want to think of the sea and the mountains.

Gurov was a Muscovite, he arrived in Moscow on a fine frosty day, and when he put on his fur coat and warm gloves, and walked along Petrovka, and when on Saturday evening he heard the ringing of the bells, his recent trip and the places he had seen lost all charm for him. Little by little he became absorbed in Moscow life, greedily read three newspapers a day, and declared he did not read the Moscow papers on principle! He already felt a longing to go to restaurants, clubs, dinner-parties, anniversary celebrations, and he felt flattered at entertaining distinguished lawyers and artists, and at playing cards with a professor at the doctors' club. He could already eat a frying-pan full of 'hot-pot' . . .

In another month, he fancied, the image of Anna would be shrouded in mist in his memory, and only from time to time would visit him in his dreams with a touching smile, as others did. But more than a month passed, real winter had come, and everything was still clear in his memory as though he had parted with Anna only the day before. And his memories were flaring up all the more vividly. When in the evening stillness he heard from his study the voices of his children doing their homework, or when he listened to a song or the organ at the restaurant, or the storm howled in the chimney, suddenly everything would rise up in his memory: what had happened on the pier, and the early morning with the mist on the mountains, and the steamer coming from Feodosia, and the kisses. He would pace a long time about his room, remembering it all and smiling; then his memories passed into dreams, and in his fancy the past was mingled with what was to come. He did not see Anna in his dreams, but she followed him about everywhere like a shadow and haunted him. When he shut his eyes he saw her as though she were as large as life before him, and she seemed to him lovelier, younger, tenderer than she had been; and he imagined himself finer than he had been in Yalta. In the evenings she peeped out at him from the bookcase, from the fireplace, from the corner – he heard her breathing, the caressing rustle of her dress. In the street he watched the women, looking for someone like her.

He was tormented by an intense desire to share his memories with someone. But in his home it was impossible to talk of his love, and he had no one outside; he could not talk to his tenants nor to anyone at the bank. And what had he to talk of? Had he been in love then? Had there been anything beautiful, poetical, or edifying or simply interesting in his feelings for Anna? And there was nothing for him but to talk vaguely of love, of woman, and no one guessed what it meant; only his wife twitched her black eyebrows, and said: 'The part of a lady killer does not suit you at all, Dimitri.'

One evening, coming out of the doctors' club with an official with whom he had been playing cards, he could not resist saying:

'If you only knew what a fascinating woman I got to know in Yalta!'

The official got into his sledge and was driving away, but turned suddenly and shouted:

'Dmitri!'

'What?'

'You were right this evening: the sturgeon was a bit off!'

These words, so ordinary, for some reason moved Gurov to indignation, and struck him as degrading and unclean. What savage manners, what people! What senseless nights, what uninteresting, uneventful days! The rage for playing cards, the gluttony, the drunkenness, the continual talk always about the same thing. Useless pursuits and conversations always about the same things absorb the better part of your time, the better part of your strength, and in the end you are left with a life earthbound and curtailed, just rubbish, and there is no escaping or getting away from it – just as though you were in a madhouse or in penal servitude.

Gurov did not sleep all night, and was filled with indignation, and on the morrow he had a headache the entire day. And the next night he slept badly; he sat up in bed, thinking, or paced up and down his room. He was sick of his children, sick of the bank; he had no desire to go anywhere or to talk of anything.

In the holidays in December he prepared for a journey, and told his wife he was going to Petersburg to do something in the interests of a young friend – and he set off for S—. What for? He did not very well know himself. He wanted to see Anna and to talk with her, to arrange a meeting, if possible.

He reached S— in the morning, and took the best room at the hotel, in which the floor was covered with grey army cloth, and on the table was an inkstand, grey with dust and adorned with a figure on horseback, with its hat in its hand and its head broken off. The hotel porter gave him the necessary information: Von Diderits lived in a house of his own in Old Goncharnaia Street – it was not far from the hotel; he lived well and was rich, he had his own horses, everyone in town knew him. The porter pronounced the name 'Dridirits'.

Gurov went without haste to Old Goncharnaia Street and found the house. Just opposite the house stretched a long grey fence adorned with nails.

'You'd run away from a fence like that,' thought Gurov, looking from the fence to the windows of the house and back again.

He considered: today was a holiday, and the husband would probably be at home, and in any case it would be tactless to go into the house and upset her. If he were to send her a note it might fall into her husband's hands, and that might ruin everything. The best thing was to trust to chance. And he kept walking up and down the street by the fence, waiting for the chance. He saw a beggar go in at the gate and dogs fly at him; then an hour later he heard a piano, and the sounds were faint and indistinct. Probably it was Anna playing. The front door suddenly opened, and an old woman came out, followed by the familiar white Pomeranian. Gurov was on the point of calling to the dog, but his heart began beating violently, and in his excitement he could not remember the dog's name.

He walked up and down, and loathed the grey fence more and more, and by now he thought irritably that Anna had forgotten him and was perhaps already amusing herself with someone else, and that that was very natural in a young woman who had nothing to look at from morning till night but that accursed fence. He went back to his hotel room and sat for a long while on the sofa, not knowing what to do, then he had dinner and a long nap.

'How stupid and upsetting it is!' he thought when he woke and looked at the dark windows: it was already evening. 'Now I've slept my fill for some reason. Now what shall I do at night?'

He sat on the bed, which was covered by a cheap grey blanket, like a hospital blanket, and he taunted himself in his vexation:

'So much for the lady with the dog . . . So much for the adventure . . . So you're stuck in this room.'

That morning at the station a poster in large letters had caught his eye. *The Geisha** was to be performed for the first time. He thought of this and went to the theatre.

'It's quite possible she may go to the first performance,' he thought.

The theatre was full. As in all provincial theatres, there was a fog above the chandelier, the gallery was noisy and restless; in the front row the local dandies were standing up before the beginning of the performance, with their hands behind them; in the governor's box the governor's daughter, wearing a boa, was sitting in the front seat, while the governor himself lurked modestly behind the curtain with only his hands visible; the orchestra was a long time tuning up; the stage curtain swayed. All the time the audience were coming in and taking their seats, Gurov's eyes were searching eagerly.

Anna, too, came in. She sat down in the third row, and when Gurov looked at her his heart contracted, and he understood clearly that for him there was in the whole world no creature so near, so precious, and so important to him; she, this little woman, in no way remarkable, lost in a provincial crowd, with a vulgar lorgnette in her hand, filled his whole life now, was his sorrow and his joy, the one happiness that he now desired for himself, and to the sounds of the inferior orchestra, of the wretched provincial violins, he thought how lovely she was. He thought and dreamed.

A young man with small side-whiskers, tall and stooping, came in with Anna and sat down beside her; he bent his head at every step and seemed to be continually bowing. Most likely this was the husband whom at Yalta, in a rush of bitter feeling, she had called a flunky. And there really was in his long figure, his side-whiskers, and the small bald patch on his head, something of the flunky's obsequiousness; his smile was sugary, and in his buttonhole there was some obscure order's badge, like a waiter's number tag.

During the first interval the husband went out to smoke; she remained alone in her stall. Gurov, who was in the stalls, too, went up to her and said in a trembling voice, with a forced smile:

'Good evening.'

She glanced at him and turned pale, then glanced again with horror, unable to believe her eyes, and tightly gripped the fan and the lorgnette in her hands, evidently struggling with herself not to faint. Both were silent. She was sitting, he was standing, frightened by her turmoil and not venturing to sit down beside her. The violins and the flute began tuning up. He felt suddenly frightened; it seemed as if everyone in the boxes was looking at them. She got up and went quickly to the door; he followed her, and both walked senselessly along passages, and up and down stairs, and figures in legal, scholastic, and civil service uniforms, all wearing badges, flitted before their eyes. They caught glimpses of ladies, of fur coats hanging on pegs; the draughts blew on them, bringing a smell of cigarette ends. And Gurov, whose heart was beating violently, thought:

'Oh Lord! Why are all these people, this orchestra around . . .'

And that minute he suddenly remembered that evening at the station, when he was seeing Anna off, and he had told himself that it was all over and they would never see each other again. But how far off the end still was!

On a narrow, murky staircase, with a sign saying 'Entrance to Circle', she stopped.

'How you've frightened me!' she said, breathing heavily, still all pale and aghast. 'Oh, how you've frightened me! I am half dead. Why have you come? Why?'

'But do understand, Anna, do understand . . .' he said hastily in a low voice. 'I beg you to understand . . .'

She looked at him with dread, with entreaty, with love; she looked at him intently, to keep his features as sharply as she could in her memory.

'I am so wretched,' she went on, not heeding him. 'I have thought of nothing but you all the time; I live only by thinking about you. And I wanted to forget, to forget you; but why, oh why, have you come?'

On the landing above them two schoolboys were smoking and looking down, but Gurov did not care; he drew Anna to him, and began kissing her face, her cheeks, and her hands.

'What are you doing, what are you doing!' she cried in horror, pushing him away. 'We are mad. Go away today; go away at once . . . I beg you by all that is sacred, I implore you . . . People are coming!'

Someone was coming up the stairs.

'You must go away,' Anna went on in a whisper. 'Do you hear, Dmitri? I will come and see you in Moscow, I have never been happy; I am miserable now, and I never, never shall be happy, never! Don't make me suffer still more! I swear I'll come to Moscow. But now let us part. My precious, good, dear one, we must part!'

She pressed his hand and began rapidly going downstairs, looking round at him, and from her eyes he could see that she really was unhappy. Gurov stood for a little while, listened, then, when all sound had died away, he found his coat and left the theatre.

IV

And Anna began visiting him in Moscow. Once every two or three months she left S——, telling her husband that she was going to consult a doctor about a gynaecological complaint – and her husband half believed her. In Moscow she stayed at the Slaviansky Bazaar hotel, and at once sent a man in a red cap to Gurov. Gurov went to see her, and no one in Moscow knew of it.

Once he was going to see her in this way on a winter morning (the messenger had come the evening before when he was out). With him walked his daughter, whom he wanted to take to school: it was on the way. Snow was falling in big wet flakes.

'It's three degrees above freezing point, and yet it is snowing,' said

Gurov to his daughter. 'The thaw is only on the surface of the earth; there is quite a different temperature at a greater height in the atmosphere.'

'And why are there no thunderstorms in winter, papa?'

He explained that, too. He talked, thinking all the while that he was going to see her, and no living soul knew of it, and probably never would know. He had two lives: one, open, seen and known by all who cared to know, full of conventional truth and of conventional falsehood, exactly like the lives of his friends and acquaintances; and another life running its course in secret. And through some strange, perhaps accidental, conjunction of circumstances, everything that was essential, of interest and of value to him, everything in which he was sincere and did not deceive himself, everything that made the kernel of his life, was kept secret from other people; and all that was false in him, a membrane in which he hid to conceal the truth – such, for instance, as his work in the bank, his discussions at the club, his 'lower race', his presence with his wife at anniversary festivities – all that was open. And he judged of others by himself, not believing what he saw, and always presupposed that every person lived his real, most interesting life under the cover of secrecy, as if under the cover of night. All personal existence rested on privacy, and possibly it was partly on that account that civilised man was so nervously anxious that personal privacy should be respected.

After seeing his daughter to school, Gurov went on to the Slaviansky Bazaar. He took off his fur coat below, went upstairs, and softly knocked at the door. Anna, wearing his favourite grey dress, exhausted by the journey and the suspense, had been expecting him since the evening before. She was pale; she looked at him, and did not smile, and he had hardly come in when she fell on his breast. Their kiss was slow and prolonged, as though they had not met for two years.

'Well, how are you getting on there?' he asked. 'What news?'

'Wait; I'll tell you in a moment . . . I can't talk.'

She could not speak, since she was crying. She turned away from him, and pressed her handkerchief to her eyes.

'Let her have her cry. I'll sit down and wait,' he thought, and he sat down in an arm-chair.

Then he rang and asked for tea to be brought to him, and while he drank his tea she remained standing at the window with her back to him. She was crying from emotion, from the miserable consciousness that their life was so hard for them; they could only meet in secret, hiding themselves from people, like thieves! Their life was shattered, wasn't it?

'Come, do stop!' he said.

It was evident to him that this love of theirs was not going to end for some time, and its end was impossible to foresee. Anna was growing more and more attached to him. She adored him, and it was unthinkable to say to her that it was bound to have an end some day; besides, she would not have believed it.

He went up to her and took her by the shoulders to say something affectionate and cheering, and at that moment he saw himself in the looking-glass.

His hair was already beginning to turn grey. And it seemed strange to him that he had grown so much older, so much plainer during the last few years. The shoulders on which his hands rested were warm and quivering. He felt compassion for this life, still so warm and lovely, but probably already not far from beginning to fade and wither like his own. Why did she love him so much? He always seemed to women different from what he was, and they loved in him not himself, but the man created by their imagination, whom they had been eagerly seeking all their lives; and afterwards, when they noticed their mistake, they loved him all the same. And not one of them had been happy with him. Time passed, he met them, became intimate with them, parted, but he had never once loved; call it what you like, but not love.

And only now when his head was grey he had fallen properly, really in love – for the first time in his life.

Anna and he loved each other like people very close and akin, like husband and wife, like tender friends; it seemed to them that fate itself had meant them for one another, and they could not understand why he had a wife and she a husband; it was as though they were two birds of passage, male and female, caught and forced to live in different cages. They forgave each other for what they were ashamed of in their past, they forgave everything in the present, and felt that this love of theirs had changed them both.

In sad moments in the past he had comforted himself with any arguments that came into his mind, but now he was beyond arguments; he felt profound compassion, he wanted to be sincere and tender . . .

'Don't cry, my darling,' he said. 'You've had your cry; that's enough . . . Let's talk now, let's think of something.'

Thus they spent a long while taking counsel together, talked of how to avoid the necessity for hiding, for lying, for living in different towns and not seeing each other for long periods. How could they get free from these intolerable bonds?

'How? How?' he asked, clutching his head. 'How?'

And it seemed as though in a little while the solution would be

found, and then a new and splendid life would begin; and it was clear
to both of them that they had still a long, long way to go, and that the
most complicated and difficult part of it was only just beginning.

1899

In the Ravine

I

The village of Ukleevo lay in a ravine so that only a belfry and the chimneys of the calico printing factories could be seen from the highroad and the railway station. When travellers asked what village this was, they were told:

'That's the village where the sexton ate all the caviar at the funeral.'

At the funeral dinner of Kostiukov, the factory owner, the old sexton had spotted among the savouries some large-grained caviar and began eating it greedily; people nudged him, tugged at his arm, but he seemed to have gone numb with enjoyment, felt nothing, and only went on eating. He ate up all the caviar, and there had been four pounds in the jar. And years had passed since then, the sexton had long been dead, but the caviar was still remembered. Whether life was so poor here or people were incapable of noticing anything, the trivial incident which had occurred ten years before was the only story told about the village of Ukleevo.

The village was never free of fever, and there was boggy mud even in the summer, especially under the fences, over which hung old willow trees that gave deep shade. Here there was always a smell from the factory effluent and the acetic acid which was used to process the calico. The factories – three calico and one leather – were not in the village itself but a little way off. They were small factories, and fewer than four hundred workmen were employed in all of them. The leather factory often made the water in the little river stink; the effluent contaminated the meadows, the peasants' cattle suffered from anthrax, and the factory was ordered to close. It was considered closed, but went on working in secret with the connivance of the local police chief and the district doctor, who were paid ten roubles a month each by the owner. In the whole village there were only two decent houses built of brick with iron roofs; one of them was the local court, in the other, a two-storeyed house just opposite the church, lived a shopkeeper from Epifan called Grigori Petrovich Tsybukin.

Grigori kept a grocer's shop, but that was only for appearance's sake: in reality he sold vodka, cattle, hides, grain, and pigs; he traded in anything that came to hand, and when, for instance, magpies were wanted abroad for ladies' hats, he made some thirty kopecks on every pair of birds; he bought timber for felling, lent money at interest, and altogether was a sharp, versatile old man.

He had two sons. The elder, Anisim, was in the police, in criminal investigation, and was rarely at home. The younger, Stepan, had gone into the business and helped his father, but no great help was expected from him, as he was weak in health and deaf; his wife Aksinia, a handsome woman with a good figure, who wore a hat and carried a parasol on holidays, got up early and went to bed late, and ran about all day long, picking up her skirts and jingling her keys, going from the granary to the cellar and from there to the shop, and old Tsybukin looked at her good-humouredly while his eyes glowed, and at such moments he regretted she had not been married to his elder son instead of to the younger one, who was deaf, and who evidently understood little about female beauty.

The old man had always a fondness for family life, and he loved his family more than anything on earth, especially his elder son, the detective, and his daughter-in-law. Aksinia had no sooner married the deaf son than she began to display an extraordinary gift for business, and knew who could be allowed to run up a bill and who could not: she kept the keys and would not trust them even to her husband; she clattered away on the abacus, looked at horses' teeth like a peasant, and was always laughing or squawking; and whatever she did or said the old man was simply delighted and muttered:

'Well done, daughter-in-law! There's a beauty for you . . .'

He was a widower, but a year after his son's marriage he could not resist getting married himself. A girl was found for him, living twenty miles from Ukleevo, Varvara, getting on in years, but good-looking, handsome, and from a good family. As soon as she was installed into the upper-storey room everything in the house seemed to brighten up, as though new glass had been put into all the windows. The icon lamps were brightly lit, the tables were covered with snow-white cloths, flowers with red buds made their appearance in the windows and in the front garden, and at dinner, instead of eating from a single bowl, each person had a separate plate set for him. Varvara had a pleasant, friendly smile, and it seemed as though the whole house were smiling, too. Beggars and pilgrims, male and female, began to come into the yard, something unheard of in the past; the plaintive singsong voices of the Ukleevo peasant women and the apologetic coughs of weak, seedy-looking men, dismissed from the factory for drunkenness, were heard under the windows. Varvara helped them with money, with bread, with old clothes, and afterwards, when she felt more at home, began taking things out of the shop. One day the deaf son saw her take four ounces of tea and that disturbed him.

'Mother's just taken four ounces of tea,' he informed his father afterwards; 'where is that to be entered?'

The old man made no reply but stood and thought a moment, moving his eyebrows, and then went upstairs to his wife.

'Varvara dear, if you want anything out of the shop,' he said affectionately, 'take it, my dear. Take it and welcome; don't hesitate.'

And the next day the deaf son, running across the yard, called to her:

'If there is anything you want, Mother, take it.'

There was something new, something merry and light-hearted in her alms-giving, just as there was in the icon lamps and in the red flowers. When at Shrove Tuesday or the local patron saint's festival, which lasted for three days, they sold the peasants tainted salt meat, smelling so strong it was hard to stand near the barrel, and let drunken men pawn scythes, hats, their wives' kerchiefs; when the factory hands, stupefied with bad vodka, lay rolling in the mud, and sin seemed to condense and hover thick as fog in the air, then it seemed less awful that in the house there was a gentle, neatly dressed woman who had nothing to do with salt meat or vodka; her charity had in those burdensome, foggy days the effect of a safety valve in a machine.

The days in Tsybukin's house were spent in business cares. Before the sun had risen in the morning Aksinia was snorting as she washed in the outer room, and the samovar was boiling in the kitchen with an inauspicious hum. Old Grigori, dressed in a long black coat, cotton breeches and shiny top-boots, a very dapper little figure, walked about the rooms, tapping his heels like the father-in-law in a well-known song.* They unlocked the shop. When it was daylight a light racing chaise was brought up to the front door and the old man got jauntily on to it, pulling his big cap down to his ears; and, looking at him, no one would have said he was fifty-six. His wife and daughter-in-law saw him off, and now that he wore a good, clean coat, and the chaise was drawn by a huge black horse that had cost three hundred roubles, the old man did not like the peasants to come up to him with their complaints and petitions; he hated the peasants and despised them, and if he saw some peasants waiting at the gate, he would shout angrily:

'Why are you hanging about? Move on.'

Or if it was a beggar, he would say:

'God will provide!'

He was off on business; his wife, in a dark dress and a black apron, tidied the rooms or helped in the kitchen. Aksinia attended to the shop, and from the yard could be heard the clink of bottles and of money, her laughter and loud talk, and the anger of customers whom she had wronged; and at the same time it was obvious that the secret sale of vodka was already going on in the shop. The deaf son sat in the shop, too, or walked about the street bare-headed, with his hands in his pockets looking absent-mindedly now at the huts, now at the sky overhead. About six times a day they had tea; four times a day they sat down to meals; and in the evening they counted over their takings, recorded them, went to bed, and slept soundly.

All the three calico factories in Ukleevo and the houses of the factory owners – Khrymin Seniors, Khrymin Juniors, and Kostiukov – were linked by telephone. The telephone was laid on to the local court, too, but it soon stopped working as bedbugs and big black cockroaches bred in it. The elder of the rural district was semi-literate and wrote every word in the official documents in capitals. But, when the telephone broke, he said:

'Yes, now we'll find it a bit hard with no telephone.'

The Khrymin Seniors and Juniors were always suing each other, and sometimes the Juniors quarrelled among themselves and began a law suit, and their factory did not work for a month or two till they were reconciled again, and this entertained the people of Ukleevo, as there was a lot of talk and gossip over each quarrel. On holidays Kostiukov and the Juniors organised races, dashed about Ukleevo and ran calves over. Aksinia, rustling her starched petticoats, used to parade, dressed to kill, up and down the street near her shop; the Juniors used to snatch her up and pretend to abduct her. Then old Tsybukin would drive out to show off his new horse; he took Varvara with him.

In the evening, after the races, when people were going to bed, an expensive concertina was played outside the Juniors' house and, on a moonlight night, the sounds sent a thrill of delight to the heart, and Ukleevo no longer seemed a wretched hole.

II

The elder son Anisim came home very rarely, only on the main holidays, but he often sent by a returning villager presents and letters written in very good writing by some other hand, always on a sheet of foolscap in the form of a petition. The letters were full of expressions that Anisim never used in conversation: 'Dear Papa and Mama, I send you a pound of flower tea for the satisfaction of your physical needs.'

At the bottom of every letter was scratched, as though with a broken pen: 'Anisim Tsybukin,' and again in the same excellent hand: 'Agent.'

The letters were read aloud several times, and the old father, touched, red with emotion, would say:

'So, he refused to stay at home, he has gone in for a profession. Well, let him! Every man to his own!'

Just before Shrovetide there happened to be a heavy storm of rain and hail; the old man and Varvara went to the window to look at it, and lo and behold, Anisim was coming in a sledge from the station. He was quite unexpected. He came indoors, looking anxious and alarmed about something, and he remained so all the time; his behaviour was far too free-and-easy. He was in no haste to leave, it seemed as if he had been dismissed from the service. Varvara was pleased at his arrival; she looked at him with a sly expression, sighed, and shook her head.

'How is this, Saints above?' she said. 'Tut, tut, the lad's over twenty-seven, and he's still leading a carefree bachelor life; tut, tut . . .'

From the other room her soft, even speech sounded like 'tut, tut'. She began exchanging whispers with her husband and Aksinia, and their faces also took on a sly and mysterious conspiratorial expression.

They decided to marry Anisim off.

'Oh, tut, tut . . . the younger brother was married off long ago,' said Varvara, 'and you still have no mate, like a cock at a fair. What sort of behaviour is that? Tut, tut, you will be married, please God, then as you choose — you will go back to your job and your wife will stay here at home to help us. There's no order in your life, young man, and I can see you've forgotten what order is. Tut, tut, it's nothing but trouble with you townspeople.'

When a Tsybukin married, the best-looking girls were chosen as brides for him as a rich man. For Anisim, too, they found a good-looking bride. He himself was dull and unmemorable to look at; though feeble, sickly in build and short, he had full, swollen cheeks which looked as though he had puffed them out; his eyes looked with a keen, unblinking stare; his beard was red and scanty, and when he was thinking he always put it into his mouth and bit it; moreover he often drank too much, and that was noticeable from his face and his walk. But when he was told that there was a very beautiful bride for him, he said:

'Oh well, I am no fright myself. All of us Tsybukins are handsome, I may say.'

The village of Torguevo was near the town. Half of it had lately been incorporated into the town, the other half remained a village. In the first – the town half – there was a widow living in her own little house; she had a sister living with her who was very poor and went out to work by the day, and this sister had a daughter called Lipa, a girl who went out to work, too. People in Torguevo were already talking about Lipa's good looks, but her terrible poverty put everyone off; people reasoned that some widower or elderly man would marry her despite her poverty, or would perhaps take her to 'live in', and that this would give her mother enough to eat. Varvara heard about Lipa from the matchmakers, and she drove over to Torguevo.

Then a proper inspection visit was arranged at the aunt's, with lunch and wine, and Lipa wore a new pink dress made on purpose for this occasion, and a crimson ribbon like a flame gleamed in her hair. She was pale-faced, thin, and frail, with soft, delicate features tanned from working in the open air; a shy, mournful smile always hovered about her face, and there was a childlike look in her eyes – trustful and curious.

She was young, still a little girl, her breasts still scarcely perceptible, but she was of marriageable age. She really was beautiful, and the only thing that might be thought unattractive was her big man's hands which hung idle now like two big crab's claws.

'There is no dowry – and we don't mind,' said Tsybukin to the aunt. 'We took a wife from a poor family for our son Stepan, too, and now we can't praise her enough. At home or in the shop she has hands of gold.'

Lipa stood in the doorway and her looks seemed to say: 'Do with me as you will: I trust you,' while her mother Praskovia, the daily woman, hid herself in the kitchen, numb with shyness. Long ago, in her youth, a merchant whose floors she was scrubbing stamped at her in a rage; she went chill with terror and there always was a feeling of fear at the bottom of her heart. When she was frightened her arms and legs trembled and her cheeks twitched. Sitting in the kitchen she tried to hear what the visitors were saying, and she kept crossing herself, pressing her fingers to her forehead, and gazing at the icons. Anisim, slightly drunk, kept opening the door into the kitchen and saying in a free-and-easy way:

'Why are you sitting in here, precious Mama? We're missing you.'

And Praskovia, overcome with timidity, pressing her hands to her lean, wasted breasts, said:

'Oh, not at all . . . We're very grateful to you.'

After the inspection visit the wedding-day was fixed. Then Anisim walked about the rooms at home whistling or, suddenly thinking of something, would fall to brooding and would look at the floor fixedly, silently, as though his eyes wanted to penetrate the depths of the earth. He expressed neither pleasure that he was to be married, married so soon, in the week after Easter, nor a desire to see his bride, but simply went on whistling. And it was obvious he was only getting married because his father and stepmother wished him to, and because it was the custom in the village to marry the son so as to have a woman to help in the house. When he was leaving he seemed in no hurry, and his behaviour was quite different from that on previous visits – he was particularly free-and-easy, and said inappropriate things.

III

In the village of Shikalova lived two dressmakers, sisters, belonging to the flagellant sect. The new clothes for the wedding were ordered from them, and they often came for a trial fitting, and spent a long time drinking tea. They were making Varvara a brown dress with black lace and tubular glass beads, and Aksinia a light green dress with a yellow front, with a train. When the dressmakers had finished their work Tsybukin paid them not in money but in goods from the shop, and they went away depressed, carrying parcels of tallow candles and tins of sardines for which they had no use at all, and when they left the village for the open country they sat down on a hillock and began to cry.

Anisim arrived three days before the wedding, in new clothes from top to toe. He had dazzling rubber galoshes, and instead of a cravat wore a red cord with little balls on it, and over his shoulders hung an overcoat, also new, its sleeves dangling.

After crossing himself sedately before the icon, he greeted his father and gave him ten silver roubles and ten half roubles; to Varvara he gave the same, and to Aksinia twenty quarter roubles. The chief charm of the present lay in the fact that all the coins, as though carefully selected, were brand new and glittered in the sun. Trying to seem grave and sedate he pursed up his face and puffed out his cheeks, and he smelt of spirits. Probably he had dashed to the buffet at every station. And again there was a casual manner about the man – something superfluous. Then Anisim had a snack and drank tea with the old man, and Varvara turned the new coins over in her hands and asked about villagers who had gone to live in the town.

'They are all right, thank God, they get on quite well,' said Anisim. 'Only something has happened to Ivan Yegorov: his old wife Sofia died. From consumption. They ordered a wake for the peace of her soul at the confectioner's at two and a half roubles a head. And there was real wine. The peasants from our village – they paid two and a half roubles for them, too. They ate nothing. What would a peasant know about sauces!'

'Two and a half!' said his father, shaking his head.

'Well, it's not like the country there, you go into a restaurant for a bite of something, you ask for one thing and another, others join till there is a party of us, you have a drink – and before you know where you are it's daylight and you've three or four roubles each to pay. And when you're with Samorodov he likes to have coffee with brandy in it after everything, and brandy is sixty kopecks for a little glass.'

'He's making it all up,' said the old man with delight; 'he's making it all up!'

'I am always with Samorodov now. It is Samorodov who writes my letters to you. He writes splendidly. And if I were to tell you, Mama,' Anisim went on gaily, turning to Varvara, 'the sort of fellow that Samorodov is, you wouldn't believe me. We call him Mukhtar because he's like an Armenian – very dark. I can see through him, I know all his business like the back of my hand, Mama, and he senses that, and he always follows me about, never far behind, we are as thick as thieves. He finds it a bit uncanny, but he can't bear to be without me. Where I go he goes. I have a reliable, true eye, Mama. You see a peasant selling a shirt in the market place. "Stop, that shirt's stolen." And really, it turns out I'm right: the shirt was a stolen one.'

'How can you tell?' asked Varvara.

'No special way, I just have an eye for it. I know nothing about the shirt, only for some reason I seem drawn to it: it's stolen, and that's all I can say. Among us detectives they just say, "Oh, Anisim has gone to shoot snipe!" That means looking for stolen goods. Yes . . . Anybody can steal, but it is another thing to keep! The earth is wide, but there is nowhere to hide stolen goods.'

'In our village the Guntorevs had a ram and two ewes rustled last week,' said Varvara, and she heaved a sigh, 'and there is no one to find them . . . Oh, tut, tut . . .'

'Well, I might have a try. I don't mind.'

The day of the wedding arrived. It was a cool but bright, cheerful April day. People were driving about Ukleevo from early morning with pairs or teams of three horses decked with many-coloured ribbons on their yokes and manes, with a jingle of bells. The rooks, disturbed by this activity, were cawing noisily in the willows, and the starlings sang their loudest unceasingly as though rejoicing that there was a wedding at the Tsybukins'.

Indoors the tables were already covered with long fish, smoked hams, stuffed fowls, boxes of sprats, various salted and pickled savouries, and a lot of bottles of vodka and wine; there was a smell of smoked sausage and of soured lobster. Old Tsybukin walked about near the tables, tapping his heels and sharpening the knives against each other. They kept calling Varvara and asking for things, and she ran breathlessly, looking distracted, into the kitchen, where the chef from Kostiukov's and the head cook, a woman from Khrymin Juniors', had been at work since early morning. Aksinia, with her hair curled, in her stays with no dress, in new squeaky boots, flew about the yard like a whirlwind, and her bare knees and breasts could just be glimpsed as she ran. It was noisy, there was a sound of scolding and oaths; passers-by stopped at the wide-open gates, and in everything there was a feeling that something extraordinary was imminent.

'They've gone to fetch the bride!'

The bells peeled out and died away far beyond the village . . . After two o'clock people ran up: again the bells rang out: they were bringing the bride! The church was full, the chandelier was lit, the choristers were singing from written music, as old Tsybukin had wished. The glare of the lights and the bright coloured dresses dazzled Lipa; she felt as though the choristers' loud voices were hitting her on the head with a hammer. Her boots and the corset, which she had put on for the first time in her life, pinched her, and her face looked as though she had only just come round after fainting; she gazed about, uncomprehending. Anisim, in his black tail-coat with a red cord instead of a tie, stared at the same spot lost in thought, and when the choristers cried out loudly he hurriedly crossed himself. He felt touched and on the verge of tears. He had known this church from earliest childhood; his late mother used to bring him here for communion; he used to sing in the choir with other boys; every icon he remembered so well, every corner. Now he was being married, he had to take a wife for propriety, but he was not thinking of that now, he had forgotten his wedding completely. He could not see the icons for tears, his heart felt crushed; he prayed and begged God that the inevitable disasters, that were ready to burst upon him any day now, might somehow pass him by, as storm clouds in time of drought pass over the village without yielding one drop of rain. And so many sins were heaped up in the past, so many sins, and everything was such a quagmire, so irremediable that it seemed absurd even to ask forgiveness. But he did ask forgiveness, and even gave a loud sob, but no one took any notice, since they all supposed he had been drinking.

A fretful childish wail was heard:

'Take me away, Mama darling!'

'Quiet there!' cried the priest.

When they returned from church people ran after them; there were crowds, too, round the shop, round the gates, and in the yard under the windows. The peasant women came in to sing songs of congratulation to them. The young couple had scarcely crossed the threshold when the choristers, who were already standing in the lobby with their sheet music, broke into a loud chant at the top of their voices; a band ordered expressly from the town began playing. Sparkling wine from the Don was brought in tall wine glasses, and Elizarov, a carpenter who did jobs by contract, a tall, gaunt old man with eyebrows so bushy that they almost hid his eyes, said, addressing the newly-weds:

'Anisim and you, my child, love one another, live in God's way, little children, and the Heavenly Mother will not abandon you.' He leaned his face on the old father's shoulder and gave a sob: 'Grigori, let us weep, let us weep with joy!' he said in a thin voice, and then at once burst out laughing in a loud bass guffaw. 'Ho-ho-ho! This is a fine daughter-in-law for you too! She's got everything in the right place; it all runs smoothly, no creaking, the mechanism is in good order, lots of screws in it.'

He was a native of the Yegorievsky district, but had worked in the factories in Ukleevo and the neighbourhood from his youth, and had made Ukleevo his home. He had been a familiar figure for years as old and gaunt and lanky as now, and for years he had been nicknamed 'Crutch'. Perhaps because he had been for forty years occupied in repairing factory machinery he judged everybody and everything by its soundness or its need for repair. And before sitting down to the table he tried several chairs to see whether they were solid, and he touched the white salmon too.

After the Don champagne, they all sat down to table. The guests talked, moving their chairs. The choristers sang in the lobby. The band was playing, and at the same time the peasant women in the yard were singing their tributes in unison – and there was an awful, wild medley of sounds which made you giddy.

Crutch turned round in his chair and jostled his neighbours with his elbows, prevented people talking, and laughed and cried alternately.

'Little children, little children, little children,' he muttered rapidly. 'Aksinia, my dear, Varvara darling, we will live all in peace and harmony, my dear little hatchets . . .'

He drank little and a glass of English bitters was enough to make him drunk. The revolting bitters, made from nobody knew what, intoxicated everyone who drank it as though it had stunned them. Their tongues began to falter.

The local clergy, clerks from the factories with their wives, tradesmen and inn keepers from other villages were present. The clerk and the elder of the rural district who had served together for fourteen years, and who had during all that time never signed a single document for anybody nor let a single person out of the local offices without deceiving or doing him wrong, were sitting now side by side, both fat and well fed, and it seemed that they were so steeped in injustice and lies that even the skin of their faces was somehow peculiar, swindling. The clerk's wife, an emaciated woman with a squint, had brought all her children with her, and like a bird of prey looked sideways at the plates and snatched anything close to hand to put in her own or her children's pockets.

Lipa sat petrified, still with the same expression as in church. Anisim had not said a single word to her since he had first met her, so that he did not yet know the sound of her voice; and now, sitting beside her, he remained mute and went on drinking bitters, and when he got drunk he began talking to an aunt who was sitting opposite:

'I have a friend called Samorodov. A special man. He is an honorary citizen, and he can converse. But I can see right through him, Auntie, and he feels it. Pray join me in drinking to the health of Samorodov, Auntie!'

Varvara, worn out and distracted, walked round the table pressing the guests to eat, and was clearly pleased that there were so many dishes and that everything was so lavish – no one could disparage them now. The sun set, but the dinner went on: they had no idea what they were eating or drinking, you could not make out what they said, and only occasionally when the music subsided a peasant woman could be heard shouting:

'They have sucked the blood out of us, the Herods; a plague on them!'

In the evening they danced to the band. The Khrymin Juniors came, bringing their wine, and one of them, dancing a quadrille, held a bottle in each hand and a wine glass in his mouth, and that made everyone laugh. In the middle of the quadrille they suddenly started to dance squatting; Aksinia in green whirled past, stirring up a wind with her train. Someone trod on her flounce and Crutch shouted:

'Hey, they have torn off the plinth! Children!'

Aksinia had naive grey eyes which rarely blinked, and a naive smile played constantly on her face. And in those unblinking eyes, and in that little head on the long neck, and in her slenderness there was something snaky; all in green but for the yellow on her chest, she looked with a smile on her face as a viper looks out of the young rye in the spring at the passers-by, stretching itself and lifting its head. The Khrymins were free in their behaviour to her, and it was very noticeable that she was on intimate terms with the elder of them. But her deaf husband was unaware, he did not look at her; he sat with his legs crossed and ate nuts, cracking them so loudly that it sounded like pistol shots.

But now old Tsybukin himself walked into the middle of the room and waved his handkerchief as a sign that he, too, wanted to dance a Russian dance, and all over the house and from the crowd in the yard rose a roar of approbation:

'*He*'s going to dance! *Him*!'

Varvara danced, but the old man only waved his handkerchief and moved his heels, but the people in the yard, leaning against one another, peeping in at the windows, were in raptures, and for the moment forgave him everything – his wealth and the wrongs he had done them.

'Well done, Mr Tsybukin!' was heard in the crowd. 'That's right, show them! You can still do it! Ha-ha!'

It ended late, after one in the morning. Anisim, staggering, went to take leave of the choristers and musicians, and gave each of them a new half rouble. His father, who was not swaying but still seemed to be leaning heavily on one leg, saw his guests off, and said to each of them:

'The wedding has cost two thousand.'

As the party was breaking up, someone took the Shikalova innkeeper's good coat instead of his own old one, and Anisim suddenly flew into a rage and began shouting:

'Stop! I'll trace it at once! I know who stole it! Stop!'

He ran out into the street and chased someone. He was caught, brought back home and shoved, drunken, red with anger, and wet, into the room where the aunt was undressing Lipa, and they were locked in.

IV

Five days passed. Anisim, who had got ready to go, went upstairs to say good-bye to Varvara. All the lamps were burning before the icons, there was a smell of incense, while she sat at the window knitting a stocking of red wool.

'You haven't stayed with us long,' she said. 'You've been bored, I dare say. Oh, tut, tut . . . We live comfortably; we have plenty of everything. We celebrated your wedding properly, in good style; your

father says it came to two thousand. In fact we live like merchants,
only it's dreary. We treat the people very badly. My heart aches my
dear; how we treat them, my goodness! Whether we exchange a horse
or buy something or hire a labourer – it's all cheating. Cheating and
cheating. The Lenten oil in the shop is bitter, rancid, the people have
pitch that is better. But surely, tell me, pray, couldn't we sell good
oil?'

'Every man to his job, Mama.'

'But we have to die, don't we? Oy, oy, really you ought to talk to
your father . . .'

'Why, you should talk to him yourself.'

'Well, I said what I had to, but he said exactly what you say: "Every
man to his job." In heaven they'll judge the job you were put to, all
right. God's judgment is just.'

'Of course no one will judge,' said Anisim, and he heaved a sigh.
'There is no God, anyway, you know, Mama, so what judging can
there be?'

Varvara looked at him with surprise, burst out laughing, and
clasped her hands. Because she was so genuinely surprised at his
words and looked at him as if he were an oddity, he was embarrassed.

'Perhaps there is a God, only there is no faith,' he said. 'When I was
being married I was not myself. Just as you take an egg from under a
hen and there is a chick chirping in it, so my conscience suddenly
chirped in me, and while I was being married I thought all the time
there was a God! But when I left the church there wasn't. And indeed,
how can I tell whether there is a God or not? We haven't been taught
right since childhood, and even when the baby sucks his mother's
breast he is only taught "every man to his own job". Father does not
believe in God, either. You were saying that Guntorev had some
sheep stolen . . . I've found them; it was a Shikalova peasant who
stole them; he stole them, but father's got the fleeces . . . So much for
his faith.'

Anisim winked and shook his head.

'The elder does not believe in God, either,' he went on. 'Nor do the
clerk and the sexton. And if they go to church and keep the fasts, that
is simply to stop people talking ill of them, and in case there really will
be a Day of Judgment. Nowadays people say that the end of the world
has come because people have grown weaker, do not honour their
parents, and so on. All that is nonsense. My idea, Mama, is that all
our trouble is because there is so little conscience in people. I see right
through people, Mama, and I understand. If a man has a stolen shirt, I
see it. A man sits in a tavern and you fancy he is drinking tea and no
more, but to me the tea is neither here nor there; I see further, he has

no conscience. You can go about the whole day and not meet one man with a conscience. And the whole reason is that they don't know whether there is a God or not . . . Well, good-bye, Mama, keep alive and well, don't think of me badly.'

Anisim bowed down at Varvara's feet.

'We thank you for everything, Mama,' he said. 'You are a great gain to our family. You are a very lady-like woman, and I am very grateful to you.'

Much moved, Anisim went out, but returned again and said:

'Samorodov has got me mixed up in something: I shall be either rich or ruined. If anything happens, then you must comfort my father, Mama.'

'Oh nonsense, don't you worry, tut, tut . . . God is merciful. And Anisim, you should be nice to your wife, and not give each other sulky looks; you might smile at least.'

'But she's a bit odd,' said Anisim, and he gave a sigh. 'She doesn't understand anything, she never speaks. She's very young, let her grow up . . .'

A tall, sleek white stallion, harnessed to a charabanc, was now standing at the front door.

Old Tsybukin leapt in jauntily at a run and took the reins. Anisim kissed Varvara, Aksinia, and his brother. On the steps Lipa, too, was standing; she was standing motionless, looking away, and it seemed as though she had not come to see him off but was there just by chance, for some unknown reason. Anisim went up to her and just touched her cheek with his lips.

'Good-bye,' he said.

And without looking at him she gave a strange smile; her face began to quiver, and everyone for some reason felt sorry for her. Anisim, too, leapt into the charabanc with a bound and put his arms jauntily akimbo, for he considered himself handsome.

When they drove up out of the ravine Anisim kept looking back at the village. It was a warm, bright day. The cattle were being driven out for the first time, and the peasant girls and women were walking by the herd in their festive dresses. The dun-coloured bull bellowed, glad to be free, and pawed the ground with his forefeet. On all sides, above and below, the larks were singing. Anisim looked round at the shapely white church – it had only lately been whitewashed – and he recalled praying in it five days before; he looked round at the school with its green roof, at the little river in which he used to bathe and catch fish, and there was a stir of joy in his heart, and he wished that walls might rise up from the ground and prevent him from going further, and that he might be left with nothing but the past.

At the station they went to the buffet and drank a glass of sherry each. His father felt in his pocket for his purse to pay.

'It's my treat,' said Anisim. The old man, touched and delighted, slapped him on the shoulder, and winked to the waiter as much as to say, 'See what a fine son I have got.'

'You ought to stay at home in the business Anisim,' he said; 'you'd be worth any price to me! I'd shower gold on you from head to foot, my son.'

'It can't be done, Papa.'

The sherry was a little sour and smelt of sealing wax, but they had another glass.

When old Tsybukin returned home from the station, for the first moment he did not recognise his younger daughter-in-law.

As soon as her husband had driven out of the yard, Lipa was transformed and suddenly brightened up. Wearing a threadbare old petticoat, with her feet bare and her sleeves tucked up to the shoulders, she was scrubbing the stairs in the entry and singing in a silvery little voice, and when she brought out a big tub of dirty water and looked up at the sun with her childlike smile it looked as if she, too, were a lark.

An old labourer passing by the door shook his head and cleared his throat.

'Yes, indeed, your daughters-in-law, Mr Tsybukin, are a blessing from God,' he said. 'Not women, but treasures!'

v

On Friday, the eighth of July, Elizarov, nicknamed Crutch, and Lipa were returning from the village of Kazanskoe, where they had gone to pray on the occasion of a church celebration of the Holy Mother of Kazan. Well behind them walked Lipa's mother Praskovia, who kept lagging behind, as she was ill and short of breath. It was getting near to evening.

'A-a-a . . .' said Crutch, wondering as he listened to Lipa. 'A-a! . . . We-ell?'

'I am very fond of jam, Mr Elizarov,' said Lipa. 'I sit down in my little corner and drink tea and eat jam. Or I have tea with Varvara, and she tells some story full of feeling. They have a lot of jam – four jars. "Have some, Lipa; eat as much as you like." '

'A-a-a, four jars!'

'They live very well. We have white bread with our tea; and meat, too, as much as we want. They live very well, only I am frightened with them, Mr Elizarov. Oh, oh, how frightened I am!'

'Why are you frightened, child?' asked Crutch, and he looked back to see how far behind Praskovia was lagging.

'To begin with, when we had the wedding I was afraid of Anisim. Anisim didn't do anything, he didn't ill-treat me, only when he comes near me a cold shiver runs all over me, through all my bones. And I did not sleep one night, I trembled all over and kept praying to God. And now I am afraid of Aksinia, Mr Elizarov. It's not that she does anything, she is always laughing, but sometimes she glances at the window, and her eyes are so fierce and there is a gleam of green in them – like the eyes of the sheep in the shed. The Khrymin Juniors are leading her astray: "Your old man," they tell her, "has a bit of land at Butiokino, a hundred and twenty acres," they say, "and there is sand and water there, so you, Aksinia," they say, "build a brickyard there and we will go shares in it." Bricks now are twenty roubles a thousand, it's a profitable business. Yesterday at dinner Aksinia said to my father-in-law: "I want to build a brickyard at Butiokino; I'm going into business on my own account." She laughed as she said it. And Mr Tsybukin's face darkened, you could see he did not like it. "As long as I live," he said, "things mustn't be separate, everyone must act together." But her eyes flashed him a look, she gnashed her teeth . . . Fritters were served, she wouldn't eat them.'

'A-a-a! . . .' Crutch was surprised. 'Wouldn't eat!'

'And tell me, please, when does she sleep?' said Lipa. 'She sleeps for half an hour, then jumps up and keeps walking about to see if the peasants have set fire to something, or stolen something . . . It's frightening to live with her, Mr Elizarov. And the Khrymin Juniors didn't go to bed after the wedding, but drove to the town to sue each other; and folks say it is all on account of Aksinia. Two of the brothers have promised to build her a brickyard, but the third is offended, and the factory has been at a standstill for a month, and my uncle Prokhor is out of work and goes about from house to house begging crusts. "Hadn't you better go working the land or sawing wood, meanwhile, Uncle?" I tell him; "why disgrace yourself?" "I'm not used to peasant work any more," he says; "I can't do any now, Lipa . . ." '

They stopped to rest and wait for Praskovia near a copse of young aspens. Elizarov had long been a subcontractor, but he kept no horses, going on foot all over the district with nothing but a little bag of bread and onions, and stalking along with big strides, swinging his arms. And it was difficult to keep up with him.

At the entrance to the copse stood a milestone. Elizarov touched it to see if it was solid. Praskovia reached them out of breath. Her wrinkled and perpetually scared face was beaming with happiness;

she had been at church today like anyone else, then she had been to the fair and there had drunk pear kvas. For her this was unusual, and it even seemed to her now that she had enjoyed herself that day for the first time in her life. After resting they all three walked on side by side. The sun had already set, and its beams filtered through the copse, casting light on the trunks of the trees. There was a faint sound of voices ahead. The Ukleevo girls had long before pushed on ahead but had lingered in the copse, probably picking mushrooms.

'Hey, wenches!' cried Elizarov. 'Hey, my beauties!'

There was a sound of laughter in response.

'Crutch is coming! Crutch! The old fogey!'

And the echo laughed, too. And then the copse was left behind. The tops of the factory chimneys came into view. The cross on the belfry glittered; this was the village: 'the one where the sexton ate all the caviar at the funeral'. Now they were almost home; they only had to go down into the big ravine. Lipa and Praskovia, who had been walking barefoot, sat down on the grass to put on their shoes; Elizarov sat down with them. If they looked down from above Ukleevo looked beautiful and peaceful with its willow trees, its white church, and its little river, and the only blot on the picture was the factory roofs, painted for cheapness an outlandish gloomy colour. On the slope on the further side they could see the rye – some in stacks and sheaves here and there as though strewn about by the storm, and some freshly cut lying in swathes; the oats, too, were ripe and glistened now in the sun like mother-of-pearl. It was harvest time. Today was a holiday, tomorrow they would harvest rye and cart hay, and then Sunday a holiday again; every day there were mutterings of distant thunder. It was misty and looked like rain, and, gazing now at the fields, everyone thought, 'God grant we get the harvest in on time'; and everyone felt cheerful and joyful and anxious at heart.

'Mowers ask a high price nowadays,' said Praskovia. 'One rouble forty kopecks a day.'

People kept coming and coming from the fair at Kazanskoe: peasant women, factory workers in a new caps, beggars, children . . . Now a cart drove by, stirring up the dust and behind it ran an unsold horse, and it seemed glad not to have been sold; then a cow was led along by the horns, resisting stubbornly; then a cart again, and in it drunken peasants swinging their legs. An old woman led a little boy in a big hat and big boots; the boy was tired out with the heat and the heavy boots which stopped him bending his legs at the knees, but yet blew unceasingly with all his might at a tin trumpet; they had descended the slope and turned into the street, but the trumpet could still be heard.

'Our factory owners don't seem quite themselves . . .' said Elizarov. 'There's trouble. Kostiukov is angry with me. "Too many boards have gone on the cornices." "Too many? As many as were needed, Mr Kostiukov; I don't eat them with my porridge." "How can you speak to me like that," said he, "you good-for-nothing blockhead! Don't forget yourself! It was I who made you a contractor," he shouts. "So what?" said I. "Even before I was a contractor I used to have tea every day." "You're all rogues . . ." he says. I said nothing. "We're all rogues in this world," thought I, "but you lot will be rogues in the next." Ha-ha-ha! The next day he'd softened up. "Don't you hold my words against me, Elizarov," he said. "If I spoke out of turn," says he, "what of it? I am a merchant of the first guild, your superior – you have to put up with it in silence." "You," said I, "are a merchant of the first guild and I am a carpenter, that's correct. And Saint Joseph was a carpenter, too. Ours is a righteous calling and pleasing to God, and if you think you're my superior you're welcome, Mr Kostiukov." And later on, after that conversation I mean, I thought: "Who is superior? A merchant of the first guild or a carpenter?" The carpenter must be, children!'

Crutch thought a minute and added:

'Yes, that's how it is, children. He who works, he who endures, is superior.'

By now the sun had set and a thick mist as white as milk was rising over the river, in the churchyard, and in the open spaces round the factories. Now when the darkness was coming on rapidly, when lights were twinkling below, and when it seemed as though the mist were hiding a bottomless abyss, Lipa and her mother, who were born destitute and prepared to live so till the end, giving to others everything except their frightened, gentle souls, may have fancied for a minute perhaps that in the vast mysterious world, among the endless series of lives, they, too, were a force and superior to somebody; they liked sitting up here, they smiled happily and forgot that they still had to go back down.

At last they were home again. The mowers were sitting on the ground at the gates near the shop. As a rule the Ukleevo peasants would not work for Tsybukin, and outsiders had to be hired, and now in the darkness it seemed that there were men sitting there with long black beards. The shop was open, and through the doorway they could see the deaf son playing draughts with a boy. The mowers were singing softly, scarcely audibly, or loudly demanding their wages for the previous day, but they were not paid for fear they should go away before tomorrow. Old Tsybukin, with his coat off, was sitting in his waistcoat with Aksinia under the birch tree, drinking tea; a lamp was burning on the table.

'I say, Grandfather,' a mower called from outside the gates, as though taunting him, 'pay us half anyway! Hey, Grandfather.'

And at once there was a sound of laughter, and then again they sang barely audibly . . . Crutch, too, sat down to have some tea.

'We have been at the fair, you know,' he began telling them. 'We've had a good time, a very good time, my children, praise the Lord. But an unfortunate thing happened: Sashka the blacksmith bought some tobacco and gave the shopman half a rouble, to be sure. And the half rouble was a false one' – Crutch went on, and he meant to speak in a whisper, but he spoke in a smothered, husky voice, and everyone could hear. 'The half rouble turned out to be a bad one. He was asked where he got it. "Anisim Tsybukin gave it me," he said, "when I went to his wedding," he said. They called the constable, took the man away . . . Look out, Mr Tsybukin, see that nothing comes of it, no talk . . .'

'Grandfather!' the same voice called tauntingly outside the gates. 'Gra-andfather!'

A silence followed.

'Ah, my children, children, children . . .' Crutch muttered rapidly, and he got up. He was overcome with drowsiness. 'Well, thank you for the tea, for the sugar, little children. It's time to sleep. I'm a bit of rotten timber nowadays, my beams are crumbling under me. Ho-ho-ho!'

And as he left he said:

'I suppose it's time I was dead.'

And he gave a gulp. Old Tsybukin did not finish his tea but sat on a little, pondering; and his face looked as though he were listening to the footsteps of Crutch, who was far away down the street.

'Sashka the blacksmith told a lie, I expect,' said Aksinia, guessing his thoughts.

He went into the house and came back a little later with a parcel; he opened it, and there was the gleam of roubles – perfectly new coins. He took one, tried it with his teeth, flung it on the tray; then flung down another . . .

'The roubles really are false . . .' he said, looking at Aksinia and seeming perplexed. 'It's them . . . Anisim brought them that time, his present. Take them, daughter,' he whispered, and thrust the parcel into her hands. 'Take them and throw them into the well . . . To hell with them! And mind there is no talk. Harm might come of it . . . Clear away the samovar, put out the light . . .'

Lipa and her mother sitting in the barn saw the lights go out one after the other, only overhead in Varvara's room there were blue and red lamps gleaming, and a feeling of peace, content, and ignorance seemed to float down from there. Praskovia could never get used to her daughter being married to a rich man, and when she came she huddled timidly in the lobby with an ingratiating smile on her face, and tea and sugar were sent out to her. And Lipa, too, could not get used to it either, and after her husband had gone away she did not sleep in her bed, but lay down anywhere to sleep, in the kitchen or the barn, and every day she scrubbed floors or washed clothes, and felt as though she were a daily woman. And now, coming back from the service, they drank tea in the kitchen with the cook, then went into the barn and lay down on the ground between the sledge and the wall. It was dark here and smelt of harness. The lights went out about the house, then they could hear the deaf son shutting up the shop, the mowers settling themselves about the yard to sleep. In the distance at the Khrymin Juniors' they were playing an expensive concertina . . . Praskovia and Lipa began to fall asleep.

And when they were woken by somebody's footsteps it was bright moonlight; at the entrance of the barn stood Aksinia with her bedding in her arms.

'It's a bit cooler here, I think,' she said; then she came in and lay down almost in the doorway so that her whole body was lit up by the moon.

She did not sleep, but breathed heavily, tossing from side to side with the heat, throwing off almost all the bedclothes. And in the magic moonlight what a beautiful, what a proud animal she was! A little time passed, and then steps were heard again: the old father, white all over, appeared in the doorway.

'Aksinia,' he called, 'are you here?'

'Well?' she responded angrily.

'I told you just now to throw the money into the well. Did you?'

'What next, throwing good money away! I gave it to the mowers . . .'

'Oh my God!' cried the old man, dumbfounded and frightened. 'Oh my God! you're a troublemaker, woman . . . Oh my God!'

He clasped his hands and went out, and he kept repeating something as he left. And a little later Aksinia sat up and sighed heavily with annoyance, then got up and, gathering up her bedclothes in her arms, went out.

'Why did you marry me into this family, Mother!' said Lipa.

'You have to get married, daughter. It's not up to us.'

And a feeling of inconsolable woe was about to overcome them. But it seemed to them that someone was looking down from the height of the heavens, from the blue sky and the stars someone saw and watched over everything that was going on in Ukleevo. And however great was the evil, still the night was calm and beautiful, and still in God's world there is and will be truth and justice as calm and beautiful, and everything on earth is only waiting to merge with truth and justice, just as moonlight merges with the night.

And both, huddling close to one another, fell asleep, comforted.

VI

News had come long before that Anisim had been put in prison for counterfeiting and distributing the coins. Months passed, more than half a year passed, the long winter was over, spring had begun, and everyone in the house and the village had grown used to Anisim being in prison. And when anyone passed by the house or the shop at night he would remember that Anisim was in prison; and when they rang at the churchyard for some reason, that, too, reminded them that he was in prison awaiting trial.

A shadow seemed to have fallen on the house. The house looked darker, the roof was rustier, the heavy iron-reinforced door into the shop, which was painted green, was covered with cracks, or, as the deaf son expressed it, 'blisters'; and old Tsybukin seemed to have grown dingy, too. He had given up cutting his hair and beard, and was shaggy. He no longer sprang jauntily into his chaise, nor shouted to beggars: 'God will provide!' His strength was on the wane, and that was evident in everything. People were less afraid of him now, and the constable drew up a formal charge against him in the shop, though he received his regular bribe as before; and three times the old man was called to town to be tried for illicit dealing in spirits, and the case was continually adjourned owing to the non-appearance of witnesses, and old Tsybukin was worn out with worry.

He often went to see his son, hired somebody, handed petitions to somebody else, presented a holy banner to some church. He presented the governor of the prison in which Anisim was confined with a silver glass-holder, 'The soul knows what is right,' and a long spoon.

'There is no one who'll lend a proper hand,' said Varvara. 'Tut, tut . . . You ought to ask one of the gentlefolk, they could write to people in charge . . . At least they might let him out on bail! Why make the lad suffer?'

She, too, was grieved, but had grown stouter and whiter; she lit the icon lamps as before, and saw that everything in the house was clean, and regaled guests with jam and apple paste. The deaf son and

Aksinia looked after the shop. A new project was in progress – a brickyard in Butiokino – and Aksinia went there almost every day in a wagon. She took the reins, and when she met people she knew she stretched out her neck like a snake in the young rye, and smiled naively and enigmatically. Lipa spent her time playing with the baby which she had given birth to before Lent. It was a tiny, thin, pitiful little baby, and it was strange that it should cry and look about and be considered human, and even be called Nikifor. He lay in his rocking cradle, and Lipa would walk back towards the door and say, bowing to him:

'Good morning, Nikifor Tsybukin!'

And she would rush at him and kiss him. Then she would walk back to the door, bow again, and say:

'Good morning, Nikifor Tsybukin!'

And he kicked up his little red legs, and his crying was mixed with laughter like the carpenter Elizarov's.

At last the day of the trial was fixed. Tsybukin had gone there five days before. Then they heard the peasants called as witnesses had been rounded up from the village; the old workman who had received a summons had gone too.

The trial was on a Thursday. But Sunday passed, and Tsybukin was still not back, and there was no news. Towards evening on Tuesday Varvara was sitting at the open window, listening in case her husband came. In the next room Lipa was playing with her baby. She was tossing him up in her arms and saying enthusiastically:

'You will grow up ever so big, ever so big. You will be a peasant, we shall go out to work together! We'll go out to work together!'

'Come, come,' said Varvara, offended. 'Go out to work, what an idea, you silly girl! We'll make a merchant of him.'

Lipa sang softly, but a minute later she forgot, and again:

'You will grow ever so big, ever so big. You'll be a peasant, we'll go out to work together.'

'There she is, at it again!'

Lipa, with Nikifor in her arms, stood still in the doorway and asked:

'Why do I love him so much, Mama? Why do I feel so fond of him?' she went on in a quivering voice, and her eyes glistened with tears. 'Who is he? What is he like? As light as a little feather, as a little crumb; but I love him; I love him like a real person. He can't do anything, he can't talk, and yet I know what he wants from his little eyes.'

Varvara was listening; the sound of the evening train approaching the station reached her. Had her husband come? She did not hear or understand what Lipa was saying, she had no idea how the time passed, but only trembled all over – not from dread, but intense curiosity. She saw a cart full of peasants roll quickly by with a rattle. It was the witnesses coming back from the station. When the cart passed the shop the old workman jumped out and walked into the yard. She could hear him being greeted in the yard and being questioned . . .

'Deprivation of rights and all property,' he said loudly, 'and six years' penal servitude in Siberia.'

She could see Aksinia come out of the shop by the back way; she had just been selling kerosene, and in one hand held a bottle and in the other a funnel, and in her mouth she had some silver coins.

'Where is papa?' she asked, lisping.

'At the station,' answered the labourer. ' "When it gets a little darker," he said, "then I shall come." '

And when it became known all through the household that Anisim had been sentenced to penal servitude, the cook in the kitchen suddenly broke into a wail as though at a funeral, imagining that this was what convention demanded:

'There is no one to care for us now you have gone, Anisim, our bright falcon . . .'

The dogs began barking in alarm. Varvara ran to the window, and rushing about in distress, shouted to the cook with all her might, straining her voice:

'Sto-op, Stepanida, sto-op! Don't torment us, for Christ's sake!'

They forgot to put on the samovar, they couldn't make any sensible decisions. Only Lipa failed to grasp what it was all about and went on playing with her baby.

When the old man arrived from the station they asked him no questions. He greeted them and walked through all the rooms in silence; he had no supper.

'There was no one to help . . .' Varvara began when they were alone. 'I said you should have asked some gentleman, you wouldn't take any notice of me . . . A petition would . . .'

'I did go and see people,' said her husband with a wave of his hand. 'When Anisim was found guilty I went to the gentleman who was defending him. "It's no use now," he said, "it's too late"; and Anisim said the same; it's too late. But all the same as I came out of the court I hired a lawyer, I paid him something in advance. I'll wait a week and then I'll go again. As God wills.'

Again the old man walked through all the rooms, and when he came back to Varvara he said:

'I must be ill. My head's in a sort of . . . fog. My thoughts are clouded.'

He closed the door that Lipa might not hear, and went on softly:

'I'm unhappy about my money. Do you remember the week after Easter before his wedding Anisim brought me some new roubles and half roubles? One packet I put away at the time, but the others I mixed with my own money. When my uncle Dmitri – God rest his soul – was alive, he used constantly to go to Moscow and to the Crimea to buy goods. He had a wife, and this same wife, when he was away buying goods, used to take up with other men. She had half a dozen children. And when uncle was in his cups he would laugh and say: "I never can tell," he used to say, "which are my children and which are other people's." An easy-going temper, to be sure. And now I can't tell which of my roubles are genuine and which are false. And I think they're all false.'

'Nonsense, God bless you.'

'I buy a ticket at the station, I give the man three roubles, and I keep fancyïng they are false. And I am frightened. I must be ill.'

'There's no denying it, we're all in God's hands . . . Oh dear, dear . . .' said Varvara, and she shook her head. 'You ought to think about this, Grigori . . . You never know, anything may happen, you are not a young man. See they don't wrong your grandchild when you are dead and gone. Oy, I am afraid they will do Nikifor wrong! He has as good as no father, his mother's young and foolish . . . You ought to transfer something into his name, poor little boy, at least land, say, Butiokino, Grigori, really! Think it over!' Varvara went on persuading him. 'He's a pretty boy, I'm sorry for him! You go tomorrow and make out a deed; why put it off?'

'I'd forgotten about my grandson,' said Tsybukin. 'I must go and have a look at him. So you say the boy is all right? Well, let him grow, please God.'

He opened the door and, crooking his finger, beckoned to Lipa. She went up to him with the baby in her arms.

'If there is anything you want, Lipa dear, you ask for it,' he said. 'And eat anything you like, we don't grudge it, so long as it does you good . . .' He made the sign of the cross over the baby. 'And look after my grandchild. I have no son, but I still have my grandson.'

Tears rolled down his cheeks; he sobbed and withdrew. Soon afterwards he went to bed and slept soundly after seven sleepless nights.

VII

Old Tsybukin went to town for a short time. Someone told Aksinia that he had gone to the notary to make his will and that he was leaving Butiokino, where she had set up a brickyard, to Nikifor, his grandson. She was informed of this in the morning when old Tsybukin and Varvara were sitting near the steps under the birch tree, drinking their tea. She shut the shop in the front and at the back, gathered together all the keys she had, and flung them at her father-in-law's feet.

'I'm not going on working for you,' she began in a loud voice, and suddenly broke into sobs. 'So, I'm not your daughter-in-law, but a hired worker! Everybody's jeering and saying, "See what a servant the Tsybukins have got themselves!" I didn't come to you for wages! I'm not a beggar, I'm not a slave, I have a father and a mother.'

She did not wipe away her tears, she fixed upon her father-in-law eyes full of tears, vindictive, squinting with wrath; her face and neck were red and tense, and she was shouting at the top of her voice.

'I don't mean to go on being a slave!' she went on. 'I am worn out. Work, sitting in the shop day in and day out, scurrying out at night for vodka – that's my lot, but being given a present of land, that's the lot of that convict's wife and her little devil. She is mistress and lady here, and I am her servant, am I! Give her everything, the convict's wife, and may it choke her; I'm going home! Find yourselves some other fool, you damned Herods!'

Tsybukin had never in his life scolded or punished his children, and had never dreamed that one of his family could speak to him rudely or behave disrespectfully; and now he was very much frightened; he ran into the house and there hid behind the cupboard. And Varvara was so appalled that she could not get up from her seat, and only waved her arms before her as though she was fending off a bee.

'Oh holy Saints! What is this?' she muttered in horror. 'What is she shouting? Oh tut, tut . . . People will hear! Keep it quiet . . . Oh, keep it quiet!'

'He has given Butiokino to the convict's wife,' Aksinia went on bawling. 'Give her everything now, I don't want anything from you! Let me alone! You are all a gang of thieves here! I've seen enough, I've had enough! You've been robbing everyone that comes, on foot or by carriage; you've robbed old and young alike, you brigands! And who has been selling vodka without a licence? And counterfeit money? You've filled boxes with counterfeit coins, and now you don't need me any more!'

A crowd had by now collected at the wide-open gates and was staring into the yard.

'Let the people look,' bawled Aksinia. 'I'll shame you all! You'll burn with shame! You'll grovel at my feet. Hey! Stepan,' she called to the deaf son, 'let's go home this minute! Let's go to my father and mother; I don't want to live with convicts. Get ready!'

Clothes were hanging on lines stretched across the yard; she snatched off her petticoats and blouses, still wet, and flung them into the deaf son's arms. Then in her fury she dashed about the yard where the linen hung, tore down all of it, and what was not hers she threw on the ground and trampled.

'Holy Saints, calm her down,' moaned Varvara. 'What sort of creature is she? Give her Butiokino! Give it her, for Christ's sake!'

'Well! Wha-at a woman!' people were saying at the gate. 'There's a wo-oman for you! She's really let fly – awful!'

Aksinia ran into the kitchen where the clothes were being washed. Lipa was washing on her own, the cook had gone to the river to rinse the clothes. Steam was rising from the trough and cauldron by the stove, and the kitchen was thick and stifling with steam. On the floor was a heap of unwashed clothes, and Nikifor, kicking up his little red legs, had been put down on a bench near them so that if he fell he should not hurt himself. Aksinia came in at the moment her chemise had been taken by Lipa out of the heap and put in the trough, and Lipa had just reached out to a big ladle of boiling water which was standing on the table . . .

'Give it here,' said Aksinia, looking at her with hatred, and snatching the chemise out of the trough; 'it's not your business to touch my linen! You're a convict's wife, and ought to know your place and who you are.'

Lipa gazed at her, dumbfounded, and did not understand, but suddenly she caught the look Aksinia gave the child, and at once she understood and went numb all over.

'You've taken my land, so here you are!' Saying this Aksinia snatched up the ladle of the boiling water and flung it over Nikifor.

After this there was heard a scream such as had never been heard before in Ukleevo, and no one would have believed that a little weak creature like Lipa could scream like that. And it was suddenly silent in the yard. Aksinia walked into the house with her old naive smile . . . The deaf son kept moving about the yard with his arms full of linen, then he began hanging it up again, in silence, without haste. And until the cook came back from the river no one ventured to go into the kitchen and see what was there.

VIII

Nikifor was taken to the district hospital, and towards evening he died there. Lipa did not wait to be fetched, but wrapped the dead baby in its blanket and carried it home.

The hospital, a new one recently built, with big windows, stood high on a hill; it was lit up by the setting sun and looked as though it were on fire inside. There was a little village below. Lipa went down the road, and before reaching the village sat down by a pond. A woman brought a horse down to drink and the horse would not drink.

'What more do you want?' the woman said to it softly 'What do you want?'

A boy in a red shirt, sitting at the water's edge, was washing his father's boots. And not another soul was in sight either in the village or on the hill.

'It's not drinking,' said Lipa, looking at the horse.

Then the woman with the horse and the boy with the boots walked away, and now there was no one to be seen. The sun went to bed wrapped in purple and gold brocade, and long clouds, red and violet, stretched across the sky, guarded its sleep. Somewhere far away a bittern cried, a hollow, melancholy sound like a cow shut in a barn. The cry of that mysterious bird was heard every spring, but no one knew what it looked like or where it lived. At the top of the hill by the hospital, in the bushes by the pond, and in the nearby fields the nightingales trilled. The cuckoo kept reckoning someone's years and losing count and beginning again. In the pond the frogs called angrily to one another, straining themselves to bursting, and one could even make out the words: 'That's what you are! That's what you are!' What a noise there was! It seemed as if all these creatures were singing and shouting so that no one might sleep on that spring night, so that all, even the angry frogs, might appreciate and enjoy every minute: you only live once.

A silver half moon was shining in the sky; there were many stars. Lipa had no idea how long she sat by the pond, but when she got up and walked on everybody was asleep in the little village, and there was not a single light. Home was probably about eight miles away, but she had neither the strength nor the sense to find her way: the moon gleamed, now in front now on the right, and the same cuckoo kept calling in a voice grown husky, with a chuckle as though jeering at her: 'Oy, look out, you'll lose your way!' Lipa walked fast; she lost the kerchief from her head . . . She looked at the sky and wondered where her baby's soul was now: was it following her, or floating aloft among the stars and no longer thinking about his mother? Oh, how lonely it was in the open country at night, in the midst of that singing when you cannot sing yourself; in the midst of the incessant cries of joy when you cannot yourself be joyful, when the moon, equally lonely, indifferent whether it is spring or winter, whether men are alive or dead, looks down . . . When there is grief in the heart it is hard to have nobody. If only her mother, Praskovia, had been with her, or Crutch, or the cook, or some peasant!

'Boo-oo!' cried the bittern. 'Boo-oo!'

And suddenly she heard clearly the sound of human speech:

'Harness the horses, Vavila!'

By the wayside a camp fire was burning ahead of her; the flames had died down, there were only red embers. She could hear the horses munching. In the darkness she could see the outlines of two carts, one with a barrel, the other, a lower one with sacks in it, and the figures of two men; one was leading a horse into the shafts, the other was standing motionless by the fire with his hands behind his back. A dog growled by one cart. The one who was leading the horse stopped and said:

'It sounds like someone coming along the road.'

'Sharik, be quiet!' the other called to the dog.

And from the voice you could tell that the second was an old man. Lipa stopped and said:

'God help you.'

The old man went up to her and answered after a pause:

'Good evening!'

'Your dog won't break loose, Grandfather?'

'No, come along, he won't touch you.'

'I've been to the hospital,' said Lipa after a pause. 'My little son died there. Now I'm taking him home.'

It must have been unpleasant for the old man to hear this, for he moved away and said hurriedly:

'Never mind, my dear. It's God's will. You're making a hash of it, lad,' he added, addressing his companion; 'look alive!'

'I can't find your yoke,' said the young man; 'it's not to be seen.'

'That's just like you, Vavila.'

The old man picked up an ember, blew on it – only his eyes and nose were lit up – then, when they had found the yoke, he went with the light to Lipa and looked at her, and his look expressed compassion and tenderness.

'You're a mother,' he said; 'every mother grieves for her child.'

And he sighed and shook his head as he said it. Vavila threw something on the fire, stamped on it – and at once it was very dark; the vision vanished, and as before there were only the fields, the sky with the stars, and the noise of the birds keeping each other awake. And the landrail called, it seemed, in the very place where the fire had been.

But a minute passed, and again she could see the two carts and the old man and lanky Vavila. The carts creaked as they went out on the road.

'Are you holy men?' Lipa asked the old man.

'No. We are from Firsanovo.'

'You looked at me just now and my heart was softened. And the young man is so quiet. I thought you must be holy men.'

'Are you going far?'

'To Ukleevo.'

'Get in, we'll give you a lift, as far as Kuzmenki, then you go straight on and we turn off to the left.'

Vavila got into the cart with the barrel and the old man and Lipa got into the other. They moved at a walking pace, Vavila ahead.

'My baby was in torment all day,' said Lipa. 'He looked at me with his little eyes and said nothing; he wanted to speak and could not. Holy Father, Queen of Heaven! I kept falling down on the floor with grief. I stood up and fell down by the bedside. And tell me, grandfather, why a little thing should be tormented before his death? When a grown-up, a man or woman, is in torment their sins are forgiven, but why a little thing, when he has no sins? Why?'

'Who can tell?' answered the old man. They drove on for half an hour in silence. 'We can't know everything, how and why,' said the old man. 'It is ordained for the bird to have not four wings but two because it is able to fly with two; and so it is ordained for man not to know everything but only a half or a quarter. As much as he needs to know so as to live, so much he knows.'

'It's easier for me to go on foot, Grandfather. Now my heart is all of a tremble.'

'Never mind, sit still.'

The old man yawned and made the sign of the cross over his mouth.

'Never mind,' he repeated. 'Yours is not the worst of sorrows. Life is long, there will be good and bad to come, there will be everything. Great is Mother Russia,' he said, and looked round on each side of him. 'I have been all over Russia, and I have seen everything in her, and you may believe my words, my dear. There will be good and there will be bad. I've been regularly to Siberia, and I've been to the Amur River and the Altai Mountains and I settled in Siberia; I worked the land there, then I was homesick for Mother Russia and I came back to my native village. We came back to Russia on foot; and I remember we were on a ferry, and I was thin as anything, all in rags, barefoot, freezing with cold, and sucking a crust, and a gentleman who was on the ferry – God rest his soul, if he is dead – looked at me pityingly, and the tears came into his eyes. "Ah," he said, "your bread is black, your days are black . . ." And when I got home, as the saying is, there was neither stick nor stall; I had a wife, but I left her behind in Siberia, she was buried there. So I am living as a day labourer. And yet I tell you: since then I have had good as well as bad. Well, I don't want to die, my dear, I'd like to live another twenty years; so there has been more of the good. And great is our Mother Russia!' and again he looked at each side and turned round.

'Grandfather,' Lipa asked, 'when anyone dies, how many days does his soul walk the earth?'

'Who can tell! Ask Vavila here, he has been to school. Now they teach them everything. Vavila!' the old man called to him.

'Eh!'

'Vavila, when anyone dies, how long does his soul walk the earth?'

Vavila stopped the horse and only then answered:

'Nine days. My uncle Kirilla died and his soul lived in our hut thirteen days after.'

'How do you know?'

'For thirteen days there was a knocking in the stove.'

'Well, that's all right. Go on,' said the old man, and it could be seen that he did not believe a word of it.

Near Kuzmenki the cart turned on to the highroad while Lipa went straight on. It was by now getting light. As she went down into the ravine the Ukleevo huts and the church were hidden in fog. It was cold, and it seemed to her that the same cuckoo was calling still.

When Lipa reached home the cattle had not yet been turned out; everyone was asleep. She sat down on the steps and waited. The old man was the first to come out; he understood all that had happened at a glance, and for a long time he could not articulate a word, but only smacked his lips.

'Eh, Lipa,' he said, 'you didn't take care of my grandchild . . .'

Varvara was woken. She clasped her hands and broke into sobs, and immediately began laying out the baby.

'And he was a pretty child . . .' she said. 'Oh tut, tut . . . You only had the one child, and you didn't take care of him, you silly girl . . .'

There was a requiem service in the morning and the evening. The funeral took place the next day, and after it the guests and the priests ate a great deal, and with such greed that you might have thought that they hadn't tasted food for a long time. Lipa waited at table, and the priest, lifting a salted milk-cap mushroom impaled on his fork, said to her:

'Don't grieve for the babe. For of such is the Kingdom of Heaven.'

And only when they had all gone home did Lipa realise fully that there was no Nikifor and never would be. She realised it and broke into sobs. And she did not know what room to use for sobbing, for she felt that now that her child was dead there was no place for her in the house, that she had no reason to be here, that she was in the way; and the others felt it, too.

'Now what are you bellowing for?' Aksinia shouted, suddenly appearing in the doorway; in honour of the funeral she was dressed all in new clothes and had powdered her face. 'Shut up!'

Lipa tried to stop but could not, and sobbed louder than ever.

'Do you hear?' shouted Aksinia, and she stamped her foot in violent anger. 'Who am I speaking to? Get out of the place and don't set foot here again, you convict's wife. Out.'

'There, there, there,' the old man said, flustered. 'Aksinia, calm down, my girl . . . She is crying, it is only natural . . . Her child is dead . . .'

' "It's only natural," ' Aksinia mimicked him. 'Let her stay the night here, and don't let me see a trace of her here tomorrow! "It's only natural!" . . .' she mimicked him again, and, laughing, she went into the shop.

Early next morning Lipa left to stay with her mother at Torguevo.

IX

At the present time the roof and the front door of the shop have been repainted and are as bright as new, there are cheerful geraniums in the windows as of old, and what happened in Tsybukin's house and yard three years ago is almost forgotten.

Grigori Tsybukin is looked upon as the master as he was in old days, but in reality everything has passed into Aksinia's hands; she buys and sells, and nothing can be done without her consent. The brickyard is working well; and as bricks are wanted for the railway the price has gone up to twenty-four roubles a thousand; peasant women and girls cart the bricks to the station and load them up in the trucks and earn a quarter rouble a day for the work.

Aksinia has gone into partnership with the Khrymin Juniors, and their factory is now called Khrymin Juniors and Co. They have opened a tavern near the station, and now the expensive concertina is played not at the factory but at the tavern, and the postmaster often goes there, and he, too, is engaged in some sort of traffic, and the stationmaster, too. Khrymin Juniors have presented the deaf son, Stepan, with a gold watch, and he constantly takes it out of his pocket and puts it to his ear.

People say of Aksinia that she has acquired a lot of power; and it is true that when she drives in the morning to her brickyard, handsome and happy, with a naive smile on her face, and afterwards when she gives orders there, you sense great power in her. Everyone in the house, the village and the brickyard fears her. When she goes to the post the postmaster jumps up and says to her:

'I humbly beg you to be seated, Mrs Tsybukina.'

A certain landowner, middle-aged but foppish, in a fine close-fitting coat and patent leather high boots, sold her a horse, and was so carried away talking to her that he knocked down his price to meet hers. He held her hand a long time and, looking into her merry, sly, naive eyes, said:

'For a woman like you, Mrs Tsybukina, I should be ready to do anything you please. Only say, when can we meet so that no one disturbs us?'

'Why, whenever you please.'

And since then the elderly fop drives up to the shop almost every other day to drink beer. And the beer is horrid, bitter as wormwood. The landowner shakes his head with disgust, but he drinks it.

Old Tsybukin has nothing to do with the business now at all. He does not keep any money because he cannot tell good from bad, but he is silent and tells nobody about this weakness. He has become rather forgetful, and if he isn't fed he does not ask for food; they have grown used to dining without him, and Varvara often says:

'He went to bed again yesterday without any supper.'

And she says it casually because she is used to it. For some reason, summer and winter alike, he goes about in a fur coat, and only in very hot weather does he not go out but sit at home. Usually, after putting on his fur coat, wrapping it round him and turning up his collar, he walks about the village, along the road to the station, or sits from morning till night on the seat near the church gates. He sits there without stirring. Passers-by bow to him, but he does not respond, for he dislikes the peasants as much as ever. If asked a question, he answers quite rationally and politely, but briefly.

There is a rumour going about in the village that his daughter-in-law has turned him out of the house and gives him nothing to eat, and that he is fed by charity; some are glad, others are sorry for him.

Varvara has grown even fatter and whiter, and as before she does good works, and Aksinia does not interfere with her. There is so much jam now that they have not time to eat it before the fresh fruit comes in; it crystallises, and Varvara almost sheds tears, not knowing what to do with it.

They have begun to forget about Anisim. A letter has come from him written in verse on a big sheet of paper as though it were a petition, all in the same splendid handwriting. Evidently his friend Samorodov was serving the same sentence. Under the verses in an ugly, scarcely legible handwriting there was a single line: 'I am ill here all the time; I am wretched, for Christ's sake help me!'

Towards evening – it was a fine autumn day – old Tsybukin was sitting near the church gates, with the collar of his fur coat turned up and nothing of him could be seen but his nose and the peak of his cap. At the other end of the long seat was sitting Elizarov the contractor, and beside him Yakov the school watchman, a toothless old man of about seventy. Crutch and the watchman were talking.

'Children ought to give food and drink to the old . . . "Honour thy father and mother . . ."' Yakov was saying with irritation, 'while she, this daughter-in-law, has turned her father-in-law out of his own house; the old man has neither food nor drink, where is he to go? He hasn't had a morsel for these three days.'

'Three days!' said Crutch, amazed.

'Here he sits and says not a word. He has grown feeble. And why stay quiet about it? He should take her to court, they wouldn't let her off in court.'

'Let who off in court?' asked Crutch, not hearing.

'What?'

'The woman's all right, she tries hard. In their line of business they can't get on without that . . . without sin, I mean . . .'

'From his own house,' Yakov went on with irritation. 'Save up and buy your own house, then people turn you out of it! She is a nice one, to be sure! A pla-ague!'

Tsybukin listened and did not stir.

'Whether it's your own house or others' it makes no difference so long as it is warm and the women don't quarrel and nag . . .' said Crutch, and he laughed. 'When I was young I was very fond of my Nastasia. She was a quiet woman. And she used to be always at it: "Buy a house, Makarych! Buy a house, Makarych! Buy a house, Makarych!" She was dying and yet she kept on saying, "Buy yourself a light chaise, Makarych, so that you don't have to walk." And I bought her nothing but gingerbread.'

'Her husband's deaf and stupid,' Yakov went on, not hearing Crutch; 'a regular fool, just like a goose. Do you think he can understand anything? Hit a goose on the head with a stick and even then it can't understand.'

Crutch got up to go home to the factory. Yakov also got up, and both of them went off together, still talking. When they had gone fifty paces old Tsybukin got up too, and walked after them, stepping uncertainly as though on slippery ice.

The village was now plunged in the evening dusk and the sun only gleamed on the upper part of the road which ran wriggling like a snake up the slope. Old women were coming back from the woods and children with them; they were bringing baskets of forest mushrooms, milk-caps and agarics. Peasant women and girls came in a crowd from the station where they had been loading the trucks with bricks, and their noses and their cheeks under their eyes were covered with red brick dust. They were singing. Ahead of them all was Lipa singing in a high voice, with her eyes turned upwards to the sky, breaking into trills as though triumphant and ecstatic that at last the day was over and she could rest. In the crowd was her mother Praskovia, who was walking with a bundle in her arms and breathless as usual.

'Good evening, Makarych!' cried Lipa, seeing Crutch. 'Good evening, sweet man!'

'Good evening, Lipa dear,' cried Crutch, delighted. 'Dear girls and women, love a rich carpenter! Ho-ho! My little children, my little children.' (Crutch gave a gulp.) 'My dear little hatchets!'

Crutch and Yakov went on further and could still be heard talking. Then the next person the crowd met was old Tsybukin, and there was a sudden hush. Lipa and Praskovia had dropped a little behind, and when the old man was passing them Lipa bowed down low and said:

'Good evening, Mr Tsybukin.'

Her mother, too, bowed down. The old man stopped and, saying nothing, looked at the two in silence; his lips were quivering and his eyes were full of tears. Lipa took out of her mother's bundle a piece of pasty with buckwheat and gave it him. He took it and began eating.

The sun had by now set; its glow died away on the road above. It grew dark and cool. Lipa and Praskovia walked on and for some time they kept crossing themselves.

1900

The Bishop

I

The evening service was being celebrated on the eve of Palm Sunday in the Old Petrovsky Convent. When they began distributing the willow branches* it was close upon ten o'clock, the candles were burning dimly, the wicks wanted snuffing; it was all in a sort of mist. In the twilight of the church the crowd heaved like a sea, and to Bishop Piotr, who had been unwell for the last three days, it seemed that all the faces – old and young, men's and women's – were alike, that everyone who came up for a willow branch had the same expression in their eyes. In the mist he could not see the doors; the crowd kept moving and looked as if it was endless. The women's choir was singing, a nun was reading the prayers for the day.

How stifling, how hot it was! How long the service went on! Bishop Piotr was tired. His breathing was laboured, rapid, and dry, his shoulders ached with weariness, his legs were trembling. And it disturbed him unpleasantly when a crazy 'fool in God' uttered occasional shrieks in the gallery. And then all of a sudden, as though in a dream or delirium, it seemed to the bishop that his mother Maria Timofeyevna, whom he had not seen for nine years, or some old woman just like his mother, had come up to him out of the crowd, and, after taking a willow branch from him, walked away looking at him all the while good-humouredly with a kind, joyful smile until she was lost in the crowd. And for some reason tears flowed down his face. There was peace in his heart, everything was well, yet he kept gazing fixedly towards the left choir, where the prayers were being read, where in the dusk of evening you could not recognise anyone, and – he wept. Tears glistened on his face and on his beard. Now someone close at hand was weeping, then someone else further away, then others and still others, and little by little the church was filled with soft weeping. And a little later, within five minutes, the nuns' choir was singing; the weeping had stopped and everything was as before.

Soon the service was over. When the bishop got into his carriage to drive home, the cheerful, melodious chime of the heavy, costly bells was filling the whole garden in the moonlight. The white walls, the white crosses on the tombs, the white birches and black shadows, and the far-away moon, which had now risen over the convent, seemed now living their own life, apart and incomprehensible, yet very near to man. It was the beginning of April, and after the warm spring day it had turned cool; there was a faint touch of frost, and the breath of spring could be felt in the soft, chilly air. The road from the convent to the town was sandy, the horses had to go at a walking pace, and on both sides of the carriage in the brilliant, peaceful moonlight there were people trudging along home from church through the sand. And all was silent, sunk in thought; everything around seemed kindly, youthful, akin, everything – trees and sky and even the moon, and you wanted to think that it would always be like this.

At last the carriage drove into the town and rumbled along the main street. The shops were already shut, but at Erakin's, the millionaire shopkeeper's, they were trying the new electric lights, which flickered brightly, and a crowd of people were gathered round. Then came wide, dark, deserted streets, one after another; then the highroad, the open country, the fragrance of pines. And suddenly there rose up before the bishop's eyes a white turreted wall, and behind it a tall belfry in the full moonlight, and beside it five shining, golden cupolas: this was the Pankratievsky Monastery, in which Bishop Piotr lived. And here, too, high above the monastery, was the silent, dreamy moon. The carriage drove in at the gate, crunching over the sand; here and there in the moonlight there were glimpses of dark monastic figures, and there was the sound of footsteps on the flag stones . . .

'Your Holiness, your mama arrived while you were away,' the lay brother informed the bishop as he went into his cell.

'Mama? When did she come?'

'Before the evening service. She asked first where you were and then she went to the convent.'

'Then it was her I saw in the church, just now! Oh, Lord!'

And the bishop laughed with joy.

'She told me to inform your Holiness,' the lay brother went on, 'that she would come tomorrow. She had a little girl with her – her grandchild, I suppose. They are staying at Ovsiannikov's inn.'

'What time is it now?'

'Just after eleven.'

'Oh, that's vexing!'

The bishop sat for a little while in the parlour, hesitating, and somehow incredulous that it was so late. His arms and legs were racked with pain, the back of his neck ached. He was hot and uncomfortable. After resting a little he went into his bedroom, and there, too, he sat a little, still thinking of his mother; he could hear the lay brother going away, and Father Sisoi, a monastery priest, coughing the other side of the wall. The monastery clock struck a quarter.

The bishop changed his clothes and began reading the prayers before sleep. He read attentively those old, long familiar prayers, and at the same time thought about his mother. She had nine children and about forty grandchildren. At one time she had lived with her husband, the deacon, in a poor village; she had lived there a very long time from the age of seventeen to sixty. The bishop remembered her from early childhood, almost from the age of three, and – how he had loved her! Sweet, precious childhood, always fondly remembered! Why did it, that long past irrevocable time, why did it seem brighter, richer, and more festive that it had really been? When in his childhood or youth he had been ill, how tender and sympathetic his mother had been! And now prayers mingled with memories, which burned like a flame, brighter and brighter, and prayers did not stop him thinking of his mother.

After praying, he undressed and lay down, and at once, as soon as it was dark, he imagined his dead father, his mother, his native village Lesopolie . . . the creak of wheels, the bleat of sheep, the church bells on bright summer mornings, the gypsies under the window – oh, how sweet to think of it! He remembered the priest of Lesopolie, Father Simeon – mild, gentle, kindly; he was a lean little man, while his son, a divinity student, was a huge fellow and talked in a roaring bass voice. The priest's son had been peeved with the cook and swore at her: 'Ah, you female ass of Jehud!' and Father Simeon overhearing it, said not a word, and was only ashamed because he could not remember where this ass was mentioned in Scripture. After him the priest at Lesopolie had been Father Demian, who used to drink heavily, and at times drank until he had delirium tremens, and was therefore nicknamed Demian the Snakeseer. The schoolmaster at Lesopolie was Matvei Nikolaich, who had been a divinity student, a kind and intelligent man, but he, too, was a drunkard; he never beat the schoolchildren, but for some reason he always had hanging on his wall a bunch of birch twigs, and below it an utterly meaningless inscription in Latin: 'Betula kinderbalsamica secuta.' He had a shaggy black dog whom he called Syntax.

And his holiness laughed. Five miles from Lesopolie was the village Obnino with a miraculous icon. In the summer the icon was carried in procession about the neighbouring villages and bells rang the whole day long, first in one village and then in another, and it seemed to the bishop then that joy was quivering in the air, and he (in those days he was called Pavlusha) used to follow the icon, bare-headed and barefoot, with naive faith, with a naive smile, infinitely happy. In Obnino, he remembered now, there were always a lot of people, and the priest there, Father Aleksei, to save time during the offertory, used to make his deaf nephew Ilarion read the notes attached to the communion bread asking for prayers for health or for the souls of the departed. Ilarion read them, now and then getting a five or ten kopeck coin for the service, and only when he was grey and bald, when life was nearly over, he suddenly saw written on one of the pieces of paper: 'What a fool you are, Ilarion.' Up to fifteen at least Pavlusha was backward and a poor learner, so much so that they thought of taking him away from the clerical school and making him a shop-boy; one day, going to the post at Obnino for letters, he had stared a long time at the post office clerks and asked: 'Can I ask how you get your salary, every month or every day?'

The bishop crossed himself and turned over on the other side, to stop thinking and go to sleep.

'My mother has come . . .' he remembered and laughed.

The moon peeped in at the window, the floor was lit up, and crossed by shadows. A cricket was chirping. Through the wall Father Sisoi was snoring in the next room, and his aged snore had a sound that suggested loneliness, forlornness, even vagrancy. Sisoi had once been housekeeper to the bishop of the diocese, and was called now 'the former Father Housekeeper'; he was seventy years old, he lived in a monastery twelve miles from the town and stayed sometimes in the town, too. He had come to the Pankratievsky Monastery three days before, and the bishop had kept him that he might talk to him at his leisure about business, about the way things were done here . . .

At half past one they began ringing for matins. Father Sisoi could be heard coughing, muttering something in a discontented voice, then he got up and walked barefoot about the rooms.

'Father Sisoi,' the bishop called.

Sisoi went back to his room and a little later made his appearance in his boots, with a candle; he had on his cassock over his underclothes and on his head was an old faded skullcap.

'I can't sleep,' said the bishop, sitting up. 'I must be ill. And what it is I don't know. Fever!'

'You must have caught cold, my Lord. You ought to have a rub down with candle tallow.'

Sisoi stood a little and yawned. 'O Lord, forgive my sins.'

'They had the electric lights on at Erakin's today,' he said; 'I don't like it!'

Father Sisoi was old, scraggy, bent, always dissatisfied with something, and his eyes were angry-looking and prominent as a crab's.

'I don't like it,' he said, as he left. 'I don't like it, I want nothing to do with it!'

II

Next day, Palm Sunday, the bishop took the service in the town cathedral, then he visited the diocesan bishop, visited a very sick old lady, a general's widow, and finally drove home. After one o'clock he had welcome visitors dining with him – his mother and his niece Katia, a child of eight. All dinner-time the spring sunshine was streaming in at the windows, throwing bright light on the white table-cloth and on Katia's red hair. Through the double windows they could hear the noise of the rooks and the singing of the starlings in the garden.

'It's nine years since we last met,' said the old lady. 'And when I looked at you in the monastery yesterday, good Lord! you'd not changed a bit, except maybe you're thinner and your beard is a little longer. Holy Mother, Queen of Heaven! Yesterday at the evening service no one could help crying. I, too, as I looked at you, suddenly began crying, though I couldn't say why. His Holy Will!'

And in spite of the affectionate tone in which she said this, he could see she was inhibited as though she were uncertain whether to address him formally or familiarly, to laugh or not, and that she felt herself more a deacon's widow than his mother. And Katia gazed without blinking at her reverend uncle, as though trying to discover what sort of a person he was. Her hair sprang up from under the comb and the velvet ribbon and stood out like a halo; she had a snub nose and sly eyes. The child had broken a glass before sitting down to dinner, and now her grandmother, as she talked, moved away from Katia first a wine glass and then a tumbler. The bishop listened to his mother and remembered how many, many years ago she used to take him and his brothers and sisters to relations whom she considered rich; in those days she did all she could for her children, now it was all for her grandchildren, and she had brought Katia . . .

'Your sister, Varenka, has four children,' she told him; 'Katia, here, is the eldest. And your brother-in-law Father Ivan fell sick, God knows of what, and died three days before the Assumption; and my poor Varenka is left a beggar.'

'And how is Nikanor getting on?' the bishop asked about his eldest brother.

'He is all right, thank God. Though he has nothing much, yet he can live. Only there is one thing: his son, my grandson Nikolasha, refused to go into the Church; he has gone to the university to be a doctor. He thinks it is better; but who knows! His Holy Will!'

'Nikolasha cuts up dead people,' said Katia, spilling water over her knees.

'Sit still, child,' her grandmother observed calmly, and took the glass out of her hand. 'Say a prayer and eat.'

'What a long time since we last met!' said the bishop, and he tenderly stroked his mother's hand and shoulder; 'and I missed you abroad, mother, I missed you dreadfully.'

'Thank you.'

'I'd sit in the evenings at the open window, lonely and alone; often there was music playing, and all at once I'd be overcome with homesickness and feel as though I would give anything only to be at home and see you . . .'

His mother smiled, beamed, but at once she made a grave face and said:

'Thank you.'

His mood suddenly changed. He looked at his mother and could not understand how she had got that deferential timid expression in her face and voice: what was it for? And he could not recognise her. He felt sad and vexed. And then his head ached just as it had the day before; his legs were racked by pain, and the fish seemed to him stale and tasteless; he felt thirsty all the time . . .

After dinner two rich ladies, landowners, arrived and sat for an hour and a half in silence with rigid countenances; the archimandrite, a silent, rather deaf man, came to see him about business. Then they began ringing for vespers; the sun was setting behind the forest and the day was over. When he returned from church, he hurriedly said his prayers, got into bed, and wrapped himself up as warmly as possible.

It was disagreeable to remember the fish he had eaten at dinner. The moonlight bothered him, and then he heard talking. In an adjoining room, probably in the parlour, Father Sisoi was talking politics:

'The Japanese have a war now. They are fighting. The Japanese, my good woman, are the same as the Montenegrins; they are the same race. They were under the Turkish yoke together.'

And then he heard the voice of Maria Timofeyevna:

'So, having said our prayers and drunk tea, we went, you know, to Father Yegor at Novokhatnoe, so . . .'

It was all 'having had tea' or 'having drunk tea', and it sounded as if the only thing she had done in her life was to drink tea. The bishop slowly, languidly, recalled the seminary, the academy. For about three years he had been Greek teacher in the seminary: by that time he could not read without spectacles, then he had become a monk, he was made a school inspector. Then he had defended his thesis for his degree. When he was thirty-two he had been made rector of the seminary, and consecrated archimandrite: and then his life had been so easy, so pleasant; it seemed so long, so long, no end was in sight. Then he began to be ill, grew very thin and almost went blind, and on medical advice had to give up everything and go abroad.

'And what then?' asked Sisoi in the next room.

'Then we drank tea . . .' answered Maria Timofeyevna.

'Good gracious, you've got a green beard,' said Katia suddenly in surprise, and she laughed.

The bishop remembered that Father Sisoi, who had gone grey, really had a greenish tinge to his beard, and he laughed.

'My God, what a pest this girl is!' said Sisoi, aloud, getting angry. 'Spoilt child! Sit quiet!'

The bishop remembered the utterly new white church in which he had conducted the services while living abroad, he remembered the roar of the warm sea. In his flat he had five lofty light rooms; in his study he had a new desk, a library. He read a great deal and often wrote. And he remembered pining for his native land, a blind beggar woman playing the guitar under his window every day, singing of love, and he recalled, for some reason, always thinking, as he listened, of the past. But eight years had passed and he had been called back to Russia, and now he was a suffragan bishop, and all the past had retreated far away into the mist as though it were a dream . . .

Father Sisoi came into the bedroom with a candle.

'Oho!' he said, wondering, 'are you asleep already, your Holiness?'

'What is it?'

'Why, it's still early, ten o'clock or less. I bought a candle today; I wanted to rub you with tallow.'

'I have a fever . . .' said the bishop, and he sat up. 'I really ought to have something. My head feels bad . . .'

Sisoi took off the bishop's shirt and began rubbing his chest and back with tallow.

'That's the way . . . that's the way . . .' he said. 'Lord Jesus Christ . . . that's the way. I walked to town today; I was at what's-his-name's – the archpriest Sidonsky's . . . I had tea with him . . . I don't like him! Lord Jesus Christ . . . That's the way . . . I don't like him.'

III

The bishop of the diocese, a very fat old man, had rheumatism or gout, and had been in bed for over a month. Bishop Piotr went to see him almost every day, and on his behalf dealt with all his petitioners. And now that he himself was unwell he was struck by the emptiness, the triviality of everything for which the petitioners asked or wept; he was angered by their backwardness, their shyness; and the quantity of all this useless, petty business oppressed him, and it seemed to him that now he understood the diocesan bishop, who had once in his young days written on 'Doctrines of the Freedom of the Will', and now seemed to have taken refuge in trivialities, to have forgotten everything, and not to think of God. The bishop must have lost touch with Russian life while he was abroad; he did not find it easy; the peasants seemed to him coarse, the women petitioners boring and stupid, the seminarists and their teachers uncultivated and at times savage. And incoming and outgoing documents came in tens of thousands; and what documents they were! The higher clergy in the whole diocese gave the priests, young and old, and even their wives and children, marks for behaviour – excellent, good, and sometimes even middling; and about this he had to talk and to read and write serious reports. And there was positively not a single free minute; his soul was aquiver all day long, and Bishop Piotr calmed down only when he was in church.

He could not get used, either, to the awe which, against his wishes, he inspired in people in spite of his quiet, modest disposition. All the people in the province seemed to him little, scared, and guilty when he looked at them. Everyone was timid in his presence, even elderly archpriests; everyone 'threw themselves down' at his feet, and not long previously an old lady, a village priest's wife who had come to consult him, was so overawed that she could not utter a single word, and left empty-handed. And he, who could never in his sermons bring himself to speak ill of people, never reproached anyone, because he was so sorry for them, was moved to fury with people who came to consult him, lost his temper and flung their petitions on the floor. The whole time he had been here, not one person had spoken to him genuinely, simply, as to a human being; even his old mother was no longer what she used to be, not in the least! And why, he wondered, did she chatter away to Sisoi and laugh so much, while with him, her son, she was grave, nearly always silent and inhibited, which did not suit her at all? The only person who behaved freely with him and said what he meant was old Sisoi, who had spent his whole life in the presence of bishops and had outlived eleven of them. That was why the bishop was at ease with him, although, of course, he was a tedious and cantankerous man.

After the service on Tuesday, the reverend Piotr was in the diocesan bishop's house receiving petitioners there; he got excited and angry, and then drove home. He was as unwell as before; he longed for his bed, but he had hardly reached home when he was informed that a young merchant, Erakin, a donor, had come to see him about a very important matter. He had to be seen. Erakin stayed about an hour, talked very loud, almost shouted, and it was difficult to understand what he said.

'God grant it may,' he said as he left. 'Most essential! According to circumstances, my Lord! I trust it may!'

After him came the mother superior from a distant convent. And when she had gone they began ringing for vespers. He had to go to church.

In the evening the monks sang harmoniously, with inspiration. A young priest with a black beard conducted the service; and the bishop, hearing of the Bridegroom who comes at midnight and of the Heavenly Mansion adorned for the festival, felt no repentance for his sins, no tribulation, but peace at heart and tranquillity. And he was carried back in thought to the distant past, to his childhood and youth, when, too, they used to sing of the Bridegroom and of the Heavenly Mansion; and now that past rose up before him – living, fair, and joyful as in all likelihood it never had been. And perhaps in the other world, in the life to come, we shall think of the distant past, of our life here, with the same feeling. Who knows? The bishop was sitting near the altar. It was dark; tears flowed down his face. He thought that here he had attained everything a man in his position could attain; he had faith and yet not everything was clear, something was lacking still, he did not want to die; and he still felt that he was missing something most important, something of which he had dimly dreamed in the past; and he was troubled by the same hope in the future as he had felt in childhood, at the academy and abroad.

'How well they sing today!' he thought, listening to the singing. 'How well!'

IV

On Thursday he celebrated mass in the cathedral; it was the Washing of Feet. When the service was over and the people were going home, it was sunny, warm, the water gurgled in the ditches, and the unceasing trilling of the larks, tender, invoking peace, rose from the fields outside the town. The trees had now awoken and were smiling a welcome, while above them the infinite, unfathomable blue sky stretched into the distance, God knows whither.

On reaching home Bishop Piotr drank tea, then changed his clothes, lay down on his bed, and told the lay brother to close the shutters on the windows. The bedroom was darkened. But what weariness, what pain in his legs and his back, a chill heavy pain, what a noise in his ears! He had not slept for a long time – for a very long time, as it seemed to him now, and some trifling detail which haunted his brain as soon as his eyes were closed prevented him from sleeping. As on the day before, sounds reached him from the adjoining rooms through the walls, voices, the jingle of glasses and teaspoons ... Maria Timofeyevna was merrily telling Father Sisoi a story with quaint turns of speech, while the latter answered in a grumpy, ill-humoured voice: 'Damn them! Not likely! What next!' And the bishop again felt vexed and then hurt that with other people his old mother behaved in a simple, ordinary way, while with him, her son, she was shy, spoke little, and did not say what she meant, and even, as he fancied, had during all those three days kept trying in his presence to find an excuse to stand, because she was too inhibited to sit. And his father? He, too, probably, if he had been living, would not have been able to utter a word in the bishop's presence ...

Something fell down on the floor in the adjoining room and was broken; Katia must have dropped a cup or a saucer, for Father Sisoi suddenly spat and said angrily:

'That child is a real pest! Lord forgive my sins! She'll break the lot!'

Then all was quiet, the only sounds came from outside. And when the bishop opened his eyes he saw Katia in his room, standing motionless, staring at him. Her red hair, as usual, stood up from under the comb like a halo.

'Is that you, Katia?' he asked. 'Who is it downstairs who keeps opening and shutting a door?'

'I can't hear it,' answered Katia; and she listened.

'There, someone has just passed by.'

'But that was a noise in your stomach, Uncle.'

He laughed and stroked her on the head.

'So you say Cousin Nikolasha cuts up dead people?' he asked after a pause.

'Yes, he's studying.'

'And is he kind?'

'Oh yes, he's kind. But he drinks vodka awfully.'

'And what did your father die of?'

'Papa was weak and very, very thin, and all at once his throat was bad. I was ill then, too, and brother Fedia; we all had bad throats. Papa died, Uncle, and we got well.'

Her chin quivered, and tears welled up in her eyes and trickled down her cheeks.

'Your Reverence,' she said in a shrill voice, now weeping bitterly, 'Uncle, mother and all of us are left very wretched . . . Give us a little money . . . do be kind . . . Uncle darling . . .'

He, too, shed tears, and for a long time was too moved to speak. Then he stroked her on the head, touched her shoulder and said:

'Very good, very good, little girl. When the holy Easter comes, we will talk it over . . . I'll help you . . . I'll help you . . .'

His mother came in quietly, timidly, and prayed before the icons. Noticing that he was not sleeping, she asked:

'Won't you have a drop of soup?'

'No, thank you,' he answered, 'I'm not hungry.'

'You seem unwell . . . now I look at you. Of course, how could you help it? The whole day on your feet, the whole day – and, my God, it makes my heart ache even to look at you! Well, Easter is not far off; you will rest then, please God, then we will have a talk, but now I'm not going to bother you with my chatter. Come along, Katia; let his Reverence sleep a little.'

And he remembered how once very long ago, when he was a boy, she had spoken exactly like that, in the same jestingly respectful tone, to a rural dean . . . Only from her extraordinarily kind eyes and the timid, anxious glance she stole at him as she left the room could one have guessed that she was his mother. He shut his eyes and seemed to sleep, but twice heard the clock strike and Father Sisoi coughing the other side of the wall. And once more his mother came in and looked timidly at him for a minute. Someone drove up to the steps, as he could hear, in a coach or in a chaise. Suddenly a knock, the door slammed, the lay brother came into the bedroom.

'My Lord!' he called.

'Well?'

'The horses are here; it's time for the Lord's Passion.'*

'What time is it?'

'A quarter past seven.'

He dressed and drove to the cathedral. During all the 'Twelve Gospels' he had to stand in the middle of the church without moving, and the first gospel, the longest and the most beautiful, he read himself. A mood of confidence and courage came over him. That first gospel, 'Now is the Son of Man glorified', he knew by heart; and as he read he raised his eyes from time to time, and saw on both sides a perfect sea of lights and heard the splutter of candles, but, as in past years, he could not see the people, and it seemed as though these were all the same people as had been round him on those days, in his

childhood and his youth; that they would always be the same every
year and till such time as God only knew.

His father had been a deacon, his grandfather a priest, his great-
grandfather a deacon, and his whole family, perhaps ever since
Russia had been converted to Christianity, had belonged to the
priesthood; and his love for Church services, for the priesthood, for
the peal of the bells, was deep in him, ineradicable, innate. In church,
particularly when he took part in the service, he felt vigorous, of good
cheer, happy. So it was now. Only when the eighth gospel had been
read, he felt that his voice had grown weak, even his cough was
inaudible. His head had begun to ache intensely, and he was troubled
by a fear that he might fall down. And indeed his legs had become
quite numb, so that gradually he ceased to feel them and could not
understand how or on what he was standing, and why he did not
fall . . .

It was a quarter to twelve when the service was over. When he
reached home, the bishop undressed and went to bed at once without
even saying his prayers. He could not speak and felt that he could not
have stood up. When he had covered his head with the blanket he felt
a sudden longing to be abroad, an unendurable longing! He felt that
he would give his life not to see those pitiful cheap shutters, those low
ceilings, not to smell that heavy monastery smell. If only there were
one person to whom he could talk, pour out his heart!

For a long while he heard footsteps in the next room and could not
recall whose they were. At last the door opened, and Sisoi came in
with a candle and a tea cup in his hands.

'You are in bed already, my reverend Lord?' he asked. 'Here I have
come to rub you with spirit and vinegar. A thorough rubbing does a
great deal of good. Lord Jesus Christ! . . . That's the way . . . that's
the way . . . I've just been to our monastery . . . I don't like it. I'm
leaving here tomorrow, my Lord; I don't want to stay longer. Lord
Jesus Christ . . . That's the way . . .'

Sisoi could never stay long in the same place, and he felt he had been a
whole year in the Pankratievsky Monastery. Above all, listening to him,
it was hard to make out where his home was, whether he cared for
anyone or anything, whether he believed in God . . . He did not know
himself why he was a monk, and, indeed, he did not think about it, and
the time when he had taken his vows had long been erased from his
memory; it seemed as though he had been born a monk.

'I'm going away tomorrow. Let them all look after themselves.'

'I should like to talk to you . . . I just can't find the time,' said the
bishop softly with an effort. 'I don't know anything or anybody
here . . .'

'I'll stay till Sunday if you like; so be it, but I don't want to stay longer. To hell with them!'

'What sort of a bishop am I,' said the reverend Piotr softly. 'I ought to have been a village priest, a sexton . . . or an ordinary monk . . . All this crushes me . . . crushes me.'

'What? Lord Jesus Christ . . . That's the way . . . Come, sleep well, your Reverence! . . . What's the good? It's no use. Good night!'

The bishop did not sleep all night. And about eight in the morning he began to haemorrhage from the bowels. The lay brother was alarmed, and ran first to the archimandrite, then for the monastery doctor, Ivan Andreich, who lived in town. The doctor, a stout old man with a long grey beard, made a prolonged examination of the bishop, and kept shaking his head and frowning, then said:

'Do you know, your Reverence, you have got typhoid?'

After an hour or so of haemorrhage the bishop looked much thinner, paler, and wasted; his face looked wrinkled, his eyes were big, and he seemed older, shorter, and it seemed to him that he was thinner, weaker, more insignificant than anyone, that everything that had been had retreated far, far away and would never recur or be continued.

'How good,' he thought, 'how good!'

His old mother came. Seeing his wrinkled face and his big eyes, she was frightened, she fell on her knees by the bed and began kissing his face, his shoulders, his hands. And to her, too, it seemed that he was thinner, weaker, and more insignificant than anyone, and now she forgot that he was a bishop, and kissed him as though he were a child very near and very dear to her.

'Pavlusha, darling,' she said; 'my own, my darling son! . . . Why are you like this? Pavlusha, answer me!'

Katia, pale and hard-bitten, stood beside her, not understanding what was the matter with her uncle, why there was such a look of suffering on her grandmother's face, why she was saying such sad, touching things. By now he could not utter a word, he could understand nothing, and he imagined he was a simple ordinary man, walking quickly, cheerfully through the fields, tapping his stick, while above him was the open sky bathed in sunshine, and he was now as free as a bird and could go where he liked!

'Pavlusha, my darling son, answer me,' the old woman was saying. 'What is it? My own!'

'Don't disturb his Reverence,' Sisoi said angrily, walking about the room. 'Let him sleep . . . what's the use . . . it's no good . . .'

Three doctors arrived, conferred, and then left. The day was long, incredibly long then the night came on and passed slowly, slowly, and towards morning on Saturday the lay brother went in to the old mother who was lying on the sofa in the parlour, and asked her to go into the bedroom: the bishop had just breathed his last.

Next day was Easter Sunday. There were forty-two churches and six monasteries in the town; the sonorous, joyful clang of the bells hung over the town from morning till night unceasingly, stirring the spring air; the birds were singing, the sun was shining brightly. The big market square was noisy, swings were going, barrel organs were playing, accordions were screeching, drunken voices were shouting. After midday people began driving up and down the main street in carriages drawn by trotting horses – in short, all was merriment, everything was fine, just as it had been the year before, and as it will be in all likelihood next year.

A month later a new suffragan bishop was appointed, and no one thought anything more of Bishop Piotr. Afterwards he was completely forgotten. And only the dead man's old mother, who is living today with her son-in-law the deacon in a remote little district town, when she goes out at night to bring her cow in and meets other women on the common, begins talking of her children and her grandchildren, and says that she had a son who was a bishop, and this she says timidly, afraid that she will not be believed . . .

And, indeed, not everybody did believe her.

1902

The Bride

I

It was about ten in the evening, and the full moon shone over the garden. In the Shumins' house evening service, ordered by the grandmother Marfa, was just over, and now Nadia – she had gone into the garden for a minute – could see the table being laid for supper in the dining-room, and Granny bustling about in her gorgeous silk dress. Father Andrei, the cathedral dean, was talking to Nadia's mother, Nina, and now, seen through the window in the evening light, her mother somehow looked very young; Andrei, Father Andrei's son, was standing by, listening attentively.

It was still and cool in the garden, and dark peaceful shadows lay on the ground. You could hear frogs croaking, somewhere far, far away out of town. There was a feeling of May, sweet May! You breathed deep and longed to fancy that not here but far away under the sky, above the trees, far away in the open country, in the fields, the woods, the life of spring had now unfolded, mysterious, lovely, rich and holy beyond the understanding of weak, sinful man. And somehow it made you want to cry.

She, Nadia, was already twenty-three. Ever since she was sixteen she had dreamed passionately of marriage, and at last she was engaged to Andrei, the young man who was on the other side of the window; she liked him, the wedding was now set for the seventh of July, and yet there was no joy, she was sleeping badly, the merriment had gone . . . She could hear from the open windows of the basement, where the kitchen was, the hurrying servants, the clatter of knives, the banging of the swing-door; there was a smell of roast turkey and marinaded cherries. And somehow it seemed to her that it would be like that all her life, with no change and no end.

Now someone left the house and stopped on the steps; it was Alexandr Timofeich, or simply Sasha, who had arrived from Moscow ten days before to stay. Years ago a distant relative of the grandmother, a gentleman's widow called Maria Petrovna, a thin, sickly little distressed gentlewoman, used to visit and ask for charity. She had a son, Sasha. He was somehow said to be a fine artist, and when his mother died, Nadia's grandmother had, for the salvation of her soul, sent him to the Komissarov school in Moscow; about two years later he switched to art school, spent virtually fifteen years there, and left after getting by the skin of his teeth a degree in architecture. He did not set up as an architect, however, but took a job at a Moscow lithographer's. He used to come almost every year, usually very ill, to stay with Nadia's grandmother to rest and recover.

He was wearing now a frock coat buttoned up and shabby sailcloth trousers, with frayed hems. And his shirt was unironed, and he looked quite frowsty. He was very thin, with big eyes, long thin fingers, and a swarthy, bearded face, and yet he was handsome. He treated the Shumins as his family, and felt at home in their house. And the room in which he lived when he was there had long been called Sasha's room.

Standing on the steps he saw Nadia, and went up to her.

'It's nice out here,' he said.

'Of course it is. You ought to stay here till the autumn.'

'Yes, I expect it will come to that. All right, I'll stay with you till September.'

He laughed for no reason, and sat down beside her.

'I'm sitting here looking at mother,' said Nadia. 'She looks so young from here! My mama has her weaknesses, of course,' she added after a pause, 'but still she is an exceptional woman.'

'Yes, she's nice . . .' Sasha agreed. 'Your mother, in her own way of course, is a very kind and sweet woman, but . . . how shall I put it? I went early this morning into your kitchen and there were four servants sleeping on the floor, no beds, and rags for bedding, stench, bedbugs, cockroaches . . . Just as it was twenty years ago, no change at all. As for Granny, forget about her, she's just Granny; but your mother speaks French, I expect, and goes in for amateur dramatics. You'd think she might understand.'

When Sasha talked, he stretched out two long emaciated fingers at his listener.

'I'm not used to things here any more, they all seem outlandish,' he went on. 'Hell, nobody ever does anything. Your mother just strolls all day like a duchess, Granny does nothing either, nor do you. And your fiancé Andrei never does anything either.'

Nadia had heard this the year before and, she fancied, the year before that too, and she knew that Sasha was bound to think that way, and this had once amused her, but now she somehow felt annoyed.

'That's all old, and I have been bored with it for ages,' she said, and got up. 'You should think up something a bit newer.'

He laughed and got up too, and they went together towards the house. Next to him, she, tall, handsome and slim, looked very healthy and well dressed; she sensed this and felt sorry for him and somehow ill at ease.

'And you say a lot you shouldn't,' she said. 'You've just been talking about my Andrei, but you don't know him, do you?'

' "My Andrei . . ." Bother him, your Andrei! What I'm sorry about is your youth.'

The family was already sitting down to supper as Nadia and Sasha entered the dining-room. The grandmother, or Gran as she was called in the household, very stout, ugly, with bushy eyebrows and whiskers, was talking loudly, and her voice and manner of speaking showed that she was the senior person in the house. She owned rows of stalls in the market and the old-fashioned house with columns and an orchard, yet she prayed every morning for God to save her from ruin, and she shed tears as she prayed. Her daughter-in-law, Nadia's mother, Nina, a fair-haired, tightly corseted woman, with a pince-nez and diamonds on every finger, Father Andrei, a lean, toothless, old man, with an expression as if he were about to say something very funny, and his son Andrei, a stout and handsome young man with curly hair, looking like an artist or an actor, were all talking of hypnotism.

'I'll get you well in a week,' said Granny addressing Sasha. 'Only you must eat much more. What do you look like?' she sighed. 'You're dreadful! You're the spitting image of the prodigal son.'

'Squandering the gifts my father gave me,' said Father Andrei slowly, with laughing eyes. 'Outcast, I grazed with senseless beasts . . .'

'I like my reverend dad,' said Andrei touching his father on the shoulder. 'He is a splendid old man. A good old man.'

Everyone was silent. Sasha suddenly burst out laughing and put his napkin to his mouth.

'So you believe in hypnotism?' Father Andrei asked Nina.

'I cannot, of course, assert that I believe,' answered Nina, assuming a very serious, even severe, expression, 'but I must own that there is much that is mysterious and incomprehensible in nature.'

'I quite agree with you, though I must add that religion distinctly curtails for us the domain of the mysterious.'

A big and very fat turkey-hen was served. Father Andrei and Nina went on with their conversation. Nina's diamonds glittered on her fingers, then tears began to glitter in her eyes, she worked herself up.

'Though I don't dare argue with you,' she said, 'you must admit there are so many insoluble riddles in life!'

'Not one, may I assure you.'

After supper Andrei played the violin and Nina accompanied him on the piano. Ten years before, he had taken an arts degree at the university, but had never held any post, had no proper job, and only occasionally took part in charity concerts; and in the town he was called a musician.

Andrei played; they all listened in silence. The samovar was boiling quietly on the table, but only Sasha was drinking tea. Then, when the clock had struck twelve, a violin string suddenly broke; everyone laughed, bustled about and began saying good-bye.

After seeing her fiancé out, Nadia went upstairs where she and her mother had their rooms (Granny occupied the lower storey). They began putting the lights out below in the dining-room, while Sasha still sat on drinking tea. He always spent a long time over tea in the Moscow style, drinking as much as seven glasses at a time. For a long time after Nadia had undressed and gone to bed she could hear the servants clearing away downstairs and Gran talking angrily. At least everything was hushed, and nothing could be heard but Sasha from time to time coughing on a bass note in his room below.

II

When Nadia woke up it must have been about two in the morning, it was beginning to get light. A watchman was tapping somewhere far away. She was not sleepy, and her bed felt too soft and uncomfortable. Nadia sat up in bed and fell to thinking as she had done every night that May. Her thoughts were the same as they had been the night before, useless, persistent thoughts, always alike, about Andrei courting her and proposing, her accepting and then little by little coming to appreciate the kindly, intelligent man. But now, somehow, when there was hardly a month left before the wedding, she began to feel dread and uneasiness, as though facing something vague and oppressive.

'Tick-tock tick-tock ...' the watchman tapped lazily. 'Tick-tock ...'

Through the big old window she could see the orchard and distant, densely flowering lilacs, drowsy and lifeless in the cold, and the thick white mist was floating softly up to the lilacs, trying to cover it. Drowsy rooks cawed in the far-away trees.

'My God, why am I so depressed?'

Perhaps every girl felt the same before her wedding. Who knows! Or was it Sasha's influence? But for several years past Sasha had been repeating the same thing, like a copybook, and when he talked he seemed naive and odd. But why couldn't she get Sasha out of her head? Why?

The watchman had long since stopped tapping. Under the windows the birds had started to sing and the mist had disappeared from the orchard. Everything was lit up by the spring sunshine as by a smile. Soon the whole orchard, warm and caressed by the sun, returned to life, and dewdrops glittered like diamonds on the leaves, and that morning the old neglected orchard looked so young and elegant.

Gran was already awake. Sasha's husky bass cough began. Nadia could hear them below, putting on the samovar and moving chairs.

The hours passed slowly. Nadia had been up and walking about the garden for a long while, and still the morning dragged on.

Now Nina appeared with a tear-stained face, carrying a glass of mineral water. She was involved in spiritualism and homeopathy, read a great deal, was fond of talking of the doubts to which she was subject, and all this, it seemed to Nadia, had a deep, mysterious significance. Nadia now kissed her mother and walked beside her.

'Why have you been crying, Mother?' she asked.

'Last night I was reading a story in which there is an old man and his daughter. The old man works in some office and, well, his chief falls in love with his daughter. I haven't finished it, but there was a passage where it was hard not to cry,' said Nina, and she sipped at her glass. 'It came back to me this morning and I cried again.'

'I have been so downcast recently,' said Nadia after a pause. 'Why can't I sleep at night?'

'I don't know, dear. When I can't sleep I shut my eyes very tightly, like this, and picture to myself Anna Karenina moving about and talking, or something historical from the ancient world . . .'

Nadia sensed that her mother did not and could not understand her. She sensed this for the first time in her life, and it even frightened her and made her want to hide; and she went away to her own room.

At two o'clock they sat down to dinner. It was Wednesday, a fast day, and so vegetable soup and bream with boiled grain were set before Granny.

To tease Granny, Sasha ate his meat soup as well as the vegetable soup. He joked all through dinner-time, but his jests were laboured and invariably had a moral bearing, and the effect was not at all amusing when before making some witty remark he raised his fingers, very long, thin, like a dead man's; and when you remembered that he was very ill and might not be much longer for this world, you were moved to tears of pity for him.

After dinner Granny went off to her own room to lie down. Nina played on the piano for a little, and then she too left.

'Oh, dear Nadia!' Sasha began his usual afternoon conversation, 'if only you had listened to me! If only!'

She was sitting far back in an old-fashioned arm-chair, with her eyes shut, while he slowly paced the room from corner to corner.

'If only you would go to university,' he said. 'Only enlightened and holy people are interesting, they're the only ones that are needed. The more such people there are, the sooner the kingdom of God will come on earth. Of your town then, eventually, not one stone will be left, everything will be blown up from the foundations, everything will be changed as though by magic. And then there will be immense, magnificent houses here, wonderful gardens, marvellous fountains, remarkable people . . . But that's not what matters most. What matters most is that the mob in our sense of the word, in the sense in which it exists now – that evil will not exist then, because every man will have faith and every man will know what he is living for and no one will seek moral support from the mob. Dear Nadia, darling girl, go! Show them all that you are sick of this stagnant, grey, sinful life. Prove it to yourself at least!'

'I can't, Sasha, I'm going to be married.'

'Oh, stop it! Who needs it?'

They went out into the garden and walked up and down a little.

'And however that may be, my dear girl, you must think, you must realise how unclean, how immoral this idle life of yours is,' Sasha went on. 'Do understand that if, for instance, you and your mother and your grandmother do nothing, it means that someone else is working for you, you are consuming someone else's life, and is that clean? – isn't it filthy?'

Nadia wanted to say 'Yes, that is true'; she wanted to say that she understood, but tears came into her eyes, she suddenly became silent, shrank into herself and went to her room.

Late that afternoon Andrei arrived and, as usual, played the violin for a long time. He was on the whole taciturn, and loved the violin, perhaps because there was no need to talk while playing. At ten, when he was about to go home and had put on his overcoat, he embraced Nadia and began eagerly kissing her face, her shoulders, and her hands.

'My dear, my sweet, my beauty,' he murmured. 'Oh how happy I am! I am beside myself with rapture!'

And it seemed to her that she had heard that long, long ago, or had read it somewhere . . . in some old tattered novel, thrown away long ago.

In the dining-room Sasha was sitting at the table drinking tea with the saucer poised on his five long fingers; Gran was laying out patience; Nina was reading. The flame crackled in the icon lamp and everything, it seemed, was quiet and going well. Nadia said good night, went upstairs to her room, got into bed, and fell asleep at once. But just like the night before, at first light she woke up. She was not sleepy, there was an uneasy, oppressive feeling in her heart. She sat with her head on her knees and thought of her fiancé and her marriage . . . She for some reason remembered that her mother had not loved her late husband and now had nothing and lived in complete dependence on her mother-in-law, Gran. And however much Nadia pondered, she could not imagine why she had hitherto seen in her mother something special and exceptional, how she had overlooked a simple, ordinary, unhappy woman.

Nor could Sasha sleep downstairs, she could hear him coughing. He is an odd, naive man, thought Nadia, and in all his dreams, in all those marvellous gardens and wonderful fountains one sensed something absurd. But somehow in his naiveté, even this absurdity, there was so much beauty that as soon as she thought whether she should go to university it sent a chill right through her heart, her chest and flooded them with joy, with rapture.

'But better not think, better not think . . .' she whispered. 'I must not think of it.'

'Tick-tock . . .' tapped the watchman somewhere far away. 'Tick-tock . . . tick-tock . . .'

III

In the middle of June Sasha suddenly felt listless and started to think about going back to Moscow.

'I can't live in this town,' he said gloomily. 'No water supply, no drains! It disgusts me to eat dinner; the filth in the kitchen is quite impossible . . .'

'Just wait a little, prodigal son!' Granny tried to persuade him, speaking for some reason in a whisper, 'the wedding is on the seventh.'

'I don't want to.'

'You meant to stay with us until September!'

'But now I don't want to. I have to work.'

Summer turned out grey and cold, the trees were wet, everything in the garden looked dejected and uninviting; it certainly did make you want to work. Unfamiliar women's voices were heard down-stairs and upstairs, there was the rattle of a sewing machine in Granny's room, they were working hard at the trousseau. Six fur coats alone were provided for Nadia and the cheapest of them, in Granny's words, had cost three hundred roubles! The fuss irritated Sasha; he stayed in his own room and was cross, but all the same he had been persuaded to stay, and he promised not to go before the first of July.

Time passed quickly. On St Peter's Day Andrei went with Nadia after dinner to Moskovskaia Street to inspect once more the house that had long since been rented and made ready for the young couple. It was a two-storey house, but so far only the upper floor had been decorated. The hall had a shining floor painted to look like parquet; there were bentwood chairs, a piano, a music stand for the violin. There was a smell of paint. On the wall hung a big oil painting in a gold frame – a naked lady and next to her a purple vase with a broken handle.

'A wonderful picture,' said Andrei, and he gave a sigh of respect. 'It's by the artist Shishmachevsky.'

Then there was the drawing-room with a round table, a sofa and arm-chairs upholstered in bright blue. Above the sofa was a big photograph of Father Andrei wearing a priest's headgear and his decorations. Then they went into the dining-room, in which there was a sideboard, then into the bedroom; here in the half dusk stood two beds side by side, and it looked as though in furnishing the bedroom the idea had been that it would always be very nice there and could not be otherwise. Andrei led Nadia through the rooms with his arm round her waist all the time, and she felt weak, guilty, she hated all these rooms, the beds, the arm-chairs, she was nauseated by the naked lady. It was clear to her now that she no longer loved Andrei, or perhaps had never loved him; but how, to whom and why she could say this, she did not and could not understand, though she thought about it all the time, day and night . . . He held her by the waist, talked so affectionately, so modestly, was so happy, walking about this house of his; while she saw nothing in it all but vulgarity, stupid, naive, unbearable vulgarity, and his arm round her waist felt as hard and cold as an iron hoop. And every minute she was on the point of running away, bursting into sobs, throwing herself out of the window. Andrei led her into the bathroom, and here he touched a tap fixed in the wall and at once water flowed.

'What do you say to that?' he said, and laughed. 'I had a tank holding two hundred gallons put in the loft, and so now we shall have water.'

They walked across the yard and went into the street and took a cab. Thick clouds of dust were blowing, and it seemed that it would rain any minute.

'You're not cold?' said Andrei, screwing up his eyes at the dust.

She did not answer.

'Yesterday, you remember, Sasha reproached me for doing

nothing,' he said, after a brief silence. 'Well, he is right, absolutely right! I don't and can't do anything. Darling, why not? Why does the very thought of ever ramming a cockade on my head and going into government service repel me so much? Why do I feel so uncomfortable when I see a lawyer or a Latin teacher or a member of the district council? O Mother Russia! O Mother Russia! How many idle and useless people you still support! How many people you have like me, long-suffering Mother!'

And his doing nothing led him to generalise and see in it a sign of the times.

'When we're married let's go together into the country, my darling; there we shall work! We'll buy ourselves a little piece of land with a garden and a river; we shall labour and observe life. Oh, how good that will be!'

He took off his hat, and his hair floated in the wind, while she listened to him and thought: 'Good God, I want to go home! God!'

When they were quite near the house they overtook Father Andrei.

'Ah, here's father coming,' cried Andrei, delighted, and he waved his hat. 'I love my dad really,' he said as he paid the cabman. 'He's a splendid old man. A kind old man.'

Nadia went into the house, feeling cross and unwell, thinking that there would be visitors all evening, that she would have to entertain them, smile, listen to the violin, listen to all sorts of nonsense, and talk of nothing but the wedding. Granny, dignified, gorgeous in her silk dress and haughty, as she always seemed when there were visitors, was sitting in front of the samovar. Father Andrei came in with his sly smile.

'I have the pleasure and blessed consolation of seeing you in good health,' he said to Granny, and it was hard to tell whether he was joking or speaking seriously.

IV

The wind was beating at the window and the roof; there was a whistling sound, and in the stove the house spirit was plaintively and sullenly droning his song. It was past midnight. Everyone in the house had gone to bed, but no one was asleep, and it seemed all the while to Nadia as though the violin were being played downstairs. There was a sharp bang; a shutter must have fallen off. A minute later Nina entered, wearing just a night-dress, carrying a candle.

'What was the bang, Nadia?' she asked.

Her mother, with her hair in a single plait and a timid smile on her face, looked older, uglier, smaller on that stormy night. Nadia

remembered how very recently she had thought her mother exceptional, and had listened with pride to the things she said, and now she
could not remember those things, everything that she could recall was
so feeble and pointless.

The stove made the sound of several bass voices in chorus, and she
even heard 'O-o-o my G-o-od!' Nadia sat on her bed, and suddenly
she clutched at her hair and burst into sobs.

'Mama, Mama,' she said. 'My darling mama, if only you knew
what is happening to me! Please, I beg you, let me go away! I beg you!'

'Where?' asked Nina, not understanding, and she sat down on the
bed. 'Go where?'

For a long while Nadia cried and could not utter a word.

'Let me leave town,' she said at last. 'There must be no wedding,
there can't be, try and understand! I don't love the man . . . I can't
even speak about him.'

'No, my darling, no!' Nina said quickly, terribly alarmed. 'Calm
yourself – it's just because you are in a bad mood. It will pass. It often
happens. I expect you've had a tiff with Andrei; but lovers' quarrels
always end in kisses!'

'Oh, go away, Mother, oh, go away,' sobbed Nadia.

'Yes,' said Nina after a pause 'it's not long since you were a baby, a
little girl and now you're a bride. In nature there is a continual
transmutation of substances. Before you know where you are you
will be a mother yourself and an old woman, and will have as
querulous a daughter as I have.'

'My darling, my sweet, after all, you're clever, you're unhappy,'
said Nadia. 'You're very unhappy; why do you say such very
banalities? For God's sake, why?'

Nina meant to say something, but could not utter a word; she gave a
sob and went to her own room. The bass voices began droning in the
stove again, and Nadia felt suddenly frightened. She jumped out of bed
and went quickly to her mother. Nina with a tear-stained face, was in
bed, wrapped in a pale blue blanket and holding a book in her hands.

'Mother, listen to me!' said Nadia. 'I beg you, think about it and try
to understand! If you could only understand how petty and
degrading our life is. My eyes have opened, and I see it all now. And
what is your Andrei? Why, he's not even clever, Mother! Oh Lord
God! Try and understand, mother, he is stupid!'

Nina abruptly sat up.

'You and your grandmother torment me,' she said with a sob. 'I
want to live! to live,' she repeated, and twice she beat her breast with
her little fist. 'Give me freedom! I'm still young, I want to live, and you
two have turned me into an old woman! . . .'

She broke into bitter tears, lay down and curled up under the blanket, and looked so small, so pitiful, so foolish. Nadia went to her room, dressed and sat down at the window to wait for the morning. She sat all night thinking, while someone kept tapping on the shutters and whistling in the yard.

In the morning Granny complained that the wind had blown down all the apples in the orchard and broken an old plum tree. It was grey, murky, cheerless, dark enough for candles; everyone complained of the cold, and the rain lashed at the windows. After tea Nadia went into Sasha's room, and, without uttering a word, knelt down by an arm-chair in the corner and hid her face in her hands.

'What is it?' asked Sasha.

'I can't . . .' she said. 'How I could live here before, I can't understand, I can't conceive! I despise my fiancé, I despise myself, I despise all this idle, senseless life . . .'

'Well, well,' said Sasha, not grasping yet what it was about. 'That's all right . . . That's good.'

'I am sick of this life,' Nadia went on. 'I can't endure another day here. Tomorrow I'm leaving. Take me with you, for God's sake!'

For a minute Sasha looked at her in astonishment; at last he understood, and was as delighted as a child. He waved his arms and began tapping his slippers as though dancing with delight.

'Splendid!' he said, rubbing his hands. 'God, how fine that is!'

And she stared at him without blinking, with adoring eyes, as though spellbound, expecting him any minute to say something important, something infinitely significant; he had told her nothing yet, but already it seemed to her that something new and broad was opening up before her, something she had not known till now, and already she gazed at him full of expectation, ready to face anything, even death.

'I am going tomorrow,' he said after a moment's thought. 'You come to the station to see me off . . . I'll take your things in my suitcase, and I'll get your ticket, and when the third bell rings you get into the carriage, and we'll go. You'll come with me as far as Moscow and then go on to Petersburg alone. Do you have a passport?'

'Yes.'

'I swear to you that you won't regret it or repent,' said Sasha enthusiastically. 'You'll go, you'll study, and then go where fate takes you. When you turn your life upside down everything will change. The main thing is to turn your life upside down, and all the rest is unimportant. And so we set off tomorrow?'

'Oh yes! For God's sake!'

It seemed to Nadia that she was very excited, that her heart was heavy as never before, that till the moment she left she would have to suffer and think agonising thoughts; but she had hardly gone upstairs and lain down on her bed when she fell asleep at once, with a face wet with tears and a smile, and she slept soundly till evening.

v

A cab had been sent for. Nadia in her hat and overcoat went upstairs to take one more look at her mother, at all her things. She stood in her own room by her still warm bed, looked about her, then went slowly in to her mother. Nina was asleep; it was quiet in her room. Nadia kissed her mother, smoothed her hair, stood for a couple of minutes . . . then walked slowly downstairs.

It was raining heavily. The cabman, drenched, with the hood pulled down was waiting at the entrance.

'There's no room for you, Nadia,' said Granny, as the servants began putting in the luggage. 'What an idea to see him off in such weather! You should stay at home. Just look at that rain!'

Nadia meant to say something, but could not. Then Sasha helped Nadia in and covered her legs with a rug. And now he had got in beside her.

'Good luck to you! God bless you!' Granny cried from the steps. 'Mind you write to us from Moscow, Sasha!'

'Right. Good-bye, Gran.'

'The Queen of Heaven keep you!'

'Quite some weather!' said Sasha.

It was only now that Nadia began to cry. Now it was clear to her that she really was going, which she still had not believed when she was saying good-bye to Granny, when she was looking at her mother. Good-bye, town! And she suddenly recalled it all: Andrei, and his father and the new house and the naked lady with the vase; and it all no longer frightened her, nor weighed upon her, but was naive and trivial and kept receding further and further. And when they got into the railway carriage and the train moved off, all the past which had been so big and serious shrank into a little lump, and a vast wide future which till then had been so imperceptible began unfolding before her. The rain battered the carriage windows, nothing could be seen but the green fields, telegraph posts with birds sitting on the wires flitted by, and joy suddenly took her breath away; she thought that she was off to freedom, off to study, and this was just like what used, ages ago, to be called going off to be a free Cossack.

She laughed and cried and prayed all at once.

'It's a-all right,' said Sasha, smiling. 'It's a-all right.'

VI

Autumn had passed and winter too had gone. Nadia had begun to be very homesick and thought every day of her mother and her grandmother; she thought of Sasha, too. The letters that came from home were kind and gentle, and it seemed as though everything by now were forgiven and forgotten. In May after the examinations she set off for home in good health and high spirits and stopped off at Moscow to see Sasha. He was just the same as the year before, with the same beard and unkempt hair, with the same large beautiful eyes, and he still wore the same coat and sailcloth trousers; but he looked unwell and worn out, he seemed both older and thinner, and kept coughing, and somehow he struck Nadia as grey, provincial.

'My God, Nadia has come!' he said, and laughed gaily. 'My darling girl!'

They sat in the lithographer's, which was full of tobacco smoke and suffocated you with the smell of Indian ink and paint; then they went to his room, which also smelt of tobacco and was covered with spittle; by the cold samovar stood a broken plate with a piece of dark paper on it, and there were masses of dead flies on the table and the floor. And everything showed that Sasha lived his personal life in a slovenly way and lived anyhow, with utter contempt for comfort, and if anyone began talking to him of his personal happiness, of his personal life, of affection for him, he would have been baffled and would only have laughed.

'It is all right, everything has gone well,' said Nadia hurriedly. 'Mother came to see me in Petersburg in the autumn; she said that Granny is not angry, and only keeps going into my room and making the sign of the cross over the walls.'

Sasha looked cheerful, but he kept coughing, and talked in a cracked voice, and Nadia kept looking at him, unable to decide whether he really were seriously ill or whether she only imagined it.

'Dear Sasha,' she said, 'you're ill, aren't you?'

'No, it's nothing. I am ill, but not very . . .'

'Oh, my God!' cried Nadia, in agitation. 'Why don't you see a doctor? Why don't you take care of your health? My dear, darling Sasha,' she said, and tears gushed from her eyes, and for some reason there rose before her imagination Andrei and the naked lady with the vase, and all her past which seemed now as far away as her childhood; and she began crying because Sasha no longer seemed to her so novel, intellectual, interesting as the year before. 'Dear Sasha you are very, very ill. I'd do anything to see you less pale and thin. I owe so much to you! You can't even imagine how much you have done for me, my good Sasha! Really, you are now the person nearest and dearest to me.'

They sat on and talked, and now, after Nadia had spent a winter in Petersburg, Sasha, his works, his smile, his whole figure had an aura of something obsolete, old-fashioned, written off long ago and perhaps already dead and buried.

'I am going down the Volga the day after tomorrow,' said Sasha, 'and then to take the fermented mare's milk cure: I mean to drink koumiss. A friend and his wife are going with me. His wife is a wonderful woman; I am always at her, trying to persuade her to go to the university. I want her to turn her life upside down.'

After their talk they drove to the station. Sasha bought her tea and apples; and when the train began moving and he waved his handkerchief at her, smiling, it could be seen even from his legs that he was very ill and was unlikely to live long.

Nadia reached her native town at midday. As she drove home from the station the streets struck her as very wide and the houses very small and squat; there were no people about; she met no one but the German piano tuner in a rusty greatcoat. And all the houses looked as though they were covered with dust. Granny, now very old, but as fat and ugly as ever, flung her arms round Nadia and cried for a long time with her face on Nadia's shoulder, unable to break away. Nina had also become much older and plainer, she had somehow shrivelled up, but was still tightly corseted and still had diamonds flashing on her fingers.

'My darling,' she said, trembling all over. 'My darling!'

Then they sat down and cried without speaking. It was evident that both mother and grandmother sensed that the past was lost and gone for ever; they now had no position in society, none of their old prestige, no right to invite visitors; so it is when in the midst of an easy, carefree life the police suddenly burst in at night and carry out a search, and the head of the family turns out to have embezzled, committed forgery – and then good-bye for ever to the easy, carefree life!

Nadia went upstairs and saw the same bed, the same windows with naive white curtains, and outside the windows the same garden, cheerful and noisy, bathed in sunshine. She touched her table, her bed, sat and thought. And she had a good dinner and drank tea with delicious rich cream; but something was missing, there was a sense of emptiness in the rooms and the ceilings were too low. In the evening she went to bed, covered herself up, and somehow it seemed funny to be in this warm, very soft bed.

Nina came in for a minute; she sat down as people who feel guilty sit down, timidly, and looking all around.

'Well, how are things, Nadia,' she asked after a brief pause, 'are you pleased? Quite pleased?'

'Yes, Mama.'

Nina got up, made the sign of the cross over Nadia and the windows.

'I've become religious, as you see,' she said. 'You know, now I'm studying philosophy, and I keep thinking and thinking . . . And many things have become as clear as daylight to me. I think that first and foremost life should pass as it were through a prism.'

'Tell me, Mama, how is Granny's health?'

'She seems all right. When you went away that time with Sasha and we got your telegram, Granny fell on the floor as soon as she read it; for three days she lay without moving. After that she kept praying and crying. But now she's all right.'

She got up and walked about the room.

'Tick-tock,' tapped the watchman. 'Tick-tock, tick-tock . . .'

'First and foremost life should pass as it were through a prism,' she said; 'in other words, life in consciousness should divide into its simplest elements as into the seven primary colours, and each element must be studied separately.'

What else Nina said, and when she left, Nadia did not hear, as she quickly fell asleep.

May passed; June came. Nadia had grown used to being at home. Granny busied herself about the samovar, heaving deep sighs. Nina talked in the evenings about her philosophy; she still lived in the house like a poor relation, and had to go to Granny for every kopeck. There were lots of flies in the house and the ceilings, it seemed, were getting lower and lower. Granny and Nina did not go outside for fear of meeting Father Andrei and Andrei. Nadia walked about the garden and the street, looked at the grey fences and it seemed to her that everything in the town had long ago grown old, was obsolete and was only waiting either for the end or for the beginning of something young and fresh. Oh, if only that new, bright life would come quickly – that life in which we shall be able to face our fate boldly and directly, to know that we are right, to be lighthearted, free! But sooner or later such a life would come. The time would come when of Granny's house, where things are so arranged that four servants have to live in filth in one basement room – the time would come when of that house not a trace would remain, and it would be forgotten, no one would remember it. And Nadia's only entertainment was from the boys next door; when she walked about the garden they knocked on the fence and shouted in mockery:

'The bride! The bride!'

A letter from Sasha arrived from Saratov. In his cheerful dancing handwriting he told them that his trip down the Volga had been a complete success, but that he had been taken rather ill in Saratov, had lost his voice, and had been in hospital for the last fortnight. She knew what that meant, and she was overwhelmed with a foreboding that was like a conviction. And it vexed her that this foreboding and the thought of Sasha did not distress her so much as before. She had a passionate desire for life, longed to be in Petersburg, and her friendship with Sasha seemed now something from the past, sweet but very, very remote! She did not sleep all night, and in the morning sat at the window, listening. And she did in fact hear voices below; Granny, greatly agitated, was asking questions rapidly. Then some one began crying ... When Nadia went downstairs Granny was standing in the corner, praying, and her face was tearful. A telegram lay on the table.

For some time Nadia walked up and down the room, listening to Granny weeping, then she picked up the telegram and read it. It said that the previous morning Alexandr Timofeich, or just Sasha, had died at Saratov of tuberculosis.

Granny and Nina went to the church to order a requiem, while Nadia went on walking about the rooms and thinking. She was clearly aware that her life had been turned upside down as Sasha had wished; that here she was, alien, isolated, unneeded, and that she needed nothing here, all the past had been torn away from her and had vanished as if it had burnt up and the ashes scattered to the winds. She went into Sasha's room and stood there for a while.

'Good-bye, dear Sasha,' she thought, and she pictured a new, broad, spacious life, and that life, still obscure and full of mysteries, beckoned her and bore her away.

She went upstairs to her own room to pack, and next morning said good-bye to her family, and full of life and high spirits left the town – as she supposed, for ever.

1903

NOTES

Ever since 1886, when major writers first noticed his talent, Chekhov had been tempted to write a serious, extensive piece. *Steppe* was written in little over two months in early 1888. It was inspired by Chekhov's first return to the south, where the idyllic landscapes of his childhood had been, where sheep and horses grazed the prairie lands and great deciduous forests stood: it was in the early 1880s turned to an industrial wasteland by developers such as the Welsh mining engineer Hughes. The story is an evocation of a two-month journey of seven hundred miles across the Ukraine, a memorial to a wild countryside that was now engulfed. It is one of Chekhov's first 'green' pieces, and equally the first work where he subordinates plot to atmospheric evocation. Already he begins to abandon the all-knowing authorial standpoint and lets the story unfold through the uncomprehending but responsive eyes of his main character, here a bewildered boy. The plot abandons many elements – the search for the wool-merchant Varlamov, for instance, peters out. While writing Chekhov was most preoccupied with 'tone', 'musicality', 'poetry in prose'; for the first time he had set out to rival Pushkin and Gogol, 'the king of Steppe descriptions': *Steppe* is literally a masterpiece.

Its success can be measured by the editor of the journal where it was published asking Chekhov to name his fee; Chekhov even toyed with a sequel where Yegorushka would become a seventeen-year-old suicide. Even critics who missed a strongly delineated plot or ideology put the work on a level with the best of Dostoevsky and Tolstoy. Tolstoy himself singled it out for its success in seeing the world through a child's eyes.

E. M. Forster admired it for its 'beauty . . . sense of completeness . . . imaginative fullness'. Professional literary scholars such as Petr Bitsilli regard it as a turning-point in the evolution of a new genre, half story, half prose poem, in which the author's lyrical digressions are inseparable from the protagonist's stream of consciousness.

The characters of the Jewish innkeeper's rebellious brother and the trouble-making Dymov were seen as the first seeds of radicalism in Chekhov. But more significant is the central role of the kindly, sensitive Father Khristofor, one of several priests in Chekhov's work who, as in the stories of Nikolai Leskov, symbolise the author and artist in their gift for communication, for inspiring trust and for responding to distress.

Steppe influenced Chekhov's later work: the combination of cherry blossom and a cemetery in the opening chapter lays the scene for *The Cherry Orchard* sixteen years later. It is also instructive to compare *Steppe* to Katherine Mansfield's masterpiece *Prelude*: they have the same intense impressionistic disoriented child's view of exotic nature and adult distress.

p. 5 Lomonosov: Lomonosov Mikhail was a pioneer poet, scientist and luminary of the eighteenth century, an example to Yegorushka: he rose to fame from humble origins by his own exertions.

p. 10 Tsar Alexandr Pavlovich: i.e., Alexander I, reigned 1801–25.

p. 20 Molokans: a sect that dissented from Russian orthodoxy; they were vegetarian.

p. 56 Old Believers: Old Believers were dissenters who rejected the reforms adopted by the Russian Orthodox Church in the 1600s and who, like the Molokans, often migrated to remote areas.

p. 65 Mazepa: Seventeenth- and eighteenth-century Ukrainian hetman, cursed for deserting Russia for her enemies the Swedes and Turks.

p. 78 Piotr Mogila: Bishop of Kiev in the first half of the seventeenth century and an important theologian.

p. 79 St Nestor: reputed to be an author of the Russian medieval chronicles.

A DREARY STORY

Also known as *A Boring Story, A Dull Story*, the work's title understates the power of Chekhov's first major 'first-person narrative'. Written in 1889 it was appropriately included in Chekhov's collection of 1890, *Gloomy People*. It was composed in the Crimea, in terrible heat, among the depressing sanatoria of Yalta, shortly after the harrowing death of Chekhov's brother Nikolai. The central character owes something to Chekhov's university teacher, the brilliant professor of medicine, Babukhin (who survived his fictional variant by only two years). *A Dreary Story* was controversial because it seemed to shadow and polemicise Tolstoy's recently published *Death of Ivan Ilyich*. The professor's scathing opinions on the theatre and Russian literature were taken to be Chekhov's (not wholly unjustifiably) and Chekhov was accused of gloom, misrepresentation, even plagiarism. The adverse critical response only deepened Chekhov's desire to escape, and helped prompt his flight to Sakhalin.

For all his unfeeling cruelty to his family the professor comes across as a sympathetic figure, because of his fight with the shadow of death and his remorseless honesty. All the stranger, therefore, is his similarity to the comical and loathsome Professor Serebriakov in *The Wood Demon* of the same year (and *Uncle Vania* a decade later): the thundery night of Chapter V in which the angst-ridden professor torments his womenfolk anticipates Act 2 of the plays, an example of Chekhov using the same material for tragic narrative and comic drama. Note too how both professors are of lowly origin and how Kharkov (a city four hundred and seventy miles south of Moscow) achieves hellish status in Chekhov's work.

p. 85 Pirogov (Nikolai, 1801–81): famous Russian military surgeon.

p. 85 Kavelin (Konstantin, 1818–85): a liberal lawyer.

p. 85 Nekrasov (Nikolai, 1821–78): the great Russian 'civic' poet.

p. 85 Turgenev . . . one of his heroines: from the *Diary of a Superfluous Man*.

p. 86 *The Song the Lark was Singing*: by F. Spielhagen, 1829–1911.

p. 91 Gruber (Ventseslav, 1814–90): Professor of Anatomy.

p. 91 Babukhin (Aleksandr, 1835–91): Professor of Medicine.

p. 91 Skobelev (Mikhail, 1843–82): Russian general, conqueror of Turkestan.

p. 91 Perov (Vasili 1833–82): Professor of Art.

p. 92 Patti (Adelina, 1843–1919): Italian soprano, well known in Russia.

p. 92 Hecuba . . .: one of *A Dreary Story*'s many references to Shakespeare's *Hamlet*, a key play in Russian culture, where Hamlet is an honorary citizen. Chekhov often quotes Hamlet's puzzlement at actors' ability to change character, a trait reflected in his Hamlet-like professor.

p. 100 Chatsky: the misanthropist hero of Griboedov's verse comedy, *Woe from Wit*. Chatsky's intolerance of Moscow fools is ironically like Nikolai Stepanovich's.

p. 114 'I look with mournful eyes . . .': from a lyric by Lermontov.

p. 115 Marcus Aurelius, Epictetus: stoic philosophers very influential on Chekhov.

p. 116 Dobroliubov style: Nikolai Dobroliubov (1836–61) was a radical idealist, a bad poet but influential literary critic, revered by generations of Russian students.

p. 117 Arakcheev (Aleksandr, 1769–1834): terrifying reactionary adviser to three Tsars, effectively prime minister 1815–25.

p. 121 Jean-Jacques Petit: perhaps Chekhov meant Jacques-Louis Petit (1674–1750), a French surgeon.

p. 121 Nikita Krylov (1807–79): Professor of Roman Law in Moscow.

p. 122 'An eagle may . . .': from a fable by Ivan Krylov, the Russian Lafontaine.

THE DUEL

Published in the autumn of 1891, *The Duel* is Chekhov's longest work of fiction and the first great work he wrote on his return from Sakhalin. (The idea came to him from his first visit to the Caucasus in 1888.) Superficially, this is one of Chekhov's most conventional works, for the basis of the tension, a duel, is almost a cliché in the plots of Russian novels and plays from Pushkin to Kuprin. Chekhov's motivation is his sceptical treatment of the 'strong' scientist, Von Koren, who greatly resembles the ruthless explorer Przhevalsky. (Chekhov had written a eulogistic obituary of Przhevalsky three years before.) Likewise, Tolstoy's ideas on work, sexuality and women are parodied in the 'weak' Laevsky's excuses for inertia. Chekhov is now free from ideologies: the protagonists argue in a vacuum that is now filled by the naïve, unthinking altruism of the military doctor, the deacon and the Abkhaz natives. The story is set in Sukhumi, then a small, new Russian garrison town surrounded by Caucasian highlanders, and is one of a handful of Chekhov's works with an exotic setting. Originally, Chekhov intended both his chief characters to be unRussian: Von Koren is clearly Germanic in his applied Darwinism, Laevsky (at first Ladzievsky) was meant to be more Polish than Russian.

Like Maupassant in *Pierre and Jean* Chekhov shows himself here to be almost a mystic poet when the sea is the setting for his story. Nature now becomes as powerful a force as it was in *Steppe*. Instinct, inspired by nature, supersedes moralising or argument. Instinctual characters, such as the deacon, like all priests in Chekhov's work, have a pivotal role.

Russian critics, then at their most obtuse, generally disliked the moral ambiguities of *The Duel* and found it ill-adapted to their sociological generalisations.

p. 136 Herbert Spencer: the English Victorian radical philosopher was highly regarded in Russia.

p. 138 Vereshchagin (V. V., 1842–1904): painted Central Asian scenes.

p. 145 Prince Vorontsov: the Tsar's viceroy in the Caucasus in the early 1850s.

p. 148 Onegin, Pechorin ... Bazarov: 'superfluous men', heroes of novels by Pushkin, Lermontov and Turgenev, all involved in duels.

p. 171 Stanley: the British explorer of Central Africa.

p. 172 Arakcheev: see note to page 117 of *A Dreary Story*.

p. 181 Rudin: idealistic hero of Turgenev's eponymous novel, unable to act out his rhetoric, dies a useless death on the Paris barricades.

p. 207 Chechens: a people of the central North Caucasus, much feared for their banditry.

WARD NO. 6

Published in November 1892, after almost a year's work, this was the first major work of Chekhov to win wide and immediate acclaim. The abuse of psychiatry was a theme well established in Russian history, with the declaration by Nicholas I in 1836 that the philosopher Chaadaev was mentally ill and must be detained for compulsory treatment. Such material was first developed in a documentary story by Leskov, *The Unmercenary Engineers*, where an officer who refuses to take part in corruption is ostracised, depressed, declared insane and driven to suicide. Chekhov had already broached the theme in *An Attack* (1888), where a student who denounces brothels is prescribed sedatives and those who condone prostitution declared to be normal.

Leskov is said to have exclaimed: 'In *Ward No. 6* we have a miniature representation of all our system and characters. Everywhere is Ward No. 6. This is Russia . . . Chekhov wasn't thinking what he had written (he told me so), but it still is so. His ward is mother Russia.' In his last years Leskov paid tribute to Chekhov's story and returned to the theme in his oddest work, *Hare Park*, where a secret policeman finally finds security and death in a psychiatric asylum and is nursed by the radical he persecuted.

Ward No. 6 begins deceptively as a first-person guided tour of a provincial hospital, before developing into a classical peripeteia, and, in its plot, a unique example in Chekhov's work of a classical tragedy: Dr Ragin shows hubris, suffers the catastrophe of incarceration and undergoes a momentary catharsis (the vision of the deer) before merciful nemesis. No other major work by Chekhov has such a classical plot: otherwise *Ward No. 6* would be just yet another argument between a quietist (the inert doctor) and an activist (the manic patient). Here, however, there is no third force, no cause for hope, only a hideous grey town (the quintessential provincial setting for Chekhov's most pessimistic work), no love interest, virtually no female presence, and both philosophers are punished beyond their deserts for daring to dissent. Stoicism, Tolstoy and Schopenhauer's philosophy all prove hollow self-deception. The story represents Chekhov at his most depressed: the political interpretation belongs to his readers. V. S. Pritchett called it 'a study of the nightmare of absolute solitude'.

p. 232 *zemstvo*: a rural district council, set up in the reforms of the late 1850s.

p. 234 **Sviatye Gory** (or Sviatogorsky Monastery): a place of pilgrimage near Voronezh; Chekhov knew it well.

p. 235 *The Doctor* (*Vrach*): a weekly journal for doctors from the 1880s to the 1900s: Chekhov was a subscriber and, once, a contributor.

p. 239 **Pirogov**: see notes to *A Dreary Story*.

p. 239 **Pasteur, Koch**: were idolised respectively for offering vaccination against rabies and promising a cure for tuberculosis.

p. 254 **Rumiantsev Museum**: later the Lenin Library, now the Russian State Library.

THE BLACK MONK

Written in the summer of 1893 and published in January 1894, *The Black Monk* is one of Chekhov's more flamboyant stories from the period of spiritual recession between *Ward No. 6* and the great efflorescence of his prose and drama in the second half of the 1890s. It too deals with insanity as inspiration and subtly combines the symptoms of mental derangement with those of physical illness. As a study of madness it begs comparison with Garshin's *Red Flower*, a story written from personal experience rather than observation. *The Black Monk* introduces *The Cherry Orchard*'s theme: an orchard is wrecked as it passes from the old order to the new. With its melodramatic use of a musical motif (Braga's *Wallachian Legend*) and a hallucination, the story is in a much more popular vein than any other mature Chekhov work. It was also acclaimed, however, by Tolstoy and Meyerkhold and was the first of Chekhov's stories to be widely known about in his lifetime (in French in 1897, German in 1901, English in 1903). Shostakovich was enthralled by it: not only did he declare that his Fifteenth Symphony was related to *The Black Monk*, but he told his biographer, 'I am certain that Chekhov constructed *The Black Monk* in sonata form, that there is an introduction, an exposition with main and secondary themes, development, and so on.'

p. 271 **'Onegin, I shall not conceal it . . .'**: from Gremin's aria from Tchaikovsky's opera *Evgeni Onegin*.

p. 273 **Braga** (Gaetano, 1829–1907): Italian composer. On their piano in Melikhovo the Chekhov's kept the sheet music for his *Serenade: A Wallachian Legend*.

p. 276 'Kochubei is rich . . .': from Pushkin's narrative poem *Poltava*.

p. 277 Gaucher: French horticulturist whose works were read by Russian gardeners, including Chekhov.

p. 285 The fast of the Dormition: celebrated by the Russian church in the first half of August.

p. 288 Elijah's Day: 20 July.

p. 291 Sevastopol . . . Yalta: Then, as now, travellers to the Crimea took the train as far as Sevastopol and crossed the mountains to Yalta by road.

THE STUDENT

Published in the spring of 1894, this Easter story seems a typical occasional, seasonal Easter piece. But Chekhov singled it out, as Beethoven did his eighth symphony, as a short work whose perfection was missed even by the critics who noted it as a transition to a new type of narrative: 'new, cheerful, life-enhancing, deeply disturbing to the reader and sometimes extraordinarily bold' (V. Albov). Bunin reports Chekhov saying, 'How can I be a moaner, a "gloomy person", "cold blood" as the critics say? How can I be a pessimist? My favourite piece is the story *The Student*.' In blending New Testament elements into his account of a priest's inner turmoil Chekhov prepares for his valedictory *The Bishop*.

p. 295 Rurik: semi-legendary ninth-century Viking, the first ruler of a united Russia.

ARIADNA

(Also translated as Ariadne.) This story was a sensation when published at the end of 1895, largely because of the inner narrator's warnings about the dangerous animal force of woman: much of his diatribe summarises Schopenhauer's notorious essay 'On Women'. (In the first version of the story the diatribes were even more Schopenhauerian in their misogyny.) The name *Ariadne* is meant to recall the spider-like heroine of Greek mythology, abandoned by her lover on a rock. But, like *The Seagull*, *Ariadna* blatantly uses the private life of Chekhov's closest friends, Lika Mizinova and the writer Potapenko, as well as features of other friends such as the actress Yavorskaia; the plot reflects Chekhov's own travels around Europe, although, unlike the fictional Shamokhin, he failed to come to the rescue of the pregnant and abandoned Lika. In the contrast between the detached author-narrator and the involved protagonist-narrator Shamokhin we might be tempted to see Chekhov resolving an inner conflict in his attitude to women: Chekhov had intended writing a thesis on the topic of sexual dominance and therefore read Sacher-Masoch, Strindberg and Max Nordau with particular interest. Strangely, many of the most appreciative readers of *Ariadna* were women, for example Tolstoy's daughter Tatiana. Chekhov had many doubts about the story and he cut a great deal before re-publishing it in the book version, here translated.

p. 299 Volochisk: the Russian border point on the Austro-Hungarian frontier. From Volochisk the narrators travel by train to Odessa and then by boat to the Crimea.

p. 300 Veltman (Aleksandr): a Russian writer (1800–70), the reference being to a story *Salome* in his collection *Adventures drawn from the Sea of Life*.

THE HOUSE WITH THE MEZZANINE

Constance Garnett entitled this story by its subtitle *An Artist's Story*, a subtitle which links *The House with the Mezzanine* with *My Life* as a first-person narrative by an outsider and a loser. What a 'mezzanine' was – an intermediate storey or a first-floor conservatory – was no clearer to Chekhov's readers than to us today, and is part of the mysterious antiquated atmosphere of the decaying household. Published in the spring of 1896, the story reverts to the ironical first-person genre Chekhov had used so successfully in *A Dreary Story*, where the narrator reveals to the reader what he cannot see in himself. The decaying estate and the contrast between an active, unlovable heroine and an inert but lovable heroine are features which Chekhov had established for all his mature drama (Masha and Nina in *The Seagull*, Varia and Ania in *The Cherry Orchard*), as are the arguments on how to realise the bright future, the artist declaring that no social activism is needed, his opponent rejecting love and art for radical intervention.

The biographical motifs (Bogimovo – friends' estate with a lime-tree avenue, the unhappy and often idle artist Levitan) are of slight importance: this is a story that deplores lack of courage and enterprise, a new existential morality that dominates Chekhov's late works. The puritanism of *Ariadna* has evaporated: most contemporary critics were dismayed by Chekhov's new scepticism towards the 'social worker' type that the anti-heroine, Lida, represents. The story had some influence on D. H. Lawrence.

p. 320 Ammosov stoves: forced-air stoves invented by N. Ammosov (1787–1868).

p. 323 Buriat: a Mongolian people living in East Siberia, east and south of Lake Baikal.

MY LIFE

Published over the last three months of 1896 in the popular monthly *Niva* (a journal particularly carefully censored), this politically controversial story was published in 1897 with most cuts restored in book form, together with *Peasants*, some of whose themes it shares. It is Chekhov's longest work of fiction after *The Duel* and, if the full range of Chekhov's genius had to be represented by one work, *My Life* would be the inevitable choice: it has the lyricism of nature, the failure of love through non-communication, the debate on whether to realise the future by self-sacrifice or by resignation, the horror of Russia symbolised by a nameless provincial town; it mingles autobiographical reminiscence with a mass of philosophical and literary topics, from Ecclesiastes to Tolstoy. It is also the finest piece of first-person narrative in any literature, a pioneer exploration of the existentialist middle-class drop-out, in which the hero-narrator stumbles on truths that the reader is allowed to guess before him. Some of its devices, such as the Turgenevian ending with an orphaned little girl, the Gogolian interview with the governor or the wise Tolstoyan utterances of Radish, and the theme of the railway as destruction, are more traditional than Chekhovian: *My Life* distils the essence of the whole of literature, not just of its author. Many stories which this anthology omits, for instance *The New Dacha*, where peasants rob their would-be benefactor, or *The Grasshopper*, with the ill-assorted wife and practical husband, are present embryonically or vestigially in *My Life*.

Critical reaction to *My Life* was dampened by all the furore around *Peasants*, and it was not until this century that its full importance was realised.

p. 338 Dvorianskaia: 'Nobility' street, a typical name for a provincial high street and an ironic commentary on the Poloznev class obsession.

p. 339 Kleopatra . . . Misail: The names of the hero and his sister are unusual to the point of absurdity, emphasising the heritage visited on them by their pretentious father.

p. 345 Jewish youths: the mention of Jews tells us that the town lies somewhere within the 'pale of settlement', i.e., in southern Russia.

p. 348 Better-than-nothing: literally 'A little bit of profit', the boyhood nickname of Aleksandr Chekhov in Taganrog.

p. 386 Pechenegs: Turkic nomads who devastated southern Russia in the twelfth century.

PEASANTS

Based on Chekhov's own observations over five years as a district doctor and landowner, this story came as shock to the public when it was published in the spring of 1897, although much of its thesis was explicit in *My Life*, i.e., that the peasantry are depraved and degenerate yet more human than their exploiters since they believe in truth, justice, and love Scripture, knowing, unlike the bourgeoisie, that drunkenness and thieving are wrong. The censors at first ordered the story to be excluded or publication of the journal in which it appeared, *Russian Thought*, to be held up, until major cuts were made. Chekhov reinstated a page which had been cut for the book edition, from which this translation was made, but he was discouraged from continuing the story. (Two chapters, X and XI, survived in draft form and I have added my own translation of them to the Garnett version.)

Like *Ward No. 6* this story aroused an uproar of both acclaim and condemnation: acclaim from Marxists, condemnation from Populists and from Tolstoy, but Chekhov was too preoccupied by his deteriorating health to respond to either side. It was one of the few stories to make an impact in France and Germany during the author's lifetime.

p. 418 Aumont (Charles): owner of the *Aquarium*, a theatre-restaurant and the *Bouffe* theatre in Moscow.

p. 419 the Exaltation of the Cross: celebrated on 14 September.

p. 433 when well-to-do peasants . . . became councillors . . .: In 1890 the electoral roll was changed to favour the rich and exclude the poor peasants from elections to the rural district council.

p. 434 Feast of the Protective Veil or The Feast of the Intercession of the Virgin is on 1 October.

p. 437 Annunciation: celebrated on 25 March.

A VISIT TO FRIENDS

This story (also known in English as *All Friends Together*) was written in the winter of 1897–8 in Villefranche for the Russian section of *Cosmopolis*, a French publication. It is based on the feckless ruination of a family Chekhov had known for a decade, the Kiseliovs at Babkino. Most of the plot and setting, even much of the wording, for instance the heroine's refusal to countenance the sale of the estate, was re-used five years later for *The Cherry Orchard*. Any or all of these facts may explain why Chekhov avoided reprinting the story in his collected works, and it passed unnoticed by his contemporaries. It appeared in book form in German in 1902. (It escaped Constance Garnett's attention, and I offer my own version.) Quite apart from the subtly condensed narrative, or the light this story sheds on the author's view of the owners of *The Cherry Orchard*, the work has a very fine 'non-proposal in the garden' scene and a sharp delineation of Moscow and provincial attitudes.

p. 444 gypsies on the Little Bronnaia . . .: This was one of Moscow's 'red light' districts.

p. 448 Straight is the line . . .: The quotations are from Nikolai Nekrasov's *The Railway*.

p. 449 Before he'd said 'Alas, alack . . .': from Ivan Krylov's fable *The Peasant and the Workman*.

p. 452 And you-ou will be queen of the wo-orld: from the Demon's aria in Rubinstein's opera *The Demon*.

IONYCH

'Ionych' is the patronymic, the middle name, of the hero: Chekhov's title has here been kept since the story pivots on this slightly absurd patronymic, which speaks of the doctor's lowly origins. (The story has been retitled in English as *Dr Startsev* and as *In the town of S.*) Published in September 1898, after a year's germination, it marks the return of the doctor as a leading character, but this time, as in the plays, a doctor who degenerates in the course of the action. Some of the scenes, including the assignment in the cemetery, recycle episodes from Chekhov's early comic writing. The cemetery itself recalls that of Taganrog, which Chekhov knew well as a boy. Russian critics, now more subtle, began to understand Chekhov's technique of suggestion rather than denunciation and the work was widely praised for its sophisticated mixture of comedy and melancholy.

p. 459 Before I'd drunk the tears . . .: from a song by Yakovleva to words from Baron Delvig's *Elegy*.

p. 460 Die, Denis . . .: supposed to have been said by Prince Potiomkin to the playwright Denis Fonvizin after a performance of *The Minor*.

p. 463 Pisemsky (Aleksei Feofilaktovich, 1821–81): novelist and playwright.

THE LITTLE TRILOGY

I *The Man in a Case*   II *Gooseberries*   III *About Love*

There is no doubt that, when he published them in *Russian Thought* in the summer of 1898, Chekhov intended these three stories as a series, and the word 'trilogy' occurs in his letters; when first published the second and third stories were numbered accordingly. The stories are linked not only by being narrated in turn by three friends (a device which Chekhov had ten years earlier planned for a novel), but by their common theme of the disastrous consequences of conformism, whether to authority, ambition or morality. Chekhov apparently intended to continue the series.

The Man in a Case (also known in English as *A Hard Case, A Man in a Shell* – the word for 'case', *futliar*, usually means a wooden box or cloth cover, whether for spectacles, an umbrella or a violin) reverts to an absurd schoolteacher, a common object of satire in Chekhov's early work: the schoolteacher is resurrected in the 1890s, notably in the plays (Medvedenko in *The Seagull*, Kulygin in *Three Sisters*). The political implications of this story were powerful in Russia, where the schoolteacher and the priest were considered by the state to be adjuncts to the police.

Gooseberries stemmed from an idea in Chekhov's notebooks for 1895, and seems to be a reply to Tolstoy's rhetorical question, 'How much land does a man need?' Whereas the Tolstoyan answer is 'enough for a grave', Chekhov's response is 'the freedom of the whole earth'.

About Love was alleged by Lidia Avilova in the 1930s to be the story of her relationship with Chekhov, but there is no corroboration in the archives: she claimed that she had lost her letters to Chekhov (which had been returned to her) and was later robbed of Chekhov's letters to her, including one signed 'Aliokhin'.

Russian critics saw the link between the stories and welcomed them as Chekhov's turn from pure art towards a moralising role.

p. 476 Shchedrin: pseudonym of Mikhail Saltykov, 1826–89, Russian satirical novelist.

p. 476 Buckle (Henry): English historian notorious in Russia for his dismissal of Russian backwardness.

p. 477 Gadiach: a small Ukrainian town in Poltava province.

p. 480 *The Man-eating Spider*: a Ukrainian play by Kropivnitsky, which Chekhov had seen in 1893.

p. 487 a serf-soldier: known as a cantonist, a peasant in a special military colony designed by Arakcheev (see notes to *A Dreary Story*) to breed soldiers who would plough by night and train by day.

p. 488 six feet are what a corpse needs . . .: Chekhov's reply to Tolstoy's story of 1886 'How much land does a man need?'

p. 491 One falsehood that exalts . . .: from Pushkin's lyric *The Hero*.

p. 492 someone standing with a hammer: Note how this image recurs in the story *On Official Duty*.

p. 495 European Herald: the best of the Russian 'liberal' monthly reviews.

ON OFFICIAL DUTY

Also known in English as *On Official Business*, this story, written in Yalta in 1898 and published in 1899, brings back a pair of professional heroes common in early Chekhov, the examining magistrate and the doctor, who normally meet only when there are cases of violent death. Notes for the story date back to 1891. Suicide among the intelligentsia was a preoccupation of Russian medical literature: Chekhov knew Dr Rozanov, the author of a standard investigation of suicide around Moscow. The story's socio-medical implications, over and above its nightmarish poetry of the blizzard, won the approval of critics and public. Tolstoy read it aloud to his family and claimed that he had earlier dreamed of Chekhov's 'conshtable'.

p. 510 'Cutting a feathery furrow': from Chapter V of Pushkin's *Evgeni Onegin*.

p. 511 Un petit verre de Cliquot: a French music hall waltz popular in Russia.

THE LADY WITH THE DOG

Chekhov's most famous and best-loved story, published at the end of 1899, is also known as *The Lady with the Little Dog*, *The Lady with the Lap Dog*, although the dog plays little more than an introductory role. It is Chekhov's most ambiguous story in its morality and its open ending: the nearer we get to the end, the more the story talks of beginnings. Is it about the conversion of a womaniser, or the last refuge of a middle-aged man? The references to, and quotations from, Nietzsche are disturbing: the story seems a pagan response to the Christianity of Tolstoy's novel of adultery, *Anna Karenina*. Chekhov shortened the story still further for his final version, reducing both Gurov's cynicism and Anna's idealism.

A number of Yalta women had to endure being labelled as the prototypes of the 'lady with the dog', but it is the scenery and meeting places of Yalta, rather than the population, which are perpetuated in the story. Chekhov appears to have used the name of his potential German publisher Diederichs as the source for the name of the cuckolded husband.

Against the current of opinion, Tolstoy found the story animal and immoral, which did not stop a trickle of imitations.

The poetics of the story are rich and subtle: note, for example, Chekhov's use of the colour grey, or the way in which the hero's and the author's reflections are blended.

p. 519 'The Scarlet Woman': Mary Magdalene, the subject of a well-known poem by A. K. Tolstoy: Chekhov has characters recite it in several stories and in *The Cherry Orchard*.

p. 520 Oreanda: a vista in the mountains above Yalta.

p. 525 *The Geisha*: operetta by Sidney Jones, very popular all over Europe, but especially in Russia (it had 200 performances in Moscow in 1899): it borrows its ideas from *Madame Butterfly*, but provides elements of Chekhov's plot both in this story and in *Three Sisters*.

IN THE RAVINE

Published in 1900, *In the Ravine* (also known as *In the Gully*) marks a partial return to the sociologically well-researched stories of the early 1890s and to the study of the disintegrating peasantry. Chekhov's approach, exploring the impact of a ramshackle capitalism on what was left of the Russian village, aligns him with Russian Marxists. (Chekhov liked to pun 'I am a Marxist now', meaning primarily that his collected works were being published by A. F. Marks.) *In the Ravine* is the longest work, and the broadest in scope, of Chekhov's last years, and is striking for its harrowing, violent action, which put paid to the cheap accusations that Chekhov's stories were effete, uneventful, unprincipled.

Gorky and Tolstoy joined the general chorus of praise, even though Chekhov's portrayal of the peasantry is no less uncompromising than before.

p. 533 the father-in-law in a well-known song . . .: In Russian folklore the father-in-law is an object of terror for the new bride.

THE BISHOP

Published in April 1902, but planned for over three years, this story was only too obviously Chekhov's farewell, his rehearsal for his own death. The bishop's rise from obscurity to fame and alienation, the mystery of the bond between him, his inspiration and his congregation remind one not just of earlier laments, such as *A Dreary Story*, but of Chekhov's own life. The story brings to a culmination the genre of *historia morbi*, where the plot is made by the fatal progress of illness, and the whole lyrical prose tradition of Russian literature from Pushkin to Turgenev. Its perfection was at first noted only by Bunin and Tolstoy and took a generation to be recognised widely.

A Russian bishop, strictly speaking 'archimandrite', was a member not of the ordinary priesthood, but of the celibate monastic clergy: the bishop of the story is a deputy to the diocesan bishop.

p. 565 willow branches: In the Russian Orthodox church the palms of Palm Sunday are substituted by willow branches.

p. 575 the Lord's Passion: In the Orthodox Easter service twelve passages are read from the four gospels.

THE BRIDE

Also known as *A Marriageable Girl*, *The Fiancée*, this is Chekhov's last story, published in December 1903. It is unique in that all the author's drafts and manuscripts survive: he died before he could destroy them. They show how complex and difficult it was for Chekhov's prose to evolve from notes to finished manuscript. If *The Bishop* is valedictory, then this story can be read as a testament to urge the living to make the best use of their time.

The Arctic setting reminds one of an equally 'feminist' work, *Three Sisters*. Here the three woman stuck in provincial ice are not sisters, but are arranged vertically, grandmother, mother and daughter. At least one makes the escape to the metropolis, even though a phrase in the last sentence 'as she supposed' casts a shadow on her hopes of permanent freedom. (An inadequate Andrei who plays the violin is another touch that recalls *Three Sisters*.) The denunciatory and cloud-cuckoo-land speeches of Sasha recall Trofimov in *The Cherry Orchard*, on which Chekhov had begun work, and the relationship between an impotent provocateur, the household that feeds him and his naïve female pupil also anticipates Chekhov's last play.

Critical approval was strong, even though many noted the scepticism of the simple phrase 'as she supposed'.

CHEKHOV AND HIS CRITICS

Most critical reaction to Chekhov's prose has focussed on one or another story. Accordingly, we cite these responses in the notes to the relevant story. For most of Chekhov's lifetime only a few Russian critics were able to generalise about his art as a whole. The first to realise his importance were the older generation who were mourning the deaths of the giants – Dostoevsky and Turgenev. By 1890 Tolstoy was prepared to declare, 'Maupassant and Chekhov are major talents.' In 1888 Pleshcheev saw *Steppe* as a major landmark, which showed Chekhov had wasted his time writing short works for periodicals: he lamented, 'you have less renown than writers unworthy to undo your bootstraps. And all this because of lousy newspapers which are read one day and used as wrapping paper the next.' Another veteran, Grigorovich, complained, 'there is unanimous sincere regret that you undervalue your talent by collaborating with the petty press and forcing yourself to rushed jobs', before proclaiming: '. . . such mastery in conveying observations can be found only in Turgenev and Tolstoy.' Russia's most popular critic, N. K. Mikhailovsky, deplored the press for 'teaching you to be fragmentary, to stroll along a road with no destination and no reason'. Just before his suicide the writer Vsevolod Garshin, whose role in the short story was that of St John the Baptist to Chekhov's Christ, exclaimed that 'such pearls of language, such life, such immediacy had never been seen in Russian literature before'.

Some of Chekhov's generation of writers, whom Chekhov loyally persisted in seeing as a guild of mere craftsman, were ready to admit: 'he is an elephant compared with the rest of us.' But the real enthusiasm came from musicians and painters who sensed their art in Chekhov's literary technique. Tchaikovsky led the way in 1889: 'Have you any idea of the new Russian talent, Chekhov? In my view this is the future pillar of our literature.' The painter Repin wrote in 1894, 'I couldn't tear myself away from your book, once I'd opened it, I read the last page with sadness.'

In the early 1890s Russia's makers of radical opinion had decided to punish Chekhov for his refusal to conform to their idea of civic conscience: 'a priest of unprincipled writing', was not the worst of their abuse. Reactionary fellow-collaborators on Suvorin's *New Times* joined the attack: Burenin declared 'the Chekhovs are beginning to fade . . . such mediocre talents have become incapable of looking straight at life around them.' Only when they needed Chekhov's contributions or when the writing was clearly too great to belittle, did they grudgingly relent. When they did so they persisted in inventing a Chekhov more like themselves: Lenin felt that he too had been 'locked up in Ward No. 6'. Gorky decided that 'Chekhov was a profound connoisseur of the psychology of little people'. Even Tolstoy complained to his son that 'Chekhov still has no definite point of view'.

In the later 1890s Chekhov's very greatest work, *My Life*, was passed over by the critics almost without comment. It was not until the 1900s that critics felt compelled to account for the affection of readers and the envy of writers for Chekhov's narrative skills. Then they understood that what they had seen as faults were in fact the virtues. The first recognisably modern appreciation was by a certain Kugel in *Teatr i iskusstvo*, 1900, 8, p. 168: 'Mr Chekhov feels, thinks, reacts to life in episodes, in details, in its flotsam, senses it, if one may say so, in endless parallels which never intersect, not at least on the visible plane. People are episodic; at first sight their fates are episodic too; life is episodic, like a fragment of an infinite process which we did not begin and which will not end with us.'

Innovative Russian criticism, the 'formalism' that has led to modern structuralism, preferred to use not Chekhov but Gogol, Dostoevsky and Tolstoy as experimental animals in their new critical laboratory. It was now foreign readers and writers who began to sense the newness: the *New Statesman* reviewer in 1916 exclaimed: 'Tchehov is, for his variety, abundance, tenderness and knowledge of the heart of the "rapacious and unclean animal" called man, the greatest short-story writer who has yet appeared on the planet.' Katherine Mansfield's whole evolution can be seen as an apprenticeship to and appreciation of Chekhov, from her first plagiarism of *The Girl who was Sleepy* to her own autonomous masterpiece *Prelude*. Thomas Mann's *Essay on Chekhov* of 1954 finally fixed on a moral rather than aesthetic basis Chekhov's claim to be the father of twentieth-century prose: 'This is how Chekhov's fiction has affected me. His irony about fame, his doubt in the sense and worth of his activity, his disbelief in his greatness have so much of modest quiet greatness. Dissatisfaction with himself, Chekhov said, is a basic element of any genuine talent.'

SUGGESTIONS FOR FURTHER READING

PRIMARY SOURCES

Anton Chekhov, *Polnoe sobranie sochinenii i pisem* (30 vols), Moscow, Leningrad 1974–1983.
Constance Garnett, tr., *Tales of Tchehov* (12 vols), London: Chatto & Windus, 1916–1921.

BIOGRAPHIES

E. J. Simmons, *Chekhov, a biography*, London: Cape, 1963 – The most substantial and literary.
R. Hingley, *A New Life of Anton Chekhov*, Oxford: Oxford University Press, 1976 – Uses material released in the 1960s, but not the letters published after 1974.
H. Troyat, *Chekhov*, London: Macmillan, 1987 – Flamboyant, imaginative, but uses a limited range of sources.
V. S. Pritchett, *Chekhov: A Biography*, London: Penguin Books, 1990 – The best written and best judged, but relies wholly on previous biographies.
Recently published and unpublished archival material are the basis for the forthcoming (1996):
D. Rayfield, *Chekhov: A Life*, HarperCollins, London.
Richard Garnett, *Constance Garnett: A Heroic Life,* London: Sinclair Stevenson, 1991.

CRITICAL STUDIES

P. Bitsilli, *Chekhov's Art: A stylistic Analysis*, Ann Arbor: Ardis, 1983 – A translation of a superb Bulgarian formalist's study.
A. P. Chudakov, *Chekhov's Poetics*, Ann Arbor: Ardis, 1983 – A translation of a pioneering Russian study of Chekhov's narrative devices.
Toby W. Clyman, ed., *A Chekhov Companion*, Westport, N.J.: Greenwood (USA), 1986 – A mixed bag of essays and articles. See its pp. 311–31 for a bibliography of criticism in English.

W. Gerhardie, *Anton Chekhov: a critical study*, London: Macdonald, 1949/1974 – An Anglo-Russian Bloomsbury writer's proselytising.

L. Hulanicki and D. Savignac, eds, *Anton Čexov as a Master of Story-Writing*, The Hague: Mouton, 1976 – A sample of the best Soviet critiques.

R. D. Kluge, ed., *Čechov: Werk und Wirkung*, Tübingen, 1990 – A gigantic polyglot assembly of conference papers, some tedious, some enthralling, some in English.

V. Llewellyn-Smith, *Anton Chekhov and the Lady with the Dog*, Oxford: Oxford University Press, 1973 – An original and faintly feminist biographical critique.

Donald Rayfield, *Chekhov: The Evolution of His Art*, London: Elek, 1975 – to be superseded by *Understanding Chekhov*, London: Duckworth, 1996.

T. Winner, *Chekhov and His Prose*, New York: Rinehart, 1966.

SHORT STORY COLLECTIONS
IN EVERYMAN

A SELECTION

The Secret Self 1: Short Stories by Women
'A superb collection' *Guardian* **£4.99**

Selected Short Stories and Poems
THOMAS HARDY
The best of Hardy's Wessex in a unique selection **£4.99**

The Best of Sherlock Holmes
ARTHUR CONAN DOYLE
All the favourite adventures in one volume **£4.99**

Great Tales of Detection Nineteen Stories
Chosen by Dorothy L. Sayers **£3.99**

Short Stories
KATHERINE MANSFIELD
A selection displaying the remarkable range of Mansfield's writing **£3.99**

Selected Stories
RUDYARD KIPLING
Includes stories chosen to reveal the 'other' Kipling **£4.50**

The Strange Case of Dr Jekyll and Mr Hyde and Other Stories
R. L. STEVENSON
An exciting selection of gripping tales from a master of suspense **£3.99**

The Day of Silence and Other Stories
GEORGE GISSING
Gissing's finest stories, available for the first time in one volume **£4.99**

Selected Tales
HENRY JAMES
Stories portraying the tensions between private life and the outside world **£5.99**

£4.99

AVAILABILITY
All books are available from your local bookshop or direct from **Littlehampton Book Services Cash Sales, 14 Eldon Way, Lineside Estate, Littlehampton, West Sussex BN17 7HE.** PRICES ARE SUBJECT TO CHANGE.

To order any of the books, please enclose a cheque (in £ sterling) made payable to Littlehampton Book Services, or phone your order through with credit card details (Access, Visa or Mastercard) on 0903 721596 (24 hour answering service) stating card number and expiry date. Please add £1.25 for package and postage to the total value of your order.

In the USA, for further information and a complete catalogue call 1-800-526-2778.